ANTONIA FRASER:
Three Great Novels

Also by Antonia Fraser

Cool Repentance
Oxford Blood
Your Royal Hostage
The Cavalier Case
Jemima Shore's First Case and other stories
Jemima Shore at the Sunny Grave and other stories
Political Death

Antonia Fraser

Three Great Novels

Quiet as a Nun
Tartan Tragedy
A Splash of Red

ORION

First published in Great Britain in 2005 by Orion,
an imprint of the Orion Publishing Group Ltd.

1 3 5 7 9 10 5 6 4 2

A CIP catalogue record for this book is
available from the British Library.

ISBN 0 75287 2907

Typeset by Deltatype Ltd, Birkenhead, Merseyside

Printed in Great Britain by Clays, Ltd, St Ives plc

The Orion Publishing Group Ltd
Orion House
5 Upper Saint Martin's Lane
London, WC2H 9EA

Contents

Quiet as a Nun

For Rebecca
Who read it first

The holy time is quiet as a Nun,
Breathless with adoration
                                        Wordsworth

Contents

1

Out of the past

Sometimes when I feel low, I study the *Evening Standard* as though for an examination. It was in that way I found the small item on the Home News page: NUN FOUND DEAD. It was not a very promising headline. Nevertheless I conscientiously read the few lines of print below. It staved off the moment when I would look round the empty flat resolving to cook myself a proper meal for once, and knowing that I would not do so.

'Sister Rosabelle Mary Powerstock,' the story continued, 'of Blessed Eleanor's Convent, Churne, Sussex, was found dead today in a locked building on the outskirts of the convent grounds. It is believed that the forty-one-year-old nun, known as Sister Miriam at the convent where she had lived for eighteen years, had been taken ill and was unable to raise the alarm. Reverend Mother Ancilla Curtis said today that Sister Miriam would be a great loss to the community of the Order of the Tower of Ivory, and would be sadly missed by her many pupils, past and present.

'Sister Miriam was the daughter of a former Lord Mayor of London.'

Before I had finished reading the short item, I had been transported back a whole generation. I knew that ruined building. It was in fact a tower. Blessed Eleanor's Retreat, as the nuns called it, in memory of the foundress of the Order of the Tower of Ivory. Sometimes irreverently referred to by the girls as Nelly's Nest.

For that matter I knew Sister Miriam. Or I had known Rosabelle Powerstock? Rosa. Had I known Sister Miriam? On consideration, no. But for a short while, long ago, I had known Rosabelle Powerstock very well indeed. For a few moments the cold elegant surroundings of affluent London in the seventies dissolved. It was wartime. A little

7

Protestant day-girl sent by the vagaries of her father's career to a smart Catholic boarding convent conveniently next door. Bewildered and rather excited by the mysterious world in which she found herself. The resolute kindness of the nuns – was there any kindness like it for the undaunted firmness of its warmth whatever the reaction of its recipient? Reaching its final expression in Reverend Mother Ancilla.

I learnt that the nuns in their religious life adopted a name, Latin or otherwise, for some virtue or religious attitude they particularly admired; failing that, the name of some especially inspiring saint. Ancilla meant Handmaid of the Lord – echoing the great submissive answer of the Virgin Mary to the angel's unexpected announcement of her coming motherhood, 'Behold the Handmaid of the Lord.' No doubt the Lord had been happy with his handmaid, Ancilla Curtis: but it was difficult even now to envisage any relationship in which Mother Ancilla was not the dominant partner.

And Rosa – the late Sister Miriam. So she had taken that name in religion. She had always declared her intention of doing so – if she became a nun. It had been a fashionable topic of conversation at Blessed Eleanor's.

'If I become a nun, and of course I wouldn't dream of doing such a thing, I'm going to marry and have six children, then I'll be Sister Hugh. After little St Hugh of Lincoln.'

'I'll be Sister Elizabeth. After St Elizabeth of Hungary who gave bread to the poor and it turned to roses when her husband tried to stop her.'

'Did the poor eat the roses?' I enquired. I was not trying to mock. I was fascinated by the whole concept. To cover up, I said quickly: 'If I become a nun, that is to say if I become a Catholic first, and then become a nun, I'll be Sister Francis.'

How lovely. The birds. The dear little animals. That met with general approval.

'No, not St Francis of Assisi.' Honesty – or cussedness – compelled me to add, 'St Francis Xavier.' I had just been reading about the origins of the Society of Jesus, and the heroic struggles of that St Francis to convert the Japanese, dying in the attempt. Like many non-Catholics I was morbidly intrigued by the Jesuits. Secretly, the one I would really like to have chosen was St Ignatius.

'Jemima should be Sister Thomas,' said Rosa sweetly. 'Doubting Thomas.'

'Isn't Miriam rather an Old Testament sort of name?' I countered. I meant rather Jewish.

'It's one of the titles of Our Lady. Our Lady Star of the Sea.' Rosa loved to snub and enlighten me at the same time about the intricacies of her religion. Humbly, I loved to listen to her. I thought of the other titles in that great litany. Star of the Sea, pray for us. Mystical Rose pray for us. Tower of Ivory, pray for us.

Like most Protestants, I knew the Bible much better than my Catholic friends. Besides, my terrifying nonconformist grandfather had been fond of reading it aloud. He was particularly fond of the Song of Solomon. 'Thy neck is as a tower of ivory,' sang Solomon – and thus my grandfather in his booming voice, 'Thine eyes like the fishpools in Heshbon by the gate of Bath-rabbim . . .' Fish pools. Not very pretty to modern ears. But thinking about fish pools, dark, with swirling depths, the phrase was not inapt to Rosa's eyes in certain moods.

Mysterious Rosa, once my Star of the Sea, was now dead – in her ruined Tower of Ivory.

I shook myself, to remove the touch of memories long buried. Wartime had brought strange schooling to many, and quick changes. After the war my parents had decided to go back to their original Lincolnshire and make their home there.

'Goodbye, Jemima,' Reverend Mother Ancilla in our final interview. She combined the roles of Reverend Mother of the convent and headmistress of the school, an awesome conglomerate of power. This time it was very much the headmistress who was to the fore.

'What a clever girl you have been. Top of your form. The nuns all say they will really miss teaching you. A very nice impression to leave behind. Don't forget us.'

'Oh Mother, I couldn't,' I gushed. That was one thing the convent taught you – how to return a soft answer. Mother Ancilla paused. I knew quite enough about nuns by this time to know that they never left you with the last word.

'This cleverness, Jemima. A wonderful gift from Our Lord. You must develop it of course. Go to university perhaps?'

A mutter. 'I hope to, Mother.'

'But there is the spirit too as well as the intelligence. The spirit which bows itself and in doing so finds its true happiness. Self-abnegation, Jemima.' She paused again. At no point had the nuns ever tried to convert me from the thin Protestantism spread upon me by my parents. It would have been quite outside their philosophy to attempt by words what example could not do. I felt her pause was a delicate acknowledgement of that restraint.

'St John of the Cross, one of our great mystics, once wrote that unless I find the way of total self-abnegation, I shall not find myself.'

'Yes, Mother.' I bobbed a curtsey.

At the time her parting words had seemed singularly inappropriate.

And later even more so to a successful career, carved, sometimes clawed out, by methods which always contained a great remembrance of self. Ironically enough, it now occurred to me that in my relationship with Tom I had probably realised self-abnegation at last.

The thought of Tom brought me back sharply to the empty flat, as it always did. He had said that he might telephone about ten.

'If I can get to my study and she has a bath so that she doesn't hear the click of the telephone as I pick it up.'

It was a proviso which had been made before.

I once said: 'Tom, why don't you get a telephone which doesn't click?' He said nothing, but kissed me gently. So it was the way of total self-abnegation. It was now eight o'clock. There were two hours to wait. I turned on the television and turned it off irritably, deciding that the critic who said in this week's *Listener* that my own programme was really the only thing worth watching these days had after all a great deal to be said for him. I picked up the autobiography of the children's doctor from Nigeria I would interview on Friday. I forgot Mother Ancilla. I had long forgotten Rosa. Sister Miriam I did not know. I even forgot Tom for an hour and a half, and the last half-hour passed not too slowly, considering it was actually an hour, and nearly half-past ten before he managed to ring.

The letter from Mother Ancilla arrived about a fortnight later. The small convent writing paper, covered clearly and carefully in a still familiar handwriting, unlocked its own memories. Nuns did not waste writing paper: waste was not only extravagant, but also displeasing to God. I was curiously unsurprised by the arrival of the letter. It was as though I had been expecting it. The previous memories had warned me: we are after you, out of the past.

Mother Ancilla's letter was complimentary on its first page, sad on its second page and astonishing on its third. The compliments referred to my own career, 'which although we did not play, I fear, the whole part in your education, we have nevertheless followed with interest. And of course like all our old girls, you have always had the prayers of the community. Our girls nowadays regularly watch your programme on television – yes, we have colour television in St Joseph's Sitting Room, the gift of an old girl. Your programme is one of the few we can safely trust to be both entertaining and instructive. Sister Hippolytus often tells the girls about your earlier triumphs in the debating society, and how she predicted a public career for you.'

It was a surprise to me that Sister Hippolytus had predicted anything so favourable in my future as a public career. Famous for her sharp tongue, Sister Hippo was one of the few – no, the only nun who had made me conscious of my alien status. Then I remembered that 'a public career' on the lips of certain Catholics was not necessarily the golden prospect it would seem to the rest of the world. Motherhood, sanctity, those were the true ideals. Neither of them had I satisfied.

The sadness referred to the death of Rosa. 'You will perhaps have read in the papers of the death of Sister Miriam, whom you knew as Rosabelle Powerstock. Perhaps like us, you felt that the coroner's remarks were a little unfortunate.' In fact I had not actually seen a report of the inquest. My newspaper-combing phase had passed. I had been busy, and besides, Tom's wife had gone to stay with her mother. Later in the month, there was the prospect of a really long trip to Yugoslavia for the two of us.

'But even in these enlightened days,' Mother Ancilla's measured letter continued, 'I suppose we must remember that the Catholic faith was once persecuted in this country. There is still a great deal of prejudice about. Poor Sister Miriam, she did not have a very happy life latterly, she had been ill, and although the manner of her death was tragic – Sister Edward blames herself dreadfully and of course unnecessarily – one cannot altogether regret the passing of her life on this earth. R.I.P.'

The third page astonished me by containing a remarkably pressing invitation to visit the convent as soon as possible. It was couched in language which, even disguised by Mother Ancilla's precise calligraphy, sounded remarkably like a plea.

'In fact, in general, these have not been very happy times for the community as a whole. I want to ask your help, dear Jemima, in a certain very delicate matter, which I cannot explain in a letter. Will you make time in a busy life to come down and see us? After all these years. As soon as possible . . .'

'*My* help,' I thought lightly. 'Mother Ancilla must be desperate to want *my* help.' But as it turned out, that was quite a sensible reaction to her letter.

2

'I want to find myself'

I arranged to drive down to the convent the following Saturday. My work would be over for the week – my programme was recorded – and by Friday I was generally filled by a post-programme adrenalin in which all things were possible, whether the programme had gone well or badly. In this case it had gone well, and on Friday night I was going to have dinner with Tom. He also said that he would be able to spend the whole night with me, in my flat.

'What if – she – telephones you at home?' I did not particularly like saying Carrie's name, or introducing her into the conversation. But the question had to be asked. In the past we had both endured some unsuccessful stolen nights, when Tom lay sleepless in my bed, wretchedly imagining the unanswered telephone and Carrie's subsequent anguish.

'She won't,' said Tom cheerfully. 'Mother-in-law's telephone has broken. She chatted the wire through. Thank God. Long may it stay that way.'

I thanked God too. The Almighty suddenly seemed to be taking a more friendly interest in my affairs. Perhaps it was the influence of Mother Ancilla and the prayers of the community? That reminded me to tell Tom that I had to be off early the next morning. For a moment I was almost tempted to postpone – no. It would do Tom no harm to find that I too had some personal commitments beyond the vicarious ones imposed on me at second hand by Carrie. Though Tom might frown.

Later, Tom did frown. After all he loved me. We were in love. He pushed back his hair off his forehead. It was a gesture almost as familiar to me as his kiss. Tom's hair, straight, floppy, unmanageable, was another of the persistent problems in his life. Still frowning, he said:

'Blessed Eleanor's Convent. Wasn't that the awful place where the nun starved herself to death? Quite mediaeval, the whole business. Nobody knows what goes on beyond convent bars, you know. It was pure chance this case got out in the open because the nun actually died. I think the coroner was quite right.'

'Oh Tom,' I burst out. 'Don't be so ridiculous. 'There aren't bars. It's a school. I was there in the war and afterwards. I must have told you. As for the coroner, I thought it was disgraceful what he said. No Popery rides again.' (I had since looked up the clippings.) 'It was accidental death, no-one denied that, and he had no business blaming that poor young nun who gave evidence. Nuns have feelings just like anybody else.'

'Well they don't look like anybody else,' said Tom.

'Really—' Mother Ancilla's letter had made me feel curiously protective, even in the face of Tom.

'Or rather they all look just like each other. I saw a couple on the tube today. Couldn't possibly have told one from the other, even if one had been my sister. Two identical black crows.'

'What extraordinary prejudice from Tom Amyas, MP, that well-known hero of liberal causes.'

Tom grinned. 'Sorry. Some rooted anti-Papist prejudice in me somewhere. Relic of my childhood I think. The Inquisition and all that. I remember reading *Westward Ho* – connections with my name – and being full of British indignation about it all. It still horrifies me: the idea of the imposition of *belief* upon others ... you should know that.'

'I hardly think that an obscure convent in Sussex full of harmless middle-aged women can be blamed for the horrors of the Spanish Inquisition four centuries ago,' I said coldly. I was oddly narked by Tom's remarks. I tried to tell myself that at the first hint of Catholic persecution returning to this country – perish the unlikely thought – Tom would be the first to throw himself into the cause of quelling it. Save The Nuns: I could see him marching now with his banner. It was one of the things for which I loved him. But we had never discussed Catholicism before – why should we – and I hated to find even this corner of prejudice in my kind and gallant Tom, the champion of all those in trouble.

I thought of telling him that Mother Ancilla too was in trouble, or thought she was. I decided not to. We dropped the subject.

But I remembered Tom's remarks the next day as I drove up the long gravel drive to the convent. It was autumn. In the sunshine the convent grounds were immaculate. It was the season in which I had first arrived at Blessed Eleanor's as a day-girl. I walked with my mother from my parents' leaf-strewn autumnal garden, which had a kind of rich self-made compost under-foot throughout at this season, through to gardens where evidently no leaf was permitted to rest for very long before being tidied away.

'The nuns must catch the leaves before they fall,' said my mother jokingly, to leaven the slightly tense atmosphere of a new school. She paused and gulped.

'My God, look at that.' We both stopped and observed a nun – young? old? who could tell? – carefully catching a leaf long before it fluttered to the ground. She put it carefully away in a pocket, or anyway somewhere in the recesses of her black habit.

'Catching leaves is lucky.' My mother was quick to seize on an occasion for optimism. 'We'll find out who the lucky nun is, and you can make friends with her.' I assented rather dubiously. But we never did find out who the lucky nun was. As Tom observed thirty years later, from a distance they really did all look exactly the same.

At that moment two nuns pulled a crocodile of small girls into the side of the drive as I passed. Identical. Two black crows. The children's uniform, a blur of maroon blazers and pink shirts, seemed singularly unchanged from my own day. I smiled. The children smiled amiably back. Both nuns smiled. The autumnal sun continued to shine, mellowing the rather fierce red brick of the convent façade. That too seemed much as I remembered it. Peaceful. Tidy. Even the creeper on the walls did not romp but climbed up in an orderly fashion. It was difficult to imagine what possible troubles could lie behind that calm exterior – troubles, that is to say, that could not be solved without recourse to the prying outside world. That was after all the world that I represented: Jemima Shore, Investigator, was how I was billed on television. It was a deliberate parody of the idea of the American detective, a piece of levity considering the serious nature of my programme. I was nevertheless an alien to the convent world. But Mother Ancilla had deliberately sent for Jemima Shore.

I stopped feeling an alien when a nun answered the door. She was very small. Ageless, as all nuns tended to be, with their foreheads and throats covered, so that the tell-tale signs of age were hidden. The short black cape covering the upper part of her body, whatever it was called, part of the nuns' uniform, also partially hid her waist. It had the effect of making her figure into a sort of bundle. She looked a bit like Mrs Tiggy-Winkle – hadn't there been one nun we named Tiggy? Perhaps all small nuns looked like Mrs Tiggy-Winkle. I gave my Christian name just in case.

'It's Jemima Shore to see Reverend Mother Ancilla.'

'Ah Miss Shore,' she beamed. So I didn't know her. 'We've been expecting you.' Into the reception room, a large room just by the front door, known for some reason as the Nuns' Parlour – although it was very much not part of the nuns' accommodation, being used exclusively for confrontations between secular and religious worlds. Here parents bringing quivering offspring to the convent for the first time were welcomed, smoothed down by Mother Ancilla, and made to feel – so my mother had told me – that they themselves were about to enter a disciplined but friendly institution.

The Nuns' Parlour really was exactly the same. The reproduction holy pictures in their dark frames, with their dully gold backgrounds. Fra Angelico seemed the prime favourite. On the table lay the familiar pile of wedding photographs, still surely dating from the forties. At any rate they were still mainly by Lenare and not by Lichfield. Perhaps the old girls of Blessed Eleanor's had abandoned their propensity for lavish white weddings, like the rest of the world? These wedding photographs, when I was at school, had exercised the same secret fascination over me as the Jesuits. I used to gaze at them covertly when my father was discussing my need for better science instruction with Mother Ancilla.

'But Mother Curtis,' he would say at the beginning of every term, finding the name Ancilla evidently too much to stomach: 'Science instruction by *post* is really not enough to equip your girls for the modern world.'

'Oh Captain Shore,' Mother Ancilla would regularly reply with a tinkling laugh. 'I keep asking Our Blessed Lord to send a vocation to a good young science mistress to help us out, but so far, He, in His infinite wisdom, has not seen fit to do so.'

'I seem to remember a saying about God helping those who help themselves,' began my father. No doubt he intended to refer to such unsupernatural expedients as advertisements and educational agencies. But no-one bandied words with Mother Ancilla and stood much chance of emerging the victor. Especially about Almighty God, someone whose intentions, mysterious as they were to the whole world, were somehow less mysterious to Mother Ancilla than to the rest of us. In the language of today, one would have referred to Mother Ancilla as having a hot line to God: or perhaps an open line was the correct term.

'Exactly, Captain Shore. Helping ourselves. That's exactly what we're doing with our postal science lessons. Just as Our dear Lord wants us to do.'

My father gave up: till the beginning of the next term. I stopped gazing at the brides. Even then I suspected that I should never make that honorific folder. God might help those who helped themselves, but he did have a habit of not marrying them off. At least not in white.

As I turned over one photograph – the face was vaguely familiar – I heard a single sonorous bell ring somewhere in the convent. I recognised the signal. All the nuns had their own calling signal, like a kind of cacophonous morse code. One ring, then another for the Infirmary Sister, two then one for the Refectory Sister and so forth. One bell on its own called for the Reverend Mother.

Silence.

A pattering of feet on the heavily polished floor. The swish of robes outside the door, the slight jangle of a rosary that always presaged the arrival of a nun, and then—

'Jemima, my dear child.' Reverend Mother Ancilla kissed me warmly on both cheeks. I reflected ruefully that probably to no-one else in the world these days was I, at nearly forty, still a child. My parents were both dead. Tom? I could not remember him using the term even in our most intimate moments. Besides Tom, as a crusader, liked to see in me a fellow crusader. He had his own rather demanding child in Carrie and, for Tom, to be childlike or childish was not necessarily a term of endearment.

I studied Mother Ancilla's face as we talked, and I answered her preliminary polite enquiries. Nuns' faces might not show age but they did show strain. On close inspection, I was faintly horrified by the signs of tension in her mouth. Her eyes beneath the white wimple were no longer the eyes of a fierce but benevolent hawk as they had been in my youth. They reminded me of some softer and more palpitating bird, the look of a bird caught in the hand, frightened, wondering.

'You never married, my child?' Mother Ancilla was asking.

I hesitated how to reply. There was still something compelling about Mother Ancilla. 'Too much involved perhaps in your work,' she said tactfully, after a minute's silence between us.

I nodded, relieved and disappointed at the same time. That would do. Besides, it was true. Until I met Tom I had been too much involved in my work – for marriage, if not for love.

'We here, of course,' continued Mother Ancilla smoothly, 'understand a life of devotion, for which the ideal of home and family is sacrificed. We too have made that sacrifice, in honour of Our Blessed Lord.' She fell into silence again. 'It can be very hard. Even at times too hard, unless the grace of God comes to our aid. Sister Miriam—'

'Yes, Mother?' I said as helpfully as possible.

'Perhaps the sacrifice was a little too much for her? Who can tell? Perhaps Sister Miriam should never have become a nun in the first place. I wondered so much about her vocation.'

This was surprising. I had anticipated some more religious bromides, as I described them to myself, about the value of the sacrifice.

Mother Ancilla took my hand and said suddenly and urgently:

'Jemima, we must talk.' This time she did not call me her child. 'We don't have much time.'

'I'm not all that busy,' I began. I realised with a faint chill that she was talking about herself.

'I'll begin with Sister Miriam; Rosabelle as you knew her.' It was a pathetic story, not uncommon perhaps in a single woman these days, a spinster. But I was conventional enough to be shocked by its happening to a nun. A decline in health. A form of nervous breakdown, culminating in a hysterical outburst in the middle of teaching. Sister Miriam was whisked away to a sister house of the convent in Dorset by the sea, a convalescent home. There she found the greatest difficulty in eating, although with the help of tranquillizers her composure returned. After six months Sister Miriam was adjudged ready to return to Blessed Eleanor's. But she was given light duties, French conversa-tion with the Junior school—

I gave an involuntary smile. 'That wouldn't have been a light duty in my day,' I explained hastily.

'We have a language laboratory nowadays. The gift of an old girl.'

A laboratory. That reminded me of the old days of my father's arguments. I wondered if God had ever sent Mother Ancilla that experienced science mistress. And was it too much to hope that God would also have inspired an old girl to endow a science laboratory?

'And the most beautiful science laboratory, by the way. How pleased Captain Shore would have been to hear that, wouldn't he, Jemima?' So she had not forgotten. Mother Ancilla never forgot an adversary.

'Did you get the science mistress too?' I couldn't resist asking.

Mother Ancilla opened her eyes wide.

'Why, of course. They both came together. Sallie Lund, an American girl. When she joined the Order in 1960 she was already a trained scientist, so naturally she could teach science here. And as her father pointed out, she could hardly teach science without a laboratory. A very dear man, and most practical about money, as Americans generally are. So he gave us it.'

I was only surprised that it had taken Mother Ancilla till 1960 to iron this matter out.

17

We had been distracted. Mother Ancilla returned to a sadder topic than her scientific victories.

'As I was saying, Sister Miriam appeared to return to normal, although she still found great difficulty in eating. Difficulty that persisted for all her valiant efforts to overcome it. She told me once that strange visions seized her, that God wanted her to die, to go to Him, so that it was His will that she should not feed the flesh . . .'

For a moment, I felt a strong distaste for the whole convent and all its works expressed in such language.

'I told her that it was God's will that she should make a good nun and eat up her supper. Such as it was,' said Mother Ancilla sharply. I remembered that uncanny attribute she had of seeming to read one's thoughts.

'A form of anorexia nervosa, I suppose.'

But the story got worse. Rosabelle began to talk of her visions, eat less, hide her food, got thinner, a doctor was called, more doctors. She got fatter again. She seemed more cheerful. She took more interest in life around her. One day when attention was no longer focused on her and her affairs she disappeared. A typed note was found: 'I can no longer hide from the community that I have lost my vocation. I have gone to London to stay with my relations. Please don't try to find me. I want to find myself.'

'I want to find myself!' I echoed. It was the phrase Rosa had used to me years ago in our teenage discussions about our future, lasting half the night.

'But of course she never went,' I said.

'No, poor unhappy Sister Miriam. She went to Blessed Eleanor's Tower and locked herself in and – well, you probably know the rest. You probably read the newspapers.' I nodded.

'What's her name? The nun who knew all the time where she was and never told.'

'Sister Edward.'

Sister Edward. She was the one I felt sorry for. But how she could have been such an idiot – 'She is young, young in religion, she has only just stopped her postulancy. I think she really believed Sister Miriam when she spoke of her vision and the need to undergo a period of trial and purgation. And then when she realised that all along Sister Miriam had lain there, that the old key had snapped off, that she had tried to escape and been too weak, the door locked, growing gradually weaker, she nearly broke down herself.'

'It might have been better not to go into the court with that story all the same.'

Mother Ancilla opened her eyes wide. 'That would have been against the law, Jemima.' I was reminded of the formidable rectitude of the convent.

'All the same, to give the coroner the opportunity to refer to the centuries-long tradition of perverse practices and cruelty of the Church of Rome, and the suggestion that Sister Edward *gloried* in Sister Miriam's death.'

'Our reputation is very low around here now I fear. They are simple people. It's quite deep country you know. Churne village has people in it who have never been to London, for all the short distance. The nuns hate to go shopping alone at the moment. Some very hurting remarks are made.'

At last I perceived why Mother Ancilla had sent for me. It was, I assumed, to rectify the convent's 'image' in the national, or at any rate, the local mind. With the touching faith of ordinary people in television, Mother Ancilla obviously thought her former pupil could do it for her.

'Jemima,' said Mother Ancilla sharply, interrupting this train of thought. 'You've got to tell us. Why did she die?'

3
Jemima knows

I realised that the object which Mother Ancilla was twisting between her fingers was not, as I had imagined, a black wooden rosary such as all the nuns wore at their side. It was a scrap – no more than that – of white paper. Mother Ancilla pushed the paper towards me.

I began to read. I recognised the handwriting immediately: it was Rosa's. I thought how little it had changed over the years. That's because she's a nun. Was a nun. Frozen. Mine must have changed beyond all recognition. Not that I really use it much these days except for the odd secret note to Tom, perhaps after a speech at the House of Commons – 'Darling. You were terrific. All my love, J.' I always imagined that he destroyed such notes instantly, for fear of Carrie finding them in his pockets. Yet, perversely, I could not resist writing them in a form too compromising to be preserved. I had a secretary for everything else and then of course there was the telephone.

Rosa on the other hand would have honed and fashioned her handwriting A.M.D.G. – *ad majorem Dei gloriam* – To the greater glory of God. It was odd how quickly that phrase came back to me. The nuns wrote it on everything. We wrote it piously at the head of Scripture papers, and on other papers too where we thought it would help.

I looked down again at the piece of paper. No, Rosa had not written this message for the greater glory of God. At least if she had, she had not thought fit to embellish it with the customary initials.

'Jemima will understand what is going on here. Jemima knows why I have to do this,' I read carefully aloud. 'Jemima knows.'

I paused. Mother Ancilla's bright dark eyes, the focus of her face, were regarding me intently.

'I don't understand,' I said after a moment's silence. My voice sounded rather flat. 'This is written in her own hand. And you said her farewell note was typed.'

'It was in her missal. Her old Latin missal she used as a child. Not her breviary. It was dated the day of her death. We only found it later. That's why the police never saw it at the time. They took the other note away of course.' Mother Ancilla pursed her lips.

'She must have been in two minds at the time. I mean, about it all . . .' I thought: she must have been in more minds than that. And all her minds distracted.

'Poor Sister Miriam,' said Mother Ancilla sharply, 'was certainly a very disturbed person.' Disturbed: and disturbing. Disturbing to the peace of Blessed Eleanor's Convent. Potentially highly disturbing to my own peace.

On the back of the little white slip was a picture of the Virgin Mary in her blue robe, surrounded by a halo of stars.

I breathed a fairly devout prayer of thankfulness – I was almost tempted to cross myself – it was odd how these practices so slightly learnt at the time were returning to me – to whatever tutelary power had kept Rosa's message hidden. Imagine the newspaper headlines. Yes, I could imagine them only too well. Jemima Shore in Dead Nun Drama. Mystery of last message. So much more appetising than the simple 'Nun Found Dead' which had originally attracted my attention. Suddenly a feeling of the craziness of it all overcame me. I had not seen Rosa for – how long? It had to be fifteen years, no, more. After school there had been some unsatisfactory meetings in London. I remembered particularly one girls' lunch in a store – D.H. Evans was it, somewhere in Oxford Street. It was definitely not Fortnum and Mason, as Rosa had suggested. I knew that was too expensive for me and had said so.

'I generally go there with my friends, but I don't like it particularly,' was Rosa's comment. She sounded rather blank on the telephone.

In any case, I could not even pay the price of the set lunch at D.H. Evans, so it was just as well we had eschewed Fortnum's.

'Don't be silly,' said Rosa easily, paying both bills. She took a wallet from her leather handbag. Fascinated I saw that it contained another thin white fluttery note – as five-pound notes were in those days. I suppose that note was the single positive object which told me that Rosa was rich. Our school uniform, strictly imposed, made us all equal just as the nuns' black imposed uniformity on them. Rosa the nun – Sister Miriam – would have seemed no richer or poorer than say that little nun who had let me in at the door. Because I did not want to think back into the past for too long, I allowed a more modern thought to strike me. Rosa had been rich. Even, perhaps, very rich. What happened to her money when she entered the convent? What happened to it now that she was dead?

'She was a great heiress of course.' Mother Ancilla's voice broke into my thoughts in a way I was beginning to take once more for granted. The words came to me on a sigh. 'All the Powerstock money from generations back came to her. She had no close relations left.'

I thought back.

'Land in Dorset somewhere?'

Mother Ancilla smiled sadly.

'Alas, no. Not just that. That would have been simple. But there were all the great London properties as well. Her family estates in London. The Powers Estate.'

I began to put two and two together.

'You mean Powers Square, Powers House, and all that. Good God – sorry Mother.' I had done a programme on it all some time back, a particularly successful one as it had turned out. Combining as it did questions of the environment (Powers Square was said to be Cubitt's finest achievement) and social policy (the poor families on the nearby Powers Estate were being ejected from decrepit but still elegant houses so that a monster high-rise development could take place). I had also managed to discover that a good many of my colleagues at Megalith Television were living in the aforesaid decrepit houses and had done them up very nicely, thank you. They too objected to being removed yet essentially were being asked to make way for working-class housing . . . It was all very confusing. So confusing that I could not immediately remember who Jemima Shore, Investigator, had finally decided was in the right. Tom of course had been full of special scorn for my television colleagues in their refurbished homes ('A series of I'm-all-right Jills and Jacks masquerading as liberals'). I think I decided as usual that justice lay in the middle – that is to say nowhere.

Then there were the Powers Project fanatics. I'd temporarily forgotten about them. They too had been represented on my admirably impartial programme in the shape of an interview with their leader Alexander Skarbek.

Before the programme went out, several of the directors of MGV had taken fright and suggested that Skarbek should be cut.

'We're not here to promote the social ideas of mad extremists,' was the general line taken. Cy Fredericks, Megalith's colourful boss, groaned to me in private:

'Jem, what are you doing to me? Lord Loggin-Smith is an insomniac and rings me up throughout the night. Dame Victoria believes in making a brisk start to the day and calls me any time from six-thirty onwards.' But in public he merely murmured a few platitudes about television being open to all sides of the question. Actually I had rather enjoyed interviewing Skarbek, who was quite young and was certainly a more sympathetic type to me, fanaticism and all, than most of the directors of MGV.

The Powers Project aimed quite simply to set up a type of workers' commune all over the Powers Estate. The Projectors, as they became known, dismissed with equal contumely the existing concept of Cubitt's Powers Square and Powers House, and the council's future high-rise blocks. I was never quite clear what kind of rudimentary housing would replace the present Victorian façades, but there would be acres of it, that was certain. I think they were going to grow vegetables there too, like the Diggers, and keep pigs and hens.

Tom poured scorn on them too.

'Darling, when we're trying so hard to institute a proper housing policy in that part of London, to have some dangerous loony advocating a return to the standards of the seventeenth century – yes, Skarbek is dangerous. Power mad. You watch out.'

'Everyone on this particular programme is power mad,' I countered. 'Or rather Powers Mad. In the sense that everyone wants something different from everyone else for the Powers Estate. And wants it like crazy, with no ability to compromise. To coin a phrase, this programme is turning out to be an allegory of our society.'

'Your programmes always turn out to be an allegory of our society,' said Tom crossly, 'and if you don't say it beforehand, the critics say it for you afterwards.'

But he had at least provided me with a title for this programme. Powers Mad it became. And Powers Mad it went out, Alexander Skarbek and all.

'And of course she owned the convent land itself,' continued Mother Ancilla delicately with a little cough.

This time she had really astonished me.

'Blessed Eleanor's. You mean Rosa *owned* Blessed Eleanor's.'

'No nun owns anything, dear Jemima,' said Mother Ancilla calmly. 'In the sense that you in the world own things. A nun has given everything to God. It is just a case of the formalities of the arrangement.' I had a vision of God's lawyers – hatchet-faced men, as Tom would have them – behind whom the warm and benevolent God was able to shelter. 'Of course it was all handled by the lawyers and made part of a trust. Set up by Sir Gilbert Powerstock long ago. You probably remember him at Parents' Day: an enormous man. I remember thinking what an imposing sight he must have made in his

Lord Mayor's robes, quite different from Rosabelle – Sister Miriam. She took after her mother. Poor Marie Thérèse was a Campion of course and all the Campions were small and dark ever since the marriage of the 1st Earl Campion to one of dear Queen Mary's Spanish ladies-in-waiting.' I suddenly realised she was not referring to the late Queen Mary of betoqued fame, but to Mary Tudor. In my convent days I had to learn not to refer to her as Bloody Mary.

'You won't remember Lady Powerstock. She died very young – the Campion chest, you know. We were going through a period of grave financial difficulty at the time. And then dear Sir Gilbert stepped in and bought most of the land on which the convent stands and endowed it in perpetual memory of his wife. But for some technical reason to do with the trust, although the convent buildings became a charity, the land itself was different. I am afraid, as his heiress, Sister Miriam still owned it outright.'

'You're *afraid* she owned it outright?'

It was an odd choice of words, even for a nun.

'Oh Jemima, I am so worried that the whole wretched business of the land drove her to what she did.' It was Mother Ancilla at her most human and appealing. She stretched out and held my hand in hers. I remembered what ones the nuns were for physical contact, hugs, embraces, kisses, hands warmly held. The contacts whose natural corollaries were denied to them . . . No, that was Tom's kind of talk. They were just a bunch of affectionate and sweet, slightly girlish women, frozen perhaps in the girlishness of the age at which they had joined the convent.

'It worried her so, the responsibility of it, on top of her illness. Our Lord certainly knew what He was talking about when He told the centurion to sell all that he had. How poor Sister Miriam longed to lose all her great wealth into the arms of God. But the lawyers, you know. Even for a nun. They wouldn't let her alone. They kept saying: we must regularise the situation. And then she began to get such odd ideas about it all into her poor sick head. Not at all what Sir Gilbert intended, I can assure you. Ah well, Our Lord saw fit to put an end to all that. He knew that she would have never got such an idea in her right mind.'

'Mother, you must tell me. What was it that Rosabelle wanted to do with the land?'

This time Mother Ancilla looked quite genuinely surprised.

'But, Jemima, don't you know? You must know. I thought she must have written to you, when I found the note. It was after your programme. She wanted to take it away from us and—'

'Yes?'

'Give it to the poor.'

'Give it to the poor,' I repeated. Then the funny side of it all struck me. There had been such absolute horror in Mother Ancilla's voice. I could not resist adding: 'Just like the centurion in fact.'

'Not at all like the centurion,' replied Mother Ancilla icily. 'The centurion, you will remember, was a responsible man in a high position. Sister Miriam was a very sick woman. Her own lawyer begged her not to perform such a destructive and – one cannot avoid the word – crazy action. It would have ruined the convent of course. No grounds, no land. Right up to our very gates. No, beyond our gates. To our front door. It seems that the chapel itself would have gone. Our own chapel! Oh, we could no longer have existed. All our work gone for nothing. So very very far from the intentions of her father and the memory of her dear mother.'

She sighed again. There seemed to be more irritation than charity about the exhalation. I felt encouraged to continue.

'The poor – that's an awful lot of people. How did she choose?' Mother Ancilla gave me a smile of great sweetness.

'The poor. As Our Blessed Lord said, they are always with us. I remember it was the title of one of your programmes, wasn't it? "They are always with us." I wondered at the time how you selected *them*.'

'I doubt if Sister Miriam used the methods of Megalith Television.' Once again I regretted the decision to strike back. Another clasp of the hand. Another desperate look. A nagging feeling that something – or someone – was frightening Mother Ancilla, returned.

'Look, Mother Ancilla,' I said in my gentlest Jemima Shore manner, 'I want to help you. Please believe that. But you must explain to me what's going on here. Or what has been going on. I'm really quite at sea. Let me state a few simple facts—' Oh that phrase! Why couldn't I resist it? Even now when I was desperately trying to be honest. A phrase parodied by satirical programmes, which generally had me following it with a load of absolutely incomprehensible gibberish. 'No, Sister Miriam, Rosabelle, never wrote to me about the programme. In my enquiries I certainly never came across the fact that a nun of the o.t.i. had any connection with the properties – why, that would have made a terrific addition to the programme, come to think of it—'

I reined myself in. This was scarcely the time for such enthusiasm.

'Jemima knows, she wrote . . . But Jemima doesn't know. You must tell me. Otherwise I cannot begin to help you.'

There was a silence. It was interrupted by a knock at the door.

'Yes, come in,' said Mother Ancilla sharply. 'Yes, Sister, what is it now?'

'Oh, I'm sorry, Reverend Mother, I didn't realise you had a visitor—'
A slightly breathless voice behind me. But I did not quite like to turn
round and stare. I waited for Mother Ancilla to introduce me. But
Mother Ancilla continued to gaze over my head at her visitor with
barely concealed annoyance.

'As you can see, Sister, I'm really rather busy at the moment,' was all
she said. The unseen visitor – a nun, evidently, but I knew no more
than that – departed.

Mother Ancilla frowned. I noticed that she suspended speaking until
there could be no question of the recent intruder overhearing us.

Then at last she explained. How Rosabelle Powerstock, in her new
life as Sister Miriam of the Order of the Tower of Ivory, had never
shown any particular interest in her previous wealth. She took her vow
of poverty extremely seriously. Naturally she brought a dowry with her
to the convent as all the nuns did.

'A substantial dowry,' said Mother Ancilla, nodding. The language
laboratory? The swimming pool? I did not like to interrupt her by
asking. 'Our Blessed Lord saw to it that at last we were able to mend the
chapel roof, which has needed the most expensive repairs since the day
of Reverend Mother Felix.' Ah. I felt reproved for the secular nature of
my speculations. But beyond that she had renounced the vast trusts
once administered in her name, the beneficiaries being a series of
Catholic charities and educational projects.

Of course, Sister Miriam had made the usual will required by a
member of the o.t.i., leaving the residue of her dowry to that
community. But that in itself was not expected to be a great fortune.
And what with chapel roofs and other religious luxuries . . . In the years
which had passed since dear Sir Gilbert's death – his dear death, I
almost thought Mother Ancilla would say – no-one had had the faintest
idea that Rosabelle Powerstock still retained outright ownership of
every single inch of the so-called convent grounds of the Blessed
Eleanor's. It was, it seemed, an oversight on the lawyers' part that the
trust deed which covered the buildings did not in fact cover the lands.
A technicality.

'One can't help wondering why, if they were to make the mistake in
the first place, Our Blessed Lord ever guided them to discover it so
many years later,' observed Mother Ancilla with something approaching waspishness. But discover it, they had. And in their interminable
way had begun the long, long process to rectify it. To establish the deed
by which Rosabelle Powerstock would hand over the grounds to the
convent, as once her father had officially handed over the buildings.

'She agreed to do so?' I interrupted.

'At first. Without hesitation. I told you that Sister Miriam cared nothing for the things of this world. In her right mind.'

'But lately, there was a change. She wanted to give these same lands away?'

'Oh, those lawyers, they took so long. And wrote so many letters. And came to see her, and insisted on explaining to her what she was doing. As if Sister Miriam was *doing* anything. She was simply being a good nun. And putting her signature to a piece of paper which should have been over and done with years ago. And then she became ill.'

'And everything changed.'

'She changed. Nothing round her changed in the slightest.' Mother Ancilla began to speak more rapidly. 'It was after she saw your programme on television. She was convalescing at the time. She wanted to give it to the poor. Not just any poor, Jemima, but those poor people in the demolished houses of Powers Square. The Powers Projectors they call themselves. She talked of the rich man and the needle's eye. But she was, alas, mad. We know that now – too late. I thought she wrote to you. I thought she must have written to you. But somehow she got in touch with that man, the leader of the demonstrators or the residents' association or whatever they were called. She wrote to him. She offered him our lands. She said they were hers to give. Alexander Skarbek his name was.'

Alexander Skarbek. The man I had secretly found more sympathetic than the directors of MGV. Secretly and not only because of my job but because he was Tom's *bête noire*. Tom once said Alexander Skarbek existed to give good causes a bad name. A man without scruple, at least in Tom's opinion: it depended of course upon what your own scruples were. A man who certainly possessed qualities of decision and leadership. A man, a fanatic, sufficiently convinced of the rightness of his cause, who would not have hesitated to accept such an offer, even made by a half-crazy nun. A man who would also have understood exactly how to beat the Powerstock family lawyers at their own game. Had he not defeated the combined efforts of the Ministry and local Council in his efforts over the Greatpark Housing Estate?

Jemima knows: but I had known nothing of this, even if my programme had been responsible for touching it all off.

'She talked of Christ's poverty. How she would settle at our gates like Lazarus and teach us the true meaning of the Christian message.'

I could see that Mother Ancilla in her capacity as Dives, would scarcely welcome such a Lazarus as Alexander Skarbek at her gates.

'But in the event, Mother Ancilla, it didn't happen,' I heard myself say in my best unemotional manner. 'For I gather she never changed her will. Blessed Eleanor's inherited everything she still possessed.' The old nun shook her head. 'So the community has – forgive me for putting it so bluntly – by the untimely death of Sister Miriam Powerstock acquired the lands for itself.' I almost said: 'Timely death.'

Mother Ancilla did not seem to notice. She merely nodded. Behind her head there was a reproduction picture of the Virgin and Child in a bevelled burnished gilt frame. By Lippo Lippi. That had not changed since my day. But then Lippo Lippi could hardly be said to date. The Virgin looked infinitely sorrowful. But detached. As though she knew that all the concern she felt for the pitiful human scene taking place beneath her calm sad gaze could not alter the course of the stream of human passion by one iota. Her high round brow, the tendrils of her perfectly delineated golden hair, gave her an implacable beauty.

Mother Ancilla's brow on the other hand was not visible beneath the white band of her wimple, and no tendrils escaped from this prison. Any hair that did show would be grey and wispy, if not white. Nuns' hair had been a preoccupation when we were at school. The delicious thrill of shock when Sister Thomas, a young nun, had appeared in class with a distinct curl of brown hair showing. She must have dressed in a hurry, poor child. As nuns were not allowed to look in mirrors, she was probably unaware of her solecism. Another delicious thrill at the idea of Mother Ancilla's tart regret when the offending wisp was glimpsed. It all added up to the fact that nuns were not bald and did not shave their heads; they simply cut their hair conveniently short.

Gazing at Mother Ancilla now beneath the tumble-locked Virgin, I found that I had not altogether lost my preoccupation with nuns' hair. Or their appearance generally.

'You know, my child, I have not been very well recently,' said Mother Ancilla. I realised that there had been quite a silence between us, although to me her little room – even the headmistress's study was not allowed to waste space – had seemed filled by a voice from the past.

'Supposing a nun just refused to have her hair cut—' Rosa, young and audacious. But one day Rosa's own hair had been chopped off. That unruly brown curling hair I loved, hair which I used sometimes to brush furiously. Cut into the shape of Sister Miriam. Buried forever, first beneath the severe black headdress, now in the perpetual blackness of the grave.

Back to Mother Ancilla, another blackness and the shadow of her health.

'I'm sorry to hear that, Mother.' The conventional gush.

'Don't be sorry. Our Lord has been very good to me. He has allowed me to spend many years at the head of this convent, trying to serve

Him. I cannot complain if now He feels that my work here is over. In many ways,' she paused, 'I shall be glad to lay down the burden.'

'Oh surely things aren't quite so serious.' Another easy riposte. Then with more conviction: 'I can't imagine this convent without you. You've made it what it is. You *are* the Blessed Eleanor's to most of us.'

'Nonsense' – briskly. 'We are none of us indispensable. I should be gravely wanting in humility if I believed what you have just said to be true.' But under the air of reproof she did look slightly pleased. I was reminded of a recently retired Trades Union leader, appearing on my programme. I had made the same sort of observation along the lines of 'You are the Union'. He too could eliminate ambition but not pleasure in the success of his work. Another admirable martinet, I suppose. At any rate the camera had caught the fleeting expression of self-satisfaction. There was no camera to catch Mother Ancilla's momentary pleasure, and now she was frowning.

'Like Simeon, I would wish to make haste to be gone. If only I could leave the community as it should be . . . Not divided, frightened.'

She began to speak much faster again.

'Jemima, something is going on here. It is not simply the death of Sister Miriam, nor the reports in the Press. Although obviously those shook the community gravely. I feel it. I have been, you know, nearly fifty years in religion. I should have my Golden Jubilee next summer if . . .' A pause in the rush of words, and then she dashed on, 'I will be frank with you. If I live that long. I have been warned by our doctor that I may not. That I *will* not, unless I take things easier. That means of course retirement: maybe to our little house at Oxford. Maybe to our convalescent home in Dorset, built incidentally on part of the Powerstock estate. Mindful of my vow of obedience I would go any time. I should go willingly. But how can I leave the community now? When they are—' A long pause. A single sonorous word: 'Troubled.'

'Jemima, I want you to help us. I told you there isn't much time.' It was a return to the old voice of authority. 'I want you to find out what is going on here amongst us. No, please don't say no, not immediately. I have prayed long and earnestly about this. Think about it.'

One bell tolled in the distance. One bell for Reverend Mother.

'My bell.' Mother Ancilla arose and with surprising alacrity for a sick woman approaching seventy, moved to the door, automatically putting one finger in the tiny holy water stoup and crossing herself. 'I have arranged for you to have lunch in the refectory with the children, dear Jemima. They are thrilled at the prospect, naturally. They are all great fans of yours. Sister Clare will give you coffee later in the Nuns' Parlour. A visit to the chapel, perhaps?'

I smiled noncommittally. Things were going altogether too fast. I wanted to retain what control I still had of the situation. The chapel represented a form of capitulation I was definitely not prepared to make.

My last sight of Mother Ancilla was of a figure like a little black bird skimming down the corridor. The corridor itself was plain except for a series of alcoves containing incongruously garish statues of assorted saints.

'Miss Shore,' said a gentle voice more or less at my elbow. I realised that a little nun, hardly more than a novice from her face, had been waiting for some minutes to speak to me. With her twitching mouth and neat nose, she looked rather like an unhappy rabbit.

'I'm Sister Edward. I must talk to you.' Sister Edward: the name rang a bell. Yes, the nun who had so unfortunately not revealed Sister Miriam's crazy plan of self-purgation. And only sounded the alarm about the locked tower when it was too late. I also realised from her voice that Sister Edward had been that intruder in the headmistress's study whose appearance had been so unwelcome.

'Talk away,' I replied with false cheerfulness, my voice unnecessarily loud.

'Not here.'

At that moment the bell sounded again, three strokes then four. Sister Edward literally blanched.

'My bell. I must go.' All the same she continued to stand twisting her hands. 'They're after me. They don't want me to talk to you—'

'Sister Edward, I really think—'

By way of reply, Sister Edward dragged me into the narrow alcove beside me.

'She killed her,' she said, panting, and poking her little face into mine. 'She wanted her dead. So she killed her.'

'*Who?*' I might have said 'What' with equal force. I had no idea what Sister Edward was saying.

'Why Mother Ancilla of course.' The rabbit's face was turned up in innocent surprise. 'Mother Ancilla killed poor Sister Miriam.' The next moment Sister Edward was in her turn skimming down the corridor towards the nuns' part of the building. Another black bird. I knew that it was Sister Edward. But of course from the back it might just as well have been Mother Ancilla or any other nun. They really did look exactly alike.

I was left alone except for a statue of St Antony holding the Infant Jesus in his arms.

4

A balanced programme

Lunch in the refectory did not last long. Actually the refectory had been turned into a cafeteria since my day, complete with counter and plastic cases for food. All the nuns behind the counter had beaming rather flushed faces. We used to divide nuns into Snow Whites and Rose Reds, as the religious life (or the wimple) seemed to have the effect of sending their complexions to one or other extreme. These were all Rose Reds.

The food was delicious. I said as much to the girls sitting with me at table. They all affected considerable surprise.

'Would you like a second helping, Miss Shore?' enquired a girl at the end of the table politely. It was the first remark she had made throughout the meal. She had a long, interesting face, with a straight nose, like a crusader modelled on a tomb. As she brought back the plate, she bent over my chair and said quite low: 'This was Sister Miriam's favourite pudding as well, you know.'

Afterwards I asked Mother Ancilla who she was.

'Why, that's Margaret Plantaganet!' cried Mother Ancilla. She sounded delighted at my cleverness in picking out such an eligible candidate for my attention. 'Lady Margaret Plantaganet,' she added in passing – no-one could throw away a title like Mother Ancilla. 'The Bosworths' daughter.'

'It's not a very Catholic name,' I muttered. In my irritation at having given Mother Ancilla such an opening, I quite forgot to ask how a mere schoolgirl could have known of my friendship with Rosa.

'It's true that her mother was—' and Mother Ancilla mentioned some incredibly grand-sounding Italian name which I had genuinely never heard before, although I should have tried to look blank in any

31

case. 'Lord Bosworth is a convert. But Margaret herself looks pure Plantaganet, don't you think?'

It was clear that Mother Ancilla regarded the presence of Margaret Plantaganet at the Convent of Blessed Eleanor as a latter-day triumph for the Counter-Reformation.

I did not go to the chapel.

I did receive coffee from Sister Clare in the Nuns' Parlour. Sister Clare was extremely plump, and the sight of her swelling front beneath her black habit tempted me to wonder anew whether nuns wore bras (another perennial topic of discussion, and one which as far as I was concerned had never reached a satisfactory conclusion). If we had been on television I would have asked her, 'Sister, there is one question I know our female viewers are dying to ask . . .' Everyone would have expected something about sexual frustration; instead of which I would have continued: 'In an age when many women are boasting of burning their bras . . .' and so forth. We were not on television. I put temptation from me. It was unlikely that Vatican II had left the topic untouched in any case, whatever the mode when I was at school.

To distract myself, I reapplied my attention to the pasteboard brides in and out of their portfolio. At least I could picture Lady Margaret Plantaganet featuring here in a few years' time, stern in white, on the arm of some suitably aristocratic bridegroom. And the convent would send them a wedding present of table napkins embroidered by the nuns in which the Plantaganet arms mingled with those of the Blessed Eleanor . . . This agreeable fantasy lasted until I had finished my coffee.

Shortly after that I made it clear to Mother Ancilla, kindly but firmly, that Jemima Shore, Investigator, was a character who existed more or less for the benefit of television. I could not undertake a special secret mission to iron out the problems of Blessed Eleanor's. My encounter with Sister Edward had nevertheless given me an inkling as to the nature of these problems. Clearly a host of celibate women cooped up together could ferment from time to time like yeast. In the middle ages Sister Edward would have seen visions. Nowadays she merely accused her superior of murder. She probably watched too many thrillers on television. The gift of an old girl. In St Joseph's Sitting Room.

As I drove back to London, I felt that the long fingers of the past had stretched out to grasp me. And I had eluded them. I was sorry for Mother Ancilla. But I could not help her.

Besides, I was shortly off to Yugoslavia with Tom.

Two days later, he took me for dinner in our favourite restaurant, a trattoria behind Victoria station, discreet, convenient for the House of Commons. I wore my treasured Hanae Mori dress. A motif of scattered hearts. The heart: my lucky symbol. I tended to scribble a heart on my notes to Tom. Not so lucky tonight, it seemed. For I was not in fact off to Yugoslavia. Or at any rate, not with him. The Welfare Now Group, on which Tom had lavished so much of his prodigious idealism, was calling for urgent meetings with the Minister before the autumn session of Parliament. In the expectation that these meetings would be unsatisfactory – and they always were – there was to be a rally in Trafalgar Square. Tom of course would be one of the principal speakers. His tall thin figure, bowing slightly in the gale of his own words, was an inseparable part of the w.n.g. platform.

'It's not that I can't get out of it,' Tom said unhappily. 'It's just that I don't want to. We've got to make them see that our demands are reasonable. You understand what I mean, darling.'

As a matter of fact I did not understand. It occurred to me that the Archangel Gabriel with the resources of Maecenas would not be able to satisfy the demands of the w.n.g. But this was not a time for saying so.

'Tell me we shall go to Yugoslavia one day.' My voice had a mournful spaniel's note which I disliked.

'I promise.' Tom was a totally truthful person, even sometimes when I wished he wouldn't be. I believed him. Perhaps it was Tom's honesty that now compelled him to let drop the news that Carrie's mother was also unexpectedly altering her plans and coming over from the States. To me at a suffering distance, Carrie's mother had the power and caprices of a Byzantine Empress. Much of Carrie's innate disturbance of personality was laid by Tom at her door. Carrie's fear of having children for example:

'Can you wonder with the sort of mother that she had, that she doesn't want to take on the role herself?'

'Why don't you adopt a Vietnamese orphan *pour encourager?*'

Tom looked reproachful. Vietnamese orphans were not subjects for humour. I was well aware of that. My own programme on the subject had been deadly serious. He also looked reproachful now when I murmured how convenient it must be for Carrie to have Tom with her after all to help stave off her mother's onslaughts. But I did not pursue the point.

That night was perhaps the tenderest we had ever known. It was also a whole night. I do not know what story, if any, Tom told Carrie. She was quite forgotten by us both, along with everything else.

The next morning at breakfast I told Tom all about Mother Ancilla and the Order's inheritance and Rosabelle's will and her intention to leave the land away from the Order. I did not, of course, mention poor crazy Sister Edward's accusation. Then, out of nowhere, or so it seemed at the time, we quarrelled violently about Rosa's right to give away the convent lands. I felt buffeted by a series of prejudices, my own and his. On the one hand Tom had clearly not overcome his innate revulsion for convents, nuns and their like. The words 'black crows', although not spoken again, were implicit in several of his remarks. On the other hand, he criticised anew a social system which allowed an individual – Rosa – to own so much land.

I pointed out several times that Rosa's ownership was an anomaly, which it was intended that time would set right. Community ownership after all was exactly what Sir Gilbert Powerstock had in mind when he handed over the buildings to the Order. I also pointed out that the nuns had worked the lands honourably for many years – generations of them – long before Sir Gilbert bought it in fact and, like the working-class residents of the Powers Estate, were now in danger of seeing the fruit of their labours handed over to another body. All this because of an arbitrary accident of birth which gave Rosabelle Powerstock the legal – if not moral – right to do so.

'Well, she's dead now. Your old friend. So you can't argue with her,' replied Tom heatedly. 'Mind you, I still think there's something fishy about her death. A little too convenient if you ask me—'

It was those last words that did it. That, and the cruel awareness of three blank weeks in my life. A week later, I was once again driving down to Churne. It was precisely the date on which I should have been boarding a plane to Dubrovnik with Tom, I reflected, as I pressed into the deep countryside. Various skeletal trees reminded me that winter was coming. How quickly autumn passed! Like every pleasure, it seemed momentary.

It was dark when I arrived at the convent. The same small hedgehog of a nun let me in at the gates. On the telephone I had been brief and reserved to Mother Ancilla. I merely told her that after all I had decided to accept her offer of a few weeks' relaxation at Blessed Eleanor's. To the curious, it might be hinted that I was contemplating a programme on women in religious orders in the modern world, i.e. post Vatican II.

'I am not sure that we are the best example of such changes,' said Mother Ancilla drily down the telephone. 'A great deal of prayer and thought has persuaded us that to move with the times is not necessarily to move according to the will of God. Or indeed the intentions of Our Blessed foundress.'

'Precisely. A balanced programme. In other words, it takes all sorts.'

I did not see Mother Ancilla that evening. The girls had already eaten. The small nun – Sister Damian – brought me supper on a tray in the Nuns' Parlour. The food was delicious. Each dish not only tasted good but was also exquisitely presented, reminding me of food in Japan. Later Sister Damian took me to the guest corridor. Botticelli (a Virgin), Titian (a Madonna with Child) and Fra Angelico (an Annunciation) were represented on the walls. By the bed I observed two books. One, bound in black leather, turned out to be the Treasury of the Blessed Eleanor, a work whose name if not its contents, was familiar to me. The other, still in its dust jacket, was the recent autobiography of a prominent Roman Catholic. I knew him from a rather unsuccessful programme of mine about birth control.

Under the circumstances, I picked up the Treasury of Blessed Eleanor.

I read: 'As a Tower points towards heaven, so should a man build his whole life in the direction of God. Yet even the highest Tower can never touch the sky; nevertheless man by the grace of God and his own Faith may expect to reach heaven one day. This is the supreme mercy of God, to set man higher than his highest buildings, to make of him a living Tower who will one day touch the sky.'

Towers clearly obsessed Blessed Eleanor. She had been born a French princess and briefly married in youth to an ageing English king. Childless widowhood had clearly suited her; she had made no effort to marry again, but had retired thankfully to Churne Palace which formed part of her marriage jointure. To the palace she had affixed the buildings of a large convent, and founded the Order of the Tower of Ivory.

It wasn't quite clear if that name actually dated from the lifetime of the Blessed Eleanor. There was some suggestion that she had already thought of commemorating her own name. Would the nuns have been called Queen Eleanor's Own, I wondered, as a modern regiment is named for royalty? Be that as it might, the o.t.i., as it had become, was certainly a very old foundation in Mother Ancilla's words. Even the vicissitudes of the Reformation period, the years of persecution, had been overcome without extinguishing the Order altogether. The Order itself transferred to Belgium, the buildings, less mobile, transferred to the ownership of a friendly Catholic-sympathising family. Then in the happier times of the nineteenth century and Catholic Emancipation, the o.t.i. was ready to flourish on English soil all over again.

As Reverend Mother, Blessed Eleanor continued to inhabit Churne Palace, leaving her nuns to the somewhat lesser state of their convent. Even her retreats had not exactly been taken in the bosom of the community. That was where the tower – Blessed Eleanor's Retreat – came in. Now all that was left standing of the ancient foundation, it had originally been constructed slightly apart from the convent for a sinister reason. Outside its extra thick walls, Rosa had ghoulishly assured me, the screams of the Blessed Eleanor, as she scourged herself remorselessly in penance for her sins, could not be heard.

'She did not want to be rescued from herself,' Rosa went on, large eyes opened wide. She loved to impress me with the more horrific details of her Faith. I shivered. It reminded me too vividly of the details of poor Rosa's own death: and I was not ready to think about those tonight. I should have to think about them and many other things tomorrow.

Let the Blessed Eleanor, dead for so many years, rest. And Rosa too. *Requiescant in pace.* But I could not wrench my thoughts so easily away from the pair of them. It came back to me, unbidden, that the Blessed Eleanor too had died in her tower. In her case there had been an Arthurian deathbed, with the dying woman carried to the tower by six black nuns, and laid on the stone flags.

I could not resist checking the story in the brief biography of the saint at the back of her Treasury. Yes, I was right. And there was something else too which I had forgotten. 'And then our blessed foundress called for her royal robes, the robes of a Queen of England and a Princess of France, and they brought them to her, whereon the lions and the lilies were splendidly entwined. Now good sisters attire me, she commanded them. And they wondered that she who had given up the riches of the world so willingly should call for them in the hour of her death. But she reproved them for their lack of understanding, saying, "Is it not thus in my finest raiment that I should go to meet my bridegroom, the King of Heaven? . . ." ' And so on, till the Blessed Eleanor with a great many last words and admonitions and pious ejaculations, finally expired. Leaving her body to perform those necessary miraculous feats of healing which ensured her beatification in the nineteenth century.

I felt rather more warmly towards the Blessed Eleanor after learning that she had insisted on dying dressed up in full royal gear. Personally, I was not deceived by the excuse she gave the nuns. Once a queen, always a queen. She wanted to sport those lions and lilies once more. Otherwise why preserve them all those years?

My attention was caught by something outside the narrow world of my own thoughts. Far away there was a small distinct sound. The sound of a door opening and shutting. No, the sound of swing doors being gently helped to close. There were two swing doors to the left and right of the guest corridor. One led to the children's dormitories and the other to the vast nuns' wing. That was quite an unknown area to me. Nevertheless I assumed it included a stairway directly to the chapel.

Then why was someone attempting to leave the nuns' wing as silently as possible, in order to descend to the chapel by the visitors' staircase? For I could now hear distinct soft steps on the flight outside my door.

It made no sense. It was not particularly late by my metropolitan standards. But it was extremely late by the standards of the convent. The whole place was plunged in darkness, except for the occasional light reflecting from a corridor window where the children slept. Moreover the night owl, whoever she was, was not moving in that busy rapid fashion of all the nuns, intent on not wasting time in the service of God. She was taking step by step very carefully, stopping occasionally as though to listen for any extraneous sounds.

I waited until I reckoned she must have reached the side door of the chapel. On an impulse, and without in any way thinking of what I was doing, I opened the door of my room and slipped out as silently as I could. I too ventured quietly, slowly, down the winding stairs. I touched the oak door to the chapel. It was not latched and pushed open in my hand. It made no sound at all as it swung forward.

At first the chapel seemed to be totally dark except for the red light of the sanctuary lamp, hanging in front of the altar. Then I realised that a group of candles were burning unevenly in front of a statue on my left. Some patronal feast day or other. I picked up one of the candles off its little spike and held it in front of me. I steadied it, and waited for my eyes to grow accustomed to the gloom. I was quite sure I was not alone in the chapel, that the mysterious visitor could not have left by any other door, and must still be lurking in front of me in the shadows.

The strangeness of her silence grew. Why did she not speak? Or at least make some signal. As fear, for the first time, began to catch up with me, there was a rush of cold air behind me and my candle went out. At the same time I put my hand down against the first wooden pew to steady myself. I found my hand touching warm flesh.

I screamed.

5

Unnatural lives

Shortly after my scream, two things happened. Someone or something rushed past me into the chapel from the outside, by the route I had used, out by the nuns' door and away.

The flesh turned out to be a face turned up towards mine in a rather dazed way. There was a nun kneeling at the end of the pew I had touched.

'Miss Shore,' said the nun in a low voice, 'I'm sorry if I startled you.'

'Who was that?'

A rustle. The nun rose to her feet. I could not see her face and did not recognise her voice.

'I'm Sister Agnes.'

'No, who was that? The other person who rushed past us.' I was still trembling and could not let go of the pew. 'Who blew out the candle?'

'There was no-one else here, Miss Shore; see, the chapel is empty.' Deftly Sister Agnes took the candle from my shaky hand and relit it at the shrine. I saw that the statue was of the adult Jesus pointing to a large red heart prominent on his breast. Sacred Heart of Jesus. *Sacré Cœur!* I felt like exclaiming it aloud as a relief to my feelings.

'I've been on duty in St Aloysius' dormitory, the big dormitory. I came here on my way down to say my night prayers. I'm sorry to have disturbed you.'

'Down the visitors' staircase?' I enquired sharply. If Sister Agnes was surprised at my inquisitorial tone, she did not show it. But she did take a moment to reply. Then she said easily:

'It is quicker that way than going back into the nuns' wing and all the way round by our own stairs. I'm making a novena to the Sacred Heart of Jesus,' she added.

'Then I'm sorry that I disturbed *you*, Sister Agnes,' I answered politely. I was recovering my poise. 'I will leave you to your prayers and peace.'

With as much dignity as I could muster I turned to go back up the winding staircase to my little room, which now seemed like a haven compared to the rustling chapel.

'Let me put on the stair light for you,' said Sister Agnes. 'No wonder you were frightened. We nuns get used to the darkness here in the chapel.'

Sister Agnes stepped swiftly ahead and flipped a switch outside the door. Light flooded the stairs. Enough light to show me an alcove at the bottom of the stairs. It was sufficiently large to conceal a person who might shrink back into it. A person who knew they were being followed and did not want to be seen.

For of course Sister Agnes could not be telling the truth. There was no question of that. There was no way in which she could have slipped out of the children's wing, down the visitors' stairs and reached the pew to be kneeling there calmly and silently ahead of me. Her story was implausible from many angles. For one thing there had not been enough time. For another, the mysterious prowler had definitely come from the nuns' not the children's wing. In any case, if Sister Agnes had arrived from the big dormitory why did she not use the ordinary front staircase to the main chapel entrance, past the refectory?

Last of all, there had been another human being there with us, someone as yet without a face, behind me in the alcove, who blew out my candle before beating a fast retreat to the nuns' part of the building. Ergo: she was a nun. Ergo: Sister Agnes must have seen her over my shoulder, her eyes accustomed to the darkness, my candle held high. Ergo: Sister Agnes was lying.

All of this occupied my mind as I passed back up the staircase to my room.

My last sight of Sister Agnes was of an upturned face wearing an expression of gentle concern. She reminded me of someone. Then I realised that she resembled a Murillo I had once admired of St Agnes with her lamb, the saint as a charming young creature with dark eyes and loosely playing locks. Perhaps it was that resemblance which inspired my new friend to choose the name of Agnes in religion. I had no idea what the inspiring virtues of St Agnes might be beyond a weakness for lambs like Mary in the nursery rhyme. Or was that merely a play on her Latin name? In any case it was tempting to think that Sister Agnes had secretly been prompted by human vanity. I was still thinking of the story of the Blessed Eleanor and her royal robes. It struck me that Sister Agnes must have been a pretty woman once.

Later, when the door of my room was safely shut, it occurred to me further that Sister Agnes probably still was a pretty woman – under that confining coif and veil. It was a commonplace at Blessed Eleanor's that one could never tell the real age of nuns. The tell-tale throats and foreheads were securely hidden. From my brief glimpse of her, I put Sister Agnes at no more than thirty. The thought of that motionless figure in the pew, waiting, remained with me as I fell asleep.

There was no doubt that the life of a nun was an unnatural one. At the age of thirty an attractive unmarried woman like Sister Agnes would be better employed meeting her married boss after hours from the office than keeping lonely trysts in a chapel. At the age of thirty, I myself had been doing just that. With the great Cy Fredericks himself, my married boss at Megalith. He had not of course been quite so great in those days. But he had been married all right. With all the heartbreak of the relationship, I doubt if I should ever have emerged as Jemima Shore, Investigator, without his help. It was not a case of string-pulling. He was just naturally infectious. You could not help catching confidence off him, like a cold.

There was no doubt that the life of a nun was an unnatural one. I drifted into sleep.

'I expect you feel that we all lead unnatural lives here, Jemima,' said Mother Ancilla the next morning, in her tiny study. It was her no-nonsense, head-of-the-school tone.

'I wouldn't say that exactly, Mother,' I replied carefully. 'From my time here I respect the logic of your existence. Even if I don't share in it.'

'I assumed that to be so. Otherwise you wouldn't be here' – even brisker. 'But that wasn't my point. I was referring to the fact that our lives do have an order, an order of their own. Which is not the slightest bit unnatural, for two reasons. First it is an order dedicated to the service of God. We are convinced that as best we may, we are carrying out God's will for *us* on earth. Secondly, it is not unnatural because we are all here voluntarily. Of our own free will.'

I received a slight jolt.

'You look surprised, my child. But what I am saying is perfectly true. We are not living in the Middle Ages. A vocation is a difficult thing to assess of course. Only Almighty God can truly see into our hearts. But we do our best to choose the members of our community with care, even today when vocations are so much rarer. That is God's will too, and we must accept it.' (But I got the impression that Mother Ancilla might have a thing or two to say to God on the subject when the twain finally encountered each other.) Meanwhile, she was marching on:

'Sometimes of course, in spite of all our precautions, our long probationary period of postulancy and novitiate, we are just plainly mistaken. Or a nun is mistaken about her vocation. And then she is released from her vows and returns into the world. You may remember Beatrice O'Dowd from your time here. She was a nun for fifteen years, and left us last year. We regretted it but we did not try to stand in her way.' All the same I got the impression that Beatrice O'Dowd, like God, was not in Mother Ancilla's best books.

'And Rosabelle – Sister Miriam?' I was thinking of Tom. What, no incarcerated nuns, no immured and helpless victims, no white faces behind grilles?

'Exactly. Sister Miriam never asked to be released from her vows. Even when she had her nervous breakdown, she begged the community not to reject her.'

I had to believe all that she said.

'Tell me about some of the younger nuns here,' I replied, changing the subject. 'I must know everything possible about the community if I am to help you. Do they not feel, well, restless, with all the changes in the modern world? Someone like,' I appeared to search for a name, 'Sister Agnes, for example.'

Mother Ancilla's eyes met mine, level, watchful.

'Ah, I see you have noticed the resemblance then. I wondered whether you would.'

'The resemblance?'

'Sister Miriam. They were first cousins – although of course Sister Agnes is considerably younger. She was born a Campion, Agnes Campion when she was at school here. She did not change her name in religion, which is of course rare in our Order. In fact,' Mother Ancilla added rather crossly, 'it used not to be allowed. Our Blessed Foundress . . .' She rolled her eyes to heaven, but so automatically that I felt her mind was distinctly on earth. 'Our Blessed Foundress commanded us to throw away all earthly things in her rule, including the names our parents had given us.'

'While keeping her own?'

'Royalty. That's different.' Mother Ancilla swept on without embarrassment. 'A symbol for leaving our own houses for the house of God. There was a technical relaxation of the rule last year' – Mother Ancilla managed to cram an extraordinary distaste into the word 'technical' – 'but I must say I was surprised when Sister Agnes took advantage of it.' After that Mother Ancilla's roving mind abandoned the subject of Sister

Agnes's unexpected independence and returned to that of Rosabelle: 'The resemblance is of course much more marked in the religious habit. The eyes are so similar, don't you think? Sister Agnes had much darker hair, really jet black. Such a pretty child, her Spanish blood—'

I felt the subject of the ancestry of the Campions looming once more and said hastily:

'I did sense something familiar.' And so I had. 'But of course I never saw Rosabelle after she became a nun. I only heard indirectly that she had joined the community.' And that, in its own way, was true too.

Hadn't there been a letter? A long, long letter, all very earnest. In which Rosabelle examined herself and her problems in her small neat handwriting for page after page. She was in effect consulting me as to whether she should enter the convent. I knew it. Her father had recently died, she wrote, and she felt herself to be alone. Alone that is, except for the love of God. And – me. My friendship. An outsider. Not even a Catholic. I would be able to bring a fresh eye to it all: I had such a clear mind. And I would remember all our discussions on the subject in time gone by.

Yes, there had been a letter. And I had not answered it. Time gone by. It had arrived some time during my second year at Cambridge, when I was in the throes of enjoying that coveted place. Won with such grim concentration, it was now to be savoured. I had put the letter aside: Rosa and her problems seemed as remote as the time of the Blessed Eleanor.

Later I heard by chance from a cousin of hers at Cambridge, Celia Campion, a cheerful type, product of another convent school and rather improbably reading Maths: Rosabelle Powerstock had entered Blessed Eleanor's. Or as Celia put it, 'Cousin Rosa has taken the jolly old veil.'

'Mother Ancilla,' I said, 'I imagine that I am free to wander as I please while I'm here, to talk to whom I please, to ask what questions I like.'

'But of course, dear Jemima.' Mother Ancilla threw up her hands. 'That's what you are here for. An outsider's eye to see clearly what perhaps we, so close to it all, have missed.'

'In that case I think I should try to talk to several of the nuns singly, on the excuse of my television programme of course, try and feel my way round a bit.' That seemed to Mother Ancilla an excellent plan. Why not start tonight? Nothing wrong with that either. It was, she pointed out, the Feast of All Saints and thus a whole holiday. This evening there would be Solemn Benediction in the chapel which I might like to attend? Yes, I would like to attend it, the music at Blessed

Eleanor's being a speciality not to be missed. Afterwards the children would be watching a film – *The Sound of Music*, as a matter of fact. Such a lovely uplifting film. Had I ever interviewed Julie Andrews? No, what a pity – but any member of the community would be free for a chat.

In this way I had intended to ask to see Sister Edward. I thought I might just as well grasp the nettle of her hysteria at the beginning of my investigations, rather than let an unpleasant and fundamentally rather pointless interview hang over me. I shall never understand what impulse led me to substitute the name of Sister Agnes for that of Sister Edward. I certainly did not believe in such split second decisions being manifestations of some divine plan. More likely it was something in Mother Ancilla's manner, a conviction that she was unwilling to discuss Sister Agnes, which prompted me.

Besides I was already falling half in love with my own cover story of a programme about women in orders. Why not, after all? Once I had cleared up Mother Ancilla's little problem for her. From the point of view of television, Sister Edward would be quite hopeless. But Sister Agnes now, so calm in a confused situation as I had already discovered. In her appearance, come to think of it, there was more than a hint of Audrey Hepburn in *A Nun's Story*. I should have remembered that I was supposed to be on holiday from my programme and not listened to the whisperings of the television devil.

Under the auspices of Solemn Benediction, the chapel seemed to be involved in some vast royal wedding service. The priests wore heavy white robes traced with gold and silver. Great golden tassels hung down from their copes. Candles filled the chapel, a series of bright tiers, which it must have taken the sacristan nun a laborious age to light. How different the chapel seemed from the menacing darkness of the night before! As the censors were swung gravely to and fro, first to the altar, then to the congregation, the heavy fruity smell of incense began to permeate the air. It would linger, I knew, in the still air of the chapel, long after those bridal candles were extinguished, and Sister Agnes knelt alone in the darkness before the sanctuary lamp, saying her novena.

> Sweet Sacrament divine
> All praise and all thanksgiving
> Be every moment thine
> Sweet Sa-a-a-crament divine . . .

People talk of the purity of boys' voices in a choir. But to me that evening there was a purity and an anguish about the female voices singing, which lingered in my mind long after the voices were still, as the incense lingered in the chapel. All that was missing was the bride: no doubt each lonely heart imagined that she was the bride in the centre of this superb ritual: the bride of Christ.

The nuns knelt or stood on one side of the chapel, the girls on the other. Visitors occupied seats at the back of the school benches. I glanced across at the nuns. It was no longer true that one nun looked much like another. I was beginning to be able to distinguish them again quite easily. Sister Damian the hedgehog, Sister Clare the plump coffee-bringer, and one or two nuns who had certainly been there in my day. That was Sister Elizabeth for sure, hardly changed, Sister Liz, the famed teacher of English, for whom Wordsworth and the lyric poets occupied roles in her pantheon not much below the saints. And Sister Hippolytus, the Hippo, who stood towards history as Sister Elizabeth stood towards English. Here the long history of the convent was the thing to conjure with, preferably in terms of the many documents and records perused by Sister Hippolytus in the convent library, to which no-one else paid any attention – foolishly, in the opinion of Sister Hippolytus. Many a history lesson had been hopelessly misrouted by a casual enquiry from Rosa or myself:

'Sister, is it true that the o.t.i. isn't really an English foundation at all? But Belgian.'

'Our Belgian sister house is a post-Reformation foundation' – Sister Hippo would begin fiercely, unable to resist the bait. Nevertheless, once concentrated on such matters as the Age of the Enlightened Despots, a strict teacher in contrast to the effusive Sister Liz. I owed a lot to them both, I had come to realise ... How could the younger nuns hope to compete with these established figures, who had enjoyed all the certainty of the old-style Church? Nuns in the modern world indeed. No wonder Rosabelle had collapsed under the strain. And Sister Edward looked like following her ... I really would have to talk to Sister Edward tomorrow. It was only fair.

My chat with Sister Agnes took place in the empty guest room next to mine, by permission of Reverend Mother. She told me that I could use it as a sitting room. The décor included the Assumption by Murillo and various other scenes in the life of the Blessed Virgin Mary. Sister Agnes did indeed have a Murillo-like air as she faced me across the mock fire-place with its single electric bar. She looked both demure and collected. She did not in truth greatly resemble Rosabelle, except around the eyes, but then, as Mother Ancilla pointed out, I had never seen Rosa in her habit.

And Sister Agnes, in response to my questions, remained demure and collected throughout. She gave the impression of a cricketer who has been instructed by his captain neither to score runs nor to let a ball pass by. Yes, these were difficult times for women in religion with so many new opportunities open to their contemporaries. No, she did not feel they were *specially* difficult times: for when had the life of women in religion been easy? You did not give yourself to God expecting an easy time. And so on and so on. Nothing I could not have written down in advance for myself.

So I was surprised that when our anodyne interview was concluded, Sister Agnes did not immediately leave the room. She stood, her hands clutching the top of the ugly guest room chair, much as I had supported myself on the pew the previous night.

'Miss Shore, there is one further thing I should tell you,' said Sister Agnes in her well-modulated voice. 'You will discover nothing to your advantage here. Nothing. Do you understand me? Nothing.' Her voice was not raised a half-tone from our previous conversation and the words in themselves hardly sounded dramatic. But it was her eyes. She could not control her eyes. They were dilated, either in fear or anger, I did not know her well enough to say.

'Why don't you go home while you can?'

With this, Sister Agnes passed swiftly from the room. According to the noise of the swing doors she had gone directly to the nuns' wing. Not to the chapel this evening for her novena, unless she had taken the long way round by the nuns' staircase.

It was not until the next morning, the feast of All Souls, that I learnt of the death of Sister Edward, suddenly in her cell, during the night.

6

The Black Nun

The feast of All Souls, following All Saints, proved as doleful a day as I could remember. It even rained. The leaves in the drive ceased to scutter in the wind but congregated in sodden heaps. More leaves were driven off the dripping trees. Altogether it was a day of lamentation in the fullest tradition of the ancient faith. Now the black vestments of the priests matched with the black habits of the nuns. The girls wore short black veils over their hair in chapel in contrast to the flowing white veils of the previous feast day. The multitudinous flowers of the night before, great pyramids and obelisks of white chrysanthemums, had vanished. Whatever happened to them? A hospital, I wondered vaguely. But the nearest hospital was miles away and Churne Cottage Hospital had been shut down.

At least that question was answered a day later. I found it macabre that the same flowers, still in their festive pinnacles, were used to flank the plain wooden coffin of Sister Edward as it lay in the chapel in the days before burial.

The Commemoration of the Dead, I reflected bitterly, was a gloomy enough subject without the additional demise of a young nun from a heart attack following an asthmatic fit.

Dies Irae, Dies Illae, day of mourning, day of weeping. As the magnificent sombre words of the requiem rang out in the chapel, I thought of Mother Ancilla in savage terms. She, with the rest of the community, would probably consider it a happy coincidence that Sister Edward's poor weak heart had chosen November the second to give up the struggle for life. While her lungs still struggled for breath. Look how her coffin benefited from the flowers of the previous day's feast: Holy economy! I was in that kind of mood.

'Her medicines were all within reach,' Sister Lucy told me desperately. There were tears in her eyes. 'If only she had had the strength to take them.' Sister Lucy was the young nun who had recently succeeded old Sister Boniface as infirmarian. I was glad to see those tears in her eyes. She was human enough for that. Sister Boniface, on the other hand, sitting like an aged tortoise at the end of the dispensary, showed no emotion. I was unfair, I was being unfair, and I knew it. But I got the impression that Sister Boniface regarded the death of Sister Edward as a kind of defeat for modern stimulants.

She had apparently expressed considerable doubts as to the wisdom of dosing Sister Edward so consistently. But Dr Mayhew, who attended the convent, had been a great believer in the therapeutic power of such things.

'He said: with all these aids, there was no reason why she shouldn't lead a normal life,' Sister Lucy repeated. 'In so far as a nun's life is normal. I mean, that's what he said.' Sister Lucy was clearly in a state of great distress. Sister Boniface snorted and twitched her rosary. Her fingers were incredibly gnarled, like the roots of trees in an Arthur Rackham drawing. Arthritis: the endemic disease of ageing women living in damp conditions. Probably the nuns' quarters were not even heated – or only for one month of the year or something mediaeval like that. I shivered. Pain did not however stop Sister Boniface being as garrulous as ever.

My new mood of bitterness towards the convent and all its works had its origin in guilt. I could not rid myself of regret that I had not chosen to interview Sister Edward, as I had intended. It was not that I felt she had now taken her secrets with her to the grave or anything ridiculous like that. Just that something so chancy as a heart attack must depend on so many elements. My interview, the relief of talking to an outsider, might have even saved her from the fatal bout of asthma.

The dispensary lay just outside the infirmary which, like the convent itself, was divided into a nuns' and a children's section. Dr Mayhew had just left, after signing the death certificate. There was no doubt about it. Sister Edward had died from natural causes – if you could call anything about a nun natural, to echo the doctor's own words.

There would thus be no need for an inquest. No further tussles with the coroner, the unfriendly magnate of Churne, he who had criticised Blessed Eleanor's and Sister Edward herself so sharply after the death of Sister Miriam. That was a relief, at least. It would not have done to have the remotest suspicion of foul play or even suicide directed towards another inmate of the convent. Even supposing the coroner held his fire on this occasion – which was unlikely – the local population would not. The sidelong glances in shops to which Mother Ancilla had referred in her original letter would scarcely diminish.

As it was, Sister Edward could be placed tranquilly in her coffin – such a little coffin. But then Sister Edward herself had hardly been much taller than Sister Damian, the minuscule portress. On the whole the teaching nuns were considerably taller than the so-called lay nuns. These latter attended to the domestic duties of the convent. For the greater glory of God. And of course to free the other nuns from such menial tasks. It occurred to me how little I knew about the pathetic rabbit-like person who had escorted me that day by the statue of St Antony.

'What was her name – before?' I asked with sudden curiosity. I hoped that was a tactful way of phrasing it.

'Veronica O'Dowd,' Sister Boniface now added a sniff to a snort. 'She was in the school here since she was six years old. I knew all about her asthma. Many's the night I sat with her, choking her heart out. And soothed her. And said my rosary. She liked the click of the beads. We used to joke together. Sister Bonnie's rosary – the patent cure for asthma.'

Sister Lucy said nothing. Her silence suggested more that Sister Boniface must be allowed the licence of her great age than any form of agreement with what she said. From time to time Sister Lucy wiped her eyes surreptitiously with her handkerchief, large, white and rather masculine in type, the sort of handkerchief that all the nuns used. Then after a bit, to distract herself from Sister Boniface, she began to type up her medical notes.

Obviously as infirmarian she too must have seen a lot of Sister Edward with her chronic asthma. As a trained nurse – Sister Lucy had worked at a big London hospital before she discovered her vocation – she was certainly likely to be right in her notion of how to treat an asthmatic. Frankly, the remedies of Sister Boniface, prayers and so forth, struck me as not so far from the practices of a witch doctor. Or a witch.

Veronica O'Dowd. The name struck a bell. Hadn't the nun Mother Ancilla quoted to me as having left the convent so amicably, been called O'Dowd?

'Yes, they were sisters,' confirmed the former nurse. 'But Sister Edward was of course much younger.'

'The first and last daughters of a lovely Catholic family. Nine of them in all. Five girls and four boys – two boys priests and the first and last girls given to God. That's the way things should be,' muttered Sister

Boniface. Given to God indeed: my indignation had not altogether left me. One sister had gone back into the world after fifteen years of wasted seclusion. The other sister was dead at the age of – what? her early twenties, I would say.

'Beatrice O'Dowd should never have chosen the name of John in religion.' There was no stopping Sister Boniface now. 'I told her. It may be the name of the disciple Our Lord loved, but He certainly doesn't love nuns called John in this convent. Sister John Brodsky died in a train crash before the war – an amazing thing to happen to a nun in those days. We hardly ever went in trains. Sister John had to have false teeth and she was on her way back from the dentist. She must have been so sad to have wasted the community's money. Being on her way back. When she got to purgatory, that is.'

Sister Boniface chomped her wrinkled cheeks.

'Sister John Megève died of diphtheria. She had never been immunised, being brought up abroad. And then Sister John O'Dowd getting all these newfangled ideas and leaving us. I warned her.'

'Edward wasn't a very lucky name, either,' I said, drily.

'Stuff and nonsense,' replied Sister Boniface. 'Sister Edward Walewska joined the Order when she was sixteen. And lived to be over a hundred. As a little girl in Poland she watched Napoleon dance at a ball with her aunt, from a balcony. I knew her quite well as a child here. What do you say to that, now?'

I had nothing to say to that. Except the obvious fact that nuns under the old order of things often lived to a ripe old age. Nowadays they often died young. Or left the convent.

Nevertheless the roots of the late Sister Edward's hysteria were beginning to be uncovered. Her sister leaving the convent after, presumably, a period of indecision and doubt would have been traumatic enough. Then there was Sister Miriam's secret, her ghastly death, the coroner's public castigation. It could all have added up to a pattern of imbalance in a much stronger person. But Sister Edward had been an asthmatic since childhood. While asthma itself was frequently of nervous origin.

Naturally I wasted no thought on Sister Edward's allegation that Sister Miriam had been deliberately killed. Not even the news that Mother Ancilla had been the last person to see Sister Edward alive sent my thoughts in any particularly sinister direction. Why should it? Sister Edward had felt faint during benediction, and later retired from the nuns' supper. It was quite proper that Mother Ancilla should pay a visit to her cell after supper. The younger nun seemed sleepy but the faintness had passed. She was certainly not breathing quickly.

No-one else saw Sister Edward alive.

Whether she called out as she fought for breath in the narrow cell could not be known. Whereas the children's wing and classrooms, together with the refectory, had been built in the late twenties in red brick, the nuns' wing and the chapel had been constructed in the throes of the Victorian gothic revival. From the outside the bland modern style contrasted with the heavily arched Gothic of the convent proper. I gathered that the nuns' cells, through their swing doors, had been recreated according to a Victorian notion of a mediaeval cloister.

The walls were thick. Not as thick as the walls of Blessed Eleanor's Retreat perhaps. But the intention was the same. Noise, human noise, was not intended to intrude into the great silence of God.

The Tower of the Blessed Eleanor was also an unexpected topic of conversation that night at supper. I had decided to eat my main meals in the refectory-cum-cafeteria with the girls. I did not fancy the solemn service of the Nuns' Parlour. Sister Damian continued to enchant me, but I found Sister Clare's portly figure, labouring along with her tray, an increasing trial. Besides, I was becoming interested in the girls themselves, the girls in general and Margaret Plantaganet in particular.

Tom would like Margaret. The thought came to me, unspoken, that evening in the refectory. She was not unlike one of his devoted acolytes at the W.N.G., a girl called Emily Crispin. Emily had come forward as a helper without pay – which was just as well as the W.N.G. were as fierce in their determination to keep all their funds for the poor as, say, the Powers Estate Projectors. It subsequently turned out that Emily could well afford the sacrifice, being the daughter of a rich man, although you would not otherwise have guessed it from her demeanour – or her clothes. Margaret had the same air of secrecy about her, an individuality which had nothing to do with her name or birth. It did have something to do with her physical appearance, the long crusader's face with its helmet of straight brown hair: and her silence. Emily Crispin, I once told Tom with irritation I did not bother to hide, sits for hours at your elbow without opening her mouth, like a dog asleep.

'That explains why I always get the impression she agrees with every word I say,' Tom replied.

Margaret Plantaganet herself never spoke much at meals. She left that to her chatterbox friend Dodo Sheehy.

It was Dodo, at supper on the Feast of All Souls, who enquired: 'I wonder if anyone saw the black nun last night?' Her tone was rather bright. Dodo was such a pretty plump little thing with fair curls and a Cupid's bow mouth, that nothing she said sounded completely serious.

But I noted a wry expression on Margaret's face, a slight compression of the lips.

'Aren't all nuns black?' I responded lightly. The death of Sister Edward had not cast a notable shadow on their spirits: she was too young to have taught them. But I wanted to get the conversation away from the events of the night before.

'I'm talking about The – Black – Nun.' Dodo gave the three last words sepulchral emphasis. 'An apparition. Did you never see it when you were at the school?'

'No – wait, I do remember something vaguely. Doesn't it haunt the chapel? Or is it the tower?'

Margaret said: 'And the convent itself. Sister Miriam told us she actually saw the Black Nun when she was a girl at school.'

'She didn't tell me. It must have only bobbed up after dark. I was a day girl. You tell me.'

'Dodo, you tell.' Dodo was nothing loath. It transpired that the Black Nun was commonly held to appear shortly before or shortly after the death of a member of the community. Yes, of course, all nuns wore black, but the point of the Black Nun was that you suddenly came across a nun you didn't recognise, a nun you had never seen before. You imagined: a novice, a transfer from another convent. But the next day you heard of the death of a nun. And of course you never saw the Black Nun, that particular Black Nun again.

I burst out laughing.

'You don't believe us,' said one of the other girls at the table rather grumpily. 'But some of us saw the Black Nun three nights after Sister Miriam ran away. And that turned out to be the night she must have died.' Much chattering followed. Yes, a strange nun, a nun they had never seen before, a nun with a strange face, passing them at night, in the corridor, on their way to . . . their way to where? Why, the chapel. To make a novena to Our Lady. And that night, they learned later, Sister Miriam had given up the ghost in the tower. Surely I had to admit it all added up.

On the contrary, it all sounded deeply implausible to me. Another enigmatic novena in the middle of the night: something I was fairly sure was not allowed by the rules.

When I was informed that the Black Nun had first appeared to Blessed Eleanor herself, goodness knows how many years ago, I scoffed openly. Six black nuns were supposed to have carried her to her tower, and at the last moment a seventh unknown nun appeared. Blessed Eleanor asked the stranger who she was, and the answer came back pat: 'I am Death itself, who comes before you as a Black Nun.'

'None of that delightful story appears in the Treasury of the Blessed Eleanor,' I commented in a fairly acid voice.

'Exactly. Sister Miriam told us about it. She used to tell us ghost stories after lights out.' I was glad to hear that in one respect at least my old friend had not changed. Ghost stories and ghoulish information generally had been Rosa's speciality.

'Anyway, somebody did see the Black Nun last night,' said the grumpy girl suddenly. Blanche, Blanche Nelligan, was her name. She did not look like a Blanche, being beetle-browed with rather a bad complexion.

'Tessa Justin, that girl with plaits in the Lower IVth. I was on prefect duty in the big dormitory and Sister Agnes was doing the rounds. Suddenly young Tessa appeared, shrieking her head off, plaits flying, saying a strange nun had interrupted her in the loo. That must have been the Black Nun.'

At this we all laughed. A minute later the chairs were scraping back for grace and supper was over. I decided not to give another thought to the Black Nun. I enjoyed my solitary tray of coffee after the girls' chatter. Then I climbed up the visitors' staircase to my own retreat. I really felt that I had quite enough problems on my hands without the question of a spectral religious haunting the junior school bathrooms. The Black Nun was scarcely likely to bother me.

Once I was installed in my room and had looked at the papers on my desk, I saw that I was wrong.

'If you don't believe in the Black Nun' – so ran a typed message on a sheet of plain paper placed on top of my copy of *The Times* – 'why don't you come to the tower one night and see for yourself? Tomorrow night for example.'

There was no superscription and no signature. Jutting out from the paper, on the front cover of *The Times* I saw a photograph of Tom on the platform at his w.n.g. rally. That looked like Emily Crispin at his elbow with some papers on her lap. Neither of them looked particularly ghostly. The photograph gave me no consolation whatsoever.

7
Forewarned

In the night the wind got up. The change of noise from the steady downpour on the chapel roof to the gusts and rattling of my windows awoke me. Lying, somnolent, I was aware of some other noise quite close at hand. The guest room next to me – my temporary sitting room – was empty. Beyond that lay another guest room, also unoccupied. Beyond that the communal bathroom. If anything the noise was located in the furthest guest room, next to the bathroom. The walls here in the modern block were not particularly sound-proof. The vigorous sound of Sister Perpetua's broom scouring my bedroom regularly disturbed the peace of my sitting room.

I felt too drowsy to investigate. Besides, I needed my sleep. For I was always awake early in the convent, what with the chapel bells and the shuffle of the children going to early mass. In London I considered myself, and allowed the world to consider me, an early riser. I prided myself on my ability to take testing telephone calls at full strength from eight o'clock onwards. But I had to admit that the need to appear fresh and purposeful for a refectory breakfast at 7.45 was another matter altogether. As I drifted into sleep, I made a mental note to explore the convent grounds the next day. Such an expedition might be combined with a talk to one of the nuns. The tower above all presented an emotional problem. It might be better not to visit it for the first time after Rosa's death, at night – and alone.

In the morning I went into Churne. I had decided to buy a torch. Sister Lucy, on her way to have a prescription made up, offered me a lift. I accepted, wondering privately whether she wanted an escort to run the gauntlet of Churne. In the event, I had no time to worry about the local inhabitants. For Sister Lucy drove with a terrifying reckless-ness, amounting almost to innocence, which robbed me of all other considerations except for a desire for the safety of my own beloved Volvo. Down Churne Hill, a notorious winding black-spot, the battered Mini Traveller driven by Sister Lucy was definitely the faster vehicle of the two.

One of my winces must have attracted her attention. I was recalling the old saying, repeated by my mother, that nuns made rotten drivers because they paid too much attention to St Christopher, too little to the Highway Code. In the car driven by Sister Lucy there was not even a St Christopher to aid us – hadn't he been demoted by the Vatican? Come back, St Christopher—

'Don't worry, Miss Shore,' Sister Lucy spoke quite calmly. 'I know this car like the back of my hand.' She did not mention the hill. Then she added rather shyly: 'As a matter of fact, though I really should not mention it, this car belonged to me once. In the world, I mean. Now of course it belongs to the community. It was my dowry to the convent. All I was able to bring them.'

'That, and your skill, Sister,' I said earnestly, trying not to look out of the window.

She blushed and looked genuinely pleased. On the way back Sister Lucy confided to me that Sister Elizabeth could hardly be trusted at the wheel of the Mini, having learnt to drive late in life. It was only then I realised she had taken my compliment as referring to her skill as a driver, rather than as a nurse.

The funereal rain had blown itself out by lunch-time. Only piles of sodden leaves and pools of water on the gravel drive served to remind us of the night's storm. But clearer sharper weather was on the way. My diary reminded me to expect a full moon that night. Surely the weather often changed around the time of the full moon.

After the previous day's *Times* had been properly perused, Tom received a quick note in my familiar style: 'Darling, your speech was *good*. I'm having a holiday away from everything, your world of the (political) poor and my world of the (television) rich, and that's good too. All my love J.' I drew a heart at the end.

Yes, his speech had been good, full of honest compassion for the poor and honest indignation against the government. The poor, if they read *The Times*, would undoubtedly be pleased. The government, who undoubtedly did read *The Times*, would not. Tom could be proud of his intervention. I gave no address and allowed the letter to be posted with the rest of the children's mail. I doubted if the postmark Churne would mean anything to Tom.

The children's letters were put on a chest outside the refectory, as they had been in my day. It was amusing to note that the letters were now sealed, while the destinations could still be read by any inspector. In my day the boarders had their letters read by Mother Ancilla. According to Rosa it was a task she performed with lip-smacking thoroughness. According to Rosa, too, Mother Ancilla was not above making pointed allusions to the contents of a letter, if it suited her purpose. Rosa proceeded to organise my services as a postman; girls who wanted to write uncensored letters were urged to place them in my trustworthy hands.

'Is this quite *all right*, do you think darling?' asked my mother anxiously one day. She was enormously impressed by the whole convent set-up: and secretly adored the idea of the glamorous high-born girls with whom her own much lower-born daughter was mixing. Mother Ancilla's references to lineage found a ready audience in my mother. We had a couple of Italian princesses in the school, whose English mother had taken refuge here in the war. They were listed merely as Pia and Vittoria. And received scant shrift from us girls, as unpopular Wops, particularly when the Italian campaign was in full swing. But Mother Ancilla always gave the whole family, mother and daughters, the full rolling due of their titles. She also liked to practise the Italian learnt so many years ago in a visit to Rome as a novice. 'Principessa' was quite one of her favourite words, I decided.

'Fancy Princess Pia being descended from the Pope!' said my mother admiringly one day.

It was probably true, given the nature of early papacies. But I was already feeling a nasty instinct to put my mother in her place whenever she got a particular starry-eyed look.

'Popes don't have children,' I replied coldly. 'I should have thought even you knew that.' Fatally my mother gave way and tried to ingratiate herself with me.

'I do envy your opportunities here, Jem. You're learning such interesting things. Daddy and I sometimes wonder if you might even, well, think of *becoming* a Roman. I mean a Catholic,' she added nervously.

Either way she made it sound like a form of career like a teacher or a gym instructor. I did not deign to answer. I quelled my mother's objections to my clandestine postal service with equal use of intimidation by coldness.

Only Rosa never made use of my services. Did she *have* no boy friends, I wondered? I never enquired. Jealously, I preferred to cherish the fantasy that Rosa did not trust me to post her love notes. She told me other things about her holidays, casually, without emphasis. But the boys, with names like Marcus and Peregrine, all turned out to be cousins. On her mother's side. The Campion family, for all its ancient blood, turned out to be infinitely more prolific and thus capable of survival than the more plebeian Powerstocks.

I did ask once: 'Do you like him, Marcus?' I tried to keep the note of caring out of my voice.

'He's my cousin,' said Rosa in that blank voice she reserved for matters which she clearly felt were too obvious to need discussing. And that was that.

Looking at these letters now, laid out for inspection, I was pleased to see that some of them were boldly addressed to males. Robin Nelligan Esq., Ampleforth College, York. Jasper Justin Esq., Eton College, Windsor, Berks . . . So perhaps freedom was on the march after all. It then occurred to me that Robin and Justin were probably the brothers of Blanche and Tessa. So perhaps things had not changed so much after all. There was also an established safe ring about most of the addresses. Tom would have been full of scorn for them.

But of course it was ridiculous to suppose then as now that any really subversive letter would be left out on the chest. Rosa's letter to Alexander Skarbek for example. The nuns' letters could be distinguished by the quality of their paper – small and thin – often by the precise handwriting also, and always by the letters A.M.D.G. in the corner. That letter to Skarbek certainly did not lie out on this chest, open to curious eyes. The extent of Alex Skarbek's participation in Rosa's tragedy was still unknown to me. How had he taken the news of Rosa's death, for example, and the consequent collapse of her property hand-over scheme? The coroner's remarks had not dealt with that side of her life and death, mercifully: there had been no need to air in public the proposed handover, which had caused such pain in private. But Alex Skarbek had the reputation, at least in Tom's circles, for rigid determination. It always amused me to see how Tom and his friends of the W.N.G. derided in their opponents exactly those qualities which led to their own triumphs.

'An extremist . . . quite ruthless in manipulating people . . . thinks anything is justified so long as it advances the Project . . .' So Tom muttered indignantly, with Emily Crispin, indicating agreement by her silence, close beside him. Yet Tom's brilliance in outmanoeuvring the government on the subject of housing subsidies for one parent families was generally acknowledged to be his greatest coup on behalf of the W.N.G. I knew all about that coup: it was the over-friendly young minister on my programme who had let slip the details of what the government was going to propose. I thought Tom's action – and my own – morally justified in view of the use we made of the information. But all the same, not too scrupulous.

Alexander Skarbek: had he simply accepted the loss of his new commune, on the verge of establishment, as one of the losses of war? In this case, the war being against society?

That was an area where Mother Ancilla might be gently probed further. After that it was tempting to contact the man himself in London. One advantage of having my own programme was that no-one with an axe of his own to grind resented my approach. He always hoped to turn my platform to his own advantage.

I walked round the hockey fields in the afternoon with my old friend and teacher Sister Elizabeth. She was not aware that I also had the key to the tower in my pocket – I had requested it from Mother Ancilla. The Reverend Mother had asked for no explanation, merely handed it to me.

'The only other key is on my belt,' she said, patting a bunch of keys. 'We don't want any more – mistakes, do we?'

Sister Liz and I paraded round the hockey fields. I watched an extremely energetic black figure hurtling towards the goal with a hockey stick wielded to deadly effect: Sister Immaculata. Surely she could not still be playing hockey after all these years. I remembered what a shock it gave me to find that nuns, at the sight of a hockey field, merely looped up their black skirts, and tackled the game with their usual brisk efficiency, veils and all. The maroon coloured figures of the girls were considerably more lackadaisical in their attitude to the game.

The only other participant showing any energy at all was wearing a short black skirt, black stockings, a black jersey with a white collar and a short black veil which revealed most of her hair – luxuriant hair. A postulant. I had to look up the word in the dictionary while I was at school. Postulant: Candidate, especially for admission into religious order. Tom I suppose was a parliamentary postulant at the general election. At least I was firmly on the side of his election. I wasn't sure what I felt about this girl's candidature. From the convent's point of view, however, it was a good thing that there were still some new vocations around: now that the Order of the Tower of Ivory was not after all to be dispossessed by the Projectors.

'She's Irish,' said Sister Elizabeth, following the direction of my gaze. 'Of course.'

Sister Elizabeth was a woman for whom I had a genuine affection, nun or no nun. Her generosity of spirit, her mad enthusiasm for literature in all its forms, endeared her to me. There was a Margaret

Rutherford touch about her zest. With her flailing arms, springy walk (signally untouched by the passage of twenty-five years), and her earnestness, she really was not unlike my idea of Margaret Rutherford, supposing she had ever played the part of a nun.

Sister Liz was the only woman in the world capable of exclaiming: 'I thanked Our Blessed Lord on my knees this morning for making Wordsworth write the *Prelude* at such *length*.'

Of course as a schoolgirl I was attracted to her, just because her values did not seem totally permeated by those of the Catholic religion. We had corresponded in a desultory way after I left. 'I shall pray for you,' Sister Liz dutifully ended her letters. But I knew she prayed for sensible things like a proper understanding of *Paradise Lost* or a real appreciation of *The Waste Land*, not lost causes like my conversion.

Now we chatted easily on literary matters. The Christianity of King Lear was one topic; Sister Liz's determination to discuss James Joyce came as more of a surprise to me. Then I realised that she must have few opportunities to discuss Joyce's work. Of the two of us, it was I, not Sister Elizabeth, who shrank from discussing fully some aspects of Joyce's nature. I was uncertain where I should draw the line in order not to shock her. Sister Liz on the other hand had a kind of sublime frankness about her remarks which left nothing to the imagination. It sprang, I realised, from innocence. My own reticence was rooted in guilt.

Only the fact that our returning steps had led us to the entrance to the nuns' little cemetery made Sister Liz draw breath. We paused and, by unspoken agreement, entered through the low gate. It was an out of the way place. The girls did not come here. The seclusion was ensured by the high dark hedge surrounding the grass. Rows of plain stone crosses marked the last resting places of the community. The inscription on each was identical in form, and minimal. Sister John Brodsky o.t.i. 1900–1935. Below the name and dates: r.i.p. And that was all.

The last cross in the sequence was the one I feared. But it could not be avoided. Yes, here it was. Sister Miriam Powerstock o.t.i. 1932–1973 r.i.p.

At my side I noted that Sister Liz crossed herself. Then she held her rosary and her lips moved silently. I felt nothing, nothing at all. Then feelings did rush in, overwhelmingly, into the vacuum. I felt fiercely that there was no connection, none at all between this plain stone cross and the young girl who had once been my friend. My compassion, such as it was, was reserved for the memory of Sister Edward who would soon lie in the neighbouring earth.

'I can't accept that this is anything to do with Rosa. I don't believe Rosa is *here*, you know.' My aggressive voice rang out in the quiet graveyard.

'Mother Church would agree with you about that,' replied Sister Elizabeth mildly. 'She's not here. Only her poor tormented earthly body lies here. May God have mercy on her soul.' And she crossed herself again.

Abruptly I asked Sister Liz if she would accompany me across the fields to the tower. I pulled the key out of my pocket. It was a bright new Yale key. The key to the padlock which now secured the tower, as Mother Ancilla had instructed me. Not the ancient rusty key which had broken off during Rosa's frantic struggles to escape her self-imposed fate. By now I needed to exorcise that tower for myself, and Sister Liz with her warmth and compassion, her understanding of people beyond the narrow prescription of the convent, was the right person to accompany me. The evening's possible adventure had quite vanished from my mind.

As we skirted the fields, trying to avoid the squelching mire left by the rain, a late afternoon sun emerged from the barred clouds, illuminating the November landscape. Sister Elizabeth began to recite Wordsworth in her special faraway poetic voice, which like her walk, had not changed. Her eyes rolled in wonder as she spoke. It was as though she was receiving a direct message from the poet, line by line:

> It is a beauteous evening, calm and free
> The holy time is quiet as a Nun,
> Breathless with adoration . . .

By this time we were in sight of the tower, black, square, shorter than I remembered – oh, the shrinkings brought about by time – the sun was beginning to sink behind it. I was reminded of a card in the tarot pack: the Tower of Destruction, depicted by a tower very similar in design, out of which spilled unhappy falling people in mediaeval dress. Yes, Tower of Destruction indeed and Rosa's destruction above all. It seemed quite inappropriate under the circumstances to contemplate a late night rendezvous with some prankish schoolgirls pretending to be ghosts. I would lay my own ghost and then depart.

> Dear Child! dear Girl! that walkest with me here,
> If thou appear untouched by solemn thought,
> Thy nature is not therefore less divine;
> Thou liest in Abraham's bosom all the year . . .

Sister Elizabeth's sonorous declamation was drawing to its close.

'Somehow those last lines rather remind me of you, Jemima,' she said afterwards. There was a charming note of hope in her voice. I realised that this literary reference was the nearest Sister Liz would ever get to probing my religious beliefs. I ignored the implied question. Besides, I had an irreverent desire to laugh at the idea of television in the guise of Abraham's bosom – Megalithic House. In any case, I was not untouched by solemn thought, rather the contrary. The sight of the Tower of Destruction was more upsetting than I had anticipated.

After a silence, Sister Elizabeth said simply: 'I love that poem. I first learnt it as a girl. I am not sure it did not influence me towards the Church, and later my vocation. The idea of a nun, breathless in adoration. So calm. So free. I'm a convert you know. I was received into the Church when I was twenty-one.'

'Quiet as a nun,' I repeated. To me they sounded ironic words. Where was the quiet in this seething community of neurotic women, many of them frustrated in one way or the other, quite out of touch with all that was good in the modern world? Many of them would do better to return to the world and find their own peace, than reside in this false quiet. As Beatrice O'Dowd had done. Only someone like Sister Elizabeth with her untouchable love of literature probably escaped a measure of frustration.

We unlocked the padlock – new, like the key – and entered the tower. The air was dank. Since the ground floor was windowless it was also dark. By the light of the open door we began to climb up the wooden ladder to the first floor. We went in single file. I let Sister Elizabeth lead the way. On the first floor there would be one window high up in the far wall, overlooking the farm lands beyond. You could neither see the convent from the tower nor be seen from it. A further window in the first floor, on the convent side, had been blocked up in the nineteenth century.

Although the tower was officially out of bounds, in my day at school it had been a fashionable dare to purloin the conspicuously large key from the portress, and pay an illicit visit to Nelly's Nest. I recalled some furniture, a wooden table, a large chair, a rocking-chair, I thought, an empty fireplace. Even in summer the thick stone walls gave off an unpleasant atmosphere of damp and chill.

'The community came and tended to the tower. After it happened,' Sister Liz observed over her shoulder as we climbed. She meant: you won't find anything distressing here, as in the graveyard. She said aloud: 'And no-one has been here since.'

I believed her. Once again my feelings had frozen. I gazed up at Sister

Elizabeth's retreating black back, her neat black feet with their goloshes over black strap shoes, black stockings, black skirts looped up at the sides for walking the muddy fields. Sister Elizabeth panted slightly. The door banged to downstairs, removing our light. But at the same moment Sister Elizabeth reached the trap door and pushed it open. She poked her head through the trap door.

There was an audible gasp and Sister Elizabeth stopped quite still on the last rung of the ladder.

Then there was silence. She did not move.

'Sister Liz—' I said after a minute, anxiously.

'It's all right, my child,' she replied, rather heavily. 'Just that I had rather a shock.'

'What *is* it?' I could see nothing from behind her.

'Nothing really. It must be the children. A silly practical joke.'

I was going frantic. Much more slowly, Sister Elizabeth lumbered up the last rung and vanished into the room. I clambered up after her at speed. When I entered the room, Sister Elizabeth was leaning one hand on the table and panting.

The only other piece of furniture in the room was a large wooden rocking-chair. Just as I remembered, in fact. Draped in the chair and over it was a nun's black habit. Including a veil and rosary and all the other accoutrements you would need if you were to dress yourself up as a nun. Or to dress yourself if you were a nun.

At first glance there was certainly the impression of a black nun sitting there in the chair. A faceless nun. But the impression did not outlast the first second. We were looking at a set of empty and thus lifeless black clothes. Except—

'No shoes or stockings,' I thought suddenly, remembering my glimpse of Sister Elizabeth's stocking and goloshes.

'The children. It must be the children. They have an innocent sense of humour. They don't realise how distressing these things can be,' Sister Elizabeth muttered. She made no move to touch the clothes, I noticed. 'I'll tell Mother Ancilla and someone will fetch the habit in the morning.'

I thought: Yes. The children. The children – with their innocent sense of humour – had prepared some kind of reception for me tonight. A sort of religious scarecrow. And I, by my early visit, had sprung their trap.

I wrinkled my nose. In the damp air, another smell disturbed me. A smell which should not have been there. For a moment I could not quite place it, although it was one of the most familiar smells of my urban life. I gazed around and my eye fell on the empty fireplace. Not quite empty. At the back of the fireplace, carelessly thrown down, were a host of cigarette stubs. No attempt had been made to conceal them.

I wondered if the nun's habit which was to greet me tonight had after all been intended to be empty. Maybe I should have to pay a return visit to the tower. It was an unlikely ghost who smoked Gauloises. And in such quantity. My spirits rose. Forewarned was, traditionally, forearmed. The Black Nun, habit and all, could expect a somewhat cynical reception from me in the late hours of the evening.

8
Secret witnesses

Supper that night in the refectory was a subdued meal. I was getting used to the tactiturn ways of Margaret Plantaganet. But Dodo's normally busy chatter was also absent. Alcohol did not play an enormous part in my life: I never drank spirits if I could help it, and I was not one of those who needed a drink or two to go on the television. In fact I avoided the pre-programme drinking as far as possible, leaving the traditional hospitality to my nubile aide, Cherry: 'Jemima's just on her way. And now won't you have another drink?' Consequently up till now I had not really noticed the total absence of alcohol from my life in the days at the convent.

Tonight I really felt the need for a drink at dinner. A carafe of wine, I reflected, would have loosened all our tongues. I remembered reading somewhere of American nuns in a newly emancipated Order who wore make-up and smoked and drank. How Americans exaggerated! Make-up did seem quite unnecessary in the brides of Christ, or perhaps that was just my Puritan streak. As for smoking – well, I had no particular feelings either way. As a non-smoker working in a profession of professional smokers, I felt more sorry for them and their addiction than anything else. But alcohol, now . . . No doubt conversation in the American refectory (if they still had a refectory, that is, not a smart French restaurant) improved as a result.

Dodo and I exchanged polite news on the subject of my contemporary of the same surname, Dora Sheehy. Dodo turned out to have been named for her: 'Both of us Theodora,' she said, with a return to her old cheerfulness. 'But who could stick a name like that? She was Dora and I'm Dodo. Aunt Dora held me at my baptism, you know, she was my godmother. And why she didn't protest against another innocent child being lumbered with a name like Theodora I shall never know.'

'And Dora is now—?' I enquired delicately. On the familiar form I expected to hear: married to a doctor, probably Irish like herself, and mother of five children. 'I haven't heard from her in years,' I added untruthfully.

I had never heard from Dora Sheehy. There had been a brief competition between us – in school terms – for the friendship of Rosabelle. When I arrived at Blessed Eleanor's, Dora Sheehy was allegedly Rosabelle's best friend. And when I left, Rosabelle was unquestionably mine. But Dora, as I remembered her, had been a dull and rather sycophantic girl, whose good quality from Rosa's point of view, had been her subservience.

I much preferred Dodo, blonde curls, giggles and all. She had confided to me that she had ambitions to get into television once she had left the convent. I was not a bit surprised. One of the odd things about Blessed Eleanor's was how few of the girls had that ambition. At visits to ordinary schools for lectures or brains trusts, to say nothing of encounters with my friends' growing children, I was quite used to the sidling approaches of pretty teenagers: 'Is there an exam or something I can take?' Dodo at least was conforming to that norm.

'But she was *Sister* Theodora,' said Dodo. 'We talked of her the other night.'

'Sister Theodora of the Angels,' put in Margaret. It was her first remark of the evening. 'Murdered in Africa.'

I felt curiously put down.

The plates were mainly empty. It would soon be the time for the traditional scraping back of our chairs and grace. Blanche Nelligan said, with a sudden very sweet smile, which lit up her heavy face:

'Would you come and have coffee with us for a change? In St Joseph's Sitting Room. We're allowed to entertain if we provide the coffee.'

'And we shall keep the odious Fourth Formers *out*,' added Dodo with a grimace. 'By fair means or foul.'

I realised that the restraint at dinner had been due to a genuine uncertainty as to whether I would accept the invitation. I was touched.

'Our coffee is much *much* better than Sister Clare's,' contributed Imogen Smith, blushing. I knew little about her so far except that she was Blanche's best friend, and always sat next to her.

'Immo brought it back from London on Sunday. Swiped from her mother's store cupboard.'

'But we'll pay her back of course—'

'Unless we decide that property is theft' – Margaret, with a rare grin.

'Oh, please let me—' I began feebly, feeling for my hand-bag. It was not there. Like the carafe of wine, that other accompaniment of life in a London restaurant, it seemed to have no place in the refectory.

'Actually the nuns don't exactly economise on things like coffee,' remarked Blanche later, pouring me an enormous mug right up to the brim with great care. It was made of thick grey china. There was no milk, and a plastic cup of white sugar had one plastic spoon sticking up out of it.

The coffee in point of fact was a great deal less nice than that provided by Sister Clare. I also thought rather wistfully of the delicate matching china in which her coffee appeared, white traced with green in a Chinese pattern. A beaker of hot milk, a jug of cold; coloured sugar crystals, tiny silver spoons – they were actually Apostle spoons, I was enchanted to notice. The tray was lined with a cloth embroidered, as only nuns could embroider, in an exact silk replica of the china's pattern. It was all no doubt arranged to the greater glory of God. But at the same time it was most delightful for mere mortals to behold.

'Yes, this is a pretty plush convent,' remarked Imogen. 'Basins in our rooms and carpets.'

'Those are your rooms,' I felt bound to point out. 'I doubt if the nuns have basins and carpets in their cells.'

'But we pay for them, don't we?' Blanche sounded plaintive. 'Out of our school fees.'

'Or rather our parents pay for them,' Dodo as usual put more energy into her complaints. 'And don't they let us know about it . . . The last time Mummy came here she told me my room was more luxurious than the room in the hotel Daddy took her to in France for a holiday. And that was a hotel *très confortable* in Michelin. I said, if that was the case I would go to France, save the school fees, much nicer and she could come here for a holiday with Daddy.'

'We are *assez confortable* here, Miss Shore, you must admit,' Margaret interrupted. 'But that's not the point. The point is, how comfortable are the nuns? How comfortable should they be?'

Her voice, the intensity of her gaze, gave the remark considerable authority. The slightly frivolous conversation ceased. We all began to talk about Holy Poverty, at once and in different ways. Holy Poverty, and what that meant. Vocations, and what they meant. There was one insistent theme: surely nuns were better off nursing in Africa, refusing to abandon the sick, nursing to their last gasp (witness Sister Theodora of the Angels) than teaching a lot of upper-class brats in an over-plushy convent. The last vivid words were contributed by Dodo. I got the impression that she was repeating something once said by someone else. Before I could pursue the matter, Margaret stopped the conversation again.

'Your friend Sister Miriam didn't agree with all this luxury, Miss Shore. She wanted to leave the convent lands to the poor.'

I was quite astonished by her words.

To begin with, I was amazed that these girls knew of Rosa's crazy plan. Admittedly they seemed to have been her intimates, what Miss Jean Brodie would have called her *crème de la crème*. How many other people at the convent had known? It opened up a whole new field of enquiry. How many of the nuns had known? Wretched Sister Edward must have known something, hence her wild accusation of Mother Ancilla. The enigmatic Sister Agnes, she of the soulful Murillo eyes, had she known? A Campion cousin, too, according to Mother Ancilla. Although the property was inherited from the Powerstock side of the family, there could have been cousinly confidences on the subject.

But there was a second point. For all their intimacy with Sister Miriam, the girls had got hold of a slightly garbled story. Rosa, according to Mother Ancilla, was determined to give away the convent lands. As soon as possible. No question of waiting for her own death. As for the question of a will, it had been the existence of Sister Miriam's unaltered will, made at the time she entered the convent, which had ensured the receipt of the property by the community.

Was Margaret testing me in some way? My instinct was at work again. I felt myself on the brink of a piece of valuable knowledge. If I trod carefully enough, I might arrive at it.

'But she didn't. She didn't leave the convent lands to the poor,' I said.

'How do you know she didn't?' Margaret, smooth, definitely up to something.

'Here we all are. Her will, I gather, for what it's worth, carried out her father's intentions, and automatically entrusted the land to the community.'

'That was her original will,' said Margaret. She let the words sink into the air of St Joseph's Sitting Room, with just enough emphasis on the word 'original' for her meaning, also, to sink very slowly but surely into my mind. I bent to my coffee, fastening my lips reluctantly to the thick edge of the china. It was by now cold and rather disgusting. But I wanted time to think. I therefore treated the rite of drinking Blanche's coffee with all the respect that would have been due to Sister Clare's superior brew.

I looked round. The furniture of St Joseph's Sitting Room did not offer much for inspection. A battered record player was the chief sign that it was a room for girlish recreation. There was a large sofa, equally battered, pushed to the back of the room, as though no-one ever sat on it. Otherwise with its pictures – Leonardo's Virgin of the Rocks, Botticelli, Fra Angelico? – I was beginning not to distinguish them in their heavy gold frames – it might have been a nuns' sitting room. The girls' notion of the unfair luxury in which they lived suddenly seemed a little pathetic to me. Once again, I got the impression that someone outside had been at work influencing their notions concerning poverty and distribution of wealth. It could have been Rosabelle herself, of course. Then Rosa had changed. I could imagine Rosa as a secret fanatic – mysterious Rosa as I used to call her – but not as a proselytiser.

At least copies of the *Daily Telegraph* and one copy of the *Daily Express* – banned in my day – were to be seen, indicating progress. The fact that they were several days old was less encouraging. Just as letters to males on the chest had seemed encouraging, until I discovered they were mainly to brothers. The *Tablet* was still the most prominent magazine displayed. Did they read the liberal press? It would have been good to have found a copy of the *Guardian* or even the *New Statesman*.

'Sister Miriam told us she was going to make another will,' confided Dodo in a rush. My long silence had had the desired effect.

'And then she died. And it was too late.'

I caught Blanche looking at Imogen. There was a nervous intensity about Blanche's normally rather impassive gaze. I thought I saw Imogen give her a very slight shake of the head. I was not quite sure. Margaret said nothing. Like me, she was contemplating her coffee cup.

'I don't think you should exaggerate all this,' I said carefully. 'If Sister Miriam wanted to give the lands to the poor, there was really nothing to stop her.' As Mother Ancilla had found – or very nearly found – to her cost.

'But if she was going to, well, put an end to it all, then she might want to leave the lands straightaway to the poor. In her will. No time for handing it over' – Dodo again.

I was in a quandary. On the one hand the girls had the whole matter ridiculously upside down. Rosabelle had unquestionably intended to hand over the lands. Rosabelle had not intended to die. It was the latter tragedy which had frustrated the former plan. The will, so convenient from the point of view of Mother Ancilla, was a rogue element coming out of the past. On the other hand, there was clearly more information to be gleaned from the girls about Rosa's state of mind shortly before her death.

Margaret's remark had been calculated, I was sure of it. I was beginning to think a great deal more about Margaret Plantaganet was calculated than met the eye.

'The sick, the mad if you like, don't always act very consistently,' I went on. 'I shouldn't worry about Sister Miriam's will if I were you. She probably told another lot of girls that she was going to leave the land to a lot of cats and dogs—'

'Sister Miriam was fond neither of cats nor of dogs, Miss Shore.' If Margaret had not sounded bland, she would have sounded rude. I was reminded a little of the stone-walling technique of Sister Agnes in my interview with her. 'And she did not talk to another lot of girls. We were her girls—' Ah, the Miss Brodie touch. 'Because she knew that we shared her concern about the way wealth is shared out. For the real poor.'

All the girls started talking at once:

'The third world—'

'As much food in a *day*—'

'No running water—'

'The convent grounds alone would house a whole estate of workers' families, hundreds of them.' It was Dodo's voice which won out. 'Instead of which upper-class drones like ourselves play hockey on them.'

I had a ghastly feeling during this cacophony that the girls were indeed great fans of my programme. Just as Mother Ancilla had said. And not only the Powers Estate investigation, the so-called Powers Mad programme. What on earth was the title of the programme on starvation at home and abroad? Food for Thought – And Nothing Else. I had interviewed Tom in the course of it to give the work of the w.N.G. in that area a deserved little puff. Now this conversation Tom would enjoy. No established complacency here.

The evening bell put an end to these thoughts. I suddenly realised that Sister Agnes was standing at the door of the sitting room. I had no idea how long she had been there. Unlike most of the nuns, her progress did not seem to be marked by either a rustle or a jangle. No doubt it was the graceful nature of her movements which enabled her to pass from corridor to classroom so quietly. Time for night prayers in the chapel. With the exception of Margaret who was on prefect duty and could say her prayers in private as a result. Later she would join Sister Agnes in patrolling St Aloysius' dormitory. St Aloysius, the patron of youth. Not a saint for whom I had ever had much affection when at school: I suppose even then I had had not much sympathy for youth as such. The sort of young I admired were those like Margaret and Dodo, who showed some signs of thinking for themselves.

For me, it was time to make ready for the night's expedition. Through the high windows of St Joseph's Sitting Room, curtainless, I was glad to see the moon shining full and reassuring over the chapel, as promised in my diary.

'Who's got my veil?' cried Imogen in anguish, 'I know I brought it down here.'

'Sister Agnes, do let her off her veil. It's only night prayers,' said Blanche. 'Two minutes flat in the chapel; as if God cared about a veil—'

'Mother Ancilla is most particular about your veils in the chapel. You know that.' Sister Agnes's tone was strictly neutral. It was impossible to tell whether she felt that Mother Ancilla and God were on the same side as regards veils or not.

'Come on, Immo, here's a veil for you,' said Margaret kindly. 'One of the Fourth Formers must have left it behind.' She pulled a rather dusty looking black veil from behind the sofa. It was caught. There was a sharp tug, the veil came away, then the noise of a scuffle and a loud cry.

'Christ!' exclaimed Margaret. It was a strictly unreligious monosyllable. 'Tessa Justin, what the hell are you doing here—'

A smallish girl, with abnormally long and thick plaits was being hauled out from the sofa. Sister Agnes made one of her rapid darts across the room and pulled the child to her feet, away from the furious grasp of Margaret. She proceeded to dust her down with her handkerchief, with little clicks of disapproval, though the convent floor was so spotless that one could not imagine even a sojourn behind a sofa resulting in much contamination.

'Tessa Justin! You were supposed to be in bed half an hour ago. I'm afraid Mother Ancilla will have to hear of this in the morning. Come along now.' Sister Agnes swept the child, by now managing a few anguished sobs, out of the sitting room.

'Those bloody Fourth Formers!' Dodo's language too was degenerating. 'They dare each other to do that sort of thing. She must have heard every word we said.' Margaret said nothing. It was the first time I had seen her look really non-plussed.

After they had gone, I tried to watch television in the sitting room. Some modern drama or other, in which adultery, offices, and adultery in offices, all featured prominently. It was no good. It failed to grip me. My mind was too closely involved with the dramas here in the convent. And the prospective drama, tonight, outside. Finally I went to my own room, both excited and jangled.

The Treasury of the Blessed Eleanor was just the thing to set me right, I decided, catching sight of it lying on my desk. I opened it at the marker:

'Within the Tower of the Church dwell many witnesses to the Word of God,' I read. 'Some of these witnesses lean out from their Tower and cry out: Here be the Tower of God's Church, to all who have ears to listen. Others of these witnesses dwell secretly within the Tower and their words are never heard in the outside world. Nevertheless the prayers of these secret witnesses are their words. These secret witnesses are most acceptable to God.'

As I finished the passage, I realised that the marker was not of my own making at all, but a typed slip of paper. Exactly similar to the first slip which had suggested the rendezvous with the Black Nun. Even the wording of the message was reminiscent.

'If you don't believe Sister Miriam made a new will,' it ran, 'why don't you look for the will yourself? And you might ask Blanche Nelligan and Imogen Smith about a certain piece of paper they signed.' And the words 'secret witnesses' at the bottom of the passage were underlined in pencil, in case I had missed the point. But I had not missed the point.

Secret witnesses ... most acceptable to God in the view of the Blessed Eleanor. Not so acceptable perhaps to Mother Ancilla and the more conservative section of the community. Grimly I wondered who else in the quiet convent might be looking for the will.

9
To the Dark Tower

As I made the preparations for my nocturnal adventure, I wasn't so much full of courage as lacking in fear. I did not believe in ghosts. As a child I had been unaffected by ghost stories. When Rosa loved to entertain me with her ghoulish tales, it was her face I watched, rapt with her own horror: I hardly listened to her words.

Night-time. I wondered what the Black Nun's interpretation of night-time might be. Eleven o'clock? Ten o'clock?

Nor was I worried by the prospect of the solitary journey. Darkness of itself had never frightened me: my terrors were all within my own breast, regrets and guilts long buried, potentially more powerful than predatory creatures of the night. Besides, I had lived on my own to all intents and purposes since I was eighteen years old. Solitariness, even loneliness, had become a condition of my life.

Boots, a thick coat and my new torch were the necessary preparations for my expedition. And the bright little key which I had 'forgotten' to return to Mother Ancilla. Whoever else had acquired the spare key to that padlock, it seemed wise to bring my own. Beside my bed lay a candle and some matches.

'For emergencies, isn't that now?' said Sister Perpetua on the first day, in her soft Irish voice, arranging the candle and matches with care on the table as though they were sacred objects on the altar.

'You like candles?'

'Ah sure candles give comfort where torches never do.' So it was more as a tribute to Sister Perpetua than with any practical intention of using them that I also slipped the candle and matches into my pocket.

My self-confidence, or perhaps in retrospect arrogance would be the right word, was complete. Like Childe Roland, I would come to the

71

Dark Tower, and sort out at least one of the mysteries which enmeshed the convent. Where Sister Liz had attempted to win converts to Saint William Wordsworth, I had always preferred plain Robert Browning. I could make Browning's melancholy my own, and also his sense of drama. As a poem, 'My last Duchess' was far more to my taste than what I privately considered Wordsworth's holy ramblings. Just as I rated the romantic marriage of Elizabeth Barrett and Browning way above the pious Wordsworth family life – as described by Sister Liz. It was years before I discovered that the relationship with Dorothy was not necessarily all it seemed: and then it was too late, the pattern was set. So now, with Browning's Roland, I murmured to myself: 'Dauntless the slug-horn to my lips I set and blew . . .' I might have no slug-horn but there was a strong possibility I would be able to make some sort of report to Mother Ancilla in the morning . . .

It was therefore in a mood of positive optimism that I padded down the visitors' stairs, ignored the left turn to the chapel and found myself facing the small side door to the gardens. It was a door sometimes used by outsiders to enter the chapel. There were certain neighbours who treated the convent as their parish church and came to mass there regularly on Sundays and feast days. Blessed Eleanor's chapel was not strictly speaking a parish church. The bishop disapproved of the practice, which was also much disliked by the parish priest proper of the diocese. Outsiders at the chapel services were supposed to be confined to parents visiting their daughters.

Mother Ancilla however turned a resolutely blind eye to both episcopal and parochial disapproval. Blandly, she assumed that it was the most natural thing in the world that everyone round Churne should wish to worship in the chapel of the Blessed Eleanor. Parishioners had been known to receive coffee and convent-baked biscuits at feast days after mass. No such hospitality was available in the chilly parish church of St Gregory.

Mother Ancilla fended off the attempts of the parish priest, condemned to serve the convent masses as well as his own, to spot errant parishioners among bona fide parents. She was once overheard assuring the caustic Father Aylmer that an old lady of at least seventy, mobled in chiffon over sparse white hair, was 'one of our dear parents'.

In my day there had been two or three priests attached to St Gregory's. Nowadays, with the universal decline in vocations, the strain of providing a regular mass at the convent must have risen considerably. No doubt the parish priest at St Gregory's, whoever he might be, loved Mother Ancilla's empire-building no better than old Father Aylmer had done. It was understandable under the circumstances that some of these errant worshippers preferred to slip in through a side door.

I had noted that at night this side door was fastened merely by an inner bolt. Now I drew the bolt back and slipped out into the convent grounds.

My moon was still shining brightly, no longer quite so high over the chapel. I hoped that its light would see me at least as far as the Dark Tower. Preferably there and back again.

Apart from the moon, casting its own eerie light, the journey across the fields was remarkable chiefly for the variety of life I saw. In theory I was alone. But I never once felt myself truly alone throughout my journey. In practice every hedgerow, the furrows of the newly ploughed fields, seemed alive with life. Small animals scuttered hither and thither. An owl hooted somewhere. And the occasional bird – were they not supposed to be asleep? – stirred in the hedges. I came to the conclusion that the so-called silence of the night was a poetic misnomer.

I was quite happy to plod on across the furrows, in my stout boots. The only person I would have been happy to have at my side at that moment was Sister Liz. Her great voice, ringing out over the dark fields, would have provided the correct musical accompaniment. I could almost hear her now:

> Great God, I'd rather be
> A pagan suckled in a creed outworn, . . .
> And hear old Triton blow his wreathèd horn . . .

Another of her favourite poems. Not one, however, which could have pointed the path to Rome. Was there something pagan abroad? Ancient gods and goddesses stirring under the sod. If so, I did not feel it. As a rationalist, I was if anything closer to the God of Mother Ancilla, the authoritarian religious system of the Church of Rome with its own precarious logic, than to whatever earthly creatures were shaking the old soil. I had no beliefs, I told myself, and thus no fears.

And that sharp, hoarse sound was, I guessed, a fox barking. Somewhere in the distance. Not even the unexpected nature of the noise caused me apprehension. There was the exhilaration in my independence, to which at that moment I was convinced that nothing, not the loneliness of the night, not nature's marauders, not even the human powers of mischief, could shake.

The owl hooted again and I stumbled over something heavy in the darkness. A log or heavy fallen branch. My boots prevented me from suffering too much damage. I declined to regard the incident as a hubristic reminder of my own mortality.

By the time I reached the tower, I was confident that nothing and no-one could check me, cause me true affright. The tower loomed up above me, quite dark. The moon was now quite far down behind it.

On my principle of being forewarned, I decided to pad softly round to the other side of the tower and see if some glimmer showed there out of the solitary window. Glimmer. The west still glimmering with some trace of day. Banquo's murderers, another nasty late night rendezvous. No, that was not the parallel I sought. I would stick to Childe Roland and his Tower. Around the back of the tower there was no glimmering whatsoever, only the darkness was more eerie, with the moonlight stronger and more diffused, reflected against the thick walls.

I returned with slightly more haste to the tower entrance. I hesitated, and felt for the sharp little key. Then I groped my way for the padlock, and switched on the torch. I had my first surprise. The padlock was still firmly shut. That seemed to suggest that no-one else had yet entered the tower. Even with a duplicate key, it was difficult to see how they could have relocked the padlock from the inside. Unless they were possessed of superhuman powers. Only a ghost would pass successfully through a padlocked door and leave it locked ... That was another nasty thought like the stupid recollection of Banquo's murderers. My impregnable spirits wavered a bit.

For the first time, I had the impression of being watched, watched by something or someone other than the owls and the foxes. This impression was extremely strong and growing since my visit to the far side of the tower; and yet I had absolutely no rational grounds to support it. Instinct. My journalistic instinct, that famous instinct, at work? Sheer suggestibility, more likely, the culminative effect of the journey and the moonlight on even the toughest spirits. I had overestimated my own hardihood. I jumped sharply at the crackle of a twig near me, and nearly dropped my little torch.

Prayer would have been nice in a situation like this, I reflected wistfully. A quick crossing of oneself as Sister Liz would have done, or Mother Ancilla. My guardian angel would come in handy at a moment like this, supposing I believed in such a thing. That prayer Rosa taught me, which little Catholic girls muttered at night time, something invoking their guardian angel to sleep not while they slept. My guardian angel, or perhaps some stout saint. Was there a Saint Jemima? Hebrew for dove, one of the daughters of Job, it all seemed a little far back and Old Testament for the saints. Perhaps Job would protect me, a most suitable patron, a man who knew a thing or two about life's rough edges . . .

Hesitating still, occupying myself with foolish thoughts, I finally resolved to put an end to my fears and enter the building. Unquestionably, my trip round to the other side of the tower had filled me with a morbid reluctance to go further. As though I was gradually being surrounded by unnamed terrors, a tide of terror lapping round me, rising. Here be monsters . . . as they used to write on unknown seas on the edges of antique maps. Here be the Tower of God's Church. That reminded me: secret witnesses. Blessed Eleanor, protect me. Were there indeed secret witnesses all round me, in the darkness? Secret witnesses, friends to the owls and foxes, lurking there beside them?

Come on, Jemima, I addressed myself aloud, come on, daughter of Job. I had not talked to myself like that since I was a child when I used to rally myself for an unpleasant task by talking aloud. Once again the ground crackled near me. But it was nothing. Absolutely nothing.

I opened the padlock quickly and competently. I pushed open the thick door into the chasm beyond, remembering the geography carefully from my visit with Sister Elizabeth. I pushed the door hard, and took care to leave it wide open.

I stepped firmly over the threshold of the tower, and clutching my torch firmly in one hand, picked out in its small precise light the wooden rail of the ladder. The rail supported me.

'Is there anyone there?' I called, looking upwards, in the most calm and masterful tone I could muster. Complete silence followed my words. The dampness which surrounded me was marked and most unpleasant. We did not seem to have aired the tower at all by our afternoon's foray. 'Is there anyone there?' Why, that was De La Mare's Traveller. 'Tell them I came and no-one answered—'

Nothing moved.

I put my hand more firmly on the rail. The next moment there was the most appalling feeling of physical assault. With a hideous noise, all the more ghastly for the contrast of the silence only seconds before, I was being attacked on all sides, beaten, murdered. Screaming, screaming unashamedly I dropped the torch and tried to beat it off, beat them off. In vain. The hideous noise, the whirr and whoosh continued.

Finally I turned and fled back outside.

Panting, dishevelled, my hair mussed, half crying, it took me some time to realise that I had been attacked, if that was the right word, by bats.

I recovered my breath slowly; on the one hand I felt idiotic at my panic, on the other hand the waves of terror had been slightly diminished by the upset.

Come on, Jemima, indeed. A few bats were not going to put me off, having come so far. The existence of the bats, my temporary breakdown, only confirmed my resolve. No doubt it was the bats, poor blind benighted creatures, who were responsible for my fears of a new hidden presence.

I stepped over the threshold once more and scrabbled on the ground for my torch. The odd thing was that I could not find it. It must have rolled away. It could hardly have rolled very far on the solid pressed earth floor. It was also odd that it had gone out when I dropped it: perhaps the bulb was broken. In which case, I decided after a moment, there was no point in bothering with it further; leave it to the bats.

The only problem was: how was I to illumine my ascent of the ladder? As a non-smoker, matches were out of the question. Now if Tom had been with me, forever slapping the pocket of his worn jacket for cigarettes and/or matches and never seeming to have them both together – matches. I dug into my own pocket. But there *were* matches here, matches and a candle. In my panic I had forgotten. The percipient words of Sister Perpetua came back to me: 'Ah, candles give comfort where torches never do.'

I found the candle, strangely soft and thin in my fingers. It had broken and bent, but when the first match flared, it was still indubitably a candle. Sister – or Saint – Perpetua, many thanks. I lit the candle, despite its droop, and began rather gingerly to climb up the ladder.

Then I heard a distinct sound above my head. This was no creature of the night. And it was no familiar sound heard during my evening's travail. Not exactly a human sound either. A scrape on the floor, an irregular jarring on the floor above my head, like something rocking above my head . . .

Rocking.

Christ, the rocking-chair.

My cry was every bit as irreligious as Margaret's had been. It was no wonder. Someone, something, was gently rocking to and fro in the rocking-chair above my head. I still plunged on up the ladder, holding my unsteady candle: at the time, it was sheer instinct not courage; there seemed no other choice but to go on upwards. Unlike my terror of the bats, my urgent instinct was to confront the danger, not to flee it. As I reached the last rung of the ladder, I think I was aware of another different sound behind me. Not the door shutting. Some new movement in the darkness of the tower's windowless ground-floor chamber. But there was no time to analyse it.

Pushing open the trap-door above my head with one hand, I prepared to make the last of the ascent. My candle flickered and almost died so that I entered the first floor chamber into what seemed like darkness, except for a square grey light – the far window. The chair was still softly, remorselessly, rocking in its corner. The candle flame righted itself. Heart thudding, I held it upwards.

I saw, unquestionably I saw, a nun sitting there in the chair. A nun waiting for me. Gently rocking to and fro.

But that was not why my heart stopped in my breast. Equally unquestionably the nun in the rocking-chair had no face. The faceless one. That old nightmare of my childhood, the faceless one who waited for you, whose face you could never recognise, because it had no face. Everything in my world had to have a face, because then it was human and ordinary and you could understand it and control it. But this black shape had no face. Even in the candlelight I could not be mistaken. There were white hands, long bony hands rocking on the edge of the chair. And a black habit stretching to the ground. And a veil and a wimple and a rosary. Even the faint rustle of a nun's skirts joined to the rocking of the chair.

But beneath the white band of the wimple there was nothing, blackness, the void.

I know that I screamed loudly, starkly. Quite different from the brief frenzied panic of the bats' attack.

And then I must have fainted. I hope I fainted. Or perhaps not immediately. Just before I fainted there were jumbled strange impressions. A blow, a sharp blow from somewhere behind me. Or perhaps I merely fell and hit my head on the ladder. At any rate the light seemed to explode and vanish, and the Black Nun whirled round in the spectrum of my eyes, white hands still clenched on the chair. Then she seemed to rise up. A voice in my gathering dream said 'Now,' very clearly. As the voice of an anaesthetist before an operation. I felt the nun's habit enveloping me, her black skirts muffling my eyes, my head, my senses sinking. After that, everything was totally black and there was no light at all and no sound.

Much, much later, I felt the habit being gently pulled back from my eyes like a bandage. The total blackness had gone, there was a little subdued light, and something white near to me.

'Miss Shore,' I heard a gentle urgent voice saying as if from a great distance. 'Miss Shore, Miss Shore.' My name sounded beautiful, like the sound of the sea heard inside a shell.

Bending over me, her wimple so close to my face that it constituted the bar of white in my darkness, was Sister Agnes.

'Miss Shore, Miss Shore.' The sibilants receded and stopped. What she was saying was: 'Miss Shore, are you all right?'

'Of course I'm all right,' I said. 'What the hell are you doing in the tower, Sister Agnes?' I added, struggling unsuccessfully to sit up.

'In the tower, Miss Shore?' replied Sister Agnes, leaning forward again, and soothing my forehead with the ubiquitous nun's white handkerchief.

'But this isn't the tower. This is the chapel, Miss Shore.'

10
Particular friendships

'Poor Miss Shore,' said Sister Agnes softly, pausing in her minstrations. 'You have quite a nasty lump here on the back of your head.' Her fingers explored my skull gently. Then she took my hand and guided it to the back of my head. There was indeed a vast lump there. Sister Agnes's fingers had not hurt me, but my own clumsier touch caused me to wince violently. And that in its turn made me realise that my whole head was in the power of a huge headache, dormant, except that, as I lay on one of the chapel's pews, the faintest movement brought it to ferocious life.

'How in God's name did I get here?'

'I think you must have fallen and hit your head. Here on the edge of the pew. See how sharp the wood is.' Once more Sister Agnes guided my fingers to the bevelled end of the pew. Her guidance was rather a pleasant sensation. But I really had to sit up. Reluctantly I did so. The effort certainly aroused all the devils of the headache inside my forehead. And I felt rather sick into the bargain. Sister Agnes also appeared to be dusting off my coat and boots – what an abnormal amount of dust for the spotless chapel to contain – they were really filthy.

Nevertheless—

'I mean, how did I get here? Into the chapel?'

Sister Agnes did not answer immediately, but performed a few more little soft efficient dabs.

'You're not quite yourself yet, Miss Shore,' she said, her face turned away. 'You've probably forgotten just how you came to be here. A blow on the head can do that, you know.'

As a matter of fact, she was right. Or had been right. Up till a moment ago, the precise circumstances preceding my unconsciousness had eluded me. But now they came back, flooding back, along with the headache. And now I felt the shape of my torch – once more back in my pocket.

What was I doing in the chapel indeed? Yes, but what was Sister Agnes doing in the chapel for that matter? I had no idea of the time. It was still dark outside. No hint of grey showed through the stained glass windows which surrounded the altar.

Under the circumstances I decided that Sister Agnes had as much explaining to do as I did. I was not disposed to make her my confidante.

'You're right. I must have fallen and hit my head,' I replied vaguely. 'I can't remember anything else.'

'That's right, Miss Shore,' replied Sister Agnes sweetly. 'Relax. Don't you try to remember. Don't strain yourself.'

She helped me to my feet. I staggered and nearly fell on her. But Sister Agnes was unexpectedly strong and wiry to the touch, for all her professional gentleness and grace of movement. She managed to support me. Then, in a passable imitation of a frog-march, Sister Agnes helped me up the visitors' stairs.

At the outer door to the chapel we paused for breath. It was bolted. Once more bolted.

'At first I thought there was an intruder,' said Sister Agnes. 'Then I heard a noise – it must have been your fall – I'm sleeping in the cubicle at the end of the big dormitory, with the door open. I came down here. That door was open. Perhaps you opened it, Miss Shore? Then I heard a groan in the chapel. And I found you.'

It was quite a long explanation from the enigmatic Sister Agnes. Particularly in view of the fact that I had not asked for one.

'Perhaps you had opened that door, Miss Shore?' she repeated, as we mounted the stairs.

'I'm afraid I can't remember *anything* just before the accident,' I said firmly. 'The last thing I remember is watching some rotten play on television in St Joseph's Sitting Room.'

I got the distinct impression that Sister Agnes relaxed. I added: 'I really think I should go to the infirmary.'

'You wait here and I'll go and wake up Sister Lucy,' was all Sister Agnes said by way of reply.

Sister Agnes deposited me on my own bed and departed, almost noiselessly. While she was away, I wondered rather groggily why she hadn't called Sister Lucy in the first place.

Time passed, or perhaps I dozed.

But it did seem an age before Sister Agnes returned. There was a frown, or something as near a frown as I had yet seen on that marble face.

'Sister Lucy wasn't there,' was all she said. 'I'll take you to the infirmary myself.' She lifted me up by my elbow, cushioning it, setting me on my feet again.

'You're surprisingly strong, Sister,' I said, 'I'm sure I'm no light weight.'

'It's not a question of strength, Miss Shore. Just how you use your body. I learnt that of course in my profession in the world.'

She made it sound extremely mysterious. We were whispering as we passed down the passage to the infirmary.

'What was your profession, Sister?' I asked her jokingly as she tucked me into a clean bed in the end cubicle of the vast – and apparently empty – lay section of the infirmary. 'Weight lifter?'

'I was trained as a dancer, Miss Shore,' replied Sister Agnes, pursing her lips slightly. 'And later I became an actress.'

'A *dancer?*' I cried.

'Shhh. I'm sorry, Miss Shore. But I don't think you should excite yourself. Before Sister Lucy takes charge, that is.'

It explained many things, her grace, her strength. Even her looks, the huge doe eyes seemed to owe something to the style of the ballet. At that moment, Sister Lucy bustled in, out of breath.

'Ah, Sister, I found your note.'

The two nuns conferred together outside the cubicle in low voices. I couldn't hear what they said. Besides, I was beginning to feel sleepy. I wasn't even able to appreciate fully Sister Lucy's night costume, the neat little muslin cap over her head, just as Rosa reported. But she did seem to have quite a lot of hair under it, no shaven head here. Pleasant auburn hair. In fact she looked a great deal more like the nurse she had been, than the nun she was.

The strain of the evening was beginning to tell, and my head ached. I felt secure and safe in Sister Lucy's care. Sister Agnes must have left because when I opened my eyes again Sister Lucy was sitting composedly by my bed, reading her little black prayer book. It was her office, I supposed, the prayers every nun had to say daily. Composed no doubt by the Blessed Eleanor herself. I continued to feel safe in her care.

The next day I was officially cleared of concussion, although commanded to spend the day in bed. Everything seemed to be back to normal – including strangely enough my clothes. I had a distinct, if groggy memory, of Sister Agnes brushing off quantities of dust from them in the chapel. Yet Sister Lucy denied finding any dust at all; it would be fair to say that she positively bristled at the idea of any contact with the chapel, however unplanned, resulting in the contamination of dust. I had another glimpse of the nurse Sister Lucy had once been, in her own way fairly formidable. I composed myself by concocting an official explanation of my fall for any interested enquirer.

The need to keep my own counsel for the time being was underlined by a discovery I had made in the pocket of the brown overcoat I had worn to the tower. Inside the pocket I found a typed note, exactly similar in appearance to the note which had summoned me to the Dark Tower. 'If you really want to avoid any further nasty bumps on the head,' it read, 'why don't you go back to London and television where you belong? You have been warned.'

An interested enquirer was not slow to manifest herself. Quite early in the morning, Mother Ancilla swept in at her familiar fast pace. Whatever her problems of health, they were not visible in her walk or her bearing.

'Jemima, my child, what's this I hear?' She clutched my hand fervently. 'When I asked you to help us, I certainly did not ask you to get hit over the head, did I? We must take better care of you—'

'I'm afraid I was very silly, Mother.' It was impossible not to feel twelve years old again. I was almost hanging my head.

'We prayed for you at mass of course. No, don't look cross. Naughty girl. We feel God should take you under His special protection since you are doing His work here.'

I was not, strictly speaking, displeased to hear I had been prayed for in the chapel.

I had not rejected Sister Lucy's urgently proffered tranquillizer either. In my philosophy, such activities came under the heading of 'Will probably do no good, will certainly do no harm.' Tom would have had a much stronger reaction to both suggested remedies; he had a personal horror of tranquillizers – having seen their effects on Carrie – and would have felt positively contaminated by the mention of his name in a Roman Catholic chapel. I was made of softer stuff. But it did not do to give Mother Ancilla an inch—

Sure enough: 'Maybe a little visit of thanksgiving?' she enquired hopefully. 'For your safe deliverance?'

'I'm sorry, Mother Ancilla,' I said very firmly. 'As far as I am concerned, I owe my deliverance to Sister Agnes.' I gave her my official story: a sudden noise in the night, an investigation in the chapel, stumbling in the darkness, hitting my head hard on the back of the pew. It was all so ridiculous, I exclaimed. My story gained unexpected plausibility from the fact that there *had* been a sudden noise in the night. It transpired that Sister Lucy had rushed through the nuns' corridor to the aid of Tessa Justin.

As Sister Boniface observed gruffly: 'That Tessa Justin causes nothing but trouble. Nightmares about the Black Nun indeed! Screaming her head off and saying a nun had tried to put a pillow over her head. And there's Sister Lucy trying to make out she's emotionally disturbed and needs talking to! Showing off I call it. Calling attention to herself. Her mother was just the same. Always showing off. When we were children here, anyone who even mentioned the subject of the Black Nun had to say all three mysteries of the Holy Rosary as a penance. Trying to get out of going to early mass. Or not done her homework . . . Showing off, I call it.' And so Sister Boniface rumbled on.

It occurred to me that Sister Lucy's position as infirmarian was not totally enviable with this old religious war-horse breathing down her neck. How different the healing of the sick must seem to her in the convent, compared to a great London hospital. Was she quite satisfied with ministering to the needs of 'upper class brats' – to quote Dodo Sheehy's evocative if possibly second-hand phrase? At least Dodo's aunt, the late Sister Theodora of the Angels, had died nursing black babies . . . How did nuns decide on the exact expression their vocations should take anyway? I supposed I should really have to ask them: it would make a fascinating part of the television programme I was still valiantly contemplating.

Not so much 'Why the Cross?' – and hadn't that been done before anyway? – as 'Which Cross?' . . .

'My recent experiences simply prove to me that I should keep to my self-imposed rule and not pay stray visits to the chapel—' I told Mother Ancilla cheerfully.

'You're incorrigible!' Mother Ancilla, throwing up her hands, almost roguish, at her best. She looked better than on the day of our first interview. Her cheeks were still white. But I had the impression that the deep lines at the edges of her mouth had softened somewhat. The frightened look had gone. I wondered what had happened to make Mother Ancilla look more cheerful.

One bell sounded. One bell for Reverend Mother. It sounded curiously loud. But then in the infirmary we were bordering on the nuns' wing. The infirmary was a kind of limbo. I had never liked the definition of that term during Religious Instruction at school – ('But Jem, you *must* go to Divinity Lessons, whatever they call them,' my mother had insisted. 'You don't want to be different from the other girls.' She meant: more different than you are already.) Limbo: a place for unbaptised babies. It had a punitive sound to it, like an orphanage for outcasts. I much preferred the easy modern usage of my own world. I used it all too often in my investigative interviews:

'So, Mrs Poorwoman, the social security services have left you in a kind of limbo, have they not?' There being a strong suggestion that something could and would be done about the matter.

Perhaps I could make some use of my own stay in this limbo. There was one untapped source of information about life in the convent close at hand ... if I could lure Sister Boniface from discussing her personal grudge against Sister Lucy and her methods. An on-going limbo, to combine two jargons.

'My bell,' Mother Ancilla sighed. 'Just when we were having a lovely talk, dear Jemima.' She sounded almost happy. Was that possible? Her serenity was particularly surprising in view of her next remark: 'It's the day of Sister Edward's funeral. Had you forgotten? Quite natural in view of last night's events,' she went on. 'That bell is probably to tell me of the arrival of the family. Mrs O'Dowd is such a dear woman and Sister Edward was her youngest. I ought to go and greet them.'

She marched away. A happy warrior. A general whose troops had just won a skirmish. But what was the victory?

'Mother Ancilla—' I called after her.

She did not stop. Perhaps she did not hear me. Nuns like ordinary women were capable of growing deaf around seventy and Mother Ancilla would be further handicapped by the head-dress blocking her ears.

Later in the morning Sister Lucy and I watched the funeral procession together out of the high thin Gothic window of the infirmary. The line of nuns, strung out, single file, paused silently under our gaze out of the chapel door in the direction of the cemetery.

'What a tiny coffin!' I exclaimed involuntarily. I had forgotten the touching smallness of that rabbit-like figure.

'Sister Edward herself was not much more than five foot.' Even wood was not wasted at the convent.

The tall male figures – her brothers? – behind the coffin looked enormous in contrast to the nuns. The nuns' eyes were downcast. The men were looking about them. But they were not carrying the corners of the coffin. Like the Blessed Eleanor, Sister Edward was being carried to her grave by six black nuns.

'How do they choose the six nuns to carry the coffin?' I enquired idly. 'The six strongest? Or particular friends of the deceased?'

'Not particular friends,' replied Sister Lucy primly. 'Nuns of the O.T.I. have no particular friends. The rule of our foundress is most specific on that point. Particular friendships within the community are not pleasing in the sight of God since they distract the religious from her work in God's holy cause and can give scandal to other godly women.'

I couldn't help laughing.

'Oh come on, Sister Lucy. You know that I didn't mean that.' Particular friendships – but had I not meant that? Wasn't a particular friendship what Rosabelle and I had enjoyed: but then Rosa had not been a nun in those days. Nothing against particular friendships at a school, surely.

'I'm afraid I over-reacted,' responded Sister Lucy. She sounded flustered by my teasing. 'As you can imagine, communities have to be very strict about that sort of thing. Even the very innocent sort of particular friendship, as we call it, can cause disharmony. And disruption.' Seeing that I looked still unconvinced, she went on: 'To the participants themselves, I can assure you. As well as being displeasing to God. Think of, well, you were a friend of poor Sister Miriam,' Sister Lucy coughed and stopped.

'I should investigate the topic for my programme.'

'Miss Shore, please—' Now Sister Lucy looked frankly horrified.

'Oh please don't misunderstand me,' I soothed her. We turned our attention back to the procession.

At a distance the noise of the singing was thin, a little sorrow, not a mighty lament as it had sounded in the chapel on All Souls' Day. In keeping with the small size of Sister Edward's coffin, the short span of her life. Even the procession itself from our lofty vantage point was like something seen at the wrong end of a telescope. The little black figures became formalised. That veiled and bowed figure between two women wearing black hats must be Mrs O'Dowd, mother of the lovely Catholic family. No Mr O'Dowd, as far as I could make out. He presumably had died years ago, worn out. Of the four men, two were in priests' cassocks and two in equally priestly long black coats. Doctors, had Sister Boniface said?

On the dull November day, no sun, trees black, there was only a single splash of colour in the procession. One of the women mourners was wearing a bright purple coat. Purple of course was a colour of mourning in the Catholic church as pink was a colour of rejoicing. Purple vestments in Lent, purple coverings for the statues in Holy Week. But there was something about this coat, its cut maybe, its swagger, which did not speak of the funeral. It was also remarkable that of all the mourners, this little purple figure was wearing neither a hat nor a veil. She was wearing shiny black boots – again not particularly funereal – but her head, a head of bubbly fair hair which made it the more noticeable, was not covered.

'Blondes really should not wear purple.' It was a judgement from another world. I said it aloud.

'I agree. Beatrice O'Dowd could have spared Mother Ancilla that at least.' The contained Sister Lucy sounded quite venomous.

My interest quickened sharply. 'So that's the ex-nun. The former Sister John.'

'That's Beatrice O'Dowd.'

A return to the flatter tone. The more you looked at the procession, the head of which was now vanishing down the soggy path to the cemetery, the more flaunting the costume of ex-Sister John appeared. A gesture against Mother Ancilla, so Sister Lucy interpreted it: yet it was hardly reverent to her mother, the priests her brothers, the corpse of her dead sister, if those were your values.

I decided that it was time to talk to Beatrice O'Dowd. In the interests of my programme, as I put it to Sister Lucy: who received the request with an impassivity which entirely failed to conceal her violent disapproval.

I did not exactly relish the idea of that flaunting purple in the white calm of my little cubicle. But Beatrice O'Dowd proved a pleasant surprise. Close to, detached from the black procession, the purple did not look so garish. Her hair was naturally sandy rather than blonde. She had the long upper lip and slightly prominent front teeth of her younger sister. It was true that the hair-style was over bouffant and the lipstick an unbecoming bright pink. Years in television had given me an automatic eye for such things. For the same reason, I could see through to the homely woman in her late thirties visible within the slightly old-fashioned trappings of glamour.

After all, fifteen years of sombre black under Mother Ancilla's eagle eye was enough to send anyone towards all colours of the rainbow. Under her coat Beatrice O'Dowd wore a tight purple polo-necked sweater (she really did like the colour). Whether nuns wore bras or not – and what a perfect opportunity to find out, from an ex-nun – Miss O'Dowd was certainly wearing one now.

Clothes apart, Beatrice O'Dowd seemed to be a straight-forward, even down-to-earth sort of woman. It was interesting how completely she lacked the demeanour of a nun: there were no cast-down eyes here à la Sister Agnes, no evidence of hysteria à la Sister Edward. She crossed her legs – rather stocky legs in their black boots – as though to the manner born, twitching down a skirt which was once again just slightly too short for the current fashion. Yet you never saw a nun crossing her legs. Rosa once told me that it was a mortal sin for a nun to cross her legs. It was more likely that nuns sat with their knees together because to cross them under the thick folds of the habit would be a difficult manœuvre.

How odd it must have been for Beatrice O'Dowd to learn such necessary feminine accomplishments as sitting in short skirts after fifteen years' freedom from these cares. Whatever it had cost her, how completely this woman had thrown off the trappings of a nun. Of course it could have been the other way around: perhaps Sister John had never properly adapted herself to them. Hence her desire to leave.

'I wanted to talk to you anyway, Jemima,' said Beatrice O'Dowd conversationally. I did not know that we were on Christian name terms. Still, television intimacy is a phenomenon which all successful performers have to endure. 'So I was glad when you sent for me. In a way it does make more sense seeing you in here.'

'In here?' I thought she meant: sick, in the infirmary.

'Here at the convent. We had discussed contacting you in London. I said: yes. The others said: wait a bit. And then lo and behold you turn up here. As young Ronnie told us. And of course that made absolute sense to us all. We realised that you were one jump ahead of us in your thinking—'

'You're going much too fast. I've been ill you know,' I said desperately. 'Why did you want to talk to me? Please begin at the beginning.'

Beatrice looked momentarily nonplussed. Then she leant forward again and said in her conversational style:

'But of course I wanted to talk to you, Jemima. Seeing that Rosabelle Powerstock was such a particular friend of mine.'

It was not, I feared, a phrase that a former nun of the O.T.I. could use by accident.

11
Will

My first reaction to the words of Beatrice O'Dowd was a sudden sharp pang. Irrational annoyance – jealousy would really be too strong a word – seized me. What had this rather plain women with her fat legs – she *was* plain and her legs were bulging over the tops of her boots – to do with my Rosa? The ridiculousness of my reaction struck me almost immediately. My Rosa was long since gone to her Tower of Ivory. Many years later a middle-aged nun called Sister Miriam had formed a particular friendship with another woman, then a nun:

'Particular friendships can cause scandal to other godly women in the community' – Sister Lucy's observation. I quoted it aloud.

'Particular friendships! Absurd phrase—'

'But you just used it.' Beatrice O'Dowd paid no attention.

'Did you know,' she enquired warmly, 'that this convent was founded on a particular friendship? Do you think that an upper-class woman like Princess Eleanor would have stuck around in this dump without the particular friendship of Dame Ghislaine le Tourel to cheer her up? And yet we were denied even the simplest of human relationships, and taught to consider them wrong. With your under-standing of people, how society really works, you must know what I mean.'

I ignored the compliment.

Dame Ghislaine. She had certainly featured in the life story of the Blessed Eleanor. A devoted *Dame d'Honneur*. One of the six black nuns who carried her in her coffin to the tower. The nun who was chosen as the next Reverend Mother by the dying wish of the foundress (no nonsense about democratic election in this community). Eleanor and Ghislaine. As Mother Ancilla would say – royalty, that's different.

It was all a very long time ago. Rosabelle and Jemima. Like Eleanor and Ghislaine that too was a very long time ago. Ancient history. Not so Sister Miriam and ex-Sister John. Beatrice's language of denunciation had a strictly contemporary ring. As contemporary for example as the passionate phrases of Dodo Sheehy on the subject of the poor. And not altogether unlike them.

'From the first moment I saw your programme,' continued Beatrice as though giving me a prepared lecture, 'I was with Rosa all the way. I like to think I may even have suggested the handover. Be that as it may.' Poor Rosa, was she not even to have the credit of her own generous idea? 'Certainly Mother Ancilla always thought so.'

She managed to get a great deal of dislike into the name of Mother Ancilla. I recalled Sister Lucy's venom in pronouncing the name of Beatrice O'Dowd.

'That's when she decided to get me out at all costs. Nothing and no-one stands in the way of Mother Ancilla when she decides to have her own way.'

'But surely you went of your own accord? You didn't want to stay – I mean, listening to you—' I really wanted to say: looking at you. In your boots with your make-up and your crossed legs and your bouffant hair.

Beatrice O'Dowd sighed.

'Oh in a sense, yes, of course. I was in a state of crisis about the whole thing for years. My vows, I mean. I would have gone sooner or later. I was way ahead of Rosa in *that* way. Although of course she would have left in the end. If she had lived.'

She sighed again.

'Poor Rosa. No, I wanted to stay here to see the thing through. Go in my own time. The handover of the land – well, you know all about that. I could have supported Rosa through it all, the lawyers, Mother Ancilla, the lot. I was so much stronger than her. She *needed* my strength. And then they took me away from her.'

A voice from the past. A letter still remembered:

'How strong you are, Jemima. Not needing any props to support you. No religion or belief or anything like that. I need so many props. That's one of the reasons I had to become a nun. To be propped up by God.'

Even in the convent Rosa had still needed strength.

'There wouldn't have been that ghastly upset,' Beatrice went on, 'that nervous breakdown – that's what it was of course, but the nuns would never admit it. Even her terrible plan to shut herself up in the tower. That would never have happened if they hadn't sent me away, using the

excuse of a particular friendship. It was deliberate victimisation.'
Another phrase from the modern world.

'Mother Ancilla told me Rosa had been very ill,' I put in mildly.

'Oh she told you that. Too late. And wrapped you round her little
finger, I'll be bound. The charm of that woman when she wants to use
it. But she didn't fool little Ronnie, my sister Veronica, she knew the
truth about Mother Ancilla.'

Beatrice O'Dowd's tone changed abruptly.

'There was another will, you know.'

'Ah.'

'You knew?'

'No. But – a hint was dropped.'

'Who by?' Sharply.

'The girls: nothing specific, just gossiping.' I did not intend to be
more explicit until Beatrice O'Dowd showed me a few of her own
cards.

'Which girls?' Even more sharply. 'There are over eighty girls here.
Counting the junior school.'

'I haven't met anyone from the junior school,' I replied pleasantly.
Which was true – except for a brief glimpse of a weeping Tessa Justin,
in St Joseph's sitting room. 'Some of the girls who were friendly with
Rosa. They seemed to know all about her plans – your plans – to give
away the lands. And they as good as indicated to me that there was a
second will. Leaving it to the poor and away from the convent, after all.'

'Oh, them. Margaret and Dodo and Co. Oh yes, Blanche and Imogen
even witnessed the will. That's how we knew about it in the first place.
They didn't read it, but Rosa told them quite frankly what it was. But I
hoped—' She stopped. 'You see, there is a girl here who knows where
Rosa *hid* the will, and Mother Ancilla knows that too—'

It was at this point that Beatrice O'Dowd and myself became aware
that Mother Ancilla was standing there at the entrance to the cubicle,
watching us. She had appeared with a silence worthy of Sister Agnes
herself. One of the reasons for this silence might well be the fact that
she was holding her black rosary crushed in her hand. So that it would
not chink. So that it had not chinked.

'Speak of the devil,' was all I could think of saying in a bright voice. It
was, under the circumstances, a singularly inappropriate remark.
Mother Ancilla showed no signs of having heard it.

'Dear Beatrice,' she cried. What an actress the woman was. I honestly
could not have told the difference between the affection with which she
clasped the former nun's hand and the love with which she mantled,

say, a princess. 'We're all so pleased you came down to see us, even on this sad occasion. The community are longing to see you.'

I really believed her. I turned towards Beatrice to see how she was taking all this. After fifteen years of Mother Ancilla's sway, I wondered how easy she found it to face her.

The answer was: not easy at all. Beatrice O'Dowd was gazing at Mother Ancilla, fascinated, as a rabbit gazes hopelessly at a snake. Gone was the forceful downright woman who had been instructing me only minutes before. Beatrice O'Dowd, purple jersey, black boots and all, looked frankly terrified. The resemblance to the late Sister Edward was suddenly marked. I remembered that fateful encounter in the school corridor.

'Thank you, Mother,' she mumbled. 'I'll be glad to see them all again.' She picked up the purple coat.

'And how is your work going, my child?' enquired Mother Ancilla, even more tenderly.

'Splendidly, Mother, thank you,' replied Beatrice with an increase of spirit. 'In spite of recent setbacks we think we have found a way round our problems.' She actually gave the Reverend Mother a challenging look. Mother Ancilla tucked in the corners of her mouth. If Beatrice could look like a rabbit, Mother Ancilla could certainly resemble a snake. Her gaze was watchful, cold. But her next words still sounded benign:

'I'm very pleased to hear it, dear Beatrice. And I mean that most sincerely. Just because your – er – plans did not work out one way, it does not mean they are displeasing to God in every way.'

'Thank you, Mother.' Beatrice sounded sardonic.

'Often Our Blessed Lord comes to our aid in the most unexpected ways.'

'I will bear in mind what you say.'

'I take it that although your project cannot go ahead in its original form, it will nevertheless go ahead in a different way?'

'You can take it that our project will go ahead, Mother Ancilla,' returned Beatrice with something of the older nun's bland sweetness. 'Rosabelle Powerstock's will shall prevail.' That sounded like a text. 'And now if you'll excuse me, I'll go and look up some of my particular friends in the community. Miss Shore, we'll be in touch.' There was no doubt of the deliberate provocation of her last remarks. And she went, I noticed, in the direction of the school wing, not the nuns'. I waited till the purple coat had disappeared from view.

'What is her project, Mother Ancilla?' But I had already guessed the answer to my own question. It was really no surprise to me to learn that

Beatrice O'Dowd now worked for the Powers Estate Projectors. Directly under Alexander Skarbek: his aide.

Alexander Skarbek. I suspected strongly that there had been some contact between Skarbek and that little Sixth Form group. Possibly through Rosa, certainly through Beatrice. How many others? And what orders had he given Beatrice O'Dowd? I might have to swallow my pride, ring up Tom, and make a few more enquiries about Alexander Skarbek.

'I wonder just what Beatrice O'Dowd intends to do now?' said Mother Ancilla meditatively. 'Poor Mrs O'Dowd was telling me that she's still completely under the influence of that dreadful man. She was always so easily led. And oh *dear* that coat and that jersey! Nuns never have any taste in ordinary clothes, you know. That's why it's so disastrous when they put themselves into short skirts.'

How strange to think that at her age in the world Mother Ancilla would now be dressed as an old lady. In her black habit on the other hand she still appeared as a dominating and formidable figure. A woman of iron will.

Will. It all seemed to come down to a question of will. Will and the will.

Will. There was a great deal of it about. Not only the will of God but a great deal of other wills including the last will and testament of Rosabelle Powerstock. The will of Mother Ancilla to preserve the convent and its work at all costs. The will of a good many other people – including Beatrice O'Dowd, the outsider Alexander Skarbek, the girls of the Sixth Form – to bring that work in effect to a halt by installing a housing project at the convent walls. The will of the Black Nun, or the sinister forces represented by that phantasmagoric figure. The will of the Black Nun was the clearest of the lot: that Jemima Shore, Investigator, should drop her investigations and get out. Her note in my overcoat pocket had made that amply clear.

I concentrated for a moment on the will of Rosabelle Powerstock, the late Sister Miriam. Or rather the two wills of Rosabelle Powerstock. One, a simple testament made at the time of her final vows, which all the nuns made, leaving her effects and modest possessions to the community. The vast Powerstock Estate, of course, long ago placed in trust and excluded. The other, written many years later, the product of an anguished mind.

The missing will.

A will leaving the lands to the poor, Margaret had hinted. But even a mentally distressed nun would hardly phrase her intentions in the language of the Bible – 'Give all to the poor' in this day and age would probably end up by giving all to the government, not the same thing at all. Or at least not in the way Rosa had intended. The poor in this case were therefore ably represented by the Powers Estate Project. I could safely assume the Project to be the beneficiary of the missing will.

Yet even here there was a mystery within the mystery. Why had Rosabelle bothered to conceal her new will before her death? Who did she wish to conceal it from? A will was there to express her intentions when she was no longer there to make them clear herself. Yet she had apparently gone to great pains to hide this will. Unless of course someone else had hidden it – after her death.

The will. Will. I continued to propound to myself these problems.

'Wilful,' said Sister Boniface. She was handling her rosary by my bed. Her chest wheezed and the fingers clutching the beads were as twisted as ever. I thought of Keats: 'Numb were the Beadsman's fingers ... and while his frosted breath etc., etc.' St Agnes's Eve: Sister Elizabeth was beginning to have an effect on me. But Sister Boniface's tongue was still vigorous.

'Wilful. That's Tessa Justin for you.' Sister Boniface seldom let a subject go. 'Now she wants to have a private interview with you, Jemima. Those were her exact words. If you please! The little madam. Says she has some private information to tell you. I said: be off with you and don't bother Miss Shore when she's sick. Besides, you were sleeping. She said: but I've got to tell her what I know. I said: you can tell her tomorrow, all in good time. And off she's gone, sulkily, to bed.'

For once I was listening with rapt attention to Sister Boniface.

'I could see her first thing tomorrow,' I suggested quickly.

'Oh she'll keep, she'll keep,' replied Sister Boniface. Her tone was comfortable. 'You still need to take things easily. Besides, she's got a busy day tomorrow. We all have. Her mother's coming down to open the school bazaar. Why don't you wait and talk to her when the excitement's all over?'

At the time I saw no great harm in the delay.

12
Worse than death

It was characteristic of the prudence of Mother Ancilla that Blessed Eleanor's Christmas bazaar took place in early November. That way, she reckoned, no-one of any decency could possibly have begun their Christmas shopping. The parents' entire financial outlay could therefore be plunged into the giddy whirlpool of the school bazaar. Mother Ancilla was in no doubt that given a choice of Harrods and the school bazaar, any sensible parent would choose the latter.

The school hall, when I poked my head rather nervously round the door, did for a moment resemble Harrods in the pre-Christmas rush. Exhausted adults were milling to and fro, many with small children attached to their hands. In other ways, however, it was remote from the great Knightsbridge store. The nuns, unlike shop assistants, spent most of the time exclaiming and clucking over the old girls, particularly those with babies.

Mother Ancilla was everywhere, kissing and clasping hands, until her fingers finally became permanently entangled with those of a handsome, rather plump, middle-aged woman with black hair in a knot, and a great deal of gold jewellery. I was surprised. She had surrendered the hand of another well-dressed parent, rumoured to be an Austrian baroness 'related to absolutely everybody in Europe'. But when she pounced on me, hand in hand with her new protegée, the mystery was explained:

'Jemima, you remember the dear princess, you remember Pia.' How satisfied my mother would have been to learn that Pia had allied herself in marriage to an Italian prince of even more exalted birth than her own!

'Geemima! So wonderful! I'm telling you.' Pia embraced me

94

ecstatically, taking me into her warm bosom, where the softness of her cashmere jersey contrasted with the sharp imprint of her myriad gold chains. She smelt delicious. She was charming.

'Gianni! Gianni! 'Ere, 'ere.' Pia's English had not improved. And Gianni, whoever he was, husband, lover, son, chauffeur, was not attending. 'Look 'ere, last night I'm sitting in Claridge's and I'm watching television, because we don't go to Annabel's, really so boring every night, and I *see* you!'

She was a fan. I wondered just which repeat she had seen in her luxurious suite: not the Powers Estate Investigation, that would be too ironic. Yet it was due to be repeated sometime. I was beginning to think of that as a lethal programme. Perhaps Princess Pia would now become infected and sell all that she had? Looking at her chains I decided that like the centurion she probably had a great deal to sell.

Mother Ancilla beamed.

'Isn't it wonderful to think of dear Pia watching you on television?' she cried. I only wished my mother could have survived to hear the news. She too would have thought it quite wonderful.

I edged away in the direction of Sister Elizabeth. At least she remained sublimely indifferent to the occasion in hand. We managed to have a quick exchange on the nature of Christian pantheism as expressed by Shelley in 'The Skylark' before a parent claimed Sister Liz to discuss the somewhat lesser literary matter of his daughter's essays.

At the secondhand book stall Sister Hippolytus was presiding grumpily. The books comprised a mixture of lives of the saints and extremely worn paperback Agatha Christies. The Agatha Christies were doing a brisk trade. I could see no way of avoiding my former history mistress; Sister Agnes, whom I wished formally to thank for rescuing me in the chapel, was nowhere around.

'You haven't bothered to come and see *me*, Jemima, with your questions about convent life,' said Sister Hippolytus, who made no pretence of being other than cross at her exclusion. 'Yet no-one else here knows anything at all about the history of this place. No-one else here even *cares* about history.'

'Tomorrow, Sister Hippolytus,' trying to sound as apologetic as I could.

'Tomorrow, tomorrow. Today belongs to God, tomorrow may well belong to the Devil. As Blessed Eleanor said to Dame Ghislaine when she was dying and Dame Ghislaine wrote it down. I've written it down too, you know. A new life of our foundress is sadly needed, don't you agree? Besides, I'm making a major historical revelation—'

I began to edge away to another stall. I could not honestly regard a new life of the Blessed Eleanor as one of the crying needs of modern publishing.

'God granted me an extra long spell in the infirmary last winter,' said the old nun, deserting crossness temporarily for complacency, 'and I was able to get on with it wonderfully well. I was able to help one or two of the Sisters to a speedier recovery by telling them stories of bygone times at Blessed St Eleanor's. They had never heard such tales before.'

I believed her, including the miraculous recoveries of those Sisters condemned to the Hippo's historical revelations . . .

'Anyway history makes much the best television.' That was Sister Hippolytus' parting shot. 'The past. Towers, ancient foundations, secret hiding-places, old buildings, that's what the public likes. You'll see. Not a lot of foolish women talking about themselves.'

The implication was: to another foolish woman. But for all her crotchety temper, Sister Hippolytus had cleared up at least one matter in my investigations.

I helped myself to some of Sister Clare's excellent coffee. Sister Clare was presiding behind an urn, aided by Blanche Nelligan and Imogen Smith. Blanche rolled her eyes to indicate how far this coffee would fall below my standards.

At a nearby stall Sisters Damian and Perpetua had arranged a series of bottles ranging from Worcester sauce to something mysterious and unlabelled in a vast black bottle. For a handsome sum of money, people were entitled to throw hoops over these bottles in an attempt to secure them. As I arrived, the little hedgehog was plucking nervously at her companion's sleeve.

'Sister, Sister,' I heard her say. 'One of these bottles is alcoholic. What happens if a child wins it?'

'Ah, never worry, Sister,' replied Sister Perpetua happily. 'They won't win anything at all, and that's a promise. These hoops are all far too small to go over the stands. That's the way we used to do it at home in Ireland,' she explained to me, without a trace of shame. 'You make so much more money that way. After all, it's all for charity isn't it? The poor little black children.'

The other stalls were run on rather less ruthless lines. The prize goods – clothes and napkins exquisitely embroidered by the nuns themselves – quickly vanished. Whereas a quantity of logs and leaves and ferns sprayed in silver by the junior school still lurked to trap the unwary visitor.

I even bought one of these festive pieces of nature myself.

'Miss Shore, can we have your autograph?' A group of giggling juniors, bored with the rest of the proceedings, surrounded me. Some proffered autograph books, others scraps of paper. The last girl lingered. She was tiny, with huge goggling eyes and hair scraped into a thick pony tail.

'Will you put: For Mandy, Miss Shore?' It was done.

'And that's my toothbrush holder.' She pointed to a large besilvered log, in which three very small holes had been bored. 'Nobody's bought it. And I took so much trouble—' A frightful expression of woe which did not convince me for a moment: I bought the toothbrush holder. After all, there were unlikely to be two like it in existence. Triumph succeeded woe on the small face.

'Mandy Justin,' said the voice of Mother Ancilla sharply, 'you should be getting ready to hold the bouquet. Your mother's just going to make her speech. And if you see Tessa tell her to go to the platform too.'

So yet another member of the Justin family was an adept at improving the shining hour. My attention was caught by a cortège of what were evidently more Justins, shuffling uneasily onto the platform. Another prudent move on the part of Mother Ancilla was to have the so-called opening ceremony performed as a closure when the stalls were more or less empty. This meant that the distinguished visitor, in this case Lady Polly Justin, had to stay to the bitter end, buying for all she was worth. And so did all but the most brazen of the other visitors. It was a bold parent who ran the gauntlet of Mother Ancilla's disapproval by leaving before the speech.

I studied the Justins.

I recognised Sir Charles Justin. He was a Conservative MP, enormously stout, very much looking the part of authority. He had once given a drink to Tom and myself on the terrace of the House of Commons when his right wing and Tom's left wing views had somehow brought them into agreement over some matter of individual liberty (Tom), freedom from state control (Sir Charles Justin). He looked remote and intensely gloomy sitting there on the platform.

I deduced that the proximity of Lady Polly Justin was responsible for much of this catatonic state. Lady Polly looked pretty as a picture in exactly the right furry hat and soft frilly blouse. Her looks, strong nose, heart-shaped face, reminding me of Romney's Lady Hamilton, gave one hope for her daughters. Perhaps Mandy and Tessa would one day turn into swans like this. Nevertheless Lady Polly succeeded in making a speech of quite exceptional incompetence. As a Tory MP's wife, she must surely have become accustomed to such things. Of course the ever-protective Tom never forced his constituency on Carrie – her nerves would never allow her to make a speech. But he was Labour.

Tories were known to be different and demanded far more from their wives.

Yet Lady Polly not only read her speech but lost her place and dropped her notes. She even made a hash of that hoary old play on words – 'a fête worse than death'. This came out as: 'I am sure this is not a death worse than a fête, even though my fate may be, trying to open it, I mean close it.' Quite. Perhaps she did it on purpose to try and gain her husband's attention? If it was a manœuvre, it failed. Sir Charles showed absolutely no interest in the proceedings whatsoever.

The lanky young man yawning beside Lady Polly was, I guessed, Jasper Justin of Eton College, Windsor, Berks. There was a miniature version of him sitting beside Sir Charles, equally spindly, in the uniform of some doubtless impeccable prep school. It was difficult to believe that Sir Charles had ever looked quite like that. But perhaps Justins put on weight, with responsibility, as they got older. Mandy Justin duly presented the bouquet to her mother, looking like a little doll, and giving a truly magnificent display of bashfulness. There was no sign of Tessa Justin.

'You must come and meet Polly,' purred Mother Ancilla in my ear. 'She's such a dear.' Like Lady Polly herself, Mother Ancilla was quite unabashed by the platform performance.

Not so every member of the audience.

'Honestly, Miss Shore, did you ever hear such rot?' hissed an indignant voice beside me. It was Dodo Sheehy. Dodo and Margaret had not been much in evidence during the bazaar. No doubt they disdained such things as being both time wasting and class ridden. It was a point of view one could share.

'Sir Charles Justin is a fascist beast,' she went on. Blanche and Imogen, standing rather languidly by, having abandoned the coffee stall, nodded as though well versed in the horrors of Sir Charles Justin's politics.

Margaret Plantaganet was standing by herself, over by the door. Her arms were folded. Her face wore its habitual stern expression in repose, what I called her crusader's look. Lady Polly, platform surrendered, stood quite close to her, twittering away and gesturing. I could not hear what she was saying, but the two of them could hardly have presented a more complete contrast in style and looks. I could not imagine Margaret opening a bazaar such as this in ten years' time, any more than she might marry a Conservative MP. That for her would truly constitute a fate worse than death. I had long ago abandoned my fantasy of Margaret among the brides in the Nuns' Parlour arrayed in white.

I decided to greet Margaret. But on reaching her, I was sucked into Polly Justin's orbit.

'I can't understand it,' she was saying with great indignation. 'Where is Tessa? I mean where is she? Why isn't she here? Why didn't she come for my speech?' It was tempting to suggest that Tessa Justin might have heard her mother speak before, and decided to keep clear. I resisted the temptation. But as the other parents melted thankfully away, a great deal of agitation was revealed among the remaining nuns. Mother Ancilla, like Lars Porsena, was sending her messengers forth, east and west and south and north, to summon Tessa Justin.

Mandy Justin was hopping to and fro at her mother's skirt sucking one finger.

Jasper Justin continued to yawn, while eyeing Dodo Sheehy. Master Justin, evidently a precocious youth, eyed a Fourth Former.

'I told you the girl wasn't here,' said Sir Charles Justin, fixing me with a belligerent and slightly bulbous eye. 'The trouble with Polly is that she's like a bitch in a thunderstorm when trying to make a speech. No sense at all.' It was the solitary remark I heard him make.

For all Mother Ancilla's enquiries, for all Lady Polly's fluttery demands, by the time the last parent had vanished, the last girl had returned to the children's wing, the Justins' silver Daimler still sat empty at the front door. By itself it seemed to constitute a great gleaming reproach to the institution which had so carelessly mislaid a member of its precious cargo.

Tessa Justin, the fact had to be faced, had utterly disappeared.

An hour later it transpired that she had not after all disappeared without trace. It was Mandy, weeping, who finally disgorged a typed note from her pocket.

'From Tessa,' she said, between sobs.

'Dear Mama and Papa,' it read, 'If you really want to know where I am, I have gone to stay with Aunt Claudia. Because I am unhappy here and she won't make me come back. I have got plenty of money. So don't worry. Your loving Tessa.' It was all typed, including the signature. Lady Polly continued her hysterics.

'Oh isn't that just typical of Tessa? Claudia Justin isn't even on the telephone. She's Charles's mad sister. Yes, Charles, don't contradict me. She is mad. Living in the Lake District and thinking dogs and cats can speak. You know the sort of thing.' But Sir Charles showed no signs of interrupting. He just looked more furious than ever.

'Why did she do this to me?' ranted on Lady Polly. 'We'll have to drive up there. No, we can't. It's much too far. And we've got the

Spanish Ambassador coming to stay. Oh it's too bad of Tessa – Charles, what shall we do?'

Sir Charles Justin said nothing. He strode forward and got to the wheel of his Daimler. It seemed as good an answer as any.

It was Jasper Justin who was left saying placatingly: 'Come along, Mama, we'll send a telegram. Mother Ancilla will iron it all out. I'm sure Tessa's perfectly all right. She always is.'

As I watched the departing Daimler, into which the remaining Justins had piled like the family of Louis XIV going to Varenne, I wished I shared Jasper's confidence. I myself was much less sure that Tessa Justin was perfectly all right. For one thing, I had recognised the typing of the note. And its style. I was positive that the same unknown source had provided all four typed notes; they had certainly been done on the same machine; three to me, one now to the Justins. Unless a ten-year-old had deposited two of the notes on my desk and secreted the third one in my overcoat pocket (which did not seem conceivable), then Tessa's note was a fake.

In which case, where was Tessa Justin? Kidnapping, I reflected with a sinking feeling, was one of the few experiences which really did justify that overworked phrase, a fate worse than death. Unless it turned out to end in death itself.

With a heavy heart, I took myself back to that room, the guest room, which I was now beginning to consider as my own personal cell. I tried, as calmly as I could, to consider the possibilities.

I was interrupted by a knock on my door.

There were few people I wanted to see at that particular moment. Certainly not Mother Ancilla, nor Margaret and Dodo for that matter. I desperately needed peace for thought before I talked to any of them.

I went to the door.

It was Sister Boniface. Her expression was almost as troubled as my own. And she was wheezing hard as she came in: she must have just climbed the visitors' stairs.

'Jemima, I'm worried,' she began without preamble, sinking down in a chair, a sign of exhaustion. Nuns rarely just sit down like that. 'I've been praying about it in the chapel. Taking my troubles to Our Lady, who lost the Infant Jesus when He went to the temple. And she's told me to come and talk to you.' More hard breathing.

'That child. Disappearing like that. Leaving a note. I don't like it one bit. She can't type for one thing. They don't learn typing till the Sixth Form. That note was beautifully typed. Sister John couldn't have done better herself, Beatrice O'Dowd I mean, when she was here she taught them typing. She was a trained secretary.'

The old nun drew breath.

'Besides, it's not like Tessa Justin. She's a show-off, you know. If Tessa was unhappy, we'd all know about it. She'd paint it on the chapel roof if she could. Not disappear. No fun, that, not seeing all the fuss for herself.

'Sister Lucy won't listen to me. Talks about a situation of sibling rivalry, I think that's what she calls it, all to do with Mandy presenting the bouquet. Hence Tessa's choice of her father's sister as a refuge. I told her that was all rubbish. But she won't listen. So I prayed to Our Blessed Lady, and she told me to come to you.'

'What about Mother Ancilla?' I had to ask that.

'I see you haven't heard yet. Poor Mother Ancilla. The strain of it all, the bazaar, the child vanishing. She's had one of her attacks. A bad one. She's lying in her cell now. They don't even want to move her to the infirmary.'

So potent was the aura of Mother Ancilla that for a moment, at the prospect of its removal, I felt quite helpless.

'I'm acting Reverend Mother. As the oldest member of the community.' Sister Boniface at least did not feel completely helpless. That at least encouraged me.

'And then – she wanted to tell you something, didn't she? Urgently. A private interview, she said. And I stopped you, Jemima, I'm sorry about that. And now I'm a frightened old woman.'

Not so strong after all. Another frightened old woman. As Mother Ancilla had been in our first discussion. No, merely that Mother Ancilla had collapsed and the burden had fallen on Sister Boniface's even more ancient shoulders.

I took a deep breath. It was time to take someone into my confidence. It looked as if my confidante, directed by the Virgin Mary or otherwise, was destined to be Sister Boniface.

As briefly and unemotionally as possible, I told her of Mother Ancilla's request to me, to uncover whatever might be evil or discordant at the heart of the convent. I did not burden her with the murkier ramifications of the whole affair. And I did not go further into the mystery of the Black Nun and my own terrifying encounter in the tower, beyond saying that there were forces of evil at work in the convent, and forces of good, in which some use was being made of the legend of the Black Nun, and I was not quite sure as yet which was which. God willing (oh fortunate phrase, that came to my tongue) I intended to find out.

But there was one vital question I had to ask her.

'Sister Bonnie,' I said, 'you know this place. You've been here, how long? Since you were a small child at the school – seventy years! Then you know everything there is to know about it. Is there any way known to you in which the tower, the old tower, Blessed Eleanor's retreat, could be linked to the chapel?'

An extraordinary look crossed the old nun's face. It was neither fear nor astonishment. It was a kind of illumination. For one instant she even looked young again. I had seen a glimpse of the young nun she had once been, not the gnarled old creature who confronted me.

'So many years ago,' she murmured. 'So many years have passed. That you should ask me that now.'

'Please, a life may depend on it.'

Sister Boniface gave me a more straightforward look, a return to her old self.

'When I was a novice,' she began gruffly, 'we knew that a secret passage joined the tower to the mediaeval chapel. That the chapel, our modern chapel, had been built over its foundations, so that the passage came up somewhere lower, into the level of the old chapel, into our crypt as a matter of fact. The idea was that the Blessed Eleanor making one of her retreats, used to come by night from her tower to pray privately in the chapel. But no-one ever talks about that now.'

'Why not? You must tell me.'

Another straightforward look.

'Because many years ago, when I was young, still a novice in short, a historian came here and talked a lot of nonsense about the Blessed Eleanor. He had been researching in some mediaeval sources he said. And he had come to the conclusion, or so he told Reverend Mother, right to her face, can you imagine it, well, you didn't know Reverend Mother Felix, but anyway he told her right to her face that the secret passage hadn't been for that at all. That it had been for Dame Ghislaine de Tourel to visit Blessed Eleanor at night, and for no good reason . . . And then, he asked if he could see the entrance to the secret passage!'

After all these years, indignation still burned.

'He wasn't a Catholic of course,' she added. 'Hardly. He was a *heathen*, in my mind. And I'll tell you what Reverend Mother Felix did. Straightaway she summoned us all and she told us that henceforth the secret passage did not exist. That we were never ever any of us to speak about it again, according to our holy vow of obedience. That we must protect the reputation of our Foundress from the attacks of the ungodly. And he went away defeated. And we never did speak about it again. And the others who knew about it then are all dead, years ago. Why, I believe I'm the only person alive who knows how to find the entrance.'

'Sister Boniface,' I said slowly. 'I'm afraid you're wrong. There is someone else still alive who knows how to find that entrance to the secret passage. Will you show me too? To the greater glory of God.' I don't know what made me add that last phrase. Convention. The convention of the situation in which I found myself.

13
Come to dust

It was nine o'clock. Looking out of the window I saw nothing but darkness. No moon tonight. It might have been the small hours. I was waiting for my rendezvous with Sister Boniface. She was adamant that she had to complete the ordained ritual of night prayers before joining me. I did not look forward to what we – I – had to do. I felt not so much fear, or the false exhilaration of my previous expedition. More a great sadness.

Whatever I discovered, whomsoever I might rescue, the status quo of the convent could not be saved entirely. But perhaps that was destined for disruption in any case. Mother Ancilla was still lying in her cell, too ill to be moved to the infirmary. She had suffered another heart attack, I learnt from Sister Lucy. The convent doctor had been and gone. That too cast a pall of sadness over us all.

I wrote a note to Tom.

I had decided to do that in case anything happened to me. It would be brief, and for once impersonal. The sort of note that he would not destroy. He could even show it to Carrie.

'Dear Tom,
    Just in case. Check up on Alexander Skarbek in London. And ask Sister Boniface where to find the secret passage in the convent. That's all.
    J.'

I addressed the envelope: Tom Amyas MP, House of Commons. I left it lying on my desk, right on top of the Treasury of the Blessed Eleanor, where it could not be overlooked.

A soft knock at the door interrupted my preparations. This time I would take two torches – Sister Boniface would provide me with a second – and in honour of Sister, otherwise Saint, Perpetua, two candles. A piece of rope (purloined from a child's trunk in the store room) and a good sharp knife (purloined from the cafeteria where it had vanished from under Sister Clare's eyes. Or so she put it. She was still making ineffectual noises of loss when I discreetly left the refectory).

Another soft knock. Clearly not Sister Boniface.

It was Sister Agnes.

'Miss Shore, please excuse me.' How polite she always was, deferential. Yet she always gave the impression of trying to put me at my ease, rather than the other way round. 'I know it's late. But I can't get little Mandy Justin to go to sleep. It's hardly surprising with all the upset of her sister running away. But she keeps saying that she has something to tell you, the television person, as she calls you. And she won't tell it to anyone else. I don't like to fetch Sister Lucy. So I wondered if you would perhaps consider coming along to St Aloysius' dormitory—'

I agreed with alacrity. Experience had taught me that it did not do to keep the Justin family waiting when they had news to impart.

Mandy Justin was presented for my inspection in Sister Agnes's own sleeping-quarters: a kind of extra cubicle on the outside of the big dormitory. That gave her freedom of movement to supervise the older children, who slept in double rooms, without disturbing the juniors in the dormitory.

This time Mandy's tears and suffering had, I fancied, been genuine. The first thing she said was:

'I'm not going to tell it to her,' and she pointed to Sister Agnes. 'I'm just going to tell it to *you*. Because you bought my silver toothbrush holder. And I've seen you on telly. Besides, I'm frightened of nuns.'

She started to sob. I touched her rather gingerly. Over her head my eyes met those of Sister Agnes.

'Sister?' It was only tentative.

'I'll go, Miss Shore,' she replied. Her expression was impossible to read. 'There, Mandy, don't cry,' she added kindly. 'You tell your story to Miss Shore, and then you can go to sleep.' She sounded even gentler than usual.

Sister Agnes withdrew. But she did not go very far. I could see her shadow outside the cubicle, the elongation of the shadow, its formlessness making her look much taller than she was.

Mandy's story was about a nun too. A strange nun, a nun she had never seen before, who had handed her the typed note. That note which she subsequently presented as being from her sister Tessa. Having been threatened that if she, Mandy, so much as opened her mouth on the subject, or produced the note until exactly one hour after the bazaar ended, the strange nun would come and take her away too. Like Tessa. The story of the Black Nun had clearly not reached the infants at Blessed Eleanor's. Otherwise Mandy Justin would have been not so much tear-stained as hysterical.

'Don't worry, Mandy, don't worry. It'll be all right.' How did one console a seven-year-old child whose ten-year-old sister had been kidnapped? I needed Sister Agnes. But there was one question I had to ask.

'The voice, Mandy; the voice. Did you recognise the nun's voice?'

'I told you I didn't know her. She was a horrid great nun. Besides, she was whispering—'

A horrid great nun who whispered. Was that what lay ahead of me in the Dark Tower? I surrendered Mandy to Sister Agnes.

'She'll sleep now.' I hoped that was true. I left Sister Agnes and the child abruptly. I went back to my room and tore open my note to Tom. I added in a scrawl: 'That isn't all. I love you, my darling. Till – death – but I do hope it won't happen. J.' I ended it with the outline of a heart. It was no longer the sort of note he could show to Carrie. But that would be his problem. I addressed another envelope and replaced the white note on top of the black Treasury.

Down the visitors' stairs, quiet as possible. Into the chapel, checking that the outside door was bolted on the way. It was. The red sanctuary lamp winked and glinted from the altar. The candles at the shrine of the Sacred Heart had burnt low since my first visit there. The statues, like living people, seemed to be making beckoning gestures in the gloom. Sacred Heart of Jesus, pray for me. Heart, my lucky symbol. St Joseph, father of the Holy Family, pray for me. Our Lady Tower of Ivory, pray for me. All the saints, pray for me. I could hear the litanies chanted in my imagination. But I did not pray myself. I merely adjured all possible saints to pray for Tessa Justin, or at least to try and guard her from on high. Tessa, Teresa – St Teresa, pray for her. No, not the great St Teresa of Avila, a woman for whom, beliefs apart, I had a great deal of sympathy. Reading a biography of her once, a composite with the other St Teresa, I had always felt that we should get on. I addressed myself not to that Eagle but to the Dove, the lesser St Teresa, the Little Flower. Sainte Thérèse, protect your Tessa Justin.

A dark form rose slowly up from the front pew.

Sister Boniface, bending and moving with difficulty. Her agility these

days was all in her mind – and her tongue. She gestured me to follow
her into the sacristy, to the left of the altar. The oak door was already
open. But there was no light. Sister Boniface's heavy breathing was the
only noise in the chapel.

Once we were safely in the sacristy, Sister Boniface shut the door
firmly. The heavy sound made me jump. But Sister Boniface spoke
naturally in the dark:

'I'll switch on the light for a moment. To find the door to the crypt
staircase. Only for a moment. We mustn't alarm the whole community.'

There was an instant of extreme brightness. Sister Boniface felt her
way round the oak panelling which lined the sacristy. I saw the priest's
robes, already laid out for the next morning's early mass. How
elaborately they were embroidered, how minutely, when you saw them
close! Even the vestments for an ordinary weekday mass, representing
so many hours of nuns' labour. Still, it was labour voluntarily given.
A.M.D.G., as I had quoted to Sister Boniface.

The furthest panel had a little iron inset. It contained a ring. Sister
Boniface twisted the ring and pulled it sharply. The panel swung back
and a narrow but well-turned stone staircase was revealed.

'I'd better turn out the sacristy light now,' said Sister Boniface. She
sounded quite cheerful about it all. I switched on my torch. 'Here's the
second one. You take that too.' She handed it over.

'When I come back, I'll leave the panel open of course. You'd better
come back before early mass. Otherwise whoever serves mass tomorrow
might go and shut it. And then where would you be? No windows in
the crypt. And very deep down—'

'Sister Bonnie, please!'

We descended.

The crypt was indeed very deep down. And not a very salubrious
atmosphere when we got there. At least I was allowed to switch on the
light: a rather dim bulb dangled in the centre of the arched ceiling from
a wire. But the floor was stone, unlike the floor of the tower, so that we
were spared that prevailing smell of damp. The crypt was also, so far as
I could see, extremely clean. The convent cleanliness extended even
underground. There were various niches in the stone walls, containing
more statues. And one large alcove, with a wooden *prie-dieu* in front of
it. A kind of shrine, it appeared. The alcove above contained a life-size
statue. I inspected it: a queen with a crown on her head – Mary, Queen
of Heaven, presumably. The features were idealised, soulful, and
reminded me of Sister Agnes. Victorian, I supposed.

'Blessed Eleanor herself,' said Sister Boniface. 'She was briefly Queen of England, you know. Wouldn't it be lovely if we had a Catholic queen again? Do you think Prince Charles—'

It was no time for this Mother Ancilla talk.

'I should think the statue is about 1860, wouldn't you?' I said hastily.

'Oh no, it's a portrait from the life,' said Sister Boniface reproachfully. 'Very, very old indeed. Anyway there are coffins here. Dame Ghislaine and quite a few of the early nuns. And they certainly are old. They stayed here undisturbed all through the Reformation, thanks to the mercy of God and the protection of Our Lady. Blessed Eleanor herself, I regret to say, was taken to Belgium. Although to be fair she did perform several miracles there in the last century. Which she might not have felt inclined to do here ... Being on her home ground.'

I was not disposed to discuss the finer points of miracle-making either. Besides, I did not like the reference to the other inhabitants of the crypt.

'I can't see any coffins,' I said nervously.

'There's a grille. Look behind you.'

I turned round. The far wall was not in fact made of stone. It consisted of a series of shelves, on which stacked coffins could be vaguely discerned. I had no idea how many of them there were. Or how far back they extended. A large iron grille stood between us and the coffins. Nevertheless I found the sight extremely creepy. But it did not seem to worry Sister Boniface at all. Perhaps it was her own strong faith, perhaps it was her inevitable nearness to death. But Sister Boniface was really quite unconcerned at her presence here among the bones of the dead.

The dust of the dead by now. They had all come to dust. Dame Ghislaine had been dead for over five hundred years. Even her dust had vanished.

'When was the – er – last?' My gaze was still riveted on the grille.

'Reverend Mother Felix. No, Reverend Mother Xavier and Reverend Mother Louise must both have been buried here after her. At my age, one gets muddled. You see only Reverend Mothers are placed here now. The rest of the community are buried in the cemetery. The grille is only opened on the death of a Reverend Mother.'

'So Mother Ancilla—'

'In God's good time, Mother Ancilla will rest here too.'

It was in both our minds that God's good time for Mother Ancilla could not be far away.

'I'm glad they're still behind a grille. The coffins. They can't get at me.'

'But, my child, it's behind those bars that you have to go,' said Sister Boniface. 'That's where the entrance to the secret passage is. Hidden by the coffins.'

14
The power of darkness

I felt quite sick. Bones, dust, what did it matter?. The fact that the last corpse must have been laid here over thirty years ago? All the same, this was a charnel-house. A grisly trap. I wanted to escape—

'Sister Boniface,' I answered in a shaky voice. 'Please show me now.'

She motioned to the grille.

'It was on the right. You should find the door in the wall on the right. It may be very dusty there. You may have to move a coffin, several. And that grille is probably very stiff. It hasn't been used for a generation.'

But it wasn't stiff at all. I tugged the handle. The grille swung back with ease. There was no dust that I could see. The door was very clearly delineated in the wall. And none of the coffins was blocking it. In short, there was no reason why the door to the passage could not have been in regular use lately. No reason at all.

I felt the door. And found another inset with a ring inside it, similar to that of the sacristy. I turned it and pulled sharply. The door opened. Another exit not to be shut against my return. Blackness yawned, complete blackness, and this time a heavy, disgusting stink of damp. Sister Boniface and I peered into the chasm.

'So it's still there,' she said after a while. 'Do you still want to go, Jemima?'

'I don't want to. I must.'

'I'll pray in the chapel till you come back,' said Sister Boniface.

'Take your torch back.'

'No need, nuns can see in the dark, didn't you know? I'll find my way back to the chapel. God bless you, my child, and preserve you from harm.'

Harm. What is it that would harm me? That evocative phrase, the powers of darkness. Darkness had no powers, I told myself savagely as I stepped into the black chasm. Come on, Jemima. The only power of darkness lay in the use that clever, unscrupulous people made of it to frighten and waylay the innocent. Darkness would have no power over me, because I would not permit it to do so.

I began to feel my way along the passage, watching the ground in the light of my torch. The passage was narrow, and the walls at the bottom crumbly. I could now understand how my coat, covering my unconscious body, had gathered dust. It struck me that I must have been carried, not dragged. There had been no bruises on my body when I was recovering in the infirmary.

But if carried – another inescapable thought assailed me. That meant two people. Two people of considerable strength. I was taller than average. It was not a conclusion to cheer a lonely traveller.

I hoped I would not find two people – two people of considerable strength – at the end of my journey.

The ground was surprisingly even. And above my head was a well-worked stone roof. It was inconceivable that this passage had been constructed in this form in the middle ages. Like the statue of the Blessed Eleanor, I suspected a much later date. It all had the workmanlike look of a well-put-together Victorian folly. Obviously whichever Reverend Mother had been responsible for building the Victorian chapel had had the passage thoroughly overhauled as well.

The existence of the passage had been common knowledge in Sister Boniface's youth: which brought us to a period before the first war. Then the threat of the historian's revelations had induced Mother Felix to impose her vow of silence. But knowledge did not die away so quickly. Sister Hippolytus, for example: did she know about the passage? Was that the revelation she promised us in her manuscript? More than likely. Poking about in the convent records, she could easily have made such a discovery.

I have no idea how far I travelled before the ground began to rise. I had the impression of walking at least half a mile, but the darkness robbed me of a sense of time and distance. As the crow flew the tower was not really so far from the chapel. It was tramping the fields which took the time to get there. No doubt the passage followed the most direct route.

The incline grew more pronounced, the ground was cut into steps. Then there were formal steps of stone, and those in their turn led to a winding staircase. Finally I found myself in front of a door. It was exactly similar to the door at the other end of the passage. The door was shut.

She who hesitates is lost. Come on, Jemima. I twisted the iron ring which held it, extinguished my torch, and pushed the door open. I stepped forward.

Immediately something very hard indeed struck me sharply on the top of my head. I ducked. Instinctively I put up my hand. It felt like stone. A broad smooth stone surface with a sharp edge. Then I heard a noise which sounded like a cat or perhaps a kitten mewing.

There was no other sound at all.

I felt upwards again. I had hit my head on a piece of stone. It was in fact the mantel of a stone fireplace. I recognised where I was: standing bent inside the fireplace of the first floor chamber of the tower. The fireplace where I had originally spotted those tell-tale Gauloises stubs. The winding stair must have come up inside the thick walls of the tower. Boldly, I switched on my torch.

The rocking-chair was still. And empty. There was no sign of a black habit there. Or a black nun.

Tessa Justin was lying on the floor in the corner. In the small light, she looked as if she were asleep or perhaps drugged. But it was she who was responsible for those sounds, the mewings of a kitten. The trap-door to the ground floor was closed.

I walked across to her. She was not asleep. Her eyes were open. I didn't think she was drugged. She was in fact sobbing, but so tiredly that only these tiny sounds emerged.

'Tessa,' I said softly, 'Tessa, don't cry.'

She didn't look up. Her body – still in its school uniform but the maroon heavily marked with dust – froze.

'It's me, Jemima Shore.' No move still. She didn't look at me. I touched her shoulder. It was quite rigid. Maybe after all she had been drugged.

'I've come to rescue you.' No move. I had an inspiration. 'I've come to hear the story you've got to tell me. Look, look at me, Tessa.'

Slowly Tessa Justin lifted her head off the floor. Her thick plaits were dusty too, whitened. Her eyes looked enormous. I shone the torch onto my own face.

'See, I'm not a nun.'

She gave a loud cry, said something like: 'Oh, oh, take me *home.*' And scrambling off the floor, flung herself at me.

At least Tessa Justin, the missing Tessa Justin, was neither drugged nor damaged. And for the time being at least she was safe. I didn't know how long that happy state of affairs would last. How soon before the powers of darkness who had kidnapped her and dumped her here, planned to return? As once they must have come to find the imprisoned Rosa in her Tower of Ivory. And seen that she never escaped from it ... It didn't do to think of such things.

We had to get back. But first I had to soothe the incoherent Tessa. I doubted whether I could carry a ten-year-old girl all that way down the passage. By myself.

'Tell me later,' I kept saying, patting her and trying to disentangle myself. But she wouldn't let me go. I longed for the calm strength of a nun, any nun. The gentle authority of Sister Agnes, the businesslike ways of Sister Lucy.

Tessa Justin would not be stopped from pouring it all out, as we sat there on the wooden floor in the dark tower. And we each held one torch. Eventually I pulled her onto my lap in the rocking-chair. And cuddled her there as best I could. The feeling of closeness grew on me. I couldn't remember when I had last held a child of any age in my arms.

'There, there,' I kept saying, and other things, endearments and tender words, until the choking finally stopped.

Like her sister Mandy, Tessa poured out a story in which there was the now familiar feature of a strange nun, a nun she had never seen. Except that Tessa, being in the Lower Fourth knew all about the Black Nun; and readily identified her as the persecutor. Mandy had spoken of a horrid great nun who whispered. Tessa described the Black Nun herself, speaking in a low hoarse voice, the Black Nun who for some time, for ages, forever, had been out to get Tessa Justin.

How the Black Nun had come to her at night and whispered to her – and nobody had believed her. And how on another night the Black Nun had threatened to put a pillow over her face and nobody had believed that either. How Sister Lucy had just given her medicine and Sister Boniface had threatened to give her a good smack. And even lovely Sister Agnes had not believed her. That's why she had tried to talk to me about it. And Sister Boniface had stopped her.

But it was true, all true. The Black Nun was out to get her. And then, the worst thing of all, just before the bazaar, as she was getting tidy, she received a message to say that her parents were waiting for her in the sacristy. She thought it was a bit odd—

'But everything about nuns is a bit odd, Miss Shore, isn't it?' she said rather pathetically. So along went Tessa to the sacristy. And the next thing she knew, the strange nun, the Black Nun, pulled her down some stairs and into a dark place and through a long smelly tunnel. And then—

'And then?'

'Well, these questions,' she cried. 'All the time these questions. And if I didn't answer I would never see my parents again, or Mandy, or Jasper, or Charlie or anyone.' More sobs. I cuddled her again.

'Questions? The will, then, Sister Miriam's will—'

'Oh yes, the will, the beastly will. Oh if you know where it is, can't you tell them, Miss Shore? I told her, I told her what I knew. But she just wouldn't believe that was all.' The head buried in my coat. I smoothed the plaits, all I could see of her.

It transpired that what Tessa Justin knew about the will was this: it was not much, I had to admit. Except that she did know more than anyone else about it. There had been this odd conversation with Sister Miriam, on what turned out to be the very day Sister Miriam disappeared. Tessa had just come back from seeing off her parents at the front door when she found herself grabbed by Sister Miriam who looked, as she put it, 'awfully odd, even for a nun'. In Tessa Justin I detected already the beginnings of an anti-nun prejudice to rival Tom's.

There was nobody much about. Sister Damian, the portress, was not at her post, and there were no other nuns visible. Sister Miriam had much surprised Tessa by suddenly putting her thin face very close and whispering to her:

'I've made a new will, you know.' Or something to that effect.

'Of course she *was* a little batty,' confided Tessa – oh Rosa! – 'We juniors knew that. Batty but rather sweet. We all liked her. So we never teased her on anything horrid. And then she said something about it being quite safe and I must remember and tell nobody. Then I think her bell rang – a bell rang, hers or someone else's, and another nun came round the corner. I don't remember who. And she started and let me go and ran off. You don't often see a nun haring along, do you?' she ended.

But Tessa hadn't really understood what Sister Miriam was talking about. Even when she was found dead. Till that day in St Joseph's sitting room where she had hidden for a dare and had been discovered. And after that Margaret Plantaganet and Dodo Sheehy had suspected something. Because she had foolishly boasted to her best friend, who was Cordelia Smith, Imogen's sister, that she knew where the missing will was. Then Cordelia told Imogen. And the big girls had questioned her. And she didn't tell them anything of course. Horrible bullies. But she had told everything to the Black Nun, and now to me. And please would everyone leave her alone?

'But where, where was it safe?'

But that alas was exactly where Tessa's childish memory became vague. All she could tell me was what she had told the Black Nun so many times, and not been believed for her pains.

'It was something to do with brides,' she said. 'Brides and nuns, or the other way round, nuns and brides.'

'Nuns and brides – nuns, the brides of Christ? That's what they're sometimes called.'

Yes, that was it. The brides. The brides of Christ. Being safe among the brides of Christ.

Safe among the brides of Christ, I thought. Safe indeed. But that might be anywhere in the entire convent . . . No wonder the Black Nun had shaken Tessa till her teeth rattled and still got nothing more out of her. And gone away and threatened to come back soon. And how Tessa must then tell her more or else . . . Yes, it was time for us to be going.

There was no point in dusting the child down. We should get dirty enough on our return journey, if not worse. I urged her to cling onto her torch at all costs—

'Tie your plaits round it if necessary.' A wan smile. 'It belongs to Sister Boniface. She's waiting for us in the chapel.' That did cheer Tessa: obviously Sister Boniface was to her, as to me, a symbol of security.

We made our way back through the fireplace. I made no attempt to close the door behind me. That was for others to clear up. Down the winding stair, stone giving way to earth, then back the way we had both come through the tunnel. The return journey seemed to take aeons of time. It was not that Tessa dragged behind. On the contrary, she was incredibly staunch considering her ordeal. The Justins had spirit, one had to hand it to them. Show-off she might be, Tessa was also full of proper courage as well.

But I was waiting and listening all the time for some noise ahead of us. The signal of the return. Even now was the Black Nun abandoning her nightly search for the will? And going back for a fresh examination of her victim? Who could tell? Perhaps she had at last found it, and would return in triumph . . .

A whole age of nervous footsteps had passed before we saw the crypt door ahead of us. God be praised, it was still open. And praise all the saints too. And St Teresa – both St Teresas. I was in a mood to be generous. I had not admitted to myself how much I had been dreading to find our exit barred.

'Come on, Tessa, not much further,' I said in a low voice.

She went through the door first with her torch. I followed, stooping. We were once more beside the coffins, in the charnel-house in fact. The grille too was still open. Swung back as it had been before. The dim light still burned in the crypt. I could see that the outer door to the sacristy was still ajar. Everything was just as it had been. We were safe. Safe indeed. Once more under the roof of the brides of Christ.

It was a piercing scream from Tessa which told me, violently, that I was wrong. Not everything was just as it had been before.

There, there behind the marble statue of the Blessed Eleanor, lay the difference. A black shape, a long shadow, now stretched out from behind the statue. Tessa's screams rang in my ears as the black shape, now growing in size, stepped out from the protection of the alcove and began slowly, purposefully, to move in our direction.

15

A crypt is for coffins

'Run, Tessa, run,' I shouted. 'Find Sister Boniface'. The little girl, still obediently clutching her torch, did not hesitate, and bolted in the direction of the open door.

She reached it. The last I saw of Tessa Justin was her thin legs scampering up the stairs to the sacristy. Then the crypt door clanged to. She must have banged it behind her.

I was alone with the Black Nun.

Black not only from head to foot in her habit but also black and faceless. In the electric light of the crypt I could see clearly that the so-called Black Nun was wearing a black mask. That made me feel no better. At that moment I would have preferred to face a ghost than this silent figure, hands folded under her cape. The characteristic gesture of nuns by which they hid their hands. I knew all about these particular hands. I had already glimpsed their long bony fingers in the candlelight of the tower.

I touched the knife in my pocket.

The Black Nun now stood quite close. Between me and the door. The odd thing was that I could smell her: a strong human smell of someone who is excited. It gave me quite a different kind of jolt: I don't think I had ever consciously smelt a nun before. Whatever the austere nature of the cleansing materials allowed to them, every nun I had known had been as immaculately clean as if no body whatsoever existed inside the habit. And there was another smell, too, a different smell . . .

I was taken quite unawares by the next action of the Black Nun. Suddenly she extended one long arm from beneath her cape and with those same strong fingers, swung down the iron grille in my face. Iron bars now separated us; on the one side of them, the Black Nun, hands once more folded under the cape. I was imprisoned with the coffins.

The Black Nun continued to face me. Then with another rapid movement, she whipped up her hand and removed the thick mask.

'Jemima Shore. We've met before,' said the Black Nun. 'That rhymes. How charming.'

It was the roll of the 'R' on the word rhyme which reminded me that Alexander Skarbek had a faint foreign accent.

When I last saw him on my television programme, I had noticed it. I thought it part of his attraction. Now it only confirmed my worst fears, and still more fearful anticipations.

He removed his other hand from under the cape. I saw that he was smoking. A Gauloise. The second familiar smell I had noted. The first smell had, of course, been that of a man. Looking down I saw that the floor was littered with cigarette stubs. He must have been waiting here for me for some time. Knowing where I had gone. Knowing that the tower was locked and that I had to come back this way. Into the crypt.

The crypt with its coffins, amongst which it seemed likely that I would stay.

'A bad habit,' said Skarbek. He flung down the cigarette and stubbed it out impatiently with his foot. I noticed that he was wearing black boots, ordinary Kings Road type of boots as I would normally have termed them. With chunky heels. His feet – for a nun – looked enormous. Yet he was hardly much taller than I was. That explained the absence of shoes and stockings when Sister Liz and I first discovered the empty habit. For one idiotic moment I recalled all those wartime stories about German paratroopers dressed as nuns and how you could tell them by their boots.

'You look quite charming surrounded by coffins,' said Skarbek. 'Are you fond of coffins, Jemima?'

'Not particularly, Mr Skarbek.' My frigidly formal tone was the best I could do under the circumstances. I suddenly had to hang on to the grille. I was shaking.

'But a crypt is for coffins, Jemima.' Another roll of the 'R'. I wondered how I could ever have found his accent attractive. Or him.

Yes, in a way he made a plausible woman, or nun at least, because of the regularity of his features: yet his light eyes and sharp straight nose, his wide mouth, had not struck me as particularly feminine when we met. More wolfish. But he seemed slight to me then. Physically it was odd how a slender man became a towering woman – or a horrid great nun, in the words of Mandy Justin. A nun who whispered, who spoke in a hoarse tone: that was to conceal the man's voice. The wimple to conceal not the signs of age, but the man's throat, the prominent Adam's apple. Then the black mask to hide the man's face to anyone who might recognise it, such as myself. But there would be no need to disguise his face to children. Especially to little girls, late at night. So Skarbek the Black Nun had been able to roam as he wished through the convent, looking for the will which eluded him. The will leaving the lands to the Powers Project.

His relief at hearing the news that this will did exist after all must have been profound. Otherwise why not let Rosabelle hand over the lands herself and endure the long battles with the lawyers?

It only remained to find it. The missing will. And then the property for which one woman had already died would belong to the poor. Or rather to the Powers Project.

'Do you think I make a good nun, Jemima?' Skarbek interrupted my frightened searching thoughts. His voice was still light, almost caressing, through the grille.

'I don't think you make a nun at all, Mr Skarbek,' I said with all the spirit I could muster. 'Nuns are dedicated to the service of God. If I believed in His existence I would say that you on the contrary were dedicated to the service of the devil.'

'Harsh words, Jemima. But like you, I don't believe in the devil. All the same, the devil and all his pomps is a good phrase. Certain pomps are quite devilish, aren't they? Places like this. Wasting money, parasites on society.'

He was playing with me. There was no point in joining in the sport. I rattled the grille.

'Mr Skarbek, are you going to let me out of here?'

'But of course, Jemima. If only because I want to come much closer to you.' With a courtly gesture towards the grille. 'Perhaps you will like me better if we are closer to each other. Or is it the habit which troubles you? That can easily be arranged. At least part of it.' Rapidly, as if born of long practice – which I suppose it was – Skarbek removed the black veil, fixed by its tiny black pins, then the stiff white wimple and white cap beneath. He placed them on the *prie-dieu*. Beneath it all his hair was unexpectedly long. Instead of a nun he looked now like a young priest, standing there in black soutane. Then he swung back the grille.

I stepped out. It was a relief to be free, free at least from the coffins.

'I'll have your torch if you don't mind.' He took it. I made no resistance. I did not want him to know about the knife. Till I was ready. Then he offered me one of his cigarettes from the blue packet. I had not smoked since I was fifteen, when I puffed out of bravado with Rosa. But I took one and lit it clumsily and drew on it as I had watched others do, as I had watched Tom do, so many times. It was an odd feeling having Skarbek's face so close to mine, now free of its habit, as he held the match. Odd. Intimate. Distasteful.

'Mr Skarbek—'

'Alex, please. You don't mind if I call you Jemima. After all I was on your programme. We're friends.' A roll of the 'R'. I wondered if he was putting the accent on. What new friendships television brought me to be sure – Pia recalling me with delight, who had hardly known me at school, Tessa and Mandy Justin who both thought of me as their ally for no better reason than because they had seen me on the box, and now Alexander Skarbek. 'I know you especially well because I saw you again last night on the programme, our programme. I thought how pretty you were all over again.'

It was sickening to think of this kind of compliment actually winning the hearts of Rosa and Beatrice O'Dowd. For myself, I had always lived in the world, and was scarcely susceptible.

'You know, Jemima,' went on Skarbek, 'I thought last night that you would make a good nun. I don't mean all that—' he gestured to the veil and wimple with his cigarette. He looked so masculine to me now that I wondered even the children had been deceived. 'But your spirit. There is something nun-like about you, something pure, withdrawn, dedicated to service.'

'The nuns you have known may have started pure and dedicated to service,' I retorted with an angry puff of my cigarette, 'but they soon became dedicated to something quite different.'

'Nun, what nun?' he said sharply. 'Put that thing out. You have no idea how to smoke it.' He took the cigarette from my fingers and threw it on the floor to join the others, crushing it with his boot.

'Rosabelle Powerstock, Sister Miriam, and Beatrice O'Dowd, Sister John, when you first knew her.'

'Ah yes. Those most sincere ladies. I certainly changed the direction of their dedication, that is true. Or rather we changed it between us, did we not? Our programme, as I call it. From the service of God in heaven to the service of the poor on earth. Not a bad swap, I would say.'

I said nothing. I was wondering, now that he was more relaxed, whether I could make a dash for the door. I put my hand casually into my pocket and closed it on the knife.

Immediately Skarbek threw down his own cigarette, grabbed my wrist and pulled it out of my pocket, knife and all. He continued to hold it up, gazing at the blade. Then he laughed and with a twist made me turn the blade towards myself.

'Don't be frightened, Jemima. A dagger to your heart? No, no, too crude. I don't work like that. Everything is natural that happens here. Natural – if unfortunate. A key breaks off in a lock. A sick nun starves to death as a result. It's all a mistake. Who is to question that?'

'So – Sister Edward too?' I said bitterly. 'Her medicines out of reach. Struggling for breath. Natural if unfortunate.'

'I did not kill Veronica O'Dowd,' replied Skarbek. 'I can assure you of that. That was – how shall I put it – purely unfortunate. She would not have lived long in any case. Asthma had weakened her heart. Her family knew that. For you, perhaps, another unfortunate incident in the tower. Jemima Shore, Investigator, is the victim of her own adventurous spirit. She investigates the passage, a door slams, too late. She can't get out. Like her friend Sister Miriam, she dies in the Tower of the Blessed Eleanor.'

'Who told you about the passage? You can satisfy my curiosity about that.'

'Ah, the passage. That was a bit of luck, wasn't it? The reminiscences, which would otherwise have been intolerably dreary, of a bad-tempered but historically-minded old nun.'

I had no difficulty in recognising the description ... Sister Hippolytus. I wondered when he had met her: how he had fooled her. It would not be so easy to pull the wool over Sister Hippolytus's eyes.

He opened my fist and the knife clattered to the floor. Then he put his hands in my pockets and brought out the rope, the candles and the matches.

'How very thoughtful of you Jemima, to bring your own rope. I was wondering what I was going to use to tie you up. Perhaps you might be wearing an exciting belt under that thick and rather unexciting coat? Or perhaps my rosary? Quite thrilling that.'

'What are you going to do?' I could not stop the apprehension from creeping into my voice.

'I'm going to tie you up. To this convenient grille I think. Inside it or outside it? Shall it be inside with the coffins? Or outside with the statue of the Blessed Eleanor? Boring woman. I've looked at copies of her Treasury once or twice, searching for the will. Incredibly tedious, don't you think? I do hope her ghost doesn't come to call on you. For your sake. She might bore you to death. Forgive me, I didn't mean to make quite such a bad taste joke—'

'Not inside. Please. Not with the coffins.

'Surely you don't seriously believe in ghosts? They're all dead, you know. Bones and nothing else in those coffins.'

'What are you going to do?' I said again.

'Just tie you up for a little while. That's all. Not forever. There's someone I have to go and see. And I don't want you to get away.' He busied himself with the rope, tying me deftly, quickly, to the outside of the grille. At least I was thankful for that. Perhaps this small mercy was some kind of good omen that he did not after all intend to deal too harshly with me. It was better to hope.

'You might try saying a few prayers if you're lonely,' he said. 'You're not a Catholic, I know. Then I could teach you a few. A Hail Mary or two works wonders for the nerves.'

'Are you a Catholic?' I asked incredulously.

'My parents were. I was brought up as such. Until I saw the error of their ways – very early indeed in my existence, I can assure you. The country where I was born is one of those where ignorance and superstition is so deeply rooted in the hearts of the stupid peasants that nothing, not even communism, can get rid of it. Poland.'

'Poland. I didn't realise you were Polish.'

'I came here as a refugee when I was very young, ironically from the new state after the war. Because I was officially a Catholic, the do-gooders here even sent me to a convent school at first – until I ran away.' It explained many things.

'So you see I know what I'm talking about when I say that you would have made a charming nun. By the way, what a pretty colour your hair is.' He put out his hand and touched it. I flinched. 'And your face. There is still something child-like, untouched, about your face. In spite of that incredibly severe expression you are trying to assume.'

He held my chin and looked at me. I turned my head away. The light, almost yellow eyes were like those of an animal. A hunting animal. Not an animal in the zoo. Of the two of us, I was the captive animal. I saw him glancing at the veil.

'I wonder how it would be—' he said suddenly. 'Do you fancy dressing up as a nun?' And he bent his head and pressed his lips hard to mine. I struggled and tried in vain to press myself further back into the grille. I was profoundly horrified.

'No,' I cried, when at last he released me.

'Blasphemy? Sacrilege? You can't believe that,' he said, smiling.

'But *you* do.'

'I must remind you that there is no God. Hence no blasphemy. All the same, it might have been interesting. For us both. I assure you, Jemima, I'm not interested in unwilling victims. No-one was unwilling.'

'Pathetic sex-starved women,' I said. 'What splendid conquests!'

'Oh, quite. Conquests weren't the point. Surely you understand that.' He lit another cigarette. 'That was all purely for the good of the cause. It meant nothing to me whatsoever. Beatrice O'Dowd is a nice woman but an awful fool, not at all my type. In any case it was not necessary to seduce her, she simply exchanged one love or passion for another, in both cases strictly platonic. As for those girls, that fat little blonde with the absurd name, Dodo, and Blanche and Imogen.' He mimicked their enthusiastic upper-class voices. 'Working for the poor in the holidays from their smart fee-paying school. Writing us eager letters, imagining they have actually joined us on the other side of the barrier. Hero-worship was what they wanted, not sex.'

'And their leader, Margaret?'

'She's different. At least she knows how to keep her mouth shut. An interesting girl. She's more like you.'

'And Rosabelle?' I had to ask.

'Ah, your friend. The heiress. A strange woman. Even for a nun. So many different impulses: no wonder she had a nervous breakdown.'

'Beatrice O'Dowd thought all that happened because Mother Ancilla got her away. They were of course great friends.' Even now I refused to use the term 'particular friends'.

'Nonsense. Rosabelle had many secrets from Beatrice, I can tell you. Including where she hid her will. Beatrice always exaggerates her importance in every situation. It makes her hell to work with at times at the Project. The others complain. It was Rosabelle Powerstock who first contacted us, I can assure you. Afterwards—' He seemed to have nothing more to say on that subject. I did not know whether to be glad or sorry. Just as I did not altogether know whether to be glad or sorry at the unexciting truth about the relationship between Rosa and Beatrice. Glad that it had been innocent. Sorry that Rosa had not even been granted the comfort of one real confidante in her last months.

'The brides of Christ indeed!' he went on angrily. 'Most of them would be a great deal better off as proper brides, bourgeois white finery, veils, orange blossom and all. At least they would perform one useful function in society; wife followed rapidly by mother. I prefer the intelligent,' he repeated. 'That's why it's a pity that you're not more accommodating. Tom Amyas is your chap, isn't he? Oh, don't worry. We make it our business to know that sort of thing about MPs who don't exactly love us. Just in case the information comes in useful. An awful ass, isn't he, always grinding on about his conscience. Does he bleat about it in bed as well?'

I did not deign to answer. Skarbek fished something out of his pocket.

'Which reminds me. We can't have this hanging about, alas. That would never do.'

It was my note to Tom. Skarbek lit a match and put the flame to the corner. The black fragments floated down to the floor to join the cigarette stubs.

I was no longer so hopeful that nothing terrible was going to happen to me. Skarbek was robing himself in the wimple and veil again. Then he took up my two candles.

'Your candles I'll leave you,' he said. 'Out of reach. But alight. No funny stuff burning the ropes. You will be like a saint, Jemima, with two candles burning to you. Your own particular shrine.'

So saying, he moved the *prie-dieu* across the crypt until it faced me. He placed one candle on either side. Then he switched off the crypt light.

'Very charming.' An elaborate roll of the 'R' again. I was certain he was putting it on. 'Saint Jemima of the coffins.' To me the whole crypt, now lit only by the flicker of two small candles, looked less charming than horrifyingly eerie.

And roped to the grille, in my own particular shrine as he called it, I no longer believed Skarbek in his protestations about blasphemy. In some corner of his being, however remote, he still believed in the possibility.

'I promise I won't be long,' he said, 'we have so many interesting things to talk about. Later. But there's someone I just have to see. Another intelligent female, as a matter of fact. I really do have a taste for them. And I must deal once and for all with that wretched child. Something natural, what was it I said, something natural but unfortunate.'

Tessa! In my fear and confusion I had forgotten all about Tessa Justin. And what on earth had happened to my old but stout-hearted sentinel, Sister Boniface, last seen departing to pray in the chapel? Why had Sister Bonnie not raised the alarm? Tessa Justin, in her filthy and hysterical state was surely sight enough to promote a dozen search parties.

'Tessa will have woken the whole convent by now,' I answered. 'I doubt if you will find it quite so easy to deal with her.' My words were bold. But I was worried by the lack of extraordinary sounds from above. In fact, no sound at all. 'Sister Boniface was there and—'

'Oh, she's been dealt with already.'

Not Bonnie—

'Nothing sinister in this case. Purely natural, dear Jemima. Not even unfortunate. Lured away from the chapel. A story that Mother Ancilla needs her. After that she will be given an assurance that you are safe. That Tessa is safe too. That you both returned through the chapel while she was absent. She won't interfere with our plans.'

Our plans. That was it. I had to face the fact – that Skarbek had an accomplice within the convent itself. A highly efficient accomplice or as he himself described her, an intelligent female. Someone who had nightly opened the crypt door to let in the Black Nun. Not Beatrice O'Dowd, who was no longer an inmate of the convent, free to come and go as she pleased. Besides, I believed Skarbek when he said that Beatrice, foolish clothes and all, was still in her own way animated by love, or at least idealism. 'Very easily led,' Mother Ancilla had said. In more ways than one, I was beginning to think that the Reverend Mother's opinions represented the most solid canon of common sense in this unquiet convent.

'And so Jemima, I must leave you. I must go once more among the brides of Christ.'

I watched the Black Nun depart. His figure in its habit soon melted into the darkness of the crypt staircase. At least he left the lower door open. The candles flickered. I prayed – yes, prayed to something or someone – that they would not go out. And leave me alone and helpless in the darkness. No smoking, no praying, where now were the principles of a lifetime, I asked myself. Come on, Jemima. It was a grim attempt at humour. At least it might help me to survive.

I had many reasons to wish to survive. For one thing, I now knew where the last will and testament of Rosabelle Powerstock was hidden.

16

Healing hands

He was gone. I was alone in the crypt with the coffins – and the statue of the Blessed Eleanor – for company. I heard the upper sacristy door shut. I was entombed.

There was silence.

Only minutes later, it could not have been more, there was a noise. It sounded like that same sacristy door opening. Yes, and now footsteps down the stairs again. Why? Had Skarbek forgotten something, or had he perhaps thought better of leaving me in the crypt? Was I destined for the tower straight away ... All these questions thronged through my mind, none of them arousing very pleasant images, as the light foot-steps descended the stairs.

A nun stood framed in the doorway. It was not, I thought, Skarbek. So far as I could be sure against the limited light of the candles. The crypt light flicked on.

'Why Miss Shore,' said a familiar voice. 'Whatever are you doing here?'

It was Sister Agnes.

A lesser woman might have screamed. Or amplified her question. At least she might have cried out: whatever are you doing there tied up with ropes, with two candles beside you, confined to a grille in a crypt, backing onto a multitude of ancient coffins. Not so, Sister Agnes.

'Oh dear, oh dear,' was all she said, moving swiftly across the crypt to my side. 'Poor Miss Shore. Poor dear Miss Shore.' From her tone she might have been sympathising with a child who had fallen over and cut her knees.

'Free me, Sister Agnes, free me please.'

'Of course, Miss Shore, of course I'll free you.' Her delicate strong fingers were already plucking at the rope.

'There's a knife somewhere. On the floor over there.' Sister Agnes bent down and came up with a cigarette stub. She wrinkled her nose. Then she found the knife. She straightened and held it towards me – for a moment, I even thought—

But Sister Agnes quickly and competently cut the rope. I was free. Dusty, stiff, still terrified, but free. She put the knife down on the *prie-dieu*.

'You must have help,' she said.

'We must both have help,' I replied earnestly. 'Tell me, first of all, is Tessa all right?'

'Tessa? But she ran away. You remember—'

'No, no, she didn't run away. Anyway she's back. Oh, God, don't tell me he's got Tessa—'

'There's no sign of Tessa Justin upstairs in the dormitory, I assure you. But we can deal with that later. First, I must help you upstairs. Why, you're in the most distressing state.'

Once more Sister Agnes began to cluck, and dust my clothes. I felt her healing hands cross my brow for the second time; she had rescued me before, and was experienced in how to soothe me. Then carefully and I thought disapprovingly, Sister Agnes blew out the candles which had constituted my shrine.

'How dreadful,' said Sister Agnes. It wasn't clear whether she meant the whole enterprise or just the candles themselves.

'Now I shall help you back up the stairs.'

I thought: we've done this before too, as the young nun put her arm round my shoulders and began to aid me back up the winding stair to the sacristy. Once inside, there was no light on. That was odd. Perhaps Sister Agnes, like Sister Boniface, had not wanted to alarm the whole convent. But in my opinion, growing rapidly in urgency, the sooner the whole convent was alarmed, the better.

Where was the switch? I felt round to the door, found it. The sacristy flooded with light. Sister Agnes moved quickly round after me and switched it off again.

'Please Miss Shore,' she said. 'Not yet. Here's your torch. I found it on the floor. Use that if you like. We nuns can see in the dark, you know.' As Sister Boniface had observed to me earlier. Sister Boniface. Surely the old nun would have sent someone by now to my rescue.

'I left Sister Boniface here in the chapel—' I began.

'Hush, hush, Miss Shore. Don't worry about Sister Boniface. If she was praying here, and has gone, she was probably needed by Mother

Ancilla. Our Reverend Mother is gravely ill and Sister Boniface is by convent tradition her deputy. Until the new Reverend Mother is chosen.'

She sounded amazingly matter-of-fact about the prospect of her superior's imminent death. But one expected nuns to be matter-of-fact about death. It was Sister Agnes's calm approach to my own predicament which confused me. To say nothing of the missing child.

'But Tessa Justin, I *found* her. And now what's happened to her? You don't understand what's going on here, Sister Agnes.'

By way of answer Sister Agnes opened the sacristy door to the chapel. We were once more in the religious light of the sanctuary and its candles. Candles in their proper place in front of a proper shrine. It was a great relief to me to find myself back in the ornate Victorian chapel, away from that mediaeval nightmare of crypts, secret passages and towers.

The chapel, so far as I could see, was empty. I devoutly hoped – not quite the cliché the phrase usually was – that no-one was lurking behind the far pillars. No Black Nun within the distant shadows.

Sister Agnes paused by the first pew.

'No, Miss Shore,' she said. 'I think it is you who doesn't understand quite what is going on here.' Then she guided me out of the chapel by the visitors' door. 'Come, we must go to your room.'

There was great authority in her low voice. I felt mesmerised by her. Far more mesmerised than I had felt while in the power of Alexander Skarbek. Her personality was hypnotic. In her mixture of tranquillity and strength, combined with her physical resemblance to my dead friend, I found all the qualities I had once sought, and sought in vain, in Rosabelle.

I tried once more a feeble protest.

'Don't you think the infirmary – Tessa—'

'No.'

We went in silence up the stairs. Sister Agnes opened the door of my room. She settled me in my chair, taking my coat, dusting the skirt of it again, and finally placing it on the bed. It look dishevelled, and as I felt, forlorn as a result of its experiences in the passage.

'Listen to me, Miss Shore. I have to leave you here for a while. There is something I have to do. Someone I have to see. Please stay here.' She paused and placed one hand on mine. It was a clasp whose warmth and firmness reminded me not so much of Rosabelle as of Mother Ancilla.

'Promise me that whatever you do, you won't leave this room until I return. Is there a key? Good. Then lock your door. And don't let anyone in.'

I was only too delighted at the idea of locking my door. I had absolutely no wish to admit any of the sinister nocturnal ramblers at Blessed Eleanor's. Above all, not the Black Nun. Still roaming somewhere loose in the corridors, the rooms, the passages. Maybe even in the empty guest room next to mine. I shivered. I would lock my door all right.

'Trust me, Miss Shore,' concluded Sister Agnes solemnly. 'It won't be for very long. I shall come back. Later. We have so much to talk about.' She was the second person that evening to use those same words.

I ought to warn her—

'The Black Nun—' I began desperately.

'Later. Lock your door.' Sister Agnes departed. I was abandoned to the three holy pictures on the walls, where the Botticelli Virgin still looked at me with her expression of detached pity, the Titian Madonna still offered cherries to her child, and an Angel was, as ever, arrested in mid act of announcing impending pregnancy to the maiden Mary. Then there was the Treasury of the Blessed Eleanor, described by Alex Skarbek as intolerably dull. I could do with a little dullness, I decided. I picked it up. No white marker this time to mark my place. I turned a few pages, was guiltily inclined to agree with Skarbek, then went to the brief life at the back of the book.

'Of all the holy women under her care, Dame Ghislaine le Tourel was the one for whom our foundress had the most tender love,' I read. 'Blessed Eleanor loved in Dame Ghislaine le Tourel the blessed reflection of Our Saviour Jesus Christ, which she loved in duty bound wheresoever she found it, and most of all she found it in Dame Ghislaine le Tourel.'

The reflection of Christ – who was I to say that was not the truth of their relationship? It was, as we all agreed, a very long time ago. The anonymous author of this charitable nineteenth-century life was just as likely to be right as a later historian. A non-believer. And a man. His insights into the mentality of mediaeval nuns were as likely to be limited as mine were. The relationship of Rosabelle and Beatrice O'Dowd had turned out to be an innocent one. Why not then give the benefit of the doubt to Blessed Eleanor and Dame Ghislaine?

I read on.

Then I saw the handle of my door turning. It turned and did not give. There was a little rattle. My visitor seemed to be disconcerted to find the door was locked.

I heard a voice, very low but not whispering, outside the door: 'Miss Shore, Miss Shore, are you there?'

'Yes, I'm here. Who is it?'

'Oh thank God you're all right. Thanks be to God. I've been so worried. I didn't know where you were. I didn't know what to do. Tessa Justin came rushing to the infirmary in the most ghastly state—'

It was Sister Lucy.

With a great sigh of relief, I jumped up and unlocked the door. Sister Lucy was outside, panting. She came in, and recovered her breath.

'You're safe. Thank Heaven. I haven't known what to think. You see Tessa Justin reappeared a while ago, running to me with some extraordinary story about Black Nuns and secret passages and the tower, and kept saying "Save her, save her" meaning you—'

Admirable little Tessa Justin.

'We were all upside down from seeing to Mother Ancilla. And then Sister Boniface came along from visiting Mother Ancilla's cell and said that it really seemed too much to have Tessa Justin calling attention to herself with a pack of lies when Reverend Mother might be dying—'

'Sister Boniface said *that*—' I was bewildered.

'Yes. And of course I knew what Tessa was saying must be nonsense. Tessa is really a most emotionally unstable child.' Sister Lucy was recovering something of her normally competent manner. 'Just the sort of story she would tell – the concept of the tower for example and the passage – full of psychological significance. I agreed with Sister Boniface to that extent, that she had made the whole thing up. At least we were as one about that. Then Sister Boniface suggested corporal punishment, a good hiding was her exact phrase. As you can imagine, I didn't go along with that. Tessa was simply mixed up in herself. So I gave her a nice soothing sedative, something strong but appropriate to a child. And she went down like a baby. Sleeping the whole thing off now.'

'But Sister Boniface knew—' I began. I stopped.

'Yes, please do explain,' said Sister Lucy. 'What is going on? Where on earth have you been, Miss Shore? I looked in here a while ago and the room was empty. Sister Agnes is missing too; her cubicle is empty.'

I hardly knew where to begin. But Sister Lucy was a nurse and must have heard some strange tales in her time, tales of humanity twisted between good and evil. Nurses, even nurses who have become nuns, knew all about the dark side of human nature.

'Oh, Sister Lucy. I've had the most terrible time.' The strain of it all was beginning to tell on me.

'Sit down again, Miss Shore. Yes, you do look – well, exhausted is hardly a strong enough word. I'll get you something. A good tranquilliser is what you need. In fact I think I've got something right here in my pocket. I was going to ask the doctor if any of these would help Mother Ancilla.'

She dug in her capacious black skirts with her healing hands, and produced a small pink box.

Sister Lucy held it out towards me with a happy smile at having solved my problem.

'I'll get you a glass of water.'

I did not take the pink box.

My eye had followed Sister Lucy's gesture automatically downwards as her arm went towards the pocket of her habit.

And stopped there.

Sister Lucy's skirts, the whole length of the hem, very deep, eight or nine inches of it, were covered in tell-tale white dust.

The crumbly particles of the secret passage showed up particularly strongly in contrast to the black of a nun's habit. More strongly, for example, than they had shown up on my brown coat, now lying on my bed, or on Tessa Justin's maroon uniform.

After a moment Sister Lucy followed the direction of my eyes. It was too late to avert them.

But Sister Lucy did not stop smiling. Nor did she withdraw the small round pink box.

'Why don't you take one all the same, Miss Shore?' she said pleasantly. 'It'll save trouble in the end.'

17
Trust

'You,' I said without moving.

'Yes. Me,' replied Sister Lucy. She remained as normal in her manner as before. The only moment of discomposure she had shown throughout our entire interview was at the beginning and then I suppose she was not totally sure of the situation. Where to find me. What I knew.

Casually she put her hand into her pocket and took out a knife – that same knife from the cafeteria which Sister Agnes had used to free me. She might have been a surgeon contemplating my body for an operation.

Her self-possession was now completely restored. With Tessa Justin heavily sedated – was she intended to survive? – and myself at the receiving end of what was doubtless a lethal pill, Sister Lucy had very little to worry about.

The accomplice. The intelligent female praised by Alexander Skarbek. Sister Lucy: the new infirmarian, the trusted nurse. Sister Lucy: the accomplice of the Black Nun. Someone who believed in medicines and pills and potions. Who argued with Sister Boniface and described her methods as old fashioned. Oh Sister Bonnie, with your rosaries and your penances, what injustice had been done to you! Sister Lucy who believed in science and psychiatry, whichever suited her book better at the time. Or did she believe in any of these things? In the end it seemed that she merely believed in power over others, and power was what these remedies had given her. And I had considered Mother Ancilla to be the power-mad member of the community . . .

'Tell me one thing, Sister'. The title sounded ironic. But I could think of no better way to address her. I didn't even know her other name. Or anything about her at all. Except that she was both a nurse and a nun. Two categories in combination that made me trust her absolutely: whereas in the past I had always been too canny to trust any nurse altogether – they're human beings like ourselves I was prone to observe; and I had certainly not trusted every nun.

'Tell me what will happen to Tessa?' I asked her.

'Nothing. Nothing at all. She'll sleep it off, just as I told you. Nightmares. Tales of Black Nuns and towers. Who will believe her, a highly strung child like that? Her parents are angry enough with her already for making herself a nuisance: they are hardly likely to listen now. Nothing will happen to her. And gradually she will forget. Especially when you yourself are no longer here to support her and feed her mind with – lies.'

'So what will happen to me?'

'Nothing. Or rather I should say: nothing more. An overdose – how tragic, such a promising career! How sad! But of course she was hopelessly involved with a married man, wasn't she? We may even type a little note of farewell to your friend Tom Amyas – rather differently phrased from your own note, though. The death of Jemima Shore, Investigator, the television star. A headline in the evening paper. A tribute on television news. And then – all forgotten. Television is so ephemeral, Miss Shore. It's quite forgotten the next day. As you will soon be forgotten.'

I felt the depths of her hatred beneath her agreeable if slightly prim voice. I kept a watchful eye on that knife. In her own way Sister Lucy was far more frightening than Alexander Skarbek, because she was mad. He was evil, but in a horrible way within the bounds of reason. She was mad, and therefore outside them.

'Television is not always forgotten the next day. Have you quite overlooked the effect of the Powers Estate programme on Sister Miriam and Beatrice O'Dowd? We shouldn't be here now if it hadn't been for that programme.'

'That wasn't television,' cried Sister Lucy. 'That was Alexander Skarbek himself. His wonderful strength and his beliefs reached out to them . . .' And so on and so on. Raving, calmly raving. With death facing me, in the shape of a small round pill box, I did not feel disposed to argue the logic of her case.

'Sister Edward?' I interrupted her. 'That was you, I suppose.'

'That was a mistake. More of an accident. He was angry about that. But she was beginning to suspect that Sister Miriam had been deliberately shut into the tower by a nun. She had seen something. She was asking questions.'

'Actually she suspected Mother Ancilla,' I pointed out. Sister Lucy did not seem noticeably regretful about the mistake.

'She was dangerous, I tell you. Sister Edward was in the infirmary when Sister Hippolytus confided to me about the secret passage and where the entrance was to be found. And I passed it on to Alexander – with everything else that happened to me in the convent. Nightly,' she said proudly. Almost with pity, I remembered Alexander Skarbek's disdain – the intolerable reminiscences of an old nun, he had termed Sister Hippo's historical revelations. And after all, he had not received them first hand. I was glad that Sister Hippo at least had not been taken in by the Black Nun. Her reputation for sharpness of character, matching that of her tongue, survived.

Then Sister Lucy added: 'If Sister Edward hadn't been such a ninny, she could have gone and found the passage for herself. As it was, she might have passed on the story at any moment. To her sister Beatrice for example.'

'You hate Beatrice O'Dowd, don't you? Why? When you both work for the same cause. The same man.'

'The same man! Beatrice O'Dowd doesn't even *know* the Alexander Skarbek that I know. Any more than those stupid Sixth Form girls knew him. Margaret and Dodo and Blanche and Imogen – he used them all. How exciting they found it: a man dressed up as a nun roaming the convent . . . so perfect for their adolescent fantasies wasn't it?' And how was it for yours, Sister Lucy, I wanted to ask, but she was continuing in the same vein: 'Playing up the legend of the Black Nun for all they were worth. Believing they were in on the secret. But they never knew the truth about him. They weren't in the *real* secret at all. Any more than Beatrice O'Dowd was. Beatrice O'Dowd is a foolish spinster who wants to do good in the world.' She made it sound the most ridiculous objective. 'What could she know of the delights, the visions, the travels of the mind and spirit which we two have experienced?'

I thought: Alexander Skarbek. He had succeeded in corrupting Sister Lucy. But the innocent he had tried to corrupt and failed. In their own way Beatrice O'Dowd and Rosabelle Powerstock had held him off by innocence. Margaret and Dodo were still innocent because they were young: long might that innocence last and protect them. Particularly Margaret. But Margaret was clever. After all, her reserve did not conceal a lack of balance. 'More interesting,' Skarbek had said. 'More like you.' All that meant was Margaret would probably end up working for someone like Tom: her resemblance to the dedicated Emily Crispin still tantalised me. I was glad that I too had held him off, although in my case it was knowledge not innocence which had protected me from corruption.

Sister Lucy was visibly controlling herself after her outburst. The surgeon's knife had begun to shake. The knife stopped shaking. Finally she succeeded in presenting to me once again that pleasing visage which, in spite of everything, I still associated with her.

She rattled the pill box gently.

'So now, Miss Shore, why don't you take one of these?'

She stood between me and the door. I was sitting down. Even a maniac armed with a knife could not, I fancied, force me to swallow a pill. At which moment Sister Lucy bent forward, grabbed my throat in a grip of extraordinary strength, and pushed me viciously backwards. She had dropped the knife. As I flailed about feeling for the knife, I felt the pill being placed roughly on my tongue. She fastened my jaw with one hand. At the same moment my nostrils were grasped and pinched so that I could not breathe. The temptation to swallow was ghastly—

The loud noise of the bell startled us both. A nun's bell quite close. One loud clamour. Then silence. Then another toll.

'My bell,' said Sister Lucy automatically. Two bells for the infirmarian. The slight release in pressure gave me my chance. I spat the pill out into my hand, and then threw it to the floor. Whatever it was, I wanted it to be no nearer to me than I could help.

'Mother Ancilla! Sister Boniface must be looking for me.'

'On the contrary it is I who am looking for you, Sister Lucy,' said a gentle voice. 'That's why I sounded your bell.' We both turned round. It was Sister Agnes who stood there, in the doorway, eyes level and steady as ever. She had a large bell in one hand. And a small pistol in the other. She really was making a habit of rescuing me. One of these days I should really have to do something for her.

'Do be careful, Miss Shore.' Sister Agnes was as ever polite. 'This pistol is bound to be loaded. I have just persuaded Mr Skarbek to hand it over to me. And I don't think he is the sort of gentleman to carry an unloaded gun around with him, do you?'

'Where is he?' asked Sister Lucy hoarsely. 'Where is Alexander?'

'He's in the car, under the trees, Sister. In the Mini-Traveller. He's waiting for you. Don't you think you should join him?'

'My car!'

'The car you brought with you when you joined the community,' Sister Agnes corrected her. 'The community's car.'

Sister Lucy looked uncertain. But she did not look nearly so uncertain as I felt. I could not believe my ears. Unless Sister Agnes was also in the plot, it made no sense to allow Skarbek and Sister Lucy to make their escape like this. In their different ways, they were two dangerous people: too dangerous to be set at liberty as if nothing had happened.

Sister Agnes still had her mesmeric effect on me. And she hypnotised Sister Lucy too, or else it was the gun. The infirmarian walked towards her as in a dream, and still in the same state turned towards the visitors' staircase. The outside door was unlocked. She walked through it. The last we saw of Sister Lucy was her black habit in the light thrown from the porch, passing towards the drive.

We could not see her face. She might have been anyone. Any nun, that is.

'Why, why, Sister Agnes?' I burst out. 'Why let them go? You're as crazy as they are.'

'He's changed back into his own clothes.' Sister Agnes did not answer my question. 'I'm glad of that. I found them in the sacristy, hidden under the priests' robes for tomorrow's mass. The insolence of it: his jersey and anorak beneath the vestments embroidered by Sister Perpetua to celebrate her twenty-five years in religion.' Sister Agnes, I noticed, was too delicate even to mention the subject of his trousers in the same breath as a priest's vestments.

Then she put her hand on my arm.

'What could I do, Miss Shore? Think about it. The convent in uproar, our work all undone. Mother Ancilla is dying. We don't want her to die like this, do we, with the good name of the Blessed Eleanor dragged through the newspapers? We went through it once with Sister Miriam, and Mother Ancilla suffered so much. What would our foundress have thought?'

Oh these nuns! Their unworldliness. The good name of the convent; had she no sense of reality at all?

'He had a gun! I know you took it away. But he's still dangerous.'

'Oh this,' said Sister Agnes, looking down at the pistol in her hand. Casually she gave it a little click. Nothing happened. 'No, this wasn't Mr Skarbek's. He didn't as far as I know carry a gun. Not the type. Preferring his own methods.' She wrinkled her nose and did not enlarge on the subject. 'No, this comes from the children's acting cupboard. We did *Murder on the Nile* last term: Agatha Christie. Really delightful – you would have enjoyed it. We needed a gun for that. I didn't think Sister Lucy would notice the difference, with the state she was in. All those pills she was always taking.'

'You're quite an actress,' was all I could think of saying.

'I was an actress once: I told you,' replied Sister Agnes with a smile. 'Not a very good one. Then I became a nun.'

'You're quite a nun, then.'

'Thank you, Miss Shore. Now that is a compliment I really value. Even though I know myself to be unworthy of it.'

Sister Agnes cast down her eyes with a modesty wholly worthy of the Murillo I had once fancied she resembled. It had been a foolish notion. Or rather Sister Agnes' appearance might be that of a Murillo, but her spirit was made of sterner stuff. Another Spanish painter, Goya, would have made a better job of Sister Agnes.

Sister Agnes bent down and picked up the knife which Sister Lucy had abandoned. 'I must give that back to Sister Clare first thing in the morning,' she said. It was evident that her sense of order was outraged by the presence of the knife so far outside its natural habitat of the cafeteria.

She was indeed quite a nun. If not so quiet as the poet Wordsworth and her own demeanour would have one believe.

The suspicions of Sister Agnes had, ironically enough, first been aroused by the prevalent nightmares of Tessa Justin. I did not know what the future might hold for that young lady: but on the form of her first ten years, I could hardly believe she would lead a trouble-free life. The attitude of Sister Lucy to these nightmares had struck Sister Agnes as strange. Sister Agnes herself was the object of Tessa's childish adoration. Like Sister Boniface, she considered Tessa to be an exhibitionist—

'But Our Lord teaches us to be especially loving to such children, does He not? The little children in the Bible who crowded round Him, whom He suffered to come unto Him, were they not exhibitionists in their own way? Asking for His love?'

As usual, Sister Agnes was probably right.

But she did not think of Tessa as being a liar. Meanwhile the evidence of her own senses began to tell Sister Agnes that someone unlawful was prowling about the convent at night. The whisk of a black skirt round a corner where skirt there should be none. The sight of a nun, seen from the back, vanishing in the top corridor. The noise of someone apparently inhabiting the empty guest rooms. A bathroom strangely occupied and then empty. Above all, a sense of a mysterious presence in and around the chapel. She began to watch.

'Your novena then – that first night in the chapel? That was a cover-up, a pretence?'

'Certainly not, Miss Shore.' Sister Agnes sounded quite shocked. 'I would never pretend to make a novena. Our Lord would never forgive me. Besides, I had a great deal to pray about, didn't I?'

It was Sister Agnes's growing awareness that a member of the community was involved in the mystery which had led her to try and warn me off on the occasion of our interview. Sister Agnes was as ever discreet in her mode of expression, but she made me understand that the presence of Jemima Shore, Investigator, within Blessed Eleanor's had constituted yet another problem – to put it at its mildest. She murmured something about the standards of television not being entirely those of the convent. I quite understood the point she was trying to make.

As for Sister Lucy – so many little suspicious things, from her movements and unaccountable absences at night, to the fact that Tessa's running-away note had been clearly typed on the dispensary typewriter used by Sister Lucy to write up her medical notes.

'She was not with us very long,' said Sister Agnes, compressing her lips in a manner once more reminiscent of Mother Ancilla. 'And Sister Boniface was never satisfied about the nature of Sister Lucy's vocation. Sister Boniface may be old, but here at Blessed Eleanor's we pay a great deal of attention to the views of the older members of the community. There will be changes here of course when Mother Ancilla dies.' Again that matter-of-factness about the inevitability of death. 'But in all these changes I can assure you that the wishes of those who understand our traditions will be consulted. And respected. Changes must be in accordance with the will of God. And some of our older members are very close to Him now after a lifetime of prayer and devotion.'

In spite of the extraordinary circumstances of our conversation, I felt that I was listening to some kind of manifesto for the future. I remembered the occasion when Sister Agnes had sought gently to dissuade me from entering the infirmary. Sister Agnes might not be a senior member of the community, but she too had never been quite persuaded of the strength of Sister Lucy's vocation.

'But you're not going to let them go?' I groaned. 'Forgiveness of your enemies is all very well, but the man is dangerous, and a murderer. While Sister Lucy is insane and probably a murdress as well. She certainly intended to kill Sister Edward even if in the end her death was an accident.'

'There is no question of forgiveness, Miss Shore,' said Sister Agnes, opening her dark eyes wide. 'Forgiveness is for Almighty God, who sees into every heart, not for us. I simply did the best I could at the time. Getting them both out of the convent precincts. Finding Mr Skarbek in the sacristy, I recognised him without difficulty – we watched the repeat of your programme last night with the Juniors – very instructive by the way, although I'm not sure I agree with all your conclusions. He had no idea of what I knew. I merely suggested that he should leave the convent instantly. As an unlawful intruder. Otherwise I threatened to summon the police. Finally I told him I would send our infirmarian down to him, Sister Lucy, as he was obviously sick, breaking in like that to a convent. And he'd better wait for her in the community car parked under the trees. And she would drive him back to the village. And get him some attention.'

'But Sister Agnes, he was dressed up as a nun,' I cried.

'Exactly. That helped to convince him. I said: "You must be sick in your mind to do such a thing." I suggested it, and he didn't disagree. Besides only his – er – body was dressed in the habit. His head was clearly visible. I simply pointed to his own garments and said, "Those are your clothes I believe. Please resume them" and I left the sacristy.'

It was difficult to believe that Sister Agnes had been all that bad an actress.

'All the same we'll have to summon the police in the morning.'

'As to that, we must trust in God, Miss Shore,' said Sister Agnes, sounding weary for the first time. 'He will dispose of it all. We must trust Him.'

Another appalling thought struck me.

'But the will, Sister Agnes. Do you realise that Sister Miriam's second will leaves all the property to the Powers Project? Even if Skarbek is nailed, the property will still go to the Project. There is nothing wrong with the Project itself: the rest of them are perfectly honest people, if somewhat extreme in their views about society. It will all be quite legal. You will be turned out, dispossessed. The workers' commune up to your front door. Your work here will end just the same.'

'The second will of Sister Miriam isn't yet found, is it, Miss Shore? Until it is discovered, her original will leaving everything to the community still stands.'

'But it will be found. Believe me, it will be found.'

I hadn't the heart to tell her that I now knew exactly where to find it.

'Then it will be found. We must still put our faith in Almighty God, Miss Shore,' said Sister Agnes. 'What else can we do?'

18
Into the future

But in the event it was not necessary to summon the police. Very early the next day the police came of their own accord to the Convent of the Blessed Eleanor. They roused a sleepy Sister Damian, and asked to see the Reverend Mother. Since that was not possible, she being far too weak, it was finally to Sister Boniface, supported by Sister Elizabeth and myself, that they broke the news of the fatal car crash on Church Hill in the early hours of the morning.

A dark night, a sharp bend on a steep hill taken too fast: it was what Alexander Skarbek would have called, for once with proper accuracy, a natural – if unfortunate – accident.

There were two passengers, both killed instantly. The police were sorry to disturb the Sisters of Blessed Eleanor's so early in the day, but the car was registered in the name of the convent. Furthermore they had to break it to Sister Boniface that one of the two dead people was a nun. Had been a nun.

'It seems that the nun was actually driving,' said the senior policeman with a sympathetic clearing of the throat.

'People always say that nuns are such bad drivers,' commented Sister Elizabeth sadly. 'Trusting in God to protect them, instead of looking at the road. And it isn't true at all. But Sister Lucy really was a bad driver. Then of course she hadn't been a nun very long.'

There were tears in Sister Elizabeth's eyes. After a moment she began to quote Wordsworth to herself.

> 'There is a comfort in the strength of love;
> 'T will make a thing endurable, which else
> Would overset the brain, or break the heart . . .'

It wasn't clear to me to which love she was alluding, the love of God, or the love of Sister Lucy for Alexander Skarbek.

When Sister Elizabeth had finished, Sister Boniface said robustly: 'Sister Lucy didn't trust in God enough.'

The policeman said: 'The driver certainly didn't look at the road.'

I thought of Sister Agnes. No doubt she would always believe that it was Almighty God who had thus conveniently disposed of Sister Lucy and Alexander Skarbek. But I did not want to think like that. To me, it was a natural accident – natural, and on reflection, fortunate. Fortunate, for everyone. Even the dead.

We were sitting in the Nuns' Parlour by the front door, the police and myself having been fortified by the coffee, delicious and hot, which even at this early hour Sister Clare had managed to produce.

I waited till the police had withdrawn and the nuns too had gone away to begin the endless sad process of untangling and sorting out all the mischiefs which had recently taken place in their unquiet convent.

Alone in the Nuns' Parlour, I too had a sad task to perform. Putting the brides of Christ out of my mind, I went over to the polished table on which lay the portfolio of wedding photographs of successfully paired-off old girls. The art of Lenare and Yevonde, Bassano and Vandyk, and the few more recent examples, had spilled out onto the table. I put my hand inside the portfolio and felt another thinner piece of paper amongst the pasteboard. I drew it out: it was an envelope.

On the envelope was written' 'This is the very last will and testament of Sister Miriam.' I recognised the hand-writing – Rosa's own. Even in her anguish, it had really not changed much since we were at school together. Here among the brides, the brides not of Christ but of wealthy stock-brokers and poor Irish doctors and foreign princes and struggling Catholic lawyers and all other types of happy Catholic grooms, the will of Rosabelle Powerstock had lain safely hidden.

It was instinct which made me now seek out the chapel. Above all I had to be at peace. There at least would be repose and silence. There would be no more prying ghosts to disturb its ornate tranquillity.

Once in the chapel I sat down in the pew nearest to the statue of the Sacred Heart. The heart, my symbol. That pew in which I had first encountered Sister Agnes keeping her watch, and saying her novena at the same time. The candles, a little forest of them this morning, flickered. It was in their light, close by the shrine, that I read the last message from my friend:

'I, Rosabelle Powerstock, known as Sister Miriam of the Order of the Tower of Ivory, being in sound mind in spite of everything that has happened to me, do hereby revoke all other wills. In the confusion in which I find myself, I have prayed to God and His saints and to our Blessed Lady to guide me.

'I wished to place my property in the hands of the poor, in accordance with the message of Our Saviour Lord Jesus Christ. Yet recently I have been aware that I have not yet found the right hands in which to place it. There are pressures all round me, within myself and without. I no longer know what is the right decision to make. It must therefore be for others, who have always been so much stronger than I, to decide.

'I therefore leave the lands surrounding the Convent of the Blessed Eleanor, in their entirety, to Jemima Shore. She will know what to do with them. Everything else I leave, as before, to the community of the Tower of Ivory, of which I die, as I have tried to live, a faithful member.'

It was signed: Rosabelle Powerstock, and in brackets: Miriam. A.M.D.G. The will was witnessed at the bottom of the paper by Blanche Nelligan and Imogen Smith.

I sat for a long time holding this piece of paper between my fingers. I thought of many things. Of the past: Rosa. A friendship from which I had taken so much, yet had abandoned. And forgotten. For Rosa a friendship which had marked her whole life; even seeing me on television in some shallow programme, calling for social reform from the security of my own detached position, had been enough to make her try and sell all that she had, and give it to the poor. A friendship which had in the end unwittingly brought about her death. A friendship founded on trust which had not failed even in her last hours when she was confident that her old friend would perform the labours which she no longer had the strength to carry out.

Of the future: the future of this convent robbed of its lands. But maybe the women within it would be released from their incarceration, find themselves playing a more valuable role in society . . . Of my own future: establishing a great settlement for the poor perhaps, helped by Tom, supported by the w.n.g. As Rosa had wanted. As Tom would want.

I thought of the present: of Mother Ancilla, dying in her bare cell upstairs.

After a bit I stretched out my piece of paper towards the shrine of the Sacred Heart and lit the corner of the will from a candle. It flared up. I felt a momentary scorch on my fingers, and then I dropped it. I felt nothing else at all.

I rose up from my pew to find Sister Agnes standing at the side door watching me. She had made one of her noiseless entrances.

'You were right to put your trust in God, Sister Agnes,' I said. 'There will be no further changes at the convent of the Blessed Eleanor.'

'Oh we shall have changes, Miss Shore,' replied Sister Agnes. 'But we shall decide on them together. I should tell you that Reverend Mother has just given me her dying voice as the new superior. My first action will be to have the choice confirmed by an election within the community. Even the lay nuns will be given votes. It will be an open contest.'

I believed her. But somehow I felt Sister Agnes would be elected all the same.

There was nothing more for me to do here now. I asked if I could see Mother Ancilla before I went back to London. She was very weak and cruelly white, but perfectly composed. Sister Boniface was looking after her, under the doctor's orders: even at her age Sister Boniface did not seem displeased to have come out of her retirement as infirmarian.

I clasped the hand which had so often taken mine in its warm grasp: it felt very cold. A crucifix above the bed was the sole decoration in the cell. The air here was chilly, not warm as the children's wing always was.

'Mother Ancilla,' I said. 'You knew, didn't you? You knew about the will.'

'Oh no, my child, I knew nothing. I only suspected. She loved you so much. She had such confidence in you. Your judgement. Jemima's so brilliant, she used to say. And she used to ask special permission to watch television on the nights you appeared. She admired you so much. As did we all, of course, dear Jemima. When no will was found, and she seemed so unhappy, so confused, I thought she might have done something like that.'

Mother Ancilla took a sip of water. I helped her.

'But of course I couldn't be sure. And I didn't know where the will was. If I had known, I should certainly have produced it. We nuns are a very law-abiding lot, you know.'

I let that pass. 'But that's why you sent for me? Tell me now.'

'Perhaps. If she had left you the property, then it was in my mind that you might get to know us all over again. And you would understand about our work. And see that it is worth preserving. And you did, my child, didn't you?' Sister Agnes had told her.

I shook my head.

'It wasn't for that. It's because you were good. And he was evil.'

Mother Ancilla smiled.

'How simple, Jemima. Good and bad. Good and evil. How do we

know ? Our Blessed Lord knows but we don't. We just have to be sure that we are doing the work that God wants us to do on this earth.'

There was a long silence. She raised herself a little on her pillows.

'Now it is my turn to ask you a question, Jemima. One day, do you think that you might ever—'

'No, Mother, never.' Very firmly. 'I'm sorry. Faith is a gift, they say. If so, I haven't been given it.'

'But you want to believe, I know it, I feel it.'

'No' – gently. After all she was a dying woman. Even so I had to speak the truth. Another silence. Then—

'My child, do you wish you believed?'

And then some ugly honesty took over, the honesty I could never defeat, part of me. Against my will, hating myself, for a moment even hating her, I said with absolute truth:

'Yes, Mother, I do wish I believed.'

Mother Ancilla smiled. A seraphic child's smile.

'Well then, it's simple, isn't it? Our Blessed Lord will see to it, won't He?'

I shook my head. It wasn't as simple as that. It was nothing. I just couldn't help telling the truth. It was nothing to do with anything.

'He'll see to it that you receive the gift of faith. Or I'll get after Him.' Mother Ancilla's voice was fading away.

After a bit a nun, Sister Damian I think, came and tapped me on the shoulder and said: 'You must go now, Miss Shore.'

I got up quietly and took a last look at Mother Ancilla before I left her – forever, as I knew it would be. She was still smiling, faintly, victoriously. She would sort it out with Our Blessed Lord. She had promised to get me the gift of faith. I felt quite sorry for Him – if He existed.

I drove back to London and repossessed myself of my empty flat. I flipped through my mail, which Cherry had left in neat piles as befitted the perfect secretary. Included among it was an official letter from Megalith Television congratulating me on the success of my repeats, especially the Powers Estate programme ('Into the top ten ratings'). It was signed by Cy Fredericks. At the bottom he had scrawled: 'Well done. The Gem of my collection.' It was an old reference. The letter also suggested a whole new series under the general title Into the Future. I tossed it aside: unlike the past, the future did not strike me as being particularly urgent.

I left a message for Tom at the House of Commons to say that I was back in London and would he ring me? My lucky dress with its motif of hearts was hanging ready in the cupboard. I picked up the Evening

Standard and began to read it. Sometimes when I'm low and waiting for a call I read the *Evening Standard* cover to cover as though for an examination. But on this occasion I threw the paper on the floor, after the Megalith letter. I decided to go for a walk.

It was a beautiful evening. And I wanted to be calm and free. It didn't worry me at all that I should be out when Tom called.

Tartan Tragedy

For Benjie
and all at Eilean Aigas

Contents

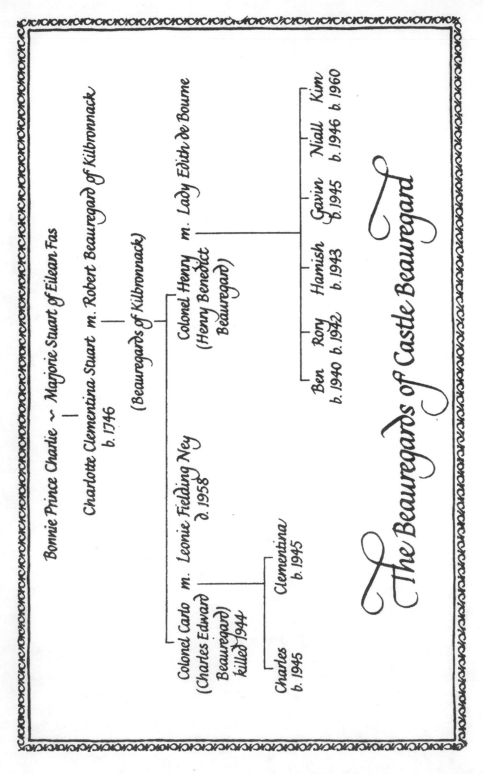

Bonnie Prince Charlie ~ Majorie Stuart of Eilean Fas

Charlotte Clementina Stuart m. Robert Beauregard of Kilbronnack
b. 1746

(Beauregards of Kilbronnack)

Colonel Henry m. Lady Edith de Bourne
(Henry Benedict
Beauregard)

Ben   Rory   Hamish   Gavin   Niall   Kim
b. 1940 b. 1942   b. 1943   b. 1945   b. 1946   b. 1960

Colonel Carlo   m.   Leonie Fielding Ney
(Charles Edward   d. 1958
Beauregard)
killed 1944

Clementina
b. 1945

Charles
b. 1945

The Beauregards of Castle Beauregard

1

A Highland welcome

As Jemima Shore arrived at Inverness Station, it was early morning but already the sun was shining. She thought: I'm arriving in Paradise. At that moment a man's voice said in her ear:

'All this way for a funeral.' It was an intimate voice. Almost purring. Jemima felt uncomfortably startled. She looked round.

Behind her a man of a certain age, tall, cadaverous, was bending down to pick up a suitcase. A younger man of much the same ilk was standing beside him. Possibly they were related. Both were dressed with extreme formality for the place – a station – and the time – it was 8.30 am. Jemima had just emerged from her sleeper. She did not feel up to such a situation, at least until she had had a cup of coffee. Whichever of the two men had spoken, it was nothing to do with her. She turned her head back and concentrated on the prospect of a porter.

'It's not all that bad, Colonel Henry,' said a second voice. 'In fact, in some ways it's good. In some ways it's very good indeed.'

Jemima shivered. She was glad she did not know, and never would know, anything more about a funeral to which it was possible to have anything but unmixed reactions of sorrow. She stepped firmly onto the platform. She had come here to get away from that sort of thing. The first sight which met her eyes was an enormous splashed scarlet graffiti on a hoarding opposite.

'Up the Red Rose!' it screamed and then something beneath in what looked like Gaelic, as well as an odd separate sort of calligraph, which she couldn't make out at all. The scarlet letters were imposed wilfully on another, more formally written, white notice. To her irritation, she found herself trying to make it out instead of concentrating on the task of finding a porter, or even a barrow. Stronger men than her, with dogs and gun cases to reinforce their claim, were apparently engaging all conceivable porterage. 'A Highland Welcome', the original notice had read. That at least was friendly.

Of course the inhabitants of the Highlands could still welcome Jemima weekly on their television sets, if they were so minded. As 'Jemima Shore, Investigator' in a series put out by Megalith Television under that title, she generally found her way into the ratings. Jemima's speciality was in fact serious-minded sociological enquiry – housing, deprived families, these were the kind of topics which interested her; but the title of the series played on the notion of an amateur detective. That title had been an early inspiration of her boss, Cy Fredericks. Sometimes she felt that it had become almost too memorable, too much of a catch-phrase for journalists and cartoonists alike. But MTV, entranced by the series' prolonged success, would not dream of changing it.

Before her departure she had recorded what seemed like a monumental number of programmes in her new series. The public would switch on. But she herself would be absent – in Paradise. The sun was still shining. In fact it had been shining all of the ten minutes since her arrival at Inverness Station and not a drop of rain in sight.

She needed a rest from curiosity. All the same, who were they welcoming? 'HRH', those were the next letters, partly obscured by the word 'Red'. After that it was easy: 'A Highland Welcome to HRH Princess Sophie of Cumberland.' So Hurricane Sophie, as television had irreverently nicknamed the young Princess, was visiting the Highlands, was she?

That was yet another fact which need not concern Jemima Shore. Funerals, royal visits, none of that was going to stop her enjoying a well-deserved rest away from it all. And on an island. Could anything be further away from it all than a Scottish island in the middle of a fast-flowing river, complete with cliffs and chasms to protect its privacy?

Two men watched her alight. Unlike the funeral party, this second pair were dressed in such a nondescript fashion as to rouse exactly that suspicion which they presumably intended to avoid.

'Look, Miller, that's Jemima Shore,' said the more stolid-seeming of the two. 'I fancy her.' He made his approval sound like an announcement from the pulpit.

'She was on the box last night,' the man named Miller spoke wonderingly.

'She's always on the box.'

'But she's not always at Inverness Station. And come to think of it, Tyne, nor are we. Where's HRH then?'

'HRH is putting the finishing touches. Plenty of time.' The man named Tyne continued to look lugubriously after Jemima Shore, whose figure was vanishing down the platform. Her hair, its pure Madonna-like style made famous by television, ruffled slightly in the breeze. 'My wife fancies her too. She's somewhat the same type, my wife. Same colouring and hair style. Once in a shop, someone came up to her . . .'

A discreet cough interrupted these reminiscences, and as a glimpse of something bright and girlish, red, a coat, a hat, perhaps, was seen through the corridor window, both men proceeded to give their full attention to the interior of the train, rather than the outside world of the platform.

If Jemima Shore noticed the heads turning at all, it was in some automatic register of her brain. It meant absolutely nothing to her. The only sign of recognition she would welcome this morning would be from her future landlord Charles Beauregard. And he was to convey her, rapidly she hoped, away from the panoply of Inverness Station *en fête* to her much-desired Highland retreat.

But twenty minutes later, sitting in the Railway Hotel, whose name belied its distinct if old-fashioned grandeur, there was still no Charles Beauregard to rescue Jemima Shore. She was now surrounded by her luggage, one of the dog-and-gun-case set having condescended to share a vast truck with her. But the effect of the multitude of suitcases distributed round her in the lounge of the hotel was to make her feel like someone who had been shipwrecked. It was expensive American luggage acquired during her last trip to the States and her enthusiastic young secretary Cherry had insisted on having it all stamped with her full name.

'Oh, Jem, you never know when it might help. Your name being so famous in every corner of the globe. In a tight corner, it might prove invaluable.' Cherry had a vivid if cliché-ridden imagination. To her, all corners were tight, and all names in television famous throughout the universe.

Now, Jemima reflected sardonically, here was a tight corner indeed. Herself sitting with her luggage in a remote corner of the world – surely the Highlands of Scotland qualified for that – with absolutely no way of getting to the holiday cottage she had rented for a month. No telephone. No directions. And an address which at the time had struck her as infinitely romantic, but now as rather ludicrously imprecise: 'Eilean Fas, Inverness-shire.'

The staff of the Railway Hotel was amiability itself. Part of this amiability extended to the fact that its members had no objection to her sitting there indefinitely; they neither pressured her into partaking of breakfast, or otherwise enquired of her intentions. But it was no good pretending that this mountain of luggage proclaiming the name of Jemima Shore was cutting any ice with them whatsoever.

Jemima took out Charles Beauregard's letter which was rapidly becoming her last link with her projected holiday. 'Beauregard Estate Office,' it was headed, 'Kilbronnack.'

Dear Miss Shore,
This is to confirm the arrangement made over the telephone with your secretary. You will rent the cottage known as Tigh Fas on Eilean Fas for one month starting from . . .

Yes, right day, right month. Not that Cherry could fail, but clearly Beauregard Estates could and in a sense had done so. The letter ended:

As Eilean Fas is difficult to find, and the bridge rather tricky, it seems simplest if I meet you in Inverness with the Land-Rover. I can explain details about the cottage, heating, etc, then and hand over the keys.

I should tell you that you won't be able to get television on Eilean Fas but if there is anything special you want to see you can always come over to the Castle to watch it.

I look forward to meeting you.

The letter itself was carefully typed, and the signature: Charles Edward Beauregard, careful – even measured – in the writing. But there was a scrawled PS, where the writing was larger and not so tidy. It gave the impression of being written under some stronger impulse than the mere details of a holiday let:

PS. There is another matter concerning Eilean Fas which I should like to talk to you about personally. It can't be put in a letter.

Jemima Shore, however, was not the slightest bit interested in the personal details of the island, nor for that matter how and when to watch television in the Highlands – perish the thought! She wanted a Land-Rover and breakfast, preferably in that order. In short she wanted a Highland Welcome, such as had been promised to Princess Sophie – or any welcome. But if not, at least breakfast.

Jemima made a decision. She went to the reception desk and said in her most pleasant, brisk manner: 'My name is Jemima Shore.'

The receptionist was quite a young girl with dark hair and healthy pink cheeks. Jemima did not pause for any possible reaction. 'And I am waiting here for Mr Charles Beauregard. If he arrives and asks for me, will you tell him I am in the dining room having breakfast?'

But the girl behind the desk continued to stare at Jemima. Her mouth was truly open, a rare phenomenon. And she said nothing at all. Jemima wasn't even quite certain she had taken in the message. As for this fan reaction, it was all that Cherry could have hoped for. So she repeated:

'Mr Charles Beauregard. You know Mr Beauregard?' The letter had stated the arrangement clearly enough: 'We'll meet at the Railway Hotel, where they know me and Alistair, the head porter, is an old friend of mine.'

The girl gave a strangled sound which could at least be interpreted as 'Aye', and immediately dived through the little door at the back of the reception desk cubicle.

Jemima passed into the dining room where a series of vast pictures of steam trains rushing through Highland gorges enlivened the otherwise tomb-like room. There were a number of scattered breakfasters. Two of them, seated at a table near the door, were conspicuous in their dark suits. Jemima recognized them from the train and that snatch of rather eerie conversation. The rest wore tweeds, jeans, thick jerseys and even – on one very stout and elderly man – a kilt.

A huge dog was roaming about among the tables. A labrador? Or was it a St Bernard? Its head came up nearly to the level of the table. Jemima was vague about dogs, the intricacies of their breeding and maintenance never having penetrated her world of television – and she herself never having led that kind of settled domestic life which would either inspire her or enable her to own one. Jemima felt an affinity for cats, cats headed by her own long-haired white-pawed tabby, with her mackerel markings, Colette.

This dog was biege, although that was probably the wrong word when applied to a dog. Jemima, however, admired the colour beige; it was in fact her favourite colour and she was wearing it at the moment. Beige, a great deal of it, including beige trousers, from a man's tailor (for free, as a discreet advertisement), beige silk shirt (Yves St Laurent, in no way for free), beige and white pullover (ditto). Even the boots beneath the tailored trousers were dark beige.

The dog, she thought, would make an artistic addition to the ensemble. The dog seemed to think so too. He came snuffling up to to the table where the waiter had installed her, wagging his tail as though he hoped to sweep the room with it, and disturbing many tablecloths round him as a result. He put his huge head in Jemima's lap and looked at her passionately.

'Jacko!' shouted the elder of the two men in the dark suits. Then with more fury: 'Jacobite.' His voice entirely lacked the purring note of that remark in the train. It had great authority, was even stentorian.

'Jacobite – Here, boy.' The dog turned and bounded with instant obedience in the direction of his master. It was an impressive performance. Although Jemima could not easily imagine anyone, man or beast, or even woman, disobeying that voice.

Moodily, she ordered a breakfast of things Scottish, more because she thought she ought to, than because she was any longer very hungry: finnan haddock, which was delicious. The coffee was awful. She sipped it, wondering whether the next step was to ring up Cherry – a confession of failure considering how firmly she had announced: I'm away for a month, Cherry. No letters which aren't urgent, which means no letters. No calls – you can't telephone me anyway and I'm not going to trudge to a Scottish call box to call you. No telegrams if you can resist it.' Cherry loved telegrams, whose language satisfied the dramatic side of her nature. No, she really did not want to telephone Cherry just twelve hours after that conversation.

How maddening for the Estate Office not to give its telephone number on the writing paper. Kilbronnack itself must have telephones even if the islanders didn't.

At that point in her musings she was aware of the older man in the dark suit standing over her. For a moment, confused, she thought he had come to say something about the dog, since Jacobite had followed his master back across the room and was once more lifting his nose to the table, sniffing the elixir of the remains of Jemima's breakfast.

'Miss Shore?' he was saying. 'Good morning. I'm Henry Beauregard.'

Jemima's first reaction was enormous relief that at last a Beauregard – if not the right one, at least a member of the family – was taking an interest in her cause.

'Ailsa at the desk was telling me you were having some difficulty in getting to the funeral,' remarked this Beauregard. He really did have a most attractive voice when it was lowered. In fact altogether Henry Beauregard was an attractive as well as a distinguished-looking man, with his bony face set off by thick hair, grey but showing streaks of what must have been the original black. Jemima thought of Hamlet's father, 'a sable silvered'. Although there was nothing particularly fatherly in the manner of Henry Beauregard. And his hair too was curiously long for a man who in other ways was so conventionally dressed. It added to the romanticism of his appearance.

However, Henry Beauregard, attractive as he might be, appeared to be under a slight misapprehension as to the reason for her presence in the Highlands.

'Oh no,' said Jemima quickly. 'There's been a mistake. I was trying to leave a message for Charles Beauregard. Your brother or cousin or something? Anyway, he's coming to fetch me. I thought the girl didn't understand at the time.'

Henry Beauregard stared at her. For such a totally poised man he looked genuinely startled.

'I'm afraid there's no mistake, Miss Shore,' he said after a pause. 'And my nephew will hardly be coming to fetch you, I fear. You see, we are on our way to his funeral. Charles Beauregard is dead.'

2
Terribly sudden

The first reaction of Jemima Shore, which she did not in fact express, was: 'Oh God, there goes my holiday...'

Instead she said in a tone of perfectly modulated regret: 'I'm sorry.' She added equally perfectly: 'Was it terribly sudden?'

Henry Beauregard continued to stare at her. Jemima felt her cool beginning to abandon her.

'I mean, I had a letter from him only the other day.' It was a ridiculous remark and the dog seemed to think so too. He looked at her with exceptional mournfulness and wandered away to another table, his tail wagging.

'You were – great friends?' Henry Beauregard was purring again. She recognized the note, both sinister and attractive.

'No, no, we'd never even met.' Charles Beauregard's uncle did not appear to know how to deal with this.

After a moment he said reverently, 'Charles was a very special person.'

'Oh, I know,' replied Jemima with equal reverence. Then she thought: This is ridiculous. I never knew him. I have absolutely no idea, no idea whatsoever, what he was like. I must step out of all this. Now.

'Was it terribly sudden?' she asked again. There was more authority, less reverence, in her voice. Henry Beauregard seemed to recognize it. He positively drew to attention.

'Oh God, yes, terribly sudden.' There was a pause while he seemed to be considering what to say next.

'Colonel Henry, we really must be going,' said a third voice, interrupting them. It was the younger man in the dark suit. The only person now absent from the party was Jacobite, currently sniffing at the feet of the elderly man in the kilt. Jemima regarded the younger man; no, he did not really have the appearance of being related to her interlocutor. Just a generic likeness in the handsome, slightly craggy features. It was the dark suit which had given them a certain funereal resemblance.

To begin with, this man was not only younger but shorter. And now she examined him, his black suit was fancy and ridiculous where Colonel Henry's was ancient but becoming, while his voice lacked both the seductive purr and the stentorian command of his companion's.

'Miss Shore,' said Colonel Beauregard. 'May I introduce our local MP, Ossian Lucas?'

Jemima Shore felt as surprised as if, with memories of Anglo-Saxon at Cambridge, she had met Beowulf's Grendel the Dragon. And failed to recognize him. Ossian Lucas!

The famed MP for the English Highlands, as *Time* Magazine would put it. And although Lucas had only occupied the seat since the October '74 election, *Time* Magazine had already found occasion to put it just like that. What with Scottish nationalism and Scottish internationalism and Scottish devolution and Scottish revolution . . . The great thing about Scotland was that it was news these days. And Ossian Lucas was news too.

His clothes for one thing. On close inspection Ossian Lucas's dark suit was waisted as though for Spanish dancing, unlike that of Colonel Henry which proceeded majestically from high neck to lower ankle without interruption as though according to some prearranged law. And was there not some hint of velvet, black but velvet all the same, on his collar and a suspicion of black frogging about the buttonholes?

Jemima, indeed, felt quite surprised that Ossian Lucas, MP, had been sitting in the Railway Hotel, Inverness all that time without one newspaper reporter making an appearance. That must explain her failure to recognize him. Of course she had not seen a copy of this morning's *Highland Clarion*. That might well contain the headline OSSIAN LUCAS IN INVERNESS.

Ossian Lucas. Was he even Scots?

There were those, all too many of them, who would swear to having been at a minor English public school with one Oswald Lucas. The trouble with these mischief-makers was that they had all been at different schools.

Ossian Lucas, like that legendary Gaelic bard for whom he had presumably been named either by his parents or himself, might be suspected of being the product of a forgery. But it was mighty difficult to prove.

Anyway he was the MP for the Highlands and Islands constituency. On the whole, Jemima felt warmly towards MPs. Her former lover Tom Amyas was a former MP – losing his seat in the October '74 election. He now worked permanently for the vociferous Welfare Now Group, where rumour had it that he had become close to his youthful acolyte Emily Crispin. Jemima believed the rumour.

Jemima's own affair with Tom had ended with one passionate and prolonged – all night – row; this took place shortly after the strange events involving Jemima at the Convent of the Blessed Eleanor, Churne. In a way they had both turned to acolytes for consolation. Tom had sought out his aide at the WNG, the silent and devoted Emily; Jemima had turned to Guthrie Carlyle, handsome, rather more loquacious than Emily, a few years younger than herself, equally devoted and her producer on the 'Jemima Shore, Investigator' programme at Megalith Television.

But she remained on the side of MPs.

She was even prepared – cautiously – to be on the side of Ossian Lucas.

'Oh God,' cried Ossian Lucas, looking at her. 'The press! Why won't they leave one in peace?' He struck his temple with what Jemima expected to be one lily-white hand. On close inspection it was not white. Merely a hand pressed to a brow in a slightly extravagant gesture. Rather a muscular workmanlike hand. With a quick look at Colonel Henry, Jemima realized that he was the one with the long artistic white hands.

'I'm not the press any more than you are,' retorted Jemima in an equally muscular tone, recalled to reality from fantasies of MPs and Scotland and long white hands. 'I'm here on holiday. Or rather I was intending to be here on holiday.' She gazed at Colonel Beauregard as beseechingly as she could.

'Colonel Beauregard,' she proceeded with a very passable fluttering eyelash, 'I was renting a cottage from your – er – nephew – we've never met – I mean we never had met – but he was going to meet me—' Oh, the English language. This was hopeless.

But Colonel Henry was already purring. There was no other word for it.

'A tenant!' He might have been saying: A Magician! A Martian! Or whatever your particular fancy was. There was such a mixture of delight and lust in his voice. 'I thought you were a *friend* of poor Charles.' Into the word friend, it had to be admitted, went a very different mixture of expressions. Contempt. Pity. Almost ridicule.

'A friend of Charles – Jemima Shore,' said Ossian Lucas. 'That's hardly likely.' There was the same ambiguity, an unpleasant irony, which she remembered from the remark in the train. How she wished, in view of all this unexpected intimacy, that she did not remember that sinister little exchange. She felt like someone who arrives to stay in an unknown house, blunders into an unlocked bathroom and finds subsequently that the invaded naked stranger is her host.

'What are we going to do about you?' Colonel Henry was purring again. Jacobite was back, sniffing. He seemed to emphasize the affectionate, even claustrophobic atmosphere produced by Colonel Beauregard's remark.

It was a question which was beginning to preoccupy Jemima Shore. She was frequently praised for her calm and quick-wittedness on television in difficult situations. For the life of her she could not think what the solution was for a situation where you arrived as the tenant of a man who turned out to be dead.

But Colonel Henry suddenly knew exactly what the protocol was.

'We must at least see that you enjoy your stay in the Highlands, Miss Shore. After this regrettable start.' He gave her an absolutely sweet smile, like a benevolent monarch. The effect of such a smile on his normally rather bleak face was delightful.

There was, then, no question of her rejection. A return to London – and Cherry – on the night train. That was the worst prospect. Jemima had not realized how much she dreaded seeing the nubile enthusiastic Cherry – before a month of recuperation was up.

Jemima, in her infinite relief, even patted Jacobite, newly returned to their side.

'And how do we get you to Eilean Fas?'

Executive problems had overcome family considerations in the Colonel's mind. 'We can take her with us, don't you think, Ossian?' he went on.

'Wouldn't look right, Colonel Henry,' said Ossian solemnly. 'Commerce before mourning.'

'You're quite right. Good point.'

'How about those dreadful hearty boys of yours? Ben, for example. Can't he help?'

'Ben! My dear Ossian, Ben has other fish to fry. Royal fish. It's the Visit. Besides, Ben and Charles . . . had you forgotten?' Colonel Henry paused and muttered. He continued more aggressively. 'And why aren't you involved, may I ask? MP and all that.'

'Oh, policy, policy,' replied Ossian airily. 'It cuts both ways. Royalty, rah, rah, on the one hand. The Red Rose, rah, rah, on the other. Most of my supporters go for both, I suspect. Much better to keep clear.

Besides, I loathe tagging along – Royals, don't you know, so inclined to upstage one – so I pleaded parliamentary duties.'

'But it's the middle of August. Parliament isn't sitting,' put in Jemima. She had become interested in this amazing creature in spite of herself.

'A good MP never rests in the service of the electorate,' replied Ossian Lucas suavely.

Ten minutes later Jemima found herself sitting in the back of an enormous estate car, surrounded by her personalized luggage.

'How pretty!' said Ossian Lucas. 'Of course I prefer travelling incognito myself.' Jemima cursed Cherry.

'Probably have to have everything marked in television,' said Colonel Beauregard safely. 'Big place. I remember in the War Office—' But Ossian Lucas was already bundling him into an expensive-looking and undoubtedly foreign car.

Jemima proceeded towards Eilean Fas in the Colonel's own car. She was accompanied by Jacobite, who settled himself on top of her, and driven by Young Duncan, a retainer whose youth, it transpired, was not in his years but in his style of driving. As they left Inverness for the west, Jemima expected pigs and hens to scatter under his wheels. As it was, he challenged successfully the vast lorries and tankers of the North's oil boom.

'What a friendly dog,' observed Jemima. She felt she had to say something. 'He doesn't mind leaving his master.'

'It's Lady Edith looks after him for the most part,' commented Young Duncan. 'What with the Colonel visiting London so often for his business affairs. She's wonderful with dogs, her leddyship, trains them herself. He wouldn't be bothering you now if Lady Edith were in the car.'

'You do know the way?' Jemima said rather nervously to the left shoulder of Young Duncan.

'Aye. Ye'll be going to the Wild Island.'

'Well, Eilean Fas, actually. Is that the same?'

'Aye. Eilean Fas. The Wild Island. And a good name for it I'll be thinking. The way things have turned out.'

Young Duncan chose that moment to overtake two cars towing caravans on the main road out of Inverness. To the right of them, very close, lay the lapping waters of the Beauly Firth. It was summer, but all the same, Jemima did not fancy total immersion. Seagulls rose and screamed. She knew exactly what they meant. Seagulls welcome careless drivers.

'Puir Mr Charles,' said Young Duncan after a pause, dramatically punctuated by feats of daring on his part, gasps from Jemima. Only Jacobite slept on unperturbed. 'Will you be going to the funeral now?'

'No, no I won't. You see we never actually met. The Colonel will be going, I understand. It must be a great shock to him. His nephew—'

'Aye, a great shock. You could put it like that. When a mon is brought up to be puir and own nothing and suddenly in the twinkling of an eye finds himself verra verra rich. A most unexpected development.' His strong Highland accent positively lilted on the last precise words.

'Are you referring to Colonel Beauregard?' Jemima was a practised interviewer. She wanted to make no mistakes on this matter – a matter of growing interest.

'Aye, Colonel Henry as we call him hereabouts to distinguish him from Colonel Carlo, his brother who was killed in the war. Father of Mr Charles Beauregard. A hero. Mebbe you saw the film—'

Jemima did dimly remember seeing some film. *Brother Raiders* it was called, or something equally straightforwardly swashbuckling. Henry Fonda and Kirk Douglas – was it? – played a couple of Scottish aristocrats. Brothers. One had ended by dying in the other's arms. There had been so much nonchalance about the place, with English butlers serving tea impeccably in desert tents, that she could hardly remember the intermittent bursts of heroic action. However, she was confident that all concerned – including the butler, possibly Ralph Richardson or maybe that was another film – had acquitted themselves admirably.

Jemima, however, was not interested in dead war heroes. She wanted to know more about Henry Beauregard now.

'And now I'm thinking he's inherited it all,' continued Young Duncan with a dramatic flourish.

The car had turned to the right, Duncan proceeding straight across the main road to achieve this change of direction without a pause. He drove over a narrow stone bridge. Now the car was at a halt. There was a gate before them, padlocked, three padlocks; a lodge to the left, small, stone-built.

Before them stretched a valley, broad but clearly defined with high mountains on either side. Glen Bronnack, valley of weeping, but looking happy enough now. Jemima knew all about it from Charles Beauregard's original letter. The road stretched forward, winding, until it vanished behind a wall of mountain. The mountains themselves were covered with dark trees, then grasses, then grass and rocks, then pure rock. There was heather – yes, it really was heather – that brilliant purple flower. The sky was still the improbably vivid blue it had been since her arrival in Scotland a few hours earlier.

There was a feeling of pristine innocence about the scene.

Once again Jemima Shore thought: this is Paradise. This is what I've come to find.

'Aye, yon's a beautiful glen true enough,' said Duncan, getting out of the car. He returned with an ever older version of himself – Old Duncan perhaps? – who was unlocking the padlocked gate.

'There's many a mon would commit murder to own a bonnie glen like that,' continued Duncan. 'And those were Colonel Henry's own words to me. The very day that Mr Charles Beauregard was drowned. And him on his way to London, and never knew the poor laddie was dead in the river.'

So saying, Young Duncan got behind the wheel again and started to drive purposefully towards Jemima's Paradise.

3
Nature red

A bird rose above them into the azure sky. It seemed to hang painted above the mountains. A hawk? An eagle? Jemima knew even less about birds, she realized, than she knew about dogs.

'Colonel Henry getting the property. Of course you'd no be agreeing with all that,' observed Young Duncan. There were silver larches, she thought, or birches – anyway exquisitely beautiful trees and in such profusion, lining the road and beginning to hide the river bed. The occasional glimpse of the water showed her, however, that the gorge was deepening, the torrent increasing. The sun still shone. Jemima felt in that kind of mood when she knew that the sun would shine for ever. For her, and never mind the fact that it was Scotland. Silver and gold. The sun on the trees and dappling the water. But in patches of shadow the water was so black that she could not guess at its depth.

'You'd no agree with that,' repeated Duncan with gloomy satisfaction.

'Inherited wealth?' enquired Jemima cautiously. Experience had taught her that radically left-wing views were frequently ascribed to those who appeared on the box, without any evidence that they actually held them. Not, however, on the whole by the Duncans of this world. More by the Colonel Beauregards. She was slightly surprised to find Duncan the victim of the fashionable delusion about left-wing trendies. Jemima herself, while she had never yet voted Conservative, had years ago inherited nearly £10,000 on the deaths of both her parents in a car crash. It had bought the lease of her flat.

'Women's rights, now. That's what you'll be for, I'll be thinking. My wife watched your programme the other night. She found it most instructive.'

The road was starting to ascend and curve at the same time. Duncan warmed to his theme, and turning his head on the word 'instructive', produced a dramatic roll of the car. It was not, Jemima felt, an ideal time for the discussion of women's rights.

'So you'll be thinking Miss Clementina Beauregard should inherit the property,' continued Duncan, nodding vigorously and slewing the wheel to navigate a particularly sudden corner. 'And so will she be thinking the same, I'll be bound. And so will she.'

He cackled. There was no other word for it. 'And there'll be others thinking that on the Estate too, mind you. Colonel Henry is a fine gentleman. I'm no saying any different. But there will be those saying that it should go to the lass all the same. Seeing as her father Colonel Carlo, who was a hero, as I was telling you, built the Estate up when he was young, and her mother, who was an American lady, verra rich, the sort they have over there, made it all into such a fine place.'

Jemima made a sympathetic noise. She was now looking over the tops of the larches. The bird, her bird, still hovered in the sky. She had no idea of its height.

'Ah the puir wee girl,' said Duncan, turning his head again to look at Jemima and adopting a sentimental tone rather different from his normally precise Scottish utterance. 'To lose her brother and home and all, in one fearful day. It's no wonder she's become a little touched.'

'Touched?' And now there was another bird. Twisting and turning with its pair.

'Barricading herself in. Says she won't give up the Castle to the devil himself. And worse. Aye, the language of the lasses these days. It's the television of course.' Aware of his solecism Duncan continued hurriedly, 'Or so my wife says. But I say they have to learn it somewhere and you can hear worse in Glasgow any Saturday night. As I was saying, Miss Clementina is possessed of Colonel Carlo's guns there. The famous Beauregard Armoury. You'll have heard of that now, Miss?'

Jemima shook her head.

Guns did not interest her, nor did shooting as a sport. Although it was August, and judging from the gun-cases on the platform at Inverness there was a good deal of it around, she had no intention of joining in anything so lethal herself. Fishing – now that was a sport for a detached and contemplative soul in a Highland environment.

I don't know whether you are a fisherwoman [Charles Beauregard had written in his original letter], but there is not much fishing at Eilean Fas. It's also rather dangerous in places. You have to watch your step . . .

Still, Bonnie Prince Charlie is said to have enjoyed the fishing at Eilean Fas, according to the legend. We even have a 14 lb stuffed salmon in a case at the Castle and firmly labelled 'Caught by HRH Prince Charles Edward Stuart (HM King Charles III of Scotland) April 15 1746'. That was Mother's doing. The only question was whether she caught the fish herself on the home beat or got the ghillie to do it for her. The Eilean Fas story has to be nonsense because no one has caught a salmon off the island in years, in spite of many efforts to do so. The river is too deep and too fast. The Estate Office will give you a prize of £100 if you do. Then we can put up the rent.

Memories of that original rather jolly letter reminded Jemima that she had quite looked forward to meeting Charles Beauregard. If not for too long or too often. Drowned. She wondered suddenly how and where he had been drowned. Not fishing, she hoped, in the dangerous water off Eilean Fas. Jemima shivered, and fixed her eyes once more on the pair of birds hovering and fluttering. Even as she watched, one of the pair made an astounding sharp, almost vertical dive to the ground. She very much hoped it was not a bird of prey.

Dogs, guns and even birds belonged to a side of country life of which she knew little. It was certainly not nature red in tooth and claw which she had come to appreciate, but Paradise, a primitive untouched Eden, a kind of Scottish Forest of Arden, in which Young Duncan could perhaps be Touchstone (a Touchstone who watched telly). She would perhaps be Rosalind in her beige doublet and hose.

Rosalind – come to think of it, Miss Clementina Beauregard was probably the true Rosalind round here. Wasn't the original plot of *As You Like It*, as far as she could recall, the dispossession of Rosalind by her father's brother? At least this Miss Beauregard was a woman of spirit. Barricading herself in indeed! Rosalind had merely taken herself off to the Forest of Arden.

Duncan swerved, apparently to avoid a rabbit. But it turned out he had swerved in order to kill it.

'Diseased. Best dead,' he said briefly.

'But not us,' Jemima wanted to add. The swerve had brought them perilously near the precipice. She thanked her lucky stars that the road through Glen Bronnack, the Valley of Weeping, had proved empty indeed. A car coming the other way would surely have been fatal. Perhaps the road was treated like a single-line railway track? With only one car on the stretch at a time.

The car screeched to a halt. They were on the very corner of the steepest turn yet.

'There, do you see it now?' cried Duncan with enormous satisfaction. To her absolute horror, Jemima saw beside the road the carcase of what had once doubtlessly been a sheep. Surely, he couldn't be—

But Duncan was gazing at the new view before him. He must have seen it – she had no idea – a thousand times, ten thousand times if he had been brought up here, but Duncan was gazing at the prospect before him with all the wonder and delight of some Highland Cortés.

The final corner had brought them into a different terrain. It was as if they had passed through a mountain barrier or pass. Below them the land dropped away down to the river. Above them still soared the mountainside, with its trees running up to the stone level, then halting. But Jemima's attention was concentrated on the new fertility of this plain, the winding placid pattern of the river, looking like something in a mediaeval psalter in which the figure of a pilgrim might be seen at various stages of his journey. In the centre of this valley the river broadened out into a wide lake, on which could be seen pine trees, rhododendrons, other bushes more domestic than wild. Overlooking all this romantic perfection in which the sun still shone with a remorseless brightness out of its blue sky – so that she was beginning to feel she was in Greece rather than the Highlands of Scotland – was a gigantic Victorian castle.

Be-turreted and be-pinnacled, it dominated the landscape. It also looked exactly like a castle in a fairy story, from which the boy adventurer might try to rescue the princess. There was much of fantasy, nothing rough, bleak or mediaeval about it. In fact it was not even grey, like the Scottish stones surrounding it, but red, rich dark red.

Castle Beauregard: a nineteenth-century structure. A previous edifice on the same site was visited by Bonnie Prince Charlie in the course of his peregrinations round the Highlands – at any rate according to the *Northern Guide*. '*Oui, c'est un beau regard*' he was supposed to have observed to some ancestor of her host's at the time. What appreciation of natural beauty historical royalty always managed to fit into the busiest schedule, and how they preserved their gracious royal good humour in the tightest corner . . .

If the view itself was tranquil, there was nothing particularly peaceful about the structure of this castle. From every red turret seemed to spring another turret like a series of acrobats. Even the pinnacles gave you the impression that, like some form of life, they might be spawning and proliferating while your back was turned. One large central layer appeared to occupy the role of keep. There was a flagpole on the highest turret and a flag which, however, was not stirring in the windless day.

'A fine property!' said Duncan with undisguised approval, smacking or rather chewing his lips. 'There's many Glasgow businessmen, or them from the South, would pay a fine price for it. An Arab, mebbe, looking for a place for his harem.'

Well, thought Jemima, that's one way of putting it. That's how he measures his approval.

'You can't blame a lass for wanting to hold onto it, now, can you?' went on Duncan.

In the foreground Jemima suddenly noticed a small white-washed church, oblong, like a child's building brick. Arranged neatly around it were some grey stone graves. And a very high fence. The fence looked old.

'That barrier,' she enquired. 'So high—?'

'The church you'll be meaning. Oh, it's the deer come and eat the flowers', said Duncan briefly. 'They're unco' fond of flowers, deer. And young trees. You'll find that quick enough on Eilean Fas.'

Jemima thought poetically she would enjoy the acquaintance of the deer on Eilean Fas. As wild creatures, they were welcome to the inappropriate flowers of civilization as far as she was concerned.

But the church – and this was the day of Charles Beauregard's funeral, as she had already discovered to her cost. Was he to be buried here? Presumably Colonel Henry and Ossian Lucas had talked of the Glen Bronnack church. And would Miss Clementina Beauregard, then, not be attending, barricaded within her be-turreted fortress? She must have a pleasant vista for a siege.

Jemima was still meditating on the prospect before her, framed by the purple mountains at the head of the valley, a few of them snow-capped despite the season, when the car screeched to a halt. For a moment she thought that Duncan had actually hit something. Then she realized that they had been quite literally waved down.

A young man with a flag had, as it seemed, appeared suddenly out of the hillside itself, and Duncan had had to brake sharply in order to avoid hitting him.

Jemima gazed at the flag, which was made easy for her by the fact that the young man in question was now holding it aloft. Like the graffiti at Inverness Station, it was emblazoned in scarlet, with the same obscure emblem beneath. 'Up the Red Rose', it proclaimed.

'Up the Red Rose,' repeated the flag-bearer.

'And may the Red run White,' replied Young Duncan with great fervour.

4
Blood on the rose

Slowly, Jemima took a measured look at the flag-bearer.

He was in fact an extremely young man. He had the black curly hair and blue eyes, the kind of bull-like looks traditionally associated with Ireland. He was wearing a kilt, and a white t-shirt on which a large red rose was emblazoned – or perhaps splashed would have been a better word – for there were splashes of red emanating from the rose. It took her a moment to realize that the rose was in fact intended to be dripping blood. Beneath the rose, also in the colour of blood, was the emblem which she had noticed on the station platform.

And behind the man's ear – improbable touch – was a real red rose. The shirt was pristine. But the flower was overblown and slightly wilting. Jemima did not think it would survive many more expeditions of this sort.

'Up the Red Rose,' repeated this unlikely dandy, shaking his flag. His expression was quite amiable.

'If you say so.' To her own ears Jemima's voice sounded over-gracious.

'And may the Red run White,' joined in Duncan for the second time.

'Quite correct. Ah, Mr Duncan, it's you driving, is it? I thought mebbe it would be Sandy.' There was a pause. 'And you'll be Miss Jemima Shore?'

There seemed no point in denying it.

'Yes, I'm Jemima Shore. And who might you be?'

'He's Lachlan Stuart from Torran,' said Duncan.

'Captain Lachlan, ADC to the Chief of the Red Rose.'

'Captain Stuart, why don't you lower the flag,' said Jemima persuasively. She was happy to give him his military rank. Captain

Stuart. Captain Shore. She thought for an instant of her father. A very different kind of military man. More like Colonel Beauregard, as glimpsed in the Railway Hotel. The image vanished. She went on, 'And then we can talk.'

Captain Stuart seemed a harmless enough crank, Scottish style.

'Aye, it will be a pleasure to talk to you,' said Captain Stuart. 'A guid talk. I've a guid deal to tell you of the greatest interest. Never you fear. But no' just now. Just now I'm inviting you on behalf of the Red Rose to view the coffin of his Majesty.' This flummoxed Jemima completely. The coffin of his Majesty. Were there two coffins? Was the glen full of coffins? No, that was going too far, even in this fantastic world in which she found herself.

'Mr Charles Beauregard's coffin . . .' she began cautiously.

'The coffin of his late Majesty King Charles Edward of Scotland. Who you'll mebbe be knowing by the name of Charles Beauregard,' replied Captain Stuart, drawing himself up into a passable military pose.

Heaven have mercy, thought Jemima. What on earth was he talking about? She wished she had a firmer grasp on Scottish history, to know what on earth Captain Stuart could be meaning, with his reference to majesties and kings. Scottish history was an absolutely closed book to Jemima apart from a few salient points like the '45. She had been busy studying Scottish topography for her holiday, and had brought with her the poems of Burns and a couple of Walter Scotts in paperback. The Burns – the love poems – had been a present from Guthrie Carlyle. He had inscribed it: 'Maybe you will invite me to your island . . .' Jemima had accepted the book and made a mental resolution to do no such thing. The Scotts on the other hand, *Old Mortality* and *The Heart of Midlothian*, had been recommended to her as 'the good Scotts' – as though there could be bad Scotts like bad people – by Marigold Milton, her brilliant if didactic girlfriend from Cambridge days, now suitably teaching English to a widening circle of terrorized but fascinated students at London University. Neither Burns nor Scott, national heroes as they might be, struck her as likely to be particularly helpful in the present situation.

It seemed that she should have been studying the ancestry of the Scottish royal family. There was some kind of Stuart pretender; she dimly recalled ceremonies in which, surely, a white rose rather than a red had been involved. But wasn't the fellow a Bavarian prince anyway?

Of course it was up to her whether she chose to discover the answer to these questions. She imagined she was perfectly free to refuse Captain Lachlan's courteous invitation on behalf of the Red Rose. She would simply express her wish to reach her destination as soon as possible (true enough) and pass by on the other side from the flag-waving self-styled ADC to the Chief- . . . Curiosity, at once her best and her worst quality, got the better of her. The funeral was hardly likely to last long, and she was keen to satisfy a certain low desire to find out more about this surprising Beauregard family in a painless manner.

But with Lachlan installed in the front seat of the car, she discovered almost immediately that she was wrong on one count: the funeral was not intended to be brief.

'We intend to see that the late monarch gets a full royal funeral,' explained Captain Stuart. 'As far as is possible in the present circumstances. And will ye be driving with more care, Mr Duncan. We don't want anything to happen to Miss Shore while she's under the protection of the Red Rose.'

Well, thought Jemima, he may be a Royalist nut, but at least we agree about Duncan's hair-raising driving . . .

'So you got yourself a job, did you now? An ADC, do you call it?' countered Duncan sarcastically to the quip about his driving. 'After you were thrown off the Estate.' But he did slow down his driving, Jemima noticed.

Lachlan Stuart gave Duncan an extremely dirty look. Jemima thought it wise to intervene.

'Look here, Captain Stuart—'

'Captain Lachlan, if you please, Miss Shore. We have no surnames in the Army of the Red Rose. For security reasons, you understand.'

Security with regard to surnames was surely an idle matter, with Duncan there to provide the necessary information, like a vindictive chorus. Nevertheless Jemima was not disposed to argue the point.

'Captain Lachlan, what on earth is my part in all this? I'm simply on my way to Eilean Fas—'

'Aye, we know that. We had the information from the Castle.'

'From whom?' He ignored the question.

'And we're taking you along purely as an observer.'

'But an observer of what—'

'Why, to tell the world of the royal funeral of his late Majesty. You'll be representing the world's press and television. And then we'll let you go to make your report. It'll be the making of your career, mebbe,' added Captain Lachlan kindly, 'to have such an opportunity.'

Curiouser and curiouser. Madder and madder. The press and television indeed! Did he imagine that she carried television cameras with her, somehow concealed in her expensive luggage, to say nothing of travelling crews.

'And what's the Colonel going to say to all this? And Mr Lucas the MP, all the way from London?' enquired Duncan gleefully. It was a question which had been vaguely worrying Jemima.

'The usurper, Colonel Beauregard as you call him, won't get here. By orders of the Red Rose,' responded Captain Lachlan confidently. 'My men are posted further down the road.'

'He was the Colonel to you quick enough. When you worked on the Estate,' Duncan put in in his sing-song voice, apparently unable to resist intervening.

'There's blood on the Red Rose now, Mr Duncan,' answered Captain Lachlan with intensity. 'You know that. Everyone on the Estate – as you call it, but I've another name for it – everyone knows that. Who killed Mr Charles Beauregard? Tell me that now. Never tell me he drowned. Him knowing the river all ways since he was a boy. Who would go fishing in Marjorie's Pool? Just when he was setting up the memorial and all?'

Duncan said nothing. His silence worried Jemima more than the presumably wild accusations of Lachlan Stuart. She had expected him to rebut them furiously. But he said nothing.

'And where was Mr Ben Beauregard on that occasion? Fishing down the river ... His own cousin, and who hated him since they were boys—' Captain Lachlan stopped. There had been genuine emotion in his voice. He seemed ashamed of having expressed it.

'Drowned,' he repeated much more calmly. 'Aye, there's blood on the Red Rose.'

Duncan's only response was to drive faster as though to get away from Captain Lachlan's passion.

'Mr Duncan, I warned you,' said Captain Lachlan after a brief silence. 'The Red Rose wouldna like it if anything was to happen to Miss Jemima Shore.'

The road was descending into the plain. It seemed appropriate that the brilliant sun, coruscating on the waters of the loch, and which had accompanied Jemima since her arrival in Scotland, had now disappeared. Clouds were massing at the head of the valley. The heads of the high peaks had vanished. Even the heather had lost its vivid purple. How very sombre was its colour without the sun, she thought. And mountains, so often allegedly blue, were actually grey, anthracite grey, or even something darker. The loch, reflecting the sky, had not so much lost its colour as gained an angry positive darkness.

By the time they reached the simple white-washed church, there was no feeling of light or sun in the valley at all.

Standing round the church were a group of men. Some wore dark clothes, but the majority wore kilts with dark jackets. She noticed that no one wore a t-shirt splashed with blood on the rose. These were presumably the mourners for Charles Beauregard. There were no women outside the church that Jemima could see. Above the church there was a small white arch with a bell inside it. And above that was a flag. In the gathering breeze, the flag stirred and fluttered. On a white background, a vast rose could be clearly seen. There seemed to be some royal arms of sorts there as well. Below that the red emblem – UR2. Of course. Up the Red Rose. Jemima had always been rather good at guessing riddles.

Now she saw that the mourners outside the church all had red roses in their buttonholes.

Where were the rest of the congregation – the Beauregard family? Jemima suddenly felt rather ill-equipped to attend this strange funeral and regretted the half-frivolous impulse which had brought her to the church.

With his debonair courtesy, Captain Lachlan ushered Jemima up the gravel path through the small lych-gate. Church of St Margaret and All the Angels, Glen Bronnack. Mass 8 am daily; 8 and 11.30 Sundays. For the first time Jemima realized that this plain little valley structure was in fact a Catholic church. Its plainness had deceived her. How very different from the ornate chapel of the Convent of the Blessed Eleanor where she, as a Protestant living nearby, had been educated during the war.

Jemima suddenly wished passionately that she had Mother Agnes by her side. Mother Agnes, the young but increasingly formidable Reverend Mother of that convent, was, she often thought, the only truly serene person that she knew. Her serenity added to her strength. Mother Agnes would know how to deal with Lachlan, of that she was quite convinced. Lacking the nun at her side, Jemima tried to imagine at least how Mother Agnes would behave in these circumstances. Calm, but forceful calm, seemed to be the watchword. As it was, she would have to content herself relating it all to Mother Agnes afterwards in a long, long letter once she had reached Eilean Fas. And peace.

There were graves on either side of the path. Most of them looked old, forgotten, mossy. But one newly dug, surrounded by red roses, caught her attention. Beyond, surrounded by a little low hedge of green bush, was a separate enclave. Here were situated a number of graves. All very freshly tended. No moss here. And there, quite clearly to her surprise, was another freshly dug grave. By its side, also, was grouped a flower-shop of wreaths, white chrysanthemums, touches of yellow, predominantly white flowers. Conventional funeral floristry. And not a sign of a red rose to be seen.

Still gallant, Captain Lachlan ushered Jemima to the front door of the church. As Jemima entered the church itself, heads, a multitude of them, or so it seemed, turned round, as though according to a single command. A blur of white faces, all quite unknown to her, all looking as reproachful as a herd of sheep in a field disturbed from grazing by a strange dog.

The small church was packed. The walls, like its exterior, were white-washed, and punctuated here and there by brass plates and other memorial stones. The Stations of the Cross were there to remind one of its Catholicism, otherwise it resembled a simple Scottish church of some lower denomination much more than any Catholic church Jemima had ever visited. But there was an extraordinary glass window above the altar. Greens and blues swam in front of her eyes like a lighted aquarium. Figures, knights on horses – perhaps crusaders – swirled among the vivid colours in what was some kind of battle scene. Gazing at it a moment, Jemima lost all sense of her surroundings.

The next moment a rich harsh voice rang out in a very strong and – for once – ugly Scottish accent:

'Lachlan Stuart, you have no right to bring your wicked flummery into the House of God. You are making a mockery of Christian burial.'

The sheep-like faces of the congregation continued to stare in their direction. Striding down the aisle towards them was a truly enormous man, his long black cassock flapping behind him. Over it, the white surplice hardly seemed to come half way down. Thick black eyebrows, in contrast to the shock of white hair above, dominated the face above the surplice. The man must be at least six and a half feet tall, thought Jemima. And he was gazing at Captain Lachlan with blazing fury. Jemima herself got a scathing look. Of all the absurd things, she was suddenly embarrassed to find herself wearing trousers in church.

'And, wummun, whomsoever you may be, will you not cover your head decently in the House of God? And in the presence of the dead.'

It was then that Jemima became aware of the coffin, draped in black velvet, behind the priest. An enormous wreath of red roses was centred on top of the black velvet. There was a surround of some kind of tartan, and tartan flags were hanging from poles at each corner of the coffin. Her eyes travelled to the altar. Once again red roses – that most unlikely accompaniment to a funeral – were here placed, defiantly as it were, in vast vases.

Jemima felt in her handbag. It was no time to be arguing about the relaxation of the Church's rules concerning head-covering. Which as far as she knew had occurred many years back in the rest of the world, but news of which had evidently not penetrated Glen Bronnack. A chiffon scarf, Hanae Mori, printed with a design of hearts, emerged and fluttered nervously in her fingers as she tried to tie it rapidly over her hair. Its pale pretty colours must make her, she thought, look even more unsuitable among the sea of black hats and veils which stretched before her.

Captain Lachlan himself was in no way discomposed by the priest's anger.

'Father Flanagan, you may now-proceed with the funeral of his late Majesty,' was all he said, with a calm Jemima envied.

'I will not be burying Mr Charles Beauregard under such flags and roses and the like,' replied Father Flanagan fiercely. 'I said it to his face when he was alive and I'll not be holding my tongue when he's dead. I denounce the Red Rose and all its works. An insult to the dead, and to Almighty God and to his sorrowing family.'

'Are you referring to me, Father?' said a clear female voice from somewhere above their heads. Jemima realized for the first time that there was a gallery in the plain church. She looked back. The gallery, which ran the width of the church, over its doorway, was totally empty except for one girl, sitting in the centre on what looked remarkably like a kind of wooden throne.

'Since I am the only member of this family sorrowing over the death of Charles Beauregard, it is my request that the Red Rose is present,' continued the high clear voice. 'I instruct you, Father, to proceed with my brother's funeral.' She paused, and looked furiously, disdainfully, at the rest of the congregation below her. 'I regard the rest of you, as you well know, as murderers.'

'Her Majesty Queen Clementina,' murmured Captain Lachlan with something like reverence. He even managed a kind of bow.

'Murderers,' repeated Miss Clementina Beauregard.

5

Dead but not buried

There was a kind of commotion in the little church, a subdued but audible buzz of horror. Jemima dropped her eyes from the improbable figure of vengeance in the gallery, and tried to form some impression of the members of the congregation as individuals.

The general image of the congregation was now dissolving into a series of portraits. Miss Clementina Beauregard was already a portrait in her own right. Or rather, sitting there, with her long fair hair under a black velvet beret and her black clothes with white frills at the neck, she had the air of a mermaid in mourning. What was that Hans Andersen story about a little mermaid who walked on knives to gain the man she loved . . . Clementina Beauregard would have done well as a mourning mermaid. Cold, even in her sorrow.

The rest of the congregation did not look as though they had come out of any sort of fairy story. They were neither fey nor frail in appearance. Or to put it another way, they were positively beefy-looking. What you might expect in a Scottish church of any denomination on a Sunday. Except that this wasn't Sunday, and Jemima was reluctantly coming to the conclusion that nothing in Scotland was going to be quite as she had expected.

The front left-hand pew had an obvious gap at its end. That, she guessed, was for the absent Colonel Henry to slip into. And it was likely now to remain empty. The woman who actually headed the row was wearing a conventional black hat. She continued to stare persistently in the direction of Clementina and her gallery.

The Colonel's lady? Presumably. It was an unexpectedly sweet face, with those kind of features – small nose, round chin – which time blurs, removing the prettiness of youth, leaving behind something slightly pathetic, distressed, in its place. 'Remember me, I was young and pretty once.' A tall young man standing next to her put his arm round her shoulders, stooping to do so. She turned her head, in its small black hat, to look at him. What a preponderance of males there was in this church on a closer inspection. There was no female in the family pew, with the exception of this middle-aged woman; then of course there was the galleried Clementina. At that moment a boy leant forward in the front pew and touched the woman on her arm. He had a fresh rather cheeky face, pink cheeks and black hair; he looked quite cheerful. Not much funereal pretence here. And then Jemima distinctly saw him give his mother, if that was who she was, a thumbs-up sign. He even smiled broadly. No, no funeral pretence here, whatsoever.

The woman turned her face once more to the gallery. Something about her expression arrested Jemima's attention. There was real feeling here. Alone of the staring faces, she seemed to display not so much anger, embarrassment or real outrage as some other emotion. Compassion, perhaps.

The tall young man whispered in her ear. His expression was quite stern. Jemima would remember that face. How tall they all were – and not every one of those beefy young men could be Beauregards.

The tallest man in the church was, however, Father Flanagan. The priest had not deigned to reply to Clementina Beauregard. He stood for a moment, a huge and rather frightening figure. Then he too turned and strode back up the aisle. Captain Lachlan handed Jemima into a back pew with his usual grace. The sheeplike faces were now all turned towards the altar.

To her continued amazement Jemima Shore, at eleven o'clock on an August morning, found herself attending a Roman Catholic Requiem Mass in a remote Highland church, for a man she had never met. By this time, in her romantic anticipation of her holiday, she had expected to be sitting tranquilly on her lonely island gazing at peaty waters, admiring the heather. Alone. As it was, she was beginning to think wryly that Megalithic House, that busy hive of television, was a better bet for solitude than the Highlands of Scotland.

The Mass proceeded.

Yes, she would certainly have something to write to Reverend Mother Agnes about.

In fact the Mass now proceeded quietly, almost quickly. There was no sermon or address of any sort, either from Father Flanagan or Captain Lachlan, which perhaps under the circumstances was just as well. There was no drama about it at all, except what Mother Agnes would call the central drama of the Mass itself.

Holy Communion. Members of the Beauregard family filed up to the altar. Jemima realized that in spite of those far-off years as a Protestant day-girl at a Catholic convent, and in spite of recent traumatic experiences at the same convent, she had never actually attended a Catholic requiem before. She was faintly surprised to see that communion played some part in it. The front phalanx of mourners left the front pew for the communion rails looking more like bullocks, and less like sheep.

But from the gallery Clementina Beauregard did not descend. Nor for that matter did Captain Lachlan leave his pew for the communion rails. It was only at the end of the requiem that Captain Lachlan made any move at all.

Then he looked up in the direction of Clementina Beauregard. She nodded. Lachlan made a gesture, once again courteous – a positively chivalrous man. Four men in dark jackets, wearing the kilt, red roses in their buttonholes, stepped forward to the corners of the coffin.

There was a faint gasp from someone – it sounded like 'Oh no' – as the four men shouldered the box. Somewhere someone wept. A woman. That vulnerable compassionate woman perhaps.

Under the implacable gaze of Miss Clementina Beauregard, the coffin, in its black velvet coverlet, still crowned with its red roses, was marched slowly out of the church.

Lachlan, motioning Jemima to follow him, fell in behind it.

'Ye'll now see the royal burial, a verra wonderful sight which the Red Rose has brought you here to witness,' he whispered. Jemima pulled off her headscarf. As she did so, she noticed a man entering the church by the side door; if he was a member of the Red Rose, he wore neither t-shirt nor flower behind his ear. The most violent splash of colour about him was his shock of bright red hair. He spoke urgently in Lachlan's ear, as though remonstrating with him. Lachlan shook his head. The red-haired man looked angry or at least discomposed; then he vanished again through the side door. Jemima and Lachlan left the church together.

No doubt the royal burial would have been a very wonderful sight. Who could tell? – since the sight that met their eyes as they left the church was totally unexpected.

Dark-suited as before, but somehow grown in stature or at least in authority since that encounter at Inverness Station, Colonel Henry Beauregard confronted them. He was flanked by a number of men – six or more – whose clothes seemed to indicate that in contrast to the forces of the Red Rose, they had not planned on attending a funeral that day. Two of the men were wearing boots, thick green boots; one wore a dark waterproof jacket; there were tweed jackets, dark brownish tweed the colour of peat, jerseys. One man even wore a tweed hat. There was no sign of Mr Ossian Lucas MP.

'Ah, Stuart,' said the Colonel easily. 'Just get your fellows to put down that coffin, would you?'

He might have been talking to the barman of a West End club, asking him to put down a whisky on the table. It was an authoritarian voice. But it was not loud.

To Jemima it all seemed totally unreal. The nonchalance of the Colonel's attitude added to the unreality. Lachlan hesitated: he looked round. Jemima had the impression that he might have been looking for his red-haired companion. But there was no sign of him.

'Her Majesty Queen Clementina—' he began bravely.

'I don't want a scene in front of the church,' said the Colonel. His tone was still easy.

'Do as he says, Lachlan,' said a voice behind her.

'Mr Rory—' Lachlan was undoubtedly losing confidence.

'I don't need any help to deal with this,' said the Colonel. The tall young man looked abashed.

Lachlan still hesitated: finally he gave a quick, rather ungracious signal to the four pall-bearers of the Red Rose who were motionless with the coffin on their shoulders.

'Aye, we'll be gone now, Colonel,' he said sullenly. 'But we'll be back. And we'll have our rights too. The Wild Island for a royal memorial. You'll see.'

Slowly, glumly, the members of the Red Rose lowered the coffin to the ground. But it was not the Colonel's motley force which now shouldered it.

'Rory, Hamish, Gavin, Niall,' said the Colonel in a much sharper voice. This time he sounded as if he was talking not to a barman, but to four dogs. And like dogs, four of the healthiest looking young men Jemima had ever seen bounded forward with ruddy cheeks, eager eyes. Just like dogs. Even the tall Rory now looked eager rather than sulky. None of them possessed an iota of the distinction of the Colonel. Their features were somehow coarsened with too much health – or was it youth? His were refined by age – or was it authority? For the second time that day, Jemima thought of her father. As she had seen him in her childhood's eye. Not the sad father of the post-war years, but the magnificent military man of her infancy.

All the same, for all her thoughts of her own father, it came as a surprise to hear one of these amiable boys say:

'Which graveyard, Dad?'

Dad. It did not sound appropriate.

'The family graveyard,' replied the Colonel in a clipped voice. 'Where else?'

'But they were digging a sort of royal grave, covered in red roses.'

'Don't be more ridiculous than you can help, Hamish,' was all the Colonel said.

'Clementina said—'

The family graveyard,' repeated the Colonel. There was thunder, not too distant, in his voice. Hamish dropped back.

The boys proceeded with the coffin towards the family graveyard. The former coffin-bearers, relieved of their burden and led by Lachlan, were shambling away down the road. Nobody seemed to pay much attention to them. The Glen swallowed them up.

'Ah, Miss Shore.' It was the Colonel again, in an exceptionally affable mood.' Awfully sorry to have got you mixed up in all this. Just a little local difficulty. As Harold Macmillan would say.'

Jemima smiled. She did not need to be told the source of the quotation.

'Look, we'll just get this sad business over. And then I'll drive you to Eilean Fas myself. I don't want,' said the Colonel carefully, 'you to think we are complete barbarians.'

'Oh, please—' said Jemima, with a regal wave of her hand. She was still aware that she was waving away a great deal. But the Colonel's courtly manners aroused that sort of response in her.

The coffin was being lowered into the family grave. The mourners stood around. Then a woman's breathless voice said:

'Henry, you must *do* something—' For one second, the Colonel frowned, a truly terrifying split-second frown. Then he continued in his usual calm way:

'My dear,' he said, 'may I present my wife? Miss Jemima Shore, my wife, Edith.'

'Henry,' went on the woman, and it was that vulnerable woman of the front pew, 'You must do something about Clementina. She won't come to the burial if you're there. I said: Poor Charles is dead, there's no point in arguing now. We can't bring him back to life. She said: Dead but not buried. In that fearfully cold voice of hers. Just like Leonie's in one of her icy moods. She's saying you murdered Charles.'

The Colonel still sounded absolutely calm.

'How utterly absurd of her, my dear. And rather absurd of you, Edith, to repeat it.' He turned away from his wife's flushed face, her hair untidy under its confining hat.

'Miss Shore, perhaps you would prefer to stay in the car, while we sort all this out.'

It was definitely a command, for all the politeness. Jemima was glad to obey. She walked down the gravel path to Duncan's car. Ahead of her lay the loch, dark grey, anthracite. Rain was beginning to beat down on the edges of the water. At that moment she narrowly missed being knocked down by a sports car, white, driven very fast. At the wheel she recognized the black beret, fair hair and pale set face of Clementina Beauregard.

She had kept her word not to attend the funeral of her brother, in the presence of her uncle. What had she said of Charles Beauregard? Dead – but not buried. It seemed an ominous start to a holiday that was to take place, willy-nilly, in the bosom of the Beauregard family territory.

6

Island of Eden

'No chance of strangers here, you see,' said Colonel Henry. It was half an hour later. By now the estate car was swaying over the narrow bridge to the Wild Island. The bridge had evidently been built of a series of wooden slats. A good many of these were now missing. The remaining slats shifted and seemed to complain under the car's weight.

It really was an astonishingly narrow bridge. Not even a parapet or a handrail. Two sagging ropes on either side. Hardly sufficient to safeguard a person, let alone a car. Had there ever been a crash here ? Jemima shivered. She shot a look at Colonel Henry's handsome hawk-like profile – how narrow his lips were – and did not like to ask.

Beneath them the water looked as black as the loch. On the left the cliffs of the Wild Island reared up, enormously high. Below the bridge, forking down to the loch, the river was deep and fast-flowing. A wide river with vast trees lining the edges of it, huge and very dark green trees whose roots must surely be in the river itself as their branches trailed in the water. Jemima thought of trees drawn by Arthur Rackham. These trees too looked menacing. There were no banks to this river, no footholds if an unwary traveller slipped into the dark waters. Something seemed to jump there below. Jump and splash. A fish? A salmon? But Charles Beauregard had said there were no salmon to be caught here, by tradition. The surface of the river recovered its smoothness.

It was still raining. Jemima looked away from the threatening trees upstream and caught her breath.

The river above the bridge was no river, but a vast waterfall caught between two rocks, forced through a chasm. The effect was startling, the pounding water as it poured down looking yellow, its spray white.

Her exclamation had caught the attention of the Colonel.

'The Fair Falls,' he said briefly.

'Fair?' The falls looked dark, neither fair of aspect nor intention, to Jemima.

'Watchful. The watchers' falls. The guardians, if you like. Guardians of the Wild Island. They are literally its guardians, you see. The falls prevent anyone crossing to the island except by this bridge.' Colonel Henry sounded more complacent than the occasion warranted.

'They could swim...' said Jemima doubtfully. She was fond of swimming herself. She remembered foolishly that she had packed a printed leopard-skin two-piece costume, bought in New York: in fact, to be honest, a bikini. Packing in her London flat, a dip in a Scottish burn from a cottage surrounded by water had seemed quite plausible. It now seemed an utterly ridiculous concept. She could not possibly imagine herself immersed in these black inhospitable waters, so turbulent, so restless.

Colonel Henry had rattled off the bridge onto the island itself.

'A Canadian once tried to shoot these rapids,' he said conversationally, 'In a canoe. To prove it could be done. In the war.'

'I gather it's impossible.'

'Oh, absolutely. As a matter of fact his head hit a rock on the way down. He's buried in the churchyard. The idea was quite ridiculous from the start.'

Jemima could think of no comment to make. It was all a very long time ago: during the war, when men were dying everywhere. And some of them under the gallant command of Colonel Henry. All the same there seemed a singular lack of regret in the recollection. The fellow had failed – and had been a fool into the bargain.

She turned her attention to the steep road – if it could be called that – which they were now climbing. It wound upwards, heavily banked by what looked like rhododendrons. Pines, Scotch firs, whatever they were, and some massive oaks poked their heads out of the shrubberies. How beautiful it must look in the spring, if all these green shrubs flowered.

Now in high summer everything was green; green and heavy. Dank even, in the rain. And so many different greens, the black green of the firs; the light pretty feminine green of the larches; the grey green of the oak trunks. But always green. It might have been some tropical scene in a Rousseau picture, except for the cold. There was nothing tropical about the temperature. Jemima was genuinely shivering now and longed for her faithful white Burberry raincoat.

There was no heather here, no stone, no flowers. Only green. Tigers or leopards might come forth from this jungle. And at that moment, even as the thought crossed her mind, a small deer broke out of the undergrowth on her left. The perfect miniature bounding creature had a Walt Disney quality.

To her amazement, Colonel Henry immediately and purposefully drove straight towards the deer.

'Little bugger,' he said, missing it. Then by way of explanation: 'Roe deer, you know. They eat the tops of the trees.' To Jemima, frankly, it did not seem sufficient explanation. She wondered suddenly if Colonel Henry was prone to the elimination of young animals. Those which stood in his way, that is.

But at that moment the sight of the house stopped her voice, and her thoughts. It was all so totally unexpected. Hardly a house, certainly not a cottage, more like a church. It was built of louring grey stone, in contrast to the rich red of Castle Beauregard, with long high arched windows.

And below the house, equally surprising, falling away, stone terraces, overgrown with grass, but still showing traces of magnificence; more rhododendrons, and a view. A view which was open and grandiose: the river below them, the mountains beyond. Above their heads loomed another mountain. Beyond them, the chasm. And at that very moment, as they arrived, the sun came out. The rain did not stop. So that when Jemima first saw Tigh Fas, with its stone porch, church-like aspect and all, it was framed in the halo of a rainbow.

'It's so absolutely – surprising,' she said after a moment. She was aware of the banality of her comment. But she could think of nothing more appropriate to say.

'We get a lot of rainbows round here,' replied Colonel Henry. Once again he sounded complacent, as though he were personally responsible for them.

'I meant the house. Is this the house? This is Tigh Fas? You see, I had expected a cottage.' Her own letter, Cherry's letter, had specified a cottage. She had *wanted* a cottage.

'Of course this is Tigh Fas,' Colonel Henry sounded surprised. 'I must say it's not exactly my idea of a cottage. Don't know what your standards are in television of course.' He shot her a doubtful look as if anything was to be expected from this unknown medium. 'As a matter of fact we'd call it a shooting lodge up here. My grandmother built it, when she first came to the Glen as a bride, before she got around to rebuilding the Castle. But there's always been some kind of dwelling on Eilean Fas: natural defensive position. Bonnie Prince Charlie is said to have rested up here after the fiasco of the '45. Believe he had a thoroughly good time.' The Colonel spoke as though the Prince had been a recent tenant.

Bonnie Prince Charlie may have been happy about his let, thought Jemima crossly, but I am not. Besides, the house looked threatening. Like the river. Like the waterfall. It was not even the size of it, so much larger than she had expected. Nor the greyness. Nor the large apparently curtainless bleak windows. It was something else: the product of her own instinct. At that moment Jemima Shore felt the straightforward impulse to flee; to turn the wheel of the estate car and immediately go back. Back to civilization, away from Paradise and this island of Eden.

She recovered herself. Then she saw a tall grey figure, grey dress, grey hair, waving enthusiastically on the steps of the house. In its own way, that did nothing to encourage her. Not a ghost. An occupant.

'Someone lives here. I didn't know—' she began.

'No, no one,' he answered with surprise. 'Oh, that. That's Bridie. Only Bridie. She cleans for you. Cooks for you. Whatever you want.'

'Would she do nothing for me?' Jemima's voice, even to her own ears, sounded slightly neurotic. Colonel Henry shot her a look of amazement.

'Do nothing for you? Well, yes, I suppose so. She's always worked for us. Now she lives in the old Beauregard Lodge, the one we call the Black Lodge. Doesn't sleep in. Comes to work on a bicycle over the bridge.' He paused. 'Besides, she'll keep the Red Rose under control.'

It was said with a faint snort, not quite a laugh, still amused. It was the very first allusion he had made to the recent dramatic events in the church.

'It's just that I do so much need to be alone—' she began to sound like a hysterical child.

'She'll certainly keep away if you ask her. Ask her first, mind you. All the Stuarts are famous workers. She won't like doing nothing.'

'Stuarts—'

'Bridie Stuart. Born a Stuart on the Estate here and married Willie John Stuart from the west coast.'

'It's a common name round here, I suppose. No relation to—' She swallowed. She had nearly said – Captain Stuart. 'She's his mother, as a matter of fact,' answered Colonel Henry in his cheerful voice. His tone alone made it clear that Bridie was not a supporter of the Red Rose. But he added all the same:

'She doesn't hold with her son's weird ideas, naturally, any more than the rest of us do. Bridie's got a good head on her shoulders. I can assure you that the very last thing she would like to see is the Wild

Island taken over by a lot of cranks, or whatever it was that my nephew had in mind.'

'Could you explain to me just what it is they want? Just for my own interest,' asked Jemima in her most tactful interrogator's manner.

'Utterly ridiculous,' was all Colonel Henry replied, without deigning to explain what it was that was so utterly ridiculous. Then he relented: 'A Royal Memorial Island!' he exclaimed with another snort, giving the words ludicrous emphasis. 'In honour of the late and totally unlamented Bonnie Prince Charlie – of all people. Why, the fellow was a disaster for the Highlands in every way. No sense of military judgement whatsoever and finally left his own men in the lurch while he went off to France. Doesn't deserve all the attention given to him at Culloden, in my opinion, let alone another memorial up here in the Glen. At least my nephew's death put a stop to all that.'

'And now?' enquired Jemima in dulcet tones.

'Oh, these men calling themselves the Red Rose, Lachlan Stuart is just one of them, they actually want me to set up the Memorial Island all the same as a kind of Red Rose wasps' nest. With the house as a museum, as Charles had planned. Had the impudence to tell me that I ought to carry out my nephew's wishes. I sent them pretty sharply about their business, I can tell you. Told them I didn't want to hear any more about it. What with that and Father Flanagan: *he* thinks I ought to make the whole island over to his church, found a mission there . . . . However, that's another story.' They had reached the house; the Colonel pulled on the hand-brake firmly. Then most courteously he helped Jemima out of the car. Bridie advanced down the steps. She was, even with her grey hair, handsome. Jemima could see the resemblance to her son. Unlike Captain Lachlan – when last seen – she was in fact smiling radiantly.

'Miss Shore, Miss Shore!' she cried. 'Welcome to Eilean Fas. And I was seeing you on the television last night. How clever you were. That terrible man and those terrible questions. And how pretty you looked—' She paused and looked extremely sharply and critically at Jemima. Her eyes, like her son's, were blue. They were extremely shrewd eyes.

'Aye, you look a wee bit older in the flesh. Mebbe it's the journey? Well, we'll soon feed you up, get some colour in the cheeks.'

'I think Miss Shore would probably like to be alone—' began Colonel Henry.

'Of course she would. You be off now, Colonel. I'll be looking after her.' There seemed no way of diminishing Bridie's enthusiasm.

'I'll just have a dram then,' said the Colonel. Jemima noticed it did not occur to him to ask her permission. 'Funerals, you know, an awful strain. What with my niece making an ass of herself. And young Lachlan. And having to shin up that dashed mountain when those absurd nincompoops tried to stop me from getting to the church. In my London shoes! What would Mr Carter at Lobbs say? Still quite fit, you know. But the shoes were a bore.'

Jemima looked down at the once handsome shoes on his long narrow feet, scuffed and scratched; no wonder Ossian Lucas had refrained from joining the mountaineering expedition. 'Nothing like a little malt after a funeral,' ended the Colonel. 'And then I'll be off.'

'Of course. Do have a drink,' said Jemima sweetly. 'But I'm not sure if – my secretary sent a list – but I don't drink whisky.'

The conversation had distracted her from taking in the equally extraordinary nature of the interior of the house. There were antlers and heads galore, some tiny stuffed Disney-like faces, close at hand, some vast animals looming out at her from overhead; most of them accompanied by brass plaques stating when and where and by whom they had been shot. The hall itself was high and arched, probably the same date as the rest of the stone-built lodge, mid-nineteenth century at a guess. But there was an astonishing lack of furniture or even carpets in the hall, and in the rooms leading off it which she could glimpse through the heavy doors. Apart from the surfeit of taxidermy, old fishing rods in mouldering covers, a stringless tennis racket and what looked like a couple of croquet mallets constituted the main decoration of the hall.

'Oh, you have to drink whisky in the Highlands,' announced the Colonel airily. 'I'm sure Bridie's got something in her cupboard.' He led her into the dining room.

Bridie beamed. Jemima gazed at the same time at the tattered long curtains in the so-called dining room and at the sparse furniture – one large very stained wooden table and three chairs, two broken. If she had not been so firmly accompanied by Colonel Henry, she would have believed that she had stumbled on a forgotten house, some dwelling unaccountably deserted which had fallen into gradual ruin. But of course Tigh Fas was not deserted: she began to wonder helplessly whether she was ever, ever actually going to be alone since Colonel Henry was bound to stay on and on . . .

In the event she was wrong. Colonel Henry drained his dram very quickly, and speedily he was in the car again and away down the steep track.

'Come to dinner on Tuesday,' were his last words. 'Give you a few days to recover. Bridie will explain everything. She knows it all. No, you can't refuse. No telephone. One of my idiot sons will come to collect you. I should add that we've got the little Princess coming. Asked herself. But that needn't bother us.' He sprang into the driver's seat as though he was mounting a horse.

Bridie gazed admiringly after him. To her slight annoyance, Jemima found her own gaze was not totally untinged with feminine admiration. It must be the Scottish air – or even the very small deceptively pellucid dram of malt whisky she had been persuaded to taste. But she had felt first protected, then unprotected by the Colonel's disappearance. Come back for one moment, she longed to cry after him.

All her fears rushed back with his departure. The house no longer seemed welcoming. It had returned to its original sullen, rather sinister aspect. His voice no longer filled it. But at least she could be alone – once Bridie had gone.

In the meantime Bridie guided her gently into another large room where there was a fire. It was still rather cold. There were engravings of lochs and stags on the walls. The engravings were mottled with damp. The ancient patterned wallpaper, equally mottled, displayed an area of green and red and blue flowery undergrowth punctuated by birds, not unlike the vegetation she had noticed on her way up the island drive. There was still very little furniture, although the single sofa, like the dining-room table, was enormous. A bookcase with a glass front had lost two of its panes. The sparse collection of books inside, although distinctly Scottish in origin, did not look as if they would appeal either to Dr Marigold Milton or Guthrie Carlyle.

'I'll be leaving you now for a wee while,' said Bridie gently. 'And then I'll be making your lunch.'

Jemima turned to protest. But she felt too tired. It had been a long time since that early-morning awakening in the sleeper outside Inverness Station.

At least she was alone.

She wondered what on earth had induced her to choose a Highland holiday, this northern Eden already proved so full of serpents. She had better enjoy her solitude while she could.

A few minutes later, or perhaps more, perhaps she had closed her eyes, there was a winching and cracking sound at the French windows which led to the grassy overgrown terrace. Someone entered.

'Well now, Miss Shore,' said the now familiar voice of Lachlan Stuart. 'And how did you enjoy the funeral?'

7

There's tragedy enough

'Look, I've brought you these,' said Lachlan Stuart. In his hands was a bunch of wild roses. Their colour was more pink than red. But the symbolism remained clear. Jemima felt herself to have conceived a hatred for all roses, since her arrival in Scotland. In any case she had always hated red roses: a violent assault on the senses. She preferred bunches of white flowers: jonquils, narcissi in spring, with perhaps a touch of yellow permitted. White flowers suited the cool blues and pale greens of her flat overlooking the trees of Holland Park where Colette was now keeping watch. Spring flowers smelt actually erotic to Jemima. People who courted Jemima Shore quickly learnt not to send anything as crude as red roses.

In any case she decided she had had enough of Captain Lachlan and his problems: it was time to strike now if her whole holiday was not to be ruined.

'Mr Stuart,' she said firmly in a voice which would have been recognized at a programme planning meeting of Megalith Television, 'I have no wish to receive these flowers from you.'

'I have come to give you a message,' Lachlan continued, paying no attention to her interruption. His tone was oddly kind. 'These flowers are a message from the Red Rose. From our Chief. We bear you no ill will. We shall protect you. You will still be our witness. When the day of setting up the royal island comes.'

Jemima pretended not to understand the allusion.

'I don't need your protection,' she countered. 'I have no interest whatsoever in the contest you seem to be having with the Beauregard family.'

'But you must be interested in the Red Rose.' Lachlan sounded almost hurt. 'Seeing you're from the television. A reporter.' It seemed impossible at this stage to disillusion him sufficiently to explain the vast difference between the useful programmes of social comment and enquiry which Jemima Shore, Investigator, was wont to conduct, and the kind of reporter he evidently had in mind. Lachlan continued: 'Aye, but contest is the right word for it, you're correct about that. For you're knowing already about the Prince's island, I'm thinking.'

Jemima said nothing. She saw no reason to recount her brief conversation with Colonel Henry.

'The royal island,' said Lachlan impatiently. 'The Bonnie Prince Charlie Memorial. Here on the Wild Island. He told you, Mr Charles. You were to witness the setting up of it. That's why he invited you here, where no tenant has been for years. It was all part of his plan, seeing you were from television. You would make a programme about it all, and the world would see that justice had been done to the memory of the rightful King of Scotland. He wrote to you—'

'I know very little about Bonnie Prince Charlie. And I know still less about Mr Beauregard's plans for setting up a memorial to him. He certainly mentioned none of this to me in his letter . . .' Even as Jemima spoke, she had a sudden vision of Charles Beauregard's last letter: that scrawled handwritten postscript, whose tone contrasted oddly with the rest of the business-like formality, typed presumably by a secretary, since his original letter had been convivial, even rambling. 'PS. There is another matter concerning Eilean Fas which I should like to talk to you about personally. It can't be put in a letter.' No, indeed. If the late Charles Beauregard had really hoped for some sort of television special on his Memorial Island, he would have been sadly disappointed. She tried to imagine the reaction of the head of Megalith Television, Cy Fredericks, to her request: 'Cy, I've discovered these charming Scottish eccentrics—' 'Most exciting,' he would say. 'Most exciting. We must discuss it.' And then, without a pause. 'As we were saying about Northern Ireland . . .'

Now she merely repeated more firmly than ever to Lachlan: 'The troubles of the Beauregard family, their finances, and indeed the Red Rose itself I am afraid do not concern me. No one here seems to understand that I'm actually on holiday.' The slightly desperate tone of the last remark echoed in her ears. To combat it, she stepped forward defiantly, picked up the bunch of reddish roses from the cracked, barely polished wooden table and put them on the fire. A few petals fluttered onto the carpet, worn and hardly still colourful, as she she did so. The petals lay between Jemima and the fire, like pale bloodstains, which

191

someone had vainly tried to wash out. Neither Lachlan nor Jemima made any move to touch them.

'This is a lonely place for a woman, I'm thinking,' said the man after a long silence.

'I've never minded being lonely. In fact I've come here to be lonely,' replied Jemima. It was true. She had never minded loneliness. Her solitary upbringing, the death of both parents when she was eighteen, her struggles, the life of a successful woman with an enviable career in London: would any of this have been possible if she had been temperamentally incapable of loneliness? Those years of her affair with Cy Fredericks, gay, hectic, tortured years of her late twenties, those later so much less gay years of her early thirties awaiting the call of the married MP, Tom Amyas ... No, none of that would have been possible if she had been dominated by fear of loneliness.

Nowadays life was good. Guthrie Carlyle, if anyone, was the lonely one. But she certainly did not feel like sending for Guthrie: something about his evident willingness to be summoned at all hours of the day and night, at all seasons, so charming in a busy London life, had seemed to make his summoning unnecessary in the Highlands. Better far to beguile herself with his presentation copy of Burns, beside the fire, alone. Once, that is, Lachlan Stuart had been quickly but firmly eliminated.

'Aren't you afraid of ghosties, then?' There was something faintly mocking about Lachlan's voice. 'If you'll no be interested in royalty. Wummin is generally afraid of ghosties.'

Jemima smiled and said, 'I'm sorry to disappoint you.' In her experience, ghosts turned out to have an all too human explanation. Beware of charms, ghosts, dreams and such like fooleries said the Catholic catechism. As Mother Agnes would say. She thought of Blessed Eleanor's Convent. Ghosts were evil manifestations in her experience, but human evil not supernatural evil.

'This is an ancient place,' said Lachlan. 'And there are ghosts here, good ghosts, bad ghosts. But you'll no avoid the ghosts at the Wild Island. That's a Druid ring yonder, they told us as boys. And Sighing Marjorie herself at the waterfall, you'll hear her voice yourself before long, above the noise of water, yearning, crying out, and other ghosts too, not so far away, ghosts they say from the wartime, the soldier killed at the falls, and now the ghost of Mr Charles, his Majesty King Charles Edward, whose memory still calls out to us. This is a Wild Island, and there are things here you from the South will never ken, but these things will not leave you in peace, even if you be from the South. There'll never be peace here till the flag of the Red Rose flies over the island, and the memory of Bonnie Prince Charlie is laid at rest. That's why you'll need to be protected.'

A strange chanting note had entered Lachlan Stuart's voice, less like the mocking note when he had first entered the room, more like the keyed-up note of his words in the church: 'Her Majesty Queen Clementina.'

And all the time the noise of water, loud, rushing water, filled Jemima's head. And behind him through the French windows, curtainless except for some tattered chintz, with their cracked and splintered woodwork, arched another rainbow. Brightly it leapt out of the soft remorseless rain which would not surrender its fall even before the many hues of the prism. The noise of the water grew louder and louder in Jemima's ears. She began to have a strange fantasy that the river was rising, invading the house, covering the island . . .

She thought, 'I can't stay here, I shall never sleep here with the noise of that water.' Then Lachlan's face swam before her eyes. The rainbow splintered and its violent colours dazzled and enveloped her. She knew she was going to faint.

When Jemima opened her eyes again, she was sitting in the rubbed leather armchair next to the fireplace. Outside the windows the sun was shining, catching the currents of the black river with gold. It was a delightful prospect. There was no rainbow. And no sign of Lachlan Stuart. She was quite alone.

The two whisky glasses had vanished. She began to believe that, exhausted, slightly drunk from the whisky on an empty stomach unused to it, she had imagined the last intrusion.

'The roses,' she thought. She looked down at the hearthrug. There were no petals to be seen. The fire itself was neatly banked with logs.

She had absolutely no idea of the time. Her little gold bracelet watch, a present from Cy – she had noticed something similar on the wrists of other bright girls at Megalith from time to time – said five o'clock. That was absurd. It must have stopped during the night. She put the delicate object to her ear. The sun was shining so disarmingly: evening could hardly have arrived.

'Aye, it's a beautiful evening we have to welcome you,' said a voice from the door. 'And I've brought you a nice tea. I'm sure you're ready for it.'

It was Bridie Stuart. She was carrying a large mahogany tray. On it were piled a series of plates containing biscuits, buns and combinations of biscuits and buns, as well as a sponge cake, evidently so freshly made that it gave the impression of still softly steaming. Within its layers were seductive glimpses of cream and jam. There was food enough on the tray for ten people.

For one horrified moment, still drugged with sleep, Jemima imagined that others might be expected—

'Och no, it's just that I looked in at lunchtime and you were fast asleep. Sleeping like a child. So, seeing you missed your nice lunch, I thought a wee cake, and some baps. With you being so thin.'

Bridie put down the tray. She was a strong woman, as well as a tall one. She carried the heavy tray without visible effort. Then she knelt down and poked the fire. Questions thronged in Jemima's head. Who had rescued her from her fainting fit? Surely she had fallen onto the floor, and not thus neatly into a chair? Lachlan? His mother? Or both? She had no idea if Bridie was even aware of her son's visit.

'The flowers—' she began cautiously. 'Those red petals.'

Bridie looked round from the fire, positively beaming.

'I knew you'd like them,' she said with great satisfaction. 'I brought them from my little garden. Seeing as there are no flowers here at Eilean Fas.'

For the first time Jemima noticed a vase beside her. It contained a quantity of lurid but clearly home-grown roses. They were each of them a different shade of red.

'But the other petals on the hearthrug,' she persisted. 'You cleared them away?'

Bridie did not stop smiling. She dusted her apron and arose.

'Och, those flowers won't fall yet awhile,' she replied. 'Look, they're freshly picked. Not like your London flowers! Lady Edith tells me they're quite dreadful, scarcely bought but they're dead.'

'Your flowers are quite beautiful,' said Jemima hastily. She could not resist adding, 'Are you particularly fond of red roses?'

'I'm powerful fond of all flowers,' replied Bridie. 'It's just that red roses grow very strongly hereabouts. The white roses now, they won't thrive. Lady Edith Beauregard's beautiful garden, all the white roses she planted there, brought from the South from her brother's place – that's the Earl of Bournemouth, she was Lady Edith de Bourne before her marriage—' pointed out Bridie in parenthesis, in her kindly way – 'and she's awful fond of flowers, flowers in every room, collecting wild flowers, making a garden. A real lady. Anyway they all died. In one night. It seems they were from the South and wouldn't grow in our Scottish soil. That's what Robbie, the gardener, said. And Mr Charles, he had the famous white rose garden up at the Castle replanted with red roses.' She paused. 'No, all the roses you'll see growing in Glen Bronnack these days, Miss Shore, will be red.'

It was impossible to tell from her expression whether Bridie either approved or disapproved of the phenomenon: a valley where a white rose would not – or could not – grow.

'Now eat, Miss Shore,' said the older woman in a kindly voice. 'These things need not concern you, you with your tea to eat.'

Jemima gave herself up to the array of Bridie's confectionery, and discovered that she was quite astonishingly hungry. Bridie continued to stand over her, talking as Jemima ate. It was clearly a situation in which Bridie rejoiced: the visitor as the grateful devourer of her wares, herself as the expositor of the ways and doings of Glen Bronnack, narrowing onto the precise details of Eilean Fas itself, and the house Tigh Fas.

As Jemima ate four baps without difficulty, Bridie gave her a quick geographical sketch. She spoke of Kilbronnack House, 'residence of the Colonel and Lady Edith,' just outside Glen Bronnack and conveniently adjoining Kilbronnack itself.

Bridie spoke of the town too, which she described as a wonderful shopping centre, in every way superior to Inverness, and in some ways infinitely better than London, as Lady Edith herself had confirmed to Bridie. She then came to the subject of Eilean Fas, the need to be careful crossing the bridge at all times. And then she spoke of Tigh Fas, the sadness that the Estate had let the house run down, no curtains, no proper furniture, and how Jemima's unexpected appearance – 'a tenant at Tigh Fas, I was awful delighted' – was thought by Bridie to herald a wonderful new era when the Estate would have to renovate the house again. She made no mention of the late Charles Beauregard's plan for a Bonnie Prince Charlie Memorial.

Finally she talked of the capricious ways of the Aga cooker which only Bridie could understand. She talked of food, food which she seemed anxious to cook for Jemima, and which she implied could be best obtained from Kilbronnack with her, Bridie's, approval, or at least connivance.

'You having no car,' said Bridie half hopefully, half accusingly. 'And the telephone not being here, it was never worth the bother, with the house so empty. And the nearest telephone being at my house, the Black Lodge that is.'

Jemima let the point go. From the South, how delightful a Paradise without telephone or car had seemed. That mood had temporarily vanished. Something about the house was still making her uneasy: the lack of telephone or transport did not help. She would have to arrange for a car at least. But she was not prepared to discuss the subject with Bridie.

'You're very kind,' she answered. 'But I shall just be camping here. I don't really eat much myself. Besides,' she attempted jocularity, 'your tea will last me for several days.'

'But you'll be having some visitors, now?' There was a new avidity in Bridie's voice. She pronounced the word visitors, as Colonel Beauregard had pronounced the word tenant – with a mixture of awe and something like lust.

'No visitors.' Then she compromised. 'I'm planning a new series of programmes for the spring. I need absolute quiet.'

The mention of hallowed television led to a temporary lull in Bridie's offers Jemima suspected it might, however, be no more than a truce.

In all this it was noticeable that one topic on which Bridie Stuart did not dwell was that of the late Charles Beauregard. Yet he had presumably been her employer – until his death. It had been made amply clear to Jemima that young Charles Beauregard, not the much older and maturer Colonel Henry, had been the owner of all this vast estate, these lodges, this castle, this house in which she found herself. Even Kilbronnack House, Bridie made it clear, belonged to the Beauregard Estates, not to 'the Colonel perrssonally' as she put it, rolling both the *r* and the *s*. It must have been an odd feeling for the Colonel and his lady not even to own their own home . . .

The omission of the name of Charles Beauregard was all the more noticeable in the case of Bridie, since she spoke at such loving length concerning her own charges, the vast, in every sense of the word, family of the Colonel and Lady Edith.

'Mr Ben, aye, what a handsome lad he's grown into, he was my first baby, the flower of the flock said Lady Edith many times to me, and flower he is indeed . . . Mr Rory then, he's much quieter of course; indeed he's awful quiet but verra charming when you know his ways, a deep one I called him as a baby, slow to walk, verra deep, but walking verra fast when he did learn with his long legs, and of course he loves it here so much. Ah sure it's a tragedy there's no work round here. But there's no work for him in the Glen, so he has to go away to get work, travelling so often, even to London. Many's the time he's told me: Bridie, I would do anything in the world to live here, maybe here right at Tigh Fas, after all it's empty, anything short of murder, he'd say with a laugh.'

As Bridie bustled on in her narrative to further descriptions of Hamish (slow both to read and to walk) and Gavin and Niall (slow both to read and to talk and to walk, this time, so far as she could make out, and now following useful unmemorable careers in outposts of the former Empire or the Army), Jemima brooded on Bridie's last words concerning Rory. Was it Rory? Yes, Rory. She would never learn to tell them apart, and hoped she would never have to. But this was the second time today that a member of the Beauregard family was quoted as having spoken yearningly of murder. Death and land. 'A Glen worth killing for,' Colonel Henry had told Duncan. Rory had said of himself that he would do anything short of murder. What a primitive lot, thought Jemima with distaste. There was one thing of which she was quite positive: not all the land in the world was worth the sacrifice of a man's life.

But the line of Beauregards seemed like Banquo's descendants to stretch till the crack of doom.

'Isn't there quite a young boy as well?' she enquired.

'Aye, that's Kim,' said Bridie. Her voice was quite doting. 'My baby. He's fifteen.'

By now the tea, the gargantuan tea, had been despatched. Bridie took the tray. Jemima followed her into the hall to the ancient kitchen with its range, like something out of a deserted mediaeval hall. Even here there were antlers, heads, lesser heads, servant class. In the hall of the house she stopped beneath one gigantic head and read the plaque:

'Shot by Charles Edward Beauregard. Cwm Fair. September 27 1930.'

For a moment the date baffled her, then she realized that the sportsman in question must have been Charles's father, Carlo. Another large plaque read: 'Shot equally by Charles Edward Beauregard and Henry Benedict Beauregard, October 2 1932.'

'They never could agree who shot that stag,' said Bridie, following the direction of her gaze. She was now attired in headscarf and mackintosh. 'So they had the plaque made for them both. What times we had here: when the house was gay, full of visitors.'

With a start Jemima realized that Bridie, for all her weather-beaten appearance, must in fact be about the same age as the brother Colonels. There had been a charming wistfulness, a youthful reminiscence in her voice, quite different from the doting maternal tone with which she had spoken of the Beauregard children she had nursed.

Outside Bridie wheeled an ancient bicycle from behind one of the thicker green shrubs. She was preparing – reluctantly – to go. Jemima herself decided to explore a little of the island while the light lasted. She had no wish for the woman to prolong her stay, still less to unleash another flood of reminiscence. Nevertheless the sight of that double plaque filled her with a sudden urge to ask at least one of the many unanswered questions which she felt still lay between her, as tenant of Tigh Fas, and Bridie Stuart, its imperial guardian.

'It must have been a great shock to you,' she said impulsively. 'I mean, the death of Mr Charles Beauregard.'

Bridie, halfon her bicycle, turned her face towards Jemima. The seamed face, till now so warmly creased, so jolly in the intensity of its recollected memories, was totally transformed. Gone was the friendly, garrulous, almost effusive woman, still essentially a servant. The woman who now faced her was a person of authority. And she was aware once more of Bridie's commanding height, standing by her battered bicycle as though a charger.

'Miss Shore, if you please,' she said after a moment's pause in a very flat voice, There are some things best not spoken of.'

Jemima felt a surge of determination. Her combative spirit was aroused. The flood of family reminiscences Bridie had given her concerning the Beauregards contrasted so ill with this wall of sinister silence. She would have accepted one or the other, but not the ambivalence.

'I didn't mean to upset you, Bridie,' she said. 'But as I had corresponded with Mr Beauregard—' She felt she might have added, 'and as I was forced to attend his funeral by your son, his existence and death can hardly be totally ignored.' In fact she said, 'I just wanted to express my regrets to you. Before walking round the island.'

Bridie said, with a return to her old and friendly manner, 'If it's round the island you'll be walking, Miss Shore, you'll best be wearing gumboots. It's wet underfoot here, even in the summer. And we've had a great deal of rain lately. It's slippery, you see, particularly at the far end of the island. Be very careful by the Fair Falls. Don't get too close to Marjorie's Pool, don't be curious—'

'Curious?' Jemima merely repeated the word.

The pool where he drowned. Mr Charles Beauregard; of whom you were speaking just now.'

Jemima was faintly appalled.

'Oh, how awful of me!' she exclaimed. 'I just had no idea he had drowned here at Eilean Fas. How clumsy of me—'

'Didn't the Colonel tell you then?' said Bridie in her previous flat slightly menacing tone. 'It was I who found him there in Marjorie's Pool. Lying face down. Drownded.' She gave the word two long syllables.

'Oh, how ghastly – and how terrible for you.'

'Yes. A terrible death. The water filling his waders, his great boots, to his thighs. Sucking him down,' replied Bridie without expression.

She was by now mounted on her bicycle. Over her shoulder she called: 'So be careful now, Miss Shore, won't you, as you go? We've had tragedy enough at Eilean Fas.'

Bridie was already riding vigorously down the gravel path, before Jemima realized that she had still expressed absolutely no regret concerning the death of the late Charles Beauregard.

8
Utmost quiet

'I must always remember this,' thought Jemima, as she set out to walk round the Wild Island. 'This at last is my Paradise. The serpent has come and gone.'

The evening sun began to create long blue shadows on her path, but it remained bright. The alternate patches of sun and shade gave a theatrical impression. The greenness of the undergrowth rustled with birds: she knew they were birds because every so often one flew out across her path, small, alien, not the sparrows of a London walk, darting purposefully.

'Birds of paradise,' she reflected. How long since she had heard bird song? Heard and listened to it. There were butterflies too. The Rousseau-esque impression returned. She felt now neither loneliness nor fear. The ground squelched under gumboots she had borrowed from the house's antlered hall. They were much too large for her. Possibly everyone in Scotland had particularly large feet: the other possibility was that no woman had ever lived in the house at Eilean Fas. The decorations certainly showed lack of a woman's touch, to put it mildly, or rather they showed the lack of any recent touch at all. The house might have been deliberately gutted to make it seem so bleak. It was in a way no wonder that Charles had thought of it for a museum and Father Flanagan for a mission: it was bare enough for either purpose.

Above her head the vast trees rose out of the undergrowth: it was this which gave the jungle impression. Every now and then an opening in the trees exhibited a brief glimpse of the mountains round her: they too were lit up by patches of sunshine, out of their spare darkness, in the same theatrical manner as the trees. To the left, beyond the green, were the cliffs which guarded the island. In fact the path was in a sense treacherously close to the edge of the cliff, the greenery which masked it only enhancing the danger.

'I must watch my step,' she thought. The noisy river, ever present, should have served to remind her of the danger. But already the waters were fading in her immediate consciousness, no longer menacing, merely soothing. She had no idea where the path would take her, except she had been told by Bridie that it would take her eventually all round the island, so long as she did not turn off to the waterfall. At one end of the island, then, lay the domesticity of the house, the terraces now overgrown but symbolic of peace, the taming of the wild by man, the imposition of a human design, surviving much as relics of the Roman Empire survived into Ancient Britain. Even the view from Tigh Fas itself had an air of arrangement about it.

Now she was approaching a much more rugged terrain. The undergrowth began to encroach across the path. She no longer felt like some lady gently wandering in her domain, but more like an explorer.

A vista of bright red berries, heavily ornamenting a slender tree, entranced her, until it occurred to her that here at least was a hint of the future dark amidst the green present. One or two of the trees were already turning scarlet. It was after all getting on in August. Even a green paradise could not be guaranteed to last for ever.

Turning a corner, the sight of a little stone building of Gothic design, a kind of folly, at the edge of a clearing, took Jemima completely by surprise. Suddenly the trees had fallen back. She was at the point of the island. The noise of the waters had vastly increased: the waterfall and Marjorie's Pool must be close, close but still unseen. The cliffs were now revealed to her, descending sheerly on either side of this sort of summer house, which had been built to perch precariously on the apex.

For the first time she understood clearly the impregnable nature of the island. The fall of cliff was steep, steeper surely than at the bridge, and looked precipitous, unfriendly. A few slender plants grew rather desperately out of the crumbly rock. But they offered little comfort to the potential climber.

Jemima decided to investigate the Gothic folly. Despite its little arched windows the interior was dark. It took her eyes some time to get used to it. No one appeared to have been inside for years. She took another step into the gloom and felt in front of her. Suddenly her fingers closed on something soft, familiar: Petals. And as her eyes grew accustomed to the interior she became aware that a vase of fresh roses, crimson, true roses, no wild roses, these, was standing on a plinth at the back of the grotto.

Jemima's shock was quite out of proportion to the situation, she decided a minute later. It was just that she had convinced herself of the utmost quiet, even isolation, of her new existence. 'Utmost quiet required for TV personality': so had begun the advertisement Cherry had placed in *The Times* with her usual desire for positive action.

'We've *got* to get Jemima to take a *break*,' Cherry was overheard telling Guthrie in the Megalith office. As usual Cherry managed to emphasize more than her fair share of words in each sentence.

'From the series – yes. After all she's not recording again till October. But from us all? I hope not.' Perhaps it was the sudden wistfulness in Guthrie's voice which irritated Jemima and inspired her to sweep into the outer office and immediately O.K. Cherry's somewhat over-dramatic advertisement, which had in its turn produced the original approach from Charles Beauregard. And now her utmost quiet was pierced once more by the manifest presence of another human being on the island.

Above the vase was a plaque, which read:

'In ever-loving and reverent and loyal memory of Charlotte Clementina Stuart, only legitimate daughter and heiress of King Charles III of Great Britain. Wife of Robert Beauregard of Kilbronnack. 1746–1764.' A rose was carved beneath the lettering, and beneath that the motto: FLOREAT ROSA ALBA.

There was a second plaque below which read:

'In ever-loving and reverent and loyal memory of Charles Edward Beauregard 1916–1944, lawful descendant and heir of the Royal House of Stuart. Placed here by his wife Leonie Fielding Ney Beauregard 1918–1958. FLOREAT ROSA ALBA.'

Looking closely, Jemima decided that Leonie Fielding Ney Beauregard's own dates had been added more recently.

She went back to the first plaque and puzzled over it: 'Only legitimate daughter and heiress of King Charles III . . . ' Working it out, Jemima realized that King Charles III must be another name for Bonnie Prince Charlie, in legitimist terms. She remembered reading somewhere that there would be a problem when our own Prince Charles of the House of Windsor ascended the throne as Charles III, since loyal Jacobites would consider Bonnie Prince Charlie to have enjoyed that title already.

At least she was beginning to have a dim understanding of the nature of the Beauregard claim to the royal throne. Or rather the claim of the Red Rose on behalf of the Beauregards. They were descendants of some eighteenth-century royal ancestress. But – 'Charlotte Clementina Stuart' – she felt sure she had never read about this particular character in the history books. Charlotte Clementina had apparently been born around the time of the rebellion of the '45, just after it, no, wait, the battle of Culloden was fought in April 1746, she remembered from her *Northern Guide*. Some time just before or after the collapse of Bonnie Prince Charlie's bold Highland effort, he was alleged to have produced this *legitimate* daughter ... And heiress.

It was the legitimacy which baffled her. Who was the mother of Charlotte Clementina? Who was Bonnie Prince Charlie supposed to have married according to the history books, come to think of it? She would have to enquire.

Then her eye fell on a further notice – not chipped elegantly in stone this time, but written in ink on a piece of white paper in large flowing black handwriting.

'In ever-loving and reverent and loyal memory of Charles Edward Beauregard, rightful King of Scotland. 1945–1975. Placed here by his sister Clementina Beauregard. FLOREAT ROSA RUBRA.'

There was, as Lachlan had said, blood on the rose now: the Jacobite white rose of the first two memorials had turned to red. In case there was any doubt about it, scrawled at the bottom of the white paper was the single afterword: REVENGE!

Jemima felt a certain sense of relief. The flowers had been placed here by that poor distressed girl, with her obsession about the death of her brother. She had, in a sense, every right to penetrate the Wild Island. She doubted if her utmost quiet would after all be much disturbed now the flowers and the pathetic paper memorial were in place.

Jemima rose from her knees, dusted her beige trousers and left the grotto. She was determined now to visit the waterfall. Retracing her footsteps carefully from the point of the island, with wary glances at the chasms on either side – the grotto was built like a figurehead on the prow of the cliffs, it was a wonder it did not fall into the abyss – she returned as far as that mossy parting of the ways at which she had noted a left-hand path. The rise in the volume of the water noise encouraged her. She pushed her way through the greenery: here was a path it was difficult to believe had been recently trodden. As if in sympathy with her desire to find water, the rain began its soft descent once more. Nevertheless the sun still gamely shone.

And it was by virtue of this combination that Jemima perceived the Fair Falls for the second time under the perfect arch of yet another rainbow. Only this time she saw the arch literally doubled: there was another rainbow described inside the first one. She was reminded of that line in the ballad: 'The old moon with the new moon in its arms.' Sir Patrick Spens – another Scottish hero who had gone at his King's command to Noroway over the foam. If not very near Dunfermline town, this was still ballad country. The foam and fine spray flew upwards into the air recklessly, as the black water poured down between the rocks into the chasm below. The pool was at a vast distance below her feet and the grass so slippery that she drew back nervously even before recalling Bridie's warning.

Could that dark and turbulent area of water really be Marjorie's Pool? Little as she knew about fishing, it seemed an odd place to choose to wade out. The pool must surely be too deep for any kind of wading, however high the boots. And in this case of course the boots had not been strong enough ... 'Drownded. Sucked down into the waters.' Bridie's flat voice echoed in Jemima's ears. She tried to shut it out. There was, to distract her also, a high singing sound above the noise of the water, which she could not quite place.

The next moment her eyes were involuntarily drawn away from the pool towards the opposite bank. She was aware of a man in long dark clothes standing there quite still, staring at her. Surprise made her unsteady, she almost slipped and had to grasp a rather inadequate bush on the cliff's edge to steady herself. Recovering her balance, she half expected to see Lachlan Stuart once more. But it was Father Flanagan.

It was not that his expression was particularly sinister or even angry. Yet with his height, his white hair and his dark clothes, he did have the air of a kind of figure of vengeance, a ghost come back from another world to demand retribution. The evening light, the rain, the spray, the rainbow whose vanishing end hovered close to where he stood, all contributed to the phantom-like impression; or was he merely gazing covetously at the island which, according to Colonel Henry, he wanted for the Church?

Father Flanagan continued to stare at Jemima. Then he sketched a sort of wave. It might even have been the sign of the Cross. His lips moved, but the noise of the waterfall, the chasm between them, prevented her hearing his words. Then he turned on his heel and vanished among the rocks. Jemima gazed down the river to the narrow bridge to see if he was intending to pay her a visit. There was no sign of anyone on the bridge. She was safe from intrusion.

Jemima gazed once more into the depths of Marjorie's Pool, thought once more, despite herself, of Charles Beauregard pulled down into its depths as his great boots filled with water, and later found – floating – by the stern and unlamenting figure of Bridie.

No, she would cast out such thoughts. She would remember only the magic of the island, her own Prospero's isle. By an act of discipline, Jemima turned from the Fair Falls and retraced her steps along the mossy overgrown path. Then she wandered more slowly in the general direction of the house.

The undergrowth still rustled, but the birds were no longer flying so freely. The hour was approaching true dusk. Twenty minutes later Jemima found herself once more gazing at that strange Gothic dwelling calling itself Tigh Fas, the Empty House.

This time her feeling of threat, danger, dread was quite unmistakable. It was not the lush green hospitable island which threatened her and spoke of danger. Even the waterfall and Marjorie's Pool, for all its connotations, spoke of tragedy rather than of danger. Yet the house, which should have been her refuge from all this, filled her with foreboding.

'An Ancient place,' Lachlan had said. Had some foul deed been perpetrated on the site of this house hundreds of years ago? Sighing Marjorie, who was she? And whose death did she lament – or was it perhaps her own? Jemima, while not believing in ghosts, was prepared, gingerly, to accept that deeds of violence from bygone times could leave behind their atmosphere of cruelty and destruction. Even the Druids' ring, she supposed, might bring some kind of atmosphere with it from ancient times. What she could not explain was, why she, rational calm Jemima Shore, Investigator, in the words of her own television series, should feel personally threatened.

The island undergrowth spelt safety. The house stretched towards her and she longed to flee from it.

Briskly, Jemima decided that these thoughts could no longer be indulged. She marched back up the gravel path, ignored the dark uncurtained windows, pushed open the studded door into the vaulted hall and switched on the light.

The rest of the house was in darkness. Clearly no one had been here since she and Bridie had departed together. Everything was just as she had left it. The old fishing rods, shooting sticks and other strange pieces of tackle still mouldered in the hall.

She was certainly alone in the house.

Jemima, with a delicious and exhausted feeling of freedom, went into the decaying drawing room and built up the fire with logs. Then she went into the kitchen and scrambled some eggs, congratulating herself at having beaten off the proffered ministrations of Bridie Stuart. She discovered the wine ordered in advance by Cherry – a sort of Highland Beaujolais, it seemed, the best the grocer could provide. Into the eggs went some smoked salmon, another present from Guthrie. ('I know how much you love it, and the lairds up there keep it all for themselves. You won't be able to buy smoked salmon in Kilbronnack.')

Later, sitting by the fire, toying with the idea of beginning *Old Mortality*, she could not imagine greater cosiness nor happiness. It seemed indeed a pity to ruin contentment by beginning the Scott at quite this juncture. Bed and a detective story – Jemima read them by the dozen for relaxation – was probably the answer.

The bath ran with rich brown water, disconcerting at first, particularly when mixed with her favourite Mary Chess Gardenia bath oil which made her London bathroom smell like a luxurious greenhouse. But in Scotland the water was already softer than any oil could ever achieve. In any case the mahogany fittings of the bathroom hardly suited such luxuries.

The bedroom was equally firmly Scottish, not to say Spartan: the chintz curtains, blue and rose-patterned, hung tattered in places, like those in the downstairs rooms. There was a general dearth of furniture and ornaments – the only picture consisted of a vast engraving over the fireplace, depicting Bonnie Prince Charlie himself in a rousing scene at the battle of Preston.

Nevertheless the large bed with its mahogany headboard was in itself extremely comfortable, because the mattress sank so deeply in the centre as to positively enclose Jemima within its warmth. There were also three stone hot-water bottles, still-warm relics of Bridie's ministrations.

Jemima listened to the noise of the water running outside. There was no moon, and the few other sounds of the night did not disturb her.

She felt secure, happy.

Jemima picked up her detective story, entitled, she noticed, *A Scottish Tragedy*, a sort of modern-dress version of *Macbeth*, which she had chosen at Euston for its cover of tartan and a dagger dripping with blood. At the time it seemed appropriate enough. Jemima felt cosier than ever as she skimmed, sleepily but still pleasantly, through the first chapter.

She was just turning the page to chapter two when the sound of someone coming stealthily up the stairs told Jemima that she was not after all alone in the house.

9
From the South

The staircase creaked. She could not be mistaken. This was no ghost, no projection of the haunted imagination. Someone was coming up the stairs, someone who would shortly reach the head of the stairs, turn towards her bedroom, softly deliberately—

Jemima Shore felt quite literally paralysed with fright. She could not even stretch out one hand. At the same time she heard rather than felt, or so it seemed at the time, her heart thumping in time to the muffled steps. It would have been prudent to have leapt out of the huge blanketed bed, maybe even to lock the door – if there was a lock. Perhaps she should turn out the little bedside light in order to gain a certain advantage over her assailant. These thoughts went through her head while she continued to sit bolt upright in bed, frozen, the thin paper pages of *A Scottish Tragedy* still clenched between her rigid fingers.

No, she definitely could not move. All she could think was that she was alone in an empty house, with no help at all at hand, alone on a wild island, and just as she thought, This is ridiculous, I'll get the police, I'll dial 999, she remembered that there was no telephone.

It was at that moment that the intruder reached the top of the stairs. There was a hesitation, a silence, then the creaking moved in her direction. In gathering desperation Jemima listened to some new softly muted sounds outside her door: then a horrible thought struck her – there were two of them. A kind of greedy whispering consultation was going on just outside her door, she could not hear precisely what, but they were dividing her up, they were deciding what to do with her, she knew it, and soon they would burst open the door—

There was the sound of scuffling, low down. Quite suddenly Jemima

207

realized that there was nothing human outside: in fact, the whispers were snufflings, there was some kind of animal outside her door. Unless it was a human being who whined and scrabbled, with sharp nails, and sniffed avidly beneath the ill-fitting door. The snuffling changed to a kind of whining. In her shaken state, that was such a ghastly thought, a human monster, a Beast come to find its Beauty, sitting up in bed in her pale satin nightdress, that she had to reject it, put it away. Yet equally the idea of a straightforward animal there outside the door, nervous as she felt, was scarcely reassuring. Jemima had a particular dread of bears who sometimes featured in her bad dreams. The image of a bear-like monster, a kind of vicious Caliban crawling out of the undergrowth of the island in search of its prey, was both persistent and repulsive.

In the meantime the snuffling and sharp, horribly determined scrabbling continued. It was just as Jemima had recovered her courage, and decided that she who would valiant be must at least confront her enemy, that two short deep barks settled the question of the monster's identity. She was thus half way out of bed already, genuinely cold now in the inadequate satin, when the feeble catch of the door finally gave before the animal's assaults.

At which point a labrador, large, beige and friendly, burst into the room. She recognized him. It was Jacobite. His strong tail wagged with continuous energy, his nose continued to snuffle, now at Jemima's bare feet. Then the labrador paused, raced to the tattered chintz curtains, sniffed, paused again, and came back to Jemima's feet. Finally with more energetic wags of his tail, the vast dog leapt onto the bed, lowered his head, transformed himself from a labrador into a circular pile of golden fur, and went to sleep.

Still too amazed for much thought, Jemima followed him back to the bed. She got among the warm blankets again. Her will sapped by a strong mixture of relief and surprise, she saw no reason not to follow the dog's example. Putting out the light, putting aside *A Scottish Tragedy* (she would not pick up that particular book again in a hurry), Jemima laid her head on the pillow. Jacobite had considerately chosen to make his nest at the bottom of the bed. The dog's heavy breathing, or light snoring, depending on your point of view, soothed rather than disturbed her. She had certainly never slept with a dog in her room before; the fastidious cat Colette maintained the privacy of her nights absolutely. In the background the noise of the river began to float away. An instant later, Jemima joined Jacobite in sleep.

When she awoke it was broad daylight. Bridie Stuart was standing over her with a heavy tray. Sleepy as she was, she could still discern a hunter's breakfast, porridge, oatcakes, eggs and bacon, and a few other items at whose nature, except that they were farinaceous, she could only guess. Jemima never ate breakfast.

She was about to murmur politely, 'Is there any orange juice?' (Cherry could never have forgotten to order that prime need), when she was interrupted by a vicious sound from the bottom of the bed. Startled, because she had completely forgotten the dog, Jemima saw that Jacobite was growling angrily and determinedly in the general direction of Bridie. The golden fur on his neck stood up in a ruff.

Bridie herself looked genuinely startled and even – for one instant – frightened. Then she looked very angry indeed.

'Ach, the wicked dog. The devil. How did she get in here, Miss Shore?'

'I really don't know. Late last night, I heard a noise—'

'Ach, the devil,' Bridie repeated. 'She's still looking for him. She won't give up. She'll never give up.'

'He was so friendly last night—'

'He?'

'He, she, Jacobite, the dog.' As if in confirmation, Jacobite snuffled again towards Jemima and even licked her hand. Then he looked towards Bridie and gave another menacing growl. The fur on his neck, which had temporarily subsided, rose again.

'That's no Jacobite,' repeated Bridie. Anger or fright or a combination of both made her sound quite scornful. 'Jacobite would'na come here in the middle of the night finding a loose window at the back like a thief. Jacobite stays at Kilbronnack House where he belongs, with his owner. He's a good dog, Jacobite is.'

'Then this is—'

'His own sister. From the same litter. But as different a one from the other as—' a pause '—Mr Charles and Mr Ben.' Jemima patted the dog's head. At the same time her fingers felt a collar and a tag. She twisted it round and discerned in highly ornamental letters: 'I belong to Charles Edward Beauregard of Beauregard Castle.' On the other side, it read: 'My name is Flora.' To Jemima the two dogs were absolutely identical.

Bridie had recovered from her fright and anger. She put down the loaded tray. The dog – Flora, as Jemima must learn to call her – gave another distinct growl.

'Why does she growl at you?' Jemima felt she had to ask. Dogs were becoming more of a mystery to her than ever. 'She must know you so well.'

'Aye, she does that,' said Bridie briefly. The smiling welcoming Bridie

209

was not in evidence at all this morning; the dog's appearance had evidently shaken her more than she cared to admit. Of the two women, yesterday's warm enthusiastic help and today's figure of indignation and scarcely controlled outrage – or was it fear – Jemima wondered which was the real Bridie.

'She was so friendly to me, a total stranger—' began Jemima Shore, Investigator.

'Miss Shore,' said Bridie, 'it's no concern of yours, mebbe, since you're only here from the South, and a tenant, to enjoy our lovely glen. But I may as well tell you the truth. I was never able to abide Mr Charles Beauregard. Nor his sister. Nor what went on up at the Castle. I did'na hold with his ways. I told them so, when they asked me to work there. Young people, yet they weren't as young people should be. Not like Mr Ben and Mr Rory and my boys—'

'And the dog *knew* this—' Jemima's voice was incredulous. She could easily believe in Bridie's disapproval of anything even remotely un-Scottish which might go on in beloved Glen Bronnack. Particularly so, since her loyalties were so clearly involved with the other branch of the family, Colonel Henry, Lady Edith, and Bridie's vast brood of former nurselings. But Flora, to have joined in the feud was clearly a dog of extra perception.

'She knew all right. And as I gazed on him in the water, and then thought how I should help him, poor drownded creature, past all human aid, she rushed at me, bit my skirts, tore at my hand. Look, it's not healed yet, the doctor gave me an injection—' Grimly Bridie held out one large, red hand on which there was a patchwork of sticking plaster.

'She thought it was I who did it. But it was not I,' Bridie's voice gathered passion. 'Not I who did it. I know who did it mebbe, though I'm not saying so, mind you, or mebbe I have my own ideas, but it was not I who did it.' Then Bridie began to shiver, as though at the vivid appalling memory.

'Bridie, who did kill Charles Beauregard?' The question sprang to her lips. Afterwards Jemima was never quite clear whether she had actually pronounced the words or not. For at that moment, the loud sharp hooting of a car's horn caused both women – Bridie in her white apron over a thick woollen cardigan and tweed skirt, Jemima still only in her shell-coloured satin – to turn their heads.

The hooting had an imperious quality.

'Ye never hear the cars arrive up at the island,' muttered Bridie. 'The river drowns the noise.' She turned and left the room. Jemima heard her heavy footsteps descending the stairs. A door banged. Now there were swift light footsteps coming up the stairs and a high female voice calling: 'Flora, Flora, good girl, Flora ... Where are you?'

The labrador leapt off the bed barking, the wag of her tail swiping the milk jug sideways. There were joyful sounds of reunion and greetings in which 'Bad girl, *good* girl' seemed to alternate.

Finally, framed in the doorway, appeared the slight figure of Clementina Beauregard. In a Mexican blouse, thin, almost transparent, with a coloured shawl round her shoulders, a long patchwork skirt, various necklaces of beads, zodiacal signs and silver fishes hanging on chains, and with her long curling hair flowing everywhere, she presented a charming if slightly in-appropriate sight for a Highland morning.

Clementina Beauregard advanced on Jemima with a smile which was so fixed as to give an impression of strain rather than genuine welcome. She was also carrying a half-smoked cigarette in one hand.

'Miss Shore,' she cried, 'I'm so terribly pleased to see you. You will help me, won't you? No, don't say you won't. I've got something most important I want you to do for me. I mean, you are Jemima Shore, Investigator, aren't you? I say, oatcakes.' Without a pause, this fairy-like creature, so thin and pale that she resembled Titania rather than something more substantial and human, began to demolish most of Jemima's hitherto untouched breakfast.

As Clementina rattled on, the timbre of her high clear bell-like voice recalled to Jemima's mind her denunciation in the church: 'Murderers ... ' Her chatter darted to and fro in its random phrases, cries, appeals, expostulations, irrelevances, catch-phrases, like a bird, and in vain Jemima tried to interrupt her. In despair she glanced at her leather travelling clock – a practical present from Tom Amyas.

Nine thirty. At least she had slept like the dead. The phrase struck her suddenly as a sinister one. She was not dead. No wild animal had molested her, only a harmless dog looking rather touchingly for its dead master.

'Perhaps, after my breakfast,' said Jemima at last, pleadingly, to try and stem the flow. At which her fairy tormentor jumped up and cried in despair:

'But I've eaten all your breakfast! Horrors! And Bridie wouldn't dream of cooking anything for me. Such a disapproving old thing. How Ben and the boys stuck her as a Nanny, I can't think, except I suppose if you have Aunt Edith as a mother, anything is preferable. Calling Charles and me depraved! I'm sure she's far more depraved with all her jealousy and wanting everything for Ben all the time and hating us.' Clementina broke into slightly hysterical laughter.

Jemima smiled with more politeness than she felt. She had a terrible feeling that she knew exactly what Clementina Beauregard intended to ask of Jemima Shore, Investigator. Why was it that everyone expected television to present its performers with a kind of magic wand, which would enable them to solve problems insoluble by mere mortals? As far as Jemima was concerned, she was beginning to think that television *created* more problems than it solved, certainly at this hour of the morning.

She was thus not totally surprised to find herself being urgently enlisted by Clementina Beauregard to solve the murder of her brother Charles.

'I'll pay you, of course,' said the girl, tossing her fair hair confidently. She seemed to have less hysteria when discussing money than any other subject. 'I've never had any money before. Everything went to Charles of course, and even when Mummy died, despite her being American, she went and left all the money to Charles too, because that's what Daddy would have wanted. But now with Charles dead, I've got it all, the money, I mean, and I want revenge, that's what I want to spend the money on.' Her voice trembled on the word revenge.

'Yes,' she went on, more calmly and coldly, 'I'm a great heiress now. My mother was an only child whose father invented something ghastly to do with machines which everyone absolutely had to have. No other relations at all. Now Charles is dead, I've inherited the lot, yet I have now no land, not even a house to my name, all that goes to the male heir,' she invested the last two words with virulent contempt. 'In fact I can think of no better use for my money than to bring my uncle Henry Beauregard to justice. After that I'll just hand over what's left to the Red Rose, which Charles would have liked, and I'll go away. Besides if I die without children, which is extremely likely as far as I can see, then any money I don't succeed in spending has to go half to the local church and half to the next owner of the Beauregard Estates. Father Flanagan, that old horror, and Uncle Henry, or Ben, still worse! Can you imagine? No, I'll give it to the Red Rose, and then I'll just go away.'

There were tears in Clementina's eyes, of anger, perhaps, lamentation for her brother, or just passion.

Jemima replied in as measured terms as she could: 'First, Miss Beauregard, you must realize that I'm here from the South and what you're saying is all gibberish to me. Secondly, there is of course no question of my investigating the death of your brother. I'm a television reporter, not a detective. Lastly, there is no question of my accepting money for it.' She was aware, even as she spoke, that there was a certain weakness of logic about the way she phrased her denial. Clementina pounced on the fact.

'Forget the money,' she said quickly. 'I didn't mean to insult you. I'm sure you're very well paid indeed.' Yes, Jemima wryly reflected, I am at least very adequately paid; in that assumption at least about television, Clementina Beauregard is accurate. The girl went on: 'I've got this complex about my money. It's so terrible, you see: I've got this money now, pots and pots of it, and I can do whatever I want, have whatever I want in my lifetime, but how did I get it? Why, by the death of my brother Charles – the only person I've ever loved. And now I've no one to love, no one to spend it on—' The tears came again, and began to flow down her pale pretty cheeks.

Jemima felt overcome by a sudden rush of sympathy for this frail spirit, crushed by the recent death of her nearest and evidently dearest relative. And as for the laws of inheritance in these parts, Young Duncan's words in the car came back to her: it was enough to turn a girl's brain to lose her home and brother in one fell swoop, and all for the accident of birth which made her female. Jemima forgot the charm of Colonel Henry's manner, as a comparatively rare feminist indignation began to burn in her breast. Why should an uncle dispossess his niece in this manner?

'Tell me all about it,' she said kindly, in her best Jemima Shore manner, laying her hand on Clementina's thin fingers. The girl was genuinely shaking. 'Maybe the mere fact of my being from the South will let me bring a fresh eye to it all. You've been through a terrible experience: I can help you get it into proportion. If you tell me all about it, I expect I can reassure you that however tragic your brother's death, nothing criminal has taken place.' As Jemima spoke these soothing words, she noted that one part of her incorrigible brain was already toying with a major autumn programme on female inheritance in the modern world and/or the problems of a Highland feudal society or both . . . And this was supposed to be a holiday.

'First of all read that,' said Clementina, 'and then see if you can reassure me that nothing criminal has taken place. Lachlan Stuart got hold of it somehow.' She fished a piece of paper out of a loose bag of vaguely Middle Eastern origin which hung over her shoulder and pushed it towards Jemima across the denuded breakfast tray, lighting yet another cigarette immediately afterwards.

Jemima read:

'Ben. Urgent. I've just heard he'll be up at Marjorie's Pool this afternoon. He's on to us. Do something before it's too late.' The signature was H.B.B.

'Henry Benedict Beauregard,' completed Clementina as Jemima handed it back. 'And that's unquestionably my uncle's handwriting.'

10
A royal link

'Now I'll explain to you what it's all about,' said Clementina Beauregard, twisting one of her many necklaces, so that the cabbalistic signs jangled. 'And then you'll help me. I know you will.'

Jemima said nothing. In any case it was difficult to interrupt the girl in her flow of rhetoric. But she felt rising within her a genuine determination, part born of sympathy, part – she had to admit it – of feminism, to help Clementina bring her brother's murderer to justice. After reading that note, she could scarcely reassure Clementina that nothing criminal had taken place.

It was essentially a tale of two brothers, that Clementina unfolded. Charles Edward – Carlo – and Henry Benedict Beauregard, born a year apart, brought up together totally from their earliest years, had unfortunately, said Clementina flatly, loathed each other. Far from being boon companions, Carlo and Henry were brothers and rivals.

And how cruelly the law of primogeniture worked to exacerbate the situation! Carlo born to inherit land, wealth, a castle, the Wild Island, the Glen itself, the fishing, the shooting, the moors, the mountains; Henry to live in Kilbronnack House by his brother's permission for the period of his lifetime and – if he was lucky, and Carlo did not want to do it himself – manage his estates.

'Can you imagine Uncle Henry accepting that for a minute?' cried Clementina bitterly. 'He always hated my father from the moment he was born.'

'You can hardly remember that,' pointed out Jemima mildly. 'By the time you were old enough to remember your father—'

'I don't *remember* my father at all,' exclaimed Clementina, in her hysterical voice. She was by now smoking frantically, wild drags and puffs, and filling every available saucer on the breakfast tray with random ash, followed from time to time by a stub. 'Don't you understand? My father was killed on D-Day. Charles and I were born over seven months later. Over seven months my uncle had to sit and wait. And wait. And watch my mother. And think – if it's a girl, I get the lot. How he used to pray in that little white church. Oh God, let it be a girl. Oh God, give me the Beauregard Estates. And Aunt Edith, she prayed harder still because she prays harder anyway. Besides, by that time, there was little Ben, and little Rory, and little Hamish on the way—'

'How ghastly for your mother!' Once again Jemima found herself identifying with the female in the situation. She could imagine no more ghoulish predicament than that of this young pregnant widow, waiting, waiting, for the birth of the posthumous child, and all the time watched over by her vulture of a brother-in-law.

'You know that I was born half an hour before Charles. And they didn't even know we were twins,' remarked Clementina in her hard voice. 'Time enough for the doctor to ring up Uncle Henry and say – "It's a girl." And he said – "Thank God!" And Aunt Edith fell on her knees and began to recite some dismal prayer or other. And then' – with savage glee, the words were pronounced – 'Charles was born, tiny, delicate, but a boy. And Aunt Edith had to get up off her knees again.'

Clementina's subsequent account of her childhood had nightmare overtones from Jemima's point of view. The idea of this isolated valley – no paradise in the difficult post-war years – occupied by a grieving widow, alien to the Highlands, but nevertheless feeling it her duty to live there for the sake of her children, and employing her own vast fortune to beautify and modernize her husband's houses and estates, out of respect to his memory. Yes, the window in St Margaret's Church was a war memorial – commissioned by Leonie Beauregard in honour of her hero husband. Jemima had rightly observed the knights. There were actually two crusader figures swimming in the blues and greens of the glass: Leonie had not denied the surviving brother his place in the epic of Colonel Carlo's death.

In the meantime that surviving brother, Colonel Henry, was in the unenviable position of actually running these same estates from day to day, a task for which his American sister-in-law was scarcely fitted. While in Kilbronnack House, Lady Edith continued to give birth to a huge family of sons – six of them. These boys were all born if not to poverty at least to a chronic lack of money; in this and in every other way their lives contrasted totally with that of their first cousin Charles – 'frail and pale like me – we are, I mean were, very alike'. The

Beauregard boys were born with guns and rods in their hands and loved both sports: but all the shooting and fishing for miles around belonged in theory to their cousin Charles.

Jemima was reminded of the line in the Christmas carol: moor and mountain, field and fountain, it all belonged to Charles Beauregard. And throughout their childhood, only one life stood between the junior branch of the Beauregard family and these far reaching and prized possessions, which they meantime watched their father control and administer.

'A situation made for murder, that's what someone once said as a kind of hateful joke, pointing at little Charles in his cradle, with Uncle Henry standing over him. My mother overheard them. Then she used to dress us up as the Princes of the Tower, in black velvet, with our fair hair, you know, the Millais picture – partly of course to tease poor Aunt Edith who put all her boys in kilts; they slept in them as far as we could see. One day someone said to Mummy: "The Princes in the Tower, eh? Aren't you afraid of Henry doing a Richard III on Charles? He's so very much in control here."'

It occurred to Jemima that the late Leonie Beauregard, in repeating these stories to her daughter, had scarcely attempted to smooth over a delicate family situation.

'What did she think of him? What did your mother think of Colonel Henry?'

'She *hated* him,' stated Clementina in her most positive and passionate voice. 'She hated him because my father hated him, and later she hated him on her own account because he was bad and wicked, and she was right in everything she said, now he's a murderer.' The trembling began again, and the sobs.

A little cool voice inside Jemima's head said: Hadn't the lady perhaps protested a little too much? In Leonie Beauregard's lifetime, Colonel Henry had done nothing so much as dedicate his life to the service of the Beauregard Estates; in short, the service of his nephew. Whatever the jokes and implicit threats, Charles Beauregard had survived more or less healthily till the age of thirty.

It occurred to her that the circumstances must have been odd in another way up in Glen Bronnack; a young widow, a handsome man, married but his wife permanently pregnant, the widow and the brother-in-law thrust together . . . She wondered if Leonie Beauregard had always hated Colonel Henry quite so much. Half of her money had been left to the next owner of the Beauregard Estates if her own issue failed: whatever her hatred, she had not thought to alter her will.

One last question, trivial perhaps, raised itself in her mind.

'That film,' she said, 'about your father and your uncle – was that all a fake?'

'*Brother Raiders*? Fake from start to finish. Except of course for the battle bits. But utterly fake about them loving each other so much. Uncle Henry went and sold the film rights of his life in a typically disgusting way to pay for the boys' school fees – that was his story. Actually it was part of his mania for self-glorification. I told you, they hated each other. And when my father got the VC posthumously, and Uncle Henry only got the MC, he said: "Even in death, I'm still only Carlo's younger brother." Mummy told me that too.'

'I'll try to help you, Clementina,' said Jemima. 'At least to live with the tragedy of your brother's death. I can't promise anything more. I'll talk to Bridie for one thing: I've got a feeling she knows something more than she's telling about what happened down at the pool. In fact she dropped me a broad hint to that effect just as you arrived. And I'm dining at Kilbronnack next week, so I'll keep my ears open—'

'I know you are. Lachlan told me.'

'Oh.' Jemima was disconcerted. 'I must say I had not quite reckoned with the excellent intelligence service of the Red Rose. I congratulate you.'

'Lachlan has a very good contact somewhere,' said Clementina vaguely. For a moment her vagueness sounded studied. Then she went on, 'All the people round here, I mean the *real* people, support the Red Rose madly. I mean, wouldn't you, against the lairds? They want a better deal, so they support the Red Rose and a new monarchy and an independent Scotland.'

'They may get that anyway,' pointed out Jemima. 'Red oil rather than the Red Rose. Do they really want a new monarchy, I wonder? I mean, would you seriously like to be Queen of Scotland?'

Clementina smiled for the first time openly and naturally, with great charm. She sprang up, still smiling, stubbing out her last cigarette, her necklaces jangling.

'Like it? I'd adore it! I'd do anything to make it happen. Queen Clementina the First. *Groovy.*'

It was on that note, which Jemima half-hoped was joking and half-feared was serious, that their interview ended.

That afternoon Jemima settled down in the empty drawing room, the grassy terraces falling away before her eyes to the river. It was raining again. But now there was no sun and thus no rainbow. Jemima wrote two letters, one extremely short and one extremely long. The short one was to Guthrie Carlyle: 'Darling, Just to say that I'm sitting here thinking about you, because I'm about to start reading *Old*

Mortality. Love J.' She added a heart, her trademark. As she sealed the envelope, she thought: That's not even true. Actually I'm sitting here thinking about Colonel Henry Beauregard and whether that handsome distinguished-looking man could possibly be a murderer.

The long letter was written to the person whose opinion Jemima most respected in this world. She was also someone who, Jemima felt, kept her in touch with opinion in the next (if indeed it existed). Not only did she owe her friend, Reverend Mother Agnes of the Convent of the Blessed Eleanor, a letter but she desperately needed the nun's lucid impartial view on the world of Glen Bronnack. It was always a relief to marshal events for the consumption of Mother Agnes. Since the strange Gothic events which had brought them together a few years back, Jemima had come to use Mother Agnes as a kind of extra-worldly consultant. Several times the nun had managed to point exactly the right path for her own television career, and all by a chance reflection in one of her letters. Goodness, Jemima supposed, meant strength. But goodness being all too often its own reward, it was satisfying how the goodness – or rather the good advice – of Mother Agnes had enabled her, Jemima, to outwit Cy Fredericks over her last contract: 'I am reminded of the parable of the Unjust Steward,' the nun's letter on the subject had begun, 'So often misunderstood . . .'

My dear Mother Agnes [Jemima wrote], I find myself in a very odd situation here. It's not exactly working out as the tranquil away-from-it-all holiday I outlined to you in my last letter. What was that warning phrase of yours about peace being an uncertain commodity in this world? And how primitive communities had a habit of being prey to primitive emotions. I've got a number of questions to put to you, and would like your considered opinion, taking into account the full teaching of Mother Church, as to whether a house can have an evil atmosphere. But I'd better begin at the beginning. In a way it's a tale of two brothers . . .

Over the next few days the island at least recovered its atmosphere of Paradise. Other than Bridie Stuart, Jemima saw no one.

She visited the shrine again. The roses had died and had not been replaced. But the sight of the shrine, and the three plaques, two engraved, one handwritten, reminded her that she had not yet ironed out the exact nature of the Beauregard royal claim. The Historical Introduction to the *Northern Guide*, beyond providing the information that Bonnie Prince Charlie had married Princess Louise of Something or Other in 1772 and had had no legitimate descendants, that royal line dying out in 1807 with his brother Cardinal Henry Benedict of York, was not much help.

The Prince's only recorded illegitimate offspring, a daughter, belonged to the period of his European wanderings, long after Culloden; she had been educated at a convent in France, and ended up as Duchess of Albany. All this threw no light whatsoever on Charlotte Clementina, born in Scotland just before or after the Battle of Culloden, and wife of Robert Beauregard of Kilbronnack. Nor did it establish who her mother might have been.

Jemima decided to swallow her pride and ask Bridie, although she dreaded the flood of family information which might follow.

She was wrong. Bridie merely smiled, faintly sarcastically; she then made some slighting reference to the nonsense talked by the Red Rose – and the late Mr Charles Beauregard – but added:

'You'd best read the American book. It's all in the book, they tell me. I never read it mesself, I've no time for such things. It's my pairsonal opinion that we've a very good Queen on the throne and no need for another one. But coming from the television, you'd be interested in such things.'

The next day Bridie silently handed her a privately printed red leather volume with a gold coat of arms stamped on it. *A Royal Link* by Leonie Fielding Ney Beauregard. So it was the author, not the book itself, who was American.

Leonie Beauregard's style certainly owed something to her native land with its enthusiasm and colourful appreciation of all things Scottish. Nevertheless the facts, such as they were, emerged clearly enough from her narrative. The mother of Charlotte Clementina was named Marjorie Stuart, the daughter and heiress of the then owner of Eilean Fas. Purely local legend had always glorified Marjorie for the major part she had played in saving the Prince after the horrifying fiasco of Culloden. Around Kilbronnack they tended to feel that the role of Marjorie Stuart had been too much neglected, that of Flora Macdonald too much cried up in the official saga of the Prince's escape. Flora Macdonald might have behaved very bravely on the west coast. But on the east coast, immediately after Culloden, when the Prince's forces were routed, and he himself transformed from a prince into a fugitive, it was the lively and courageous Marjorie who had been largely responsible for his early getaway. As the legend had it, it was on Eilean Fas, secure in the secret depths of Glen Bronnack from the searching red-coated soldiers, that the young pair had lain out together. They were to all intents and purposes alone, Marjorie's father having fallen in the battle, and the property having passed to his daughter.

Fortunately or unfortunately, depending on your point of view, Marjorie was both prettier and more yielding than Flora Macdonald. According to tradition again, when the Prince finally got away to the west coast he left Marjorie behind with a permanent royal souvenir in the shape of his unborn child. But it was generally believed that both mother and child had subsequently died cruelly at the hands of the English soldiers: the baby first thrown into the pool beneath the Fair Falls, and the mother, jumping in to save her child, drowning in her turn. Hence the name of Sighing Marjorie: it was no wonder, after such a grim tale, that her phantom haunted the pool.

But it was here that the Glen Bronnack version as related by Leonie Beauregard in *A Royal Link* deviated from the accepted story. In the Glen it was said that the baby had not in fact been drowned but miraculously survived her experiences in the water. Like an infant Moses, she had been rescued by her loyal Stuart relations and baptized Charlotte Clementina, brought up among them as a supposed orphan. At the age of seventeen she married Robert Beauregard of Kilbronnack, dying a year later giving birth to a son. From this marriage the present-day family of Beauregards were directly descended, the blood of Bonnie Prince Charlie coursing through their veins together with that of a sound but otherwise undistinguished Scottish family.

Furthermore, and here was the delicious crux of the matter, by digging about further into old tales and legends and traditions handed down from generation to generation by word of mouth, the enthusiastic author had reason to suggest that the Prince had actually *married* Marjorie Stuart in secret when he discovered her to be pregnant. 'Is it fanciful to suppose that our brave Prince and our courageous Marjorie thus planned to safeguard the royal Stuart descent, should he be captured and executed by the English . . . ?' enquired Leonie Beauregard boldly.

So there it was. A royal pedigree   of sorts – for the Beauregards.

After finishing the book, Jemima contemplated leaving her own offering at the shrine, some of the yellow bog plants she had found on the island. She decided that it would be a sentimental gesture. She was no American romantic. Besides, she was only a tenant. She did not want to be permanently possessed by the island or its history, nor indeed the Beauregard family and its feuds. She was a bird of passage. In particular she did not want to be possessed by the house, Tigh Fas.

She read *Old Mortality* – the good Scott – alternating with Burns. On her walks at least, she felt a new balm being applied to her spirit. Warming towards Guthrie (because he had once suggested it) she even began to contemplate some kind of Highland retreat of her own, a cottage of course, a real cottage this time; it might even mean marrying Guthrie, but that too might not be an utterly impossible venture. Guthrie was in love with her, an attractive lover, *and* unmarried, a rare combination indeed. It was certainly an ideal combination in Guthrie's own opinion: he sometimes appeared quite disconcerted when Jemima rejected the occasional proposal with which he punctuated an otherwise exceptionally easy and loving relationship.

'I can't think why you *won't* marry me,' he would say. 'Millions would ... ' He was only half joking. There was of course the question of freedom. But no freedom lasted for ever and Jemima had enjoyed great freedom. Yes, she was beginning to feel very warmly towards Guthrie in her Highland Paradise.

In a way the prospect of dinner at Kilbronnack House was a tiresome interruption of this personal reverie.

The island was particularly peaceful that afternoon. The occasional small plump bird strutted on the terrace. Bridie, who had threatened to return to make her tea, despite Jemima's protests (she still could not accept this strange tenant's proclaimed self-sufficiency), did not in fact reappear.

Jemima changed into a long dark green jersey dress, elegant, discreetly sexy (she hoped): Jean Muir, a designer in whose clothes she always felt she could face the unknown. She awaited the arrival of whichever Beauregard would drive her to dinner at Kilbronnack House. Her escort was late. Perversely, this had the effect of making anticipation grow. She had succeeded in banishing Colonel Henry from her mind for the time being in favour of Guthrie and the possible future they might have together. Now, as she waited, she found herself hoping that the Colonel had not forgotten his invitation. As she put it to herself, quite apart from anything else, she had a mission to perform for Clementina Beauregard.

When the car finally scrunched on the gravel, the river noise masking its approach, it seemed to come to rest with an extravagant squeal of brakes. She suspected a very young man must be at the wheel.

The man who burst in through the door a moment later was young, if not very young. He was wearing a kilt, topped by a black jacket, and looked at first sight the pattern of a romantic Highland figure.

But his opening words were in no way romantic:

'Miss Shore, I'm Ben Beauregard, something absolutely ghastly has happened.' It was all said in a rush. Ben Beauregard's face, with its full mouth and wide-set eyes, was twitching as he spoke, twitching uncontrollably. His eyes still met hers as he went on: 'It's Bridie. I've just found her body. In the river among the weeds, all tangled up with her bicycle. She must have fallen off the bridge. Miss Shore, she's dead. Bridie's dead.'

Before Jemima's horrified gaze, his features began to break up further. Finally, putting his face in his hands, Ben Beauregard began to sob, the harsh painful sobs of someone who has not perhaps wept since childhood.

11

Is she safe?

After a time the sobs stopped. When Ben Beauregard had regained control of himself, he said, 'Sorry about that. The shock, you understand. She was our nanny, we all adored her. The bridge *is* very slippery in the rain, we all used to tease her about her bicycle, it was so ancient, and how unsteady she was on it. She must have tumbled in. Then of course she couldn't swim: we used to tease her about that too when we went over to the seaside. Poor old Bridie.'

His words faded away. Quite a different expression crossed his face, verging on anger, or perhaps irritation was the correct word.

'Oh God, whatever's going to happen now? The royal visit. We've got Hurricane Sophie coming to dinner at Kilbronnack.' The contrast between his genuine feeling at the old woman's death and his laird-like exasperation at the inconvenience to his plans was almost ludicrous.

And when an hour later Jemima Shore found herself sitting in the drawing room of Kilbronnack House, she was still torn between admiration for Ben Beauregard's cool, and suspicion that he was fundamentally able to carry off such a distressing situation with such verve.

Ben Beauregard was certainly an efficient organizer, like his father. Somehow estate workers were conjured up out of the Glen, including Young Duncan, who lived on a croft just beyond Bridie's lodge. Jemima herself was driven directly on to Kilbronnack by Duncan, while Ben stayed behind to 'clear up a few details here' as he put it – which presumably meant dealing with the body and all the other paraphernalia to do with sudden and accidental death.

The last thing Jemima heard Ben say to his aides was: 'Lachlan. We must let him know.'

'There was'na much love lost between those two,' answered an older worker dourly, one of those who had escorted Colonel Henry at the church.

'They were still mother and son,' was Ben's reply. He spoke with authority. His voice momentarily resembled that of his father. The men exchanged looks. Nobody made any immediate suggestion as to how to contact Lachlan. As Jemima was driven away, she reflected that the intelligence service of the Red Rose was so good that the news of the tragedy would probably reach Lachlan long before Ben Beauregard's official message got through. She decided to say nothing. It was Duncan, tragedy not having diminished his enthusiasm for reckless driving or conversation, who broke the silence:

'Aye, it was the dog that did it,' he observed. 'It was the dog knocked puir Bridie Stuart from the bridge. She couldn't forgive her for the death of Mr Charles.' There was a horrible kind of relish in his voice: it was as though he was enjoying the excitement of it all. Perhaps if you lived long enough in a remote valley, it was more exciting than distressing when your nearest neighbour fell off a bridge and drowned? Or was pushed off a bridge?

'Flora?' enquired Jemima in a startled voice.

'Aye, Flora. I was seeing her by and by, bounding down towards Eilean Fas, just there by the bridge, looking for Bridie Stuart she was. And she so clever, knowing how the bridge was slippery, and Bridie going to make your tea, and it was there she would be able to upset her. Aye, Flora has more intelligence in her paws than most humans in these parts have in their heads.'

It was a nasty picture that his words conjured up. Jemima tried to drive it from her mind. Still, it was strange that the dog should have been sighted near the bridge that very afternoon, in view of her manifest hostility to Bridie. Unless of course she had been in attendance on Clementina; but Duncan had spoken as though the dog was alone. She decided not to encourage Duncan's conversation on the morbid subject further.

Nevertheless it was impossible to dismiss altogether the sinister image of the malevolent animal bent on drowning its prey. And when she arrived at Kilbronnack House, it was recalled to her by the sight of Jacobite. Admittedly the Kilbronnack dog was lying fast asleep by the log fire. He did not even acknowledge Jemima's entrance by a wag of his tail. At the same time, Jemima decided to give him a wide berth: she did not think she would easily learn to trust dogs again.

The welcome of Colonel Henry Beauregard was on the other hand a masterpiece of active charm and implicit tact. He managed by a diplomatic remark both to convey his distress over Bridie – 'Forty years with our family' – and to dispose of the subject: 'We mustn't worry our little Princess about all this, must we? We want her to have a good time in the Highlands.' He cut an astonishing figure in his kilt, black jacket with silver buttons, and silver-buckled shoes: having reluctantly admired his figure and bearing in his London suit, Jemima now came to the equally reluctant conclusion that in Highland dress Colonel Henry Beauregard was one of the best-looking men she had ever seen in her life. Perhaps it was the effect of the kilt ... Yet the Colonel successfully put in the shade not only all those of his sons present (kilted themselves) but even the image of the more dashing black-haired Ben, by far the best-looking of the sons. Perhaps Highland lairds, like Scottish whisky, improved with age?

She tried to distinguish the names of the other Beauregards present: three, the remainder having departed after the funeral of their cousin. Rory seemed pleasant enough, with nice regular features and thick brown hair. Hamish's kilt and sporran both looked rather long to Jemima's inexpert eye. That gave a stolid impression. The boy Kim, whom she had noted in the chapel, looked bright. But he was clearly in a great state of tension, probably over Bridie's death. He was in fact engaged in an argument with his mother, which only ceased when Jemima came near the group.

'Hush, darling,' murmured Lady Edith, but in vain. Kim continued to press his argument, whatever it was. Jemima recognized both the other male guests. One was Ossian Lucas MP, who waved his hand languidly in her direction. He was wearing a tight-fitting suit made entirely of some improbable tartan; frills exuded from his sleeves, and torrented out at his neck. His strong face topping the bizarre costume provided a remarkable contrast. The other male guest was Father Flanagan. The tall priest was lecturing – or perhaps hectoring would be a more accurate description – Ossian Lucas on the various failings of those people who were at one swoop Lucas's constituents and Father Flanagan's parishioners. He had angrily refused a drink, which might have softened his mood. 'I tell you, I'm consulting the bishop as to whether it may not be an actual sin to belong to the Red Rose,' Jemima heard him say earnestly.

'With no employment hereabouts, and those great big wages up at the rigs for the Southerners, you can hardly blame them if they turn to the Red Rose,' observed Ossian Lucas; but he sounded fairly indifferent to the problem.

Jemima was surprised that a Catholic priest should be asked to dinner to meet Protestant royalty: and the more so when there turned out to be an extra man at dinner. It transpired that Lady Edith had rushed over in a panic to fetch him, on hearing that Princess Sophie was bringing her lady-in-waiting to dinner, Father Flanagan being the only conceivable extra man available at short notice around Kilbronnack. At which point Kim announced that he too had been promised to come to dinner to meet the Princess, 'ages ago, you *promised*, Mum, so long as I wore my jabot'. Having got into his jabot he was not inclined to surrender his place at dinner. As Lady Edith was clearly much too weak to insist on his withdrawal – to the evident disgust of his brothers – they had to make do with an extra man at the table. As Rory said *sotto voce*, 'Mum always makes things worse when she tries to straighten them out.'

There was further trouble with Kim when Rory suddenly grabbed a glass out of his hand, sipped at it, and put it down with a highly disapproving expression. Whatever the boy was drinking, it was obviously not in accordance with the older brother's notion of what was suitable for his junior.

Touched by her hostess's discomposure, which was hardly surprising in view of the closeness she must have established with Bridie in the past, Jemima listened patiently to the stream of inconsequential questions Lady Edith asked her about television. Which was more than Lady Edith herself did: she asked the same question three times: 'Don't you find it very difficult about clothes?' In vain Jemima tried to give her stock answer to this particular stock question:

'I try to wear very simple things which won't distract the viewer . . .' Like Jesting Pilate, Lady Edith did not stay for the answer, but always darted away and was found fussing in another corner of the drawing room, now straightening Kim's jabot, now bending down to dust Rory's shoes with her handkerchief.

'The dress you're wearing tonight certainly distracts the viewer.' It was Colonel Henry handing her a glass of champagne. To her surprise Jemima found herself blushing, something she was sure she had not done for many a year. To cover her embarrassment she admired Kilbronnack House, the beauty of whose classically plain early eighteenth-century façade had struck her on arrival.

The plainness of the exterior of Kilbronnack House was matched by the extreme plainness of the décor. In fact the large room was decorated more by people than anything else. There were a few dark oil paintings of forebears – kilted – on the walls. Over the fireplace, surveying Jacobite's sleeping head, was an inferior copy of the best-known portrait of Bonnie Prince Charlie.

'Our distinguished ancestor,' observed the Colonel with a quizzical smile, following the direction of her eyes. 'What nonsense all of that is! The Red Rose, I mean, pretending we're the real kings of Scotland. Damned unsuitable topic to discuss, just as Princess Sophie is about to bob up. But I must say I've no patience with all that rubbish. Of course when my idiotic nephew Charles took up with it – purely to madden me – every lunatic, deadbeat and drop-out on the Estate followed him. And as far as I'm concerned that's the whole story of this blasted Scottish Nationalism in a nutshell. People who just want to stir up trouble. Came across them in the war: knew the type. Quickly got them out of the regiment, just as fast as I could. Don't want to go into battle with people like that.'

Jemima looked up at the portrait of the Prince. There was a resemblance somewhere . . . the pale youthful face surrounded by its tumbling hair. It teased her. Why yes, it must be Clementina Beauregard. So no doubt there was royal Stuart blood to some degree in the Beauregard veins, even if the Colonel was right and it was conceived on the wrong side of the blanket.

They were interrupted by the arrival of the Princess. From the flurry and commotion outside Jemima imagined that the local constabulary were in attendance in force. The small figure who entered, escorted by Ben Beauregard, was for a moment an anticlimax. But Princess Sophie was dressed in brilliant red – her favourite colour, according to the press – and upheld by platform shoes to match. And even without her eye-catching dress, she would have commanded attention. Pop-eyed, fair-haired, a true Hanoverian in her looks, and not even a particularly pretty one, she nevertheless radiated confidence and, as a result, her particular brand of charm.

Hurricane Sophie she was to the press, her vitality having earned her the nickname. Strong men in the gossip trade had wilted away trying to keep up with the pace of her social life; 'does she never go to bed?' they had been heard to groan. Indeed it was all very unsatisfying from the scandalmonger's point of view, for when the young Princess did go to bed, it might be 6 am more often than not, but she was invariably alone.

That same vitality made her now the automatic centre of attention in a way Jemima suspected would always have been so, royal birth or no royal birth. Princess Sophie also had excellent manners. She was quite delightful to Lady Edith, instantly admiring the flower arrangements, whose beauty and choice Jemima had only just begun to notice. From Lady Edith's obvious pleasure, Jemima concluded she had arranged them herself.

To Jemima, the Princess expressed the most knowledgeable appreciation of her recent series:

'Actually, whatever the press says,' she added disarmingly, 'I spend most of my evenings sitting at home at Cumberland Palace, watching television.'

'Yes, Ma'am, that's perfectly true. But with twenty-five people sitting round with you watching as well.' It was one of the middle Beauregard boys.

The Princess, not in the slightest bit put out, pealed with laughter.

'Rory, don't give me away,' she cried. 'I'm trying so hard to make a good impression on Miss Shore. I'm her fan.' Princess Sophie rolled her round blue eyes flirtatiously in Jemima's direction, then in that of Rory Beauregard. Jemima was surprised to notice that within the bounds of good manners, this flirtation was kept up all the evening. She would have expected Ben Beauregard, so very much better looking, to have been the focus of the Princess's attentions.

Perhaps there was more to Rory Beauregard than met the eye. What had poor Bridie said about this particular nurseling? His deep love of Scotland and things Scottish: 'A deep one,' she had said. Perhaps it was this quiet strength which appealed to such a volatile character as Hurricane Sophie. And wasn't it Rory who had once told Bridie he would do anything in the world to live in the Glen? A whole series of declarations came back to her. Clementina: 'I'd do anything to be Queen.' Colonel Henry and the Glen: 'A land worth killing for.'

Her Highland Paradise had not after all cast out the serpent. The snake still lurked, the serpent of covetousness, the primitive passion for land: land, wealth and position. Could it ever be eradicated? One had to realize that while Charles's death had made Ben heir to the Estate, Rory Beauregard was still in the position of a second son to Ben.

The evening itself was rather jolly. It was Colonel Henry, not Princess Sophie, who put an end to it. Regardless of protocol (to a background noise of Lady Edith protesting, 'Henry, you really can't, Henry, please' – 'Can't I, my dear? Just watch me'), the Colonel said firmly at 11 o'clock: 'Now, Ma'am, we all know you've got to be up at six and open that dam on the west coast. We mustn't take advantage of your good nature and keep you up.'

Princess Sophie took her dismissal gamely, remaining flirtatious to the last: 'Oh, Colonel Henry, I believe you're trying to get rid of me—'

'Ma'am!' exclaimed the Colonel in gallant horror.

'Oh, I'm so frightened of the Red Rose on the way home,' went on Princess Sophie artlessly. 'You know they've told the press they're going to kidnap me while I'm up here. It was headlined in the *Express*: IS SHE

SAFE? So horrid for one to read with one's breakfast.' She did not look at all frightened.

It was true that the *Daily Express* had led off that morning with a tumultuous denunciation of the Princess's security arrangements while in the Highlands, based on the notorious reputation of the Red Rose in those parts. They were acting, they said, on a tip-off received from an undercover agent who had daringly succeeded in penetrating this extremist organization. To most of their readers, Jemima suspected, and possibly to the *Express* itself, the news of their Princess's danger and the very existence of the Red Rose had arrived at one and the same moment.

'Such an unfortunate royal title, Duke of Cumberland,' the Princess added. 'Papa should never have been landed with it. I mean, he *adored* the Highlands, but knew no history at all so he could never understand why he was always hissed whenever he got out of his sleeper at Inverness. If I was Princess Sophie of Surrey, no one would pay me any attention at all.'

'How many police—' began Ossian Lucas.

'So I thought Ben and Rory and Hamish would come with me back to the Railway Hotel,' continued Princess Sophie, 'and beat off the Red Rose. You too, Mr Lucas, you can tell me a little more about the lovely Highlands, and dams and things. As it's so early. Come along, Clarissa.'

The lady-in-waiting, a thin rather exhausted-looking girl, correctly described by Rory as 'high-born but downtrodden like all Sophie's slaves', leapt to her feet. It was a royal command. And for that matter, a royal victory.

'Henry, you really shouldn't have—' began Lady Edith, immediately the much-enlarged royal party had left.

'Brilliant, Dad,' said Kim Beauregard.

'Shut up, Edith,' replied Colonel Henry in a perfectly equable voice. 'Kim – bed!'

Jemima wondered who on earth was going to take her home. She gathered Father Flanagan was staying the night in order to say Mass in the morning at Kilbronnack. She watched Colonel Henry at the drinks tray. She distinctly saw him put a bottle of whisky in his pocket before he turned round.

'And now, Miss Shore, I shall escort you back to the Wild Island,' he said. Lady Edith's mouth opened and then shut. For an instant Father Flanagan was seen to frown. But nobody, including Jemima Shore, had the courage to contradict the Colonel.

Jemima thought of the *Express* headline quoted by the Princess: IS SHE SAFE? At that moment it seemed more appropriate to her own fate, returning alone to a deserted place with a man she strongly suspected of being a murderer, than to that of the pampered Princess, surrounded by her youthful admirers in the Railway Hotel.

12
Midnight and after

Colonel Henry relaxed with a whisky in his hand. It was his third since their arrival at Eilean Fas.

Jemima stretched out one leg towards the fire. The green jersey of her skirt fell away, revealing her dark sheer stockings and green slippers – neither of them particularly suitable for Scotland. With the tip of her slipper she had just drawn a heart in the dust now thickly forming in the grate. A dirty mark resulted on the toe of her slipper: in London her precise soul would have felt sullied by the imperfection; here she felt strangely uncaring.

Several plans had been made, all delightful, for Highland diversions, from fishing (Jemima was not too keen, with her memories of Charles Beauregard and his waders), to grouse-shooting. But what about the poor grouse—

'Oh, there aren't any worth mentioning to feel sorry for up here,' said the Colonel airily. 'We only talk about them in the first place in order to let the shooting for a decent rent. To be frank,' he added, 'it's the tenants you should feel sorry for. At our rates.'

Finally, on discovering that it was her birthday at the end of the week, the Colonel settled on some form of expedition then. 'August 30th. Virgo,' said Jemima lightly. She did not imagine the Colonel paid much attention to the stars. Nor indeed did she, except to enjoy from time to time the double image of her own sign, the cool white maiden on the one hand, the harvest goddess reigning over the most fertile time of the year on the other. Sometimes she was aware of these two images, the desire for self-preservation and for self-abandon, combining, even fighting in herself.

She was wrong about the Colonel.

'I'm a Scorpio,' he informed her. 'Very sexy.' It was said as a statement of fact. He added: 'August 30th. I think old Edith's birthday is somewhere around there. Might even *be* August 30th. Anyway, we'll do something.'

'And if it is Edith's birthday?'

'Edith and the boys. Oh, they might have their own picnic,' he replied vaguely. 'With Father Flanagan. That's what Edith and the boys would like.

'You know, Jemima,' he said, in his curious individual clipped diction, 'I loved my brother Carlo more than anyone on this earth. And since he died, nothing has ever been quite the same again. I believe I loved him even more than this glen – because to me he *was* the Glen.'

On hearing this surprising – because it was so deeply affectionate – remark about his brother, Jemima withdrew her leg, lazily.

'I thought you hated each other,' she said. The whisky the Colonel had persuaded her to share was taking effect.

'Ah.' The Colonel paused and looked reflectively into the fire. His own even longer legs were also stretched out in the direction of the smouldering logs. They were both seated, at a suitable distance, on the same sofa. 'Ah,' he repeated, 'I detect the hand of Clementina.' Then: 'She's unbalanced, of course, my niece. Deranged. Mad. Whatever you like to call it. Like her mother before her. Like her lunatic drug-taking brother.'

He poured another whisky. 'All that rot about hating Carlo and hating Charles, and finally murdering him. What absolute nonsense! Don't tell me she actually took you in, woman of the world.

'My God, I've given my whole life to looking after this place for Charles, haven't I? Could have got a good job in the City, chap I knew in the war offered me one, more money, better for poor Edith in every way. But no, I thought it was my duty to stay up here and look after the Estate. What Carlo would have wanted . . .

'I tell you, it was the happiest day of my life when Leonie told me she was pregnant. Made the terrible blow of Carlo's death bearable, d'you know, to think there would be something of his to carry on. I was always sure it would be a boy, quite convinced of it. All that time, nearly eight months we waited, I was sure I was holding the Estate in trust for little Charles, my brother's son. No idea Leonie was having twins, of course. My family have never had twins.' There was even a shade of indignation in the last remark.

'Wasn't Clementina actually born first?'

'She was. Oh God, I said, when the doctor told us. And Edith fell on her knees and prayed.' He paused again, sipping his drink, lost in the contemplation of that strange scene thirty years ago.

'Getting back to my unfortunate niece and her ravings, I really don't know what to do about it. Getting to my wits' end with her, especially now she's got the Red Rose behind her, letting them use Castle Beauregard as their headquarters. Lachlan's not a bad lad at heart, he was corrupted by my nephew, father a very decent type, served with me in the war, but some of the people with Lachlan I don't like the look of.

'I wanted to ask your advice about it all, as a matter of fact. Do you think she should see a doctor of sorts? An analyst perhaps? That kind of thing. Did think of a doctor for Charles, but that was different. But maybe a trick cyclist would straighten out Clementina and remove this obsession about her father, and me, and her brother's death and the whole damn shooting match. There was a fellow I knew in the war, wonderful when the troops cracked up under fire. I don't know if he's still around.'

It was well after midnight. Otherwise this complete reinterpretation of family events in Glen Bronnack might have come as even more of a shock to Jemima Shore.

As it was, she allowed herself to be poured yet another whisky. She suspected it was going – had already gone – to her head. Whose version was to be believed? It all reminded her of *Rashomon*, a film she was apt to recall in any case from time to time when carrying out one of her television investigations.

On the one hand Colonel Henry painted a most plausible if painful picture of a young heir growing to manhood under his uncle's loving tutelage. On the other hand he delineated a character, from the start gravely flawed, and furthermore spoiled to death by his unbalanced American mother.

'She must have had bad blood in her, poor Leonie, and passed it on to the twins. God knows she was unstable enough,' exclaimed the Colonel bitterly. 'As for Charles, no Beauregard was ever like that before. I tried to understand, tried to be tolerant. Even Edith thought I was too soft with him. I certainly treated him much softer than my own kids. Fatherless boy and all that, my own brother's son. Always difficult to be the son of a hero into the bargain. But the rot started early. He was vicious, my nephew Charles, no other word for it. Either he couldn't stick the school or the school couldn't keep him. In the end I prevailed on poor Father Flanagan to give him a few lessons up here, up at the Castle; at least he could put the fear of God into him from his enormous height. Charles was not much taller than Clementina, whereas the men of my family have always been over six foot tall.

'Later of course it was hopeless. Drugs, that sort of thing. Don't really want to go into it now, *de mortuis*, don't you know. In spite of that, in spite of the Castle becoming a kind of cesspool, a refuge for every addict and long-haired pansy with nowhere else to go, in spite of the Red Rose – why, he even uprooted the famous Beauregard white rose garden, the white circle, and planted some fearful crimson number, some appalling floribunda of the most dreadful vulgar colour! Edith nearly had a fit. Wonderful gardener, old Edith. Loves flowers. Leonie never had a clue about what you could and couldn't do in that respect. Have you noticed how American gardens are never quite right? Where was I?'

The Colonel was visibly bristling. In a calmer voice he went on, 'Yes, in spite of the Red Rose (and all his foul red roses) I still didn't want him dead. He was my own brother's son,' Colonel Henry concluded for the third time.

That was the Colonel's version of events. On the other hand there was Clementina's directly opposing story of a wicked uncle waiting his chance to scoop his nephew's inheritance. How on earth was she to decide?

'The film, *Brother Raiders!*' exclaimed Jemima.

'Oh, did you see it?' A pleased smile crossed the Colonel's handsome face. He arched his neck and shot the frill of his shirt still further out of his sleeve. 'I was pretty good, wasn't I?'

'Kirk Douglas—' began Jemima hesitantly.

'Gregory Peck!' replied the Colonel indignantly. 'Kirk Douglas looks nothing like me.'

'Sorry,' she said with haste. 'Yes, you were very good indeed. What I wondered was – you must have made some money out of it all, at least I hope you did, it was a colossally successful film, what happened to it?'

'Of course I made money out of it. Not a complete fool. That was the money that paid for the Beauregard Memorial Hall at Kilbronnack. Somewhere for the people round here to meet on Saturday night; show films, dance. What Carlo would have wanted. So much better than Charlie's idiotic notion of a museum on an island, incidentally: who needs that? Leonie was going to build it originally, but after we – er – fell out—'

He paused, evidently at a slight loss how to phrase his next remarks. 'Such a pretty woman,' he went on. 'When she was young, a little fairy. Clementina looks just like her. And talks just like her. But mad. So intense about everything she did. No lightness. She seriously thought I would leave Edith for her; well, how could I? Four boys already, another on the way, my sister-in-law, the Catholic Church, and all that. It was never on.

'Of course I was an idiot too, come to think of it,' added the Colonel reflectively. 'I should never have got involved. Father Flanagan really pitched into me about it all. He was a young priest then, but with a tongue like a whip-lash which he didn't hesitate to use. The trouble is I've never been able to resist—' he coughed. 'Well, anyway, after that she hated me. Used to shout things at me if I met her in Kilbronnack. Then it calmed down. And then – well, she died.'

That too sounded very plausible. Jemima Shore was beginning to suspect that wilfully or otherwise Clementina Beauregard had conned her into believing a totally false version of events. No doubt Clementina herself had been conned in the first place by her own mother, and later by her brother. It still did not add up to a very pretty story. Even the girl's dog was half mad if not vicious. If Flora really had sprung at Bridie on the bridge, could Clementina even have encouraged her to do so?

The fire, which they had relit on their return, was beginning to die down. Colonel Henry bent down and threw on another log. Sparks flew up, and his silver buttons flashed in the sudden bright light. He sat back and looked directly at Jemima. For an instant it was an extremely level look, half sardonic, half tender. Then he smiled:

'Finish family,' he said. 'Now tell me about you.' Leaning forward, he took Jemima's glass from her fingers.

'You've had enough, I think.' So saying, he poured himself another large dram of whisky.

A detail struck Jemima.

'The note!' she cried. 'Your note to Ben, telling him that Charles would be at Marjorie's Pool the afternoon he died; you said he was beginning to suspect something.'

The Colonel looked startled, but not particularly perturbed. 'Oh, that. How did you hear about it?' he said. 'Well, that little plot was overtaken by events all right. Ben was going to tackle Charles about seeing a doctor to help him get off drugs. And Ossian Lucas had arranged to bring this doctor, this friend of his, up to the Highlands, as though on holiday. The point was, we didn't want Charles to think there was a conspiracy to help him, particularly not with me involved. The choice had to come from him, the doctor said.'

Once again, the Colonel sounded plausible enough.

'Now I really insist on talking about you,' he said. 'You're a very beautiful woman. Hair like sunshine. And eyes like a cat: what an extraordinary colour they are. But you've been told that before many times, I've no doubt.'

He touched her cheek, and then her hair lightly. Jemima noticed once again that he had the most surprisingly long fingers and elegant hands for such a masculine-looking man. For a moment she thought he would touch her further. She felt herself tremble.

'Never before in the Highlands of Scotland,' she replied in the lightest tone she could muster. Jemima was still trying to decide what she would do if the Colonel tried to kiss her – scream? struggle? remain coolly passive? – when he moved suddenly and pressed his lips down very hard on hers, thus making further decisions on the subject unnecessary. In the event, she neither screamed nor struggled, nor, she discovered, did she remain coolly passive.

'I've been longing to do that for the last half hour,' said the Colonel, when they were finally apart, and gazing at each other, each panting slightly. 'I've been drinking all this whisky, and talking about the past, and all the time I've been trying to muster up courage to make a pass at you. I must have drunk at least five whiskies.'

'Mightn't *too* much whisky be a slight mistake? Under the circumstances,' queried Jemima, her boldness surprising herself.

'Certainly not. Whisky is mother's milk for us Scots,' replied the Colonel. Then he placed his hand on her left breast, the nipple prominent under the thin wool, and bent his lips towards it. With his other hand he began to caress her thigh, from the point of the suspender upwards.

Much later Jemima said, 'You were right about the whisky. It didn't make any difference at all.'

'How can you tell?' answered Henry Beauregard sleepily. 'You don't know what I'm like without it.'

'When shall I know that?' enquired Jemima in an equally lazy voice. The fire had died down. The lights were out. The room she knew must be strewn with such diverse objects as buckled shoes (his), green slippers (hers), dark stockings (hers), tartan socks (his), a variety of white underwear, some satin and lacy, some plain and poplin. To say nothing of larger objects like a black kilt jacket and a green jersey dress. The kilt itself had been thrown lightly over both of them by its owner, when he felt for a cigarette, 'Nothing like a kilt for warmth.' It *was* warm. Altogether Jemima felt very warm indeed and secure.

'In the morning of course. No whisky around at that time of day. Come along. I'm going to take you and myself upstairs to that enormous and, as I remember it, very comfortable bed. You'll find out what I'm like in the morning.'

But Jemima Shore never did find out. In the morning, when she awoke, she was alone in the enormous bed. It was Ben Beauregard, not the Colonel, who was bending over her, touching her shoulder.

'Miss Shore,' he was saying. 'I'm terribly sorry to disturb you like this. But where's Dad? He's completely disappeared.'

13
'I'll be back'

Because it was – for her – early in the morning and because Jemima was not immediately awake, her first thought was a purely feminine pang of regret. Sleepily, confused, she thought: he has gone, but he promised to stay. Morning had come and her night lover had fled as Cupid had fled from Psyche to avoid the dangerous contact of the dawn, and yet he had promised . . .

Then Ben Beauregard was saying something of more immediate import: 'We think the Red Rose has got him. We found a bunch of red roses on the doorstep of Kilbronnack House this morning. Plus their ridiculous sign: UR2. Ugh, reminds me of some kind of nuclear weapon. And their slogans: Long Live Queen Clementina the First! Down with the Usurper Henry Beauregard! Eilean Fas the Royal Island.'

Her mind began to clear. The Red Rose had struck indeed: not after all at a Princess guarded at Inverness by her police and detectives and minions, but at the hated local laird, the man they regarded as the purloiner of his niece's rights, the murderer of his royal nephew . . . It all made a kind of hideous sense.

Then her mind cleared still further. He had gone. A new aspect of it all struck her. Where he had gone was one question due to be investigated, but, to be blunt, *when* he had gone was now her paramount concern. She gazed at Ben, at his handsome face with its thick crest of dark hair. She did not, for the moment, have the courage to look at the bed beside her.

'He brought me home last night—' she began rather uncertainly.

'Oh, we know that,' Ben appeared to dismiss that episode with carelessness. 'Mum told us that. But you see, it's so unlike Dad not to be home for breakfast. Even if it's a very late breakfast.' He spoke rapidly, almost impatiently, as if this simple fact must be well known to everybody. The picture conjured up by this generalization was more than Jemima felt able to contemplate for the time being.

'Then there came the call—' he went on. 'Anonymous. Didn't recognize the voice. But the message was clear enough – "If you want to get back the usurper Henry Beauregard, you had better come over to Castle Beauregard straight away." '

Jemima decided that there were two, no three, things that she needed immediately to fortify her before she faced further shocks to her system. What was it indeed about the north of Scotland that she was constantly being aroused by dramatic events brought literally into her very bedroom? Poor Bridie, Lachlan, Clementina, now Ben, there was scarcely a minute's peace in her Paradise. The first two things were orange juice and coffee. The third was a dressing-gown. Jemima was suddenly aware that beneath the thick hairy blankets of the old-fashioned bed she was wearing nothing at all. At least Clementina had found her in a satin nightdress. She decided to shoo Ben Beauregard downstairs.

'Look, I'll meet you in the drawing room and tell you all I know. But do you think – possibly – some coffee? And there's some juice in the larder . . .' Smoothing her remarkably tousled hair back, Jemima smiled beguilingly at Ben. But where Guthrie Carlyle would have leapt to her command – no, to be frank, Guthrie would have already brought the juice, he never ever called her without a glass of chilled orange juice in his hand – Ben Beauregard simply stood there gazing at her.

'Coffee?' he said blankly. She might have been asking him to grow the stuff. It occurred to Jemima that this fashion-plate of Highland masculine beauty had probably never in his life been asked to perform such a mundane task. She spared a cross thought for the cosseting Lady Edith, whose gift to the modern world was apparently six totally undomesticated sons. As well as being herself a highly understanding wife . . . Although it was a pity that Carrie Amyas, wife of Tom, had never had the accommodating nature of Lady Edith Beauregard. Jemima – the memory of those inevitable if late breakfasts still rankling – wondered for the first time whether it was not possible for wives to be too understanding. Ignoring that line of thought as unprofitable before coffee, she decided it was not part of her business to teach Ben Beauregard what his mother had signally failed to do. Particularly at such a critical juncture.

'Wait downstairs then.'

He went.

It was while Jemima was in the process of tying her dark blue silk kimono tightly round her that she found the note. It was written on a scrap of paper which looked like a fly-leaf torn hastily from an old book. She recognized the handwriting from the note which Clementina had shown her. It said quite simply: 'I'll be back. H.B.B.'

And that was all. Which got her precisely nowhere, except to inform her that the Colonel's departure had evidently – if unflatteringly – been voluntary. It was not even all that unflattering if you took into account his avowed intention, not yet carried out, to return. As for his departure being voluntary, that was not exactly a surprise: deep sleeper as she might be, particularly under certain agreeable circumstances, including the unaccustomed draughts of whisky, she could never have believed that Colonel Henry had been abducted literally from her side without waking her.

So why had he gone voluntarily into the power of the Red Rose? And who had summoned him? And how?

Later in the drawing room, over coffee for two made by Jemima and drunk happily but not particularly gratefully by Ben, she said, 'And since then, no word?'

'You were our last hope. Mum said I should check first.' Ben's tone changed. 'He wasn't – of course it sounds silly – I suppose he wasn't taken forcibly from here, was he?' For a moment Jemima did not understand why he sounded embarrassed. She looked down. He was holding one of the Colonel's silver gilt buttons in his hand; he was not exactly extending it towards her, more twisting it in his hand. He had, presumably, found it on the hearthrug or thereabouts.

'No, nothing forcible took place here,' replied Jemima in her most even voice. Their eyes met. Behind Jemima's ironic regard lurked the ghost of a smile. Ben Beauregard returned it.

'Then I'd better tackle my fair cousin Clementina in her castle lair. No, correction, in our castle lair.'

Jemima took a decision.

'No, we'll both do that. I have one or two questions to ask Queen Clementina myself.'

She did not at this point care to mention the commission given to her by Clementina Beauregard, and, it had to be said, tacitly accepted by Jemima Shore: a commission of investigation into the murder of Charles Beauregard in which Henry Beauregard was the prime suspect. Now not only was Henry Beauregard vindicated by his transformation into the victim but, as regards the second local death – the apparently accidental death of Bridie Stuart – Jemima was beginning to have hideous doubts as to whether Clementina herself might not be implicated. The presence of the dog Flora could not be easily dismissed. The girl was surely crazy enough for anything, with her accusations, her obsessions, and now her involvement with the more way-out form of Scottish Nationalism, including a possible kidnapping.

Charles Beauregard had taken drugs; during Jemima's one and only encounter with Clementina, the girl had depended on nothing more lethal than a vast quantity of Rothmans cigarettes in a very short time. That proved nothing. The habit of drug-taking was easily inculcated.

In jeans, brown cowboy boots and a thin cream-coloured jersey under her white Burberry, Jemima hoped she would present a formidable aspect to Queen Clementina.

It was, however, Castle Beauregard which presented the formidable aspect. Seen from the shores of the loch, as they drove up the winding path to its eminence, it began to remind her of the castle in the Disney film *Snow White*, the first film she had ever seen and thus she supposed inevitably one of the formative visual influences in her life.

Whoever built it had not spared a Victorian/mediaeval detail. Quite apart from the flowering and springing buttresses and turrets, there was even a drawbridge and a portcullis. From the battlements hung a flag together with various other trophy-like objects of indeterminate nature.

'Imagine building this!' exclaimed Jemima. 'One wonders what the original castle looked like.'

'The site of the old Castle Tamh was slightly different. To the north: like all old Scottish dwellings, seeking shelter from the wind, as well as the enemy. Where the garden now is. The old castle itself was knocked down in the sixteenth century. The Frasers or some local despots came and blitzed it during one of their endless feuds. A heap of masonry was all that remained on the site. Bonnie Prince Charlie and Sighing Marjorie are supposed to have trysted in the ruins – before Culloden, when her father was still alive and too busy chaperoning her for any hanky-panky to take place at Eilean Fas. By now all the stones have been used for garden seats and grottoes and sun-dials, etc etc, in the white rose garden.'

He paused and said very angrily, stepping on the accelerator of the Land-Rover, '*Red* rose garden. But it won't be for much longer. We'll change all that. The white roses will be back at Castle Beauregard next summer. Even if it costs a packet to replace them. You'll see.' As Colonel Henry had said, he would be back. The Beauregards had a taste for return.

'Tell me about the Beauregard Armoury. Young Duncan mentioned it,' Jemima said to change the subject.

'Collected by my great-grandfather,' replied Ben. 'Worth a fortune.'

Jemima noticed with curiosity that the value of absolutely anything was never far from Ben's conversation: the relic no doubt of his poverty-stricken over-brothered childhood. Or was it a Scottish characteristic? But she had never heard Guthrie Carlyle make a single reference to the monetary value of anything – only to the artistic value of anything and, late at night after a good deal of red wine, to the moral value of everything.

'God knows what Clementina and her gang of local layabouts led by Lachlan have done with the guns,' he concluded. 'Sold them no doubt.'

As if in direct and contradictory answer to Ben's offhand remark, there was a sharp crack, and then another, a sound more like an explosion than a bullet. At what seemed to be one and the same moment, the Land-Rover slewed violently to the left and into the ditch beside the narrow road leading up to the Castle. Jemima was jolted violently and ended up falling across Ben Beauregard.

There was the sound of running feet and a group of men appeared, surrounding the Land-Rover. Among them Lachlan was prominent. He went to the driving seat. Another man, whom Jemima vaguely recognized, opened the door of the Land-Rover from the left and made a grab towards her. He had red hair and a thin face, paler than the rest of his associates – or perhaps it was the hair which emphasized his pallor.

The familiar rose-and-bloodstained t-shirts were back in force. But it was symptomatic of the new violence of the occasion that there were no flowers now behind their ears. There was one much older man present, inappropriately dressed in a t-shirt. Jemima suddenly recognized Young Duncan.

At the wheel Ben Beauregard was struggling violently, and so frenetic were his gestures that Jemima was terrified the already listing Land-Rover would heel over completely. Above their heads the portcullis gate yawned; could those heavy iron spikes which fringed it actually be for real? There was another flag, a placard with something written on it in Gaelic, and a dangling heavy object supporting another placard.

'Aye, Lachlan, tie him up and take them both into the Castle,' said the red-haired man in a tone of authority. 'Then we'll pull up the drawbridge.' Jemima suddenly remembered him as the somewhat mysterious figure who had entered and left St Margaret's by the side door on the day of the funeral.

'Leave us alone,' cried Jemima, desperately beginning to struggle in her turn as she saw some hefty ropes being applied – not gently at all – to Ben Beauregard. One of the ropes, intentionally or not, was drawn across his mouth and acted as a kind of gag. 'Leave him alone. You're tearing him. Oh God. Wherever is Colonel Henry?' she added in a voice more like a wail than a cry. 'Colonel Henry would soon sort you all out.'

'Aye, you may well ask that, Miss Jemima Shore,' commented Lachlan, 'seeing as you have now joined the ranks of his numerous wummin and strumpets.' There was a note of vicious prurience, a horrid gloating delight in his voice. He came around the Land-Rover to her side and, taking her two hands, jerked them quite savagely behind her. His eyes, small, cold and blue, gazed at her in a way which was both disapproving and covetous. The respect he had shown to her on all previous occasions had quite gone. He addressed her, Jemima thought suddenly, in a confused mixed image, as John Knox might have addressed the woman taken in adultery. Half disapprovingly. Half lustfully.

'How dare you touch her?' Ben's voice under the rope was glottal, strangled, but still violent.

'If we were mindful to touch her, which we are not, there's no' a thing you can do about it, Mr Ben Beauregard,' said the red-haired man in a voice full of contempt. 'It's the Red Rose is in power here, not the laird, I'll have ye know.'

'In the absence of Colonel Henry, where is Miss Beauregard herself?' enquired Jemima in the coolest voice she could muster. 'I demand to be taken before her.'

The men exchanged looks. Lachlan whispered with the red-haired man. There appeared to be some form of divided command.

'Aeneas and I agree that we'll take you to her,' said Lachlan.

'And what's going to happen to Mr Ben?' pursued Jemima.

Lachlan, the man called Aeneas and the rest, even Young Duncan, favoured Ben with a sardonic quizzical stare. There was a short laugh from someone.

'Him. Aye, mebbe we'll send him to join his father,' said one of them.

'And where might that be?' The pretence of boldness had made Jemima actually feel bolder. By way of reply, Lachlan jerked his thumb upwards.

With a feeling of total nausea, Jemima realized that the heavy object revolving slowly in the wind above them, hanging upright from the battlements, was in fact a body: a body wearing a jacket of black velvet on which no doubt there were silver buttons, a body wearing a kilt. Colonel Henry Beauregard would not after all be able to keep his promise to her to return.

14

Danger

Rope serrating the corners of his mouth, Ben Beauregard continued to stare upwards at the body of his father swinging above their heads from the portcullis. To Jemima, he seemed extraordinarily cool.

'It's the dummy,' he said, his voice strangled but still audible. 'The dummy from the castle attic. Uncle Carlo and Dad had it made for target practice when they were boys. She dressed it up. A shabby trick.'

Jemima found she was trembling violently. Tears had begun to form in her eyes. She wanted to control them.

'It's maybe a dummy, a grand stuffed body, but it's a warning to you all the same,' commented the man called Aeneas grimly. 'So shall all the lairds hang one day from the battlements when the Red Rose reigns over Scotland. And the Scottish people shall enjoy the freedom of their own land: with no lairds to harry them and drive them from their crofts.' It sounded like the beginning of a speech.

'A new Scotland under the rule of their new sovereign her Majesty Queen Clementina,' added Lachlan quickly, rather too quickly, interrupting him.

'Up the Red Rose,' chimed in Duncan, 'and may the White run Red. Colonel Henry was ever a reasonable man. I'm sure he'll be joining the Red Rose any day now and giving us our lodges for our own. There's no one I'd sooner work for than the Colonel, if I owned my own wee lodge.'

Relief was gradually calming the trembling of Jemima's limbs. Her mind too was regaining its alertness. It was clear to her that even within the gun-laden party now marching towards the vast baronial door of the Castle there were three shades of opinion. While Aeneas, surname and origins unknown, concentrated on the land-for-the-people aspect of Scottish independence – in Jacobin as well as Jacobite terms – Lachlan had from their first meeting shown a kind of romanticism, even reverence, of a very different order. As for Young Duncan, Jemima remembered his fervent recitation of the slogan of the Red Rose on her original journey up the valley. What she had then taken for sycophancy was evidently conviction – of a sort. But Young Duncan's conviction was strictly from the point of view of his own prosperity. He had no further axe to grind, no animus against his employer Colonel Henry and no particular reverence for Queen Clementina.

The man called Aeneas equated the Red Rose with the Red Flag – social revolution, in short. For Lachlan Stuart, son of the dead Bridie with her Beauregard loyalties, the two flags were worlds apart.

So must the earlier army of Prince Charles Edward Stuart also have been divided, into revolutionaries, romantics and self-seekers . . .

The sight of the enormous entrance hall to Castle Beauregard obliterated these thoughts for the time being. Here was the Beauregard Armoury in all its martial splendour. Circles, whorls and cascading spirals of guns and other weapons were pinioned to the walls. Guns were not the sole weapons displayed. Gleaming knives, long pikes, vicious-looking bayonets demonstrated the long history of the art of war. The few weapons of defence exhibited – a shield or two from an earlier age – looked oddly out of place. The martial spirit as interpreted by the Beauregard Armoury was pre-eminently one of attack, not defence.

Here and there the elaborate artistry with which the armoury had been arranged on the walls had been despoiled. A number of guns were missing from their positions as the spokes of a series of rising wheels directly abutting the general's picture. These were the guns in the hands of Lachlan, Aeneas and their companions which continued to menace Ben and Jemima as they trod warily through the hall.

The impression of mediaeval vastness did not fade as the party left the hall and began to ascend a broad stone staircase, on the walls of which huge flags of indeterminate royal and Scottish nature were hung. No expense of royal Victorian spirit had been spared in building this fantasy palace.

Lachlan stuck a thumb in the direction of a narrow arch giving a glimpse of descending stone steps.

'That way to the dungeon,' he said. After a moment Jemima realized that he was not joking. As they reached the crest of the great staircase, two portraits dominated the entrance to what was presumably the Great Drawing Room. Or the Great Library. It scarcely needed the gold label affixed to the ornate frame to inform Jemima that here was the founding father of the Beauregard family – if you believed the legend – Bonnie Prince Charlie himself.

Only, this portrait was in itself a Victorian fantasy. Magnificent in tartan, many different shades and patterns of it combined, bedizened with sporran, plaid, dirks and daggers, Celtic brooches and the rest, as well as Victorian whiskers, moustache and beard, his Majesty King Charles III (as the label termed him) was depicted as a portly nineteenth-century Coburg, more an Edward VII than an eighteenth-century Stuart. The background of the picture contained a large red velvet throne and a couple of dogs, too lean for labradors, straining at leashes held by a couple of tartan-clad retainers. No, thought Jemima, life up the Glen for Bonnie Prince Charlie was never like this; but the picture would do very nicely on a whisky bottle.

There was a companion piece, equally splendidly Victorian in its concept and execution. Here Sighing Marjorie – for it could be no other – with flowing chestnut hair, a baby in her arms, delicate white gown and tartan shawl, cowered over a waterfall while a force of red-coated soldiers stood rather woodenly by. The background of this picture consisted of a vivid impression of Castle Beauregard at sunset. Looking at the leading soldier's stolid expression, Jemima was irresistibly tempted to caption it: 'Go on, jump then.'

Entering the Great Library, her first surprise was to rediscover immediately the red velvet throne featured in the Prince's picture.

Clementina Beauregard was seated negligently on it, her pale face and hair set off by the crimson canopy louring over her head. She was smoking the stub of a cigarette. The curtains, heavy, somnolent-seeming plum-coloured curtains, were still drawn. The room was full of smoke and had a recognizable semi-sweet reek. As the heavy oak door to the library swung open, the sound of a Rolling Stones record, not in its first youth and played very loud, blared in their faces.

In all this noise and smoky darkness, for a moment the fairy-like delicacy of Clementina provided a strange contrast. Yet there was a hint of fancy dress in her own costume. On second thoughts, she did not look so out of place in the Great Library after all. In spite of the hour, Clementina was wearing a long red dress of panne velvet, too big for her and slightly Edwardian in cut, with a type of bustle and tight leg o' mutton sleeves from which most of the buttons were missing. She also wore a black hat, even more dilapidated, but with traces of grandiose feathers and flowers on its brim. Ropes of pale pink pearls hung down across her tiny bosom, which swelled out the red velvet hardly perceptibly. Some of the pearls were peeling or had lost their pinkness altogether.

Above her loomed another vast portrait, this time of an imposing female rather than a male. Built on a far ampler scale, this former Beauregard beauty was wearing identical costume to that of her descendant Clementina, seated beneath her imperious gaze. Did this adoption of the semi-regal outfit of her ancestress indicate that Clementina had decided to put on some sort of show to receive her captives?

If so, the impulse had passed. Clementina's eyes were fixed unwaveringly on Ben. She did not seem to take in the presence of Jemima. Swiftly, she knocked rather than switched the record player into silence. It was lying on the corner of the dais to the throne; there was a morass of records, none of them looking particularly well cared for, within reach.

'So, Ben, come to take over, have you?' she said in a voice which was considerably slowed down from her usual frenetic diction. 'Castle first, then the island, and last of all pretty cousin Clementina.' Her voice trailed away. She took a brief drag on the cigarette stub in her fingers. From the smell of the room, clinging round the dark drawn curtains and recesses of the library, not strongly but unmistakably, Jemima guessed that she had been smoking the marijuana for hours, maybe all night.

Lamps with dark green pleated shades illuminated the library and there were other pictures to be seen among the books. The exquisite fair-haired lady over the fireplace, a romantic post-war portrait with the Castle in the background – John Merton perhaps? – was so strikingly like Clementina as to be readily identifiable as Leonie Beauregard. There were photographs as well. One pair of portraits, carefully juxtaposed, demonstrated the rakes' progress of the Beauregard twins. On the one hand a carefully posed picture, unmistakably by Cecil Beaton, showed them as soulful and curly-haired angels at their mother's knee: Charles in frilly shirt and satin page's trousers, Clementina in high-waisted flounced dress and sash. The second portrait, by David Bailey, showed a couple of unadorned faces, placed close together, the expressions both pagan and mocking.

Everything in Castle Beauregard, however ancestral, was also highly painted, decorated and where appropriate varnished. The pictures looked as if they had been newly cleaned. The plum-coloured curtains, with their magnificent dark swags of material and tasselled gold fringes, did not look old. The carpets were thick and soft, as well as being tartan, a combination which put the thought into Jemima's mind that Leonie Beauregard's American money must be responsible for the splendour. For one thing, the interior of the Castle, stonebuilt as it might be, was not particularly cold. The library was positively hot, yet the log fire was not lit. Was it possible to centrally heat a castle, and in August? There was a strange southern warmth about the place.

Not only the warmth but also the good, even brilliant, state of repair of the Castle itself contrasted markedly with the shabbiness of that other Beauregard residence at Kilbronnack, to say nothing of the ruined state of Eilean Fas. Every visit to the Castle by the junior branch of the Beauregards must have rubbed in the contrast epitomized by Dives and Lazarus – Dives: Charles, the heir; Lazarus: Ben and all his siblings.

'Have a smoke,' said Clementina suddenly, extending the stub to Jemima, who shook her head. At which Clementina half minced, half staggered towards Ben and stuck the stub between his lips. Ben did not move. Jemima admired his control once more: the only uncontrolled thing about him she could detect was a vein beating on the side of his temple. After a moment Clementina removed the stub and, standing on tiptoe, put her velvet-clad arms round her cousin's neck. Then she kissed him lightly, on the lips. Ben still did not move.

'Pretty pretty cousin Clementina,' she repeated. 'Don't you want to kiss her now, Ben? So pretty.' Once again her words sounded slurred.

She turned to Jemima.

'He wanted to kiss me once. He wanted to very much. I didn't tell you that, did I?'

'There are quite a lot of things you didn't tell me,' answered Jemima grimly. 'In fact I'm beginning to think you told me a pack of lies the other day at breakfast. Though why you should take the trouble—'

Clementina giggled, tottered back to the huge sofa by the fireplace – Jemima noticed she was wearing black satin buckled shoes, much too big for her – and threw herself backwards onto it.

'Then I'll tell you the truth now,' she said, still laughing. 'We've plenty of time. While they're getting Uncle Henry to sign the paper giving Eilean Fas for a Memorial Island. And cousin Ben here to back him up. We need that island, the Red Rose needs it. Good for morals. I mean morale. That's what he says. Good for morale.' There were more giggles.

'I'll be glad to hear the truth,' replied Jemima carefully. 'But why don't you get Lachlan to release Ben while you're talking? These ropes surely aren't necessary inside the Castle.'

'But I adore ropes!' cried Clementina with enthusiasm. 'So kinky. Don't you adore ropes, cousin Ben, darling?' Then there was another change of mood and she said quite sharply: 'Lachlan, untie Mr Ben at once. Untie him, I said. And then go and get us some champagne from the cellar. The crystal champagne. We must have some champagne to celebrate. And fetch Uncle Henry too – if he's being good that is – he can celebrate too.'

Celebrate what ? Jemima wondered.

'I've got no orders to fetch the Colonel from the dungeons,' said Lachlan in what for him was a surly voice. He looked at Aeneas, who shook his head.

'Orders, whose orders are you talking about?' replied Clementina petulantly. 'It's my orders now at the Castle.' She tapped her small foot in its bent black shoe, so that the paste buckle rattled. Then it fell off. Clementina paid no attention.

'Our Chief's orders, your Majesty.' Lachlan gazed quite steadily at Clementina as he spoke.

They were interrupted by the shrill sound of the telephone, a sound to which Jemima found that she had grown so unaccustomed that the ordinary urban noise made her start as though at a tocsin. Clementina seemed uncertain what to do. Then she staggered over to the instrument and picked up the receiver. She said nothing. Someone was speaking rapidly at the other end. Jemima could hear the voice, but not the words.

'Is it the Chief now?' asked Aeneas intensely.

Clementina gave one of her high laughs, nodded, said into the telephone, Then you'd better give the warning straight away.' She listened briefly and dropped the receiver without saying goodbye.

'Fancy that,' she added to the assembled company. 'Fancy that. The Chief is a very worried man. He's coming over here himself. Says he's got something very important to tell me. Danger. He's talking about danger. I may be in danger. What does he mean? How can I be in danger? I'm with the Red Rose, aren't I? I'm their Queen. Cousin Ben's in danger and Uncle Henry's in danger. Even Miss Jemima Shore is in a little bit of danger if the Red Rose turns nasty – naughty Miss Shore carrying on with wicked Uncle Henry. But how can Queen Clementina the First be in danger? Oh, Lachlan, do get the crystal champagne, I want to celebrate. I want to celebrate my accession.'

Ah, thought Jemima, so that's what we're celebrating.

'He mustn't be seen,' said Lachlan in a hard voice. 'He won't want the prisoners catching sight of him. You know his orders. That would be dangerous.'

'Danger! Danger! Give me your answer do. Who's afraid of the big bad danger, the big bad danger,' Clementina sang in a high, rather pretty voice. 'I think I'll put on another record.'

She put on the record of 'Satisfaction'.

'I can't get any danger out of you,' Clementina sang above the notes of the record.

Jemima thought they were all in danger, from Colonel Henry in his dungeon to herself in the power of a nest of lunatics. Even Clementina, the alternative Queen of Scotland, had apparently something to fear. She also wondered who the Chief might be – and whether his existence increased or diminished the danger.

15
Official action

'Where was the Chief telephoning from?' asked Lachlan aggressively.

'There were pips,' said Clementina rather vaguely. 'Pip, pip, pip. So it can't have been,' she stopped, 'you know where.'

With a jerk of his head, Aeneas left the room taking Ben with him, the gun held to his back. Ben offered no resistance. It was difficult to see how he could have done so: he had presumably gone to join his father in the dungeons. That left Lachlan – and his gun – against Jemima. Clementina, who had wandered back to her throne, plucking some of the flowers from her hat as she did so and casting them aside in an Ophelia-like gesture, remained an uncertain quantity.

'So you'll be staying quiet, Miss Shore,' said Lachlan after Ben had gone, reverting to his vicious tone. 'Till we decide what to do with you. That'll be understood, will it not? Otherwise it's your paramour, the Colonel, who will suffer.'

Jemima did not deign to answer.

None of the various bibelots in the library was particularly delicate looking. They included a hunting knife with a golden stag's head as the handle. Both ends looked lethal. The knife reposed on a table entirely made up of twisted antlers' horns. Above the table an enormous glass case, placed between two bookcases, contained a regal stuffed salmon, swimming amidst some brilliant reeds. The label beneath it read: 'Caught by HRH Prince Charles Edward Stuart (HM King Charles III) off Eilean Fas . . .' Jemima recalled the jolly note struck in Charles Beauregard's original letter, 'My mother's doing . . .'

'Mummy caught that herself,' volunteered Clementina. 'On the home beat. She told me.' Clearly her concentration had not gone entirely. 'That's why she never put it in her book about BPC. Because it wasn't true. She didn't pretend the rose garden was planted by BPC or Sighing Marjorie either, like some people. She was very serious about her history.'

Jemima shot another stealthy look at the stag's-head knife.

'I've never seen this famous white rose garden.'

'Red rose garden.' Clementina glared at her. Jemima cursed herself. Clementina's moment of weakness – or intelligence – had passed.

'Where the hell's the champagne?' she cried petulantly. 'Hasn't Duncan come back with it yet?'

'Not with the Chief on his way!' exclaimed Lachlan in a shocked voice. 'It would never do for him to find us drinking at this hour in the morning. You know how strong he is against the drink.' The Puritanism was unexpected: she wondered again who the Chief might be, and whether she might get to glimpse him. His identity was doubly intriguing now that the display of guns, the abduction of Colonel Henry, the detention of Ben and herself, had rudely jolted her complacency concerning the Red Rose. She was obliged to take them seriously as a force: it was no longer possible to dismiss them as a mildly eccentric but fundamentally harmless bunch of royalist fanatics.

After a while Clementina began to wander round the library again. She played some more music, loud, aimless. The champagne did not arrive. Nor for that matter did anyone else. Jemima considered it her duty to edge in the direction of the knife. Lachlan, showing signs of nervousness, put down his gun and demanded a cigarette from Clementina. She tossed him one out of her woven handbag. It was presumably an ordinary cigarette.

The time passed very slowly, according to the ornate golden clock, French perhaps, supported by rampant stags in baroque attitudes, on the heavily carved mantelpiece.

'I could do with a dram myself,' observed Lachlan wistfully after a while. 'Chief or no Chief. I'm no too fond of the champagne, you understand.' He sounded apologetic.

'You drank enough of it with Charles in the old days.' Clementina was cross.

'I was preferring the ancient whisky, though. The great old barrel.'

'You certainly were. I've never seen anyone as drunk as Lachlan on our last birthday. It's extraordinary stuff. Dark brown. Lays people out like flies. One hundred and twenty per cent proof, or a thousand and twenty per cent proof, something like that. Over a hundred years old, Uncle Henry told us. He nearly had a fit when we started to lay into it, the moment Charles was twenty-one, and slosh it about to the ghillies and Lachlan and other good souls like him.'

At very long last – they had surely waited much longer than an hour – the noise of a car was heard. Distant at first, then growing stronger as it puttered up the valley.

Clementina gave a surprised little cry and stepped back from the window.

'Oh, it's not him. It's—' Lachlan sat up sharply, threw down his cigarette and grabbed the gun. In the split second his attention was diverted, Jemima made a dive for the knife with the stag's-head handle and stuffed it down her boot. She blessed the fashion for wide-cuffed cowboy boots. It felt uncomfortable, but safe.

'How *weird!* Where's the Chief, then?' Clementina sounded genuinely puzzled. The noise of the car grew louder and Jemima reckoned from the bumping, grating sound that it was just crossing the drawbridge; then the most extraordinary sound of singing from downstairs greeted her ears, followed by running footsteps and cries, mixed with protests and more snatches of a very drunken, very Scottish song which as it grew nearer sounded increasingly obscene. Then Aeneas burst into the library, hauling Duncan by his collar. The old man was still trying to sing.

'He's got out,' he panted. 'The devil. He's gone. Bribed him with the whisky and went.'

'It wasn't the drink at all, so it wasn't. It was the paper. We was just celebrating the paper.' As the tears coursed down Duncan's cheeks, he held out a crumpled piece of paper.

'You drivelling old fool,' snarled Aeneas, shaking the old man by his collar. 'What good will this paper do you? Do you think the laird will honour that?'

'He's promised me the lodge. The Colonel would'na break his word. He's a man of honour.'

'He'll break you more like,' commented Lachlan. 'You'll never stay on the Estate now. Not now you've tried to force the Colonel to sign that paper.'

As an expression of maudlin horror and dismay crossed Duncan's features, Jemima saw her chance. The library door was open. She pelted out of it, slamming it behind her. A vast key, shining and brassy like everything at Castle Beauregard, rattled in the lock as she did so. She turned it. It worked. The lock clicked fast as frantic shouts from the three men trapped inside reached her together with, a moment later, the strong rattling of the door itself. But the door held. Thank God for Leonie Beauregard who had refurbished the Castle in such a splendidly robust style. No rusty keys in locks here.

Jemima ran as fast as she could down the broad stairs to the arched entrance to the dungeon, scrabbling and hobbling in order to remove the stag's-head knife from her boot as she did so. At that moment the sound of other voices, urgently talking – in the armoury, or at any rate inside the Castle – reached her. The unknown visitor – the Chief or another – was within. Jemima was taking no chances. She shrank behind the arch and began to creep as quietly as possible down the stairs.

Footsteps, it sounded like a single man, went past her and right on up the main staircase. Let the unknown, whoever it was, cope with the imprisoned men and Queen Clementina. She had not dared to pause long enough to remove the key from the lock. It was up to her now to find Ben Beauregard.

Dungeons? There was now a maze of new staircases facing her below the level of the ground. But her task was made unexpectedly easy by the mint-new condition of even the subterranean regions of this castle. There were actually notices in Victorian Gothic directing her. TO THE CELLARS – she found herself by the entrance to a large room, vast in style, door open, clean, white-washed, vaulted. Not only the racks of bottles but the stink of whisky emanating from an outsize barrel convinced her that here had been Duncan's downfall.

Then she heard a noise behind her. She stopped. The noise stopped too. Someone was following her. Heart thumping, Jemima wondered why, if her pursuer were a member of the Red Rose, he did not immediately brutally grab her. She started to walk on gingerly, extremely gingerly, in the direction indicated for the dungeons. There was no sign of a guard or sentry. Had they left Ben quite unguarded in the furore of his father's escape and the unknown's arrival?

Another stealthy noise behind her. She tested it by stopping. But her follower was quick to follow suit. As Jemima proceeded along the narrowing passage, it was like playing an elaborate game of mediaeval grandmother's footsteps. Then she saw the dungeon – clearly labelled. The door was open. A body – Ben – was slumped in one corner. The ropes were wound round it. He looked horribly inert.

She gave a little cry and tried too late to stifle it. Then a strong muscular arm reached at her from behind and stifled her voice completely. Jemima tried to scream and could not: then she struggled in earnest.

'Keep still, darling,' said a voice in her ear. 'I told you I'd be back. I didn't expect *you* to come looking for *me*.'

At the same moment as Jemima recognized the voice, deep even in its low tones, she also felt a wave of violent recognition for the physical touch of Henry Beauregard.

'Ben,' she mouthed.

'Shh,' he said, not letting her go. 'It's only the dummy. Ben's got away.'

Jemima felt her body relax. She realized how corpse-like the body in the dungeon had looked to her. First the father, then the son . . . The dummy had a lot to answer for. The Colonel took his hand from her mouth and kissed her. It was done with a certain carelessness as one might kiss a child who has been soothed.

'You poor darling,' he said gently, stroking her cheek, and pushing back the hair which had fallen over her face.

'Ben's gone to get help?' asked Jemima, still panting slightly from her journey, her fright and now the reassuring kiss at the end of it all.

'Help? I *am* help, aren't I?'

'I mean, *help*; proper help. The Red Rose, I mean, aren't you going to do anything about them – they kidnapped you,'

'For God's sake, girl, I am doing something about them!' exclaimed the Colonel, his voice getting louder as he struck a note of real indignation.

'What about the police? You must send for the police. First they kidnapped you, then they locked you up. They locked us up. Besides, they've got guns, they were firing shots over the Land-Rover.'

'They didn't kidnap me, as a matter of fact. There was a signal outside the window. A kind of whistle: family signal, something we use out in the woods. I don't know how they found it out. You were asleep. I left that note and went downstairs. And they jumped me. Three against one. As for the police, these are the sort of blackguards who simply need a good thrashing from some of my stronger ghillies,' he responded robustly.

'The guns—' began Jemima again. He ignored her.

'Besides, it didn't take me very long to outwit them. Duncan never has had a head for drink. None of his family can take it.'

'And you promised him the lodge. For ever. And he believed you.'

'All part of his general idiocy when he's had a drop. As if I'd ever give him the Old Lodge – we need the lodge. He knows that perfectly well: it's right in the heart of the Glen. He can whistle for his lodge. The old fool.' The Colonel sounded almost as contemptuous as Aeneas had done.

'But you're not going to sack him?'

The Colonel looked at her as if she were insane.

'Sack Duncan Stuart? But he's worked on the Estate all his life. Besides, his son's a rotten type. Have to look after poor old Duncan, y'know. Can't go sacking him at his age.'

'His son—'

'Aeneas Stuart. Red-haired bastard – in every sense of the word. You must have seen him. He's the one who's really behind the Red Rose up here. Too clever by half. A real Red. Went to Aberdeen University and came back with a lot of half-baked ideas about land for the people, and knew less about the land and farming round here than his own grandfather who was an illiterate crofter. Not Duncan's fault: no brains to speak of there. The brains came from his mother Ishbel who was head housemaid before the war: wonderful head on her shoulders, but always causing trouble with the rest of the servants. You know the type: we never could keep a cook when she was around. Eleven cooks in one year, till we sacked Ishbel. You've probably been through the same thing yourself.'

Jemima had not.

'Trouble-makers have to go,' went on the Colonel. 'Same thing with Aeneas. Talk about the perils of educating people above their station. In the end I had him thrown of the Estate, told Duncan I wouldn't have him up the Glen. Suggested the Army, but of course he wouldn't go. Then my precious nephew Charles, he brought him back to spite me.'

'And you're still not going to take any official action?'

'In my own glen,' replied the Colonel grimly, 'I am the official action. This is between the Red Rose and me. No outside interference. Round One to them. Round Two to me.'

In short, to her utter amazement and, it has to be said, considerable dismay, Jemima found that the Colonel had worked out a plan by which they would now both leave the Castle together, as Ben had done, via the ruins of Castle Tamh. At which point the Colonel would joyously put into effect his proposals for defeating the Red Rose by his so-called 'official action' – it had exactly the opposite sound to Jemima – while she herself struggled back to the Wild Island on foot.

'Meet you there later,' said the Colonel. 'I'll be in touch.' He might have been discussing a London rendezvous, such was his insouciance.

Jemima was torn between admiration for his spirit and a gloomy presentiment, the product of an innately law-abiding nature, that it would be both better and safer in the long run to hand over the Red Rose, Clementina Beauregard and all, to the Inverness-shire police. Let them iron out exactly what charges covered the somewhat strange circumstances; assault, the use of an offensive weapon, they would certainly not lack for material.

But Jemima found that her own sense of propriety and law and order was no match for the Colonel's sense of adventure and challenge. He was quite determined not to be personally done down by the Red Rose:

indeed he hardly listened to her arguments concerning the police, which he seemed to regard as charmingly feminine – and as such deserving a reassuring caress rather than any more serious consideration.

Jemima gave up. In England, she knew, she would not have given up. She was not in England.

Meekly, she followed the Colonel through a maze of corridors in the well-dusted dungeons.

'Played in them as a boy with Carlo. Know more about this castle than the Red Rose ever will,' he said by way of explanation.

The little arched side-door by which they eventually left the Castle was swinging open, giving a broad path of light. Ben had left it open. As they approached the door, Jemima caught her breath: framed in the stone arch was an extraordinary vision of crimson, a great slope of roses, slipping away from her eyes to wards the loch, like some field of poppies in the violence and concentration of its colour. She was seeing for the first time the famous Beauregard rose garden.

She ducked and stepped into daylight. They were among the ruins of the old castle, once again neatly finished off with new masonry, and adorned here and there with wooden identifying tags in the grass: The Great Hall, The Chapel, and so forth. The stone was grey, like Eilean Fas, in contrast to the dark red brick of the nineteenth-century edifice behind them, and the crimson roses which lay ahead.

The beds of flowers stretched almost as far as the loch, which curved round to meet the Castle on this side; but the garden itself was sheltered from both the wind and the view, which explained why she had never before glimpsed this monstrosity either from the road or the castle library. For monstrosity it was: seeing what must once have been an exquisite grey and white vista transformed into a fiery demonstration of family hatred made Jemima understand for the first time the nature of Colonel Henry's personal outrage against his nephew and his followers.

She kept these thoughts to herself. She felt the Colonel needed no encouragement in his feud.

They parted at the side of the loch, still hidden from view from the Castle. Equally Jemima could not see the courtyard, nor whose car it was which had arrived at the Castle while she was in the dungeons – assuming she would have recognized it.

As she tramped, wearily but curiously elated, along the road which led down to the Eilean Fas bridge, she thought about cars and how sometimes, though not always, they were significant expressions of the personality. Her own Volvo sports car expressed a passion for fast but safe driving, a recklessness which did not find many other expressions in her character – except possibly in the present instance, in her submission to the adventurous plans of Colonel Henry, against the judgement of the cooler part of her nature.

She was meditating on this and allied topics concerning her nature and that of Colonel Henry, as she reached the narrow wooden-slatted bridge. The noise of the water was loud in her ears. She reached out for the sagging rope which served as a handrail.

It was only at that moment that she became aware, quite suddenly, that a car had come up right behind her, was in fact touching her with its bumper nudging at her – the rushing of the water had totally masked its silent approach. Jemima stepped instinctively sideways to get out of its way, nearly slipping off the wet bridge as she did so. She clutched once more at the rope, for a moment swaying perilously over the water, fighting for her balance.

'Why, my dear Jemima,' said the drawling voice of Ossian Lucas. 'I hope I didn't startle you. I was just coming to pay my respects. Don't look so frightened.'

16
Appearances

The last stretch of the journey up to the Wild Island, in Ossian Lucas's car, was a silent one. Neither the MP (wearing velvet trousers and an exgravagant silk shirt, patterned with lilies) nor his passenger had anything to say. Jemima Shore, as she watched his strong hand in its fanciful cuff on the driving-wheel, was glad to leave the rickety bridge behind.

She looked back at the black waters as the car climbed the winding gravel path – waters which had already claimed two victims in the shape of Charles Beauregard and Bridie Stuart and might even just now have claimed her. After her recent experiences, she badly needed a sense of security, protection; she wasn't quite sure whether the presence of the enigmatic Lucas provided it.

As if in answer to a prayer – an analogy which seemed peculiarly apt under the circumstances – there was a letter waiting for her on the stained and cracked hall table. She did not know what agency had brought it here, but since the house had been generally tidied, she imagined wearily that since life must go on in the Highlands, some substitute for Bridie had been found.

Jemima recognized the neat precise handwriting and thin, cheap paper immediately. There were the initials A.M.D.G. – *ad majorem Dei Gloriam*: To the Greater Glory of God – in the corner. Mother Agnes had written from her convent, that ivory tower from which she saw so many things so much clearer than ordinary mortals.

'Excuse me,' she burst out impulsively to Ossian Lucas. 'I must read this – a very valued friend – a nun as a matter of fact. A really good woman. Then I'll find you a drink; only wine, I'm afraid.'

But as they proceeded into the drawing room, a quarter of a bottle of malt whisky, neatly placed beside two clean glasses, contradicted her words: Colonel Henry's residue. Ossian Lucas helped himself, a dram, no water at all, and drained it.

Jemima was busy scanning her letter. It was extraordinary; one of these days she would really have to accept the powers of divine inspiration. Or rather, one of these days she would really have to examine the whole subject of religion seriously, i.e. *not* from the point of view of television programmes . . . As she had once told Mother Agnes, only half joking: 'I never seem to get time to think about God. It's all right for Him – if He exists – He's got all the time in the world.'

Mother Agnes had merely smiled politely.

Divinely inspired or not, Mother Agnes's present letter showed an extraordinary percipience about the situation in Glen Bronnack, although she had no means of knowing how much of dramatic import had taken place since Jemima wrote her letter recounting a tale of two brothers.

On the subject of the family:

. . . At its best an incarnation of the highest principles of human conduct, a source of wonderful comfort. Yet isn't it distressing how the Devil will never leave even the most sacred institutions alone? He is so determined to spoil things, if he can. Members of a family are also subject to special temptations of jealousy towards each other. Remember Cain and Abel, Jacob and Esau in the Old Testament. Passions so often run high in big families; such feelings are of course intended by Almighty God for the preservation and protection of His ordained unit, the family, but in certain cases, as with all human passions, the instinct, being perverted, can go awry. It can be turned towards evil. Sometimes I think Our Blessed Lord tests a pair of brothers with special temptations. He Himself of course was an only child . . .

It was Jemima's turn to smile at the last sentence.

'Christ,' said Ossian Lucas suddenly, interrupting her thoughts. 'I hate this house. I don't understand how you can stay here, and alone. There is such a feeling of sadness about it. A sort of doom hangs over it.'

'More than sadness: menace, threat,' responded Jemima

'Then you feel it too. You didn't say.'

'You are the first person who has mentioned it to me.'

'An unhappy woman. Maybe she haunts it now, poor soul. God rest her too.' He poured and drank another dram of whisky.

'Sighing Marjorie?'

Ossian Lucas looked surprised. 'That's a long time ago. I meant poor Leonie Beauregard.'

'What?'

'Didn't you know? She committed suicide in this very house. Upstairs. When the twins were about twelve or thirteen. Shot herself with one of the guns from the Beauregard Armoury. A shot-gun: an appalling death for a pretty woman. The worst of it was that Charles found her. It was no wonder that the poor boy turned odd as he did. And they left this house to rot. That's why Father Flanagan has always wanted to take it over for the Church – put matters right, in his not so humble opinion. As you may or may not know, and it's of absolutely no relevance now, our Henry and his beautiful American sister-in-law were not unattached in those far-off days. Father Flanagan first tried to persuade Charles himself to found the mission ostensibly in memory of his father; but of course for Charles the experience of being tutored by the turbulent priest was enough to lay the foundations of a most sincerely felt dislike for him and all he stood for. Seeing as he had a hatred of authority in any form, and Father F. seemed a particularly large and grim embodiment of it.

'Now Father F. is going on at Henry about it, but Henry knows how to deal with him all right. He replies most smoothly that if he had Clementina's money, coupled with the Beauregard land, he would be only too delighted to found a mission; as it is, with large estates to handle, a vast family, and not a great abundance of cash, it's out of the question for the time being. One day perhaps . . .'

'Is he sincere?' asked Jemima curiously.

Ossian roared with laughter.

'Absolutely not. Frankly, now he's managed to inherit it all, I can't imagine Henry handing over anything, let alone an island in the middle of the Estate. But the point is that Father Flanagan is kept quiet and the old dragon keeps hoping and waiting without too many sermons on the subject of sin and expiation in Henry's unwilling ear.'

A sort of doom hangs over it: his phrase echoed in her mind. There was certainly a sort of doom over Eilean Fas, with violent death polluting her Paradise down the ages from Sighing Marjorie and her baby to the widowed Leonie Beauregard two hundred years later.

Not a lucky house: the words of Mother Agnes suddenly appeared more relevant. Passions intended by nature for the preservation of the family had indeed in this case turned to evil, the evil of self-destruction.

Had the suicide been on account of Henry Beauregard? In that case it was no wonder that the twins had grown up to hate and resent him.

Jemima tried to tell herself that the house no longer felt evil to her, only tragic, now that she knew its secret. But she was happy all the same to accept Ossian's invitation for a stroll round the island, out into the mellow sunlight, the dancing yellows and greens of the afternoon.

'The land, the island,' said Jemima at one point. 'How obsessed you all are with the island.'

'Land equals the lure of gold in a primitive community. Are you surprised? Besides, it's our history. It's difficult to understand from outside. Take a previous tenant of Eilean Fas, in a manner of speaking – Bonnie Prince Charlie. Did he really come to rescue the people of Scotland from English thralldom? Or did he come to set up yet another form of dominion? Admittedly Catholic where the Hanoverians were Protestants, but since not everyone in Scotland is or was a Catholic by a long chalk, he could have represented slavery too.'

'I suppose he represented independence,' suggested Jemima hopefully; once again she cursed her English ignorance of Scottish history.

'Wouldn't true independence have been represented by setting up an independent kingdom of Scotland? Ignoring the English throne for better or for worse. As King James the Sixth and First might perhaps have ignored the throne of Elizabeth, and his mother Mary too.'

It was the most beautiful clear day she had yet experienced on the island. The misty beginnings, during which she had, as it were, stormed the castle perilous, had given way to unusual heat. The dampness of the undergrowth still exuded a jungle atmosphere. The cliffs fell away beneath them through the frondy bracken and other foliage. Her island Paradise was once more in evidence. Yet glancing at Ossian's face beside her, in profile strong, even goat-like above the striking silk shirt and purple trousers, she thought how little she knew of this stranger. How little she knew of any of them in this part of the world, a primitive community as the MP had said, obsessed by so many things: land and inheritance and history and a view of the past and the future which she did not understand.

'You don't take that point of view, surely,' Jemima countered. 'You're a democratically elected representative, for a Scottish constituency, sitting in an English Parliament.'

Ossian Lucas smiled: the satyr-like impression was enhanced and then faded.

'British Parliament,' he corrected her.

'But you don't share the wish for independence—' she persisted.

'You have to see all the sides of the question when you are a Scottish MP. If you want to survive. It's called the pragmatic approach. Come, let's look at the Fair Falls.'

The torrents of water dashed away from beneath their feet like a suicide's desperate jump. Sunlight played on the corner of Marjorie's Pool: they could both hear the high mourning sound of the water in the rocks, the voice of the Prince's lost love.

'You're very brave to come here among us like this,' said Ossian suddenly. He spoke in a low voice, but she could still hear him above the waters. 'Aren't you afraid of the passions you might stir up? As that waterfall stirs the dark waters of Marjorie's Pool.'

'There were passions enough before my arrival.'

'True enough. But perhaps there was a kind of balance, evenly matched forces—' He broke off. 'Jemima, I don't want to say more at the present time, but I do want you to be very careful whom you trust. Even the best of us, the good ones, can come to believe that the end justifies the means. Things here are seldom all they seem. I have a feeling that, coming from your world of television, sophisticated as it may be, and don't forget I'm no stranger to it—' he smiled as though in pleased personal tribute to his own publicity-seeking image – 'you may trust too much to appearances.

'Take our evening at Kilbronnack, the dinner party for the Princess. Perhaps you saw Colonel Henry only as the ideal of the handsome laird, Ben his dashing son, Rory the quiet good sort, Kim the charming young boy and so forth. Don't forget that the Glen has also brought forth the hysteria of Clementina Beauregard, the bitterness of Aeneas Stuart, to give only two obvious examples. If this were a television programme – and once again I'm by no means averse to these things – appearances would be everything. But we are far from television, are we not, in this particular closed-in valley? Besides, there is such a thing as the manipulation of appearances, is there not, even through the ever-truthful medium of television?'

He was teasing her. 'If you were to make a programme about me, for example – and don't let us rule it out for a minute by the way, the eve of the next election would suit me best, just outside the electoral period, suggested title "The Tales of Ossian Lucas", all aspects of Highland society – if you were to do that, do you not think I would manipulate my own appearance? Beginning but not ending with my wardrobe, I should certainly try.'

'And I should certainly try to stop you,' replied Jemima with spirit. Still, 'The Tales of Ossian Lucas' was not to be rejected totally; it might be nice to get something positive out of her Highland holiday, weird experience as it had turned out to be.

Ossian Lucas had become serious again.

'I warn you: there's something going on in this glen, something dark and primitive working itself out. I'm not even sure about it myself yet. You could be hurt. Come, let's see the shrine.'

He took her arm and gave a light push. Jemima gasped. Ossian immediately steadied her. 'You see what I mean? You too could be hurt as Charles was and Bridie was. You nearly slipped on the bridge just now. Be careful. Watch your step.' His words gave an extraordinarily sinister impression. 'Go back to London,' he said, 'before it's too late.'

Then they walked in silence down the soft path to the shrine. Something red and fiery glowed there through the Gothic windows. Jemima stepped inside. Beneath the shrine to Charlotte Clementina Stuart was a bunch, an enormous bunch, of blooming red roses.

She touched the petals, damp and velvety.

'Why, they're quite fresh,' she said in a startled voice.

'So they should be,' Ossian's voice came from directly behind her. She turned round. His figure filled the doorway, another pattern of red against the bright light.

'I only put them there this morning. The dew was still on them. Don't you like red roses?' His tone was mocking.

'Not particularly, as it happens.' She added, 'And it seems rather an inappropriate gesture to come from you.'

'Oh, do you think so?'

'Don't you?'

'Hardly. As a loyal member of the Red Rose, I find it very appropriate indeed.'

There was a long silence between them.

'I warned you, Jemima Shore, things up here are seldom all they seem,' said Ossian Lucas at length.

'I was beginning to guess,' she began in rather a faint voice. 'Your appearance just now. So timely. I'll alter my charge. I find you a very inappropriate member of the Red Rose.'

'Why so?' Against the light she could scarcely discern his face above its frilly shirt, but she suspected that his lips were still curving in that Pan-like smile. The long narrow bony face and curly fair hair were hidden. 'The local MP and all that. Why, you're not even from these parts!' she exclaimed. In her nervousness, she was aware that she had uttered two contradictory statements. 'Where *are* you from?' she demanded in her most brusque interviewing manner. 'You really can't get away with having "mysterious origins" in this day and age.'

'Jemima Shore, Investigator, is back, I see,' commented Ossian. He was quick to see and mimic her change of manner.

'My dear girl,' he went on, most blandly, 'but of course you're quite right. My origins are not particularly mysterious to me – though I may

choose to present them as such to the rest of the world. If I told you –
with perfect truth – that I, not Henry Beauregard, was the real
descendant of Sighing Marjorie and Bonnie Prince Charlie, would you
find me an appropriate member of the Red Rose then?'

'The baby,' stammered Jemima, 'drowned in the river by the soldiers.
Or rescued and brought up to marry a Beauregard.'

'Neither,' said Ossian. 'Nonsense – both stories. A child there was, a
daughter Mary, as a matter of fact, brought up not far from here by
foster parents and married later to a man called Lucas. I have the
documents to prove it by the way, if I so wished. But for the time being
I don't.'

'But Charlotte Clementina – the memorial on the island – she
couldn't have been *invented.*'

'Oh, she existed all right. There was no need to invent her. A Stuart
cousin, orphaned at Culloden as so many were, brought up by her
relations – where was the drama in that? She may even have been the
Prince's god-daughter, hence the choice of names. She exists all right in
the Beauregard family tree.

'Her father was a Stuart, probably Marjorie's cousin, since everyone's
related up here, but there is no direct connection with Eilean Fas.
Getting back to my Mary Lucas who really did have royal blood – she
was of course illegitimate. The marriage story is equal nonsense. Can
you imagine a Prince in desperate straits bothering to marry some
obscure Scottish girl? About the only chance left to him was to make
some rich and grand continental marriage.'

'Then the Beauregards – how on earth did they get the idea?' Jemima
felt herself to be quite bewildered. The folly, the legend, the claims of
the Red Rose, where did it all fit in?

'The answer to that, my dear,' said Ossian Lucas with a laugh, 'is
really quite simple. A mixture of two common Highland failings of the
past, self-aggrandizement and self-deception. I'm not sure they could
even be described as failings at a time when life was so hard hereabouts
that survival at any price was the local motto. Plus a strong dose of
American romanticism in our own day, to provide the finishing touches
to the mixture.

'You see, for a long while after Culloden and the '45, everything
round here was in complete chaos, with punitive government measures,
estates forfeited and all the rest of it. Somehow, towards the end of the
eighteenth century, when times got better, the Beauregards emerged
not only with Castle Tamh and a good deal of the Glen restored to
them, and Kilbronnack House which they owned already, but also
Eilean Fas, the missing part of the Glen. It rounded off the property

and they had long coveted it. In the nineteenth century, a more orderly period, it was necessary to explain exactly how this had come about and the answer was simple: Charlotte Clementina Stuart must obviously have been the Eilean Fas heiress. And that made her the missing daughter of Sighing Marjorie, and that gave the Beauregards royal blood as well as a proper claim to the island. The royal blood side of it was all very vague and pleasant and word-of-mouth to the Victorian Beauregards: they gave their children Stuart names like Charles Edward and Henry Benedict, but the property was what mattered.

'And then of course Leonie Beauregard came along and in one of her mad fits of enthusiastic refurbishment and sorting out and clarifying, which she applied to the whole Castle and the Estates, decided to get the whole thing down between hard covers. Including her own ingenious – or perhaps ingenuous would have been a better word – theory of the marriage, which had certainly never been mentioned before. She it was who put up this folly, copied in the original style of the house, and the plaques. Naturally the story of the marriage was meat and drink to the Red Rose, it provided them with a proper monarch of their own, right here in Glen Bronnack. In a way I rather admire the taste for fantasy in them all, from the Victorian Beauregards' clever legalization down to Charles Beauregard's exotic pretensions to be King of Scotland. Without, I'm afraid, being able to share it.' He looked down at himself, the velvet trousers whose hem was now bedraggled with grass and dew. 'My clothes express my only taste for fantasy I prefer it that way.'

'But that changes everything!' cried Jemima She suddenly realized that Ossian even looked quite like his royal ancestor, a less handsome but also a less effeminate version. It was the resemblance which had teased her in the drawing room of Kilbronnack House that night before dinner, gazing at the portrait.

'Does it?' answered Ossian in his quizzical style. 'I find it changes absolutely nothing so far. Nothing about the state of Scotland, which is what happens to interest me Of course,' he added, 'it is true that Eilean Fas actually belongs to me, as the only living descendant of Sighing Marjorie, not to the Beauregards. If I chose to claim it, that is.'

17
Remember me

As Ossian and Jemima walked slowly back up the path towards the house, there was a violent thrashing in the undergrowth beside them.

Jemima screamed and clutched Ossian's arm. Then she regretted it: there were too many shocks, that was all. A deer, small, graceful, with little pointed ears and antlers, leaped across the path just in front of them.

'A roe,' said Ossian briefly. 'I wonder who or what put it up.' He did not seem surprised.

'Colonel Henry tried to kill one my first day here,' said Jemima more calmly than she felt. 'He told me they ate the tops of the young trees.'

'But there are no young trees at Eilean Fas, except the self-seeded ones,' replied Ossian. 'Nothing planted since Leonie Beauregard died here. Henry Beauregard just believes in extinguishing things which may get in his way for the principle of the thing.'

Jemima said nothing.

There was more noise among the leaves and bracken.

'Ah, so it was you,' continued Ossian. A dog bounded towards them, as though in very slow pursuit of the vanished deer.

It was Jacobite. As they came in sight of the house, a Land-Rover was seen to be standing there: Colonel Henry's.

'It seems that you have a caller,' said Lucas in an expressionless tone. 'I'll be off. I have a meeting tonight. No, not the Red Rose. My constituents: the above-board lot. They're really all my constituents of course. I shall discuss a Scottish assembly and all that sort of thing, wisely and sagely.'

'Is it wise to be quite so sure that I won't give you away?' she enquired. It was the first question she had asked him out there at the shrine: 'How do you know I won't give you away.'

'Two reasons, my dear.' He touched her cheek. There was something strong but sexless about his personality, as if his masculinity was held in abeyance by other stronger needs and interests.

'First, you're curious. An observer. A journalist. It's in your nature. You want to investigate mysteries – no, I'm not just punning on your series – you really do, I recognize it in you, above all you want to be in on things. Second, rather more practically, you have absolutely nothing to gain by so doing. I doubt if you could even prove it – I've kept my tracks pretty well covered, you may be sure, and Aeneas, Lachlan and Co. would never give me away; even the Colonel himself, don't forget, begged you not to interfere between himself and the Red Rose.'

'Oh, that's his heroism,' said Jemima. '*Brother Raiders* and all that. I'm no heroine. You may do harm—' she began.

'We did you no harm. As a matter of fact we've never done anyone any harm.'

'Aren't you forgetting Hurricane Sophie?' she asked pointedly.

'Oh, that. Threats and counter-threats. A few slogans and counter-slogans. The brave little Princess, blue eyes popping, chin held high against the Highland fiends ... That made everyone happy, including the *Daily Express* which gave it a headline. And of course as a publicity lover, it made HRH very happy indeed. I happen to know that she had no objection. There was never the remotest chance of action.'

'But they actually grabbed Colonel Henry, they tied up Ben—'

'Kidnapping Colonel Henry wasn't a bad idea except that they bungled it. One might have asked a ransom or at least got some nice anti-laird publicity. Tying up Ben was pointless and to involve you was ridiculous.'

'But will the Red Rose *never* do any harm?' she pressed him.

'I very much doubt it,' he said. The words were cynical, but Ossian Lucas sounded calm rather than cynical. 'Not the Red Rose itself: it's a gallant body of men, when all's said and done, just as gallant as the Beauregard brothers in their own way, romantics all, with their signs and signals and passwords and their Queen, and before that their King. The absurdity of it all,' he went on. 'Who wants to be a king? No, that's not where the power lies, in the empty shadow of royalty. What power did that little Princess have the other night? A minor royalty, a cousin of the monarch, daughter of a dunderhead duke, good for opening a dam or two, or closing down a regiment. Henry Beauregard the laird has more power up the Glen now that he's inherited it than HRH Princess Sophie of Cumberland has in the whole of Great Britain.

That's why I'm interested neither in my royal blood, nor in my claim to Eilean Fas. Neither can forward my own cause in the slightest.'

'Power is what interests you?'

'Precisely. True power. Not the myth of it, the outward show. As a member of the Red Rose I keep an eye on my most obstreperous constituents, consolidate my own position up here and whichever way the wind blows for Scotland in the future, why, I'm ready to blow with it. Either as the guerrilla turned statesman or the politician turned nationalist leader, depending on your point of view.'

'You're a wise man,' she said sarcastically. 'And a worthy Chief of the Red Rose.'

'Ah, my dear,' replied Ossian Lucas, adjusting his wide lily-patterned collar with perfect aplomb. 'You do me too much honour. I never for one moment said I was the Chief, did I? I am indubitably *not* the Chief of the Red Rose, as it happens. Now that really would be indiscreet. A nationalist leader in good time – yes. A guerrilla leader at the present time – no. But if you did know the identity of the present Chief, you would certainly understand for the first time, if I dare make the comment, how things really work in this part of the world.'

He would not be drawn further from this, to Jemima, both irritating and enigmatic remark.

'Oh no, my dear, I've sworn the most exotic oath, full of Gaelic words, of whose meaning frankly I didn't have the faintest idea. It would be most dangerous to break it under the circumstances; one might be turned into a toad, or even a crofter or something.' And from this maddeningly frivolous point of view he refused to budge.

In revenge, and to herself, Jemima wondered whether the genuine Red Rosers and their mysterious Chief were not more attractive than this ambivalent man – born losers as they might turn out to be. Ossian Lucas, as he had indicated, was a survivor. He could not, and therefore would not, lose.

Now, standing before the house, the MP prepared to jump into his own car with a wave through the window to the Colonel, but Henry Beauregard was gesticulating at him.

'We'd better go in then,' said Lucas. 'But don't forget what I said—'

'I won't betray you. Yet. Never fear. You're right. There's nothing to be gained, so long as the Red Rose steers clear of violence.'

'Oh, it's not *that*,' Ossian shrugged off his dual roles – and who knew, maybe there were more – with indifference. 'Don't forget. Trust those least who are above suspicion. It's a good motto.'

Inside the house, Colonel Henry looked wonderfully spruce; he had all but finished his own bottle of malt whisky. He was wearing an immaculate dark suit of the kind which hung so well on his tall figure. His handsome silvered head was held high, chest thrust out. It was in fact the suit in which Jemima had first seen him – his funeral suit.

But on this occasion it proved to be his London suit. Henry Beauregard was off that evening on the overnight sleeper to London.

'Flying visit. Business meetings. Back in the morning. Sleepering both ways.'

'It's called doing a Colonel Henry in these parts,' observed Ossian *sotto voce.* 'He has lunch with his current lady friend, does his business and is back after two nights in a train looking a great deal fitter than you and me. He thinks Edith won't notice anything if he doesn't actually spend the night in London.'

To say that Jemima felt chagrin was a mild estimation of her feelings. Wearily, she remembered that this was the man who had left her in the middle of the night for the lure of a family signal. Would it always be so? she wondered with childish disappointment; money, land, the island, the Glen, coming before . . . she stopped. She did not know how to finish the sentence. After all, what did she represent to Colonel Henry? She had not yet had even the briefest time to find out. A phrase from a long-buried programme, one of her first independent ventures, about South America, came back to her. Some handsome gaucho had told her that on the pampas the motto was *Primero el cavallo, después la doña.* First the horse, then the woman. In the Highlands, the same motto seemed to apply, roughly translated as: First the land, then the lady.

Jemima wondered if Colonel Henry had altogether forgotten that Saturday was her birthday, that he had promised to take her on an expedition—

'And I'll be able to buy a birthday present in London,' said Colonel Henry with a charming smile. 'That's really why I'm going. Nothing worthy of you in Kilbronnack.'

'There's always Robbie Mack's Tartan Shop,' suggested Ossian. 'The pride of Kilbronnack.' His voice was not without malice.

'On the contrary, I was thinking of Burlington Arcade.' And with that the Colonel dismissed the subject. In his usual slightly mocking manner, Ossian then made his farewells and left the island.

'What *about* the Red Rose?' she began as soon as he had gone. 'What about Clementina, the guns?'

'The Red Rose!' snorted Colonel Henry. 'We sorted them out pretty quickly, I can tell you. Sent over Jamie Mackay and the men. That soon sent them packing, vanished – the lot of them – at the hint of authority, just as they did at the church. I doubt if we shall see much more of

Aeneas Stuart up here. Had the cheek to tell me he had got some job in an American university as a lecturer! Can you beat it? Damned Red. I've a good mind to tip them off. I've still got a few contacts in the military intelligence. At least it's not *our* money that's paying him. Bloody fools, the Americans.'

Colonel Henry clearly derived some gloomy satisfaction from the notion of Aeneas Stuart subsidized by a campus in the United States.

'And Lachlan?'

'Ah, Lachlan. Going to work on the rigs, I hear. He'll earn a fortune. But he'll be back one day, I'll be bound. He was born in the Glen. He could never keep away long from the Glen. Let that be. I've still got a score to settle with Master Lachlan. Let him come back with his ridiculous Red Roses and see what kind of welcome he gets.'

Jemima thought that Lachlan probably would return; but as Ossian had predicted, it would be under a new if equally romantic banner, the Black Thistle, the Red Lion. No doubt he would once again be defeated by Colonel Henry – up Glen Bronnack at least.

She forbore to point out that by the same token Aeneas too, son of Young Duncan and the housemaid Ishbel, would be back one day to re-engage the Beauregards. She was less certain about the outcome of that particular struggle: but perhaps the next contest would turn out to be between Aeneas and Lachlan.

'Their Chief,' she began uncertainly. 'They talked of their Chief.'

'Oh, talk, talk,' Colonel Henry airily dismissed the subject. 'Told my niece Clementina that if she didn't behave herself I'd have her certified,' continued Colonel Henry. 'Gave her a good fright. Then I left a couple of men with her to stand guard and stop the Castle being used in future as a refuge for those kind of ruffians. Edith'll go over later and calm her down – woman's work – and all that. Besides, old Edith has got to organize the move into the Castle sooner or later; she'll hate leaving Kilbronnack House no doubt after all these years, and her garden. Still,' he brightened, 'plenty of scope for gardening at the Castle. For one thing the rose garden. Get rid of those bloody red roses. Oh yes, Edith will be much too busy to mope.'

'Poor garden-loving, mope-forbidden Edith,' thought Jemima, but the Colonel was still pursuing his own line of thought.

'No, we shall hear no more of the Red Rose in these parts, I can assure you.' He sounded extraordinarily confident.

'Look – on your birthday, I thought we might have a picnic for you, here at Eilean Fas, with Edith and the boys, and then a sort of private stalk afterwards. It's a game we used to play when they were small. Stalking round the island. Someone suggested we should do it again.

Father Flanagan, as a matter of fact, put it to Edith. It turns out August 30th *is* her birthday. Wouldn't that be jolly?'

'Awfully jolly,' said Jemima in her most polite voice.

'I'll get Ossian, even ask Clementina. Heal the breach. Good idea? Blood is thicker than water and so forth.' There was a vague quality of embarrassment about his remarks. Jemima suspected the influence of Father Flanagan.

And that, it seemed, was that.

The island became very quiet again while Colonel Henry was away. It returned to its feeling of Paradise. Although Jemima never quite got over her fear of the house. 'Rest, rest, perturbèd spirit,' she thought of Leonie Beauregard. But the house still seemed to her melancholy, obscurely evil.

She wrote to Guthrie Carlyle in answer to a long letter from him, and found that she had nothing much to say except to thank him for feeding Colette in her absence. She missed Colette and thought that it would be nice to enjoy her cool undemanding company at Eilean Fas; she no longer felt the same about Guthrie Carlyle.

She received three visits from Ben, Hamish and Kim Beauregard respectively. They came, with a nice sense of hierarchy which seemed appropriate to their family structure, in order of age.

Ben suggested wistfully once again that a programme about the Beauregard Estates ... He also suggested taking her out in London. Despite his good looks, Jemima remained non-committal. She felt that one Beauregard in her life – if indeed he was in her life and not rattling to and fro in a sleeper 'doing a Colonel Henry' – was enough.

Hamish Beauregard did not suggest taking her out. He arrived with Jacobite. He was extremely polite but, like his appearance, his conversation was stolid rather than exciting. In fact the whole purpose of his visit was a little mysterious to her. He related various anecdotes – not in themselves very interesting to her   about pigeon-shooting with his brother Rory in the woods round Eilean Fas whenever both happened to be up in the Glen at the same time. It was only as he was leaving, and she was thanking him for his call, that he suddenly blurted out quite abruptly a remark about duty. Didn't she think it was difficult at times to know where one's duty lay? He was half inside the Land-Rover. It seemed a singularly inappropriate moment to discuss duty. His head bent over the steering-wheel, he said:

'If one knew something, something horrible about someone one knew, a little thing, but it might be a big thing really, if one thought about it, the more one thought about it, the more one might wonder, one might think one ought to do something?' The 'ones' and 'someone' and Hamish's peculiar upper-class circumlocutory manner of expression made it almost impossible to understand what he was talking about; but it was possible to understand that he was worried, under strain. He ended quite abruptly with a simple question: 'How long have you known my cousin Clementina, Miss Shore?' then immediately and hastily brushed his own question aside and put the vehicle in gear.

'Why don't we talk?' Jemima felt that it was her own duty to suggest at least that, despite her need to get back into the house, to be alone.

Hamish straightened up and smiled a sweet boyish smile.

'Oh, I'm probably imagining things,' he said. 'Pure imagination. I don't know why I'm going on like this.'

But after he left, Jemima reflected that he did not seem to her the sort of person who would easily imagine things. Long afterwards she wished she had pressed Hamish Beauregard further at just that tiny instant of his weakness, and not allowed her own selfish desire for solitude once again to prevail, to permit his departure.

Kim Beauregard's visit was altogether more pleasant and straightforward. For one thing he proved the most tremendous chatterbox. He arrived on his bicycle and left half an hour later having eaten and drunk most of the supplies in the house, without ceasing to talk except to take an occasional breath between food and gossip. The sulky teenager in his jabot of the royal dinner party was quite absent. Jemima learnt a great deal from Kim, including the nature of the projected private stalk on Saturday.

'It's a game we play on Mum's birthday. Father Flanagan invented it. Stalking Dad,' he explained. 'Otherwise known as the Getaway, getting away from Mum, that is, with all her fussing over the picnic things and food and not getting Dad into too much of a bait and us now drowning ourselves and shooting ourselves. It's terrific: this is the first year we've been allowed to play it on Eilean Fas – oh, since Aunt Leonie did herself in. You see she did herself in on a picnic. And cousin Charles found her. I wasn't born then of course, I'm known as The Afterthought, but Bridie told me about it afterwards.' Jemima shivered and quickly changed the subject.

Apart from that, life on Eilean Fas was calm; Father Flanagan, for example, could not exactly be classed as a visitor, since he paid no actual visit. But during an afternoon stroll to the Fair Falls Jemima did glimpse once again the tall black figure of the priest on the opposite bank as she had done during her first tour of the island.

Once again she had the impression that he was gazing covetously at the green and private territory. On this occasion he did not wave but turned away, the shape of his dark soutane gradually disappearing amidst the trees. The noise of the water drowned all other sounds and had the effect of making the odd little episode like something out of a silent film.

On Saturday morning Jemima had a fourth visitor in the shape of Colonel Henry himself. He arrived very early in the morning before she was awake and came straight upstairs.

She said, very sleepily, from the bed, 'What is it?' In her dream someone was calling her, time to dress, go to Megalith House, record the programme, time to get up, yet she was asleep.

'Your birthday present. As promised.'

'You?'

'And that's not all. Look.' She raised herself on one elbow. He had placed an enamel box in the shape of a heart on her pillow. She read the two words: *Remember Me.* The lettering was curly and held aloft on the lid by two cupids.

'Remember you,' she said some time later, when the room was once more scattered with masculine clothes thrown down in a way which she was beginning to think was actuated not so much by amorous passion as by the natural arrogance of one who was sure someone else would pick them up. 'Yes, I'll certainly remember you.'

Remember me. In this house Leonie Beauregard, his former mistress, had died. Did he remember her? There were so many memories here, around her, near her. For one instant the message, the pretty charming little birthday message painted on the enamel box, struck her as sinister.

'Will you remember *me*?' she asked fiercely.

'Till my dying day,' replied the Colonel. But he was already hunting around the room crossly for his clothes as though someone should really have come into the room and tidied them while he was in bed. 'Till my dying day. That's a promise.' His tone was debonair, preoccupied.

But his words did not reassure her. She felt the ghost of the past suddenly most present between them.

18
Outdoor manœuvre

There were no rainbows on the Wild Island that day; Jemima had hoped for one on her birthday. There was no rain either: but the weather on the birthday picnic lost the brightness it had retained since morning at exactly the moment that Colonel Henry proposed a toast to Jemima in champagne.

There was one bottle. Previously the 'boys' had drunk beer, Colonel Henry whisky and Jemima and Ossian Lucas white wine. Now Colonel Henry distributed the champagne according to some clearly ordained notion of precedence. A full glass for Jemima, a full glass for himself, a full glass for Ossian, half a glass for Ben (the heir), for Clementina (a lady), correspondingly smaller amounts for the rest of his sons, down to a mere drop for Kim (with a frown from Rory). Nothing for Father Flanagan. Nothing for his wife.

'Edith does not drink.'

Lady Edith smiled apologetically as though this was in some way her fault. She was busy clearing away the remains of the cold grouse which, together with smoked salmon, had constituted the feast. The salmon, caught and smoked on the Estate, was very good indeed, much better than that presented in London by Guthrie. But the grouse had been despatched north by those sporting sons who were currently missing, from more productive moors than those pertaining to the Beauregards. Jemima was ticked off by Kim for feeding pieces of abandoned grouse to the dogs: it was apparently the wrong thing to do, because of the splintery nature of the bones. Otherwise the picnic itself had been without incident except for a suddenly erupting fight between Flora and Jacobite.

The language of dogs was incomprehensible to Jemima. One

276

moment both animals, identically golden, were lying placidly. The next, hair risen on the scruff of the neck, they were growling and fighting, aiming literally at each other's throats (the old cliché was true). Jemima could only assume the dogs carried through the feud within the Beauregard family.

Colonel Henry separated them, coolly and rather crossly, with some well-aimed kicks, saying, 'Clementina, Edith, control your dogs.' He seemed to think their ferocious behaviour was nothing to do with him.

Now he repeated, draining the bottle of champagne into his own glass, 'Edith doesn't drink.'

'She *does*,' said Kim in a fierce voice, 'Mum does drink. Besides, it's her birthday. She ought to have some champagne.' He glared, not at his father but at Jemima as though she were in some way responsible for abrogating his mother's birthday. As usual, Lady Edith bent herself to hushing him. Colonel Henry said nothing. All the same, the moment for Jemima was spoiled, just as the weather had clouded and darkened.

'Rain?' Ben looked at Rory.

'More like the Haar will come up from the river.'

Clementina shivered. She was wearing a cheesecloth top, and the long patchwork skirt she had worn on the occasion of their first meeting. She wore no shoes. Her feet were white and small on the damp green grass. She looked extremely beautiful but fragile When Ben put his kilt jacket round her shoulders, she did not object After a bit she put it on, looking more delicate than ever, swallowed up in the rough tweed material.

'If the mist comes up, perhaps we should cancel the stalk,' suggested Lady Edith. 'You might all get lost' Colonel Henry looked sharply at his wife, then at Jemima and smiled. He gave the impression that the idea of a mist or Haar on the island, in which people might lose themselves, was not totally unacceptable to him.

'Of course we must have the stalk!' cried Kim. 'The Haar will make it better, not worse. A ghostly figure will loom out of the mist and before you know where you are you'll be dead! Much more exciting.'

'Ugh, how horrible,' exclaimed Clementina.

'Oh, not really dead,' said Kim impatiently. 'Don't you remember the rules? *Named* dead Clementina, I name you, you are dead.' He began to wave his hands in front of Clementina's face in a ghoulish manner.

'The position of Eilean Fas, lying in the river bed, means that you can get those incredible mists, quite local, during the warm weather; something to do with two bands of air meeting each other. They can last for days when the rest of the world, even the rest of the Glen, is bathed in sunshine,' Rory explained politely to Jemima.

'I always think the charm of our dear Scottish weather is its changeability,' Lady Edith threw in.

'It's true,' said Clementina, 'you can look out of the windows of Castle Beauregard and find the Wild Island has quite vanished from one moment to the next.'

'I don't think we should stalk if it gets too thick,' Ossian Lucas spoke languidly but with conviction all the same. 'I agree with Lady Edith. It could be dangerous. Someone could blunder over the cliff edge.'

'Oh, nonsense. We've all been playing this game since childhood.' Ben sounded quite angry.

'Miss Shore hasn't, said Rory.

'That she hasn't,' Father Flanagan threw in grimly. The inference of his remark was quite plain: Jemima was a stranger in their midst. Up till now the priest had maintained a somewhat grumpy silence throughout the picnic. His birthday present to Jemima, proffered with a fierce aside – 'Ye may like to glance at this or again ye may not' – consisted of the current parish circular of St Margaret's. It included a passage from the Bible which, by coincidence or otherwise, happened to be the story of the woman taken in adultery. Jemima had a feeling that Father Flanagan's own approach to such a situation would have smacked more of the Old Testament than the New.

'Exactly,' said Ossian Lucas. Jemima got the distinct impression that camps were forming: Ben was keen on the stalk; Rory not. Kim dead keen; Hamish, who had evidently recovered from his fit of neurosis earlier in the week, keen as mustard, judging from his sole sporting comment – 'Jolly good fun if somebody does go over a cliff!' Lady Edith was increasingly and openly worried about the consequences to her brood; Father Flanagan, despite Lady Edith's plaints, had become obstinately for, as though determined to spite Jemima. Clementina Beauregard, who throughout the picnic had remained perfectly pleasant but passive, as though drained of all her frenzy by the recent events at the Castle, showed no signs of trying to make such a difficult decision. Ossian Lucas was positively against. But Colonel Henry was for, and in the end, as usual, it was his will which prevailed.

He explained the rules of the stalk briefly but lucidly. Looking at him standing over the picnic scene – they were on one of the neglected terraces below the house, quite near the river – Jemima thought that this was how he must have briefed his men in those far-off heroic days of *Brother Raiders*. The same notion struck Clementina, who came to life for the first time.

'Uncle Henry, you sound so military,' she giggled. Her voice had changed slightly, very slightly but perceptibly. Jemima, becoming alert to her moods, looked at the cigarette in her fingers; at some point she had swapped a Rothman's for the familiar small white stub.

Colonel Henry was to be the focus of the stalk, designated as the Prey. All those present were his stalkers. Like a stag, he was aiming for sanctuary, in this case sanctuary being the Gothic shrine at the other end of the island. He would set off shortly from the terrace, being given fifteen minutes to get away and conceal himself. In order to kill the Prey, the stalkers had to touch him, the conventional words being: 'Colonel Henry Beauregard, you are my Prey!' But they had to do this unobserved, since in this hunt at least the stag also had the right to turn on his attackers. Unlike the stalkers, the stag did not have to touch to kill. If the Prey merely spotted any of his stalkers and was able to name them correctly, then that stalker was held to be dead, killed by the stag.

'How long does it all last?' enquired Jemima.

'Ages,' answered Kim gleefully. He was definitely the most enthusiastic member of the stalking party.

'The Prey must reach sanctuary by dark. He has to make a run for it then, if he hasn't got there already,' explained Colonel Henry. 'I should explain that there's a fifty-yard radius round the shrine where the stalkers can't lurk and the Prey can't hide. Once he enters it, he has to belt for sanctuary. The stalkers have to stalk him properly, up hill and down dale – I can safely promise you a great deal of exercise.' He smiled at Jemima again. 'There are all sorts of dips and caves at the top of the island. You can get quite lost in the bracken too. I've every intention of hiding myself for a good long time.'

'We can't wait till dark in this weather,' Ossian spoke softly but firmly.

'We're guid Scots – the most of us. We'll not mind a drop of moisture', was Father Flanagan's typically gruff contribution. But he found no further support. Even Ben, an advocate of the stalk, joined in on the other side.

'Yes, Dad,' agreed Ben. 'It's much better if we have a fixed time.'

After some discussion and some slightly pettish flashing of his watch by Colonel Henry – 'Is this accurate enough for you? Gift of my brother officers when I got married' – the time of six o'clock was agreed. Colonel Henry did not like the idea of the afternoon's sport being cut short. Nevertheless by six o'clock, if the Prey had failed to reach the shrine, victory was to be declared to the stalkers.

But already dark was coming in the form of a thickening of the atmosphere. The mist had begun to roll up from the river just as Rory had predicted. The swirling clouds, light at first, but deepening, were grey: the effect was deadening, depressing, shutting out light, and reducing the colours of the island itself. The many greens became one rather dank green. The glimpses of yellow and purple – the wild flowers – the occasional brilliant berry were no longer prominent without the sunshine to pick them out. The house's dark Gothic shape loomed above them, floating out of the mist.

Quite soon the river itself vanished from view; but you knew the river was there from the perpetual sound of running water, the noise which never ceased on the Wild Island, and higher up too you could hear the soft roar of the Fair Falls plunging into the pool where Sighing Marjorie had perished ...

And Charles Beauregard.

Clementina. His sister – and his heiress. The warning; the mysterious Chief's warning: the girl's high voice repeating it from the telephone: 'I'm in danger, he says.' And Clementina was invited to Eilean Fas, taking part in the Beauregard family picnic for the first time in years. Wasn't it odd, after the incident of the Red Rose, how first Colonel Henry had genially invited her, then Ben had looked after her in such a courtly fashion? Clementina Beauregard, if she no longer owned the Castle in which she lived, was still an extremely rich young woman. Other words floated back: 'I'll give it all to the Red Rose ... If I die without children, half the money goes to the next owner of the Beauregard Estates, Uncle Henry or Ben ....' An appalling notion struck Jemima. Land itself was good, but land with money is better. Just who was the intended Prey of this delightful family game?

She dismissed it with horror at herself. But just as the stalkers began to move off, fifteen minutes after the Colonel's disappearance, his tall figure last seen striding away up the terraces into the mist, she heard Rory say urgently to someone beside him:

'You must stay close to Clementina. Don't lose her. Don't forget.' Jemima was not sure whether to be reassured or otherwise by this remark.

As the mist continued to thicken, she herself resolved very firmly if unadventurously to stay on the path and head in the general direction of the shrine. Let the young Beauregards scramble over the hill if they wished. As for stalking Colonel Henry, she had a strong inkling that he on the contrary would be stalking her.

Like their Prey, the stalkers vanished quickly. Afterwards Jemima would recall perfectly the exact order in which they left. Lady Edith, aided by a reluctant Kim, and followed by a now submissive Jacobite, left first to deposit the remnants of the picnic in the Land-Rover before setting off to join the stalk. They would go separately – Kim having brushed off Lady Edith's suggestion that they should stalk together for safety with a furious 'Oh, *Mum.*' Father Flanagan strode off too in the same general direction. Jemima personally felt relieved once the mist had swallowed up his tall black figure with its aureole of white hair. He had the air of a prophet going off into the wilderness – a prophet in a bad mood.

Hamish said, 'Dad mentioned going up the hill, didn't he? I think I'll follow.'

'Please yourself,' said Rory. 'Knowing Dad, he'll try to trick us. He'll expect us to go up the hill, so he'll lurk close to the house until the last moment. Then he'll dash very fast, over the hill towards the shrine, in order to make it before the deadline. He'll take the rest of us by surprise, kill us from behind, so to speak. No, I'll stay down by the terraces near the house, somewhere in the bushes.'

He went off.

Ben, like Rory, voted for exploring the hill but suggested searching the far side, away from the main path, where the cliffs were steepest.

'I've a notion there's a small cave on the underhang ... Worth a look.' He too set off, saying as he went, 'Coming, Clementina?' But she did not follow him, announcing her intention rather vaguely of going towards the Fair Falls 'because they are so pretty'.

Jemima was reminded briefly and nastily of Duncan's sons in *Macbeth*, dividing their ways for security after their father's death. But no death had yet taken place, had it? The Prey was still at large.

Jemima was left alone with Ossian Lucas. She half expected him to volunteer to stay with her. Instead he exclaimed, 'Henry and his absurd games! I'll just pad around and keep an eye on things.' And he too was gone.

Jemima was now aware that although it was not actually raining, the mist had brought a kind of dampness of its own into the air. Moist globules were forming on her face and clothes. She yearned for her Burberry and jeans. Her honey-coloured suède skirt and waistcoat were hopelessly impractical for a stalk. Nor did she fancy chancing her long suède boots, which she had not been able to resist displaying, in the island rough.

Of course it had been firmly laid down that the house itself was out of bounds to everyone.

'This is a bracing outdoor manœuvre, not a damned house party,' Colonel Henry announced. 'No one goes into the house without my express permission.' Jemima had been amused: he had evidently forgotten that she was the house's official tenant. Then she found Colonel Henry looking at her. He gave her a faint smile and lifted his eyebrows. So the gallant Colonel intended the house, not the bracken, as their rendezvous. Well, why not? Feeling rather reckless – besides, she refused to spend three hours combing the hill for a human stag – Jemima gave him a nod. Then she found that both Kim and Rory were looking at her. Kim was glaring again; Jemima felt slightly embarrassed.

Now she slipped rather furtively into the house to change her clothes. The rhododendrons near the house did not stir. She was fairly sure no one had spotted her.

The mist was not lifting. From her bedroom window she could see that even the first of the terraces was lightly swathed in it. The course of the river bed had become marked by a thick belt of fog.

Jemima threw the honey-coloured suit on the bed and began to pull on a black polo-necked jersey as rapidly as possible. It was while the jersey was over her head that she heard – or thought she heard – the sound of someone else in the house. Once her head had emerged, and she was zipping up her jeans, she heard nothing more. Muffled in the wool, it was difficult to be precise exactly what sort of noise it had been: a door shutting or banging somewhere? The front door? It seemed to come from that area. Once again there was complete silence. She did not feel frightened: but her instinct told her quite strongly that she was not, or had not been, alone in the house.

Surely no one else had cheated? She decided to leave the house herself as soon as possible and honourably join the stalk. Then she found the note: it was scribbled and only just legible. 'See you here in half an hour? H.B.B.' So it had been him.

Her heart lightened. Jemima was about to leave the house once more to join the stalk, when another faint sound attracted her attention. This time it indubitably came from the back quarters of the house.

19
The Prey

The back offices of Tigh Fas, if you could use such a house agent's term for them, were surprisingly extensive and even rambling. They lay beyond a communicating door which shut them off from the front area of the house. Besides the large old-fashioned kitchen with its temperamental Aga there were not one but two deserted pantries, with cracked brown wood surrounds to their sinks where now Formica would have been obligatory; a larder with a cooling grille to the outside world reminded Jemima equally of the pre-refrigerator age; finally there was another spacious room, furnished solely by a broken sofa out of which horsehair tumbled; this Bridie had described without batting an eyelid as 'the staff sitting room: a verra nice room indeed, getting all the afternoon sun'. Outside the back door there were a series of outhouses and sheds, some containing practical needs of the day like wood, some relics of the past like a child's bicycle and a pram without wheels.

To tell the truth, Jemima herself never penetrated much beyond the kitchen; she did not care for these forgotten service areas haunted not so much by people as by a vanished sybaritic way of life. Now she hesitated. It was possible that Colonel Henry, having deposited his note, had gone out the back way. Yet unless her imagination was playing tricks, she was fairly sure that some vague movement was still going on in the house.

Her curiosity got the better of her. She opened the communicating door slightly and listened. There was someone there   more than one person, for she could hear talking. So she was not the only member of the stalk to disobey Colonel Henry's instructions not to enter the house (other than the Prey himself). She would investigate; it was after all her house – rented.

Cautiously Jemima went towards the kitchen. It was empty. She was obliged to pad further down the corridor, until she was brought to an abrupt halt by the fact that the door of the so-called staff sitting room was open, and she could see inside.

Lachlan Stuart was standing there. He was wearing a thick jersey instead of the familiar t-shirt, with its flower stain. But he was holding an enormous bunch of roses of the most violent bright crimson in his arms. They must have been plucked from the castle garden. He was saying something about remembrance. He was not looking in Jemima's direction, but fixedly and rather angrily at someone else concealed from her view behind the door.

Jemima froze.

'Aye, I ken right well the Red Rose is no more,' he went on, his voice rising slightly. 'But someone must remember us; we must'na be forgotten. And seeing as she's from the television, she'll remember us. Not let the world forget us. Surely you don't want us forgotten, now: you're our Chief.'

There was a pause. Jemima could not hear what was said.

'You *were* our Chief, then! But to me and the others you're still our Chief,' countered Lachlan angrily.

There was some answer from the person hidden by the door, but Jemima could not hear it. Lachlan looked increasingly distressed and clutched the roses; but there was nevertheless an expression of reluctant obedience on his face. It reminded her of the incident at the funeral when he had been commanded to abandon the coffin. Finally he flung the roses furiously away and out of sight.

He muttered something which she could not hear and then said more strongly, 'I'll be off now, right. I'll be off to the rig. I know: I must'na be seen here now. Dinna worry, Chief, the Haar will cover me as I go.' He strode to the door. His hands were empty. He said defiantly and quite loudly into the room, 'Up the Red Rose! Captain Lachlan salutes the Chief,' sketched some gesture with his fist, and vanished out of the back door into the mist.

There was a movement inside the staff sitting room. Jemima suddenly and desperately felt that it was essential for her to know who the Chief of the Red Rose was — or rather had been. She had to see, and not be seen, to satisfy her own sense of completeness concerning the weird tale of the Red Rose.

She shrank back into the larder; the room was both dark and chilly, with no proper window, only its grille to the wooded bank outside. Footsteps approached, calm unhurried foot-steps. Jemima peered through the crack of the wooden door; the former Chief of the Red

Rose passed so near to her that she was afraid her breathing would be heard. But he did not look back.

She watched the tall figure of Rory Beauregard walk easily away down the corridor into the house beyond.

Immediately Rory was gone, Jemima tiptoed back into the staff sitting room and saw the abandoned roses on the floor. There was a white card attached to them. She picked it up and read: 'Farewell to Jemima Shore from the Red Rose. Remember us.' She dropped the card and left it lying with the flowers.

Then she sank onto the sofa with its broken springs.

Rory Beauregard. The quiet deep brother who travelled about mysteriously; Rory Beauregard, in his own way a second son just as his father had been. The second son, siding with his cousin against his elder brother as being the lesser of the two evils. The second son who would do anything to gain Eilean Fas and had presumably organized the Red Rose to that end. Land hunger or land passion once again lay at the heart of it all . . . As Ossian Lucas had said: If you knew who the Chief was and why, you would understand more about this part of the world than you do at the present time.

A vignette came to her: Rory Beauregard commanding Lachlan to abandon his plan for the coffin. The words of Lachlan, 'Mr Rory . . . ' Then he obeyed. Another vignette: Rory commanding his brother Kim to stop drinking, and Lachlan again at the Castle: 'You know how strong the Chief is against the drink.' Rory Beauregard: a silent determined man, determined not to stay in the secondary position to which he had been born.

The sofa's springs hurt her and reminded her that it was neither pleasant nor politic to remain inside the house. Time was passing. She would have to think about it all later; perhaps one day, with tact and circumspection, she could induce Rory to unbend and tell her everything. Now that really would be a programme worth making, even if he sat with his back to the camera, like a terrorist. In the meantime she really must join the stalk.

Jemima left by the back entrance of the house, as Lachlan had done, carefully inspecting the bushes surrounding it to make sure she was unobserved. She decided to set off down the path which led to the Fair Falls.

She knew that Clementina had gone that way because the girl had advertised the fact; Jemima might be able to keep an eye on her. It was true that it was also the most exposed route from the point of view of the stalker. There was no cover to the right of the path, where the hill began to ascend, only low scrub, and Jemima had no intention of cowering to the left, within dangerous reach of the cliff edge, even to avoid the Prey's piercing gaze. But she had every reason to suppose that the Prey would not 'name' her and thus 'kill' her even if he did see her. The Prey was expecting her, alive and well, back at Tigh Fas in the not too distant future. He had no reason to draw attention to her whereabouts.

She proceeded, as discreetly as possible, along the crunchy gravel path and turned down the silent mossy track which followed the contour of the island. How different the Wild Island looked now from that first idyllic ramble! It was all very well for Lady Edith to talk about 'our dear changeable Scottish weather', but the swiftness of the transformation from sunlit Paradise to Wagnerian haunt still amazed her.

There were the usual rustlings and bustlings in the undergrowth, but she guessed they were animal not human. She felt rather happy and, now, not the slightest bit alarmed. After all, compared to her usual solitude, she was surrounded by people, even if most of them were invisible; she was enjoying her birthday—

At which point someone screamed very loudly and sharply just ahead of her on the left. Then there was a splash. Then silence. Jemima ran forward. Somebody else broke cover from behind her. She did not pause to see who it was. After running about fifteen or twenty yards and stumbling slightly, she ran round a corner and slap into Clementina Beauregard who was sobbing and being comforted by Ben. Kim too had come from somewhere. Then Ossian Lucas joined them. Clementina was saying something like this:

'I tell you, I nearly fell in! I was pushed, shoved, I tell you, I nearly went over the bloody cliff! The actual log I was sitting on went in, didn't you hear it?'

'What happened exactly?' Ossian Lucas was breathing heavily but sounded calm as ever.

'I sat down. On a log. I decided to light a cigarette. I began to rummage in my handbag. Flora lay at my feet. The first thing I knew Flora was growling slightly and I knew someone was coming. Then a voice said in a whisper: "Clementina, I name you. You are dead." And then I was shoved, shoved from behind and shoved bloody hard.'

'D'you mean *Dad* shoved you? Why, that's impossible,' said Ben.

'I don't know who shoved me. That's the whole point.'

'I don't believe you were shoved at all,' exclaimed Kim.

'I never said it was Uncle Henry. But someone gave me a push. Whispered and then pushed.'

'You're exaggerating as usual, Clementina,' said Kim scornfully.

'It couldn't possibly have been Dad,' continued Ben in a worried voice. 'He's just named Hamish on the other side of the hill by the far cliff. We both spotted Dad and started to stalk him in the bracken. Hamish like an idiot lifted his head and Dad turned round and bagged him. So I skedaddled as fast as I could back through the bracken. Dad did try a long shot after me! "I name you, Rory. You're dead." But as I wasn't Rory, I naturally paid no attention. I've no idea where Rory was. Then I heard Clementina scream. So it couldn't have been Dad.' There was a pause. 'It couldn't have been Dad anyway,' Ben added rather belatedly.

'She's made the whole thing up as usual to get attention.' Kim remained contemptuous. 'I'm getting back on the trail. If Dad was by the cliffs, I'll trail him round the other way, giving the shrine a wide berth...'

In the absence of any visible proof of Clementina's ordeal, Jemima had to concede that Kim was probably right. Clementina was in a sufficiently nervous state to have imagined the incident. It was eerie in the mist, near the falls. The high sighing noise made by the rocks did not help matters. When Ben promised to stay close to Clementina for the rest of the stalk, Jemima decided it was time to back away. Perhaps she should retrace her steps; the time of the rendezvous was approaching.

As she reached the gravel path once more, she had the impression that the mist was receding somewhat: at any rate she could see the shape of Tigh Fas distinctly, black and church-like in its outline. In a way she would rather not have glimpsed it at that particular moment, since the familiar feeling of foreboding concerning the house returned more sharply than ever; surely a lady should be feeling joy at the idea of an encounter with her lover, on a romantic Scottish island?

It was more with the idea of galvanizing herself into appropriate feelings of joy, than with any real zest, that she ran up the house steps, through the open door (she must have left it open) and into the hall. There was silence. She heard a movement in the bedroom, then Jacobite came happily tumbling down the stairs, licking her hand gleefully and positively nipping – in a playful manner – at her jean-clad ankles, as though to shepherd her back up the stairs again. Resisting slightly and looking round, her eyes fell on a piece of paper on the hall table; for a moment she thought it was the original note. Then she read: 'I'm upstairs, H.B.B.' He was here!

In her relief, excitement filled her, happiness, and she ran with the dog, up the stairs, and threw open her bedroom door.

'Colonel Henry Beauregard, you are my Prey,' she began to say according to the traditional formula. The phrase was already out of her mouth, the word Prey dying away foolishly, desperately, on her lips, when she realized that the inhabitant of her bedroom was not in fact Colonel Henry.

'On the contrary, Miss Shore, it is you who are my Prey,' said Lady Edith Beauregard in her most pleasant manner. She might have been greeting a guest at Kilbronnack House. But she was standing by the large bed holding a double-barrelled shot-gun which was pointing directly and not at all shakily at Jemima's head.

20
Before you die

'I'm so glad you managed to come,' continued Lady Edith, the gun unwavering in her hands. 'I've been waiting for this. You see I'm going to shoot you like the other one. Like my sister-in-law Leonie. Isn't it odd,' she said with a fleeting smile, 'that was on my birthday too. But I'd have done it anyway. I'm awfully determined when I set my mind to anything. You have to be, when you have a family like mine to look after. The maternal instinct, you know. No, of course you don't know, do you? And now you never will.'

The sinister phrase struck a reminiscent note. 'The instinct, being perfected, can go awry. It can be turned towards evil . . .' Mother Agnes's letter, which she could see still lying on her dressing-table where she had left it. Oh, Mother Agnes, you who can see into the human heart. Not Colonel Henry, not Ben, not Rory – but all the time Edith the mother, the centre of it all.

Jemima felt quite frozen, numb. For one thing Lady Edith continued to talk in her familiar nervous voice, as though apologizing for some fault of whose exact nature she was unaware, while accepting without reservation the fact of her own culpability. The whole situation remained quite unreal. How could Jemima reconcile the fussy, placating personality of Lady Edith with the extraordinary revelations which were now – without hesitation – pouring from her lips?

But even as these revelations were being made, Jemima's mind at least gradually unfroze, and a series of terrible and telling points occurred to her.

Lady Edith babbling on about Leonie Beauregard, horrible, mad:

'She tried to break up the family, you see, so I had to do it, didn't I? Getting hold of my Henry like that.' But then she turned on Jemima:

289

'And that's why I'm going to kill you too, We're such a happy, happy family, you see. And Henry and I were really the perfect couple, everyone says so. Of course he has to have his little bit of fun from time to time, I do realize that you have to let men enjoy themselves in their own way, which isn't ours, don't you? You know what husbands are...'

She paused and gave a little laugh, apologetic as before.

'But how rude of me! You've never been married, have you, Miss Shore? So you don't know what husbands are.' She sounded for one instant quite spiteful, like an unkind child. 'Ladies in London, oh yes, I know all about that. Their letters, sent to the Estate Office, their calls when they think I'm out, their assumed voices when they find I'm in. Silly creatures. I know it all.

'But she was different, Leonie was different. She wanted him to marry her. And so she died. And afterwards we had Kim. That just shows how happy we were really. And you're different too, Miss Shore, and so you will shortly die too.'

'Why am I different?' whispered Jemima. She was ashamed to find that her voice had temporarily deserted her.

'Because you're so tempting, aren't you, Miss Shore? To a man of his age; my Henry isn't young any longer. But you make him feel young, I can see it: he looks more vigorous, he's happier, he laughs, he's even less impatient with me and the boys. Oh, I know. And you're clever and witty and everything he likes, not like those other fools, married women indulging their stupid passions. Why, you're not even married! You're quite quite free. Father Flanagan pointed it out to me in one of his talks. Oh yes, Miss Shore, you're far too tempting to be allowed to stay in the path of my Henry.

'Besides,' Lady Edith's voice never lost its affability as she spoke; 'besides, you came here. You came to Glen Bronnack. You came into our very own glen, I never allowed any of the others to come here. The glen belonged to us, to me, and the boys. But you brought it all here, your beauty and your brilliance, you polluted our beloved glen. You came to Eilean Fas on purpose. You wanted to seduce him. You could have had any man in the world, but you chose my Henry. It was all your fault. And I shall kill you here in the house where you did it.'

Jemima felt one single very strong pang of guilt.

Then she reminded herself that there had been other deaths. Ossian Lucas had spoken of the passions that she might stir up, as the waterfall stirred up the dark waters of Sighing Marjorie's Pool. But there had been other deaths before she arrived in the Glen to upset its primitive and precarious balance. Leonie Beauregard, Charles Beauregard...

Nevertheless, that single pang of guilt would remain with her, hidden but ineradicable: it was the voice of Mother Agnes, the voice of her conscience.

She turned her mind, deliberately, as coolly as she could muster, to investigate the truth of those other deaths. Charles Beauregard, drowned deep in the river, sucked down – what had happened to him, Jemima wondered, in cold appalled amazement. Tremble as she might, she noticed that Lady Edith's grip on the gun remained steady, even vice-like. Jemima made a very slight movement, hardly perceptible, in the direction of the door, still open behind her in the empty house where the mist was now beginning to float lightly in the very air of the interior. At once there was a furious growl, pronounced, minatory, from the dog beside her. She looked down.

'Yes, Jacko, hold her,' said Lady Edith sharply. 'Hold, boy. Now wait.' The dog obeyed her instantly. His teeth closed, without biting or tearing, on Jemima's jeans. He looked up at her, his eyes as soft, as brown, as apparently sympathetic as those of his mistress.

Jacobite. Not Flora but Jacobite. Not Clementina's dog, not Colonel Henry's dog, but Lady Edith's own dog. The well-trained dog; Duncan's words on their first meeting. 'She's wonderful with dogs, her ladyship, trains them herself.'

The details of another death came into her mind. Bridie Stuart, so devoted to Edith Beauregard – who suspected the murderer of Charles but said the truth would never pass her lips ... What had she seen, what had she known? The dog named by Duncan as Flora, seen near the bridge on the day of Bridie's death, the dog which might have knocked Bridie into the water. How easily that could have been Jacobite! The two dogs were identical, certainly at such a distance.

And Rory, the Chief of the Red Rose, trying to warn Clementina on the telephone. 'I'm in danger.' What had he known? Jacobite the bad, Flora the good dog. She had once mistaken the respective characters of Charles and his Uncle Henry Beauregard, making the wrong one good, the wrong one evil. Now she had done the same with the dogs.

She felt she had to know the truth. Jemima Shore, Investigator, might be about to end her days, her pretty telegenic face blown to pieces by a madwoman armed with a shot-gun. But she had to know the truth of those deaths.

'The others,' she began, when Lady Edith had finished her fearful disquisition. 'Your nephew Charles, Bridie ... ?' But Lady Edith was delighted to explain. Her characteristic anxiety, her air of wishing to justify herself, was macabre. She even managed to sound sincerely regretful about Bridie – 'I was awfully sorry about that, but you see it just had to be done to protect the family.'

She went on: 'My nephew Charles – well, you could hardly expect me to sit by, could you, while he inherited everything and my own lovely boys got nothing ? It was so easy; pretending to Charles that I wanted a rare bog plant growing just above the water line of the pool. I'm famous for collecting wild flowers round here: I knew he'd wade in and get it for me. Charles, in spite of everything,' she said brightly, 'had awfully nice manners. Oh, I knew he'd fall into the trap. We watched. He waded in immediately. And then: so dangerous, those great boots – the times I've warned my boys to take care. We looked after him.'

'We?'

'Jacko and I. Didn't we, Jacko boy? There's a good boy.' The great dog thumped his tail. 'A quick command, in he went, the good dog, swam out, and then so easy to pull a man down in those boots—'

'And Bridie saw you—'

'She saw the dog all wet and coming out of the river as she was bicycling over to Eilean Fas, from the bridge. She didn't know Charles was dead then. She thought it must be Flora. But she found Flora, dry, up at the house, waiting for Charles who never came back. Before she found the body in the river later Flora followed her down to the river and attacked her. So she knew the first dog must be Jacko. Where Jacko goes, I'm likely to be. And she began to put two and two together. She may even have seen me on the island. I was never sure.'

Jemima thought sadly: But Bridie would never have told what she knew. Lady Edith, after all those years, had not trusted her. How quickly evil – and madness – corrupts the mind.

'So I dashed out of the house on the afternoon of our little royal party, giving as an excuse that I needed Father Flanagan to make the numbers even. And good clever Jacko and I solved the problem of Bridie on that nasty slippery bridge.'

So many clues, thought Jemima. Jacobite – not Flora – seen by Duncan near the bridge on the afternoon of Bridie's death. Lady Edith apparently mismanaging the dinner party so that there was one man over, and actually coolly planning yet another murder to cover her tracks.

'Rory and Hamish did see me training Jacobite, in the woods round Eilean Fas, when they were out pigeon-shooting. But they had their guns with them and were busy arguing about who had just shot what. You know what boys are,' she added indulgently. 'I don't think they suspected anything. Sport means so much to them: why should they bother about what their silly old mother was up to?'

It was not the moment, thought Jemima, to point out that on the contrary both Rory and Hamish had been separately worried – if disbelieving – about what they saw. Rory, in his capacity as Chief of the Red Rose, had imagined that Clementina might be in some kind of danger and had warned her on the telephone. Hamish had paid his inarticulate visit to Jemima, somehow trusting that the magic powers endowed by television would enable her to sort out this mute appeal. The trouble was that the brothers had not consulted each other. The suspicion in each case had been too horrible to be given tongue – to another member of the family.

Lady Edith moved a little. The gun now rested on the brass bedrail. Jemima moved too. The dog growled. Jemima stopped moving.

'Time for you to join the stalk, Jacko,' said Lady Edith in an indulgent voice. 'We don't want them to find you here, do we? That would give the game away. Go on, boy, find him, find him.'

Instantly the great golden dog rose and padded out of the room. Jemima could hear him padding down the stairs and out of doors, onto the gravel and away.

'Would you have killed Clementina too?' Jemima put it in the past tense.

Lady Edith smiled warmly. 'I may.' She spoke in the future. 'All that money. After all I've got six hungry boys to provide for. Five, if you don't count Ben, who's provided for now as the eldest. But on the whole, no. Enough is enough. There will have been enough deaths – including yours,' she added. Her tone was wise and compassionate. Jemima was reminded of her first sight of Lady Edith in the church, a face once pretty, blurred by time, the only one showing emotion over the death of Charles Beauregard. Under the circumstances, it was no wonder that she had appeared moved, except that she had been moved by exultation, secret glee, not compassion. But who could ever tell what went on in the crazed murderous mind which lurked beneath the disarming façade of Lady Edith?

'But just now Clementina was pushed. A log fell in. She herself nearly fell in.' Jemima was puzzled. She found it difficult to work out how Lady Edith had managed to get back from the falls in time to greet her.

'Nearly,' repeated Lady Edith with complacency. 'Then that wasn't me at work, was it? I don't make mistakes, do I? You can't make mistakes when you've got a family to look after. I dare say that naughty Kim was teasing her; he told me he planned to give her a good fright for being so awful to his father in the church. That was why he was so keen on the stalk. I knew I could safely pretend to try and stop it; I could even ask Kim to stay with me for safety's sake. I knew he would never agree. He's such a handful, that boy! Being the baby, I'm afraid he's got a tiny bit spoilt. Still, a miss is as good as a mile, as we used to say in the nursery.'

The silly catch-phrase galvanized Jemima from the strange lethargy into which she had fallen.

'Anyway, Colonel Henry will soon be here to rescue me!' she cried. 'Your husband. I'm expecting him. What are you going to do about that?'

'Oh, please don't bother yourself about Henry,' answered Lady Edith. 'You see I wrote both those little notes to you myself. I don't have your brains, Miss Shore – you couldn't imagine silly old me on television for one moment, could you? – but one thing I can do is imitate Henry's writing quite well after all these years.'

A modest expression of satisfaction crossed her face. 'And I can even imitate your writing too. You wrote me such a sweet note after our little royal party,' said Lady Edith. 'So thoughtful. Such charming manners. It's ridiculous to say people in the press and television are always rude. I shall always remember how good your manners were. "Miss Shore had beautiful manners," I shall say. "Such a pity about her unfortunate death. Trying to handle a gun when she wasn't used to it. We shall never know quite how it happened, or why. We had all grown to love her – Henry, the boys and I. Such a lovely unaffected person."'

Her tone changed abruptly.

'Look, here's the suicide note you've written.' Lady Edith threw it on the bed with her left hand. Her right hand did not leave the gun's trigger. 'I am sure you'd like to see it. Before you die.'

Jemima leant forward and gingerly took the note from the bed. She read the first few words: 'I can't go on—' She had time to think with the beginnings of panic: 'But they'll never believe this, they won't, Guthrie, Cherry, it's impossible. I'm not like that. I'll tell them. But I won't tell them. It'll be too late, I'll be dead—'

There was a noise behind her on the stairs.

Lady Edith raised the gun. After that, Jemima could never be quite clear about the precise order of events. Lady Edith levelled the gun straight at Jemima. There was a small click – afterwards she realized that was the safety catch being released. Then:

'Edith, don't shoot!' The cry, loud, frantic, almost a bellow, came from directly behind her. It was Colonel Henry's voice. But later the noise of his voice and Lady Edith's own cry: 'No, Henry, not you,' would mingle in her memory with the explosion of the gun, thunderous, enveloping, the force of the explosion which seemed to knock her backwards, sideways. But which in fact turned out to be

Colonel Henry knocking her sideways, or possibly rushing in front of her or possibly throwing himself at his wife. She would never know for sure.

All she did know was that when all the noise was over – what seemed to be a million years later, but could only be seconds – she was picking herself up, stunned but physically undamaged, from the bedroom floor. While Colonel Henry continued to lie there. And Lady Edith – with a terrible scream like a tortured animal, a scream she would never forget – had cast down the gun and was running, running down the stairs and away; her footsteps light, fast, sounded on the gravel dying away. Then there was silence. She was gone.

Still Colonel Henry did not move. Delicately, gingerly she touched his black jacket. It was damp. She opened it up. A whole area of the white shirt beneath was stained red, the stain spreading all the time.

'Help, I must get help,' she thought desperately. 'I ought to find someone – but I can't leave him.' She pulled the coverlet off the bed to try and bandage his chest. Then she felt a faint pressure on her fingers. Colonel Henry's hand was on hers. His lips were moving.

'Poor Edith,' he was saying. She could just hear, 'Poor woman.' Jemima continued to staunch desperately at the wound in his chest.

Colonel Henry's lips moved twice more before he stopped moving altogether and lay still. The first time he said something like: 'Till my dying day' – Jemima could not be quite sure, but she hoped he had said that.

Lastly, he said again, 'Poor woman.' Or was it 'Poor women'? She would never know. She only knew that Colonel Henry died as he had lived, a chivalrous man – in either case.

21

A Highland farewell

Much much later Jemima was aware of someone else coming up the stairs with slow steps and then standing over her. She looked up. It was Ossian Lucas.

'Is he dead?' he asked.

Jemima nodded. She had put her little gold mirror to his lips. There was no breath. Then she had closed his eyes gently. She could not bring herself to speak.

'An accident,' said Lucas very firmly, looking at her. 'It was an accident with a gun. You must remember that. We ought to get Father Flanagan and he'll administer the last rites.' Then he said in a softer voice, 'I tried to warn you. I wasn't sure. But I was beginning to suspect. Yet I couldn't believe she would strike again twice in the same way.' There was a pause.

'But to the outside world it was and always will be an accident with a gun.' He repeated in his previous firm tone, 'You must remember that. Close ranks. Protect the family. It's what he would have wanted.'

'Protect the family! Close ranks!' The tears were beginning to pour down her cheeks uncontrollably. 'What about her—' she began. 'It was her, all her—'

'Don't speak,' said Ossian Lucas. 'Not now. Besides, she's gone. Gone for ever. She slipped over the edge of the cliff at the Fair Falls into the pool below. In the fog, you understand. Clementina thought she saw her actually jump over the edge. Absolute nonsense, of course, but Clementina is so excitable; Father Flanagan definitely saw her slip. He tried to save her. It was a tragic accident, like the death of Colonel Henry. That's all.'

'That's all,' repeated Jemima dully after him as if it were a lesson.

She did not stay for his funeral. For after the endless police formalities had been fulfilled and the inquest was over, there was a family funeral.

'What Dad would have liked,' said Ben. No one liked to gainsay Ben now. Besides, he was becoming more authoritarian by the minute. So there would be a piper playing a last lament: a proper Highland farewell.

There was no funeral as yet for Lady Edith because there was no body. The body of the dog Jacobite was discovered floating in Sighing Marjorie's Pool beneath the waterfall. They assumed that the faithful animal had leapt in after his mistress to try and rescue her. But the black depths of the pool refused to give up the body of Lady Edith, and no corpse was ever recovered from the waters into which she had plunged, to forget what she had done, to immerse herself. Later, perhaps, there would be some form of memorial to her in the church of St Margaret's or a mention of her on Colonel Henry's own gravestone. That too was for Ben to decide.

And Father Flanagan would pray for her, as he prayed for Colonel Henry, and Leonie, and Charles Beauregard, and all sinners in the eyes of God.

Later still, as Ossian Lucas observed to Jemima Shore, driving her to Inverness to catch the night sleeper, the myths would begin to grow up. Like the bracken at Eilean Fas, they would gradually cover up the neglected truth.

'In another hundred years I dare say it will be called Lady Edith's Pool.'

Jemima thought he was probably right. In another century up the Glen, the legend of the devoted wife and mother, dying to save one of her children, or even her husband, would have succeeded the truth of the jealous, covetous murderess.

Already the deliberate covering-up process had begun. Whatever the police thought privately, it was difficult to shake the combined evidence of the Beauregard family, Father Flanagan the parish priest, and Ossian Lucas the local MP.

'An awful lot of deaths,' said the Kilbronnack constabulary dourly, and later higher police officials echoed the same sentiment. There were enquiries, and doubts, and statements. But in the absence of evidence to the contrary, in the end the verdict was accidental death – on both of them.

After the inquest, Jemima wired Cherry that she was taking the night sleeper south, and wanted to be met (after her experiences which no doubt had been fully reported in the southern press – the family picnic which went wrong and ended in a double tragedy). But she preferred the welcome of a discreet and anonymous chauffeur from Miles and Miles. She made it quite clear in her telegram that the attentions of Guthrie Carlyle would not be well received at that hour in the morning. There would be time for Guthrie – later that day. Or perhaps the next day. Anyway, there would be time for Guthrie in the office, when they were planning the new series, slightly ahead of schedule owing to the abrupt curtailment of her holiday. The trouble with Guthrie was that he was so young. Or did he just seem young to her – now?

She did not want an acolyte. She wanted – she had wanted – she stopped these thoughts. The new series: she would concentrate on that. It was work, not sleep, which had always knitted up the ravelled sleeve of her own particular care.

She received the offer of another set of attentions before she left the Glen. Ben Beauregard paid her a state visit at the Castle, where Jemima had been offered a bed and had accepted a temporary refuge. Ben too seemed a bit young; although Jemima realized afterwards with surprise that they were very nearly the same age.

In a roundabout and graceful manner he attempted to discover whether such attentions would be welcome. Equally gracefully she indicated they would not. At the end of the conversation, Jemima exclaimed impulsively:

'I think you really need someone who would care about land above all else. Or anyway understand the feeling. I could never do that – not feel it, not understand it.' She paused and said in a softer voice, 'In any case, should you not take on Clementina?'

'One way or another, I'll have to take her on,' Ben said musingly. He did not seem put out by Jemima's rebuff. She remembered the scene in the Castle when the girl had taunted him with 'pretty, pretty cousin Clementina'. She thought – in the end – he would take her on. She had once compared Clementina to Rosalind, also a dispossessed heiress. In the end Rosalind had married her Orlando, another victim of a family feud. This Rosalind had found her Orlando. And they would be happy.

She gazed at his handsome, heavy, sombre face so like yet so unlike his father's. At least he would be happy with Clementina, and with her money, and their castle. Gradually the memory of the past would fade – the memory of his mother, her brother. Clementina would be happy, and have children, a clutch of sons perhaps, the pattern repeating itself – or at least she would be as happy as any woman could be in this man's valley.

Then Ben broke it to her that one woman at least intended to be very happy there.

'Rory and Hurricane Sophie — did you guess? Of course it's a dead secret, more than ever now. As it was, the dreadful snobbish Duchess of Cumberland nearly had a fit when she heard the news and she's the one who controls all the money which will go to Sophie one day from her rich Dutch relations. Roman Catholic! Non-royal! A younger son! They've had to promise to wait till Sophie is twenty-one. And now — well, the only thing to be said is that Sophie is even more obstinate than her mother and for some extraordinary reason she's mad about Rory, so I dare say she'll get her own way in the end.

'I'm going to give them Eilean Fas, by the way. Unbelievably, Rory actually wants to live there, says it's his boyhood dream, and the past makes no difference. The whole of the Highlands is stained with bloody dramas, he said, Eilean Fas no more than anywhere else. Myself,' Ben paused, 'I'd rather die than live there, as you can imagine. But I suppose if anyone can exorcize the ghosts of the Wild Island, it's Hurricane Sophie . . .'

So Rory had achieved his dream after all. If he could not achieve it one way, he would achieve it another. And he had kept every option open; he had evidently never abandoned his courtship of the spritely Hanoverian princess, while at the same time leading the forces of romantic Stuart reaction on behalf of his secret followers. He had even managed to gratify both parties with the same bold if empty gesture, by making threats against Princess Sophie's personal safety in the name of the Red Rose. The publicity thus generated had been thoroughly welcome on all sides. A very determined if not exactly single-minded man. Or as Bridie Stuart had said long ago, deep.

'Father Flanagan's idea of a mission at Eilean Fas really isn't on — under the circumstances,' Ben added vaguely. 'I've told him I'll do something about it as soon as possible.' But Jemimna had a feeling that the day of Father Flanagan's much-desired mission up the Glen would still be long in coming.

At Inverness Station there was another enormous placard in red letters: 'A Highland Farewell to HRH Princess Sophie of Cumberland.' But on this occasion no one, not the Red Rose in mourning, nor some newly formed Black Thistle, had chosen to deface it.

Jemima Shore thought: Unlike Princess Sophie, I won't be coming back to the Highlands. But she was glad that for someone at least Eilean Fas retained, and would always retain, its magic aura of Paradise.

For her the magic was gone. She knew, as she rocketed south in her sleeper, that it was gone, vanished, gone for ever. The very colours of her memories were not the bright clear colours of the Wild Island in sunshine, but other darker shades of regret and loss.

Paradise was not for her. She would not seek it again.

The sleeper swayed and rattled, and the rails beneath the carriage seemed to be carrying out a kind of quadrille which kept her from falling into unconsciousness, exhausted as she felt. After a while, she put one hand into her handbag to find the ever-present paperback thriller. Her fingers closed unexpectedly on a small cold object. Jemima brought out instead the enamel box which Colonel Henry had given her on the morning of her birthday. She read once more the message held aloft on the lid by two cupids: *Remember Me.*

Yes, she would remember him. Jemima Shore fell asleep still clutching the little box in her hand, so that when she awoke in England, the cold enamel had become warm. But her cheeks were quite wet; she must have been crying in her sleep, a thing which had never happened to her before.

A Splash of Red

Author's Note

Adelaide Square, either designed by Adam or ruined by Sir Richard Lionnel, does not exist. For the purposes of this story, I have placed it to the West of the British Museum, sandwiched between Bedford Square and Tottenham Court Road.

Contents

For Damian
and other family voices
heard at Praia de Luz

1

'No noise'

'At least you'll be very quiet up here,' said Chloe. 'All on your own. Except for Tiger, of course. And in his own way he's very quiet too.'

'Like all cats. Part of what I love about them. The silent comings and goings.' Jemima Shore spoke comfortingly, and gave a long hard rub to Tiger's back as she did so. Tiger arched and his tail went up; he was not to be won so easily. Jemima stopped and Tiger shot away. His departure was soundless on the thick beige furry carpet which covered Chloe Fontaine's flat.

'All the same, you're sure you won't be lonely?' Chloe asked anxiously, putting down her mug of coffee on the wide glass table. The mug was the colour of oatmeal, like most of the furnishings in the flat; the milky coffee blended with the other subdued colours. Even Tiger, a long-haired golden cat, fitted in with the décor – or perhaps, reflected Jemima, it had been chosen round him. Everything in the flat was not only very light but also very clean. Of course Chloe had only just moved in; nevertheless Jemima knew from previous experience of Chloe's houses and flats that the cleanliness was something spritual in her – a protest of the soul, she sometimes felt, against the disorder of her private life. Mind against Body.

Meanwhile Chloe was looking round her, still anxious, as though, unexpectedly, the flat might reveal some hidden source of either noise or comfort – it was not quite clear which.

'I want to be lonely,' thought Jemima Shore. 'That's why I'm here. Pure selfishness. Not really to help you out at all.' Aloud she said in the kind of bracing voice she had been using to Chloe since they were at Cambridge together: 'I'm never lonely, Clo. You know me. I shall love it here. It's so tranquil. And looking after Tiger will cheer me up.'

Jemima's beautiful and beloved tabby Colette had had to be put down six weeks earlier. Jemima still found the return to her own flat, now empty, intolerable. It was one of the reasons she was happy to move away from it for the time being. 'It's so tranquil here,' she repeated.

As she spoke, Jemima Shore's eye was caught by a splash of colour through the open door of the pale bedroom. For a moment it looked as if red paint – or even blood – had been dashed on the wall. Then she realized that she was looking at an enormous canvas slurred with red. A woman's figure was involved. The picture gave Jemima a momentary sense of discomfort, the first since she had entered Chloe's cloistered off-white apartment.

Chloe followed the direction of her eyes and smiled.

'You're surprised to see it?'

'Well, everything else is so—'

'I decided to keep just one. And that was the right one to keep. The most violent one of all. To remind me. Never ever again. "A Splash of Red". No, that's its title. No matter how many calls, how many evening threats, midnight pleas, how many early-morning demands . . .'Jemima realized that the red-splashed picture was by Chloe's lover – or rather her former lover – Kevin John Athlone. This fact did not make her feel any warmer towards the picture. Besides, Chloe's reason for hanging it was not totally convincing, in view of her famous fastidiousness. Jemima wondered, rather wearily, whether somewhere in her soft heart, Chloe was still in love with the appalling Kevin John.

Yet Chloe's whole reason for leaving her pretty little house in Fulham to live in this new block of history-less flats in Bloomsbury had been as she phrased it tearfully on the telephone 'to put the past behind me. I've had it, Jem, absolutely *had* it. I can't stand it any more, the noise, the shouting, the rows, the *blows* – yes, of course there were blows, can't you see it just by looking at him? – no of course I didn't call the police, Jemima, no point, in any case the noise of it was almost worse than the blows. Anyway I'm just off, off to a new flat, just Tiger and me, somewhere where there's no Kevin John and above all *No Noise*.' This conversation had ended on a note of rising hysteria.

Chloe Fontaine's new flat was in a large Georgian square near the British Museum. It was certainly an extremely quiet area. Most of the other houses contained offices; but they were offices belonging to solicitors, architects, publishers and other sober professional people. During the day the bustle of business was subdued and scarcely likely to disturb. Even nearby Tottenham Court Road provided little more than a dull reverberation. At night, Chloe told Jemima, there was really nothing to be heard at all. The flats below Chloe's were still empty.

'At least he doesn't have your address. Or I very much hope not!' exclaimed Jemima, stretching out her long legs, tanned from the hot summer, across the carpet. Happily they toned with it. Unlike the picture.

'No, of course he doesn't,' Chloe said quickly. 'I believe he's gone back to Cornwall, to that studio he used to have. And he's living with a Vietnamese girl. Vietnamese? No, probably not. Balinese? Siamese? Something oriental and' – a pause – 'no doubt submissive.' There was a small silence.

'Listen,' Chloe went on in a much brisker voice. 'I've always liked that picture. For itself alone, believe it or not. I think I was rather exaggerating its significance in my life. Now the main point is, will *you* be lonely? I'm sorry about Rosina packing up, by the way, although you may not be. Rosina is a good sort but she's a compulsive talker. In the six weeks since I moved here most of my work has been done in a vain attempt to ward off her conversation. She said she'd be away about a fortnight – but she's not a very accurate prophet about her own movements; I suppose she has to be back before I am. Depends on the wretched child's progress. How long do you take to recover from tonsils, darling? Little Enrico is not even a good sort like his mother but he has inherited the art of conversation from her, so whatever you do – for your own peace, don't let her bring him.'

'As usual it's all immaculate,' began Jemima. 'There would be nothing for Rosina to do.'

But Chloe was rattling on, and jangling some keys at the same time. 'One thing, whatever you do don't forget your keys. The separate flat buzzers which open the front door aren't ready yet, so it's left open in the day, locked in the evening. And there really is no one within earshot at night. Believe it or not, I did that last week – forgot my keys – and had to spend the night out in Adelaide Square, after climbing over the railings. I know it's a fabulous summer. Even so – but what could I do?'

Chloe sighed, laughed, and continued. 'Still it was an interesting experience in its own way. Rather a surprise altogether. Might have altered the course of my life if I didn't already have a new angel, the most divine angel in *heaven*. As it was, it was just a little, a very little, adventure. A casual encounter you might say. A carnal encounter, perhaps. Rather naughty of me under the circumstances. But I couldn't resist it.'

Jemima felt relieved. All was explained, including the slightly frenetic quality in Chloe's conversation. A new lover. Not an old fear. No, this was not at all the distraught neurotic Chloe of months back, but the mercurial creature whose changing romances were the wonder of her friends. Like the ordered décor of her houses, Chloe's fragile appearance was belied by the tempestuous nature of her private life. Since Cambridge, when Jemima Shore had been drawn to Chloe's delicate Marie Laurencin looks – sloe eyes in a pale child's face – she had wondered at this contradiction.

What was more, no hint of it appeared in Chloe's work. In her writing Chloe was the reverse of tempestuous: on the contrary, she gave the impression of one wittily in command both of herself and her characters.

'Even Tiger's life is not as crammed with incident as Chloe's,' Guthrie Carlyle had once remarked rather crossly to Jemima. 'And he's a tom cat. What's more, Tiger is a lot more discreet. Is it possible that Chloe's cat actually wrote *Fallen Child*, do you suppose? When I think of that exquisitely honed prose and those finely judged characters, and then this latest scrape of Chloe's . . .' They were discussing Chloe's decision to leave her husband for Kevin John Athlone at the time – 'I know it only adds to the fascination,' he added hastily.

Guthrie Carlyle was Jemima's devoted assistant at Megalith Television. He had once been more than that – Jemima's devoted lover, but the affair had come to an end after Jemima's involvement in certain events, both passionate and strange, in Scotland. The tragic outcome of it all had killed in Jemima any desire for anything except work – work and oblivion. Guthrie had accepted this tacit dismissal from one of his two roles in Jemima's life with that air of whimsical sadness which he used to cover up his deepest feelings; however, Guthrie and Jemima remained close friends as well as colleagues.

Jemima Shore was the writer and presenter of one of the more popular serious television programmes. She was billed as Jemima Shore, Investigator, and the title had appealed to the popular imagination as though she were some kind of amateur detective. In fact the title was merely a catchphrase and the kind of thing Jemima investigated on television was more likely to be slum housing or the fate of unmarried mothers or some combination of the two with perhaps the medical risks of the Pill thrown in for good measure. Nevertheless the title had caught on in the minds of the public and in recent years a number of people had appealed to Jemima Shore to solve their problems – with success. Curiosity was a habit of mind to her. It was tempting even now to try and work out the identity of Chloe's lovers by considering the clues. But she must restrain herself. She had a purpose in coming to Bloomsbury. Distractions were to be avoided.

She concentrated on Chloe's future plans.

'Do I take it then that you're not after all going on this famous holiday alone?' she asked. 'I'd rather imagined that since Kevin John there hadn't been anyone, well, serious . . .'

'Oh, darling, it's absolutely not a holiday, not in that sense.' Chloe was busy scribbling down a list of local shops ('I advise plunging down into Soho for anything decent: cross Tottenham Court Road, down the Charing Cross Road, avoid the dirty bookshops and it's nearer than you think'). 'No darling, I would hardly ask you to come over here, all of a sudden, just like that,' she continued, 'if I was off on a spree. No, it's work, and God knows I need it. Do you know that my last book sold exactly four thousand copies, in spite of Valentine's gallantly porno-graphic jacket. And Jamie Grand's angelic review; no, not him personally – though he *is* an angel – but his deeply pompous and deeply powerful paper. So loyal to give it to Marigold Milton, who absolutely adores my work, when you think what some of his other lovely ladies might have made of it.'

Jemima recalled the jacket of *Fallen Child* and shuddered: some kind of naked bathing scene had been depicted, a sort of *déjeuner sur l'herbe* including all the family. It crossed her mind that Valentine Brighton was not to blame, and that the artist had not penetrated Chloe's elegant prose beyond the first twenty-five pages . . . still, as publisher, Valentine should have known better. Or perhaps he did and considered the end (sales) justified the jacket.

Jemima murmured sympathetically but without committal on the subject of the jacket. She herself felt on strong ground on the subject of Chloe's work since she genuinely admired it, and had done so since Chloe's first novel was published shortly after they both left Cambridge. She liked the mixture of precision and sensibility; the particular sly humour which regularly inspired critics to compare Chloe to Jane Austen. They generally added: 'And I do not use the comparison lightly.' To which Chloe would regularly respond: 'No, they undoubt-edly use it very heavily.' But Jemima suspected that in her heart of hearts Chloe was not quite so displeased.

Comparisons to contemporary female writers, however distin-guished, on the other hand maddened her. 'Another Olivia Manning' was one comment which had provided weeks of irritation; nor was Chloe more satisfied when reviewers in the United States mentioned the name of the ironic and brilliant Alison Lurie, and suggested that the latter had provided an inspiration.

'Anyway I found the round figure highly suspicious,' Chloe was rattling on in her attractive breathless voice, an attribute which underlined further the childlike quality of her appearance. 'And I told Valentine as much, but he swore, in that utterly convincing honour-of-the-regiment way of his which always makes one even *more* suspicious – he swore it was exactly four thousand. In the meantime I'm in a load of trouble over my new book – believe it or not, *libel*, quite ridiculous how sensitive people are, of course there's nothing in it – but he, Valentine that is, is hanging on to the advance. He says the best he can do to tide me over is to pay me a flat sum if I edit an anthology of women's letters down the ages. *The Quiet Art* – no, not heart, art, don't laugh, I know it's pretty desperate, but I'm trying to make something of it. Even I have been investigating the Reading Room of the British Library in my own quiet and, we hope, artful way . . . However, as usual I need more.

'So this is good old *Taffeta* in the ample shape of Isabelle Mancini, commissioning me. *Taffeta* Schmaffeta. But at least it never lets you down. Off to France. I think Isabelle has in mind rippling tensions between a woman and a horse, with her usual optimism, whereas I see it as a lonely woman rides in Camargue. Pictures by Snowdon if we're lucky, the insufferable Binnie Rapallo if we're not. "Thoughts suggested by white chargers," cried Isabelle: she never learns. And she always adds: "Do something about the *food*, darling, don't forget." It's a hangover from her days as a cookery writer. What do horses eat in the Camargue? If I found out, would that satisfy her? Still, I'm going ahead for ten days to sit alone and perhaps wander and get new ideas. The photographer – Binnie, I have no doubt – follows.'

'Alone, Clo?' Jemima jumped up to pace round the apartment.

'Absolutely alone. I am definitely *not* taking my new angel with me. The news of my romance, by the way, is a heavy secret till I come back. I haven't broken it to the last angel, who was of all things – well, perhaps that had better be a secret too till I get back. Why give you a quick blurb on my life when a full-length novel is so much more fun? It might spoil it. A married man – no more for the present.'

Chloe was certainly right back in her old form. Two new men at least in her life – or rather new to Jemima's list of Chloe's involvements – two new men and something catalogued as an adventure. Jemima could not quite resist running through a few possible names in her head. Then she was distracted by the majestic view from the vast picture window which ran the length of the room.

Jemima could see across the tops of the great trees of Adelaide Square to the elegant eighteenth-century houses on the opposite side. Chloe's new residence was in a concrete balconied block. To Jemima's mind its style was somewhere between the Mappin Terraces at Regent's Park Zoo and the National Theatre, less charming than the former, more appealing than the latter. Its position turned its architecture into an affront.

It also seemed peculiarly unfair that the occupant of this horror would have the advantage of looking at its beautiful neighbours, whereas they in turn had to contemplate the monstrosity. Unfair indeed – she suddenly remembered the furious protests at the building of the new landmark, or rather the demolition of the great house which had preceded it. Very understandable, but somehow the protests had either been got round or muffled.

That was, perhaps, because Sir Richard Lionnel was involved: an exotic saturnine gentleman whose tweeded figure – he did not affect the normal dark suit of a tycoon – was to be glimpsed in as many government corridors as boardrooms.

'So I shall be quite out of touch and alone, as lonely as you will be here, in a different way. No angel and no telephone calls,' Chloe was saying.

'What happened to those protesters, Clo?' Jemima interrupted. 'I'm looking into Adelaide Square. The ones who threatened this building – it was this one, wasn't it? I do see their point – if it doesn't sound ungrateful, living in your luxurious eyrie.'

'Oh, I believe the original house was riddled with dry rot, in a terrible state. I know for a fact that squatters and what-have-you were imminent. No way it could have been preserved. The façade perhaps – but that would have cost the earth.'

'So the protest just died down?'

'Oddly enough it hasn't quite. I meant to warn you, except that it's not very serious and certainly won't bother you at night. They still feel strongly about Lionnel himself. That's because they're frightened he'll do the same thing elsewhere. Notably next door. You saw the scaffolding? That battle's lost but you know what demonstrators are. You may get the odd rude note downstairs, but it will just be addressed "The Occupant", so pay no attention. There are sometimes people with placards – "The Lion of Bloomsbury, seeking whom he may devour". "Don't let the Lion eat Bloomsbury", that sort of thing. I see them there most days. But they won't bother you. Some of them are quite attractive, if you like that sort of thing. Long hair, beards and very narrow hips, if you know what I mean.' Jemima did. It was not an attraction she had ever felt. Involuntarily she frowned.

'They don't make any noise, I'm glad to say. As a matter of fact, with some rather picturesque lions on their placards, they rather cheer up the pavement.' Chloe gave a little smile, rather sly, at Jemima's disapproval. 'I adore lions, don't you? I always want to hug them at the zoo. Ever one for danger in love.'

'"The Lion of Bloomsbury" – quite a title for a programme,' muttered Jemima, adding swiftly: 'But I'm having a holiday from all that. The series is resting and so am I.' Then she couldn't resist asking: 'Always the same lot? Of demonstrators, I mean?'

'To tell you the truth, I don't think I look very closely.'

'I would get rather fascinated by them if I saw them every day,' Jemima admitted.

'You would, darling, you would!' cried Chloe. Now it was her turn to abandon the vast sofa and gaze into the darkening square across the trees. Jemima noticed her slight body instinctively fall into a graceful attitude, almost that of an actress or a dancer, so that the window framed her, and her faintly leaning head. Chloe did have exceptionally long legs for such a tiny woman – a dancer's legs. Looking at her, Jemima considered that she hardly looked any older than when they were at Cambridge together; she was perhaps just a little fatter with a certain roundness of the bosom absent in extreme youth, which only added to her femininity. But her face, if anything, was thinner.

'But then you are Jemima Shore, Investigator. And I'm Chloe Fontaine, with my limited range, my domestic palette with its few and unexperimental colours as my critics frequently tell me.'

'I never underrate your range,' said Jemima. 'Not since our first day at Cambridge when I discovered to my chagrin that the prettiest girl at the Freshers' meeting was also the top scholar of the year. Your heart is another matter, but you have an excellent head, Clo, so long as you manage to keep it somewhere not too far from your shoulders.'

'No, I haven't always done that, have I?' For a moment Chloe sounded quite melancholy. The graceful head in question sank still further. She looked quite white for a moment, or perhaps it was a trick of the light. 'Memo: keep my head, lose my heart. This new romance, Jem, it's so perfect, or rather it's going to be perfect, so long as I do keep my head. Sorry to sound so mysterious but for once that's all I can say. I'll tell you all when I get back from the Camargue.' Chloe wheeled round, facing the open bedroom door.

'I lost my head and my heart over him, didn't I? You see what a warning that painting is. No more splashes of red for me. No, don't turn on the lights. I love the dusk falling over the square. Do it when I've gone. Let me enjoy my flight from responsibility. I've shown you where they all are. Dimmers and everything for a late night rendezvous. Have a good time, a very good time, darling.'

'I'm going to be working in the Reading Room of the British Library by day,' protested Jemima, 'and trying to write at night. It's my chance, while the programme's not on and before we start gathering material in the autumn. No high life at all. I promised Valentine that I would let him have an outline at least and the first chapters of my famous book by September.'

'Ah, Valentine. If we kept all our promises to him!' cried Chloe slightly petulantly. 'Anyway he doesn't expect it. So long as one is frank about it. I always tell the truth to Valentine, however awful. He can't resist that.'

It crossed Jemima's mind that in the nicest possible way Chloe might be slightly jealous of her own more recent relationship with the publisher. Jemima did not flatter herself that Valentine Brighton had commissioned her book entirely for its own sake: the image of Jemima Shore, Investigator, was a strong one in the public's eye. Jemima's name would look good on a book jacket, particularly as television books so often headed the bestseller lists.

Chloe on the other hand had supported herself by writing alone, all her working life, none of her books having been made into plays, films, or even serialized for television. It did not matter that Jemima's projected *opus* was not in fact a spin-off from her television series, but a serious study of Edwardian women philanthropists. It was possible to argue that even with her first book Jemima Shore, Investigator, would start with an unnatural advantage over Chloe Fontaine, lady novelist of some years' standing.

'Well you could always have Valentine over here,' said Chloe with a slightly mischievous smile. 'That would be work. His office is in Bedford Square, almost opposite Cape's and his *pied à terre*, his foot on the earth as he insists on calling it, is over there, on the other side of this square. The elegant bit, behind the trees. Very handy for keeping an eye on me – that's *another* story I shall tell you on my return from the Camargue. Quite interesting. We shall make an evening of it – I shall be Scheherazade.'

'Like Garbo, I want to be alone,' replied Jemima firmly.

Jemima watched while Chloe locked the discreet white cupboard in the corner of the sitting room.

'Sorry – locking habit. You know me. Anyway I've moved most of my London clothes in there, leaving room for yours in the bedroom. I'm taking virtually nothing on holiday.' She popped the key in her pocket.

Light and charming as a fairy in her movements, Chloe was even now gathering up her bag, and in a moment was flitting down the staircase. It was a beautiful staircase, broad, even to the penultimate flight where it twisted neatly upwards to the penthouse like a piece of barley-sugar. There at least his architect had done Sir Richard Lionnel proud. The lift did not yet work however: 'Don't go near it. You don't want to take that kind of risk,' Chloe had said, quite unnecessarily. 'And I advise you not to venture into the basement either – unless you have to plunge after Tiger who adores it. Dark and unfinished.'

Jemima stood at the door and listened to Chloe clattering down the stairs in the very high heels she always wore. Chloe was six inches shorter than Jemima; even in the Camargue, Jemima imagined that her riding boots would have very high heels.

Down to the bottom went Chloe's tapping heels, gradually growing fainter. It sounded a very long way down. Jemima continued to listen, deciding, for some reason she could not quite analyse, to wait until she heard the front door bang. After a while she thought she heard a noise – that must be the door. It all took longer than she had expected. It was like listening for a stone dropped into a well: the splash was surprisingly long in coming.

Finally, Jemima turned away and went back into the flat. Still she did not put on the lights. The sky was extremely beautiful, a Tiepolo-like sky, with turquoise and gold and areas of mauve and pink. Going to the window, she thought to watch Chloe passing across the square to the other side where she had left her car. Jemima could see the car – or thought she could. It was a bright green Renault with a hatchback, and Chloe was driving to Dover that night, before taking the ferry the next day.

However, she had evidently missed her. There were a few people about, odd passers-by, foreigners mainly; a few Japanese tourists but the tourist crowds were diminishing in the fine August evening. It was more surprising to see that Chloe's car remained untouched. For a moment she was quite puzzled. Then she gave a brief laugh and turned away. Jemima suddenly remembered that she had no idea of the colour of Chloe's new car. She was thinking of the old one, and she knew that Chloe had acquired a new car recently – 'bought out of the royalties Valentine assures me I haven't earned, the pig!' Someone quite different got into the green car and drove away in the direction of Tottenham Court Road.

It was time to turn on the lights. Something soft and furry rubbed at her knees. It was Tiger returned. His tail was up, but in friendly fashion. He must have come in through the balcony window which, Chloe had informed her, must always be left open at least five inches ('you would hardly have intruders at this height – cats are more likely than cat burglars').

Chloe had already installed some tubs, filled with grey foliage – senecio, artemisia – and trailing white geraniums with silver-green leaves shaped like ivy. The cool tones of the plants completed the feeling of serenity. Jemima drew the French window back to its fullest extent. It was hot. She stepped out onto the balcony. The sight of the ugly concrete parapet jarred upon her once again, after the harmony of the plants; perhaps it was just as well that the Lionnel architect, preferring his artistic design to safety, had made it slightly lower than might have been expected, in order not to interfere with the view.

She inspected the rest of the area. She had not realized before that the next-door house was not yet completed, the scaffolding still present. It was to be another Lionnel enterprise. There the balcony was still in embryo. To her right was one of the great houses of Adelaide Square. Here the top floor, in its original state, was not graced with a balcony.

It was immensely quiet.

Her peace was disturbed by the sound of the telephone in the flat. Jemima stepped back in, noticing once more with irritation how the picture – 'A Splash of Red' – disturbed the harmony. She, after all, did not need reminding of the value of avoiding Kevin John Athlone. She might even take it down ... Tiger would hardly object. So far as she could remember, Tiger had shown a cat's good sense in regularly ramming his claws into the wretched Kevin John.

The telephone rang persistently. Jemima picked it up. According to Chloe, most of the calls would be wrong numbers. She had not yet sent out her new telephone number to her friends.

At first, therefore, Jemima assumed that she was listening to a misdirected call. She stepped back all the same and handled the instrument gingerly. It was a mean little white object, giving a rather shrill 'pip-pip', as opposed to a full-blooded ring.

Jemima intended to give the correct number in a cold and reproving voice, but did not have time to do so.

'You whore,' said the voice quite distinctly. Jemima, urban born and accustomed if not indifferent to such things, began to put the receiver back hastily, when the voice said, equally distinctly:

'Supposing there was a real splash of red on the carpet. Or would you prefer it on the bed?'

2

Disappearing in London

Automatically, Jemima replaced the telephone receiver. She stood in the white flat, quiet again after the persistent odious ringing, and looked at the miniature instrument. She considered whether to leave the receiver off the hook.

It was now nearly nine o'clock. She had deliberately not left Chloe's number with the American girl to whom she had lent her own flat in a very different area of London. Jemima had told her tenant rather vaguely that she was 'going away' and to get in touch with Megalith Television if there were any crises. She had told Guthrie Carlyle that she was 'going somewhere to have some peace' without mentioning that this peace was to be found in Bloomsbury. Her secretary, the nubile Cherry, the toast of Megalithic House, was herself on holiday in Corfu. There were no family demands likely to be made upon Jemima, no sorrowing widowed mother, no helpless bachelor father, no sister in the process of leaving an intolerable husband who might wish to call her.

Jemima Shore had many close friends, many admirers and numerous acquaintances, quite apart from the vast public who assumed they were her intimates from seeing her image on the television screen. But she was one of those rare people who, as far as she knew, had no living blood relations or, at any rate, no close ones. She was herself an only child. Both her parents had been only children and they had died together in a car crash when she was eighteen. Since then a couple of elderly spinster cousins, living together in the New Forest, who had briefly attempted to supply a family for her – without success, for she had not wanted another family – had also died. Jemima Shore was alone in the world. She preferred it that way. She had the freedom, as she saw it, to choose her own friends.

A London holiday had struck her at the time as a brilliant idea for escaping into peace. There was the Reading Room of the British Library, waiting like the belly of a whale to swallow her up during the day. Then there was none of the commitment and disruption of country life; to say nothing of the problems of reaching the country on a summer's day. Her own holiday journey had taken twenty minutes on the Underground from Holland Park station. She deliberately left her precious new Citroen behind – that too was a kind of freedom – and travelled with one piece of highly expensive, highly efficiently packed Lark luggage, navy blue piped in red, sitting at her feet. Her two other Jean Muir dresses in the thin silk jersey she loved, would emerge from it as immaculately as they had gone in – and would scarcely need the long white bedroom cupboard allotted to them by Chloe.

Jemima loved to travel light. Watching the impassive faces opposite her in the Tube, lit up occasionally by the sort of recognition she had learnt to accept without enjoying, she had thought with delight: 'You're going to work. I'm going on holiday. I'm disappearing in London.'

Jemima Shore, with no ties, thought that yes, she would take the telephone off the hook.

She certainly saw no necessity to receive the threatening calls of Kevin John Athlone. For such, she had realized, the identity of the caller must inevitably be. Who else would have made such unpleasant play with the title of the picture? And there was something quite nastily sexual about the last innuendo – 'Or would you prefer it on the bed' – which put her in mind, uncomfortably, of Chloe's last remarks, her hints of violence, her use of the word 'submissive'. A moment's crossness against the careless Chloe swept through her. To have deliberately stated that he did not have the number – and then to be caught out almost immediately after she had left the flat!

Nevertheless Jemima was surprised. For one thing it was quite unlike Chloe to lie. Eighteen years of friendship – yes, it had to be nearly as long – had included numerous intrigues, mysteries. Jemima had also provided a good many alibis in the course of Chloe's two marriages; one lasting eight years and one a bare twelve months before Chloe had been swept off her feet by Kevin John. Naturally lies had been told in that period. Yet Jemima was convinced that fundamentally Chloe was not a liar. In most ways – except where adultery had been, briefly, concerned – she was abnormally candid and truthful. 'Scheherazade' – Jemima remembered Chloe's words – 'I'll tell you all.' Jemima had had experience of Chloe's frank confessions before; they justified the title.

It was true that Chloe had been holding something back, to be revealed hereafter; but it was hardly something as trivial yet irritating as the fact that Kevin John Athlone had recently discovered her new telephone number. The mystery tantalized Jemima for a moment, and then she dismissed it.

On the glass table in front of the white sofa lay two books. Jemima glanced at the publisher's colophon on the spines. A golden helmet with a B set in it: Brighthelmet Press, Valentine Brighton's publishing house, the name a combination of his own and that of his home in Sussex, Helmet Manor. She looked inside the top book: a quick note was scribbled on the publisher's slip inside, where the golden helmet was repeated. She read: 'Tuesday. To the marriage of true minds. Love V.'

Jemima was surprised for the second time that evening. Valentine Brighton, that famously polite young man, was fond of sending round books to his authors or people he sought to *become* his authors. Whimsical notes beneath the sign of the golden helmet generally accompanied these gifts, which had begun to arrive on Jemima's desk as soon as Valentine Brighton realized that she might possibly be persuaded to write a book for him. The symbol of the golden helmet always reminded Jemima of Valentine Brighton himself with his sleek poll of thick fair hair. It was hair which always looked neat and clean and brushed, even when fashion dictated that it would sweep the shoulders of his polo-necked jersey; and, despite its length, it irresistibly reminded her of the kind of hair possessed by the young officers who went out to die in the trenches in the First World War.

Jemima's book parcels arrived at Megalithic House conveyed by Lord Brighton's chauffeur, driving the Brighton Rolls-Royce. 'Old as the hills,' said its owner airily. But it was not in fact all that old. It was just that, like all Valentine Brighton's possessions, it looked rather old – and rather good. The chauffeur also figured in Valentine Brighton's airy *dicta*.

'Used to be a gamekeeper at Helmet. But it turned out that he loathed everything to do with potting birds and loved machines. So, a wave of the Brighton fairy wand – and lo and behold, the best chauffeur in London. What luck it is to be a feudal landlord, particularly in these difficult days of staff problems.'

Jemima was never quite sure how serious that kind of remark was meant to be. It certainly *was* lucky to have inherited as a child an Elizabethan manor house, both famous and inhabitable, in a fold of the Sussex downs near the sea; plus a great deal of rich farming land surrounding it. Yet, given such a 'lucky' deal from life, why had Valentine Brighton elected to work extremely hard in Bloomsbury building up a publishing firm? Presumably, like his chauffeur, he had winced from a life of 'potting birds'. Yet at the same time Lord Brighton showed no desire to throw off his background. Jemima had never detected in him the faintest gleam of fashionable guilt at his – considerable – inherited wealth. On the contrary, the remark concerning the chauffeur was merely typical of a whole host of such allusions.

Jemima wrenched her mind from Valentine to his note. Marriage. Valentine and Chloe. Was it possible? Anything was possible with Chloe, that she had long ago learned. But Valentine? He could hardly be Chloe's new lover – already a married man by her own account. Or was it her former lover who had been married? Her last words had been ambiguous.

'Tuesday' – and today was Friday. The position of the books suggested that they had not been there very long. Was Chloe really contemplating marrying Valentine Brighton? It was odd, if so, that Chloe's remarks about Valentine, her sales, and the likely problem of her new book had had a genuinely cross rather than a romantic tinge. For that matter, the note itself was ambiguous. 'The marriage of true minds' did not necessarily refer to holy matrimony.

Yet there had been something to the relationship. 'Quite riveting', Chloe's words. Scheherazade would inform her on her return. Still, Chloe might perhaps cast some light on the topic which had troubled the gossip-mongers in literary London of the past. Exactly what if any were Valentine's sexual proclivities? On that subject, Valentine himself generally took refuge in a cloud of what Jemima privately termed his 'feudal' references: 'Mummy simply won't *let* me marry the sort of girl who can tell one end of a book from the other.' On another occasion: 'Mummy says the library at Helmet was full up at the end of the eighteenth century and a bookish girl would only ruin it, by rearranging things, or worse still *reading* the books.' It was easy to put all this together, the allegedly dominating figure of 'Mummy', Valentine's bachelor state and the pseudo-comic references, to make of him a homosexual. If so, Valentine was an exceptionally discreet one, surprisingly and surely unnecessarily so for the times in which he lived.

On the other hand there was the question of his health. 'This weak but well-bred heart beats for you' had been his characteristic way of proposing a publisher's contract to Jemima. It was common knowledge that Valentine's father had died young of a heart condition and that his mother dreaded the same fate overtaking her only child. 'Mummy positively panics when I play the third set at tennis.' That at least was a modest smoke-screen, for Valentine Brighton, far from being the effete performer his appearance might promise, was an exceptional athlete, at least by the standards of the set in which he moved.

ANTONIA FRASER

Perhaps 'waiting for Lady Right' – another of his teasing phrases – was indeed what he had been doing. And Chloe Fontaine, twice married already, had turned out to be the chosen she. The picture of Chloe queening it at Helmet was indeed a seductive one – even if her reign might prove shortlived. How long would she stand it? A year? Two years? There was still something odd about the whole business. At this point Jemima decided that she had spent enough time in one evening on Chloe and her amours. Resolutely, she ignored both Brighthelmet Press books. They belonged to an elaborate History of Taste, whose main object was to induce feelings of guilt in the purchaser, pangs to be assuaged by buying (but not necessarily reading) the books.

Jemima picked up her own Nadine Gordimer novel, and went to the wide balcony, hoping that there would be light enough to read in the comparative cool of the summer's evening. However, she found an outside switch and turned it on. Suddenly the balcony was flooded with light: for a moment she had the impression of being on a stage in a darkened theatre when the lights are switched on. The dark balcony to the right and the equally dark scaffolding to the left, gave the irresistible effect of theatrical wings.

Jemima felt totally vulnerable, even at that great height over the square. She was exposed to whatever strange malignant forces were out there in the darkness. Moreover, an extraordinary fear seized her – she, not given to such things – that there was someone waiting in the wings. Someone perhaps in the obscurity of the scaffolding to her left.

As a result, an unexpected soft thump very close to her made her give a light scream until she realized it was Tiger, returning from some nocturnal prowl. The ghost of the dead Colette, who had so often glided into her flat at night through the cat flap, a small unmistakeable sound, called to her. But she had not come here to listen to the mew of Colette's ghost.

Resolutely Jemima gave herself up to concentrate on Nadine Gordimer. She was immediately carried into another far-off and sombre world. When she next squinted at the elegant little gold bracelet watch she always wore, it was 11.30.

Time to sleep and be fresh for the Reading Room of the British Library tomorrow. The intoxication of having disappeared in London overwhelmed Jemima with childish delight. She would read – or perhaps she would not read – in bed. She would read, but she would abandon Nadine Gordimer for the night and read John Le Carré; she had spotted one by Chloe's bed. It was a great help that Jemima had read this Le Carré before, and would thus, in her sleepy state, have a

320

head start with the plot. It was, in its own way, delightful that she was not in her own luxurious but somehow demanding bed at home, with all its little pleasures and appurtenances about it, books, photographs, articles to read, paraphernalia. Last thing, she put the telephone back on the hook in the sitting room.

Afterwards she was not quite sure whether she had actually fallen asleep or not over Le Carré (it was in fact no help to her that she had read it before; the plot remained dazzling but impenetrable) when she was startled by the plaintive peep-peep of the little telephone by the bed.

'Dollie?' It was a woman's voice, anxious and quite elderly. 'Dollie? Is that you, dear?'

'I'm afraid that you have the wrong number,' began Jemima. 'There's no Dollie here.'

'Is that 6368471?' quavered the voice. Jemima glanced at the dial.

'Yes, but this is a new flat: the number must have been reallocated.'

Jemima had just said again: 'There's no Dollie here', when she suddenly remembered, feeling rather remorseful, that Chloe Fontaine's mother always called her Dollie. Jemima, having been at Cambridge with Chloe, was dimly aware of this fact. As far as she could remember Chloe, formerly Dorothy or Dollie, had changed her name on arrival at Cambridge but, as she occasionally complained, had never succeeded in getting her somewhat elderly mother to acknowledge the fact.

'I see, dear. I'll just go on calling you Dollie, if you don't mind,' was the most her mother could be persuaded to comment.

'Is that you, Mrs Fontaine?' said Jemima hastily. 'I'm afraid Chloe's gone away.' She did not feel like entering the Dollie charade herself; considering Chloe's ancient annoyance at her mother's obstinacy, it seemed somewhat disloyal to her friend. Chloe had after all lived as long under her new name as her old, and had written a great many books under it (for which reason she had never adopted either of her two married names).

'I'm her friend, Jemima Shore,' she threw in. 'You may remember: we met once at Cambridge. I'm borrowing her flat while she's on holiday.'

There was a moment's silence. Jemima had a picture of an old person at the other end of the telephone, grappling with unexpected information. And Mrs Fontaine, having, as far as she could remember, borne Chloe when she was something like forty, must be in her seventies by now.

'Not Mrs Fontaine, dear. Mrs Stover,' said the voice at last. It was less plaintive, much firmer. Further Cambridge memories came back to

Jemima. The trouble with Chloe's change of name was that she had changed both her Christian name *and* her surname on arrival at university. Fontaine was the name of her real father who had been killed early in the war, and Stover the name of her stepfather who had adopted her. Presumably the reversion represented some kind of protest; at this distance Jemima hardly remembered. Where 'Chloe' came from, Jemima had absolutely no idea; it was an unlikely middle name for Dorothy Stover. At all events, Mrs Stover had persisted in addressing letters to Miss Dorothy Stover at first, until Chloe defeated her by sending them back unopened: 'Not known at this College.'

'Jemima Shore. Well,' went on Mrs Stover, as though digesting this information in its turn. Jemima heard her say to someone quite loudly: 'Dad. Did you hear that? Jemima Shore Investigator is in Dollie's flat. I'm talking to her on the telephone.' A strong and very angry man's voice could be heard saying: 'I don't care who you're talking to on the telephone, not even if its Michael Parkinson himself or the Queen of England. I want to know where Dollie is, that's what I want to know.'

'You see, Dollie said she would come down here and spend the night with us.' Mrs Stover was now speaking directly into the telephone again: 'And she hasn't come. And Dad's worried.'

'Worried!' came a shout from the background. 'Tell her I'm not *worried*. I'm bloody fed up, that's what I am. She rings up her mother the other day, out of the blue, haven't seen her for ages, too busy, that's what she says, busy with what, says I, she rings us up, says she'll be late, so we sit up for her, Mrs Stover prepares a meal, and now her royal highness doesn't even turn up before midnight. Worried. I should bloody well think I am worried.'

'Whereabouts do you live, Mrs Stover?' enquired Jemima cautiously, when this tirade appeared to have stopped.

'In Folkestone – "Finches", Bartleby Road. Near the park if you know Folkestone. She was going to spend the night here and take the ferry to the Continent tomorrow morning. She did say she would be late. But now it's nearly twelve o'clock.'

'It *is* twelve o'clock,' came the voice of Mr Stover in the background. 'It's tomorrow already, that's what it is.'

Jemima gave Mrs Stover her most soothing television voice. 'How very worrying for you – both,' she said diplomatically. 'Chloe left here about nine so she certainly should have reached Folkestone by now. There wouldn't be much traffic. She didn't however mention that you were expecting her. She told me she was driving to Dover. I just wonder if she could have forgotten.' As she spoke Jemima – rather wearily, for she agreed with Mr Stover that it was tomorrow already – was rehearsing the familiar routine of checking for the non-arrival of a person. She would, she supposed, have to telephone the hospitals and the police, in case Chloe had had an accident or breakdown on the way.

There was another silence. Jemima half expected a roar from Mr Stover: 'Forgotten! She'd bloody well better not forget.' Slightly to her surprise there was silence from both Stovers. Then she realized that Mrs Stover was whispering to her husband. A moment later she heard Mr Stover himself take the receiver before speaking in a more conciliatory tone.

'Well you see, Miss Shore, it's like this. It is just possible that she, Dollie, as Mrs Stover and I are in the habit of calling her, has overlooked the appointment. The reason being—' another brief silence of hesitation – 'I may as well say, to save your time and ours, that I indicated to Dollie that she had better be here by six o'clock in the evening or not come at all. And she said she couldn't, why I don't quite know, but still we'll leave that one. So I said, I indicated to her, that if she couldn't be here at six in the evening to eat supper with Mrs Stover and myself she had better not come at all, under the circumstances, if you understand me. It's true that she still said to her mother that she *would* come—'

'I understand.' Jemima felt relief. Chloe had quite clearly not gone to Folkestone, but had driven directly to Dover. It made no sense to leave so late, to spend her time in Bloomsbury chatting to Jemima, if she had been intending to have supper in Folkestone. Why not mention casually to Jemima that she had to visit her parents?

'Look, I think she probably decided in the end not to come,' Jemima went on. 'Not wishing to keep you up late.' That was a diplomatic way of putting it. 'Will you ring me in the morning if you have any further problems?'

The Stovers, both of them, rang off. Jemima turned off her light. But sleep did not come. She lay for an hour, rather irritated by the whole affair. In the end she decided that it was because she was not quite convinced that Chloe had not set off for Folkestone. A responsible person would ring the police.

Jemima Shore rang the police, and after being put through to the various exchanges, established that there had been no road accidents involving a Miss Chloe Fontaine in central London or on the Folkestone or Dover roads that night. A call to the hospitals? No, at this point; that was really going too far. It was quite the wrong way to spend her 'disappearing in London' holiday, trying to track down Chloe Fontaine. She drifted into sleep.

The next time she was woken by the telephone, she was aware that it was morning. The next thing she was aware of was that the anonymous caller was back again.

At eight thirty in the morning, to her amazement, Jemima Shore found herself listening to words which began something like: 'Shall I come and give it to you in that great bed? I could, you know. Or shall I just watch you through the walls, my private view? I haven't made up my mind. Have you made up your mind? How do you want it, Jemima Shore?' The mention of her own name broke the spell and Jemima slammed down the telephone.

It rang again instantly, as though the slamming action had set off the ringing. Trembling more with annoyance than anything else, she picked it up ready to swear at her anonymous friend.

'Look here—' she began in a loud and furious voice. Then she stopped.

'Miss Shore?' someone was saying at the other end. 'This is Mrs Stover, Dollie's mother. Miss Shore, we don't know what to think now. We had a letter from Dollie this morning. You know what the posts are – it was posted three days ago. First class too. She left out the road number, of course, she always does, although I've written to her about it over and over again, and sent her the Post Office's communication that the name is no longer sufficient, you need the number, and you have to put in Lethermere Road as well as Bartleby Road. Still, as she writes so seldom, I suppose – anyway "Finches" ought to be enough after seventeen years. There's really no call for marking it "Insufficient Postal Address".'

Jemima thought she distinguished a cry of 'Bloody ridiculous' from the background. Mrs Stover continued hurriedly.

'Anyway, she said she was sorry she had to be so late, to tell Dad not to be too angry, she was sorry about their words, but she'd definitely be with us by eleven. She said she had something special to tell us. She had to tell it to us personally, couldn't write it. We didn't know what that was, of course. So, Miss Shore, she's not here, her bed's not been slept in, she didn't come in the night. Miss Shore, wherever can Dollie be?'

3

'Care for a visit?'

The next voice on the telephone was more vigorous. Mr Stover also sounded angry, as though Dollie had deliberately failed to arrive during the brief period of forgiveness he had extended and must now take the consequences. But his actual words were jovial enough, if hardly likely to cheer Jemima herself.

'I've just said to the wife,' he half-shouted, 'we're dealing with the Press here. This is Miss Jemima Shore we've got on the other end of the telephone. Jemima Shore, Investigator, no less. People round here would be queuing in their thousands to speak to her about the slightest thing, and we have her on the end of our telephone. She'll find Dollie for us, Mother...' But Jemima had not, she reminded herself, established a singularly successful career in television without being able to deal with the likes of Mr Stover.

She interrupted him firmly as he was still relating at some length his dialogue with his wife.

'I advise you to call the police, Mr Stover. That is, if you're really satisfied that Chloe—' she refused to adapt to Dollie; the persistent use of the name seemed to her part of the Stovers' fantasy about their daughter – 'if you're really satisfied that Chloe was intending to visit you and not go straight to the ferry.'

Jemima heard Mrs Stover's more plaintive voice in the background. It was still unfortunately clear.

'Show her the letter, Dad,' she was saying. 'We must show her the letter.' Strangled sounds from Mr Stover. A pause and an even more plaintive cry. 'You're *wearing* your spectacles, Charlie.' Mrs Stover added something which sounded like: 'But the telephone is cheaper on Saturday, Charlie. Your cousin Poppy told us.'

The image of the two old people in Folkestone – 'near the park, if you know the town' – worrying over their daughter and their telephone and their spectacles made Jemima feel increasingly desperate. Her holiday, her disappearance in London, was being melted away by the most unwelcome compassionate feelings.

It was not at all difficult for Jemima to imagine the Stovers at home in 'Finches' because she had just completed a programme on the special loneliness of elderly parents whose successful offspring had moved up the cultural scale, leaving them financially secure, but desperately, uncomprehendingly, lonely on their lowly rung of the ladder. It had been called *The Unvisited*. Chloe Fontaine had not contributed to it. She was, involuntarily and rather too late, contributing to it now.

'Read it over to me.' It was the best she could do. Yes, Chloe's letter sounded positive enough about her arrival as Jemima listened and the clear light of the August morning filtered delicately through Chloe's Japanese blinds. She imagined 'Finches', an immaculate little home, breakfast long since finished, crockery washed up, beds made, house garnished. The rooms would be small, unlike Chloe's airy palace. There would be plants in rows in unequal pots on the window sills, all green and rather bushy, with a small red flower or two, all quite unlike the graceful symmetrical white and grey shapes of Chloe's floral décor.

She could imagine photographs. A dark-haired Dollie with plaits winning prizes at her local grammar school. Dollie – now Chloe – in the group photograph of their first year at Cambridge. Dollie/Chloe marrying Lance Strutt? Chloe marrying Igor? Jemima had been to both weddings and not met the Stovers. It was more likely that one of those large romantic photographs of Chloe by Snowdon and Bailey and Lichfield and, best of all Parkinson, which adorned the backs of her novels and almost swamped the paperback versions, causing sardonic grief to reviewers, one of those must surely grace the Stovers' piano. Chloe in a picture hat, nestling on a swing, modern Fragonard, rising out of roses, corrupted Boucher; on one fabulous occasion actually surrounded by a flight of doves – only Binnie Rapallo could have decided to make a pastoral Greuze out of the author of *Old Miss Stevenson*, a wry tale about a spinster and her past.

Piano? A memory of Chloe at Cambridge: 'My mother actually wanted to send the piano along with my trunk. A chastity symbol I can only suppose. Certainly it would keep anything more tactile from entering this fearful room.' So the piano waited for Chloe in Folkestone. Like its owners. There would be much waiting done in that house. Waiting for Dollie.

In Chloe Fontaine's new Bloomsbury apartment on the other hand no waiting had been done at all; Chloe had not even waited to tell Jemima that she intended to visit her parents. She had hardly waited to move into the flat itself before setting off for the Camargue. Jemima heard again the light clack-clack of her high heels and her characteristic rather breathy voice: 'No, no, down the stairs, there's no lift. I'm in a hurry.' A further pang of pity for the unvisited voices on the other end of the telephone seized Jemima; an atavistic pang perhaps for those dead parents of her own, dead before Jemima took her first steps into another world. Might they too have become the unvisited?

'Look, Mrs Stover—'

'Mr Stover here. The wife's gone into the kitchen to make us some tea. All this is very upsetting to her, Miss Shore. Her nerves have been all to pieces, I don't mind telling you.' He sounded reproachful and on the verge of rehearsing the events of the night before all over again. Jemima was once more engaged in cutting him short when she heard him say:

'One thing directly following upon another if you understand my meaning. First Dollie's call out of the blue, quite unexpected, equally unexpected, and then she doesn't make an appearance—'

Jemima with a sinking feeling heard the story all over again – all this still before her first cup of coffee (a time when Jemima always felt that the whole world should know that she was to be treated with circumspection).

'I'll call the hospitals in London,' she proffered. That could no longer be avoided. She did not mention having checked with the police the night before. 'You call them in Folkestone and Dover. I'll call Chloe's editor at *Taffeta* if I can find her home number. There's probably a perfectly simple explanation for all this. If not, it's up to you to decide whether you call the police. What with Mrs Stover's nerves,' she added in a slightly less crisp tone.

All this took some time although Jemima, uncombed hair flowing over her navy blue silk kimono, did at least manage to drink a mug of coffee while dealing with the little white telephone. She also took time to feed Tiger. But Tiger's presence, golden and expectant, was not as comforting as it should have been to a confirmed cat-lover. He crouched in the middle of the carpet, haunches raised, paws forward in the attitude of a slightly aggressive sphinx. His eyes were half closed, as if he did not want her to know he was watching her and regarding events of which he did not approve. When he did abandon this stance, it was only in order to stalk through the wide balcony windows, inspect Adelaide Square or perhaps the tops of the giant trees where inviolable pigeons might be expected to lurk, and then return to the same sphinx-like position. Once only he mewed at the front door of the flat.

Tiger did not coil himself or curl up with his paws under his cheek or slumber like a thrown-away toy as Colette would have done at this hour in the morning, dreaming of the night's adventures. Jemima, efficiently telephoning the hospitals – no, no one of that name admitted since yesterday evening – was vaguely disquieted by Tiger and tried to remind herself that the animal was not only new to her but comparatively new to the Bloomsbury flat. All the same, Tiger's restlessness perturbed her. She began to have a feeling of something not altogether explained quite near them both, the woman and the cat.

She went through to the large light bathroom with its shadowy flowers on walls and shutters, as though projected imperfectly by an unfocused lens. When she returned to the sitting room she reckoned that it was finally late enough to telephone Isabelle Mancini, the editor of *Taffeta*, without sounding a note of panic.

Isabelle Mancini was a notorious gossip. The trouble was that she liked to spend her night hours in company – when taxed on the subject, she was wont to point out that chic loneliness was hardly becoming or even useful to the editor of *Taffeta*. Gossip was Isabelle's personal contribution to these night marathons. She would certainly regard Jemima's present venture into loneliness as 'utter madness, dulling.'

This gossip was never intended to be malicious. On the contrary, the creation of legends (living) – that was Isabelle's business, and the business of *Taffeta*. If trouble was the outcome, no one was more distressed and even injured than Isabelle Mancini. But her very loyalty to Chloe might lead her to broadcast in Tasha's or Dizzy's or one of the other ludicrous smart discos for the young that she affected, that Chloe Fontaine was burdened with aged, tiresome parents 'to whom she was quite wonderful'.

Isabelle would never have heard of Chloe's parents and so would know nothing of their characters; nevertheless to Isabelle all her geese were swans, and since Chloe had parents, aged parents, apparently poor parents, it must inevitably follow that she was 'wonderful to them'. Jemima thought that Chloe would probably prefer to be spared Isabelle's loyalty on the subject of her parents.

Isabelle Mancini's private life, or to be more exact, her sexual inclinations, were like those of Valentine Brighton, a subject of occasional amused speculation among her friends. It was generally believed that she had been married, once, long ago, in Paris or possibly Rome, and that Mr Mancini had been abandoned along with residence in these capitals; nowadays she was resolutely Miss Mancini in public.

What Isabelle patently did admire both in the pages of *Taffeta* and her own conversation, was the female sex.

At *Taffeta*, she patronized women writers, particularly talented women writers who were photogenic, with enthusiasm. Chloe, for example, owed a great deal to Isabelle's encouragement, particularly when her finances were low as in the present instance. So for that matter did Binnie Rapallo, a deliciously pretty photographer who had begun a successful career by celebrating these same writers in *Taffeta*. Were Isabelle's 'little passions' ever reciprocated? Or did her continuous emphasis on 'loyalty' – 'All my friends are completely loyal to me and of course I'm so loyal to them' – hide an aching heart because 'loyalty' was never equated with love?

It was Saturday. It was while looking for the telephone directory with Isabelle's home number that Jemima first noticed the piece of bright red paper lying on the carpet near the door. It was square, garish, made of card. Tiger had moved and was crouching near it. For one instant Jemima imagined that he had pushed the card to that position with his paws, had somehow delivered it.

She picked up the card rather gingerly and turned it over. 'A Splash of Red' was printed in black letters on the other side. Above it the words Aiglon Gallery, directors Crispin Creed, Peter Potter, and below: 'Recent pictures by Kevin John Athlone will be shown at the Aiglon Gallery February 1–28.' It was now August. With relief Jemima realized that she was merely holding an official – and out of date – announcement of an exhibition. It was printed, formal, innocuous. She turned the card over again and saw for the first time that there was a message scrawled along the bottom in bold handwriting: 'Care for a visit?'

It was by now far too late for any London post. Indeed no letters had arrived that morning; the flat was both too new and too cut-off for that. Letters and circulars, if any, were probably mouldering downstairs in the empty hall with its freshly cut marble floor where a 'grand porter', Chloe had assured her, was shortly to be installed. The thought of this impending porter was not much consolation now, if in the meantime Kevin John Athlone was to be paying her unsolicited visits as and when he wished.

It struck her that the card must have been delivered while she was in the shadowy bathroom; she could hardly have missed the little red flag on the pale sea of the carpet while she contemplated Tiger's aggressive crouch. The coincidence made her both uncomfortable and angry.

Jemima would endure no more of this. The Stovers struck some chord in her heart; Kevin John Athlone nothing. Grimly, she went to the door to fling it open and if necessary confront him – only to be checked by the second lock. Jemima remembered too late that she needed a key to get out of the flat as well as into it.

Tiger sidled forward and gave a little plaintive mew beside her, something more like the cry of a baby in distress than the conventional cry of a cat. She was reminded unpleasantly of the cautionary tale of Harriet who played with matches: 'Miaow, Mioo, we told you so.' Perhaps after all it was better to dispose of the Stovers first; undoubtedly they were waiting anxiously by the telephone to hear from her. That meant calling Isabelle Mancini to get some kind of address in the Camargue for Chloe. She only hoped she was in England and not on a Greek island or in the South of France or somewhere else where at this time of year in Isabelle's opinion it was all happening.

The telephone was answered immediately – but not by Isabelle. 'Miss Shore, Isabelle would just love to talk with you,' said a voice at the other end of the telephone warmly. Either its owner had just visited the United States, or she felt that only this kind of voice was appropriate to one who answered the telephone for the editor of *Taffeta*. The accent was not quite perfect but the expression of impersonal rapture at the mere sound of Jemima's name was well done – that she, Jemima Shore, should somehow have managed to get through to Isabelle Mancini's number without succumbing to the nameless perils which lay in wait for users of the telephone system! So was the sincerity of the disappointment which followed: 'But I'm afraid Isabelle is not available right now. May I take a message? This is Laura Barrymore, Isabelle Mancini's personal assistant. As of now, I am also her house guest. I am between apartments. I should be so happy . . .'

'She's in England?' Jemima spoke with relief. It was after all August.

'Why no, Miss Shore, she's not in *England*.' For a moment the voice sounded just a little disappointed in Jemima, as though the daring act of telephoning must have slightly blunted her sensitivity. 'Isabelle has been in Paris for the Collections. I meant that she's not available to speak with anyone till noon. She's at L'Hôtel, in conference with Princess Wagram, then she would be available to take your call, then she expects to lunch with—' a Japanese name followed. 'She plans to return on Sunday.'

'Of course,' cried Jemima hastily. Then with all her television warmth, 'I should so hate to bother Isabelle personally at such a critical moment. In fact I naturally did not expect to speak to her. It's just that I'm trying to contact Chloe Fontaine rather urgently. Something to do with the autumn series—'

'Chloe Fontaine?' The voice was suddenly raised several tones higher and much sharpened; its native South Kensington origin was audible. 'I hardly think that Isabelle would be able to help you with Miss Fontaine's address, Miss Shore.' Warmth had also fled, along with transatlantic softness.

As sweetly and as rapidly as possible, Jemima explained her mission. The result was surprising. Coldness in the voice gave way to genuine astonishment.

'A piece on the Camargue? Chloe Fontaine for *Taffeta*, Miss Shore?' The implication of the last remark was clear: have you, Jemima Shore, made the unforgiveable mistake of confusing *Taffeta* with *Vogue* or *Harpers & Queen*, or *Cosmopolitan*, or *Woman's Journal* or – beyond that the possibilities were too horrendous for one such as Laura Barrymore to contemplate. But Jemima knew that she had not made a mistake. She had an excellent memory for that kind of thing. She could hear Chloe's breathless voice: 'Good old *Taffeta* . . . commissioning me', and then: '*Taffeta* Schmaffeta, but at least it never lets you down . . .' What interested her was the implication in Laura Barrymore's rapidly rising tone that the very combination in itself of Chloe and *Taffeta* was unthinkable.

Jemima had to concede that a commission to Chloe Fontaine, involving both a handsome sum of money advanced and a subsequent rendezvous abroad with a leading photographer, was hardly likely to be quite unknown to Isabelle's personal assistant, one close enough to the editor to be her 'house-guest' while she was 'between apartments'. However, for the sake of the Stovers, she persevered. Laura Barrymore was adamant.

At the end of Jemima's enquiries, however, Laura clearly felt it necessary to round off the conversation in her warmer manner. 'I should just love to take this opportunity to tell you how I adored your last programme, Miss Shore,' she murmured. 'That twilight home. The old lady and the old gentleman, both knitting, it was his knitting which just reached out to me. Like a Dutch picture sprung to life.' Jemima remembered that particular phrase since it had occurred in the *Guardian* review, and the paper had also referred to the programme in the third leader. 'A Dutch picture sprung horribly to life, showing the despair masked by an outwardly harmonious composition.' That was how it had actually read.

Still, it might just be worth making some use of Miss Barrymore's enthusiasm.

'You've been so kind . . . hardly worth bothering Isabelle with all this . . . quite, quite, so busy at this time of year.' She took a breath. 'Just one thing . . . I was contemplating, you know, an in-depth profile of

Isabelle, allied to the development of *Taffeta*, in my autumn series. You know, the serious side of fashion ... people never quite realize ... the part played in the British economy, why exports alone ... social significance.' Jemima murmured on, and ended quite quickly: 'The only thing is that I was proposing to invite Chloe Fontaine to write the programme, so much her style in a way, and she brings her own elegance to these things. But if by any chance that would be unacceptable to Isabelle – this conversation is quite between ourselves, naturally.'

'Believe me,' said Laura Barrymore, 'Miss Fontaine would be *quite* unacceptable to Miss Mancini. There are some trusts which if betrayed—' She stopped, aware that she had abandoned the swanlike supremacy of the perfect friend and assistant. My God, thought Jemima, so Chloe had quarrelled with Isabelle – the fool, and then to suppose that *Taffeta* would give her a commission – no, wait a minute, had Chloe ever indeed really tackled *Taffeta* for work?

'Particularly from a writer who had been such a very close friend. Isabelle had been so *good* to her.' Laura Barrymore was continuing as if her indignation would not quite let her stop, despite her better judgement. 'And a writer of Chloe Fontaine's stature. Her previous stature, perhaps I should say. Why did she need to draw on her friends' private lives? Surely her own provides quite enough ... It was so terribly *disloyal*. And then the letters – Isabelle felt she had been nurturing a viper.'

My God, thought Jemima again, the novel; the libel which Chloe had dismissed as petty but which worried Valentine Brighton. Chloe's new book must in some way have impinged upon – if that was the right word – the Mancini sensibilities. Disloyalty. No wonder the ultra-loyal Laura Barrymore, the faithful assistant, had frozen at the very notion of Isabelle commissioning Chloe.

'I am of course Chloe Fontaine's house guest,' Jemima put in as diplomatically as possible at the end of this tirade. The reminder had the desired effect. Laura hesitated.

'You're actually in her flat? Her new flat? I hadn't quite appreci-ated—'

'Exactly.'

For a moment the honey returned. 'In that case, Miss Shore, it occurs to me that it might be helpful if I came by, maybe I could talk with you on the subject of Isabelle and Miss Fontaine, put you in the picture—'

'No, no!' cried Jemima hastily. 'Really, it's of no consequence.' She had absolutely no wish to be further embroiled in Isabelle Mancini's row with Chloe. The solution to what she was rapidly beginning to rate as the Chloe Mystery, certainly did not lie in the files of *Taffeta* magazine.

Jemima must now put that mystery away from her thoughts. Easy now to sign off her brief relationship with the Stovers. Clearly Chloe was in some enigmatic way in control of her own destiny. She had lied to Jemima about the Camargue, or at any rate misled her. Undoubtedly for the same strange reason she had also misled her parents. In fact, Jemima reflected wryly at the end of her long-drawn-out telephone call to Isabelle's flat, if anyone had succeeded in disappearing in London without trace, it was Chloe Fontaine rather than Jemima Shore. But that was no longer her concern. It was time to gather a notebook and depart for the British Library.

When she telephoned Mr Stover and told him that *Taffeta* had no trace of Chloe's whereabouts, and he must use his own judgement whether to summon the police, Jemima made it clear from her tone that she thought the step unnecessary. Mr Stover too sounded heavier and almost resigned.

'The wife always said I was too fierce to her on the phone', was his first comment. 'Thank you, Miss Shore, we'll look out for you on television in the autumn. If she does phone you—' He stopped. 'Mrs Stover, she does worry, in spite of everything, she can't help it. But she's led her own life for too long, Dollie, we don't really know her any more. That's what I tell her mother. Now if we'd had one of our own—'

It seemed an appropriate moment for Jemima to bid them a polite goodbye. She did not expect to hear of or from the Stovers again; she retained a tiny flicker of interest in what would happen to that old, unvisited couple, that worrying old woman, that old man who felt now that he had been too fierce and driven off the golden bird who was their only link with youth. Concentrated study would soon extinguish even that flicker.

But Chloe – that was different. Jemima was full of natural and cross curiosity about her wayward friend's inexplicable behaviour. If she gave full rein to it, she might ruin this whole promised day of earnest research, by mulling, pondering, even making a checking telephone call, when she, Jemima, was supposed to be incommunicado. Time to be gone. Wearing one of her favourite dresses, silk jersey in the beige she loved with its own little splashes of red and navy blue, practical enough for the British Library, elegant enough to give her spirits a lift, she picked up her notebook. It was a pretty Italianate thing which appeared to be covered in wallpaper whose unsuitability for serious research, like the delight of the flowing dress, she found both soothing and cheering.

This time she remembered to use the second key to unlock the flat door. Tiger sidled towards her and rubbed himself against the high-heeled golden sandal which, on the principle of the notebook, Jemima had decided to wear to the British Library. Jemima shooed him away. 'Back for dinner. Enjoy your balcony, there's a good cat.' And she was still in fact addressing the cat when the door swung open, and she felt both her arms roughly seized. The keys were twisted from her grasp.

'Didn't she get my visiting card?' said Kevin John Athlone. He was so close to her that Jemima could see the slight sweat on his cheeks. She noticed involuntarily that he had not shaved. 'Care for a visit?' He was flushed as well as sweating. 'Well, now she's getting a visit, whether she likes it or not. And you too, Miss Jemima Shore.'

Pushing her back into the flat, he deftly relocked the door. From the wrong side of it, Tiger gave a long unhappy mew.

4
Irish accent

'Where is she?'

Jemima thought Kevin John Athlone had been drinking: drinking all night. His breath smelt sour with a nasty tang of acid in it, mingling with the smell of the sweat which beaded his cheeks and damped his bright blue towelling T-shirt. He wore light blue jeans which did not fit particularly well. They sagged on his hips; the broad leather belt which supported them had given up beneath the curve of his belly; the jeans look more rumpled than creased.

He was still startlingly handsome. He ran rather than lumbered to search the remaining rooms of the flat; his movements were surprisingly light.

'Where's she hiding?' he demanded, grasping both her arms firmly.

The huge circular eyes which gazed into hers like those of a drugged but hostile animal being taken away to market, were of an astonishing blue. The bulging red veins visible in the white only set off their immaculate sky colour. His lashes so close to Jemima's own – for he still held her tight – that she could see them quivering as the sweat ran down the corners of his eyes, were as long as a woman's. His hair, although greasy and falling round his face, far too long for elegance, was dramatically dark and thick.

Kevin John had always looked far more like a young Irish actor than a promising English painter. His father, not half such a handsome man, had in fact been quite well known on the Dublin stage; Jemima fancied that his mother too had been an actress. At this moment he resembled some actor flung out of the Abbey Theatre Company, or perhaps just a member of the company after a hard night.

335

'Where is she, I said.' It was quite surprising to find that he spoke without a trace of an Irish accent.

'How the hell do I know?'

By way of reply Kevin John simply twisted her arms sharply. Her bag and notebook dropped.

'Find her then.' The stink of his breath was even more offensive than the pain. 'Jemima Shore, Investigator.' The sneer with which he pronounced her name infuriated her.

'Let go of my arms, you drunken slob.' This time Kevin John let go of her arms and gave Jemima a wide swinging blow on the side of her face. The pain of it was so unexpected that tears came into her eyes. Her whole head felt dizzy. As Jemima reeled, he struck her again on the face but harder this time. She staggered. He hit her again and as she felt herself sinking he shouted something which sounded like 'harlot'. Or perhaps it was 'harder'.

'It's no good,' she heard herself saying faintly. He seemed to go on hitting her. Then she toppled or sank onto the carpet.

The next thing she knew Kevin John was kneeling over her. He appeared to be crying or perhaps it was merely the sweat pouring down his face. His breath still smelt terrible.

'Oh, sweet Jesus,' he was saying. 'I'm sorry, I'm sorry.' Now he was crying in earnest. He sat down beside Jemima on the thick carpet, put his enormous handsome head on his arms and started to blubber. Jemima heard words like: 'I love her, I love her,' mingled with apologies, louder cries, and confused insults, of which 'effing whore' and 'tail-wagging bitch' were about the mildest. At any rate the words 'whore' and 'bitch' were prominent amongst them. Dizzily, Jemima wasn't quite sure whether he meant Chloe or herself.

After a bit Kevin John stopped crying, raised his head and stared at her: 'I'm drunk.'

Jemima said nothing.

'Could you be a sweetheart and make me some coffee? I must talk to you.' Jemima rose unsteadily from the floor and held onto the edge of the sofa. She was glad she had not hit her head on the edge of one of Chloe's smart little glass tables as she fell. All the same she wondered what her face looked like as she walked, still unsteadily, her head aching, into the kitchen. She looked out of the window which was at the back of the building. The kitchen had a small modern fire escape attached to it; the door was merely bolted. Chloe had shown her the key, while recommending her not to use it, except in emergency. But Jemima decided that even if the situation demanded escape, she felt far too dizzy.

She peered into the kitchen mirror (there were mirrors everywhere in Chloe's flat). Although there was a large red mark on one side of her face, as though she had slept on it, otherwise it did not look too bad. But the sting and the ache were fierce.

Jemima made some coffee, the one thing she always boasted of being able to do automatically, even half-conscious. Under the circumstances, that was fortunate.

When she came back into the living room, Kevin John was sitting on the sofa. He did not look at her as she placed the mug of coffee beside him. Jemima went and sat in the big white chair near the window, as far away as possible from the sofa; the roar of the traffic below and the occasional sharp little tooting reached her from far away, as though from some remote shore.

'Don't worry, I'm not going to hit you again.' He gulped the freshly made coffee as if it were spirits – he seemed indifferent to its heat. 'Have you got a cigarette?'

'I don't smoke. You can look around.'

'She never has any cigarettes.' But he heaved up his body and started to prowl about the room, disarranging the huge downy cushions as though packets might be disgorged. Then he vanished into the bedroom. The keys of the flat were lying on the table. Jemima wondered rather hazily whether she should grab them and run down and out into the square. She was still contemplating the move when Kevin John returned, smoking a black cigarette. The new harsh smell made Jemima feel nauseous.

'These yours?' He held out a box of Black Sobranies, and a lighter.

'I told you I didn't smoke.'

'They're not hers. The——' He added a crude description of Chloe.

Jemima remained silent. She was fairly sure such conspicuous cigarettes had not been visible in the bedroom the night before since her own distaste for cigarettes, above all in a bedroom – even unsmoked – would have caused her to remove them. He must have routed them out from some drawer, exacerbating his own hurt; still it was pointlessly provocative to say so.

'Look at this.' The lighter was dumped down in front of her. It was a pretty little object, striped black and white enamel, with an opaque reddish-brown jewel – a beryl or a piece of agate – set in its head. 'Recognize it?'

'No.' But even as she spoke, a memory stirred; she felt she had seen the lighter or something very like it before. For one thing it was the kind of personal detail Jemima noticed automatically about people whether she was interviewing them or not, a professional habit of observation. Placing the precise person was more difficult because during the last month, both setting up programmes for the autumn series and clearing the decks for her own holiday, Jemima had spoken to, eaten and drunk with an inordinate number of different people, types jumbled together.

It was also possible that she had marked down the lighter at Megalithic House. Cy Fredericks, her boss at MTV, had a fine taste in gold accoutrements, and was fond of throwing any new little bejewelled toy at her as a joke at the expense of what he supposed to be her Puritan streak: 'Fancy it, Jem? Gems for Jem? Yours if that programme wins the prize at Amsterdam.' The last time Cy Fredericks indulged his taste for that particular pleasantry, he had been referring to *The Unvisited*.

But the lighter was, she had to admit, in rather too good taste for Cy. It was really very attractive, with a feeling of modern Fabergé about it. Where *had* she seen it? Never mind, it would come back to her.

'Where is she, Miss Jezebel Fontaine, the bitch of Bloomsbury, the fuck of Fulham, the harlot of the Brighthelmet Press, the curs' delight—' And Kevin John proceeded to embark upon a string of imprecations in which terms of Biblical denunciation and suggestions of animal congress were mingled. His language had always been appalling – if colourfully so – but what had seemed rather amusingly vivid in the jolly young painter Chloe had run off with, was now merely the gratuitous thrusting of his untrammelled anger on the world.

At the same time, despite his outburst, it was clear that Kevin John was rapidly becoming less drunk. But the expression on his face being no less threatening and his wild round blue eyes still dilating, Jemima had no confidence that temporary sobriety would prevent him beating her up again if he was so minded. It had been a bad mistake not to run while she had the opportunity.

'I tell you again I haven't the slightest idea!' Jemima almost shouted the words. Despair, brought on not only by an aching head but also by a sense of the ludicrous unfairness of his question, to say nothing of his behaviour, made her abandon caution. She proceeded to tell Kevin John, furiously but succinctly, exactly what had happened since Chloe tripped so lightly out of her own flat the previous night, allegedly en route for the Camargue, leaving Jemima as her house-sitter for a month. How the Stovers had telephoned, expecting a visit; as a result of which call, Jemima had investigated the Camargue expedition and found it to be a fabrication; how there was therefore no record of Chloe's present whereabouts.

Jemima left nothing out of the story except for Laura Barrymore's strictures on Chloe's new novel.

She ended: 'All this and your calls too!' She wanted to say your 'filthy calls' but thought it impolitic.

'It was the picture she liked. It was the only thing of mine she took from the Fulham house. She sent the rest of my work down to Cornwall in a van. I found the card in the pocket of my jeans.' He spoke more flatly. 'I suppose I kept it for the Aiglon number. When I come to London, I generally try to wrench some of his ill-gotten gains – gotten at my expense – out of Creeping Croesus or his side-kick Pansy Potter. Dropping the card in was the only way I knew how to reach Chloe.'

'I meant the telephone calls.' An immense weariness was overcoming Jemima. She wished Kevin John would go away, find Chloe or not as fate – Chloe's fate – would have it, and leave her to crawl back into the white bedroom, shutter out the dry blazing Bloomsbury sunlight and sleep.

'How could I call her? She wouldn't give me her number. I only got the address in the first place by charming the pants off that new woman in Fulham. Little Chloe, sweet little Miss Delilah, paws-in-the-air have-me-any-time-you-want, God rot her for the lying scheming Dutch-doll-faced bitch she is, had been oh, oh, so sure that she didn't want anyone to have her address. "One's public, Mrs Ramsbotham, how they haunt one, don't they? One is never alone. An artist needs peace . . ."'
He gave quite an accurate parody of Chloe's breathless little voice, even if the words were ridiculous, and caressed his untidy black head with exactly the same delicate air as Chloe was apt to pat her own, as though too much pressure might bruise it.

'An Irish accent.'

Kevin John gave her his angry red-blue stare.

'Those telephone calls; obscene telephone calls. You had an Irish accent. *He* had an Irish accent. Not very pronounced but it was there.'

'Look, Miss Jemima Shore, Investigator' – he took perverse pleasure in reciting her public title and every time he used it his anger increased – 'I don't know what half-arsed Judas you're talking about or what calls either. Christ, I could use a drink. No cigarettes, no drink.' A black Sobranie was in his fingers as he spoke; he had been chain-smoking them. The packet was half full; he didn't seem to notice.

'There's some white wine in the fridge.'

'Oh, I bet there's some lovely chilled *vino blanco* in the fridge . . . And I'll pour it in long green glasses just for us two.' Once again the imitation of Chloe was at least recognizable. 'Well, I don't want any of Chloe's delicately scented ladies' piss. I want a whisky.'

'Find it. If you can. I've no idea if there's any whisky here or not.' Jemima confined her own drinking strictly to wine.

'It's too early. It's much too early for whisky. Quite the Delilah yourself, aren't you? Do you want to make me drunk at this hour in the morning? Want to control me? Bring me down? Well, I can tell you this, Miss Jemima Shore, Investigator, no one brings me down.' He glared at her. 'So what was that about the telephone?'

Jemima told him about the two calls. It seemed the safer topic of the two. She still wasn't convinced that he hadn't made them himself. She might have imposed an Irish accent because her abiding mental image of Kevin John Athlone was as being Irish – and rough. If he had been drunk enough, he might easily have made the calls and forgotten the next morning.

'But I didn't know her number. How could I do such a terrible thing?' he remarked at the end in an injured voice. His long eyelashes fluttered slightly; there was something mechanically boyish about his manner, something wheedling about his tone. Jemima glimpsed with no particular favour the handsome and indulged young man Kevin John had once been. She still didn't know whether to believe his assurance or not.

Suddenly he leant forward and to her absolute surprise and horror planted a kiss full on her lips. The stubble on his chin grazed her skin and she wriggled backwards in her chair without being able to speak or do more than mutely struggle. His mouth was enormous; it was as if a gigantic fish were trying to gobble her up.

'You're a darling, aren't you? A real sweetheart. You'll forgive me, won't you, sweetheart, because I'm going to say sorry so nicely to you. I'm going to be so utterly, utterly charming and pleasing—'

For a moment Jemima thought he meant – no, surely even he—

'I'm going to have a shower and a shave – I'm sure that' – he paused and then said in his naughty-boyish voice – 'that *lady* has a razor somewhere about. Then I'm going out and I shall buy you the biggest bunch of flowers in the whole of London, this bitch of a city, which frightens the daylights out of your poor honest artist even on a fine summer's morn.'

'I don't want any flowers.' Her voice was low. 'I have no idea where Chloe is and now will you please go away and leave me alone.'

'Oh, you'll never be quite alone here, sweetheart. Never quite without me. I'm a match for you, darling. Look – there's my picture looking down on you. A great wonderful splash of red for you. Still, if you really don't want me further, I'll leave you. Maybe my old pal Dixie is still in London; I have an idea we were drinking somewhere together last night. I couldn't get an answer from Creeping Croesus.' He passed his hand over his head as if the recollection pained him. 'He'll give me a razor and a bath. And then I'll buy you the flowers. Splashes and splashes of them. All red. Cheer up this whited sepulchre of hers.'

Jemima hated red flowers.

'You really have no need to apologize further,' she said coldly. 'You were drunk.'

'Ah, sweetheart, the flowers won't be an apology. They're to woo you, to please you, and then with your matchless wits, Miss Jemima Shore, Investigator, you'll find Miss Chloe Fontaine for me. I know you will.'

'*Please* go away. Unlock the door and go away—'

And then to her further surprise he did. He unlocked the door, deposited the keys carefully on the table, and left. She noticed once again the lightness with which his shambling body could move. Kevin John did not, however, shut the door behind him and she lacked the energy to get up. She heard his footsteps on the uncarpeted stairs, loud, thumping all the way to the front door. It was a long way down. The street door was opened. She did not hear it shut.

Jemima regained her energy and walked unsteadily to the balcony. She looked over. Amidst the desultory passers-by on the pavement of the huge Bloomsbury square below, Kevin John in his bright blue shirt was easy to pick out. He wove through the traffic and disappeared in the direction of the British Museum. It was not much more than twelve hours since she had looked for Chloe in the same square and missed her.

He was definitely gone. She was alone. Except for—

'Tiger!' she cried aloud. 'Tiger!' Oh no! Tiger, last heard mewing with outrage when Kevin John had precipitately pushed her inside the door and relocked it, leaving the cat either by design or mistake on the wrong side of it. She had no clear memory of hearing any further mews, but then the ensuing scene had been sufficiently violent to drown the plaints of an excluded cat. Tiger was certainly nowhere to be seen or heard now. He had not chosen to return by the balcony window. She wondered whether a cat would ascend the scaffolding of Adelaide Square all the way from the street. She must go downstairs and look for him. Perhaps he had vanished into the darkened basement area, the last lap of the long staircase.

Remembering to take the keys, and deciding it was prudent to lock the flat behind her – she wanted no more unscheduled visits – Jemima set forth rather gingerly down the first flight of stairs. After the airy brightness of the penthouse, the light was dim.

'Tiger – Puss, Puss, Puss—' Her voice echoed rather queerly in the well of the stairs, occupied by the lifeless lift cage.

There was no other sound. It was Saturday, and the rest of the building was of course quite empty. Even the noise of the traffic from Adelaide Square and its echo from the Tottenham Court Road was subdued.

It was as Jemima was passing the door of the third-floor flat – a substantial mahogany door, preserved no doubt from the original house, set incongruously into the concrete – that she heard quite distinctly the mew of a cat.

5

The Lion's Den

Jemima called and the cat mewed again.

She banged heavily and tried to turn the handle. It was ornamental. The cat began to cry quite plaintively, that odd infant's cry she had remarked as a curiosity before. Now it drove her frantic. She banged harder.

'Is anyone there?' she shouted.

Absolute silence from whatever lay behind the polished darkness of the mahogany. Then further mewing. This was the moment for those powers of reasoning first praised, if warily, by the nuns at her convent school, more enthusiastically by her tutors at Cambridge, finally lavishly admired by her public, as well as treasured by Megalith Television; that logical faculty, in short, incarnated in the title which Kevin John Athlone so much despised – Jemima Shore, Investigator.

But it did not in fact need supreme detective gifts to work it out. The cat could only have passed through the door if the door was open; *ergo* the door had opened. It was unimaginable that such a door should have blown open, flown open, and unlikely that it had been left open (she would certainly have noticed on her way in; Chloe on her way out, and Kevin John, lurking, could hardly have missed it). Therefore some human agency had opened it, and moreover had done so in the comparatively short time since Tiger had been shut out of the top-floor flat.

The only other possibility was that Tiger had after all tried to scale the outside of the house, and miscalculating, had entered an open window on the third floor. That raised the question of why he didn't depart by the same window on finding the flat empty – if indeed he *had* found it empty. In any case, if Tiger had after all already accustomed

343

himself to climbing the heights of Adelaide Square, during Chloe's short tenancy of the flat, why did he not of his own accord return to his natural home in the top flat?

Nevertheless the point could be quickly established by inspecting the majestic façade of the house for an open window. It might be worth looking at the back of the building too; the third-floor flat must also be connected with the fire escape.

She called encouragingly: 'Puss, Puss, Puss' and decided to give the mahogany door one more bang, partly to keep contact with the cat inside, partly to make quite sure that it had not actually jammed. After that she foresaw a routine with the police – and firemen – if no visible window presented itself.

As a loving cat-owner of many years' standing, Jemima had had her share of such experiences. Blanche, the disdainful white cat who had preceded Colette, had had the capacity of a feckless aristocrat for getting herself into scrapes and then expecting other people to busy themselves rescuing her. Jemima had a vision of Blanche, white and fluffy like some garment which had come to rest high up in a tree, gazing at the firemen hired to rescue her with implacable condescension. Life with Blanche had been an expensive and demanding business; life with Tiger and his mistress Chloe was so far proving equally demanding. Yet unlike the erring Chloe, Tiger could not be consigned to his fate over the weekend.

Jemima gave the door one last bang and almost fell over as it swung open silently at her blow.

As Tiger, a golden streak of fur, dashed between her legs onto the staircase, Jemima found herself faced with a huge cave of a room. It was carpeted in something navy blue or even black which looked like felt, but otherwise contained no furniture whatsoever. Three of the walls were painted a shiny dark cobalt blue, a pretty colour in itself, but one which scarcely relieved the sombre floor. The third wall was in fact a vast window of darkened glass, of the sort generally seen in the windows of discreet cars; it was this smoky area which gave the room its feeling of a cave.

The contrast between the summery textures of Chloe's flat and this vault was remarkable. Even the ceiling here gave the impression of being low, whereas in reality it must be considerably higher than that of the flat above; the effect of the various blues was subterranean. Jemima could see that this flat, like Chloe's, did enjoy some form of concrete balcony, somewhere behind the smoky window. Here too, the feeling of trees and space, if untrammelled by darkened glass, would be spectacular. Jemima speculated on the weird mentality of someone who would rent a very modern flat on the third floor of a Georgian square and then deliberately exclude the view.

The proportions of this flat in general, whether because of the colours or not, seemed to lack the harmony exhibited by Chloe's above it. Perhaps Sir Richard Lionnel's architect was more accustomed to designing penthouses than third-floor flats which had to be fitted into the site of a former Georgian mansion.

Grotesquely, a marble mantelpiece of classical design was stuck into the middle of the left-hand blue wall although there was no grate within it. It had the air of an old-fashioned oasis in a very modern desert.

'Adam,' said a low voice behind her.

Jemima jumped and gave a little scream. Her heart beat loudly and unpleasantly. The word, almost whispered, sounded right in her ear. She wheeled round and found she was gazing straight into the eyes of a young man who had been standing in the angle of the door, neatly concealed by it as it swung open. He was smiling at her.

'Adam,' he said again and then with a further grin at her bewilderment pointed at the mantelpiece.

'Adam. Made for the *piano nobile* of this house, I'll be bound. Doesn't it look ghastly hoiked up here? Particularly, stuck in the middle of that hideous wall. They might just as well have papered it with PVC or even cut up some plastic macs to secure the same effect. Why bother with paint?' He was rattling on, but it seemed to be natural garrulity rather than nerves. 'Nice cat that, by the way. Matches the colour of your hair. The eyes are different, though. You do have the eyes of a cat, of course, undoubtedly you've been told that before, but it just happens to be a different cat.'

During this colloquy, Tiger, as though encouraged by the direction the conversation was taking, had ventured back into the room and was rubbing himself against Jemima's legs and purring. She was touched that their short acquaintance had made such an impression on him – considering the way he had been treated – until she was aware that the stranger was being similarly honoured.

'It wanted to come in, by the way, and as I believe in liberty of the individual I permitted it. I also gave it some milk.' He waved towards an open door, presumably the kitchen. 'I was worried about letting it out in case the cars would get it. Squeal, whoosh and Goldilocks is no more.'

'Tiger. Male.'

'Seventeen-eighty, the original house, to speak of loftier matters,' continued her interlocutor warmly as though she had not spoken. 'One of the finest things Adam ever did. This was named for him originally, you know, Adam Square; they changed it fifty years later for Queen Adelaide on the accession of her old man. I've got all the original drawings, I copied them in the British Museum as a matter of fact. I had the idea of blowing them up and plastering them all over the PVC walls as a kind of reproach when I leave. What do you think?'

'Aah. A squatter.'

His smile became even more friendly.

'Certainly. What are you? Though I detest the word, don't you? It has an unfortunate association with the position Indians adopt to perform their natural functions. I prefer to term myself a Friend of the House. Like Friends of the Earth but a bit more upright. Literally. No offence meant to the Friends of the Earth; excellent people; in fact we Friends of the House deliberately copied their title and took it further – upward. Officially we're FROTH – Friends and Re-vivifiers of the House – but I myself think there's something altogether too bubbly about that title. It hardly expresses the calm and repose which we Friends of the House aim to spread about us.'

There was something curiously relaxed about the house's self-styled friend; this, despite his loquacity. His most striking physical characteristic was an aureole of reddish-brown hair. His eyes were exactly the same colour. But the hair itself, although abundant, was not unkempt and the beard which framed his chin was neatly trimmed; the Friend of the House's looks certainly showed more recent signs of care than those of Kevin John Athlone. The Friend was also taller than she had supposed at first sight; about as tall as Jemima herself. Although he was also exceptionally thin – she could have put both hands round his hips in their worn jeans – his shoulders were broad and the arms in the white T-shirt well muscled. With his curly mouth, smiling even in repose, and pointed ears, there was something of Pan or some other sprite, Robin Goodfellow perhaps, about him, not exactly malign, but distinctly mischievous.

Jemima also observed how white and clean the stranger's feet were in their thonged sandals, and indeed his skin generally. She wondered suddenly how old he was. Like his height, his age might be deceptive. For that matter, who *was* he?

'Adam. Adam Adamson.' She had the impression that the bright squirrel's eyes had read her thoughts. 'May I introduce myself since I take it we are neighbours? Adam Adamson. I know it sounds affected and maybe it is, but maybe equally it is a poor thing but mine own. In this interesting world of make-believe and make-forget in which we live, who knows or cares what I was originally called? My intense

admiration for Robert Adam obviously makes my patronymic peculiarly appropriate, although I cannot claim to be descended from him.
At least I am descended from Adam, straight descent all the way down,
no one can question that particular aspect of my pedigree. So that
Adam Adamson, whether my own legal name or not in the opinion of
our literal-minded authorities, is at least a name to which I can morally
lay claim. I made exactly the same point to the magistrate last time I
was arrested,' he added conversationally.

'For squatting? Sorry to use that vulgar term but I can't remember
exactly what it is you call it.'

'Revivifying is what we prefer. I am for example revivifying seventy-
three Adelaide Square and so, I fancy, are you. How pleased Adam
would be incidentally, to think that you, someone so classically
beautiful as you—' He cocked an eyebrow at her. 'What is your name
by the way?'

'Eve,' replied Jemima Shore in the same light tone. To tell the truth,
she wasn't quite sure whether or not the request for her name was a
further affectation. Jemima was too level-headed to allow her instant
recognizability to affect the course of her life. On the whole she
regarded her popular fame as a convenient weapon to be wielded when
necessary in the cause of her serious work of television reporting.
Nevertheless it was rare that she was not recognized by someone of
Adam's particular television-watching age group.

'No, no, you're not,' replied Adam Adamson. 'You're not Eve at all. I
know perfectly well who you are. I've known all along. You're a classical
goddess. Grey-eyed Athena, found on a pillar perhaps; not nearly solid
enough to support one, no caryatid you. Something to be worshipped;
or a fifth-century Demeter, perhaps; with your strong straight classical
lines—'

'You're talking about me as a building. And I'm generally told my
eyes are green.' Jemima couldn't help smiling back at him. Something
about Adam Adamson appealed to her. Besides she had made at least
two major programmes over the years centred round squatters, their
various ideals and projects and in most, if not all, cases, had respected
them. Nor did she lump all squatters together. The Friends of the
House, for example, clearly had a high standard of hygiene – not an
attribute possessed by all squatters whatever their idealism – for the
echoing modern cobalt blue cavern was very clean. Unless Adam
Adamson had only just moved in.

'A few weeks back,' said Adam, repeating his uncanny trick of
answering a question she had not yet put, 'we were demonstrating as
usual outside this revolting monument to Sir Richard Lionnel's

maniacal vanity, when someone tipped me the wink that a key could be had to the third floor. No questions asked. Perhaps some enlightened human being took the line that I would be a desirable tenant. Or perhaps some fellow son of Adam had conceived a violent hatred for the devouring lion's ornamentation of his own den. Oh, didn't you know?' He waved his hand. Again Jemima observed its whiteness, set off by a few red-gold hairs; the nails were clean and scrubbed-looking. 'This was to be Sir Richard Lionnel's own home.' Another wave.

'Yes, I'm squatting in the Lion's Den – and for a den I suppose the word squatting might be appropriate for once. I'm revivifying the whole house, but I doubt if much revivifying could go on in this blue hell. Cleansing fire would be more appropriate.' A further Pan-like smile.

'Still, it's the principle of the thing, and it's for the principle of bearding the lion in his den – please note the beard specially grown for the occasion – that I have deserted my previous salubrious accommodation in Chelsea. I deserted that to suffer quite dreadfully here. Oh, my aesthetic sensibilities in the excrescence of Adelaide Square!'

He showed no signs of stopping. 'The Lion is making us suffer every time we charge round Adelaide Square. Arriving at the demo in the morning causes a true ache in my heart, especially if you look at the sort of thing the Lion has recently devoured, as illustrated on the opposite side of the square. So why should he not suffer a tiny little pang at finding his own personal domain occupied? I suppose the Lion's jackal-in-chief, Judas Turpin, will let him know on Monday morning. Too late to ruin his weekend in Sussex by the sea, but a splendid sobering start to another week of swallowing houses whole in his maw. You know that he intends to devour the corner property as well? Regurgitating it as something similar to this, but worse. He's had the whole structure condemned as rotten. Ah well, he has a surprise coming.' Adam took a breath.

'Now tell me about yourself,' he continued kindly. 'And by the way shall we sit down on the Stygian carpet as we get to know each other better. Or would you prefer to entertain me in whichever corner of Hades you have chosen?'

'No, no, not upstairs,' said Jemima hastily. She had had enough of unwanted visitors for one day; even though Adam Adamson might prove an amusing addition to her life. Caution also dictated the minimum of involvement with squatters – even revivifiers.

Chloe Fontaine was after all a legal tenant at 73 Adelaide Square. No revivifier she, as *Time* magazine would put it. Having leased or bought such an expensive flat – Jemima wasn't sure which but if it was a lease presumably it was a long one, acquired with the proceeds of the sale of the Fulham house – Chloe had a vested interest in the maintenance of law and order in the building.

So far Adam Adamson presented an orderly front; but this was on the basis of one day's occupation. Jemima had seen what the most amiable squatters could do to an interior within a very short space of time. Did Adam intend to dwell here alone and if so for how long? A single rather slight man would not be very difficult for Sir Richard Lionnel's minions to eject. Perhaps he envisaged moving in some allies. On the other hand it was possible he contemplated a mere token occupation and would depart, leaving as he had suggested blow-ups of the original Adam designs on Sir Richard's dark blue walls as an artistic reproach.

Jemima's loyalty was towards her old friend. If squatters occupied number 73 in earnest, so that there was a prolonged siege, the value of Chloe's property stood to diminish drastically. Chloe, with all her faults, was a woman alone in the world supporting herself by her own – hard – labours. She probably also contributed to the welfare, if not the happiness, of the Stovers of Folkestone. Since it was not suggested that number 73 was to be left empty – indeed the Lion of Bloomsbury was intending to occupy one portion of it personally – she was not at all sure that a squat was morally justified by her own standards, if it proved financially damaging to Chloe. This was after all an aesthetic protest, not the housing of the homeless.

At the same time the architecture of this latest addition to Adelaide Square *was* brutally displeasing. If Sir Richard proposed further similar intrusions and had somehow bamboozled the powers-that-were into accepting them, there was a case to be made for popular protests. That might secure what lawful authority had failed to protect.

Jemima found herself toying with the problem, despite herself, in professional television terms. 'The Lion of Bloomsbury or Sir Richard the Lionnelheart?' (She had read some colour magazine article about the tycoon under the latter heading.) Excellent visual material available; an entertaining interview with Adam Adamson; a cool deliberately low-key one with Sir Richard Lionnel: let him damn himself out of his own mouth if necessary: Jemima Shore, Investigator, knew exactly how to conduct that kind of interview. Guiltily she remembered the claims of the British Library and the Edwardian lady philanthropists.

Gathering Tiger into her arms, Jemima said hastily: 'No time for the present to talk about me. But I've much enjoyed hearing about *you*.' Tiger wriggled in her arms and his fierce green eyes gazed at her with indignation. 'Look, I must be off. I have an appointment.' Let her sort out her correct attitude to Adam Adamson and his fellow Friends of the House in peace, rather than under his enquiring squirrel's gaze. She did not, for one thing, like the sound of that future project, whatever it might be, planned by the demonstrators. It might be her duty to Chloe to find out a little more about it.

'Yes, why don't you think it over by yourself?' said Adam with a smile as though she had spoken. 'And then, my dear goddess, I am convinced that you will join us in our cause, bringing all the powers of your fellow gods and goddesses to our aid.' Was he mocking her and was that a glancing reference to the might of Megalith Television?

'But do tell me before you go, exactly what brought you, you with your archaic smile, to Adelaide Square from Mount Olympus? Or wherever it is you generally inhabit. I sense a mystery here.'

'I had better tell you plainly that I am not a squatter – revivifier,' Jemima said quickly as she left the flat. 'I've been lent the penthouse by a friend as a matter of fact. A straightforward tenant. They do exist.'

She did not wait to see Adam Adamson's reaction to this bold announcement. Back in the penthouse she deposited Tiger, fed him and checked that the balcony window was open for his egresses during her absence. How delightful and bleached and open the penthouse seemed! Like a glorious sandy seaside after the murky cavern of the third floor. Not all the works of the Lionnel Estate were bad.

She would have preferred to have eaten a quick meal there; but she had finished all the salad the night before. Jemima decided on a local café instead, somewhere where she could enjoy a glass of wine and read a book. *Fallen Child* might be dipped into again, as a tribute to her hostess. She selected a copy from the neat little row of Chloe's novels, stored modestly and inconspicuously at ground level. As usual, she admired the author's photograph which occupied the entire back of the jacket. Chloe really was amazingly photogenic: Valentine was right to take advantage of the fact. All the same, why on earth had a lace parasol seemed an appropriate accessory for this particular picture? No wonder the reviewers sometimes sneered.

Jemima carefully locked the flat behind her with the second Chubb key.

But as she returned down the stairs to re-enter the outside world, she found Adam Adamson waiting for her on the landing of the third floor. He was not smiling quite so broadly, a mere curve of his lips saluted her. He was in fact blocking her way.

'Just one more thing, green-eyed Pallas Athena, oh wisest one. What is the name of the obliging friend who lent you the flat?'

There seemed no point in keeping it from him. For all she knew, there were letters addressed to Chloe in the hall below.

'She's called Chloe Fontaine. The writer. You may have heard of her.' She was carrying *Fallen Child*. 'Look, you might recognize her, even if you don't know the name. She sometimes appears on television.' Chloe's large sloe-like eyes gazed at them, provocative, enigmatic, beneath the white frame of the absurdly pretty parasol.

Adam Adamson gazed down at the photograph. He looked utterly disconcerted. He still smiled but as she analysed it later it was a smile of genuine surprise, even disbelief. In some way she had astonished him.

All he said was: 'Chloe: a nymph's name. But for a writer, one of the muses might have been more appropriate, Calliope, perhaps, the muse of tragedy. Still, she's certainly very beautiful.' And on that enigmatic and faintly disquieting note, Adam Adamson went back into the flat and closed its heavy mahogany door.

6

B for Beware

The Reading Room of the British Library, lying inside the British Museum, was very hot. Not unlike the summer streets of Bloomsbury through which she had passed, the Reading Room exuded an atmosphere of dust; it was also airless being without air-conditioning or open windows, the sun beating on the great glass dome which surmounted it. As a result, an aroma of faint dampness met Jemima as she presented her pass at the entrance. For a moment she was tempted to abandon this humid temple to literature in favour of the cooler halls of the Museum itself, presided over by huge wide-mouthed slant-eyed Egyptian monarchs and eagle-headed Assyrian deities. Other vast feline figures were guarding temples which had long ago disappeared. Here tourists worshipped with wondering eyes.

The Reading Room on the other hand was full of up-to-date activity. No one wandered. People strode. Unlike the tourists, the readers, carrying briefcases and rolled copies of the *Guardian*, gave an unmistakeable air of knowing where they were going. Because the Reading Room constituted its own busy little world in the midst of the great sprawling castle of the Museum, with its staircases and salons and guards, it always seemed to Jemima peculiarly appropriate that it should be built in the shape and design of a spinning-wheel in a fairy story. So one might fancifully imagine its toilers bent over intricate webs.

There were however a great many toilers already present this Saturday afternoon in August, and that particular idle fancy quickly gave way to irritation as Jemima embarked on the notoriously long-drawn-out process of finding an empty seat. Doggedly, she inspected the rows of seats, which radiated out from the central enclosure, forming the spokes of the wheel. After a while she gazed at those fortunate enough to possess them with the hostility of one searching for an empty taxi. The trouble was that the British Library system of sending for a book from the stacks necessitated the possession of a seat before you could fill in a request slip.

In the past, Jemima had enjoyed one concentrated and instructive spell working in the Reading Room. During a temporary lull in her television career, she had supported herself for three months researching in the Reading Room on behalf of an enterprising publisher who wished to launch a series composed of abridged versions of Victorian classics – out of the public mind, and also out of copyright. The series had never appeared and the publisher had disappeared. Jemima had gone back to television. But during the long days, Jemima had surreptitiously begun to study, on her own account, a topic more congenial to her own taste. This was the genesis of the book on the Edwardian lady philanthropists.

She still remembered the curious stifling anonymous freedom of working in the Reading Room every day, as though going to some office where one was at the same time totally unknown and yet expected. She had also, during that original sojourn, learnt the Reading Room rules about looking up books, which had their own logic, not readily assimilable on the first visit, but like riding a bicycle, once learnt never forgotten.

Jemima turned left and began to pace round the semicircle of seats radiating out from the central desk. They were arranged alphabetically, and she found herself beginning at L. The despised little central row of seats between each spoke were marked double L, double M, and so forth. The first three or four sections were too full to be inviting.

From an old girlhood habit, she began to tick off the letters of the alphabet in her own personal superstitious terms – L for Love, M for Marvellous, N for Naughty but Nice, O for Optimism, P for Peace, R for Romance . . . But as she searched for an empty seat, aware of a few people looking up at her with an air of vague disapproval as she passed on her high heels (or perhaps it was recognition or perhaps in the Reading Room the latter quickly turned into the former) she found imperceptibly that her litany was turning into something more macabre. V is for Violence, said the voice inside her head, and double V is for Victim of Violence. But V in Jemima's alphabet had always been for Variety, one of her favourite words, so much more diverting to the curious mind than the certainty of Victory, the bull-headed sound of Valour.

And then as she crossed over the entrance to the corridor which led to the North Library and began the alphabet again – this time at the beginning – she found herself reciting A is for Accident, B is for Beware ... C is for Chloe ... she found her mind automatically continuing. But at B for Beware and before C for Chloe was reached, Jemima suddenly found that B9 – the first end seat and thus her favourite for its slight extra feeling of space – was empty. Someone must have recently vacated it, for such a desirable position to be available so late in the day, by British Museum standards.

August after all was notorious for an influx of overseas scholars. Valentine Brighton had warned her as much when she announced her intention of using the summer season to work on those ladies inevitably christened by him, with his characteristic penchant for trivialization by nickname, 'Goodies of the Golden Age'.

'I assure you that you will find a mob of sweating scholars from Minnesota: they run package tours to the Reading Room in August.'

'You've never been seen in the British Library in August,' retorted Jemima. 'You simply sit at Helmet in the world-famous Elizabethan garden, having patrician nightmares about the proletarian professors.'

'My God, how wrong can you be? And I thought you were supposed to be an acute social observer, Jemima Shore, Investigator. I shall think twice about entrusting my Golden Goodies, to you, let alone old Aunt Emma Helmet's deeply philanthropic diaries about stamping out sex among the Sussex poor. ["But the book was my idea, Valentine," thought Jemima.] My dear girl, throughout the whole of August, I just can't wait to leave my world-famous Elizabethan garden for the ordered tranquillity of my Bloomsbury office. Those same sweaty professors from Minnesota also hie themselves inexorably to Helmet. Weekends, when the office isn't functioning, are pure hell. It's not so much them asking questions about the history of Helmet – Mummy always insists on answering them by the light of invention anyway – as *telling* me things about the place. And there I am, at one and the same time a cringing victim and the unworthy possessor. At Helmet in the summer they have me at their mercy; I much prefer the anonymity of Bloomsbury.'

It struck Jemima, glancing from her new vantage point of B9, that for the purposes of disappearing in London, the Reading Room would be ideal; for everyone, that is, except the very few physically famous. It was not ideal for Jemima Shore, for example.

As she looked up the press marks of the books she needed in the lumbering leather catalogue, a girl with long brown hair and a sharp nose spoke softly at her elbow.

'Miss Shore, I simply loved *The Unvisited*. It's all true, so true; the artificiality of our geriatric culture . . .'

'Thank you so much,' said Jemima hastily, beginning to move away.

'Just one question. It's rather personal I'm afraid; in fact I did think of writing to you—'

Firmly, Jemima filled in SHORE J. on the white book slip, gave the reference number, hoping devoutly she had got it right, and beat a quick retreat, murmuring: 'Yes, why don't you?'

The girl stared after her. Her gaze was both annoyed and vulnerable. Jemima posted her slips, six of them, in the little brown tray at the central desk and settled down in the harbour of B9 to await her books. One to two hours was said to be the average delivery time: perhaps on a Saturday she would be luckier. B for Beware – yes, indeed, beware of strangers accosting you in the British Library.

But then it seemed that no place was absolutely ideal for Jemima Shore's planned disappearance. The tomb-like weekend quiet of the concrete Bloomsbury block had been disrupted already by one visitor and one squatter – no, revivifier, but the interruption was the same; what was more the revivifier showed no signs of leaving, and the visitor might be lurking anywhere in the district. There had been that cacophony of telephone calls both from the pathetic Stovers and a so-far-unidentified male of presumed Irish extraction.

Only Chloe Fontaine possessed the magic art of disappearance, eluding a persistent ex-lover, worried elderly parents, and her great friend Jemima Shore with equally maddening grace.

Jemima had a book of her own with which to while away the waiting time – *Fallen Child*, which she had begun to reread with pleasure while in the Pizza Perfecta – but the heat and stickiness made her more inclined to put her head in her hands and rest. As for B for Beware, V for Violence and the rest of it, she put that down at Kevin John Athlone's door. The British Library was, if anywhere, a safe refuge from physical violence; no possibility of assault here (except verbally by importunate strangers).

As a resting-place it was also unparalleled, if you could stand the airless atmosphere. The man – or was it a woman – next to her had already given up the struggle for consciousness. The fair head was bowed onto the desk and the pile of delivered books ignored. Jemima recalled other people sleeping on their hands in the Reading Room in the past, on a hot afternoon, but they had been older; retired professors perhaps, turned out by their wives to graze peacefully in these quiet pastures. But there was something different about the attitude of this slumbering flaxen poll. The figure was utterly slumped, giving the impression of total abandon, even despair. It was almost as if its owner were dead rather than asleep, had found his or her last resting-place in the Reading Room, not merely a convenient situation for a quick kip.

'Hamilton? Your books.' A handsome Asian with a cultivated voice deposited five books carefully on the desk beside her, and was whisking out the white slips poked into them. He was wearing a dazzling green T-shirt with the single word BOMB on it. The books were about chemistry.

'B for Bomb,' she thought automatically. 'Beware the Bomb. Ban the Bomb. Beware the British Library.' Why were her thoughts so insatiably morbid today? She said aloud:

'No, I'm Shore, J. Shore. These aren't mine.' At that moment the fair head next to her raised itself and a pair of light rather narrow eyes were gazing at her. The long mouth twitched; the lips, like the eyes, were rather narrow but the general effect was not unhandsome in a conventional English fashion.

'Jemima Shore! I do declare!' The Asian glanced at the slips, picked up the books and went away. He seemed unconcerned by the mistake. In that respect the British Library had not changed. Jemima wondered how long it would be before her own books arrived.

'B for Brighton,' said Jemima, wondering how she could have mistaken Valentine Brighton's sleek thick fair hair, even recumbent, for anyone else's – let alone a woman's.

'Naturally it's B for Brighton, my dear. Where else should I sit? You know my obsession for my own initial, expressed in so many fascinating ways, not the least of which is the famous colophon of the Brighthelmet Press. But what good fortune that you too should have chosen to honour this humble row. Welcome to B—'

'But, Valentine, what on earth are *you* doing here? It's a Saturday in August. Even the professors in Minnesota can't have driven you this far.'

Valentine looked at her. For a moment he did not seem to understand the reference. Jemima saw that he was rather pale and there was perspiration on the fine fair skin of his brow.

'Can't you guess?' he said at length in his usual bantering tone. 'Three guesses. You won't need three hundred.'

'Hardly. You're the most unlikely sight here I can assure you.'

'I'm waiting for Chloe.'

'*What!*' In her amazement, Jemima's voice had risen above the sibylline murmur adopted by Library readers. The woman in the seat next to Valentine looked up crossly and clicked her tongue. 'Where is she, then?' Jemima hissed.

'I am hardly the person to ask, my dear girl, since I have been waiting here, pinioned to row B, for longer than I care to remember. Hence the state of torpor, not to say stupor in which you discovered me on arrival.'

'We must talk. Can you come outside for a moment?'

'That sounds as if you are challenging me to a duel, or are going to knock me down or something. However if the encounter is to be non-violent, I shall be delighted. What is the time? Can we get a drink or something?'

'It's after two o'clock. No, I don't need – want – a drink. I've just had lunch. Pizza, salad and one glass of white wine. Perfect scholar's meal and as a matter of fact I had it at the aptly named Pizza Perfecta. But as the mystery of Chloe's whereabouts deepens, I can't lose this opportunity of getting one or two things straight.'

They both got up.

'Aren't you going to leave a note?'

'Ah. Good thinking.' Valentine wrote with a flourish in red pentel on one of the white book request slips: 'C. Gone for a good chat with Jemima Shore, Investigator. Hope to iron out your problems to both our satisfaction.' He signed it: 'V'. The red writing sprawled across the printed slip, a splash of red.

'V for Violence' floated through Jemima's mind automatically. It was an inappropriate thought. Of all the men she knew, Valentine Brighton was the least redolent of violence; he seemed to lack even the smallest trace of that natural aggression which goes with masculinity, hence his oft-discussed lack of sexuality. Not that Valentine was in any way effeminate. Adam Adamson, with his youth and slightness, was the more girlish looking of the two. Yet it occurred to Jemima that oddly enough, he was also the more attractive. Even the odious Kevin John had a kind of forceful demanding sexuality which she could appreciate, while shuddering away from it. Yes, that was it. It was Valentine's polite lack of demand towards either sex, so far as could be made out, which caused the question mark to be raised. Besides, he really did not look at all well, perhaps the rumours of his heart condition were something more than maternal fussiness.

Jemima walked with Valentine out of the Reading Room in the direction of those cool Egyptian and Assyrian halls, the memory of which had originally tempted her. As they left the Reading Room, Jemima's handbag was searched in case she should have slipped out a rare book or two. Valentine was ignored, like all the other men without briefcases.

'So *why* were you meeting?'

They stood amidst the vast deities, one or two sufficiently markedly feline to remind her of Tiger, now prowling perhaps on the roofs of Bloomsbury.

'I intended to give Chloe some good advice.'

'An odd choice of venue.'

'Not my choice, I can assure you. I needed to catch my wayward author before she set off on her secret trip and this was the only rendezvous she would consider. Don't ask *me* why.'

'But I must ask you why. And for that matter – what secret trip? To the Camargue, I take it.'

'Ah. You knew then. I thought—' For an instant a look akin to surprise or even possibly apprehension marked Valentine's normally bland face. 'I thought she kept it a secret from you,' he finished. It caused her to remark once again on his uncharacteristic pallor.

'In a sense she did. She told me she was going on a solitary mission, researching an article for *Taffeta* and it was only when that turned out to be a fabrication—'

'*Taffeta!*' This time there was no mistaking the surprise. 'What an extraordinary choice of alibi.' Valentine gave a wry laugh. 'But how absolutely typical of Chloe, for reasons you probably won't appreciate, and if I get my way, never will.'

Jemima reflected that she already had a pretty good idea what those reasons might be, thanks to the ladylike indiscretion of Laura Barrymore, but she felt less interested in boasting of her involuntary detective work than getting to the bottom, once and for all, of Chloe's holiday plans. She also felt no particular need to obtrude on Valentine exactly how her discovery of Chloe's mendacity had come about: the Stovers' vigil was no concern of his. Yet, a vague feeling of hurt possessed her that Chloe had chosen to tell the truth – whatever it might be – to Valentine, a friend of far more recent standing, and concealed it in an elaborate tale about *Taffeta* from her old friend Jemima. It encouraged her to press Valentine further. Her hurt was slowly turning to anger, an anger further fuelled by recollection of the hours of the day already wasted on Chloe's complicated intrigue, to say nothing of Kevin John Athlone's assault.

'Where was she really off to? You'd better let me know. There's been quite enough lying already.'

Valentine considered, or appeared to consider. Jemima suspected that in such a deliberate man, the decision to confide in her had probably already been taken. 'She's off to the Camargue all right, but not until Monday, I gather. She's spending the weekend in London.

Then she's going to the Camargue with her latest lover. You know Chloe. You must have guessed that part of it at least.'

'But she specifically swore she wasn't! "Not my new angel." Why the lie? Why not tell me? Why the need for the cover-up?'

'Dearest Jemima, you're her alibi, don't you see?'

'Yes, I should bloody well think I am her alibi!' Jemima burst out. 'I seem to be her alibi for the whole world this morning. But what's the point of the secrecy to *me*?'

'Jemima Shore, Investigator,' said Valentine brightly.

'Investigator nothing. I've been her alibi enough times in the past, I can assure you; all through those two marriages. She could have trusted me. We've been friends for years; nothing about Chloe could shock me now. We're both adults, to put it mildly.'

'*She* could have trusted you. It was her lover who couldn't.'

'Did he need to know I was in the secret? It would have made things so much easier for her, as it happens, if she had trusted me.' And the Stovers, Jemima added mentally. 'It's all so unlike Chloe, not the intrigue itself, but the lies surrounding it.'

'This whole affair is all very unlike Chloe,' Valentine commented. 'Besides she – he, if you like – needed your innocence. In case the Press got wind of it. You are Press yourself in a kind of way. You could convince them quite genuinely that you didn't know where she was.'

'Oh, Isis and Osiris!' exclaimed Jemima with a groan. 'I'm going to sit down.' They sat on a stone bench, hard and rather uncomfortable.

'Mind you, I'm still not quite sure you wouldn't have been sufficiently fascinated by her new involvement to investigate it *just* a little,' continued Valentine. 'I could see quite a programme shaping up there. The intricate ways of love: A Woman's Choice, exquisite lady novelist and – well, no, perhaps I had better not tell you.'

'Beware my aroused curiosity,' said Jemima coldly. 'B for Beware, as well as Brighton. Besides I don't work on that kind of romantic and gossipy trash.'

'Beware, beware,' repeated Valentine soulfully. 'How often did I beg Chloe to beware . . . It was so terribly indiscreet, the whole thing, right *there*, under everyone's nose. But I'd better say no more.'

Jemima realized with increasing irritation that not only was he playing a role but he was also enjoying it. 'Valentine, I'm not sure if murder has ever been done in the British Museum, but I am convinced that these sinister Assyrians have seen a thing or two in their time. How cruel their expressions are. Gods crossed with birds. A terrible combination. At least those colossal crouched lions remind me of Tiger. Anyway, unless you tell me who Chloe's lover is, and why she was meeting you in the Reading Room, I shall behave like Ninurta armed with a thunderbolt and drive you, for the demon you are, out of my temple.' She pointed to the label above their heads.

'There, there. I only did it to annoy, I've every intention of telling you, now that Chloe hasn't turned up. I need your co-operation to get hold of her.'

'*Where is she?*' It suddenly seemed more important than anything to know immediately the whereabouts of Chloe Fontaine; more important even than the identity of her lover.

'Seventy-three Adelaide Square, I think the address is. You would know. First-floor flat, I believe. *Piano nobile*, they call it, or did before it was wrapped in concrete. She's shacked up there for the weekend with her love, Sir Richard Lionnel. Do you feel like paying a call?'

7

Scheherazade

'I don't believe it!' That was Jemima's first startled exclamation. Afterwards, as she trailed her way back to Adelaide Square and thought over the whole strange encounter with Valentine, she realized that the words had not really been true, even as she spoke them.

Under the circumstances Jemima felt a certain reluctance to re-enter number 73. The garden in the centre of the square on the contrary looked inviting. The huge trees waved their heads far above her in the sky, level with the penthouse. She remembered that a key to the square was on the ring with the keys of number 73. She entered the garden. It was quite empty, a green enclave; no summer flowers, merely a series of flowerless shrubs planted round the edges of the garden; their function seemed to be those of guardians; to protect the inhabitants of the gardens from prying eyes, rather than anything more elaborate. Here at last was the privacy she craved. A locked garden: no one could get at her here. Where the penthouse and the Reading Room had proved insecure refuges, the square garden would surely remain inviolate.

Of the benches available, all empty, she chose one which faced the block of number 73. That would, she felt, concentrate the mind wonderfully. In fact, her first impression on sitting down was to be struck anew by the full monstrosity of Sir Richard Lionnel's concrete cuckoo in Robert Adam's neo-classical paradise. Renewed sympathy for the twentieth-century Adam and the Friends of the House filled her. Adam Adamson, the revivifier, was presumably still lurking somewhere within the third-floor flat. Was his surprise at the name Chloe Fontaine now more explicable? The memory had teased Jemima ever since, for she hated pieces of a puzzle which refused to be placed. Could it be that Adam actually knew of the romantic tryst taking place two floors beneath his and intended to make some sinister use of that knowledge? If so, it was odd that Adam was at the same time unaware that Chloe was the tenant of the penthouse flat.

As she watched and pondered, she saw the front door of the concrete block open and the figure of Adam Adamson emerge. The evening sun touched his curly head and bright jaunty beard and made it look quite fiery. He looked straight in the direction of the gardens, but showed no signs of having seen Jemima; she was in any case partially concealed by one of the ubiquitous shrubs. Then he walked in a leisurely manner away in the direction of Tottenham Court Road. He gave the appearance of being a man very much at his ease. He might have been the owner of 73 Adelaide Square instead of a squatter – revivifier. Jemima looked at her little gold watch. It was 5.30. She found she felt rather sorry to think that Adam Adamson had abandoned number 73.

She ticked off the remaining inhabitants of number 73 in her mind. Up above, golden Tiger crouched on his balcony. The curtains of the broad first-floor windows, she noticed, were closed; they had scarlet linings, a series of red bars lit up in the evening sun. Within them Richard Lionnel and Chloe were presumably cosily installed, or at least Chloe was. That left the second floor: no blinds as yet, merely large blank windows. And the basement. Tiger's haunt. Goodness knows who may be hanging about there, thought Jemima crossly. After Chloe's behaviour in that place, anything is possible.

'I don't believe it.' But suddenly, startlingly, she did believe it. It was as though Chloe's whole character and exploits, past and present, were lit from a completely new angle, the red evening sun falling upon them. Chloe had lied to her parents at Cambridge about her sex life – well, all my friends did that, thought Jemima, except me who had no parents. But Chloe had lied throughout her adult life, if you chose to analyse her behaviour in that light (up till now Jemima had not done so).

Those alibis, those affairs, those passionate plunges into love, marriage, adultery, divorce, and worst of all emotion – a great source of lies, emotion; the whole involvement with Kevin John, so incomprehensible to Jemima; did it not all add up to a cool capacity for concealment as well as a reckless capacity for love? Adultery in Chloe's case had not been the first step to deception but only one of a number of steps.

There was no doubt, now that her surprise was fading, annoyance was beginning to take over. Jemima Shore had been used and she did not like the feeling. The implication that she, Jemima, had been deliberately *chosen* – out of all the gullible fools available – to occupy the penthouse flat while Chloe cavorted with her prestigious lover on the first floor – no doubt laughing the while at Jemima's ignorance – well, to say the least of it, it was irritating to Jemima Shore, Investigator.

Chloe's anxious phrases floated back: 'You're sure you won't be lonely?' 'No noise.' Chloe so beguilingly helpful when Jemima confided her own distress at the death of Colette. 'You need a change of scene. Borrow my new flat while I'm away.' Chloe so carefully establishing that Jemima intended to receive no visitors, was not in the mood for company.

Chloe had used Jemima as, to be honest, she had been using people all her life. Jemima began to think of both the Stovers and Kevin John in rather a different light. Chloe had come as an upsetting force – 'out of the blue' as Mr Stover had put it – into the Stovers' neat sad lives last week; that much was clear. Chloe, who had ostentatiously abandoned the name of her youth, thus taking from the couple who had brought her up the consolation of her public fame, had first threatened the unvisited Stovers with a visit and then withheld it for reasons of her own which were doubtless connected with her new romance.

Isabelle Mancini now – the enthusiastic patron of Chloe's work through all the years when Chloe was lovelorn and financially desperate: how had she been repaid except, it seemed, by some fairly ruthless portrait in Chloe's new novel?

For Kevin John, it was possible to argue that he had been a promising young painter, his violent impulses confined to his canvasses where they properly belonged, until Chloe like Pandora had let out his evil spirits of drink and assault.

Taking the thought further, Jemima had to admit that she too had been just a little deceived by the precision and irony of Chloe's work. Yet all Chloe's friends, most recently Guthrie Carlyle, were fond of commenting on the contrast between the work and the woman. There was pride involved too: her own. Only yesterday she had been describing Chloe to herself as fundamentally candid. Jemima, who was a professional judge of character, had made a bad mistake about one of her oldest friends. Jemima thought again of that pale bedroom in which hung the scarlet picture. Symbolic of all the violence she intended to eliminate from her life, had been Chloe's breathless comment. Was that not yet another piece of deception?

'I don't believe it.' But Valentine's story did make a kind of bizarre sense. He had recounted it to her in the British Museum with some relish after his original revelation about Chloe's whereabouts. He related how Chloe, caught up in a passionate but secret love affair with Sir Richard Lionnel, had sought his, Valentine's, advice.

'Why me?' he had enquired in his airy rhetorical manner. 'Simple. Because I found out about it by chance, sloping round to Adelaide Square one day on a publisher's rounds. Chloe needed a confidant of course and I know Lionnel since he lives near Helmet. More to the point I also know the dread Francesca Lionnel, who's a great buddy of Mummy's but also a first-class candidate for the role of Medea. Already she exudes wronged beauty with every pore, without, so far as I know, anything specific to exude it about. So I can advise on *that* score. Besides, Chloe is a story-teller. She positively enjoyed telling me all about it.'

'Scheherazade.'

'Scheherazade in reverse, since I believe the ambition of that lady, being married, was to hold off the evil day of her own death. Chloe's ambition was, as I shall tell you, to achieve the first stage of the process.'

To herself Jemima commented: I suppose that the original Scheherazade told some pretty tall stories too, as the Arabian Nights wore on. Still, that was self-preservation.

'You see, dearest Jemima, our Chloe's decided to settle down. She plans to become the second Lady Lionnel.'

'What? She must be mad!' Several tourists jumped.

'There I personally entirely agree with you. Marriage – what a ridiculous aim! Babies, children, an establishment, ugh – you know how resolutely I have avoided the former, babies absolutely horrify me, and the latter, of which I do have first-hand experience, is pure purgatory. Why not *carpe diem*? Accept the free flat and any lolly that's going, the new car – he gave her that, naturally – and enjoy, enjoy . . . I begged her to forget about marriage. But Chloe wilfully didn't agree. A strong sexual attraction – I was assured in terms much stronger than those of Chloe's novels that this is the case. Plus that essential in all Chloe's plans, novelty. Lionnel offers her the earth – a new earth, as she put it to me. On being informed that it was a marriage of true minds, or intended to be such, I offered my help.'

'The marriage of true minds,' repeated Jemima. 'How on earth did they meet?'

'It was a media romance. They happened to be on the same television programme—'

'Good God!' exclaimed Jemima. 'I arranged it. Chloe wanted some publicity for her new book. Some kind of round-table chat to do with industrial sponsorship of the Arts. Isabelle Mancini was the chairman. I knew she would be managing one of her wonderfully poised plugs for *Taffeta* – somehow she always makes that magazine sound far more

socially committed than the *New Statesman*. As she adores Chloe' –
Jemima hesitated and Valentine said nothing – 'I thought she would
hardly object if Chloe plugged her new book. I watched most of it to
see how she made out. Wait. The lighter. I suppose it was his, Lionnel's.
That's where I saw it – on telly.'

'Afterwards Lionnel whirled her away for dinner at the Mirabelle.
Coup de foudre was the expression used; I was far too frightened to
enquire any further.'

'And not a whisper in the Press. No goggling in the gossip columns.
No daring speculations by diarists. Perhaps Lionnel fixes them.'

'On the contrary. He's very worried about it. The Press hate him,
serious papers as well as muck-rakers. That kind of gentleman-
buccaneer always tots up a number of enemies among the less
piratically minded. No, he's particularly keen on silence at the moment
because he's hoping to go respectable. I mean really respectable. He's
being tipped as the new Chairman of the Committee for Arts and
Caring Industry. Now that could be *very* big indeed in the respectability
stakes. You know how keen the Royal Family are on the CARI. They
may not be crazy about the arts or industry separately but they find the
combination quite devastating. The mere thought of CARI sends them
into ecstasy. Lunch with Prince Philip every other day. The Prince of
Wales to breakfast. Jogging with Princess Anne. You know the form.'

'Hence the Camargue and that *Taffeta* cover story, I take it. But why
the clandestine weekend in London first?'

'At the last minute Lionnel was called for some meetings at number
ten; couldn't of course refuse. He suggested a kind of romantic
breakaway in his official suite, attached to the office, since Lady L was
hardly likely to rumble him there, so blatant it's actually safe. As for
Camargue, Chloe plans that to be a trial honeymoon – Chloe will be
doing the trying. She intends trying to persuade Lionnel to commit
himself to a divorce after the CARI announcement has been made. Her
view is that she's already got her man wriggling on the hook. He says he
hasn't felt this way for years, youth returned and all that sort of rot.
Now she reckons on landing him in the Camargue. My view,'
concluded Valentine in a pious voice, 'is that for something the size of
the Lion of Bloomsbury you need a net and not a fishing-rod. But
Chloe never understands anything about the animal kingdom. Her
novels are full of mistakes in that respect.'

The colossal figure of a winged lion couchant which faced them, so
much mightier than the bird-gods, leant picturesque credence to what
he had just said. Such creatures were not to be captured lightly, but by
stealth and imagination.

'Scheherazade, indeed. I can't help hoping she gets away with it.'

'That's just the trouble. At this very moment she's in danger of getting away with nothing. You see Lady Lionnel may well have rumbled the Camargue plan, and it's all my own silly fault.' Valentine gave a theatrical gesture of putting his hand to his forehead and smoothing back the fair hair. 'Or shall I blame country life in August? Nothing to do. Mischief made. First step: over comes Francesca Lionnel to tea with Mummy. Second step: she tells Mummy that Sir Lionnel's gone to the Camargue to have a real holiday, and as they're opening the gardens to the public, he's taken Tommy McKenna.

'The Camargue!' cries Mummy over the teacups, not really interested, but showing a fine natural instinct for making trouble where Chloe's concerned, since she's decided long ago – quite wrongly, alas – that Chloe's After Me. "What a coincidence. Valentine was just telling me that pretty little writer of his, that one who's always getting divorced, what is her name, darling, Clara, yes, Clara Fontaine, she's off to the Camargue. I wonder if they'll meet," she adds for good measure.

'As Francesca is beginning to burble most graciously something to do with admiring her books and isn't her name Chloe, I butt in: "Oh Mummy, the Camargue is not like a restaurant; you don't bump into people there." But the damage has been done. For one moment I've seen the glint in Medea's eye and, my dear, she *knows*. She must already know that Lionnel has met Chloe; he may even have told her about the original jolly dinner at the Mirabelle, in a burst of adulterous put-you-off-the-scent nothing-to-hide-you-see honesty. Possibly she knows about the penthouse flat. My dear, Tommy McKenna's story had better be good, otherwise murder might be done, starting with Chloe and probably going on to include that hapless stooge, Tommy McK. And it was in fact to warn Chloe of just that, that I rang her and arranged to meet her this morning. I couldn't come to seventy-three because of Lionnel, you see, or for that matter you.

'So here I am. And here she isn't,' Valentine had ended plaintively. 'Jemima, as you're living there, do you think you could—'

'No,' Jemima had said very firmly. 'Warn her yourself.' But in the end of course she had agreed. While finishing her work in the Reading Room, she was rather looking forward to the confrontation with Scheherazade.

When she had thought things through to their logical conclusion, Jemima found her usual calm restored. Valentine's role in Chloe's romance still intrigued her, and one or two aspects of his story struck her oddly, but that might have been the presence of his mother as a character in the tale; never having met the famous Hope Lady Brighton, she was never quite sure whether Valentine romanced about her peculiarities or merely reported them accurately.

Jemima would confront Chloe and of course warn her about Valentine's indiscretion. She felt controlled and tranquil in the sinking light of the evening, heat still rising from the pavements, but something tranquil in the atmosphere, or perhaps in her own attitude, very different from the wild imaginings and images of the Reading Room that morning. It would not do for the marriage of true minds to founder at the outset; and the hackneyed quotation which still never lost its power, suddenly reminded her that Valentine had also used it on the slip of the Brighthelmet Press book in Chloe's flat. Valentine's story gained plausibility.

Jemima unlocked the gate and let herself out. There were hardly any cars about as she crossed the broad road to the western side of the square. Nor did any demonstrators lurk outside the concrete block, for which Jemima was thankful. She was beginning to feel such personal distaste for the architecture that she was honourable enough to be ashamed of being seen to enter the building. The outer door was closed but not locked; she hesitated a moment on the doorstep. A cool collected conversation with Chloe, that was the best policy. But Jemima had already decided that she would not need to leave the penthouse flat in protest – hardly. First of all, to be honest, it would be most inconvenient to her plans; secondly, it would smack of moral protest towards Chloe's romance, which was the last thing she intended. She would merely make it clear that she could not be involved personally in any prolonged deception, be it towards Lady Lionnel (whom she did not know) or the world's Press (which she did).

Thus bolstered up, she opened the front door. It was oddly dark inside the marble hall, after the golden light of the evening. Jemima made for the stairs, and stumbled over something. It was heavy, sacklike, and apparently lying half on the floor and half on a chair. Frantically, Jemima reached for the unfamiliar light switch, and as she did so, the sacklike shape stirred and groaned. Her eyes too were getting accustomed to the twilight. But in the end it was her nose which told her the identity of the person before her.

At last she found the time switch which illumined the hall for a given length of time. She found herself gazing once again at Kevin John Athlone. The smell, that same sour masculine smell of the morning, brought back the events of violence and a sense of her own battering sharply to her. She felt for a moment quite sick. His eyes were shut. He looked more dishevelled than ever. The blue T-shirt was marked with dust; it could even be that he had been in a fight. He was snoring or gasping slightly.

Furiously, Jemima shook his shoulder. Sickness and fear left her. She was aware of nothing but a desperate need to get this intruder out of the house before he somehow suspected the presence of Chloe. Then, indeed, murder might be done. Francesca Lionnel was at least graciously presiding over Parrot Park in Sussex. Kevin John Athlone, packing no mean punch as she herself could testify, was right here in the building. His long eyelashes fluttered and his eyes opened. Immediately Kevin John gave her the most ravishing smile and jumped to his feet. He appeared in no way drunk and, if dirty, indifferent to it.

'My little sweetheart! You're back. And I meant to vanish before you returned, like the good fairy I am, leaving you all to your surprise. It was just that it was all too much for me, the climb, the excitement, the fun, and I probably had a drop or two at lunch with my old mate Dixie, otherwise I wouldn't have done it at all.'

'What on earth are you doing back here?' exclaimed Jemima wearily.

'Wait and see. Wait and see. Just wait and see what a splash of red awaits you in Chloe's white heaven. I climbed, I climbed, all the way up the scaffolding, on the inside mind you, didn't feel like attracting attention, although there was no one about, might have been a ghost town, and I've left you the most magnificent present. All because I was something less than a gentleman this morning. I've copied down the telephone number by the way, so I'll be able to be in touch.'

'Oh no.'

'Oh yes, darling, oh yes. Up the scaffolding, clutching my gift, in through your balcony window, conveniently left open – just for me. In. Deposit. Out. Await you. Fall asleep. Awoken by a maiden's kiss.'

'No kiss,' said Jemima. 'No kiss at all.' But then, somewhat to her surprise, Kevin John actually did give her a kiss, not one of his rubbery kisses but a gentle kiss. It was also a kiss which preceded his departure.

'I'm a gentleman at heart,' was his parting shot, as he lumbered down the steps. 'You see if I'm not.'

Jemima closed the front door thoughtfully. She waited for five minutes in the hall in case there should be a spontaneous return of the ebullient artist. Then she climbed the broad stairs to the first floor. She knocked and called gently:

'Chloe. It's me, Jemima.' She felt extremely foolish doing so but she had her duty to do. 'Chloe. It's me, Jemima. I've got a message from Valentine.'

There was a bell. The neat plate beside the door read: Lionnel (Sussex) Offices Ltd. Hesitating, she rang the bell. The sound was extremely loud on the landing and startled her. Was it startling those within? There was no sound at all. She wondered whether this door would suddenly fall open, as had the door of the third-floor flat. Sheer curiosity about her friend's daring plan to storm the heights of marriage to Sir Richard Lionnel had brought with it a modicum of amusement. She was back on Chloe's side. Deception was, once more, forgiven.

After ringing once more and knocking twice, Jemima realized that Chloe must either be out or asleep; the warning would have to wait for the next day. If Chloe and Richard Lionnel were in bed, they were best left to it, without a visit from Jemima Shore, Investigator. If she suddenly interrupted some highly romantic moment, then another form of murder might be done! Jemima had absolutely no wish to be seen in such a tiresomely prurient light.

She decided to go up to the penthouse and find out what Kevin John had deposited for her, like some huge puppy leaving an unwelcome gift for its master. She gave the door of the third-floor flat a wide berth. There was no sound from there either. Indeed, the whole building had fallen silent since the departure of Kevin John. Its silence oppressed her. Perhaps it was the contrast with the busy low whispering of the Reading Room in which she had spent the afternoon. Still, silence was what she craved. It was odd how worrying it now seemed.

She opened the door quickly and a look of horror crossed her face.

A great scarlet geranium of the most violent hue possible sat in its pot in the middle of the white carpet. Already there were dirty marks round it. Earth, dirty footsteps and some water. The red glared at her. It was revolting. The bedroom door was shut. Jemima's loathing of scarlet flowers came back to her with force. A splash of blood indeed: she was reminded of Sylvia Plath's brilliant blood-stained poem about red tulips in hospital. How on earth the heavily built and debauched Kevin John had managed to scale a scaffold clutching this object was another matter. He did seem to have dropped it once or twice for she saw that the pot was slightly cracked, hence the earth and water which were seeping out. A note next to the pot read:

'A Splash of Red. Red roses would have been better, but this was all I could find in this urban desert.

The mess was distasteful, almost as bad as the garish scarlet colour of the plant. Serve Chloe right, perhaps, for fooling around with Kevin John's affections. Now, thought Jemima, she will have to have her virgin carpet cleaned. Chloe will be utterly furious about that.

She opened the door into the bedroom. Jemima stood absolutely still. She could not stop staring. Through her head ran idiotically the continuation of the same thought. Oh God, the mess, the terrible red mess, all over Chloe's white bed. But this time she did not think that Chloe would be furious about it. Chloe would never be furious about anything again.

For Chloe, little white Chloe, one high-heel dangling from a foot which had fallen over the side of the bed, was lying with her eyes open and an enormous red gaping wound across her throat. There were other red marks on her body. Blood had splashed across her white cotton broderie anglaise petticoat. Blood had formed pools on the bed. Compared to the blood on the bed, the great picture hanging above it now looked quite flat and tame. Chloe had told her last story; this time it had not saved her. Scheherazade was dead.

8

Who, Who?

For several moments Jemima stood quite still in the doorway, burned with pity. Chloe looked so tiny, there on her huge bed, her still face and the terrible gash giving her the air of a murdered child. Jemima moved forward and touched one little white hand where it had fallen on the counterpane. Her foot encountered something sharp and she saw a razor lying on the floor by the side of the lace valance. The hand, though cool, was not stiff and for a moment she thought – but no one could have survived a great gaping gash like that – something so violent, brutal and efficiently executed must have killed her more or less instantly. Besides there were other lesser wounds. Jemima felt automatically for the pulse. There was none.

Her eyes were wide open. From that sad simulacrum of life, Jemima at last accepted that Chloe was dead. She closed them with gentle fingers, knowing with one part of her mind that she should touch nothing. But still she could not bear to leave her friend with her huge eyes gazing blindly at the destruction which death had wrought on her once immaculate bedroom.

Jemima turned away and, ignoring the rise of tears and nausea, both of which were trying to claim her, ran back into the sitting room, knocking over the scarlet geranium as she passed so that more earth spattered over the carpet.

She dialled 999 and within a few seconds, in a voice which surprised her with its calm found herself asking for the police. To Scotland Yard she gave no details other than the fact that it was urgent. All the time through her head was running the question: Why, Why? It was not until Tiger suddenly awoke from the somnolent eyes-shut crouch he had adopted in the sunlight on the pale carpet, that his slow sleepy

371

stretching mew-mew changed the note of the refrain in her head to something quite different: Not Why, Why? but Who, Who? . . .

At that very moment she heard the sound of a police siren in Adelaide Square. While she was still talking to the female voice on the other end of the telephone, a policeman in uniform – no jacket but his bright white shirt looked equally formal – came sharply into the flat. His voice and movements were brisk but not hurried, with that special kind of negative courtesy – an absence of all kind of delaying emotion, good or bad – she associated with the police. He was quite young with very smooth pink cheeks.

'Mrs Shaw,' he began. 'You dialled nine-nine-nine? We answered your radio call.' Then he recognized her. 'Ah, Miss Jemima Shore. It was your call—'

'The body's in there. I found her. I can identify her. This is her flat.' Suddenly Jemima felt she could not re-enter the bedroom until she had fought down both her pity and her nausea. 'I don't think there's much to be done for her.' He went swiftly through. Jemima picked up Tiger. She could not endure the idea of the cat picking its delicate curious way into that sullied chamber. She put him, scrabbling in her arms, onto the balcony and regardless of the heat, shut the window. As Kevin John had reminded her, she had left it unlocked. He had entered the flat by that route. And who else?

Who, Who? . . . was beginning to beat in her head with more force as the cat mewed angrily against the glass.

She heard the policeman talking into the black radio link on his shoulder, the thick black plastic wiring curling out of the machine like a snake. He was talking to Bloomsbury Police Station. In between crackles and other little squeaking sounds, she heard him calling for the CID. And a police surgeon. At that moment, he returned to the sitting room.

'I'm afraid I closed her eyes,' Jemima said rather woodenly. 'I shouldn't have touched anything.'

The policeman was kind.

'The shock. I presume you and the deceased were acquainted. Detective Chief Inspector Portsmouth will be here in a few minutes. In the meantime, Miss Shore, it is Miss Jemima Shore, Investigator, isn't it?' He gave a faint rather embarrassed smile. 'No question of *your* identity – I'll leave the questions to him.' He was writing in his notebook.

He looked round the flat.

'Excuse me, Miss Shore, is this all there is?'

'And the kitchen.' She waved her hand, and he trod in his quick authoritative way towards it, his heavy black shoes making no noise on the carpet. His manner, and his confidence, belied the extreme youth of his appearance. Through the open kitchen door, Jemima saw that the glass kitchen door leading to the fire escape was still shut and bolted.

The police and their work, including that of a murder squad, were familiar to Jemima Shore. In particular she enjoyed good relations with Detective Chief Inspector John Portsmouth (Pompey as he was familiarly dubbed) of the Bloomsbury Police. It was a friendship which had begun several years back when it had suited Pompey's purpose to issue an appeal on television for information concerning a missing child. Later he discussed the case in a brief interview. Jemima had handled both appearances.

Still later, in view of the unusual nature of the case, there had been a discussion group on television in which Pompey had featured. Even the *Guardian*, in rather a dazed way, had described Jemima's organization of this as 'fascinatingly fairminded'. Pompey had evidently agreed with the *Guardian*, since with his help, Jemima had been able to make a programme about women detectives, and another about detectives' wives. A friendship had been struck, based on the odd drink, the odd chat, the odd consultation from both sides about each other's work. On at least one occasion these conversations had resulted in the solution of a mystery temporarily baffling to Pompey. No, the arrival of Pompey held no fears, only a kind of reassurance for Jemima.

Nor was death itself a stranger to her. She had seen it in many guises, and helped to track down its begetter in her private investigative capacity. But this time it was her friend who was dead, murdered in that very room where only twenty-four hours before the living, graceful Chloe had moved lightly about in her high-heeled shoes, packing her bag. After so many years of friendship, it was as though something of Jemima's own past had been slain.

Who, Who? – the question was still going through her head when the police surgeon in the shape of a local GP arrived, followed by a police photographer; another policeman, identity and role unknown; a young man in plain clothes, probably a detective; someone she recognized as the fingerprint expert from Bloomsbury Police Station; and presiding over it all, Detective Chief Inspector John Portsmouth – Pompey – who with great urbanity took over the whole case and, as it seemed, the whole flat.

He shook his head when he saw Jemima, that gently placatory gesture which their various forays on television had made famous. Nothing ever surprised Pompey; his manner suggested that he had all along predicted that one Saturday night Jemima would find her best friend with her throat cut.

The police surgeon, a nice rather weary man, duly pronounced life extinct – to Jemima's view slightly unnecessarily, but she knew the careful ways of the police. However the doctor did summon up some enthusiasm when discussing the cause of death. He also proved to be a connoisseur of modern painting. 'Cause of death cut throat. That's clear enough. The first blow killed her, very well done, severed the windpipe immediately, that accounts for all the blood, main arteries you know, must have spouted like an oil well. By the body temperature, about six hours ago. *Rigor mortis* only just beginning to set in – the hot weather. Nothing to do with that razor by the bed of course; clumsy, aren't they? I much prefer the electric sort myself.' He smoothed his own chin appreciatively.

'They'll have to look for something else. Good picture over the bed by the way. It's an Athlone, isn't it? I thought so. There's one in the Tate rather similar. I'm very glad to have had an opportunity to see *that*.' He might have been visiting an art gallery in a provincial town.

He added in a much brisker voice: 'Most unsuitable for a lady's bedroom, I would have thought.'

'How about this, sir?' It was the young detective, addressing Pompey. He was holding in a gloved hand one of Chloe's long sharp kitchen knives. It was part of the *batterie de cuisine* which Jemima had admired the night before. According to Chloe – could one believe her? – it had been a housewarming present from Isabelle Mancini. Chloe, the domestic cat, had once been an excellent cook; now her gleaming *batterie* had been literally the death of her. The blade of the large knife looked as if it had been dipped in rust.

Jemima was familiar with the slow grinding of the police methods. She recognized the need for the endless questions and the establishment of apparently obvious facts. Nevertheless she was relieved when Pompey suggested that she should think about taking herself elsewhere – a police car would be provided – where they could continue their essential conversation in some greater comfort.

Powder was now everywhere. Everything in the flat had been dusted and tested for fingerprints. Jemima's own – fingerprints 'friendly to the environment' as Pompey put it – had been taken for elimination. It proved quite a jovial procedure, accompanied by some grave shakes of the head from Pompey.

Jemima repeated her basic story. How she had left for the Reading Room at about 12.30, going to the Pizza Perfecta *en route*. How the flat had certainly been empty when she left, since it was very small. She had visited the kitchen just before leaving to see if she could find anything interesting to eat. She was sure the *batterie* was then complete because she had used one of the smaller knives to cut a piece of cheese, before suddenly deciding in favour of the Pizza. She had returned at approximately 5.30.

Finally Chloe's little body, wrapped in hygienic black plastic, was carried away down the stairs, off to the local mortuary, at the orders of the Coroner's office. There, like the rest of London, it would spend a quiet weekend – no noise, no disturbance – awaiting its post-mortem from a pathologist on Monday morning. The efforts of the police photographer, first taking shots of the body, and then general shots of the flat, punctuated the proceedings. He might be an ardent *paparazze* trying to nose out a juicy scandal with his flashing camera, thought Jemima: but then, of course, that's exactly what he *is* trying to do.

It was illogical, but she still minded the desecration of her friend's pale paradise. It was better to concentrate on the notion of scandal, and *that* was a thought which led directly to the subject of Sir Richard Lionnel, a topic temporarily eliminated from her mind by shock. Who, Who? ... As though on cue, yet another policeman appeared in the doorway and whispered in Pompey's ear.

Pompey left the flat abruptly. His expression was enigmatic, with only the unexpected severity of the shake of his head to give some clue that for once perhaps he was very slightly surprised. Jemima was deciding to organize herself into an hotel – there must be some quiet private room in Bloomsbury of a Saturday night – when the telephone rang. Cocking an eyebrow at the remaining policeman, she answered it. She was greeted by the sound of pip-pips and then a loud voice bellowed in her ear.

'Dollie, is that you? Dollie, this is Dad.' But Jemima had already recognized the arbitrary tones of Mr Stover. Oh God, she thought, have I got to tell him? 'I'm at the station,' he went on.

'Which station?' said Jemima in a shaky voice.

'Tottenham Court Road tube station,' Mr Stover sounded extremely testy. 'That's where. Not Folkestone station I can assure you, which I left some hours ago at your personal request. Awful journey by the way. British Railways ought to be ashamed.' Pause for emphasis. 'Tottenham Court Road tube station that's where. Where you said you'd meet me at six o'clock. And it's now six-fifteen precisely.'

Jemima covered the mouthpiece. 'Officer, I think you'd better deal with this. It's the dead woman's father ... stepfather, I mean. I mentioned earlier that her mother was probably her next of kin. He appears to be here in London.'

The police officer began to address Mr Stover in that same voice of neutral courtesy which had characterized all the proceedings.

'I am a police officer, sir, at your daughter's flat; dealing with a certain matter. No, I am afraid I cannot discuss it with you on the telephone. No, sir, I cannot at the moment give you any information. If you would just stay where you are, sir, a young lady police officer will arrive to look after you.'

'He's an old man,'Jemima thought dully. 'A confused and angry old man. This shouldn't be happening to him.'

The man Pompey brought back with him was one to whom she felt confusion was quite unknown. Sir Richard Lionnel immediately dominated the scene by his mere presence. It was partly his physique – the Lion of Bloomsbury was well named.

Lionnel was urbanely dressed in a light tweed suit, so well cut that it did not even look out of place on this summer evening; the colour complemented his tanned skin. He was not in fact particularly tall, a little taller than Jemima herself perhaps, but his shoulders in the tweed suit were broad, giving an air of authority, and he himself, if not exactly heavy, was certainly a substantial man. Beyond that, everything about Lionnel exuded extraordinary life and force, from his black curly hair, tonsured by baldness like a monk, but still black and growing very vigorously, so that the curls seemed to be springing from his head, like a devil's horns, to his bright black eyes, definitely the eyes of some attendant devil at Lucifer's court. As they snapped from side to side, taking in Jemima, the flat, the policeman, the mess, they created their own energy. Even Lionnel's tan – or perhaps it was merely the native olive of his complexion – added to the air of natural force by making him look vigorously healthy.

The Lion of Bloomsbury, yes, indeed, a powerful animal. Instantly, Jemima understood what had attracted Chloe – not novelty, not sex, not security, although doubtless all these elements had been present, but command. Sir Richard Lionnel, the powerful pirate vessel, would carry along Chloe's frail little craft in his wake, and supply that command which somehow, Chloe, through two marriages and innumerable love affairs, had failed to find. For a moment Jemima, the cool, the collected, the independent, found herself irrationally jealous of her dead friend.

What was further remarkable about Sir Richard Lionnel under the circumstances, was that he was absolutely and totally at his ease. Yet, thought Jemima, taking refuge from her instinctive moment of jealousy in a meaner mood of sardonic satisfaction, when all is said and done, he has a great deal of explaining to do. A mistress in his office flat of an

August weekend. How will that be kept from the papers? Or for that matter Lady Lionnel? No question of gossip columnists now or the satiric snipings of *Jolly Joke* – headlines would be the order of the day for the beautiful slain Chloe Fontaine, romantic lady novelist. Sir Richard Lionnel's desire to go respectable had met an untimely end – as had his mistress. The pirate ship would not find a safe port at CARI after this. Of course – she looked down at his strong hands – he may have even more explaining to do. Who, Who? . . . She shuddered.

Lionnel introduced himself to Jemima with perfect gravity. 'Richard Lionnel. I own the building. I came back to my office flat downstairs to find the police. You were her tenant, I believe. I understand you found her. This must be terrible for you. Where will you go?' He did not even pause on the second word 'her'; nor could Jemima decide whether his avoidance of the name Chloe Fontaine indicated stress or total self-command. Lionnel certainly seemed indifferent to the fact – he could hardly be unaware of it – that it must also be terrible for him. The only conceivable sign of strain he exhibited was the fact that he was smoking as he entered the flat – although he stubbed the cigarette out immediately.

The black stub receded from her view into the pale glazed pottery ash-tray; it was shortly joined by another. Neither cigarette was fully smoked, a habit Sir Richard had in common with Kevin John Athlone; it was the image of the latter, stubbing out ceaselessly the black Sobranies he had found in Chloe's bedroom, which confirmed to her that this man before her had known her friend well, had from time to time shared that bedroom with her, had stored his cigarettes there, had perhaps stored a razor as well. Now she was dead, murdered.

Jemima did not of course know what had transpired between Lionnel and Pompey downstairs. Had he made a statement or were matters not that advanced? Which did he fear more – the Press or the police? These questions tantalized her as she replied with composure to match his own: 'I'm going to an hotel near here, I hope. Then I shall try to find something else. My own flat is let and I need to be in this area to get on with my work in the British Library.' She glanced at Pompey, who gave a very gentle shake of his head, and added firmly: 'And of course I want to give the police all the help I can.'

'Naturally,' replied Lionnel, as though she was offering to help him rather than the police. Once again he did not apparently feel it incumbent upon him to express the same helpful attitude. They stared at each other. 'Whatever the police know at this point about your relations with Chloe,' thought Jemima, refusing to let her own green eyes fall before his black ones, '*I* know. But do you know that I know?'

'Excuse me, sir,' said the young policeman, with a deferential cough. 'There's the question of this pet.' He was holding in his arms the golden bundle of Tiger, whose wild green eyes, rather the colour of Jemima's own but far more baleful, gazing with savage outrage at his imprisonment, made the policeman's description of him seem singularly inappropriate.

'Oh God – Tiger – I'd forgotten. Who will feed him?' began Jemima, just as the infuriated so-called pet eluded his captor's arms. Delivering a vicious scratch to the policeman's shoulder, protected only by a white shirt, he leapt away and to the floor. From this point he then leapt with equal precipitation right up on to Lionnel's tweed-clad shoulder. It was as though in his feline language, he was pointing directly and threateningly to their secret acquaintance. If so, Lionnel's reaction was equally significant. Without any visible annoyance, he simply struck the clinging cat off his shoulder, as one might brush off a beetle or some other flying insect. Tiger let out something closer to a squawk than a mew.

'Cats in their place,' said Lionnel pleasantly, but without a trace of apology. This was how Jemima had witnessed the Lion of Bloomsbury coping with television. 'Lionnel Estates will definitely be building further high-rise blocks – Lionnel Estates will be demolishing unsafe Adam houses – Lionnel Estates will do this, do that – wherever the permission is granted.' And then at the end, an unexpected grin, making him look like a happy satyr. He was not grinning now. 'But there's no need for them to starve. Cats, Miss Shore, not the masses. By repute, as you know, I'm less particular about the latter. Besides you might not get into a very salubrious hotel at this hour, and at the height of the tourist season. I'll call my people on Monday and see what we've got on offer to accommodate you. In the meantime, Miss Shore, why don't you stay downstairs? I've an office flat,' he went on blandly, 'which I'm using till my own flat on the third floor is decorated. Quite comfortable. Yes, really quite comfortable. I take it you're alone.' He looked round.

'Yes, quite alone,' said Jemima in her most poised voice. 'How very kind, Sir Richard. But what about—' she phrased it diplomatically 'your own plans?'

'I'm going back to the country. Now.' And to Portsmouth he added: 'You have my number there of course, and I'll be available at any time.'

'Thank you, Sir Richard. I should like to have a further word with you before you go.' Equally noncommittal.

'So why not, Miss Shore?' Why not indeed? It was true that Jemima felt a growing obligation towards Tiger, as though tending him was her own expression of mourning for Chloe. She could not abandon him now to his wildness. Who else would tend him? Adam Adamson? Was he yet back from that mysterious errand? Ah, that was a thought. The whole question of Adam Adamson, to say nothing of Kevin John Athlone, brought her back to the persistent refrain Who, Who? . . .

To deal with it, she needed two things. First of all, time and space for a clear think. And that the first-floor flat would provide. Second, and of this she was quietly optimistic, she needed a good long talk with her friend Detective Chief Inspector John Portsmouth, otherwise known as Pompey. She had after all a great deal of information for Pompey. Jemima, spirits rising as the habitual curiosity quickened in her, thought Pompey, unofficially of course, might have some for her.

One last encounter remained before she could descend to the abstract peace of the first floor. In its own way it was as surprising as anything which had yet confronted her that day.

Mr Stover was an unexpectedly little man. From his fiercely resonant voice, Jemima had anticipated more physical substance. He stood in the doorway, panting slightly from the climb, felt hat in hand, mackintosh over his arm – careful on even such a blazing day of what sudden rains might lie in wait in the capital. He was quite dwarfed by the policewoman at his side; she was rather pretty, with neat fair hair pinned up under a cap and a pleasantly freckled face; her black and white tie and rolled-up sleeves, revealing freckled arms, gave her the air of a school prefect.

The smallness of Mr Stover depressed Jemima once more. But then Chloe's so small. No, Chloe *was* small. She tried to put aside the memory of that frail corpse on the bed. And anyway, he's only her stepfather.

But Mr Stover was still talking quite fiercely and the eyes, in the lined face, under the white hair, were bright and even angry.

'We never came here, you know,' he was saying. 'Her mother and I were never invited.'

He looked round at the wreck of the pale flat, which now, under its police occupation, looked like some kind of abandoned film set.

'Very plush, I must say.' It did not seem the right word. 'No garden, of course.'

'There's a nice balcony, sir,' said the policewoman brightly.

Mr Stover shot her a sardonic glance. 'I can see that, my dear, I can see that. Seventy-seven next birthday and still got my own eyes. Can't say the same about my teeth, mind you, but then I don't see with my teeth, do I?'

'No, sir,' said the policewoman in a voice of friendly encouragement, as though he might if he tried hard enough.

'Those your teeth, by the way?' Mr Stover suddenly barked at Jemima, reminding her of the voice on the telephone. His small stature was certainly delusive.

'I believe so.'

'Funny. Always thought they ripped them out if you went on television and gave you new ones. That's why I never accepted any of their numerous offers to appear, you see.' Then the little spark subsided; there was something automatic about it as though Mr Stover was comforting himself with his familiar witticism.

'A balcony, yes,' he went on in a much less energetic voice. 'All very nice. But you couldn't put a baby on a balcony, could you? Not for very long. Her mother said, "Charlie, I'd like to know about the accommodation." That's the last thing she said. "Is it suitable, Charlie? You must tell Dollie to make quite sure she has a little garden."' Then he choked and Jemima realized that tears were running down his cheeks, had been running down his cheeks while he talked of Dollie and her garden, and twisted his felt hat in his hands.

'She was so happy, the wife, when Dollie telephoned. We quite forgave her all the waiting. The second letter, cancelling the visit, never arrived, you know. Some problem with the address, I suppose. It will come—' He gave a little dry sob. 'She was so happy. In spite of the, well, somewhat unusual circumstances, least said soonest mended in that direction. "A grand-child at my age!" she said. Dollie was her only one, and we never had one of our own.'

Mr Stover turned to Jemima, as though the police were not present and she, and she alone, must hear this news.

'Yes, Miss Shore, Dollie was going to have a baby. That's what she wanted to tell us. And this morning she was so happy.'

As Mr Stover still stood there, having delivered this bombshell, Jemima found the old question coming back in force. Who, Who? Not only the murderer but the father of Chloe's child. One person or two. Who, Who?

9
Fallen Child

'Yes, she was pregnant all right. About three months, according to the police doctor,' said Detective Chief Inspector Portsmouth. 'We got on to the mortuary immediately in case anything could be done to save the child, which of course it couldn't.' He was sitting, nursing a pale whisky and water, in what was designated as the receiving room of Sir Richard Lionnel's office suite.

The décor was quite unlike that of the shocking cobalt blue aquarium upstairs. Here it was most obviously gracious: a great many well-polished surfaces belonging to furniture which could have been photographed as it stood for the pages of *Country Life*. Lamps were huge, marble based with wide shades. The sofa on which Pompey was sitting was discreetly covered in tobacco-coloured material, with appropriately tawny cushions. The flowers, a huge arrangement on the bow-fronted sideboard which otherwise bore only cut-glass decanters containing a variety of rich red liquids, consisted of gladioli and roses. Red and orange predominated. Jemima expected to see *Country Life* itself lying in sheaves on the low table in front of the sofa (such planning, with its lack of any personal element, recalled irresistibly the dentist's waiting-room). Whoever had decorated this suite, it was certainly not the same hand and imagination at work as had been rampant on the third floor. Perhaps the Lionnels merely hired the most fashionable decorator of the time, regardless of style.

Only Jemima herself, still in the rippling beige dress with its tiny splashes of red and navy blue in which she found herself spending this strange day, brought some lightness into the picture. Pompey noted once again Jemima's gift – and the gift of her clothes – of seeming unruffled and elegant even in the most bizarre circumstances. It was something to which his wife had first drawn his attention. Pompey merely thought Jemima an unfairly pretty girl for one who was so markedly – even awkwardly – intelligent. Every time they met he had to adjust to the combination all over again. Shaking his head, he expressed something along these lines.

'I don't believe it!' Jemima burst out. 'Oh thank you, Pompey,' she added quickly. 'No, I meant Chloe and the baby. I can't quite believe it. But then I'm always saying that about Chloe now. I'm beginning to think I never knew her at all.' Jemima took a long cool sip of white wine – a Muscadet happily found in Sir Richard's office fridge; but then many people drank white wine as an aperitif nowadays not only Jemima herself – Chloe, for example . . .

'Tell me about her. A rather adventurous young lady, I take it.' A gentle shake of the head. 'A bit of a slip-up, that about the baby. Didn't she watch your famous programme, then, about the Pill?' Pompey's references to Jemima's programmes were generally jocular; Jemima was glad of this indication that he was in a relaxed – and therefore confidential – mood.

'Adventurous, yes. Young, well, you're always so chivalrous, Pompey. She was exactly my age.' Pompey spread his hands expressively. He looked quite roguish. The omens were good for a rather jolly discussion, if any discussion on such a painful subject could be jolly; it was one which involved Pompey's keen wits and Jemima's devouring curiosity.

Jemima had already described what she knew of the last twenty-four hours of Chloe's life. She had kept nothing of importance back, relating quite straightforwardly the various episodes of the telephone calls (including those of the Stovers), and the morning intrusion of Kevin John Athlone as she was about to leave for the Reading Room. Her description of her encounter with Adam Adamson had incurred quite a fierce headshake from Pompey but he did not interrupt her. She passed on to her unexpected meeting with Valentine Brighton in the Reading Room and her subsequent return first to the square gardens where she had spied Adamson leaving, and then to the house in Adelaide Square itself, where she had found Kevin John Athlone.

Jemima left nothing material out. She knew that if she was to pursue her enquiries successfully, she had much to gain from being very frank with Pompey in the hope that he would to some extent pool information. Only with regard to Valentine Brighton's mission to London did she tread somewhat circumspectly. This was for two reasons. First, Jemima had her own reservations about Valentine's story, told amidst the Assyrian gods. His whole presence in Bloomsbury needed further explanation so far as she was concerned; the image of that slumped figure – like a dead man as she had thought at the time – in the seat so providentially next to hers, remained to tantalize and disturb. Second, Chloe's alleged ambition to marry Lionnel was, by the rules of evidence, merely hearsay.

Jemima therefore contented herself for the time being with telling Pompey that Valentine had had a rendezvous with Chloe, and that Chloe had not kept it. On the subject of Lionnel generally, she kept her peace. Here was an area where Pompey possibly had something to tell her.

He did. Or rather, he was able to confirm a substantial part of the Brighton story out of Sir Richard Lionnel's own statement.

'She was his mistress. Oh, yes.' Doleful shake. '*And* he didn't know she was pregnant, so he says. He also swore, by the way, that *she* didn't know; he thought the old man was making it up, had got the wrong end of the stick.' Pompey coughed. 'This is before the report from the mortuary confirmed that she *was* pregnant, of course!' Another cough and a shake. 'Yes, a very adventurous young lady. Because you see, Jemima, if Sir Richard Lionnel's statement is to be believed, and we have no reason at this point to doubt his word, he could not be the father of her child.'

'I've just been working that out for myself,' Jemima said slowly. 'Three months pregnant. And the programme on which they met was at the beginning of June – I'll fill you in on that if Lionnel hasn't. Certainly not earlier, because I was in Japan until the second week of May, and Chloe's book – *Fallen Child* – must have been published at the end of the month. The programme came after that. She only moved here in June. She was already pregnant then. It wasn't visible, even the night she died, except – yes, maybe the figure just a little fuller.'

'*Fallen Child*, eh?' The title seemed to confirm Pompey's gloomiest supposition about the late Chloe Fontaine. 'Well, she was certainly fallen, poor lady. In the old-fashioned sense of the word,' he added gallantly, as if Jemima were far too young to have heard the expression.

'And to the last I always found something rather childlike about her –' Jemima hesitated, recalling their last conversation. Chloe framed in the window, the waif-like face and the newly rounded bosom, which at the time had seemed to indicate increased voluptuousness, but was now revealed as something far more vulnerable.

'You've called her adventurous, Pompey. She was, obviously. But she was also greedy, greedy like a child. Grabbing at things, people, experiences. I see it much more clearly now, now that she's no longer here to charm and woo me – Chloe wooed everyone, you know. This last grab, at Lionnel I mean, it must have been terrible for her when she found out she was pregnant. A child with child. Perhaps that's why she panicked.'

'Someone panicked, not necessarily the deceased. She didn't cut her own throat with a kitchen knife, you know. No question of that. This was a swift and quite expert piece of work. The stabs came after and were extra to requirements. Sign of a lover, more likely than not, all that frenzy.'

'I was referring to her future. Did Lionnel give any indication—'

'Said they were off to France. Taking the ferry and driving down to the South. Quite open about it. That they were spending the weekend in London because he had to be at number ten – quite open about that, too. Still, it's a very good alibi. The second best alibi in the world you might call it, the best being only half a mile away up the road.'

'D'you think the Queen's actually at home on a Saturday?'

Dubious shake and Pompey continued: 'He left this flat at ten o'clock and returned at six-fifteen according to his statement. It will be checked, of course. Unexpectedly free at lunch so telephoned Miss Fontaine at twelve-thirty. No answer. Rather surprised. Still it was a lovely day – she might have been in the gardens. The first-floor flat, as you see, does have a balcony, but she would have heard the telephone from there. Went to a restaurant in Soho. Ate his lunch. Telephoned again at two. No answer – by that time of course she was probably dead. We think she was killed between one and two o'clock. Shortly after you left the house. Back to his meeting and arrived here soon after six to find the police. That's all except he doesn't remember the name of the restaurant, something Greek was all he gave us, but that's no problem. We shall find it.'

'He's certainly highly recognizable.' There was something confusing to Jemima about her own relief that Lionnel was in the clear; was it for his own or for Chloe's sake – her last love not her killer – that she was pleased?

'But did Lionnel make any statement about their future?' Jemima ventured. 'I know this sounds a trifling question, Pompey, but it might be relevant in piecing together Chloe's past if I knew when she was telling the truth and when she wasn't.' It was also relevant to the past of her friend and publisher Valentine Brighton.

'He gave us as much as he had to, and he knew he had to, sooner or later. No more, no less. Quite straight. He's a man of the world. No point in fooling around with the police, now, is there? Not for a man in Sir Richard Lionnel's position. Too much to lose. He needs us, doesn't he, to keep the Press off his back—'

'Ah.' Jemima was wondering about the Press, so far – mercifully from her own point of view as well as that of Lionnel – absent. She knew it could hardly last.

Pompey sipped his whisky appreciatively; his whole attitude was one of melancholy but unsurprised regret at the perpetual foolishness of human nature.

Her own 999 call had been sufficiently uninformative to elude the interest of some stray listener-in to the police radio link. Saturday night was a dead time in Fleet Street, with the Sunday papers not only printed but already despatched to the provinces; it needed an emergency to alter the leading stories of the London editions. But on Sunday Scotland Yard would be notified of what had occurred and that notification would reach the Press Bureau. Then the second tornado, that of the Press following that of the police team, would strike. Chloe's murder would certainly be announced on the Sunday evening television news and splashed across the morning papers.

'In so far as that can be done,' continued Pompey, 'and in so far as we want to co-operate, which for the time being, in view of the connection with number ten, and the incomplete nature of our enquiries, perhaps we do. Of course they'll be right on to the fact that he owns the building, particularly as there's been all this fuss about it, but he didn't own her flat, the flat where she was killed. As to the relationship, well, they may suspect, may have heard rumours, but they've got to be very careful about what they print. This is a murder case, Jemima, not your average juicy scandal of adultery in high places.' From Pompey's prim tone, you might have thought that Pompey actually preferred murder to adultery. He added: 'He's made his statement and he's gone back to Sussex.'

'To Lady Lionnel. I wonder what *her* reaction will be?'

Pompey rose to his feet. For all his natural authority he was not a man you would pick out in a crowd – a fact in which he took some pride – and even after Jemima's original television interview, people had not immediately recognized him in the street. Even his age was mysterious; for all his paternal manner, he was probably not so many years older than Jemima herself. Indeed she sometimes darkly suspected that his paternalism – and his chivalry – was a professional ruse to instil confidence, and thus elicit it. Yet when one studied his face closely it had at least one highly memorable feature: a pair of curiously bushy eyebrows rising to tufted points over bright rather small eyes which together gave him the look of an inquisitive fox. Jemima could only suppose that because Pompey did not want to become instantly recognizable in television terms, he had somehow willed himself to remain anonymous. Talking to him face to face she was instantly aware of his presence. Certainly of all the men Jemima had interviewed in depth for television Pompey had adapted most naturally and unselfconsciously to the medium. Television to him had been merely another problem to be solved and he was certainly not going to be surprised or fazed by it.

'Now *that* you can tell me, Jemima, better than I can tell you. You know the old saying – Hell hath no fury like a woman scorned. Not, I am sure,' he added with another gallant nod, 'that you have ever been scorned.'

'But *was* she scorned?' murmured Jemima. 'Was Lionnel really intending to divorce her and marry Chloe?'

'Ah, now how about a woman's intuition to solve that one?' Pompey's expression was positively humorous. 'Me, as a mere man I shall take myself down to the station to see about the more mundane matter of fingerprints, eliminating those friendly to the environment. That's my next job. Then there's the question of the cleaner; the woman Rosina Whatnot, you say you never met her. My boys will interview her in the morning and take *her* prints. We'll be contacting Lord Brighton in Sussex or at his Bloomsbury flat, and we'll pick up that squatter fellow when he returns, if he returns. Myself, I want to see if my men have raised that bruiser of an artist for me yet.'

So, shaking his head in a fatherly manner, Pompey departed, taking care to leave Jemima the number of his direct line 'in case of need'. The need was unspecified. Jemima guessed that Pompey had chivalrous doubts about leaving her in the gaunt building, with only Tiger, now in a highly restless mood, as company. She herself had no such fears.

It was only after Pompey had gone that something extraordinary and on the face of it quite illogical about her own attitude to the case struck Jemima. Regardless of what Pompey might discover, why was it that she herself had not immediately concluded that Kevin John Athlone was responsible for the murder?

He was the obvious suspect. And Pompey had taught her in the past that the obvious suspect was very often the right suspect – she accepted the logic of the position, unexciting as it might be to the more tortuous mind. Kevin John had arrived at Adelaide Square that very morning with the avowed intention of doing Chloe some violence and had then proceeded to beat up Jemima. He had later quite gratuitously admitted to shinning up the scaffolding and entering the penthouse itself; depositing a geranium right next to the room where the murder had been committed. He thus had motive – by his own lights – and opportunity. What was more, Kevin John Athlone was certainly strong enough to wield that brutal knife, with the efficient hands of one whose profession was to live by them. Had he not begun life as a sculptor? Jemima had a dim memory of some unwieldy sculptures in Chloe's Fulham house, attributed to Kevin John in youth.

It was true that there were certain inconsistencies in the idea of Kevin John as the murderer. First of all, it had to be faced that the revelation of Chloe's pregnancy did complicate the issue. The obvious theory of Kevin John as the spur-of-the-moment killer need not be abandoned; but it needed expansion. If Kevin John had indeed struck her down, his motive was likely to have been jealous rage at this – to him – highly inflammatory piece of news. The repeated stabbing when Chloe was already dead, or at least visibly dying, did indicate some storm of passion. But if one accepted this as Kevin John's motive, that led to further questions. For example, why had Chloe elected to break the news to Kevin John in the first place? When did she tell him? When, and above all why, had Chloe re-entered the penthouse in her white broderie anglaise petticoat?

The alternative was to accept that Kevin John had murdered Chloe in a fit of rage quite unconnected with her condition. It did not do, as Jemima knew, to insist on neat solutions where murder was concerned. It might just possibly be that the two facts – the murder and the pregnancy – bore absolutely no relation to each other.

At the same time, Jemima was aware that her curious presumption of Kevin John's innocence antedated Pompey's confirmation of Chloe's pregnancy. For the second inconsistency in the theory of Kevin John as murderer centred round his known behaviour during the late afternoon. There was something implausible in the notion of a man who had cruelly slaughtered his ex-mistress settling down for a nap in the hall of the same house where the deed had taken place; having first advertised his forcible entry to her flat, not only by the presence of a glaring pot plant, but also in conversation thereafter with Jemima Shore.

According to Pompey, the bedroom – and the knife handle – had been wiped clean of fingerprints. That showed a deliberation, an instinct for self-preservation, at variance with Kevin John's general behaviour in the last twenty-four hours. Jemima could, unfortunately, believe that Kevin John had flung himself on Chloe like a mad bull, and as it were gored her to death rather as he had uncontrollably beaten up Jemima. But after that, what would have happened? Was it not far more in character for Kevin John to collapse weeping?

'I love her, I love her.' His distraught words in the flat that morning, as he blubbered, virtually round Jemima's neck, now rang in her ears.

She would have expected Kevin John, the fell deed done, to have cried out like Othello: 'O Desdemona, Desdemona O!'

But Chloe's murderer had coolly wiped the kitchen knife handle; had wiped prints from the bedroom; and had donned gloves to clean up his own traces. Jemima told Pompey that Chloe's kitchen gloves were missing; and she could not envisage Kevin John pausing in his path of mayhem to don a pair of kitchen gloves. Rather, like Othello, he would have slaughtered Chloe in a fit of passion; killed first, wept afterwards. Either way, it was difficult to imagine that Kevin John would choose to slump down in the hall of 73 Adelaide Square and fall stertorously asleep.

There was yet another inconsistency – that anonymous and Irish voice issuing threats in the late-night and early-morning telephone calls. Kevin John, despite his name and lineage, had no trace of an Irish accent, but rather an unexpectedly cultured English voice. Jemima had been tempted even at the time to acquit Kevin John of responsibility for these calls, impressed by his denial. If not Kevin John, then who?

The obvious suspect, leaving out of account Kevin John Athlone, was Sir Richard Lionnel . . . yet, if the police doctor was right and Jemima's dating of the crucial TV programme was accurate – a reasonable assumption in both cases – there was another inconsistency here. Sir Richard Lionnel could hardly be the father of Chloe's child. The old question arose: if not Lionnel, then who?

Chloe's own attitude to her pregnancy had been, to put it mildly, ambivalent. She had certainly not entrusted Jemima with the secret – but then Jemima, the latter reflected bitterly, had been destined for quite another role in Chloe's scheme of things than that of confidante. Yet Chloe had deliberately arranged to visit her elderly parents – unvisited for many months – in order to break the astonishing and perhaps shocking news. Failing to make the expedition on her way to France, because of Lionnel's date at number ten, she had then proceeded to summon her aged stepfather to London, having broken the news of her condition in advance on the telephone.

What sort of meeting had Chloe envisaged between Mr Stover, in his seventies, bowed but dignified and still capable of fierceness, and her new lover, the Lion of Bloomsbury? Was old Mr Stover intended to arrive with some form of metaphorical shot-gun and force on the union? In short, was Chloe, in one of her intricate seemingly artless schemes, intending to palm off the baby on her new lover, using it as a weapon to persuade him to marry her?

Certainly the summons of Mr Stover to the same building as Lionnel, indicated that some kind of confrontation had been planned. At the same time, these thoughts reminded Jemima how very much Lionnel had to lose from this revelation of Chloe's pregnancy – if he believed himself to be the father. According to Valentine, Lionnel feared any type of scandal at any time before the announcement of his new CARI appointment; the brooding Lady Lionnel, Valentine's Medea, could hardly be expected to take such news calmly. To say the least of it, Chloe's death had come at a convenient moment for her latest lover. Lionnel, like Kevin John himself, would do well to produce a cast-iron alibi for the lunchtime hour when the murder was committed.

Jemima yawned. She felt it was very late, although it was in fact only ten o'clock according to her little gold watch. The ormolu clock on the mantelpiece told some fantasy time of midnight which belonged to another world where the Lion of Bloomsbury had lain down with his pretty lamb of a mistress. Tiger who, once Pompey had departed, had decided to crouch on Jemima's lap, had gone to sleep. Jemima used his inertia as an excuse to let her own curiosity roam once more back over the known facts. She knew from experience that this curiosity, once aroused, would not let her sleep until everything, at least within the confines of her own mind, was ordered.

Fallen Child, Fallen Angel . . . but Chloe if she had remained a child, had been no angel . . . Angel – yes – angel, that was the word which was important, 'My former angel' . . . Chloe's soft breathless voice, so penetrating despite its capacity to sound as if it were borne on the wind, came back to haunt her. 'My former angel who was . . .' Yes, that was the clue which was teasing her. What *was* the identity of Chloe's former lover? Who was also, presumably, the true father of her child . . .

Restlessly Jemima fingered the telephone, more because it was within her reach without disturbing Tiger than with any clear idea of who to telephone. Who on earth at this hour would provide her with the background information she sadly needed about the last months of Chloe's life? Valentine Brighton she ruled out; she had had his story already. But it was the thought of Valentine which drew her on to the subject of the ill-fated novel, and so, inexorably as it seemed to her afterwards, to the subject of Isabelle Mancini.

At the time she felt it was pure inquisitive impulse which led her to dial Isabelle's home number for further interrogation of that transatlantic acolyte, Miss Laura Barrymore. That and the fact that Jemima, who had a good head for telephone numbers, remembered it from the morning. She was nevertheless startled when the telephone was answered immediately and by Isabelle Mancini herself.

'Isabelle, I thought you were in Paris . . .'

'Jemima, oh my God!' cried Isabelle, as though Jemima had not spoken. 'I've just heard the news. Oh my God!' she repeated. 'Oh my God!' Possibly she was crying or had been crying very recently.

The richness of her French tones was unmistakable. It called to mind instantly not only her warm personality, but the full rich French figure which matched it, wide-hipped, generous-bosomed; even Isabelle's thick black bun, with its elegant silvery streaks, had a special wealth, a heaviness about it. For Jemima, the habitual floating grey of Isabelle's clothes – she wore no other colour – conveyed more warmth than other women's pinks and reds.

But there was nothing warm about what she was now saying, only despair, a mixture of passion and despair.

'I wanted to ke-e-el 'er,' Isabelle was saying. 'I came back from Paris to ke-e-el 'er. And now she's dead.' The rest of her words were swallowed up in prolonged and convulsive weeping.

390

10
A carnal encounter

Isabelle's hysterical sobs suddenly stopped. It sounded as if the receiver had been taken away quite sharply from her. Another voice came over the wire – that of Laura Barrymore. In contrast to Isabelle, she sounded smoothly calm; it was as if she were spreading her own remarks like butter over Isabelle's previous utterances.

'Isabelle is naturally very upset at hearing the news of Miss Fontaine's death. She's also not quite herself since she's been working so very hard in Paris. She had to come back early to get some rest. And she was of course quite unprepared to take your call at this late hour.' Through the politeness came a slight implication of reproach. 'I've been trying to get her to take a sedative—'

'Who told her the news? I'd like to speak to her again.' Jemima knew how to inject a certain authority into her own voice.

'I'm not sure—'

Isabelle grabbed the telephone, her French accent more pronounced than usual: 'Valentine 'as told me. And 'e was told by the police. 'E's in 'is flat in Bloomsbury—' It was a word to which Isabelle brought her own special pronunciation. 'And so 'e telephones me. Just like zat. My 'eart, I think it stop. Because I 'ave come back from Paris *exprès*, no Laura, cherie, don't stop me, eeet's true – to ke-e-el 'er—'

'I thought you weren't coming back till Sunday – I spoke to Laura this morning.'

In the background Jemima could hear the sound of some angry expostulations from the formerly cool Miss Barrymore. Isabelle resumed in a slightly less emotional tone: 'Silly child. No, not you, dulling, *la petite Laure*, e-e-diot child. She thinks I am telling you things which are dangerous. So swe-e-et. So loyal. No, no, dulling, what I am telling you is this. I came back at lunchtime specially to ke-e-el Chloe, she was a monster that one, wait till you 'ear, I wanted to choke her, strangle her for what she's done to me.' Dramatic pause and change of tone. 'And another thing, Jemima, Laura tells me an absurd story about Chloe going to the Camargue for us. For us? With Binnie? Who, by the way, is in Capri, with some terrr-r-rible pr-r-r-ince. More terr-r-r-ible even than her usual pr-r-r-inces. Chloe in the Camargue for us?' Isabelle wheezed with rich indignation. 'Had the child gone mad?' she repeated.

'I suppose that would be quite out of the question.' Jemima sounded tentative. She was anxious not to cut off this helpful but sensitive source of information by an unfortunate word. But Isabelle by now was in full flood.

'That book,' she was exclaiming. 'It was so 'or-r-r-ible, so disloyal, something precious laid out like that for all the world to see. I shall never, never agree, I said. Over my dead body. I pleaded with her. I wanted to ke-e-el her.' Isabelle's vehemence became strangled. 'Oh God, dulling, and now she's dead,' she concluded in the calmer of her two voices. It was impossible to know whether she had realized the significance of what she had said.

Jemima decided to come out into the open. She assured Isabelle that she had not read the offensive book, knew of its existence only from Valentine, and furthermore no one would ever read it now. 'But, Isabelle, tell me one thing, Chloe's style was generally so cool, so carefully ironic, hardly full-blooded, you know what the critics say about her, used to say. I'm rather puzzled you were quite so upset.'

'Upset, what are you saying?' Isabelle's voice rose perilously. 'She used my letters, my own letters to her; foolish, foolish letters; there they were, written down for all the world to see, the letters of a foolish old woman.' Jemima tried to interrupt, but Isabelle was in full Gallic flood.

'And Valentine, too, what did he do, the terr-r-r-aitor, he asked her to edit a whole book of letters, and so she laughed, that pretty laugh, she too a terr-r-raitor, and said she would put them, some of my letters in her anthology. Letters of an Unknown Woman—' At this point Laura evidently intervened again. Isabelle's voice, still audible despite the fact that either she or Laura was now masking the telephone, was fierce.

'E-e-ediot child!' Jemima heard her say. It was the opposite to Isabelle's other famous cry: 'Swe-e-et boy (or girl)'. 'Non, non Laure no, of course not, why should I be such a fool, I? Not murder her, kee-e-el her, you understand me.' Isabelle was now speaking directly to Jemima. 'And when I come back I 'ear she is dead.' A pause. 'And then of course

I am sorry.' Isabelle was sobbing again. 'Little Chloe dead. What fiend could have done that?'

Jemima listened as Laura Barrymore recovered the telephone and in her politest manner attempted to enlist Jemima's help in securing the return of the aforesaid letters – a task she thought Jemima would be able to perform with some ease since they must, surely, remain in Adelaide Square. Miss Barrymore's tone implied that this small favour was something in the nature of passing on the name of a good hairdresser.

Jemima decided to press home her advantage. Laura Barrymore was assuming that Jemima was still in Chloe's flat; Jemima did not disabuse her of the notion. She had brushed aside an earlier warm invitation from Isabelle to join them in their own cosy apartment without comment on her present whereabouts. She realized that she had something at least to trade in return for further information from Isabelle. Personally she saw no reason why Isabelle should not have her pathetic letters back – 'the letters of a foolish old woman' – as soon as possible, although Pompey might take another view as he conscientiously unravelled the webs spun by Chloe, the fallen child. Still, even if the police read them and analysed them (Pompey had probably removed them by now in any case) she, Jemima, might be instrumental in securing their discreet return at the appropriate moment.

She assured Laura Barrymore to this effect, and in return was able to put one last question to Isabelle without having the Barrymore vigilance interrupt her.

'I suppose poor Valentine is very upset about Chloe,' she ventured.

'Oh, Chloe was so terr-r-rible to him. She behaved so badly to him,' Isabelle expostulated.

'I'm beginning to think Chloe was terrible to all her lovers.'

A Gallic exclamation. 'Lover, dulling, Valentine, no. A peck on the cheek, perhaps, no more. Too well br-r-red, too much of an ar-r-r-ristocrat.'

'It doesn't necessarily follow,' murmured Jemima, with memories of certain encounters of her own in the past. Isabelle gave an unexpectedly bawdy chuckle. Jemima had forgotten her propensity for gossip; Isabelle had taken the allusion.

'Ah, wicked Jemima. No, this was different. Valentine adored Chloe, he loved her in his own sad way, the way of a moth perhaps, fluttering towards the—' Isabelle paused before the cliché and rushed on – 'star. Yes, that was it. Kisses like a moth, don't you think, there is something so swee-e-eet about Valentine. But he was much too ar-r-r-ristocratic to think of marrying her, too frightened of *la Maman*, perhaps, and so he would torture himself hearing of her *affaires*. I tell you, she was ter-r-rible to him.'

Privately Jemima considered that Valentine had sought his own fate; she had no great sympathy with emotional masochism herself. Still, it all made sense. Whoever Lover Unknown was, he was not Valentine Brighton; thus Valentine as the father of Chloe's child could be eliminated. All the same, Valentine's movements on this particular Saturday still needed further examination – had he for example an alibi for the crucial hour between one and two o'clock when the murder had taken place? It had been just after two o'clock when she found him slumped in the Reading Room, and the police were inclined to favour an earlier rather than a later time.

Reassuring Isabelle that she would work on the problem of the letters, Jemima put down the telephone.

Isabelle? Was it possible? Should she be added to her list of potential suspects? A lot depended on the time when Isabelle Mancini had actually returned to London from Paris. 'Lunchtime' was sufficiently vague to make anything possible and in this case covered a very important area of time. Isabelle's alibi if any – that was one for Pompey and his boys to iron out. The investigation of movements was easy for them, their speciality. But all these hysterical threats – how were they to be regarded? The character and probably the behaviour of Isabelle Mancini – that was in Jemima Shore's line of business. Jemima reflected wryly that the distinction between ke-e-elling and murder was not one that the man in the street or for that matter her friend Pompey would readily accept: but it was also true that the word 'ke-e-el' was frequently on Isabelle's lips in the most unlikely conjunctions, as all her friends would testify. The word testify brought Jemima up short. She hoped, most sincerely, that it would not come to that. There had been enough havoc already, wreaked by Chloe – or Chloe's death, whichever way you liked to look at it.

Time to sleep. Jemima supposed that she must soon retire to the so-called office bedroom suite, where Sir Richard had displayed, without comment, an Empire bed, imperial eagles on the bedhead, upholstered in rich dark green; the walls were hung with the same material. The room seemed to show yet another decorative hand at work – a far more successful one. Its atmosphere was deliberately grand as well as masculine; Jemima felt her own intrusion into this room to be exotic enough as to be exciting – Chloe, had she too felt that?

Jemima yawned again and wondered which of the three rooms if any represented Sir Richard's own taste; she hoped it was not the modern horror on the third floor.

Here the balcony onto the square had a high concrete edge, making the front area of it dark and cavernous. It was time to push Tiger off her lap – he had endured the long telephone conversation without movement – and retire. The balcony windows were wide open, and for Tiger's sake, Jemima decided to leave them that way. She knew that a policeman was posted at the entrance to the building; Pompey had taken away the keys to Chloe's flat in his pocket.

Tiger stretched, that long lazy movement which completely altered the shape of his cosy domestic body into that of a hunting animal, and then vanished into the shadows of the scaffolding, lit up from place to place by the street lights. Jemima heard the cat scurrying about making little sounds, scratching.

For a moment she stood looking at the square, listening to the faint rustle of the wind in the trees. Then she leant over the concrete parapet. It was a comparatively short drop into the square itself; she could not actually see the police sentinel, perhaps he was under the eave of the porch. It was typical of the meaningless modernity of this building that whereas the parapet of the penthouse was too low for absolute security, here on the first floor it was too high for comfort.

Jemima looked idly into the shadows. The proximity of the scaffolding would have made a lesser woman nervous, but she herself had never been frightened of the dark, or indeed of solitude. She thought of her more highly strung friends – poor Chloe, for instance, had always been intolerably nervous when alone: perhaps that was the true explanation of her amazing promiscuity ... Chloe would have made anxious patterns out of these shadows and backed hastily away from the balcony for the safety of the lighted flat. In particular the shadows threw into relief one patch of greyness amid the scaffolding, very close to Jemima, which an over-imaginative person could well have fashioned into some lurking face.

Jemima's own eye travelled casually downwards. On the floor of the balcony was a pair of shoes. They looked like white gym shoes. So convinced was she still that this was purely a trick of the light, that it took her several seconds to take in that she was actually gazing at a pair of white shoes, shoes with real feet inside them, with bare ankles rising from them into the darkness above. And it was several seconds more before she finally realized that someone was actually standing in those shadows, motionless, staring at her, face almost touching hers, and had been standing there all the time, face a grey moon, face level with her own.

Jemima stood absolutely still in her turn. It was as though their two figures were engaged in playing a game of statues with each other. The hidden figure was the first to move.

'How amusing it is meeting like this,' said Adam Adamson, stepping out into the light. 'You've seen me at last. I was wondering how long I could hold my breath. My heart was beating like a mad gong, I'm amazed you didn't hear it. I seem destined to give you delicious shocks, don't I? Now, goddess, we can have a good talk, without interruptions.'

He bent down and patted Tiger.

'You, me and, of course, Puss. Goddess as you may be, you have a great deal of explaining to do to a mere mortal like myself. Never mind, the night is young.'

Putting a courteous but firm hand across Jemima's shoulder, Adam Adamson wheeled her into the lighted drawing room of the first-floor flat.

'You fool!' Jemima's momentary panic made her sound both crosser and more intimate than she intended. 'Don't you know that the police are here?'

'Raffles the Gentleman Cracksman at your service.' Adam Adamson drew off an imaginary hat with a flourish. 'I did see a stalwart bobby standing at the front door of the concrete prison; nevertheless it proved the work of a moment for your humble servant to elude his stern but straight-forward gaze and shin up the ever-convenient scaffolding. Courtesy of the Lion of Bloomsbury. Then, lo and behold, what do I see, illuminated in the first-floor window, like the goddess you are, fit for worship, but Pallas Athena herself. Ho ho, thinks I, has our fair goddess set the sleuths upon me? And for that matter what might she be doing in the Lion's official den? So I decided to pay a call—'

His grip on her shoulder remained firm.

'Let me go.' But Adam Adamson didn't let her go. Instead he guided her further into the room and sat her down on the deep comfortable tawny sofa. Then he sat down beside her, quite close. She could have touched the golden down on his freckled cheeks and stroked the curly chestnut-coloured beard had she so wished.

'First question, why did you shop me to the police? I had quite an unpleasant moment seeing yon arm of the law standing there.'

'You fool,' Jemima repeated. 'I didn't shop you. Don't you *know* why the police are here?' Jemima felt herself breathing heavily, even panting; Adam Adamson's physical presence, which once she had found oddly attractive, now seemed to threaten her. Perhaps it was the late hour, the tantalizing and rather sinister circumstances of his arrival.

'I rather imagined that they had rumbled the salubrious presence of the Friends of the House, as symbolized by your humble servant and were e'en now making sure that he did not effect any further revivifying entrances.' He put his hand on hers; she noted the golden hairs on the back of it. It was a strong hand with a spatulate thumb.

'My dear Adam—' Jemima stopped. Both their intimacy and the situation itself were developing too rapidly for caution. Jemima Shore, Investigator, was in danger of losing a key opportunity of making a few pertinent enquiries of her own, before Pompey reached Adamson.

'Where have you been, then?' She tried to stop her voice sounding too brisk. 'I saw you leave the house about half-past five just as I was coming back.'

'I like to walk round London at night. Like Puss here I see the sights and smell the smells. Especially this part when it's empty. A little spying perhaps for the organization. Some beautiful empty houses doomed for demolition, no lights on, no security. We reconnoitre them at night.'

'A long walk. But then I suppose you'd been cooped up in that terrible flat all day. You must have enjoyed the change of scene.'

Adam did not answer the implied question. His expression was hard to read. Jemima feared that hers must be more open. She remembered Adam's apparent ability to read thoughts.

'So what are the police doing here?' He spoke more abruptly.

Jemima balanced the advantages of telling him – and thus proceeding further in her enquiries in a straightforward way – against the advantage she still possessed of surprise. While she still hesitated, Adam moved even closer to her:

'No, don't tell me, you're going to lie to me, goddess, I can see it in your green eyes. And your archaic smile. Let me do this instead.' Adam Adamson, putting one hand on her breast, pinched the nipple quite hard. Before Jemima could cry out, she felt her lips impressed by his and he half kissed, half bit her.

'No,' she panted when at last she had freed herself.

'Why not? I rather thought you might like that kind of thing,' replied Adam coolly. 'More fun for us both than your telling me lying stories about the police. I hate being lied to, don't you? In fact I take very great exception to it. It's the one area where I generally take my revenge.'

'I've no intention of lying to you.' Jemima carefully checked the collar of her dress as though it was that not her breast which had suffered the assault of his hand. 'Someone was killed here today, killed, murdered. In the upstairs flat. The police are guarding the building.'

'No chance of its being Sir Richard Lionnel, I suppose?' Adamson sounded extraordinarily composed; of the two of them, she was the agitated one.

'It was Chloe Fontaine, as a matter of fact. The owner of the top-floor flat. My friend.'

He stared at her in silence.

'Ah. I'm sorry. I'm sorry your friend died.'

After a long pause, Adamson sounded conventionally sad, no more than that. 'Chloe the Tragic Nymph. There's probably a curse on this building you know, since I tried to put one on it myself. I'm sorry it was a nymph that died and not a villain. She should never have come here.'

'You didn't know her?'

'I didn't say that. I didn't know her real name until you told me yourself this morning. Dollie, she called herself to me, Dollie Stover. Then I saw her photograph on the back of a book you were carrying and recognized it. Dollie – Chloe – you see, was a nymph by nature, a Nymph Errant, and I – sometimes – am a Knight Errant. We met, as such characters are prone to do, somewhere in the mazy land of the Errant where the most wayward one is king.'

Memories of Chloe's breathless words came back to Jemima – 'A little, a very little, adventure ... a casual encounter you might say, a carnal encounter perhaps.' Was this little adventure then shared with Adam Adamson? If so, Jemima had filled in two names out of the three she had listed as the most recent admirers of Chloe Fontaine.

'A casual encounter?' she asked. She tried to make her tones sound equally offhand.

'I like them, don't you?' Adamson had in the meantime placed his arm along her shoulders; it was a more overtly friendly gesture than the fierce advance he had just made. Nevertheless Jemima still felt threatened; she could not deny that she also felt increasingly excited by his presence, his proximity.

Jemima Shore returned to business.

'So you had a carnal encounter with Chloe?' She stopped, slightly embarrassed by the Freudian mistake. It was all very well for Chloe. Jemima proceeded more firmly. 'Did you meet in the gardens, by any chance? She was locked out, she told me. Forgot her key. Climbed into the gardens and had what she called a *casual* encounter.'

Adam smiled. 'Ah. An indiscreet girl, my Dollie, or at any rate it appears that your Chloe was indiscreet. I didn't know that she was in the habit of confiding her errantry. Yes, if you want me to say so, I'll say I met her in the gardens. I'll tell you something else about my Dollie which may or may not apply to your Chloe. It was she who told me about the empty flats here. Slipped me the key. Said she got it from a friend who was a decorator. Said she was living here as a kind of superior squatter. So it was you, Jemima Shore, goddess of wisdom, who informed me not only of the rather surprising news that my Dollie was your Chloe – literature's Chloe so far as I can make out – but also even less pleasingly that she was a lawful tenant in this concrete prison.'

'Did you see her after that?' Jemima persisted. 'Your Dollie?'

'A goddess of wisdom should know everything without needing to ask.' His hand was placed on her thigh, where it rested; with his other hand, he touched her cheek. 'No, I never saw her again. I don't think I would have been interested to do so. It wasn't, you know, a great romance. Only what you so aptly called it just now, a carnal encounter. A pleasant phrase that, by the way.'

'It's hers, Chloe's. It *was* hers.'

'Ah. Pleasant phrase all the same, pleasant phrase and pleasant activity. No, I didn't see her again. But I can see that your sleuth-like instincts are aroused and as I'd rather like to arouse a different set of instincts in you, I'll begin by setting your curiosity at rest. Here goes. I stayed in the upstairs flat all day, I slept, I read Dante – it seemed appropriate to the inferno in which I found myself – also some Petrarch, but that was for a different reason, and went out about five-thirty to get something to eat. When you, I gather, saw me. No, I heard nothing. Enough?'

'You'll have to tell this to the police,' began Jemima. A terrible feeling – or was it so terrible? Merely exciting or, in dead Chloe's own phrase, carnal? – was stealing over her that the conclusion of the evening was going to be exactly as Adam Adamson planned, and not as Jemima Shore intended.

A little later she made no protest when Adam took her by the hand and led her into the dark green Empire bedroom. He stripped off the heavy rustling bedspread, and the soft white bedclothes tumbled out.

His slight body – the hips round which she could have put both hands – looked quite different naked; not vulnerable as so many naked bodies did, especially those of the young, but powerful and triumphant.

'Goddess,' he said facing her, 'it's your turn to worship me.'

11

Curiouser and curiouser

When Jemima finally awoke the next morning, it was with an instant sense of happiness, content. That sensation quickly vanished when she first felt, then saw, the figure of Adam Adamson, lying across the Empire bed. He was fast asleep. He looked everything he had not seemed the night before; innocent, uncorrupted.

'Oh Christ,' said Jemima Shore aloud. He did not move.

She longed absolutely and passionately for him to be gone, magicked away from the flat; as much as she had longed for him to make love to her for ever the night before. Why could not such a mythologically minded man bear in mind the story of Cupid and Psyche? Cupid had insisted on leaving the mortal maiden Psyche before the light came. Very sensible of him. After all, dreadful consequences had ensued when Psyche had attempted to defy the ban by lifting her lamp of oil to view her unknown lover.

In this case Cupid had overslept.

'Oh Christ.' Unbidden the visage of Detective Chief Inspector John Portsmouth came into her mind; unlike the Cheshire Cat he was not smiling, but deprecatingly shaking his head. It had to be admitted that there was something to shake his head about ... shades of Chloe Fontaine (although that too was an unfortunate phrase).

She became more resolute. After all *in its own way* it was an investigation. Jemima was fond of using the phrase *in its own way* on television when attempting to justify the unjustifiable. The Press sometimes mocked her for it. The memory of such – affectionate – attacks compelled her to admit, fair-minded person that she was, that given the opportunity she would undoubtedly behave in exactly the same way all over again.

Given the opportunity: but not however on Sunday morning. This particular Sunday morning at any rate. No one was going to be given any opportunity this morning. Adam Adamson, great casual encounter as he might be, was going to the police. She, Jemima Shore, was going to – well, first of all – have a cup of coffee.

She stepped gingerly from the white bed on which there were now no bedclothes at all and pulled her navy blue silk kimono from her suitcase. Adam did not stir as she left the room.

Some minutes were occupied in searching out first the coffee and then the method of making it in the immaculate but curiously ill-appointed kitchenette. In the end Jemima discovered a tin of Nescafé stuck behind the rows of clean cocktail glasses and made do with that, there being no apparent method of filling or making work the elaborate gleaming Italian coffee machine.

She sat meditatively on the single kitchen stool – uncomfortable and the wrong height. Was this kitchen intended for anything except getting ice cubes from the fridge? The coffee was too weak and tasted disgusting. As she sipped it, she heard the noise of the front door opening. Someone was coming in.

'Oh Christ,' she said for the third time.

The intruder had to be Sir Richard Lionnel. The police, so far as she knew, did not have a key to the flat and would in any case have rung first. Awkward and embarrassing as it might prove for him to use his own key without ringing the bell first, she supposed she could hardly object. The kitchen did possess a small digital clock. It was 11.30.

Jemima tied the sash of her kimono still more tightly round her and stepped out into the little hall with its Georgian mirror and table – the prettiest and simplest room in the flat. There was no one there. The drawing room was empty and the door to the office remained locked. It took her a few moments to realize that what she had heard was the sound of someone leaving the flat rather than entering it.

It was true. The green bedroom, now lit in a theatrical manner by one shaft of intense sunlight coming through the gaps in the heavy swagged curtains, was empty.

The light fell upon a note, written on a piece of paper headed 'From the office of Sir Richard Lionnel'.

'Dear Psyche,' it read, 'I'm afraid Cupid overslept but at least you didn't pour boiling oil over him. Thanks for everything. A. P.S. I've taken all the rest of this headed paper. Rather useful in the cause of revivification, don't you think? P.P.S. Don't worry, goddess, I'm going to the police.'

The rest of Sunday was much less exciting. Jemima forced herself to read an Edwardian diary taken out from the London Library; the small print acted as a special kind of discipline.

The call she awaited was from Pompey. It came about four o'clock that afternoon.

'Well, my dear,' he began, 'we've talked to your squatter friend.'

'*My* friend?'

'The one you met in the third-floor flat. Adam Adamson he calls himself. That's not his real name by the way. He's Adam all right but the rest of it is not quite so plain English. He tells me you advised him to go to the police. And very proper, too.' Pompey chuckled.

'Naturally. You know me, Pompey, Honest Jemima Shore. The good citizen.' All the same Jemima was not totally happy about all this jocularity. She could picture Pompey shaking his head.

'One thing did surprise me a little. He said *you'd* asked him no questions about his movements. Simply told him what had happened and said it was his duty to go to the police. And so, being a squatter – he calls it some funny name, doesn't he? – but not a slaughterer, those were his words, along he came to the station. Now, I wondered, where was the natural human curiosity of Jemima Shore, Investigator? *No* questions about his movements, alibi if any, connection with the deceased?'

Pompey might be wondering about her incuriosity but Jemima herself was speculating how Adam Adamson had eluded the policeman at the door; not so much last night but this morning in broad daylight.

Pompey answered that question for her.

'Mind you, our chap on the door, PC Bland, is still rather baffled as to how *your* friend got into the building last night. Your boy—' Jemima wished Pompey would stop the emphasis – 'swears he just walked in, and has indeed made a statement to that effect. He noticed no policeman and, in so far as a squatter can be said to do so, minded his own business. Spent the night upstairs, emerged this morning, met you, you told him – but then you know the rest of it, don't you, my dear?'

'And the murder period?'

'His statement says that he spent the day in the third-floor flat. He even had an alibi for the first period, though we haven't checked that out yet. Says he heard nothing, neither the deceased woman entering the flat with her companion whom we assume to be her murderer, nor any sounds of a struggle or cries. You wouldn't expect the latter, not with that slash across her windpipe, she would have died more or less instantly. Says the door is exceptionally thick and the flats – he called them some very rude name and tried to incorporate it in his sworn statement – are soundproof, at least above and below. Left the flat at about five-thirty to get something to eat, confirmed by one Jemima Shore. Did know the deceased woman but as Dollie Stover, not Chloe Fontaine. No prints of his in the bedroom but the murderer wiped that clean in any case.'

Pompey did not pause before adding in a completely different almost official voice: 'Ah, well, all this is of no great moment, because you see, we've picked up the artist.' Immediately Jemima's professional curiosity drove out all other considerations. 'Beyond that, we've checked out two alibis. Sir Richard Lionnel – he does prove after all to have an alibi, quite a good one as a matter of fact. The restaurant was called "The Little Athens", and he did have lunch there, no question of that, with a lady – now that's amusing – not your friend, naturally, seeing as her throat had been cut at the time, but a lady, A Nonny Mouse.' Pompey chuckled. 'Second alibi, Mrs Mantovani, Mancini, whatever, the female editor. You mentioned her. Perfect alibi. Plane lands at Heathrow at one-fifty. Bus reached the airport proper – due to delays – at two-ten. She can't be in Central London before two-fifty and that's stretching it. She's out – as we see it.

'And I've another piece of news for you,' he continued remorselessly, 'my boys have spoken to the maid, Rosina Whatnot or whatever her name is. Visited her this morning. Another funny piece of deception there. No sick child. Very healthy child bawling away out of sheer bloody-minded healthiness according to my boys. They don't know how to bring up kids without spoiling them to death, Italians, do they? Be that as it may, *your* friend Miss Fontaine gave her a few weeks' holiday. Out of the blue. Said you didn't want anyone disturbing you.'

'I probably didn't,' Jemima felt bewildered. 'But I certainly didn't say so. I never had a chance. No, wait, Pompey, don't you see? She, Chloe, didn't want Rosina Whatnot hoofing about, talking to me perhaps about Lionnel, or about anything. Much safer not. She's a great talker, I gather. Is that true?'

'One of the greats. Screamed, cried, screamed again, told my boys everything, absolutely everything they wanted to know. All about Lionnel. The Sir she called him. The Big Sir – isn't that a hippy place in California? And one or two other details which may be useful. However, she's no good for the actual murder, of course, because she'd been on holiday all the previous week. Still she is valuable background material.'

'I might visit her: I should perhaps sort out financial arrangements with her, cleaning up the flat and so on. I hardly imagine old Mrs Stover will want to do that.'

'Why not visit her, my dear?' Joviality was the order of the day.

'And Athlone?'

'That's a very different story. Picked him up in a pub this morning. Twelve o'clock. Opening time. Very much the worse for wear. Slept rough I should imagine, or as near to it as you can get. You could smell the drink a yard off. No alibi for the vital time, beyond a confused story about drinking with someone called Dixie. Then we picked up Dixie in the next-door pub and he was the worse for wear too, but not so much that he was prepared to vouch for his mate. Very shifty character, Dixie, and knew which side his bread was buttered where the police were concerned; no alibi there, oh no. Won't swear beyond the fact that he met Athlone some time before lunch, but rather fancies it was between eleven and twelve. Very damning, Dixie. Particularly the last part of his statement.'

'Which was?'

'Athlone asked him for a razor.'

'Ah, the razor.' Jemima let out a long sigh. The whole question of the razor on the floor by Chloe's bed could not be pushed to the back of her mind for ever.

'Dixie couldn't help. Did the silly bugger think he carried a razor about with him to every pub he visited? Those were Dixie's exact words. Not the words of the sworn statement, however. Besides, Dixie has an enormous beard which shows no sign of having had a razor near it in years. Athlone swigs down two double Scotches, departs, swearing that he'll first find a razor to make himself beautiful for her Royal Highness the Lady Jezebel, and then tear her to pieces like the cur he is. And he won't even need the assistance of all the other curs in her life.'

'The latter being a Biblical reference, as I don't need to remind you,' was Jemima's tart comment.

'As well as hearsay evidence, as I don't need to remind *you*. Dixie – I repeat, a nasty piece of work – only tells us that Athlone made those remarks.'

'Go on. Kevin John certainly never made any secret of his violent intentions towards Chloe and even had a dress rehearsal with me. What's his story about the razor?'

'Athlone takes the line that he doesn't need a story about the razor because he obviously hasn't shaved for several days. That at least is true. Athlone fervently denies returning to the building until about four o'clock. According to his own statement, he spent the intervening hours wandering about Soho looking for flowers. Wanted red roses. Red roses not available. Finally found a pot plant, to wit Exhibit J.H.P. 10, one red pelargonium found on the floor of the lounge of the deceased, climbed up the scaffolding, found the balcony window unlocked, deposited the aforesaid plant and let himself out of the door. Felt a little weary after the climb and maybe the drink, as he used to be an athlete but described himself as none too fit these days – accurate that. Slept in the hall. Never went into the bedroom.'

'And of course he *didn't* need the key to get out of the flat. Because it wasn't double locked. You've suddenly reminded me that when I returned from the Library I didn't need to use the second Chubb key. Yet I'm almost certain I double locked it when I went out.'

'We found the deceased's own set of keys in the bedroom. Two keys to the flat, one to the front door of the building, and two more which we have identified as fitting the office suite.'

But Jemima pursued the subject of Kevin John. 'And *never* looked in the bedroom? When he was searching for Chloe?' This time Jemima was incredulous and Pompey was calming.

'Ah, my dear, but according to his statement he wasn't looking for Chloe Fontaine. He'd already cased the flat in the morning, hadn't he? No, he thought you might be resting in the bedroom. Being a gentleman he didn't like to disturb you. Deposited the plant and quit. As you have pointed out, the second lock was not in operation. It was easy to let himself out.'

'In its own way I suppose it does make sense. If true,' said Jemima slowly. 'Tell me, how did he take the news, the news of her death?'

'I can only say that he howled. Gary Harwood, one of my lads, good-looking young fellow, you'll remember him – was with me. He can confirm that. A howl like a dog. And then blubbered like a baby. Still, that means nothing. You'd be surprised at the ways of some murderers. Cry like babies on being shown a corpse they themselves have battered to death. No my dear, it must be said that things do look rather black for him. First of all, lack of alibi. Then attempt to get a false one out of his friend. Between ourselves, we picture it this way. He returns to Adelaide Square. Meets Chloe Fontaine, perhaps on the stairs, perhaps in your – her own flat fetching something. More likely the latter. She has let herself in with her spare set of keys. She gets him the razor, takes it into the bedroom, they have a quarrel – perhaps she breaks him the news of her pregnancy – and he grabs a knife from the kitchen and stabs her to death.'

'Why is she in her *petticoat*?'

'Very hot day. Everyone is out of the building. More like a dress than a petticoat, wasn't it?'

'For obvious reasons, I don't remember it too well. Perhaps you're right. It's still unlike Chloe to wander round any building in her petticoat. She is – was – always very neatly dressed.'

'Maybe he and she were going to' – cough – 'you know. She *was* an adventurous lady, after all.' Pompey broke off discreetly.

'Anyway, continue—'

'He leaves the flat. The second half of his statement about bringing the plant and so forth is true. We've found his prints all over the scaffolding by the way.'

'I find it psychologically unconvincing, the return of a murderer – and why linger in the hall?'

'Murderers are funny people.' Pompey's voice sounded solemn down the line. Jemima could picture the shake of the head. 'Besides, he was drunk. Drunks are funny people too. And drink leads to murder. The demon drink. None of this would have happened, would it, if your friend Kevin John hadn't had a great deal more Scotch than was good for him?'

'You still have to prove it.'

'Certainly we do. Proof not psychology or feminine instinct – with due respect to you *and* Mrs Portsmouth – has always been my motto. Beyond all reasonable doubt, what's more. And we shall, we shall. He may well confess. I know the type.'

'Is he still at the station?'

'No, we let him go for the time being. We have to tie up the loose ends first. You know the form. He's staying in Chelsea now; we have the address – rather a good one: he's got rich friends as well as rough types like Dixie. No, he won't go far. I know the type.' Pompey coughed and then gave a particularly rich chuckle.

'By the way, my dear, there's something else which might interest you about your late friend's flat. Quite a way-out piece of information. We don't think the artist is involved in this. But my boys have found a spy hole through the bedroom wall. Small but perfectly formed. Behind a loose brick and right through that indecent red picture. There's modern building for you. Anyone applying their eye to it would have a good view of what went on in that bedroom.' He chuckled again. 'Easy for an outsider to come up the fire escape onto the small kitchen balcony, remove the loose brick and – er – apply the eye. The reason we don't think Athlone is involved, is nothing to do with its being his own picture, he might even enjoy damaging that in a good cause – you know artists. No, it's because there are a lot of fingerprints. We're just checking them out, but we already know two things. They all belong to the same person and that person is not Athlone.'

'What?' This time Jemima was genuinely shocked. 'My God, the caller – the anonymous caller. My secret view, he called it, something like that. It's in my statement.' She said in a controlled voice, 'curiouser and curiouser.'

'Exactly,' said Pompey with great satisfaction. 'Curious is exactly what it is.'

'To think that I slept there!'

A cough. 'I take it you *were* alone on that occasion?' Jemima reminded herself that this was to be taken as one of Pompey's little jokes, and not as a dig.

'Not only that, but you can take it that I never did like that picture,' was her fervent reply.

Pompey had had his fun. 'Now, my dear,' he continued in a graver voice, 'I'm afraid you're going to have the Press round you any minute if you haven't already. The death will be announced on the early evening news. But you'll handle that with your usual charm. They can't get into the building itself. No point in that.'

After Pompey had rung off, Jemima went to the balcony and peered discreetly over. It was true. A little knot of photographers was grouped on the pavement; there were also a few anonymous women, like extras in a crowd scene. PC Bland was staring straight ahead.

There was of course nothing to be seen except an ugly modern concrete building. The lure of murder had brought these people together; if the demonstrators returned on Monday would they mingle with this tourist crowd, still bearing their placards which vowed destruction to the Lion of Bloomsbury? In principle Jemima preferred the applied spirit of the demonstrators to the prurient curiosity of the women outside; but she wondered whether the demonstrators were as idealistic and the spectators as ghoulish as she conventionally imagined. Perhaps some of these spectators would shed real tears for the lurid death of Chloe Fontaine, beautiful, defenceless, fragile, slain by a brutal murderer, even as they goggled at the site of her death. While probably not one of the demonstrators – engaged in saving bricks and mortar – would feel much of a pang for the death of a human being, given that she had been the mistress of the Lion of Bloomsbury.

The presentation on the news programmes of both television channels was comparatively restrained. The BBC showed that still picture of Chloe under her parasol which had attracted Adam Adamson's attention. It looked highly incongruous alongside the announcement that the police were treating her death as murder. ITN rather more dashingly showed a short clip of Chloe chatting soulfully about literature, her face framed by a stiff white lace collar like a ruff; the clip must have been taken from that same programme where she met Sir Richard Lionnel. But he was not included so most likely the connection was unknown; even if there were rumours, ITN would not have risked making such a libellous inference. ITN did refer to the title of Chloe's last novel as *Fallen Woman* – a mistake corrected later in the programme – but that was probably carelessness. The BBC referred to the same novel as *Fallen Children* and did not correct their mistake later.

Nothing else happened that evening till about ten o'clock. Jemima deserted the slightly frivolous narrative and small print of the Edwardian diary for the more rewarding discipline of Nadine Gordimer's novel.

When the telephone rang, she found that with concentration on such a spare and stern book had come peace. She therefore received Valentine Brighton's late-night call with equanimity. It had been, all things considered, a bloodless Sunday. Not that Valentine himself sounded bloodless. He was breathing heavily; his voice was agitated and quite jerky compared to his usual airy tones. He did not sound at all himself.

He began at once: 'I've got something I've really got to heave off my chest about all this. I need advice, your calm approach, Jemima darling. You know about the police, don't you? That man Portsmouth, I seem to remember you worked with him in the past. You see, I've always given them a wide berth – in London that is. Our local man at home is quite a decent fellow. Mummy does the Right Thing and asks him to lunch at Helmet from time to time. But up here I've always tended to agree with Mrs Madigan in *Juno and the Paycock* that "the Polis as Polis in this city is Null and Void".'

His badly rendered accent represented a ghastly attempt at his usual light-heartedness: there was nothing properly light about Valentine's approach.

He proposed a meeting the next day. 'Now how would you like to do it? I hardly want to come to Adelaide Square. Poor divine Chloe. Surrounded by Press, I daresay. The building I mean. I don't expect you want to come to the Brighthelmet Press. How would you like the Reading Room of the British Library? I imagine you'll be trying to get back to work on the Golden Goodies.' He gave the impression of having planned it all out in a way she could hardly refuse.

It was while listening to Valentine's unaccustomedly emotional accents, and above all his rendering of O'Casey, that Jemima made a discovery. In not sounding like himself, Valentine Brighton had not exactly sounded like a total stranger. Curiouser and curiouser. Taking into account Pompey's final rich revelation of the peep-hole through the picture, it was not too difficult to make the connection.

The Irish accent clinched it; this was the intense voice of the anonymous telephone caller on the night before and the morning of Chloe's death. One phrase in particular was almost identical: 'Now how would you like to do it . . .' 'Now how would you like it . . .' had breathed the unknown caller. 'In that bed . . .' Yes, she would certainly meet Valentine Brighton in the Reading Room the next day. She had become very curious indeed about the role of Valentine Brighton in the life of Chloe Fontaine.

12
Shattered

Jemima, heading straight for Row B at the end of the Reading Room by pre-arrangement, spotted Valentine's fair head from a long way off. He was engaged in reading something which looked like a typescript. On this occasion he was not slumped down upon the dark polished desk. Nor, for that matter, was Jemima herself disturbed by premonitions of violence. The habitual mental litany, as she ticked off the rows of seats, manifested itself in words of comfort: A for Adorable, B for Better and Better . . . This time no secret shapes of dread intervened to kidnap her private alphabet.

On Monday morning, early, the Reading Room was already filling up rapidly. But as readers strode about purposefully looking for a seat, interweaving amongst assistants carrying piles of books marked by white slips, the confusion and slight noise created a favourable impression upon Jemima. The Reading Room, on this occasion, offered a haven even for Jemima Shore.

The noiseless surface of Adelaide Square had been shattered for ever by the murder of Chloe. Whatever the interior turbulence of the building before her death, it was as nothing compared to the maelstrom which now held it in its sway. It was as though the doll's-house front of the building had been stripped away, leaving Jemima, the last inhabitant – except for Tiger – exposed to the prying gaze of the outside world.

Thanks to the jolly camaraderie which existed between Fleet Street and the police, Jemima's own role in the discovery of the corpse had become known. Her present location, even the private telephone number of Sir Richard Lionnel's office suite, had also not proved beyond Fleet Street's powers of discovery.

Since she had a great many friends in Fleet Street, Jemima regarded the approaches of the journalists as quite inevitable. As a professional herself, she certainly wasted no time in resenting them (although her own kind of journalism was very different). She was after all quite capable of looking after herself, giving pleasant noncommittal answers where necessary, as well as confirming facts. She refused for example to be drawn on the question of Chloe's colourful private life beyond what was known already.

'I only know what I read in the papers,' Jemima would say charmingly. Having time and space at their disposal – unlike the television channels the previous evening – the morning papers had indeed provided their readers with some titillating details of *la vie bohémienne* as it had been apparently lived by the late Chloe Fontaine. Chloe's taste for having herself so frequently and so dramatically pictured, made love to as it were by the camera, brought unexpected financial benefits to the photographers concerned, who found their studied romantic portraits, veterans of Chloe's book jackets, pressed into service once more in the coarser medium of newsprint.

'Isabelle's pet, young Binnie Rapallo, must have made a killing,' thought Jemima. 'Evidently she was still able to sell her pictures even from darkest Capri surrounded by wild princes.'

The word Bohemian was employed quite lavishly to describe Chloe's life style. Her two marriages provided some of the material. Lance Strutt, an actor who had been at Cambridge with Chloe and Jemima, was on tour in Canada. He described himself as 'utterly shattered' in the *Mail* and 'very shocked' in the *Express*. Both statements were probably true. The further statement that he and Chloe had remained good friends after their break-up was to Jemima's certain knowledge not true.

Lance, at any rate until he became wise to Chloe's errant conduct, had been a nice but rather dim character. Igor, on the other hand, although his travel books and articles never quite raised him out of the medium-dim class as a writer had not been nice at all. About the only thing to be said for him was that he had at least been more satisfactory than Kevin John Athlone for whom Chloe had left him. Igor speaking from Venice was however nice enough to be 'shocked' in the *Mail* and 'shattered' in the *Express*. And he was honest enough to admit to having been on bad terms with his ex-wife.

The 'live-in' relationship with Kevin John Athlone (no comment available) also received a great deal of publicity. A photograph of him in a white polo-necked jersey, wonderfully handsome and somewhat thinner than of late, received almost as much prominence as photographs of Chloe. Kevin John in his turn was described – but not by himself – as being 'shattered' at the break-up of their relationship and 'emotionally distraught'. Hints of his drinking, also employing the word 'emotional', were fairly heavy. The very detailed but soberly phrased account in the *Telegraph*, ended: 'Mr Athlone, whose present whereabouts are unknown, is believed to have volunteered a statement to the police on Sunday.'

The inference, to those used to such things, was obvious. Jemima fancied she detected the hovering hand of the police in these mentions of Kevin John. A word in time, of a discreet nature, from the police, helped the Press to direct their eager noses in the right direction; and the Press in their turn helped on the police by their own enquiries. It was after all only an amplified version of Jemima's own relationship with Pompey.

Unlike the television channels, the Press gave no significant mention to Chloe's literary works. The measured warmth of Jamie Grand in the *Guardian* was the honourable exception (J.S. Grand, editor of *Literature*, writes: 'A talent to observe . . .'). Otherwise the person was considered so much more newsworthy than the *oeuvre*. Jemima thought that Chloe would have found in that personal concentration matter for regret, despite the vast publicity given to her death – but could she be sure of anything to do with Chloe any longer? Perhaps her friend would have relished the street fame, the passionate popular interest . . . No, surely not, a writer must always hope for the elevation of the work over the personality. And Chloe, whatever her other qualities, had been at heart a writer. In that at least Jemima had not been deceived.

There was not even the merest hint in the Press of Sir Richard Lionnel's connection with Chloe. Even the fact that she had lived – and died – in that controversial modern building, creation of the Lion of Bloomsbury, 73 Adelaide Square, received little emphasis. Only the *Telegraph* seemed remotely interested in the subject, and this interest was limited to the phrase: 'recently in the news due to student protest at the demolition of Adam's work'.

Did she also detect the hovering hand of the police here? More likely the hovering hands of Fleet Street's eagle-eyed libel lawyers. No point in going for the (almost certainly) innocent Sir Richard Lionnel, armed with his own equally watchful lawyers, when the (almost certainly) guilty Kevin John Athlone, a picturesque enough killer for any editor, was there for their delectation.

Jemima's favourite editor, Jake Fredericks – brother of her own boss the ebullient Cy – did ring her up from the *London Evening Post* and suggest a piece about Chloe.

'I gather that handsome brute of a painter finally went over the top and did it,' he observed cheerfully. 'I never could stand him myself. Irresistible to women, I am assured, blows and all. Maybe I should deliver a blow or two myself. I must check with Eveline sometime. Anything to please. I used to meet Athlone at Cy's parties when he was with Sophie and he used to beat her up something terrible then. She went to hospital, needed stitches, all that kind of thing. And I think Oonagh Leggatt had something of the same experience. Ugh.' Jemima repressed a smile at the thought of the charming rather motherly Eveline Fredericks entering into some kind of sado-masochistic relationship with Jake. Unlike Cy, Jake had been happily married as long as Jemima could remember. 'Good painter, though,' he added. 'Still it's not quite enough, is it? We can't have our lady novelists dying like flies, can we?'

Jake Fredericks' notion was, as he expressed it, that Jemima should set the record straight about Chloe. 'After all she was a very good writer, as well as a grand horizontal, wasn't she? My colleagues have concentrated so far on the latter angle. Here at the *London Evening Post* we have always believed in a woman's right to be both.'

Jemima was not to be drawn. Thanking Jake politely, she declined and headed for the British Library. She felt depressed. Things were getting blacker for Kevin John. A known record of violence towards the women in his life was not going to help his case forward with Pompey – or, if it came to that, with a jury. It remained to be seen whether Valentine Brighton, in heaving something off his own chest, would also relieve Kevin John Athlone in some way of the burden of guilt.

But Valentine Brighton, pale but composed, speaking in a low voice in view of the regulations of the Reading Room, did no such thing.

'I saw him.' It was as bald as that. 'I was shattered. No, no, not doing the murder—' His voice rose slightly. 'Just afterwards. It must have been just afterwards.'

'Sssh' came very angrily from the middle-aged woman of foreign appearance at the desk next to Jemima's. 'Here iss not a place for talking.' Jemima, in her own state of shock at what Valentine had just said, vaguely resented the interruption but made no effort to curtail Valentine's stream of words.

'And further I must tell you, you are sitting in the place of Professor Leinsdorf,' hissed the woman, after a moment, plucking at Jemima's sleeve. It was true. Jemima had been waved to B10 by Valentine, but Professor Leinsdorf's books, as they presumably were, were neatly stacked in the corner. The theory of economics, mainly in German. As Jake Fredericks would say, ugh.

Valentine Brighton was at this moment saying: 'Jemima, I've got to use you as my mother confessor. Do I go back to the police and tell them? How on earth do I explain what I was doing there? My God, do I have to explain about – well – I mean will it all come out, be in the papers? It will kill Mummy, I tell you it will kill her—'

His voice, never particularly deep, rose to an accompanying angry 'Sssssh' from the friend of Professor Leinsdorf.

'It *did* kill Chloe Fontaine,' Jemima hissed back furiously. 'Or rather someone did. And of course you must tell the police what you saw. Besides, they already know a good deal of it – look, Valentine, I may as well tell you now. They found the peep-hole.' Pompey had confirmed the prints as being Valentine's that morning.

For a moment Jemima thought Valentine was actually going to faint. His slightly sweaty pallor increased dramatically and his eyelids closed and flickered. He swayed in his seat.

'Oh God, poor poor Mummy,' he groaned. Professor Leinsdorf's friend stood up and regarded the pair of them with extreme disfavour; she arranged her own books and belongings all over her desk as though to prevent the possibility of any further territorial infringement by Jemima. Jemima noted the label on her briefcase, a surprisingly smart object of black leather, considering its owner's own careless appearance: Dr Irina Harman, it read, and the address was somewhere in Cambridge.

'I go to have a coffee,' Dr Irina Harman announced. Then: 'Those are the books of Professor Leinsdorf. It iss not in the rules to sit at that desk.' As Jemima did not react, she said in a louder voice: 'It is occupied.' Then Dr Harman stumped away.

'If it gets into the Press, I can't bear it. I simply cannot bear it,' Valentine was saying. 'I'll go and live abroad.'

'Oh for Christ's sake, Valentine. This is not the nineteenth century and you are not the wicked Lord Byron. *Do stop thinking about yourself.* What's a little harmless voyeurism among friends?' She forbore to remind him that she herself had received two of his calls.

Valentine groaned again. Jemima's furious flippancy only seemed to make him feel worse. For her part, she wanted to shake him.

'I take it you saw Kevin John Athlone – in Chloe's bedroom.'

'I don't know why I do such things. It started when I was a child. Perhaps because I was lonely. Anyway, where Chloe was concerned it all began one day by accident. I found the way up the fire escape when her buzzer didn't answer. There was a loose brick – I was looking for a key.

She was somehow so provocative, Chloe, wasn't she? I mean I almost felt she *wanted* me to watch her. But how can I tell the police that? As for Mummy—'

'Valentine,' Jemima whispered as calmly as she could. 'What did you actually see? The police aren't interested in your private tastes, they're only interested in you as a witness to murder.'

'I went up the fire escape and I looked through the peep-hole,' he said. 'Chloe hadn't turned up here. I had some vague idea of warning her about Francesca Lionnel. I'm not quite sure what I expected, I never am when I do these things. I suppose I also thought I might see you. I called you, you know, the night before and in the morning.' He spoke quite flatly. He seemed to have no shame where Jemima herself was concerned. Perhaps he imagined that life in television had inured her to such things.

'Leinsdorf? Your books.' An Asian carrying two large grey volumes was standing over Jemima. He deposited them without waiting for a confirmation. He was handsome and quite young; and was wearing a red T-shirt with the face of Marilyn Monroe on it. Jemima recognized him. He had tried to deliver some books to her desk – commissioned by someone called Hamilton – on Saturday. This time she accepted the Leinsdorf books without comment.

'Go on.'

'I saw him, Kevin John Athlone. In her bedroom. He was alone. At least I think he was. He was holding a razor in his hand. You can't see the top of the bed you know. The hole is too high. Only the bottom of the bed, the rest of the bedroom and the door. He was just standing there. Looking right at the picture. At me. I was terrified he'd see right through it and see me. And she'd promised me it was all over. I felt quite sick. I went away. Then I saw you walking towards the British Museum and I followed you. I followed you right into the Reading Room. I watched you looking for a place. I moved someone else's books just ahead of you and sat down. I made a place for you. You see – I wanted you to find me. I pretended to be asleep so you wouldn't suspect. I was still feeling sick.'

'Ah. The wrong books which were delivered—' Jemima began.

'Oh, Jemima, couldn't *you* tell the police? Explain I'm not feeling at all well, and I'm not, absolutely not up to it. Poor Mummy, how will she bear it—'

'You *must* make your own statement; it's vital, don't you see that? I can't give *your* evidence.'

'Pardon me, but I believe those are my books,' said a polite soft female voice above Jemima; this time the accent was not mid-European but American. 'Since I had not purposed to vacate this seat, you should provide yourself with another one. And adjust your seat number accordingly on any request slips you may have already filed.' Professor Leinsdorf spoke in the terminology of a firm but courteous public notice.

But contrary to Jemima's mental image, the Professor besides being female was comparatively young. She wore a neat white blouse and pale grey skirt, with a soft grey chiffon scarf at her neck. She might have been a member of some modern nun's order, which wore contemporary dress. She was also rather pinkly pretty with full lips and a high natural colour: although she wore no visible makeup, she hardly needed it to enhance her wholesome and attractive appearance.

'I'm so sorry,' said Jemima hastily, leaping up. 'Valentine, we have to talk. Let's go outside. Right?'

Valentine made a movement she interpreted as a nod. Professor Leinsdorf also nodded with the confident air of one who was used to restoring things to their rightful order wherever she went, and sat down.

She heard Valentine's voice calling rather faintly after her and returned. This time his message was only whispered: 'Give me five minutes to recover, old girl.' The sobriquet was somehow pathetically sportive. 'I won't rat on you,' he added, in the same Kiplingesque idiom.

'Sure. Meet you by the head of Rameses in, say, ten minutes' time? I'll fill in a book slip or two for when I return.' Valentine gave a rather more vigorous nod in which she discerned relief.

Jemima took herself off to find a new seat, succeeding finally among the Ls; a rather noisy position due to the presence of a row of machines behind her being cranked by readers to show microfilm. Still L for Love had good connotations; she speculated whether Valentine's dogging her footsteps on the fatal Saturday had not been responsible for the strange aberration of her mental alphabet on that occasion.

On her way Jemima passed Dr Harman who shot her a look of malevolent triumph. The doctor's heavy figure, ill suited by her brightly flowered skirt and green blouse, stockingless white legs in flat sandals, together with her mouse-coloured hair scraped back into a tight bun, made her the prototypical figure of the earnest female scholar of the old style, just as the fresh and soignée Professor Leinsdorf (who could have been photographed for *Taffeta* in one of its serious moods, just as she stood) epitomized the new. Yet it was possible that the two women were in fact about the same age.

'It is not good to take the seat of another person,' said Dr Harman in a loud voice. 'You will learn.' Jemima ignored her.

Finding the press mark in the catalogue – a list of numbers – and filling in a white slip to order a book was a famously aggravating task. In another area of her mind Jemima, as she coped with the heavy catalogues, was also turning over what Valentine had told her. She too was shattered. A few minutes' respite for them both was perhaps not a bad thing.

Moreover the catalogue appeared to have taken on a life of its own; it was a creature of mood, and in this case a peculiarly perverse mood. It sent her scurrying from one quarter of the alphabet to the other – a shift of numerous volumes – as a book written by one Marion Miller frustratingly turned out to be listed under her maiden name of Evans. As Mill*er* had also proved to be Mill*ar* – a shift of another volume – and the literary Evanses were innumerable – more than one heavy volume of entries – the whole operation took a great deal of time.

Jemima concentrated on filling in the order slip accurately; a mistake in the catalogue number would send her back to the start of the whole ponderous process. Slip finally filled and deposited in the box provided, Jemima made for the exit. On her way she glanced towards Row B. Valentine had gone on ahead. The typescript he had been perusing in his capacity as a working publisher was however still there, sheets spread about the desk. Clearly he intended to return and collect it.

Jemima hoped that Valentine's pause for recovery would only have crystallized his intention to make a clean breast of his story to Pompey as soon as possible. Valentine's own first-hand evidence – rather than her second-hand report of it – was both crucial and devastating where Kevin John was concerned. So far as Jemima knew, this was the first positive proof that Kevin John had been at the scene of the murder during the lunch hour. Under the circumstances her own irrational belief in Kevin John's innocence was fast fading. To say the least of it, Kevin John had lied about his movements to the police in his sworn statement (and to Jemima herself on the afternoon of the murder, for that matter).

Jemima was amused to see that Professor Leinsdorf and Dr Harman had also abandoned Row B. Perhaps some economic conference of their fine minds was being held elsewhere in the building? Their respective papers and books however were spread about ostentatiously; no chances were being taken of another alien invasion.

She wended her way to the end of the Reading Room and proceeded to the checkpoint where a couple of uniformed officials, one woman and one man, maintained a search of bags and belongings to ensure that the valuable rare books of the British Library did not stray.

Jemima's prettily patterned notebook was always subjected to a peculiarly rigorous search as though some exciting rarity was being smuggled out, although half the pages were blank and the other half filled with her own hand-written notes. Jemima was just giving her automatic speech – 'That's my own hand-writing; no, it's not the property of the British Library; look, no press marks; yes, it's my *own* notebook' when she was interrupted by a familiar guttural voice – speaking even louder than before.

'*Ja, ja,* it iss her! It iss she who took the seat of Professor Leinsdorf.' Panting heavily as though she had been running, Dr Irina Harman was standing at the exit and pointing in the direction of Jemima. 'Stop her!' A middle-aged man in a jacket and tie stood at her side.

It was really too much. Jemima, already tense about her rendezvous with Valentine – she suddenly feared she might have allowed him enough time to change his mind – felt her patience beginning to snap. The whole incident was so absurd.

'For God's sake,' she began angrily as the official stepped forward. He looked acutely embarrassed, particularly when he recognized Jemima; Jemima for her part rather thought she recognized him; he was the superintendent, or held some other fairly responsible position, and they had met in a discussion group about the future of the Reading Room.

'Excuse me, could I have a private word with you?' he asked in a low but firm voice. 'It's Jemima Shore, isn't it? We've met.' His embarrassment deepened still further. 'And you were sitting in Row B just now, and holding a conversation—'

'For God's sake,' Jemima repeated in a furious voice which she did not bother to moderate. 'It was only a tiny episode and I've already apologized. This lady seems to be quite obsessed—'

'No, no, you don't understand, Miss Shore. I'm afraid the gentleman you were talking to just now collapsed very suddenly at his desk. We're trying to track anyone who knows him—'

'Collapsed! But I only just left him—'

'I know. It was very sudden, according to this lady here. Some form of heart attack, I fear. We've summoned an ambulance. But I ought to prepare you—'

'He iss dead,' interrupted Jemima's quondam accuser in a heavily lugubrious voice. 'He spoke to uss, said some words which are odd, then he iss dead. There iss nothing even Professor Leinsdorf could do for him. She had tried respiration immediately. Your friend iss quite dead.'

13
Strong women

'Fatal heart attack. Could have happened any time. Heart in a terrible dickey state. Mother – strong woman that, by the way, remarkable fortitude – confirmed it.' Chief Inspector Portsmouth gave a shake of the head which under the circumstances was positively blithe. 'Mind if I do?' He poured himself another pale whisky and water, courtesy of Sir Richard Lionnel. 'What about you?'

Jemima in turn shook her head.

'But why did it have to happen *then*?' she asked despondently. 'When he'd told me so much – but not everything. Not every detail. And he hadn't told you – second time round – anything at all. No sworn statement.'

'My old mother, another woman of remarkable fortitude, always used to say, "Into each life a little rain must fall."' Pompey was maddeningly cheerful. You would not think, to look at his spare relaxed figure, once more installed in the gracious *Country Life*-style drawing room of Sir Richard Lionnel's flat, that he had just lost a prime witness in a murder case.

It was Tuesday evening and Pompey had invited himself over for an 'after-work chat' as he put it. Jemima envied his aplomb. She herself was suffering from a feeling of irrational guilt that she had prematurely frightened Valentine to death by dragging his story from him, instead of letting him tell it all to Pompey. She knew that it was ridiculous: Valentine needed, indeed had deliberately sought out, her encouragement. Yet she was haunted by the memory of his pallid face, his groans as he contemplated the exposure of his private tastes to a mocking world.

'And you won't even pay attention to his last message,' she

concluded in a gloomy voice. '"He came back" – maybe someone came back to the flat, someone we don't know about.'

'Certainly he came back. Athlone came back. Your voice from the grave is most convincing,' Pompey responded happily.

Jemima's depression over the death of Valentine – and after all they had been friends long before Valentine proposed a professional relationship – was increased by the grotesque circumstances which had accompanied it. The detached kindness and carefully worded statement of Professor Leinsdorf hardly compensated for the irritation engendered by further contact with Dr Harman. What was more, the two women were not only staying in the same hotel, close to Adelaide Square, but as Dr Harman made absolutely clear, actually sharing a room.

'It iss, you understand, a very large room,' she stated in her usual ponderous manner which seemed to convey some threat even when the words were palpably innocuous. 'Professor Leinsdorf iss most generous. Each year we meet like this. We see only each other. And off course we do our work.' She shot a look of ferocious devotion in the direction of her companion. 'Each year it is Professor Leinsdorf who pays.'

All the same the two women proposed to give Jemima tea in the hotel lounge, an arrangement for which Jemima was duly thankful. Intimate contact with their domestic arrangements would only bring further embarrassment. Already Dr Harman could hardly allow the Professor to pour the tea without patting her hand; at one point she even pushed back one of the Professor's soft brown curls which had strayed onto her cheek.

'Yeah, it needs a good cut. I know it,' was all the younger woman said; she gazed speculatively at Jemima's corn-coloured bell of hair.

'John of Thurloe Place—' said Jemima hastily, hoping to fend off further intimacies from Dr Harman (whose own hair could have done with some attention).

The passions of others being notoriously unfathomable, Jemima reflected that she would probably never understand what drew the Professor, a charming woman by any standards, towards her uncouth watchdog; it was much easier to sympathize with the latter's evident infatuation. The attraction had to be in Dr Harman's mind, since in Jemima's humble opinion it could hardly lie in her personality or her appearance; no doubt the appeal of Dr Harman's thoughts on German economics, or whatever the Professor's special subject might be, was overpowering . . . although an annual idyll with the good Doctor would hardly be Jemima's idea of amusement, it had to be admitted that this intellectual approach was also to the Professor's credit. She was interrupted in these frivolous thoughts by a loud and almost girlish laugh from the Professor.

'I guess Irina has just never got over her younger sister earning more than she does!' she exclaimed. 'Why if she came to the States, she could put us both up at the Savoy . . . As it is I have to leave Henry once a year to look after himself. I'm always on at her to make the switch. It was just my good fortune I went to the States when I did.'

'Ach, no, Poupa—' Jemima could not help being extremely relieved that the adoration in Dr Harman's eyes had now been revealed as sisterly in origin. It was still slavish.

At Jemima's request Poupa Leinsdorf – as she must now learn to call her – ran through Valentine's last actions and stumbled words yet again.

'He looked very sick. He gave some kind of cry, more like a cry than a groan, would you say, Irina?' The doctor nodded, her enchanted gaze held to her sister's face. 'He half put out his hand, I guess he wanted water or something. I jumped up. You got up too, Irina, at that point.' The Doctor nodded again. 'I asked him if he needed some assistance. He didn't answer right away, just said nothing at all for approximately twenty seconds. Then he said, and this is my precise recollection, and I believe Irina will confirm it: "He came back." Those three words. Then: "I've got to tell her." Quite distinct, wasn't it, Irina? Then he slumped forward. The rest you know. He didn't speak again, nothing that could be understood as more than a groan. Irina thinks he muttered something like "Mother" or "Mummy" but I would not want to be too positive about that.'

Back with Pompey, who had already perpetuated the Professor's information in the form of a statement, Jemima tried rather hopelessly to think of any way in which Valentine's words were not peculiarly damning to Kevin John. Her heart was no longer in it. Even without the help of Valentine's last words – to which Pompey refused to pay attention – it was going to be very difficult to persuade Pompey that Kevin John had not committed the murder: the prime suspect now known (if not proved) to have been present at the scene of the crime.

'We'll get him,' said Pompey of Kevin John. 'Other witnesses will come forward. He'll confess. You see if he doesn't. You, my dear, have been most helpful in what you have remembered. Good memory inside that pretty head.'

'I hope so, Pompey,' said Jemima in a pious voice. 'It's a question of the trained mind rather than the pretty head, by the way. Like Dr Harman.'

'Oh myself, I like women to have both beauty and brains; no objection to that at all. I've made that quite clear to Mrs Portsmouth from the very start of Women's Lib. Any time she wants to go to the Open University, Adult Education, evening classes – you name it. No holds barred. Instead of which she prefers to direct *my* gardening out of articles she's read in the evening paper with her feet up. I ask you! Women simply won't grab their opportunities.'

Pompey then abandoned the elaborate teasing which appeared to give him much pleasure and reverted to his brisk manner.

'The Coroner's inquest opens tomorrow, by the way. Purely formal – you won't be needed. In view of our current enquiries, we'll suggest an adjournment. You see, now we know exactly what questions to ask Athlone. We know, for example – without being able to prove it, naturally – that he lied about his lunchtime visit to the flat. The net is closing, my dear. The net is closing. We're bringing him in for questioning again, right away. The only fly in our ointment at this stage is Punch Fredericks. He's been brought in on the act.'

Jemima whistled. 'Punch Fredericks! Very impressive. How did that come about?' The youngest of the three Fredericks brothers was a well-known radical solicitor interested in a number of social causes, including law reform; he was notorious, at least to the police, for believing in bail-for-everyone-including-murderers (as Pompey sardonically put it) and armed with the traditional will and energy of the Fredericks family, very often secured it.

'Friend of the gallery owner who looks after Athlone, I believe. Very rich, very left-wing, lives happily in Chelsea, you know the type. Creep? No, that's wishful thinking. Creed. At all events Creed is putting up Athlone, so he's probably hired Fredericks at the same time. Bail-for-every-one, indeed!' Pompey shook quite fiercely.

For the rest of the week Jemima abandoned her research in the British Library. This was not only the result of an aversion towards the scene of Valentine's death – Jemima would have thought it her duty to conquer that kind of feeling. No, the fact was that Jemima was in some doubt as to whether the Brighthelmet Press itself would survive with the sudden demise of its energetic proprietor-cum-chairman-cum-managing director. In its future the survival of her own contract was only one petty problem. Jemima herself was constitutionally incapable of working without, as it were, a deadline. She had once been prepared to toil unsociably for the whole of August, disappearing into a noiseless borrowed flat. The flat was no longer noiseless, thanks to the furore engendered by Chloe's murder. Now her actual motive for research had been removed by the death of her publisher. And what was more, she had lost two friends in a week.

Work being Jemima's cure, she badly needed a substitute if this disastrous summer holiday was to be rescued. Fortunately there was work of a sort to hand: good useful work which might at least avenge Chloe's death and unravel the mystery of her last hours.

And if work was Jemima's cure, curiosity was her stimulus. The first-floor flat at Adelaide Square was still at her disposal, Lionnel Estates having not yet proffered an alternative although Jemima received twice-daily calls from a Miss Katy Aaronson, describing herself as Sir Richard Lionnel's private assistant – 'No, not his secretary, Miss Shore, his private assistant.' She was reminded of Laura Barrymore, Isabelle Mancini's cool 'personal assistant'.

In fact Miss Katy Aaronson turned out to have a secretary of her own, who put through her frequent calls to Jemima in an important voice; that again reminded Jemima of Laura Barrymore.

The call which Miss Katy Aaronson made on Thursday morning, apart from being made at 8.20 am – half an hour earlier than Miss Aaronson's wonted hour which was early enough – brought with it an additional surprise in the shape of an invitation to lunch from Sir Richard Lionnel.

Miss Aaronson did indeed apologize with her usual suavity – another Barrymore touch – both for the earliness of the hour and the shortness of notice. Her use of titles as opposed to Laura Barrymore's transatlantic employment of Christian names possibly indicated the difference between a personal and a private assistant.

'Unexpectedly Sir Richard finds himself free for a late lunch in London, since he is taking an ordinary commercial flight from Glasgow to Heathrow . . . before going down to Sussex by helicopter later in the afternoon to join Lady Lionnel at Glyndebourne. And the Minister, that is to say Lord Manfred, accompanied by Lady Manfred, hopes to join them by car from Hastings, where the Minister will have inaugurated . . . So if we sent the car for you at one-forty-five . . . There's a Greek restaurant in Percy Street just off the Tottenham Court Road where Sir Richard likes to lunch late . . . He finds the ambience . . .'

What on earth made tycoons' assistants imagine that the complicated social arrangements over which they themselves were destined to toil were of equal interest to the rest of the world, Jemima wondered irritably. The stately movements of Sir Richard Lionnel across the British Isles both dispensing and pursuing culture were no concern of hers; but Miss Katy Aaronson took care to inform her that Sir Richard had been lecturing at some Festival of Scottish Industrial Architecture in the presence of the youthful arts-minded Prince Frederick of Cumberland as well as other notables.

The apology, for all its suavity, was purely ritual. Jemima was not expected to refuse; if she had any other arrangements she was expected to put them off – in fact she had invited Isabelle Mancini to lunch to talk about Valentine and she did put her off; nor was Jemima expected to cavil at the late hour or the choice of Greek 'ambience'.

What would have happened, she wondered, if she had firmly opted for the Savoy, stating (untruthfully) that she hated Greek food? But Jemima always preferred other people to make the choices, not so much out of indecision as out of an observer's interest in the tastes revealed.

She contented herself with one flash of independence: 'No car, thank you, I'll walk to "The Little Athens". It's only a few minutes away. I know its ambience well.'

Imagining she would have quite a wait for Sir Richard, whose Scottish plane would inevitably be delayed, Jemima brought her Nadine Gordimer novel with her. The prospect of a concentrated read in the pleasant little restaurant, with its wide plant-filled window embracing Percy Street, was not displeasing. But when she arrived, she recognized the unmistakable figure of her host – well-cut fawn tweed suit, white shirt, black knitted silk tie – seen through the window as though in a frame. He was reading a magazine and laughing.

From its format, Jemima recognized *Jolly Joke*. Its pages were perpetually filled with rather crude satirical attacks on Lionnel and his ilk – this week's issue was no exception. For a man supposedly sensitive to Press criticism, Sir Richard was certainly showing remarkable *sang-froid* in laughing quite so freely. However at her approach Sir Richard covered *Jolly Joke* with a copy of Christie's catalogue illustrating a sale of antique clocks. Still the impression remained of a man in one way at least indifferent to public hostility.

Was Lionnel sufficiently indifferent to it to go further, divorce his wife and marry Chloe? And at the same time aim at respectability and the chairmanship of CARI? Perhaps Lionnel would not recognize the conflict: he would simply see it as a problem to be managed.

Chloe had been so specific about the marriage to Valentine, it was difficult to believe there was nothing in it. Just as this thought had formed in her mind – against a background of urbane conversation, quick efficient ordering of whatever she cared for in the line of food and drink, almost as though Miss Katy Aaronson had previously reconnoitred her tastes – Sir Richard surprised her still further by openly contradicting it.

Jemima had anticipated – obviously – that they would discuss Chloe; she did not flatter herself that Sir Richard had taken a sudden irresistible fancy to her on the strength of one brief meeting under traumatic circumstances. Nevertheless the directness of his approach confused her.

'The most attractive woman in the world. I was absolutely mad about her, don't you see?' he was saying, leaning forward and fixing his mesmeric black eyes upon her. The black ring of curls lifted in the faint breeze of the window, but Jemima had the impression that they were also flickering with his own personal electricity.

'But of course I would never have left Francesca. No question of that.' He was not only direct but, as on the night of the murder, strangely lacking in embarrassment. 'She's wonderful, Francesca. Wonderful hostess – you've never seen Parrot, I suppose? You never stayed there with the Hampshires? Retta Hampshire is beautiful in somewhat your style – cat's eyes – she's much older, of course.'

'I've never even met the Duchess of Hampshire.'

'You must come down, you positively must. What Francesca has done there is quite amazing; everyone says so. Even our match-boxes are eighteenth-century adaptations, I believe. The Hampshires had let it go terribly down hill.' The thought of match-boxes reminded Sir Richard to strike up yet another black cigarette; he used a lighter very similar, if not identical, to the one Kevin John Athlone had discovered in Chloe's bedroom. Jemima wondered if the police had returned it to him – or did he perhaps have quantities of such elegant *objets*? Had they also returned the razor which had been found by Chloe's bed?

'Did you read the article in *Taffeta*?' he was saying. '"Francesca goes Lionnel-Hunting"? – they meant all the original furniture she dug out of antique shops. Marvellous photograph of Francesca by that jolly little girl photographer, do you know her? Short black hair. Dresses in knickerbockers for some extraordinary reason, but very fetching.'

'I know Binnie Rapallo.' Jemima had definitely not come to lunch, chucking Isabelle for the occasion, to discuss the lissome but curiously irritating Binnie Rapallo. She was therefore somewhat startled to hear Sir Richard declaring himself 'mad about' Binnie Rapallo, in much the same language as he had used to express his admiration for Chloe. Even the tone in which he expressed enthusiasm for his own wife's taste – hardly a fault that, it had to be admitted – was remarkably similar. These repeated enthusiasms, couched in terms which were almost schoolboyish, gave an overall impression of lack of passion rather than the reverse.

Surely there was some difference of degree – between Binnie and Chloe at least, even if Chloe and Lady Lionnel were mentioned in the same breath. He was astonishingly open about it all. Throughout the conversation Sir Richard chain-smoked his black Sobranies, but otherwise showed no sign of embarrassment.

When he had finished the packet he requested the proprietor of the restaurant, a handsome but sad-eyed man with the heavy fleshy build of a successful opera singer, to request another from his chauffeur.

'Sir Richard is feeling better today?' said the man conversationally when he returned.

Thank you, Stavros. I certainly am. But it was my wife who was ill not me,' replied Lionnel with a flash of the satyr's grin. 'Now I bet you're never ill,' he said looking at Jemima as the proprietor turned deftly away, too experienced to look embarrassed at the mention of a wife, but somehow conveying apology for having instigated a conversation about one lady in front of another. 'Francesca has rotten health. London for example simply doesn't suit her. She feels right as rain at Parrot – sea air and all that kind of thing.'

'But I take it she comes up sometimes? Here, for example?' Jemima's curiosity about Sir Richard's domestic arrangements was aroused in spite of herself.

'Oh absolutely. In fact we had lunch together here on Saturday.' It took Jemima a second or two to realize that he was referring to the day of the murder.

'I thought you were alone—' she exclaimed, startled.

He grinned.

'Alone except for my wife. What can I say? Lunch with my own wife. Embarrassing, wasn't it? Originally I told the police I was alone in order to keep Francesca out of it. And I kept vague about the restaurant. Chloe never knew; I only rang her beforehand, to be frank, to check she was safely stowed inside the flat. Not to invite her out. As you know, she never answered. The police know now, of course, and our friend Stavros here has vouched for me. For some reason Francesca insisted on coming up to see me before I went on holiday and I got the lunch hour off from number ten.'

But Jemima knew the reason which had brought Francesca Lionnel pell-mell to London: the information about Chloe Fontaine's trip to the Camargue, carelessly or maliciously passed on by Valentine's mother at tea the previous day. Exactly what had transpired that fatal lunchtime? If Francesca had become 'ill' in the restaurant there must have been some kind of scene. Had she taxed Lionnel about the affair with Chloe and had he confessed? But Jemima realized she was unlikely to be told the truth of that now and it was – probably – no longer important. Sir Richard had clearly mended his fences with his own wife since Chloe's death, if not before.

She understood however what Pompey had meant when he told her that Lionnel had proved 'after all' to have an alibi – 'Quite a good one as a matter of fact. A lady. A Nonny Mouse.' Then Pompey had chuckled. He was right. There was a kind of grim humour about Sir Richard deceiving his mistress with his own wife.

Jemima decided to wrench the conversation back to the subject of Chloe Fontaine. She was still uncertain whether Lionnel was carefully rewriting history. With Chloe no longer around to contradict him, he was busy making it clear that their affair had never amounted to more than 'one of my little flings' as he put it. 'I fall head over heels in love, don't you?'

Jemima in response gave her famously enchanting smile, made famous that is to say by television, curling the corners of her wide mouth, and revealing the perfect white teeth with which Nature had thoughtfully endowed her for the purposes of her chosen profession. It was also a mechanism for concealed emotion. The real answer is – yes, I do fall, and head over heels, from time to time, she thought, her mind on Adam. But not in love. Love is another matter.

The mention of Lady Lionnel and her talents for decoration suddenly concentrated Jemima's mind. The flats, the various styles of decoration, how were they to be explained if they were not the creation of that paragon of virtuous good taste, Francesca Lionnel? In response to Jemima's careful probing questions, Sir Richard was even more startlingly frank.

'Katy Aaronson did the office suite, I think,' he said rather carelessly. 'You know Katy, don't you? She keeps me straight, rules me with a rod of iron all day then home to mother and father in Highgate in the evening – well, most evenings, anyway. No personal life at all, well, nothing outside work, awfully pretty too, first-class brain and legs like Betty Grable. Pity in a way they didn't let her go to Cambridge like her brother. Still it's been my good luck. What more could a man ask in his private assistant? I think she decorated the office suite – she's always wanted to do something like that, it seemed. Something more feminine than her usual work. I chose the mirror and table in the hall – picked them up for a song when I was quite a young man and had time for those things. Then who did the bedroom? Was it that smashing Czech Countess I met at Jane Manfred's? Or did Katy do the bedroom and the smashing Czech do the drawing room? Do you know that Czech girl? I'm absolutely mad about her. Quite beautiful and she does it all herself with a spray-gun and scissors; amazing. Come to think of it, she certainly pinned up all that green stuff on the bedroom walls.'

'And the third-floor flat?' Jemima hoped Lionnel would not ask her how she had penetrated it. He did not.

'Oh that. The photographer. You know, we were just talking about her. The one who wears knickerbockers.'

'Binnie Rapallo,' suggested Jemima in her coldest voice.

'Ghastly, isn't it?' Sir Richard gave one of his happy grins; his black eyes flashed and bulged, like the eyes of a wrestler in a Japanese print. 'That never did work out.' Did he mean the relationship or the décor? While Jemima was still trying to puzzle this out, Sir Richard Lionnel leant forward and picked up her hand where it lay on the tablecloth, sharing it now only with a large ashtray and some untouched turkish delight on sticks, thoughtfully provided by Stavros.

He turned it over and gazed at the palm. What he saw there either reassured or inspired him. The next thing he said, black eyes fixed hypnotically upon her, was:

'Miss Shore, Jemima – may I? My friends call me Dick by the way – why don't you redecorate it for me? Any way you like. Just let Katy know about the bills. Don't worry about the expense, just talk to Katy as and when it's necessary. She looks after all the empty flats.'

The role of decorator of Adelaide Square in the life of Sir Richard Lionnel had suddenly become alarmingly clear to Jemima. Hastily she extricated herself from what might have been an embarrassing situation, – although for one moment, was she perhaps tempted? . . . No, definitely not, she reminded herself sternly, definitely not to clear up the area of decorative disaster created by Binnie Rapallo. And she would not call him Dick either. Which meant she could hardly revert to Sir Richard without being rude; she would have to call him nothing at all for the time being.

'What will become of Chloe's flat?' she asked at the end of lunch in a suddenly sad voice. She had the answer to her original question now: Chloe, the great deceiver, in her last relationship had been deceived. Or at least had deceived herself. This man had never intended to marry Chloe Fontaine.

'The lease belonged to her. Not the freehold of course. Katy tells me there's probably no will. No husband, no children. That means it goes to her parents, and they will presumably want to sell it. We'll buy it back – we have first refusal. I'm trying to persuade Katy herself . . . time for even the nicest Jewish girl to leave home . . . Highgate can be quite awkward sometimes . . . Stifling environment, no wonder the brilliant brother dropped out.'

Sir Richard Lionnel was shown the bill by Stavros but was evidently too grand even to sign it; he waved it away with a smile, merely adding to it a large note.

'It would never have done,' he said, leaning back easily in his chair. 'Not because of me, but because of her. She was so wayward, wasn't she? That's what attracted me in the first place. You see, I'm surrounded by strong women. Francesca – very strong in her own way; Katy, a Tartar; my mother – still as strong as a horse at eighty-three. You're a strong woman, we should get on very well together—'

Jemima smiled at the flattery. But the compliment proved to be double-edged.

'Love is another matter. I've always been fatally drawn to the other type. A dash of adventure in my life – I need it. There was nothing strong about Chloe, was there? She was like an eel. And a liar! She lied as she breathed. She was pregnant, did you know that?'

Jemima nodded. A splash of red. Kevin John to Chloe, Adam to her, Chloe to Richard Lionnel. Apparently they all needed it.

'Not my child. Then who was the father?'

'You're sure? I know the dates make it improbable—'

'Quite sure. We have no children, Francesca and I. It's not her fault, it's mine. Boyhood illness. It's never bothered me; and Francesca has come to terms with it – as I told you, she is a strong person.' He paused. 'Then who was the father? I would like to know that before I close the books.'

'I haven't the slightest idea,' replied Jemima quite truthfully. She really did have no idea who might have been Chloe's lover, or even her partner in a casual encounter, about three months ago. At least Adam Adamson was out of the question since their relationship had developed only within the last few weeks.

'I suppose the bastard killed her.'

Afterwards Jemima refused the offer of a lift; it was after all only a step from 'The Little Athens' to Adelaide Square. She watched Sir Richard's Rolls-Royce purr away in the direction of Whitehall. Sir Richard himself, bent over some papers, was accompanied by an exceptionally attractive young woman with auburn hair who apparently had been waiting for him in the back of the car. Katy Aaronson? Or any one of the other innumerable women Lionnel surrounded himself with. As far as he was concerned, the incident of Chloe Fontaine was clearly closed. His attempts to pump Jemima about Chloe's lover having failed, he would probably spare the dead woman no further thoughts.

When Jemima let herself into the office suite, the telephone was ringing. Detective Chief Inspector Portsmouth was in a jovial mood.

'The artist fellow, Athlone,' he said merrily. 'We're charging him with murder tomorrow. Witness saw him leaving the building between one-thirty and two. Besides, he's admitted it. He was there all right.'

14
Back to Athens

Lunch with Isabelle Mancini the next day, Friday, was dominated by the news of the arrest and charging with murder of Kevin John Athlone. After a brief early-morning appearance at Bow Street Magistrates' Court, he was remanded and taken to Brixton.

As Jemima walked once again in the direction of 'The Little Athens' – for her own reasons she was minded to pursue her acquaintance with that restaurant – she speculated on Kevin John's present whereabouts. She hated the thought of that great handsome bull's head butting against fate; horns now tangled officially with the police. It was curious how sympathetic to Kevin John she had become, now that he was in a sense Chloe's victim as well as her alleged assassin. It was particularly odd, since she had never felt even covert sympathy for him before, and regarded the memory of their two encounters in Adelaide Square with distaste. The fact was that as Chloe's webs-after-death began to pull him down, she saw his involvement with her late friend in clearer colours.

Whatever a jury would find – and they were hardly likely to view his undeniably violent proclivities with favour – she would always believe that Kevin John had struck down Chloe in the face of some kind of intolerable provocation.

Oddly enough, Isabelle Mancini shared Jemima's view: another woman who had never been a fan of Kevin John's in the past and had, for example, never dreamt of featuring the artist in her cherished *Taffeta*.

''E was forced to ke-e-el 'er' she declared passionately after their first contretemps over the menu at 'The Little Athens' had been resolved. 'Chloe made everyone who loved 'er want to ke-e-el 'er. Danger – it turned 'er on . . . Ah, Chloe, ee-ee-diot child.'

Isabelle's eating was temporarily afflicted by two quite different considerations. In the first place the ethnic nature of any given restaurant had to conform to her somewhat confusing but strongly held political views. Laura Barrymore having made the new appointment and dropped her employer at 'The Little Athens' in her chic smoky-glassed black Mini, Isabelle was apparently unaware of the nature of the venue. There were some moments of difficulty while Isabelle sorted out her political attitude to that particular geographical area represented by this particular restaurant. And where might that be?

'You know, Athens, darling,' murmured Jemima sardonically, 'Athens, Greece.' Her voice was not heard as Isabelle eagerly questioned the proprietor. Stavros, handsomer, heavier and gloomier than ever under this treatment, was transparently in a mood to agree with whatever opinion it was that Isabelle so strongly held. The exact nature of this was however rather more difficult to elicit. At last Isabelle relaxed.

'*Bien.* 'E agrees with me about l' Arménie, 'e says, and 'e's never 'eard of l'Albanie,' she declared. 'Agh, eet's probably not true—' She stopped. Jemima did not dare ask what agreeing with Isabelle about Armenia involved – was that really a topic of the day? But by now Isabelle's attention was distracted by her second consideration, that of food.

Isabelle was on a diet, a diet almost as particular as her political views. Furthermore, as a former cookery writer and restaurant guide, Isabelle was not to be fooled by bland discussions of ingredients. Stavros' courtesy remained impeccable throughout their long-drawn-out negotiations, while Jemima covertly drank a great deal of retsina, a wine that Isabelle, it seemed, despised both for its content and its political implications.

Finally, with a rather good French wine to reassure her – how fortunate it was for Isabelle that France, her native country through all its vicissitudes remained mysteriously politically and gastronomically OK – Isabelle settled herself back in her chair and turned back to conversation. In her flowing grey draperies she made a dignified if substantial figure; the pretty pearl handled fan with which she cooled herself ('Perfect for zose boiling collections, darling') was perhaps a little too delicate for her looks, which were, like those of Kevin John, on a large scale. The heavy silver bracelets which clanked in time to the airy motions of the fan were more suitably massive. But as the talk flowed, Jemima derived all over again that pleasure from Isabelle's company in which her ample physical presence was merely the outward manifestation of her generous spirit. The loyalty Isabelle demanded, she certainly also dispensed.

'Paris – a nightmare. Where was I, darling? Yes, Kevin John – 'ee was forced to ke-e-el 'er. For 'e loved 'er. Valentine too, 'e loved 'er; she wanted that, you know, violence, she loved it; that's what poor Valentine could never give 'er. Swee-e-et boy. Even I—' Isabelle paused only for a moment. 'Even from me she wanted something, some 'atred perhaps, when all I 'ad for 'er was love. Why be so cruel to me? Why? I ask myself now, with zat book, zose letters – steell, we don't want to talk about that now, do we?' Isabelle rushed on, 'Poor Valentine. If only 'e 'ad been able to give her something like that. If only . . . But then 'e would not have been so sw-e-et, would he? And life – ah life—' Isabelle paused again and then plunged on, 'Life would 'ave taken a different turn for Chloe.'

At the end of lunch, Laura Barrymore arrived to fetch Isabelle. She was wonderful and long-legged in grass-green trousers and matching T-shirt, down which irregular green glass beads set in gold cascaded, revealing every tense sinew of her muscular but graceful body, she must have been every inch of six feet and barely weighed more than eight stone. Jemima watched Laura coiling herself back into the black Mini like an elegant green snake.

Through the smoked glass Jemima could not even discern the heads of the two women, as she had been able to watch Sir Richard and his female companion being borne away on Thursday. Nevertheless it occurred to her that both Isabelle and Lionnel, highly successful in their respective spheres, understood the necessity of binding their acolytes to them. A loyal acolyte was something Chloe Fontaine had not even desired unless one counted poor Valentine and even he, rightly or wrongly, had detected in her a provocation: 'She made me watch her. I had a feeling she wanted it.'

Jemima was due to visit Chloe's domestic acolyte, Rosina, later that afternoon: perhaps there would be a loyalty there. In the meantime she had some unfinished business at 'The Little Athens'.

'Mr Stavros—' she began, flashing her television smile. But it was hardly necessary. Stavros was quite enchanted at the presence – two days running – of Jemima Shore, Investigator. The exact significance of her title did not bother him as he brought some more wine – 'a present for a lovely lady', given with a smile as wide and ravishing as Jemima's own. He also banished the restaurant's traditional sweetmeats on sticks at Jemima's request – what would Isabelle have made of these glutinous lumps, politically and gastronomically? With the departure of Isabelle, and in the absence of Sir Richard Lionnel, Stavros' melancholy had quite vanished. He became a mine of information on the restaurant trade, on which he was delighted to think that Miss Shore might be planning an autumn programme.

The transition to the subject of Sir Richard Lionnel was made without too much difficulty and somehow even Lady Lionnel was introduced ... Stavros rolled his eyes. After all he had had to answer similar questions from the police; a television enquiry was not so different after all, just rather more comforting to its subject. Jemima made it clear that in her case lunch with Lionnel had been in the line of business ... since she was not concerned to pump Stavros about Lionnel's ladies, but only his movements on that particular Saturday, the task proved relatively easy.

Yes, poor Lady Lionnel had become ill. 'She was a little upset, yes, upset, definitely.' Yes, Sir Richard had summoned the chauffeur to take her to the station but it was too early, the chauffeur had not yet come back. In fact he had only just gone for his own lunch.

'About half-past one?'

'Something like that. It was a one o'clock booking. But Sir Richard was early. He always is.'

'I noticed.'

'And Lady Lionnel arrived soon after that. She just had time to taste some taramasalata – then, pouf—' Stavros' face was expressive. 'Tears.'

'And – how did she leave then?'

'Ah, then no car. He looks angry. He does not say so. I know it. He thinks, the car should be there all the time. He goes out, himself, I cannot stop him. He moves very quickly that man, and looks for a taxi. He comes back and puts her in it. Face of thunder. Both Sir Richard and the lady. He comes back, sits here. "No reason to waste an excellent meal, Stavros," he says. But he eats and drinks nothing. Later he says: "I'm afraid I'm not feeling very well, Stavros." He reads a magazine, a book maybe. Very calm. When the car comes back he is no longer angry. He waits reading until about two-thirty, and then his car takes him away.'

'To number ten Downing Street', concluded Jemima thoughtfully. 'And you told all this to the police, just as you told me.'

Stavros smiled and flung his hands open.

'I told it, yes, most of it. But I am a businessman. I do not tell them about the tears of Lady Lionnel. That is private to Sir Richard. Besides they are not interested in her, only in him. And the fact that he is here from twelve-forty-five to two-thirty. To that I swear and so do Nicky and Spyros.' He indicated two further melancholy men, younger and thinner, but in somewhat the same mould as Stavros. 'Sir Richard Lionnel, he too is a businessman. It is a pleasure to see him here. He know what he wants – we give it to him. The other lady – please forgive me, Miss Shore – your guest. What does *she* want?' Jemima left hastily, before she should be drawn into discussing the political-gastronomic ideals of Isabelle Mancini. She also paid the bill in cash: despite Stavros' evident desire to make that another present 'for a lovely lady'.

Jemima remained thoughtful on her journey to see Chloe's daily woman. She was haunted by a feeling that she had received an odd and valuable piece of information in the course of her visit to 'The Little Athens'. It was as though an insignificant chip in a jig-saw had been handed to her; if she could only place it correctly, the whole pattern might become clearer.

Jemima enlivened the walk to Tottenham Court Road tube station by re-running her conversations with both Isabelle and Stavros through her mind like a tape.

As she came to Stavros' revelations, she realized that the striking piece of information she had received concerned the precipitate departure of Lady Lionnel – the Medea of Parrot Park – from 'The Little Athens' at about 1.30 – back to the station. An item of information as yet unknown to the police, who had contented themselves with establishing Sir Richard Lionnel's alibi – lunch with his wife – with the aid of Stavros and his waiters.

That needed further quiet thought. Lady Lionnel? It was odd to think that this Medea who unquestionably had a motive for wishing Chloe removed from her husband's path, had also been vouchsafed an opportunity to effect this removal.

Something else – less obvious perhaps – some remark of Isabelle or Stavros – continued to haunt her.

She was still re-running the scene in her mind when she reached Tottenham Court Road station and bought a copy of the *London Evening Post*. A recent photograph showed Kevin John's face, anguished, pop-eyed, slightly reproachful, staring out at her from the front page. His huge eyes with their improbably starry eyelashes, seemed to be imploring her help.

Jemima shivered and turned down the steps to the moving staircase. The text accompanying the report was short: there was after all very little to be said. There was however a short interview with one Miss Kim Lee Ho, who described herself as the 'steady girl-friend' of the accused, and was also temporarily lodging with Kevin John's artistic patron, Crispin Creed, the owner of the Aiglon Gallery.

A joint photograph was provided. Inspecting it with interest, Jemima could see a dark pretty Oriental-looking girl; her small figure was almost masked by the robust presence of Creed, a man whose affectionate nickname of Creeping Croesus had been earned by a combination of inherited wealth and commercial perception. This then was the submissive girl of Eastern origin to whom Chloe had so casually referred. Jemima was vaguely pleased that Kevin John had some feminine support. It made her feel less guilty in the face of those reproachful eyes. Kim Lee Ho, who give or take her Oriental ancestry, had a certain disquieting resemblance to Chloe herself, was described in the evening paper as a model – whether artist's model or fashion model was unspecified. Chloe, despite her photogenic looks, had always rejected the fashion offers which had come her way, even when poor and out of work after Cambridge. 'I'm a model nothing,' she used to say.

She had not, it seemed, been a model employer. Mrs Rosina Cavalieri received a rather hot and fussed Jemima in a small depressing street north of Tottenham Court Road, a neighbourhood with little else to commend it except the convenience of the tube for working in Bloomsbury. Rosina was indeed as Chloe had pointed out and Pompey confirmed, a compulsive talker; her son, Enrico, no more charming than Chloe had predicted, clung to his mother's skirts and regarded Jemima with enormous baleful eyes set in a full white face.

Enrico's distinctly plump figure, however, was immaculately dressed notwithstanding the heat in a white silk shirt which buttoned on to grey silk trousers, white socks and black patent shoes. Despite his tender years, Enrico had an excellent sense of when the conversation was taking an interesting turn, and at this juncture infallibly grabbed his mother, demanding a biscuit, some other comestible, or orange juice. Thanks to these interruptions, it took Jemima longer than she had anticipated to elicit Rosina's impressions of life with Chloe Fontaine.

First, as Pompey had indicated, Rosina was most impressed by 'the grand Sir' – Sir Richard Lionnel. Second, she was not impressed, rather the reverse, by the fact that Chloe had apparently shared her favours with others during the same period. This kind of disloyalty, Rosina made it clear, was unthinkable in the particular society in which Rosina moved. At one point she even clutched the sulkily acquiescent Enrico to her breast, sticky chocolate biscuit and all, to emphasize the point.

With flashing eyes and heaving bosom – indeed, in more ways than her emphasis on loyalty, Rosina bore a general Mediterranean resemblance to Isabelle Mancini – she enquired how such matters as 'bambine' could be managed with ladies of such wayward tendencies. If her language was not quite so high flown as that of Isabelle, her English accent was an improvement. It was clear what Rosina meant especially as she appealed from time to time to the example of little Enrico, the son indubitably of his father, big Enrico, who would kill anyone, and she, Rosina, would also kill anyone if they suggested . . . This dramatic monologue on the subject of marital fidelity was broken only by the protests of Enrico, who, biscuit finished, struggled free from his mother's arms and demanded 'Orange! orange!'

But Rosina had not expounded in vain. Jemima derived the very definite impression that Rosina, by some means or other – a doctor's letter left carelessly about, a telephone call overheard – had suspected Chloe was pregnant. It was true that Rosina had denied all knowledge of such a distasteful subject to the police – but then Miss Jemima Shore was so very different, wasn't she, to the young male detective who had interviewed Rosina. Handsome as Pompey's protegé – the dashing Gary Harwood – might be, he was no substitute for a real-life television star. Miss Shore was so very friendly, so very famous ... There was an enormous television set in pride of place in the tiny sitting room which presently Enrico insisted on having switched on for his own delectation. Miss Shore, Rosina declared, was like someone she had known all her life, her own sister, for example.

More than prepared to accept this helpful hypothesis, Jemima narrowed her questions to Chloe's other callers, expecially those prominent in the period when Chloe had first moved into Adelaide Square, which had coincided with Rosina's arrival to work for her. Since Chloe had been roughly three months pregnant when she died in the first week of August, the father of her child must have been someone she knew long before the move to Adelaide Square towards the end of June; conception had to have taken place at the beginning of May.

Rosina, predictably, was gracious about the 'poor lord', meaning Valentine Brighton, whose sudden death had been brilliantly brought to her attention by Enrico when he recognized Valentine's face on the television news with a shriek. The 'poor lord' had helped Chloe with her move into. Adelaide Square, putting his Rolls at her disposal.

No, Rosina was full of approval for the poor dead Lord Brighton: 'Che gentile! Che simpatico!' and so on. At any point Jemima expected her to join Isabelle in her cry of 'Swee-e-et boy'. It was an approval which did not however extend to someone she termed the 'studente'. Jemima, despite herself, felt her heart give a little jolt.

'Studente, there was a studente?' she probed hoping that Enrico would not choose this moment – there was a commercial break – to demand another orange. She need not have worried: advertisements as well as programmes held Enrico entranced.

'Ahdum,' Rosina pronounced the name with scorn. 'Ah-dum Ahdum: he was a studente. A foolish name.' She implied that his youthful status was no excuse.

'Not then, Rosina, surely.' Jemima knew that she sounded agitated.

'Not in June. Not when she first came to Adelaide Square. It was later, wasn't it, a week or so before she died that she met the student?'

'But no! It was the end of June like I tell you.' Rosina's indignation rose. 'It was the day after the birthday of Big Enrico, June twenty-six. It was then I tell you. The *studente*. In the empty flat with her, that first day, no furniture, no bed even. They were in the bedroom, all the same. I knew. She just called out: "I'm resting. Come back in an hour!" And later when I do come back, all those stairs again, I pass him. The *studente*, with his little red beard, his *barba*, you understand? She was running down the stairs and calling: "Ahdum! Ahdum!" Then she saw me and stopped. She said: "Mrs Cavalieri, this is Ahdum, a friend of mine from Fulham. He's been helping me with the move." But the room, it was still empty.'

'What did he say?'

'Ah, he spoke in a funny voice, funny words. He was young, too young for her. He said he liked it here, better than in Fulham, and he might come and live here himself if she asked him. He laughed. They both laughed.'

At this point Enrico, maybe in a jealous rage at the thought of the laughter of others, let out a prolonged and angry bawl. 'Ma-aama!'

'He is tired with our talking,' said Rosina apologetically. 'And the television is tiring – when they are young,' she added hastily in case she seemed to denigrate Jemima's profession. 'Perhaps you will come another day, Miss Shore. I would like to ask my neighbour to tea, Mrs Pollonari, she likes television *very* much.'

Jemima was left to wend her way home by tube in the Friday rush-hour, missing for the first time in a week the easy passage her Citroen gave her through weary London.

She pondered a world in which not only Kevin John Athlone had lied to the police about his lunchtime movements but Adam Adamson had also lied – if not to the police at least by implication to Jemima Shore. He had definitely allowed her to believe that he had met Chloe for the first time a few days prior to her death. Now it emerged that they had been friends – no, more than that, lovers, long before Chloe moved to Adelaide Square. They had been lovers in Fulham, Fulham where Chloe's child had been conceived.

'I suppose the bastard killed her,' Sir Richard had said of the unknown father of Chloe's child. With a heavy heart, Jemima acknowledged that it was a possibility at least worth exploring: and Kevin John's large imploring eyes gazing out at her from the folded front page of the evening paper, called on her mutely to proceed.

15
A white petticoat

Jemima planned to move out of Adelaide Square over the weekend. On Friday evening Miss Katy Aaronson telephoned with the offer of a furnished flat – another penthouse – in Montagu Square. Under the circumstances Jemima decided to take it. She felt she had had enough of Bloomsbury; nor did she particularly wish to approach her own American tenant with a view to shortening the let by a couple of weeks. That way lay the possibility of an unwelcome intimacy with the need to ask a favour. Anonymity in Montagu Square, near Marble Arch, an area without associations, away from friends and strangers alike, if not quite the holiday she had planned, was at least the most dignified way of ending it.

Shortly afterwards a Lionnel chauffeur came round with the keys of the Montagu Square apartment. Miss Katy Aaronson had very politely excused herself from a Saturday rendezvous. She liked to spend the day with her parents in Highgate, starting with a Friday eve-of-the-Sabbath supper.

'And since Sir Richard is generally at Parrot Park on Friday nights – although house guests are invited in time for Saturday lunch, but in any case the housekeeper is at the disposal of Lady Lionnel for those arrangements – and Sir Richard's personal assistant, Mr Judah Turpin, has the flat in the old stables, should business matters arise—'

Jemima was happy to cut short this catalogue of undoubtedly admirable arrangements and arrange to arrive at Montagu Square at leisure, at a time of her own choosing, and under her own terms. She rejected the offer of a Lionnel car to convey her. The anonymity of a taxi was another personal choice. Making it clear that at Montagu Square, for the next week, her privacy was to be regarded as sacrosanct,

438

Jemima arranged to leave behind her own keys to the Adelaide Square office suite. The efficient Miss Aaronson possessing several spare sets, would arrange their collection.

It was a pity that Tiger would have to make two moves in rapid succession – for Tiger would be coming back with Jemima to Holland Park Mansions. It was as though he had been pre-ordained to replace Colette. No one else showed the slightest interest in the fierce golden cat. Mr Stover, on being consulted on the telephone, had revealed the existence of a rival Stover pet, Nipper, a terrier of great age and uncertain health—' although where cats are concerned, he's still pretty much on the ball, I can tell you that'. Mr Stover obviously regarded the possible incursion of Tiger into his dog's declining years—' mind you, he's not called Nipper for nothing' – as symbolic of the whole catastrophic confusion wrought in his own existence by the death of Chloe. Jemima was left to reflect that Mr Stover and Nipper were no exception to the oft-quoted rule that over the years pets and their masters grew to resemble each other.

Jemima did not flatter herself that she had in any sense won Tiger's affections – Colette had been from the first a far more domesticated animal – but she recognized their alliance as inevitable. And that kind of recognition was often more binding than a sentimental attachment.

Fortunately Tiger had already shown himself to be a survivor where moves were concerned. He had adapted himself to Bloomsbury after Fulham; carefully treated he would survive the short-term stay in Montagu Square, the final move to Holland Park.

Fulham and Tiger: Jemima caught her breath suddenly at the memory of Adam Adamson and Tiger on that day of their first acquaintance. Had she not sensed something strange even then about Tiger's eager disappearance into the third-floor flat? It was obviously explained by the fact that to Tiger Adam was a familiar figure. Adam had not exactly lied to Jemima in this respect: indeed, throughout their conversations he had shown a remarkable, jesuitical regard for avoiding the direct lie, while not telling the whole truth.

He had not actually denied knowing Tiger, only: 'Nice cat . . . it wanted to come in' – followed by compliments about her own appearance. No wonder Tiger, accidentally excluded from the upper flat, had peregrinated towards the least hostile terrain.

Jemima however still believed that Adam had been genuinely puzzled over Chloe's true identity. Was it possible that he could have been fooled by the pose of Dollie Stover? On consideration it was: Chloe, the mistress of deceit, had presumably conducted her carnal encounters with Adam elsewhere than in her Fulham house – in his own former dwelling, whatever kind of revivified pad that might have been. Adam's menacing comment about Chloe and her deception—' I hate being lied to' – was, she would swear, genuine.

Perhaps their carnal encounters within Adelaide Square itself had taken place on the third floor? And literally so, in view of its lack of furniture, Jemima reflected wryly; her slight sense of crossness was almost proprietary, but since all proprietary feelings about Adam Adamson were so clearly a mistake, she dismissed the whole train of thought as unworthy of her. Back to the question of Adam and the penthouse: by keeping him ignorant of her lease of the top floor, Chloe would have run no danger of him ferreting out the incriminating copies of her own works, those exquisite tell-tale photographs on the back.

Besides, now that Jemima – far too late – was coming to some new understanding of Chloe's character, she had an intuition that the encounters in the empty flat, with her own immaculate penthouse above, and Sir Richard's secure opulence below, would have given Chloe exactly that rich spice of danger she sought.

As Jemima waited for Pompey to bring her back the keys to Chloe's flat, in order that she might pack up her remaining belongings over the weekend, she continued to ponder on the subject of Adam. Adam – 'my former angel' – Adam, presumably the father of the unsought child, Adam with his fertile youth and impetuosity giving Chloe the child which she had either avoided receiving or refused to accept from two husbands and at least one steady – ridiculous word in the context – lover in the shape of Kevin John. There had been at least one abortion, possibly two, in Chloe's past, hadn't there?

Jemima was a little hazy about the details: Chloe's marriage to Lance breaking up, impossible to bring a child into the world under such circumstances, Chloe desperately writing her second novel, trying to support herself financially as a meagre-selling novelist, impossible to take on the burden of single parenthood. Jemima, not closely involved herself, knew that Chloe had always had plenty of excuses to offer – and goodness knows Jemima herself did not believe dogmatically in unwanted children coming into the world, having investigated too many of the resultant miseries. At the same time Jemima had always suspected that Chloe's deep-seated reason for avoiding motherhood was her unwillingness to tolerate the arrival of a child in her life while she herself remained in so many respects wilfully childish and irresponsible.

That left open the question of the carelessness ... the lethal carelessness which had lead to at least two, possibly three pregnancies. What precautions had Chloe taken? One had to assume that she had not been on the Pill, or at least not regularly. It was certainly true that there were plenty of medical reasons to be quoted against the continuous longterm use of the Pill for any woman. Jemima herself had quoted them – as ever giving both sides of the question – in that programme about the Pill, to which Pompey had alluded. Yet Jemima wondered once again at the surprising contrasts evinced by Chloe's character; the neatness and domesticity of her surroundings, the meticulous care of her writing, versus the dangerous abandon of her private life, carried surely to excess in her reckless attitudes to the question of her own fertility.

It did not affect matters that on this occasion Chloe had tried to turn her pregnancy to good account as part of her intrigue to get Sir Richard Lionnel – hitherto childless – to marry her. Chloe had gone to her death without knowing how that particular plot was always doomed to fail. She died, with her stepfather on his way to London as a kind of angry witness to the confrontation. Jemima was glad that at least all three parties had been spared that dreadful moment when Chloe would have been denounced as a liar, and furthermore a promiscuous one. Lionnel had to live with the knowledge now; he clearly did not find it easy. Yes, dangerous abandon had certainly been what Chloe had displayed.

Dangerous abandon – the thought suddenly struck Jemima that if Adam was Chloe's former angel, that left the identity of her casual – carnal? – acquaintance from the square gardens still unknown. Was there some mystery to be unravelled there? Or was the whole episode of that nocturnal spree as unimportant to the world now as it had been to Chloe at the time?

That certainly was the point of view taken by Pompey. He was in a joyous mood. He had rounded off a hardworking Friday, which began with the formal charging of Kevin John with murder at the police station, by having 'a jar with the lads', as he put it, of a mildly celebratory nature. And he seemed to regard his visit to Jemima as a further postponement of his return to Mrs Portsmouth and the intellectual principles of gardening.

'The lover in the gardens!' he exclaimed, shaking his head repeatedly like a mechanical toy – a fox perhaps, in a man's suit – which had just been wound up. 'Sounds like a Sunday newspaper headline to me. No my dear, Athlone did it. No question about that now. His second statement was a great deal more to the point, as well it might be. You see, your squatter friend made a statement saying he had seen him leaving the building between one-thirty and two; looked out from the third-floor balcony where he happened to be, *not* minding his own business, still it's convenient for us that he was. Described him exactly. Not only does he have his own little alibi for that period, as I told you, but *his* story was confirmed by a very different kind of witness.

'One Flora Elizabeth Powell, fifty-eight, spinster, who came into the station in response to our enquiries and made a voluntary statement. No, my dear, not a hysterical spinster, just a hard-working citizen, employed in a local caff on the early shift who was on her way home, some time after one-fifteen when she knocked off work in Great Russell Street and two-five pm when she noticed a local clock in Hammersmith, where she lives, and reaches by tube, when she saw him coming out of a house in Adelaide Square. Can pinpoint the house of course: "It's the lovely modern block, isn't it? Which the Queen Mother declared open the other day. I saw the crowds. I couldn't quite get to see her, but my friend said she looked lovely." Never mind the fact that the crowds she saw were demonstrators *against* the building.' Pompey chuckled. 'And the Queen Mother was at University College round the corner. Flora Elizabeth is our witness all right. Very particular about the blue T-shirt. Better still, she remembers seeing someone in a white shirt – that's the squatter of course – on the upper balcony. Came out with it on her own accord; couldn't have made that up; didn't know we were interested, you see. Remarked that she was happy to think the building declared open by the Queen Mother was already occupied, not like that Centre Point, since it might have worried the Queen Mother to know – but I'll spare you the rest.'

Pompey chuckled again. 'What does feminine instinct say to all that?'

'My feminine instinct has nothing to *say*. It never does. It just nags at me in the watches of the night. I don't doubt you. I don't doubt either of them for that matter – my squatter and your spinster can hardly be in league to fool us,' said Jemima rather wearily. 'It's just that I like the loose ends being tied up. The identity of the lover in the gardens – I love the headline, by the way – continues to intrigue me, although I dare say you're right and it's not important. Tell me at any rate, before I read it in the newspapers of the trial, about Athlone's second statement.'

'He admitted it. To being there, that is. Still utterly denied killing her. But that's par for the course.' Pompey shook gently, as if confirmed once again in his low – but not necessarily contemptuous – view of human nature. 'He came back at lunchtime – to apologize to you. Felt he'd behaved like a cad – well he had, hadn't he? All that violence towards a woman,' said Pompey in stern parenthesis. 'He was surprised to find the penthouse door open *with* the keys in the lock.'

'*Open?*'

'Exactly. Listen, this is his statement, not mine. In he goes. No one there – not you, and not at this point, his ex-mistress, Chloe Fontaine. He decides, believe it or not, to have another go at finding a razor.'

'I do believe that!' exclaimed Jemima. 'That razor was obsessing him. He left Dixie in the pub saying he was going to find a razor.'

'Believe that if you like. It's immaterial to our case. But a rational woman like you, Jemima – in the daylight hours' – a gallant shake – 'may find the rest of it a little more difficult to accept. Athlone finds a razor – right?'

'The same razor, we assume, which is later found beside Chloe's bed—'

'Exactly. In some drawer or other. His prints were all over the bathroom and bedroom anyway – except in those areas wiped clean by the murderer – as a result of the morning's search for that same razor. He decides to shave. And not before time—' This was clearly the reproving voice of Pompey speaking. 'But he's still pretty angry, he's drunk a good deal of whisky, feeling not only angry but violent as he himself tells us. At this point his eye lights on the picture – "The Red Paintpot", whatever it's called. He decides suddenly that she, the deceased that is, is not worthy of "my effing work of genius". His exact words.' Pompey paused. 'Except he didn't say effing.'

'So, listen to this.' Pompey's tone was now more portentous. 'He takes a kitchen knife, yes, the same knife we assume to be the murder weapon – for he remembers deliberately choosing the biggest of the knives available. He goes back into the bedroom. He proposes to massacre the aforesaid work of art. Again his own words. He is going to slash it to effing pieces and throw them over the balcony to feed the lions of Bloomsbury.'

Pompey leaned back. He gave the impression of being rather pleased with his imitation of Kevin John, which did not however in Jemima's opinion contain any of the sheer craziness of the original; there was too much devilry, too little dash in Pompey's delivery.

'But before he can carry out this felonious plan – it's not his property' – Pompey shook – 'although it's not exactly like desecrating the Mona Lisa, is it, not exactly – he's disturbed.'

'Disturbed? By whom?'

'By her, of course. The recently deceased Miss Chloe Fontaine. I'm anticipating her state somewhat, it's fair to say. So there he is, razor in one hand and effing great kitchen knife, to borrow his phrase, in the other.'

'And there she is,' cried Jemima, 'in a white petticoat, I suppose. It reminds me of that nursery riddle:

Ninny nanny petticoat
In a white petticoat
The longer she goes
The shorter she grows.

The answer's a candle by the way. Appropriate to Chloe, a flame, snuffed out. But why, Pompey, why?'

'Now that's very sharp of you, Jemima,' said Pompey approvingly. 'Because that's the first thing he said to us about her. "The C-blank" ' – cough – ' "wasn't even dressed." He objected particularly, you know, to her parading round the building in her petticoat. Thought it unseemly, or as he put it, effing disgusting'.

'And then?'

'*He* says they had a flaming row. I can't recall the precise colourful phrase he used to describe it. She, the deceased, absolutely refused to explain her presence in the penthouse beyond telling him, Athlone that is, that she had borrowed the first-floor flat from "a friend" – identity not revealed – in order to have some working peace for this anthology she's supposed to be editing. She had returned to the top floor to fetch some forgotten necessity for her work like a notebook; cat slips out; she goes to rescue cat, leaving keys in the door. They're her own keys, having given you, Jemima, the second set.'

'Pretty thin story,' commented Jemima gloomily. 'Except for the bit about the cat. That's probably true. Tiger did that to me. A restless type, I fear, like his former owner. If the cat went down to the basement, that would give Kevin John time to get up the staircase without passing Chloe on the way.'

'Athlone thought the story was pretty thin, too.' Pompey sounded equally gloomy. 'He wasn't too interested in the subject of the cat, one way or the other; but he was interested in the identity of the helpful "friend" who had lent her the first-floor flat. Thought it was certain to be male, and a lover.

'Hence the row,' he went on. 'She tells him to get out of the flat. Taxes him with following her about, harassing her, when everything is over between them. He accuses her of having a rendezvous upstairs and wants to know when and with whom. Then she really insults him, goes for him, past present and to come. Never loved him in the first place, you know what ladies can be like' – cough. 'Anyway at those words, it all changes. He drops the knife. He just leaves. Leaves her there.'

Jemima let out her breath. Pompey went implacably on: 'After that he sticks to his original statement. Had a few more drinks. Decided much later to drop in the flowers. For you or her, that's not quite clear.

Probably for you: he'd promised you flowers. Admits to being pretty drunk by now. Climbs the scaffolding, deposits the pot plant. Opens the door from inside – it's shut but not doubled locked. Bangs on the first-floor door. No answer. Goes on down to the hall. There he collapses. Has some vague idea of waiting for her to come back, or emerge from the first-floor flat. He may trap her new lover. That's not quite clear. Collapses anyway. The next thing he knows, you're standing over him.'

'And he never looks in the bedroom? On that second visit?'

'So he says. We, of course,' said Pompey gently, 'think he killed her on the first.'

On Saturday evening, Jemima found it took more determination than she had expected to mount the stairs to the penthouse flat again. Yet it had to be done, before she could shake the dust of No. 73 from her feet. She opened the door of the office suite. The stairs stretched upwards as though pointing to her duty; seeing how they curved out of sight towards the top floor gave her an odd presentiment that the end of the Chloe story was likewise still hidden. Yet the clues which pointed to any killer other than Kevin John were so extremely slender that only instinct – and natural obstinacy – prevented Jemima from abandoning her consideration of the case altogether, in favour of Pompey's rational certainties. Pompey for example was convinced that Kevin John had returned via the scaffolding only in order to clear away all incriminating traces of his earlier presence – which was certainly more logical than his own explanation.

Jemima let herself into the penthouse flat, using both keys. She was not a nervous person; nevertheless the atmosphere seemed to her not so much silent as sepulchral. That was the right word: the penthouse was now like a tomb for all Chloe's hopes and works and plans and lies and plots.

The murder charge arising from Chloe's death meant that no burial order had yet been given for her poor little body, once the giver and receiver of many strange pleasures, lacerated first by her murderer, then by the pathologists. Frozen in death, it remained waiting for the possible trial of her murderer. In the meantime would there be some kind of memorial service?

The obvious arranger of all such matters would have been Chloe's publisher, Valentine, especially since Chloe had no literary agent, preferring to trust herself entirely to what she had termed Valentine's 'aristocratic but mercenary mercies – still, in his own way, he can be an angel you know – I hardly need *more* mercenary mercies from an agent'. But Valentine was dead.

In the meantime this flat, until it was dismantled by the combined offices of Miss Katy Aaronson and the Stovers – certainly more the former than the latter – remained Chloe's true sepulchre.

The images of Chloe were everywhere. Lying flat on their backs, faces of Chloe, under her parasol, on her swing, the provocative *Fallen Child* pictures, stared up at the white ceiling from the jackets of her books. They were ranged round the pale carpet. Had the police stacked them so? Presumably. Other belongings were neatly piled and sorted. Everything was immaculate. The comparison to the hideous dust and mayhem which had possessed the flat a week ago was inevitable; Jemima did not find it particularly comforting. But she had to admit that the police had cleaned up after themselves most professionally.

The flat, if clean, was airless. Putting off the moment when she must open the white louvred double doors to the bedroom – for that gesture reminded her too clearly of the past horror – Jemima concentrated on pushing back the balcony windows. They were not locked; but the lock itself was not conspicuous and whoever shut them – the police? Katy Aaronson? – might have thought they were self-locking.

Something soft and furry caressed her legs. Tiger, on his noiseless pads, had followed her up the stairs. He put his golden paws up on the scaffolding to the left of the balcony, and sniffed delicately. Jemima rejoiced constantly in the inquisitive tendencies of cats; it reminded her that her own curiosity was in the natural order of things.

Then she observed that the earth in the pots containing the grey-leaved plants and white-flowering geraniums which had pleased Chloe's bleached sense of decoration, was quite hard and dry. What happened to plants when people died? These had been sufficiently loved by Chloe for her to bring them from Fulham to Bloomsbury. Jemima could not imagine the Stovers conveying such plants back to Folkestone, any more than they had welcomed the intrusion of Tiger. She pictured Mr Stover's large crimson roses – Ena Harkness perhaps – bristling at the arrival of these sophisticated urban cousins.

As for Jemima's own taste in such things, she recognized it to be prettier but somewhat less tasteful – pale pink roses in her case, New Dawn and Albertine, ran riot in huge dark green tubs on her own balcony, with purple pansies and gypsophila, daffodils and blue hyacinths in the spring. She certainly felt no impulse to adopt Chloe's primly matched plants, but the Rousseau-like savage Tiger was a different matter. In the end, it was the abandoned side of Chloe's nature which magnetized her.

As if to emphasize his freedom from constraint, Tiger was now bounding about the balcony and tossing a leaf, a pretended mouse, in his paws; it was a game at once playful and sinister.

The plants in comparison, if not exactly wilted, looked depressingly arid. Jemima sighed. Whatever their ultimate fate it was not her nature to leave them unwatered. One way of getting herself through those bedroom doors was to fling them open, march through and fetch a watering-can from the bathroom – she had a memory of something rather charming and painted, a kind of Marie Antoinette of a watering-can, in the corner there.

Then she would organize her own belongings into a suitcase. It was now about nine o'clock. The air over Adelaide Square was sultry. Scarcely a rustle disturbed the mighty trees. It had been about that hour of the evening that she had looked in vain across the square for Chloe's departing figure. Oppressed by the memory, Jemima turned away and, striding firmly across the thick sitting-room carpet, flung open the bedroom doors.

Then she heard herself scream, and that scream was succeeded by another, and another, and another. The sound seemed to come from outside, so that she was still listening for further screams, even while she stood panting, and now silent.

On Chloe's white bed, motionless beneath his own violent red picture, vast bulging blue eyes staring fixedly towards her, lay Kevin John Athlone.

16
Straw into gold

An instant later, the vast blue eyes shut. Relieved of their intense stare, Jemima lost her panic and moved gingerly forward. A rumbling noise – yes, it was really a snore – greeted her astonished ears. Kevin John Athlone, whom she had imagined for one feverish moment to be dead, was actually sleeping. The fixed stare which had greeted her corresponded to nothing so much as a coma, an unseeing coma.

It was an appalling thought, but had he actually escaped from Brixton?

He was wearing a white shirt, two or three buttons undone; a black tie, carelessly half unknotted, still slung round his neck; light grey trousers which belonged to a suit because a matching grey jacket was roughly slung over the back of a nearby cane peacock chair. In the top pocket of the jacket, incongruously neatly folded, was a white handkerchief. Black shoes, demonstrably polished, were disposed near the bed. Kevin John's feet, sticking out across the bed like those of the corpse he somewhat resembled, were still covered in dark socks.

The formality of the sleeping man's attire struck Jemima forcibly since she had not seen him previously in anything save jeans, T-shirts, and the most rugged polo-necked jerseys. She presumed they were the same clothes in which he had been remanded at the Magistrates' Court: Crispin Creed was probably responsible for them. In the photograph printed in the evening paper Kevin John had looked heavily handsome, like some debauched film star leaving the divorce courts for the third time. In the flesh he looked younger.

Jemima looked at the sleeping figure with more irritation than horror. Her vague intellectual feelings of the necessity of justice towards an innocent man had quite melted away in his physical presence. And even the first feeling of dread at her predicament if he *had* escaped from prison, was less strong than her sheer annoyance at the sight of this great snoring bull, lying so inconveniently prone before her.

It was essential to cope with the problem he presented – and at once. Jemima took another delicate step forward.

The next thing she knew there was a noise, an eruption rather like a mountain in blast, and Kevin John had uncurled himself off the bed, bounded forward, and was clasping her in both shirt-clad arms.

Slightly corpulent as he might be, he was astonishingly muscular. There was no escape. Jemima stood there mutely while Kevin John gave her two quick succulent kisses on the cheek with his rubbery lips.

Then he panted: 'You'll save me, sweetheart, won't you? You'll save me?'

He did not let go of her hands. He continued to stare at her. The blue of his eyes was even more amazing than she had remembered; the numerous red veins in the eyeballs were bright and clear as though running through white marble. His long, ridiculously long black eyelashes fluttered slightly; but his gaze itself did not falter. Coquetry was absent; on this occasion Kevin John Athlone was in deadly earnest.

Alcohol, the pungent disgusting smell of stale alcohol, a great quantity of it, came reeking towards her on his breath as on that fatal Saturday morning a week ago. Only the new formality of his clothing was a present reminder of all that was tragic which had happened in between.

'And if you won't save me, Jemima Shore, Investigator,' said Kevin John, puffing slightly as he spoke, but in no way slackening his grasp, 'I'll keep you here till you do.' From the severity of his tone, the new sound of purpose, Jemima had to assume that the flutter of his lashes which accompanied his words was purely automatic. She also wondered exactly how drunk Kevin John really was, despite the odour of alcohol palpitating from him with every breath exhaled.

'A hostage,' he added, 'in case there's any doubt about my intentions. A hostage to misfortune – mine.' He smiled in what was obviously intended to be a winning manner; this time the flutter of his lashes was deliberate; nevertheless it was all a cold parody of the flirtatiousness which he normally exhibited to the female sex. 'I've an idea, sweetheart, that nothing too bad can happen to me while I've got you here.'

A surge of fury filled Jemima. The memory of her previous sympathies for Kevin John merely enraged her further. She wrenched her hands free from his. She particularly disliked the notion of physical imprisonment, both in theory and practice, when it was allied to injustice.

'How the hell did you get in here?' were the first words she managed to say.

'I knew you were living here. I thought you would help me. You're famous for helping people.' The threatening note beneath the wheedling was still more marked. 'So back up the scaffolding I came. Window not locked again.'

'I'm not living here—' Jemima broke off. She did not propose to give him any more information than he had already. 'Anyway I thought you were in Brixton. For God's sake, don't tell me you've been fool enough to escape.'

Kevin John gave a dreadful leer, into which he appeared determined to inject as much boyish innocence as he could muster.

'Now would I do a thing like that?' he cried. 'Not your Kevin John. No, sweetheart, for me it was the jolly old Judge-in-Chambers.' He pronounced the words proudly and with enormous care. 'The jolly old High Court judge his very self. Saturday afternoon and all, when you would have thought all decent judges were at the races or denouncing vandalism at football matches . . . but not my judge. The merry old soul sat up all night, I mean sat up all the afternoon to receive the application of my solicitor, the well-known Red, Punch Fredericks, God bless him and all other Reds, – and what did he say? He said: Yes. Kevin John Athlone shall go free. On bail, of course, but Creeping Croesus was very handsome about that, as well he might. Anyway, out I popped from Brixton. It was just like the prisoners' chorus in *Fidelio*. And I was singing a pretty merry song myself, I can tell you. Now *that* is no place for a gentleman and an artist . . .'

Reluctantly, Jemima came to the conclusion that Kevin John, in his circumlocutory fashion, must be speaking the truth. His temporary release seemed to have been secured by the energetic action of Punch Fredericks, rightly classed by Pompey as belonging to the bail-for-everyone school. A receptive High Court judge had done the rest. As far as Jemima could make out, Kevin John had merely been requested to surrender his passport: Crispin Creed had been required to go surety for some vast sum, and also put up with Kevin John as his official house guest in Chelsea.

Jemima suspected rather cynically that Creed was animated by more than philanthropy in coming to the aid of an artist in which his Gallery had such a large stake. She only hoped that he would find the bargain worth while.

These thoughts were rudely interrupted as Kevin John suddenly pounced upon her. He shoved Jemima down hard upon the white bed, and felt deftly in the skirts of her thin silk jersey dress. From the hidden pocket he took first the keys of the first-floor flat which he rejected, then the keys of the penthouse.

He held them up.

'So! I recognize these. The keys of the kingdom! Our kingdom. No departure for either of us until you've solved the problem of the day. In short, who killed Chloe Fontaine?'

So saying, with that light athletic walk which his figure belied, Kevin John headed for the front door of the flat. He shut and double-locked it. Then he held up the keys once more.

'Shall I make you beg for them? On second thoughts not. There is no need, is there, for that kind of game between us? With your brains and my assistance, you should easily find the answer to the conundrum. Don't discount my assistance, will you? My charms are a snare; I'm not nearly as witless as I look. I shall lend you plenty of help, my celebrated hostage.'

Jemima put out a hand. Afterwards she was not quite sure what she had intended. Was it to grab — or perhaps simply possess — the keys from this unwelcome invader?

Kevin John stepped back one pace. 'One last thing to encourage you.' The broad sitting-room window was open. Without looking behind him, he tossed the keys upwards and outwards in a great arc. They swung heavily through the air, tinkled against the edge of the scaffolding, and touched something else, probably the low concrete parapet. Then, before Jemima's eyes, they vanished from sight downwards.

'Now we're all locked in for the night, as the old lady said in the ghost story,' observed Kevin John conversationally. 'No, no, you don't—' As Jemima lunged in the direction of the balcony, Kevin John neatly fielded her with his broad strong grasp. 'No maidenly cries for help, if you please. When you've solved the problem, Jemima Shore, Investigator, we'll telephone the police together. Till then — silence.' He put his finger to his stretched smiling lips.

The first few hours of Jemima's imprisonment at the hands of Kevin John passed very slowly. The manifest absurdity of her situation, kept like some latterday Rapunzel in the concrete tower, did nothing to reconcile her to it.

Rapunzel was the wrong fairy story to bear in mind. Jemima Shore was not being asked to let down her rippling corn-coloured hair for any likely prince to climb up it. The appropriate fairy story was that of the unfortunate peasant girl married off by her father to the king on the boastful (and erroneous) grounds that she could spin common straw into gold. Once wed, so far as Jemima could remember, the wretched girl had been shut up by her royal husband into a tower room well stocked with straw and told: 'Spin!'

In much the same way Kevin John seemed utterly convinced that if only he kept Jemima incarcerated long enough, she too would spin the few straws of evidence at her disposal into the gold of liberation.

The time also passed slowly because for the first few hours of her imprisonment, Jemima refused to listen to Kevin John's harangues and protestations. Nor would she discuss the case.

Kevin John let her sit down on the sofa. He shut the balcony window but – Jemima noted – did not lock it. Perhaps he too imagined the catch was, as it appeared to be, self-locking.

'I don't want anyone else coming up the route I took,' he remarked casually. Jemima did not deign to answer.

Kevin John took one of the large white armchairs and placed it opposite her, with his back to the balcony. He gazed at her with his curiously unwinking blue stare.

'He'll fall asleep,' thought Jemima scoffingly, 'and then I'll grab the telephone. The police will break the lock.' She was not carrying Pompey's private number with her since all her personal possessions, including – how foolish! – her handbag, were still in the first-floor flat. However under the circumstances, 999 would do just as well.

But Kevin John did not go to sleep. For some time he kept up a long self-pitying monologue on the subject of his relations with Chloe. He referred entirely to the past. The events of the last week were ignored as though they had not taken place: or perhaps he was hoping to tease Jemima into posing some pertinent questions. As it was, she did not respond. And not only was there self-pity; there was a perpetual air of self-justification in all he said.

'Beat her up!' he said at one point. 'Of course I beat her up. For one thing she was a' – obscenity – 'a Jezebel, a ruiner of good men's lives. And for another, mark you, she liked it.'

Jemima, thinking that in some twisted way that was probably true – Chloe had both hated and been fascinated by the violence she produced in Kevin John – still would not answer.

But in the event it was Jemima who fell asleep, not Kevin John.

When she woke up, the sitting room was lit by candle-light – one short thick white candle in an opaque holder was standing on the glass table. It was dark outside except for the glow of the street lights. Kevin John was bending over her, or as it turned out, he was bending over the table itself, depositing a tray. It contained a bottle of wine, opened, two glasses, some digestive biscuits, and a large plate of sardines.

'Nothing for me to cook for our candlelight supper. Pity: I'm a wonderful cook. Almost as good as Chloe – was. But I've done my best. Not many provisions you've allowed yourself, by the way, something less than perfect as a housekeeper, aren't you? Do your television fans know? Fridge turned off as well. Warm wine—'

While he was talking, Jemima made a quickly planned dive and succeeded in grabbing the little white telephone. She was frantically dialling the second digit as Kevin John disentangled himself from the tray by dropping it and sprang towards her. In the mêlée the bottle of wine rolled over and liquid started flowing fast along the glass table, then splashing off it onto the carpet. Biscuits and sardines were mashed together into the thick pile.

Neither gesture – neither her lunge nor his counter-spring had any point. Kevin John wrenched the receiver out of her hand and listened to it; then it dawned on him that there was no dialling tone.

It was Jemima who said bitterly: 'Cut off. This flat is empty, you know.' Momentarily she became reckless as to what information she gave Kevin John.

'Then you – what are you doing here?' It was his first visible moment of uncertainty.

'Packing up. I moved downstairs after – after she was killed.'

'It was luck, then, me finding you up here.'

Jemima favoured him with her ironic smile, not the lovely open smile which made the public adore her on television, but the other smile, the one which made government spokesmen, for example, with weak cases to defend slightly uncomfortable in retrospect. 'That Shore woman, not all sugar and spice, is she?' they would murmur questioningly in the direction of their wives once the interview had been shown.

'Luck, indeed.'

'So who *does* know you are up here?' He was quick to pick up the point.

'The police,' replied Jemima smoothly. 'They gave me the keys. A police officer will be along to collect them shortly.' Even to her own ears, the lie did not sound convincing. She did not dare consult her little gold bracelet watch, but she was aware it must be nearly midnight.

Kevin John snorted. His disbelief was clear.

For the first time Jemima found herself wondering rather desperately exactly when and by whom she would be missed. Not by Pompey, alas, nor by any member of the police force, or at any rate not for a very long while, longer than she cared to contemplate. The keys to Chloe's flat destined for Miss Katy Aaronson, were to be left downstairs in the office suite.

Pompey had not taken the Montagu Square number although he could easily ascertain it if he so wished. The trouble was that Pompey and Jemima had made no precise plans for a future meeting, their relationship in general depending on *ad hoc* consultations on either side. Besides Jemima had a shrewd suspicion that with the arrest of Kevin John, Pompey would be free and thus obliged to spend the weekend taking cuttings for the autumn in his greenhouse under Mrs Portsmouth's direction – for such he had predicted to be his fate.

'The gardening columns really get going at this time of year,' he had confided to her with gloomy resignation. 'And Mrs Portsmouth gets going with them.'

Miss Katy Aaronson was happily immured in the bosom of her family in Highgate enjoying the ritual of the Sabbath. Sir Richard Lionnel had picked up the broken threads of his life with astonishing ease and was at his home in the country – how quickly that abortive holiday with Chloe had been forgotten: the waters of fresh official engagements, such as entertaining that peregrinating minister, Lord Manfred, had already closed over his diary.

Frankly Jemima could not envisage anyone else likely to enquire about her whereabouts with any urgency. It was not that she did not have friends, lovers, admirers in plethora; just that she had taken the fatal decision to disappear in London … What an absurd ring the words now had in their original meaning!

Neither she nor Chloe had succeeded in bringing about any kind of effective disappearance. Something – no, someone – had caught up with Chloe in the flat she had pretended to abandon and pinned her down to it for ever like a butterfly in a case. Only in this case the pin had been a long sharp kitchen knife.

As for Jemima, her disappearance out of her own background, away from Holland Park Mansions and Megalith Television, had only succeeded in plunging her into the far murkier waters of her friend's life. Now Jemima was human enough to wish profoundly that some zany impulse would cause her assistant at Megalith Television, Guthrie Carlyle, to question exactly where she might be, and pursue that thought with his usual executive efficiency. For that matter, when was her secretary, the ebullient Cherry, Flowering Cherry as she was sometimes admiringly known within Megalithic House, due back from Corfu? Jemima, who had so often suffered from Cherry's over-zealous arrangements, was depressed to remember that she was not in fact due back until the end of August, shortly before Jemima would be repossessed of Holland Park Mansions.

Jemima Shore had finally succeeded, quite inadvertently, in disappearing in London. It would be many days before anyone missed her in earnest and, so far as she knew, many days before anyone came to unlock the penthouse flat. Not that she really expected many days to pass in this ludicrous form of captivity. But Jemima was honest enough to admit that the unpleasant prospect was not absolutely out of the question.

It seemed even less out of the question the next morning when Jemima awoke into the dawn. An exhausted grey light filled the sitting room, more reminiscent of a long night past than redolent of the promise of day. She squinted at her watch. Close on five o'clock. The candle had guttered to a standstill. Congested wax had spilled onto the glass table. It joined the debris of the crashed tray which Kevin John had not allowed her to clear up the night before.

She was aware that some noise had caused her awakening. Kevin John was still sitting opposite her – for they had finally fallen asleep as they sat, she rejecting with unrepressed horror the offer of Chloe's bedroom. His eyes were closed; he was emitting gentle half sighs, half snoring sounds which reminded her of how many bottles of wine he had consumed the night before – unaided but also undisturbed by her abstinence. The penthouse was at least well stocked with wine. His sighs, however, were not responsible for her waking.

It was Tiger, a dark golden blur outside the balcony window, who had roused her with his delicate infant's wail. He looked and sounded reproachful. Jemima guessed he was hungry. Knowing that she could open the balcony window, her first impulse was to let him in and feed him with the remnants of the sardines from Kevin John's tinned supper. Then she realized that here was a possible opportunity to summon help – supposing there was anyone around to summon at 5 am in Bloomsbury of a Sunday morning.

A note dropped, perhaps? One thing she did not propose to attempt was a descent via the scaffolding; and she had a gloomy feeling that the kitchen door to the fire escape at the back – poor Valentine Brighton's voyeur's route – would have been well and truly locked by the police.

'Don't do it, darling,' said Kevin John with only a flicker of his eyelashes to indicate wakefulness. 'If I'm the bully boy the police say I am, I wouldn't hesitate to cast you off the balcony after the keys would I, rather than let you yodel for help? Wait till you've solved our little problem. Then we'll both celebrate together.'

He put out his arm, brown, hairy, and very strong-looking, exposed from the sleeve of his white shirt, which was now like his grey trousers in a very crumpled condition.

'I was going to feed the cat.'

'Let him starve. I loathe cats: selfish little buggers. When do they ever put down a saucer of milk for you and me? Even worse than women.'

'He might appreciate the sardines more than I did.'

'Not a fishy sniff shall he have till you come up with your solution.'

But it was not until nearly eight o'clock, when the slight Bloomsbury bustle indicated the beginning of modest Sunday traffic, that Jemima finally agreed to listen.

Under the promise of coffee – thank God the remaining stores in the flat did not consist solely of white Muscadet – she bent her weary mind yet again to the problem of Chloe's murder. It had after all obsessed her all the week, until Kevin John's bullying had brought about a counter-reaction.

Besides, she had in mind asking for a bath once he was sufficiently mollified. The hot water system was still working. Tiger by this time had vanished, and she hoped that he had managed to scavenge a meal elsewhere.

'If not you, then who?' It was the old question: Who, Who? 'I'll accept your premise that you're innocent for the time being. Hostages can't be choosers. So long as you let me have another cup of coffee.'

'The bitch – I refer to your late friend – was meeting someone up here. I never believed that crap about looking for her notebook. Passed it on to the police, mind you. I could see it only made things worse for me if they thought I'd surprised her with someone else. Then I really might have done her in.'

'And him, too, I suppose.'

Kevin John favoured her with a boyish smile. 'Not necessarily, darling. We men stick together. We'd probably have a lot in common if she treated him as badly as she treated me. You know, the sweetness, the sex – she was very keen on that by the way; breathless, begging for it – then the torture of it, the infidelity, never knowing where she was. Oh Christ—'

He put his great black head in his hands.

'She's dead now,' said Jemima in a softer voice. 'And we're going to find out who did it. Look, I'll buy that,' she went on more rapidly, 'the fact she was meeting someone else. I've had my suspicions all along. Little things – the petticoat she wore, for example. Chloe was so particular, wasn't she? When she was working,' she added hastily. 'Then there's the question of her other lovers. Three of them. Bear with me—' She raised her hand as he gave a half groan. 'You want the truth. You promised to help me.'

Kevin John poured himself yet another glass of white wine. 'Shoot, sweetheart,' he said. Jemima herself swigged her coffee in great gulps from the oatmeal-coloured mug.

'After you split up, Chloe had three lovers. I'll call them, with great originality, A, B and C. A was a young man, a kind of drop-out, squatter, whatever you like, she knew him in Fulham. He also came here with her, to this building, probably not to this flat, squatted on another floor—'

To her surprise, Kevin John interrupted her: 'A is for Adam,' he said heavily. 'I know that. She told me about him. She boasted about him – the young body, like a Greek god, all that kind of shit. She could be very cruel, you know. That was the last time we met. In Fulham. So he was here, was he? Well, why the hell don't the police think he killed her?' His indignation was gathering momentum. 'Why pick on me?'

Jemima hesitated. Kevin John obviously did not know that Adam had sworn to seeing him leaving the building, evidence corroborated by an outside witness.

'Lack of motive chiefly. And lack of proof. I believe he has some kind of alibi. The police also don't think he did it because they think you did, I suppose. He *could* have killed her. He could have come up the fire escape from the third-floor flat.' Jemima briefly described Adam's hideout.

'And what do you think?'

'I suppose I think he's not the killing type.'

'And I am? Poor Kevin John, a lambkin among mankind, to be labelled a killing type just because he lays about him with his fists when the drink is in him—'

'Did you know Chloe was pregnant?' Jemima interrupted the tirade.

Sudden tears came into his eyes. 'The police told me. Asked me if I was responsible. Of course I wasn't. The only child we had, we could have had, *she* killed. That was a killing – a real killing – she said we weren't getting on, I was drinking – true enough, but it was *her* fault – she drove me to it.'

'I believe this Adam was the father.'

'There's your motive then!' The change of mood was mercurial. 'The young fellow doesn't want to be a father, kills her to avoid the responsibility. You know what the young are.' He gave a ghastly parody of a Harrods' matron's accent.

'A bit far-fetched, isn't it? In an age of abortion on demand. Besides, you haven't heard about B and C yet.'

'Get on with it then!'

'B was a man of substance, a famous man, whom Chloe hoped would marry her. We think she intended to palm off this baby on him;

she certainly intended to use it to lure him away from his wife. B certainly had a motive to murder Chloe, scandal, a lot to lose. But unlike A who had opportunity but not motive, B had no opportunity. B, you see, was having lunch in Soho with his wife. It is also unlikely that B would arrange a rendezvous in the penthouse – but that's another matter.'

'I suppose you won't tell me who B was?'

'Correct. You haven't heard about C yet. I think I ought to call him X rather than C because X is the man of mystery in all this. Someone unknown whom she met in the square gardens. One night when she was locked out of here, forgot her key. A casual encounter she called it. Supposing she was meeting that person, X, up here.'

'And he goes and does her in? Why?'

'I don't know yet. Maybe he sees her with you, gets the wrong impression.'

'And that might be anyone!' exclaimed Kevin John. 'That bitch was capable of having it off in the bushes with anyone, man, woman, in between—'

'You've no clues? Nothing she said?'

'My God!' he stopped. 'No, that's impossible.'

'Nothing's impossible. It's not even impossible that *you* killed her. Anyone leaving the building? Anyone she talked about?'

'What I was going to say, that's what I meant is impossible. But, wait, another train of thought. A famous man you said, a man of substance. Another impossible thing. That man, the tycoon, Lionnel—'

'You *knew* then—'

'Wait, Lionnel, the monster who put up this appalling building, but not such a monster after all, a man of taste and judgement, since he bought one of my pictures. Binnie Rapallo fixed it and since she has no taste whatsoever, he must have some himself. That Saturday, morning, lunch-time, whenever it was – I was so pissed, *and* pissed off – I saw him. I ran away from him. Didn't want to talk about any damn modern art under the circumstances, as you may imagine. You know what tycoons are, buy your work, and think they own you, including your merest conversation.'

'Where was he?'

'Outside this building. Coming from the Tottenham Court Road. Walking very fast. I thought he was coming towards me. I had the impression he ducked. Perhaps he saw me, or someone else he knew. I veered off. I was pissed as a newt, as I told you.'

'The time?'

'How the hell do I know? As I left the building. Whatever the police say. It was odd that he was walking so fast. I remember thinking that. I thought tycoons were unhurried. Or else had chauffeurs. Or both.'

Silence fell between them. Kevin John poured yet another glass of wine. Through Jemima's orderly mind were proceeding the following thoughts: not Lady Lionnel leaving the restaurant early in a taxi, but Sir Richard fetching that taxi for her; Sir Richard running out into the street in the absence of his chauffeur; evidence not given by Stavros to the police because it touched on a family row and Sir Richard was a good customer; Valentine's dying words – 'He came back'; Lionnel walking fast to Adelaide Square from 'The Little Athens', only a few minutes away across the Tottenham Court Road, and back again . . . About 1.30, the time Kevin John left the building . . . About the time Chloe Fontaine was killed. Above all, Valentine's 'He came back.'

Sir Richard Lionnel with motive *and* opportunity . . . Had the queen, shut up in her tower, succeeded in spinning straw into gold?

17

Lovers in disguise

'Now let me go,' said Jemima. 'I've kept my word.'

'You think he did it – that art-loving tycoon. Why is it, incidentally, that all the worst of them are art-loving?' Kevin John still sounded lugubrious. But he did not stop her when she walked to the balcony and pressed the catch to open it. 'Puss – Tiger—' she called into the morning air. Its freshness was a relief. But Tiger, once scorned, did not reappear.

'I need to prove it. The police too will want proof. I need to talk to Stavros, the owner of the restaurant.'

'A Greek colonel, eh? All those bastards are in league together.'

'No, an honest man. But a businessman.'

'If I let you go, what happens if you shop me to the police?'

'Shop you! You're on a murder charge already. Have you forgotten?' Dazed with wine and lack of sleep, perhaps Kevin John had forgotten. 'Next problem,' Jemima continued briskly, 'is how we get out. Do you recommend hollering blue murder – sorry, red innocence – flying a white flag, or dropping a brick on the head of the nearest passer-by in Adelaide Square—'

A mumble sounding like: 'You've promised, Jemima Shore, Investigator,' was his only reply. And then: 'You'll see me all right.' Jemima had an awful fear that the drink was overtaking him. True to her dread, Kevin John slipped further down the chair and finally onto the floor. He had fallen asleep or at least into that coma-like state which with him passed for sleep.

Oh my God, she thought, now how do I escape? Hollering was the least attractive of the alternatives. She did not wish for public attention at this moment: she needed to get to 'The Little Athens', re-examine

Stavros, work out a few times precisely, and then perhaps call Pompey with new evidence.

It might be easier to break a lock. Jemima inspected the kitchen door to the fire escape. The bolt she could draw back, but the police had also locked the door, and the key was missing. The glass was reinforced with wire. The front door was out of the question.

There was nothing for it but the balcony. Kevin John did not move as she stepped onto it. She was grateful for that. If she had to cry for help – with all the possible public consequences – she would prefer not to be accompanied by a drunken artist out on bail for murder.

Inspection of the scaffolding provided a happy surprise. Jemima had imagined that Kevin John's successive scalings of it had been an example of exaggerated intrepidity possibly due to inebriation. Now she saw that anyone even moderately athletic, with a head for heights (or the self-discipline not to look downwards), could have achieved this feat. The scaffolding was stoutly built, a credit to the Lionnel Estates. Even Kevin John's ability to elude public notice during his climbs was now more explicable. The scaffolding was quite deep as well as securely slung together. A man could well have worked there, in the shadow of the building, and not been spotted by a random passer-by.

Right. Where a drunken Kevin John Athlone could ascend, a sober Jemima Shore could descend. Slipping off her golden thonged sandals, which laced up her legs, Jemima tested her toes against the metal. Her dress remained a problem. Was a Jean Muir silk jersey dress, with all its virtues, really the right apparel in which to shin down scaffolding? It was tempting to strip to her bra and pants – but the arguments against reaching the ground in her underclothes, like those of crying for help accompanied by a man on a murder charge, were conclusive. Jean Muir it would have to be.

With brilliant improvisation, or so it struck her at the time, Jemima belted the flowing dress twice round her narrow waist with the gold thongs from her sandals. Barefoot, she embarked.

The journey was not so much long as, in spite of the solidity of the scaffolding, nerve-wracking. With relief, Jemima flopped down onto the staging-post of the concrete third-floor balcony. It was fortunate that she did not suffer from vertigo; she felt she might do so in future.

She was immediately aware – with another spasm of relief – of the presence of Tiger. Sleekly, he rolled onto his back at her feet, revealing the pale yellow fur of his tummy, and began to purr. This unprecedented friendliness was no doubt to be explained by the presence of a large bowl of milk in the corner of the balcony, and another bowl of something chopped, white enough to be chicken. There was a smaller saucer of water.

All in all, Jemima was not totally surprised – but once more relieved – to find the balcony window slightly ajar. At least she would be saved further perilous descent.

She peered through the smoked glass without being able to discern anything very clear except the confused swirl of that subterranean blue and something which looked like low modern furniture on the floor, cushions perhaps, which had not been there before. She inched the window open.

Then and only then the confused shapes of the cushions separated themselves and became white or rather pale; they also became two shapes. A Laocoon-like figure, writhing legs and arms, on the floor, resolved itself into Adam Adamson, naked; some unknown figure, equally naked except for a string of gold chains, rose hastily but gracefully from the floor, like some greyhound starting, gave a much less elegant squawk of dismay, and vanished in the direction of the subterranean bathroom.

Adam Adamson, undismayed, lolled back on his elbow.

'Pallas Athena,' he said. 'What strange moments goddesses choose to call. I was just tangling with the goddess Artemis, as you may have noticed.' He gazed at her.

His body had that confidence of nakedness associated with statues of the gods.

He went on: 'Yes, in that strange tunic effect and bare feet you really do look like a goddess. Why don't I imitate you and slip into something similar?' He rose, strolled into the bathroom in his turn and re-emerged with a towel knotted round his waist. Only the ugly geometric design, in keeping with the rest of the flat's aggressively modern décor, disturbed the picture.

Behind him, at least an inch taller, and clad in a bright green cat-suit, lurked a young woman with a highly sulky expression. From her small head, disdainfully carried on the long neck, and excessively long legs and narrow flanks, she might have been a model.

'The goddess Athena, the goddess Artemis,' Adam waved his hand.

'Miss Shore and I have met,' said the goddess Artemis; her accent was more gracious than her expression. Extending her hand, whose long fingers were serrated in gold rings, in a parody of a bountiful greeting, the girl in the green catsuit said: 'I'm Laura Barrymore, Isabelle Mancini's assistant.'

Had they ever met? Jemima really did not remember. There were many Laura Barrymores in the world. Nor did she particularly care, for that matter, why and wherefore Laura Barrymore was passing the time of day with Adam Adamson. Her concern was to find her way out of this flat and to a telephone. Then she could raise Stavros, Pompey, even Sir Richard Lionnel himself. The keys to the firstfloor, which now seemed like a paradise of a refuge, were still in her pocket.

Baldly, she addressed herself to Adam: 'Get me out of here. I don't care what you're doing here, by the way, just let me out. No questions to you, none to me.'

Adam raised an eyebrow but it was the measure of his unhurried self-confidence that he seemed prepared to do as she asked without further ado. It was Laura Barrymore who disturbed this amity.

'Miss Shore, I am truly aware that you must be wondering,' she began in a rush, 'but on my honour, I swear to you that I first came here with the absolute firm intention of rescuing Isabelle's letters, letters from that dreadful woman, well, of course one doesn't want to speak ill of the dead—' she paused, having evidently lost track of her explanation, then continued more firmly. 'That Saturday morning, you remember, when you telephoned. I thought that if *you* were in Miss Fontaine's flat, we could search together, you're famous for being so warm and understanding about human problems, I could explain to you—'

Jemima shot Laura Barrymore a look which was anything but symptomatic of those warm qualities recently ascribed to her.

Adam, who continued to regard Jemima with a slight smile, threw in: 'It's true you know,' he said. 'Our friend was fairly on the prowl. The trouble was she came to the wrong flat, and then, as they say, one thing led to another. I read her some Petrarch when I discovered what her name was and that seemed to turn her on. I never could resist goddesses you know. That coldness, that aloof air—'

'She was here – a week ago—' exclaimed Jemima incredulously.

'Oh yes, for a couple of happy hours. She went back and found her friend – shall we call her the goddess Hera, another jealous type – had arrived back unexpectedly from Paris, was there waiting for her.'

Jemima addressed herself directly to the girl.

'Is that true?'

But by this time Laura Barrymore, who had been knotting her long streaky blonde hair the while and pinning it on top of her head, had fully recovered her poise.

'And if it is,' she enquired coldly, 'what the fuck is it to do with you?' The refinement of her voice, from which all the mid-atlantic was now missing, made the obscenity sound far worse than it might have done, for example, on the vigorous lips of Kevin John Athlone.

'The police knew. I told them,' contributed Adam in a tone of mock helpfulness. 'You particularly instructed me to tell them everything.'

Yes, thought Jemima, not the killing type indeed; although there might be something to be said about Adam Adamson along the lines of not loving wisely but too often. And too precipitately. Still, as Miss Barrymore had so aptly observed, it was nothing to do with her. Adam's alibi, in its full irony, was now revealed; and the future of Isabelle Mancini and Laura Barrymore was even less her concern than that of Adam and Laura.

For her, another chase was on. The fox was Sir Richard Lionnel.

Adam Adamson went to the door, and towel-clad as he was, swept it open with style.

At this point Jemima observed with some surprise that the third-floor flat, the dark-blue subterranean cave, bore more rather than fewer signs of occupation than when she was last inside it. The image of the writhing white furniture had not been totally illusory. There were two new white plastic shapes on the dark floor; pushed together they might serve as some form of armchair or even sofa. Recently, however, they had been pushed widely apart; Jemima had a mental image that this had been effected by the athletic coupling of Adam and Laura.

There were other new traces of domesticity including a small table and some lamps. Yet by any reasonable calculations Adam should have given the place a wide berth once he had made his statement to the police. That had taken place on Sunday morning. A week ago. Even the most ardent revivifier might have twitched his cloak and passed on to fresh squares and buildings new after an experience like that.

Disregarding Laura Barrymore, who was now coldly buffing a long and glittering pearlized nail, Jemima said abruptly to Adam: 'You come and go as you please. Revivifying – squatting – whatever you call it. That's not quite the picture I get. You *live* here. That furniture wasn't here before. Explain if only to satisfy my curiosity. Then we'll both go out of each other's lives.'

'Why shouldn't he be here?' Laura Barrymore had glided to the position she seemed to prefer, which was just behind Adam's shoulder, her small snake's head clearly visible above it. 'It's his flat, isn't it?'

'Oh come now,' Jemima spoke coldly – the interjections of this grass-green Lamia were beginning to irritate her. 'To call it actually his – isn't that carrying revivification rather too far? Does Isabelle plan an article on the subject in *Taffeta*? "Back to Adam – modern style" with photographs?' These remarks, Jemima realized the moment she had uttered them, were not exactly those of the all-wise goddess she wished at this moment to personify. Adam clearly shared her opinion.

'I realize now to the full the difficulties presented by life upon Olympus,' he remarked plaintively.

Jemima smiled, her own sense of the absurd restored. 'How do you cast yourself then?' she could not resist asking. 'Please don't suggest Dionysus. No one I assure you is going to tear *you* into pieces . . .'

'Something in disguise,' he said gently. 'A minor god in a minor disguise. Perhaps I should reintroduce myself. We are all sons of Adam, as I told you, but I am also the son of Aaron. Adam Adamson by choice, preferring the old Adam to the old Aaron, but Adam Aaronson by birth.'

'Ah!' A short pause. 'Adam, brother of Katy. The brilliant one who dropped out from Cambridge.'

'Where he was studying architecture. The same.'

'How much of the rest of it was lies?'

'It depends on one's attitude to the truth. I first had the idea of revivifying this building from listening to my sister. She's an admirable girl, but no lover of the arts, to be frank. Listening to her endless disquisitions on the subject of Sir Richard Lionnel – she's madly in love with him of course – she and Francesca Lionnel have an unspoken alliance to fend off the rest – and thinking him only slightly less monstrous than his own building, I started to demonstrate. Katy didn't like it: she never really likes anything I do, ever since I got a scholarship to Cambridge and then dropped out, the scholarship she wasn't allowed to take. But she loves me all the same – in spite of everything – Adam, the baby brother, the only son, the boy. There's family life for you. You have a family?'

Jemima shook her head.

'How wise. To return to the sad story of this benighted building: at which point my late and lightsome friend, Miss Dollie Stover as was, quite coincidentally persuaded me to move in. From the street to the third floor. One of her reckless gestures, I suppose. Slipped me a key. She also seemed to dislike both the décor of the third floor – good thinking – and the woman who was responsible for it. A woman with a ridiculous name. Bunny something or other. I was her secret vengeance on this Bunny.'

'Binnie,' murmured Jemima.

'Nothing loath, I took the hint. I didn't reveal my connections. Nor for that matter did she reveal hers. We both as it were pulled the thickly woven expensive wool carpet of fantasy over each other's eyes. She, the mistress of the tycoon, posing as the skittish little-girl-loose; me, the brother of the tycoon's assistant posing as the squatter-in-danger-of-the-law.' At this point Laura Barrymore attempted to put one long serpentine arm round Adam's neck. Laura *entière à sa proie attachée*, thought Jemima. But Adam disengaged himself with a brisk movement and said: 'Not round the neck, I can't bear being strangled by women.'

It did not sound as if he was altogether joking. Then he went on: 'After I spoke to the police, Katy fixed it for me. Made it legitimate. That's her secret aim in life, I suppose, and this time I let her have her way. This is my flat now. The Lion's Den is now Adam's Garden of Eden: you see, Sir Richard did not care for the décor for some odd reason.'

'Isn't it funny, Katy Aaronson and I were at school together?' Laura put in suddenly, with a return to her gracious manner. 'Quite a coincidence.'

But Jemima did not care to stay and examine the coincidence. She did not think Adam would linger very long in Miss Barrymore's snake-like embrace; she had probably served her purpose, as Katy Aaronson had in a sense served hers. Unlike Chloe Fontaine, née Dollie Stover, formerly of Folkestone, Adam Adamson né Aaronson, formerly of Highgate, was a survivor.

Back on the first floor, Jemima knew the first telephone call she had to make.

'Sir Richard,' she began in her most formal manner. 'This is Jemima Shore, Investigator.' To her surprise he had answered the telephone himself. Perhaps by Sunday Sir Richard was bored in the country. It was certainly the impression given by his alacrity in answering her call.

'I would like you to talk to me; to come up to London and talk to me.' Whatever the rival claims of the minister and Lady Manfred – or the Medea-like Lady Lionnel – Sir Richard showed no hesitation in accepting her invitation. Nor did he hesitate when she named Chloe's penthouse flat as their rendezvous.

'You have the keys?'

'Yes, the police gave them to me so I could pack up my things.'

Jemima did not think it necessary to add that she had recently repossessed herself of them, having found them lying untouched in the gutter of Adelaide Square where they had fallen from on high, hurled by Kevin John.

With some strange feeling of the relentless pursuit of coincidence, Jemima found the rendezvous fixed for one o'clock. Or between one and two, depending on the traffic. Sunday. Eight days since Chloe had died.

She put down the receiver; she thought to make two other telephone calls. The first was to Stavros, already at 'The Little Athens'. The second call was to Isabelle Mancini.

She did not call Pompey.

Then she went for the last time onto the balcony of the first floor and gazed into the gardens. At this level the trees were more like barricades than floating galleons with the tops of their masts visible. The over-high parapet was like another barricade. It was odd how depopulated the gardens remained: in the other Bloomsbury gardens roundabout people desported themselves, lay on the dry and yellowing grass, looked upwards and imagined themselves on a perpetual bank holiday in the country. The bars which surrounded the gardens of Adelaide Square – a virtual cage with two gates, one at either end – constituted an effective discouragement. One could not readily imagine a passer-by climbing the railings.

Yet someone *had* climbed them – two people in fact. Chloe Fontaine had climbed them one hot summer's night, locked out without her keys including her own resident's key to the enclosure. And there she had on her own admission indulged in a carnal encounter with someone described by Pompey in his vein of wit, as a Sunday newspaper headline: The Lover in the Gardens. As Jemima gazed towards the forbidding railings and slightly depressing late summer shrubs, other memories floated back to her, not only Chloe's voice from the past – 'Still it was an interesting experience . . . rather a surprise altogether' – but other murmurs, from the people linked to Chloe in her life, now cruelly linked to each other by her death – for as long as the identity of her own murderer should be unknown. Once it was known, then the links would be broken.

The identity of that lover – another lover in disguise as Adam had been her, Jemima's, lover, and also Chloe's lover, in disguise – had it perhaps been staring her in the face all along? An identity which gave not only motive but opportunity.

Certain things for the first time became clear to her. More than ever, Jemima needed to confront Sir Richard Lionnel.

18
That fatal Saturday

As she re-entered the penthouse, Jemima felt all the old dread returning. Yet on this occasion it was tension for the role she knew she had to play rather than fear of the unknown which gripped her. For her, there were to be no more surprises in the short sad tale of the Chloe Mystery, only an unravelling which would also bring sorrow and a new form of tragedy in its wake. All the same, tension and a kind of nervous excitement would not be banished. It was almost as if the flat itself was aware of the strange concourse of people which Jemima, like Hagen in *Gotterdämmerung*, had summoned to the cause of revenge.

She herself was no longer the tunic-skirted, bare-footed goddess of the morning's flight. Immaculate in a plain navy-blue dress with white collar and short sleeves, she was deliberately presenting her most unruffled image, what Cy Fredericks of Megalith was apt to term 'your Jemima of Arc bit'. Golden bell of hair carefully controlled, dark stockings on her long legs above the high-heeled scarlet sandals, she smiled grimly at the irony of this single, unavoidable splash of red. Her gold sandals, thongless, were still in the penthouse flat. She did not wish to present herself as the avenging angel, not quite in that lurid light; but her television training had made her automatically select those elements in her small wardrobe which would make up the appropriate passionless appearance.

Already thus attired, she had called on Adam Adamson on her way up and invited him to attend some kind of mystery conference. Where he was concerned, mystery was, she knew, the right note to strike. Standing at the door of the third-floor flat – now his own domain – he was wearing the same clothes in which he had first waylaid her: white T-shirt, as pristine as Jemima's own dress, and jeans which looked newly washed. Should his cleanliness have made her more suspicious of his credentials as a squatter? On the other hand it had seemed logical that a revivifier should present a clean face to the world, and Adam himself had always rejected the label of squatter.

'You can bring Laura with you, too, if she's around. And Tiger, for that matter, who seems to have grown attached to you. Though I should warn you that Isabelle Mancini is due to arrive upstairs at any minute. And she's apt to be rather strong on the subject of disloyalty as she sees it.'

Adam smiled and indicated the floor of the flat with that grandiose wave of the hand he generally used to indicate the works of Sir Richard Lionnel. It looked like a very expensive luggage boutique: suitcases of all shapes and sizes, burgundy-coloured Cartier, Gucci, Hermès, any brand of luggage where initials were apt to be strewn all over the cloth or leather or tapestry, including innumerable small dressing-cases, were spread about.

'I think I've discovered that for myself,' he said. 'These came round in a taxi with a letter which should by rights have ignited the paper it was written on. Laura tells me that Dollie – Chloe – wanted to make use of Isabelle's love letters. I can only suppose she had never received her written insults else she would have made use of them. This one was definitely worthy of inclusion in some anthology or novel.'

His next words reminded Jemima that Adam, among his other qualities, had always been able to read her thoughts.

'Not very long, I think,' he went on. 'The luggage, I mean, its stay on this particular floor. Laura should really share a flat with Katy, don't you think? They both, in their different ways, need to strike out. Thank you for the invitation: Laura and Tiger and I will be happy to attend your mystery conference.'

To Kevin John, Jemima merely said, much more briskly: 'There's going to be a reception. A reception and an explanation. Are you up to it?'

'Who am I going to receive?' He had greeted her return with a cry of joy and the words: 'I knew you would come back and rescue me.' Then he gazed at her mesmerically with those vast blue eyes, which only the depth of their hue rescued from being cold and even calculating.

Otherwise her entry was something of an anticlimax after the dramas of her previous arrivals. It was a relief merely to find Kevin John sitting in the white armchair, alive, and even fresh-looking. His hair, which was flopping over his forehead, gave the impression of being newly washed. Not much could be done about his crumpled white shirt and grey trousers, but his tie was fastened, and the jacket of his suit flung over his shoulders with some attempt at style.

Jemima's first thought was of relief that he was no longer drunk. He did not even smell of alcohol, but, Jemima noticed wryly, of her own Mary Chess sandalwood bath oil which he must have found in the bathroom and poured out in quantities. Her second thought was to be surprised all over again, now he was tidied up, by his amazing good looks, undiminished by Time's rough hand.

Kevin John had also done some kind of tidying-up job on the flat itself. The mess of sardines and biscuits had been eliminated – quite efficiently; but then Kevin John, who had boasted of being a good cook, was no doubt a good cleaner as well.

There was one further change. On the floor, Chloe's own novels had been turned over onto their backs. Now all there was to be seen was the title *Fallen Child, Fallen Child*, over and over again. Jemima wondered if Kevin John, rather than the police, had been responsible for the original montage of accusing helpless photographs which she had found when she re-entered the penthouse. If so, he had repented of the gesture.

'*You* are not going to receive anyone,' she told him, 'But through this door will come in a matter of time a small procession. Then we'll have a reception followed by an explanation. As for the guests – why not let their identity remain a surprise? But first I have to test something.'

Jemima opened the cupboard in the corner of the sitting room, looked in then shut the door again, leaving Kevin John murmuring rather dazedly: 'A party, does she mean there's going to be a party – here? Maybe I should ask Dixie – no, Dixie's a bastard, ask Croesus, Croesus is a good fellow.' He found the word Croesus very difficult to pronounce clearly.

Shortly after Jemima returned, the door was pushed open and Adam Adamson stood in the doorway. Tiger, a golden familiar, crouched on his shoulder. Laura Barrymore, another golden familiar, followed him. She had obviously dug into her expensive suitcases, since she had changed the bright green cat-suit for a pair of scarlet and black printed tigerskin trousers and a transparent scarlet chiffon blouse; across this her numerous gold chains and red beads acted as a necessary breast plate. She no longer looked like a serpent, but with her spare curved body and hair now braided, she looked like some blonde Indian warrior.

Before Laura had time to construct one of her gracious greetings, there was a noise behind her as though of some vessel propelled forward by a series of noisy gusts of wind. Isabelle Mancini, when she appeared, puffing heavily from the effort of the stairs, did indeed resemble some kind of stalwart ship, a trireme perhaps, her flailing arms in their grey draperies representing the oars. She also retained a certain splendid dignity as, chin well forward, black hair strained back, she swept rather than pushed Laura out of the way, ignoring Adam altogether, and entered the penthouse flat.

Then and only then did Isabelle judge the moment right to give a scream, as though at some monstrous sight, a freak of nature: 'Terr-r--rible child! Tr-r-raitor! What are you doing here? Tell me! Speak! I demand you speak at once! Speak! Talk to me of your disloyalty, your t-r-r-eachery . . .' It would never be known whether Laura Barrymore would indeed have spoken on these interesting topics, let alone whether Isabelle Mancini would have drawn breath for long enough for her to be allowed to do so. For at that moment there was a new, and in its own way more dramatic, arrival.

Sir Richard Lionnel, perhaps because he was the owner of the stairs, positively bounded up them. There was no trace in his energetic manner and fit stride of the gravity with which he had entered the flat a week ago, accompanied by Pompey. His tonsured ring of black curly hair sprang from his head in its devil's horns, and his black eyes snapped and glittered with something which looked very like anticipatory joy.

I am sorry, Sir Richard, thought Jemima, when she had received him, crossing her dark-stockinged knees discreetly and tugging at her short navy-blue skirt, these red shoes – which it was impossible to underplay – are not a portent. This is not a rendezvous. Nor do I wish to decorate the third-floor flat, or this flat, or any of your dwellings. Nor even live permanently in Montagu Square which no doubt you would offer me.

But Sir Richard, if disappointed or even quite simply amazed by the array of people he found before him in the white sitting room, now with its balcony windows drawn right back, remained imperturbable. He greeted each person in turn with great urbanity as though welcoming directors to a board meeting of uncertain temper. Isabelle Mancini found the article on his wife and Parrot Park in *Taffeta* enthusiastically recalled – 'the best photographs of Francesca ever taken – what was the girl's name?' Laura Barrymore, who it transpired had acted as editorial assistant on this feature, got a polite salute but no more, which led Jemima to suppose that she was one of the few members of the female sex Sir Richard did not find personally fascinating. Laura, visibly pulling herself together after Isabelle's assault, managed a sketchy imitation of her former gracious manner.

The encounter which had caused Jemima most anxiety in anticipation was that between Sir Richard and Kevin John. But once again a diversion robbed it of its full flavour. It had to be faced that the ugly look had returned to Kevin John's face, making him more bull-like and less overtly handsome in his decayed film-star fashion. Also he loosened the tie at his neck, an automatic gesture which Jemima did not like the look of, and there was a knotted vein beating at the corner of his temple. But at this moment Laura Barrymore, someone with an obvious gift for choosing the dramatic moment for her appearance – and in this case her disappearance – gave a shriek, and clutched her gilded throat.

'Isabelle – Adam – together?' she cried through a series of sobs in which her accent became more and more refined like that of the transformed Eliza Doolittle. 'This is utterly intolerable.' And throwing out her long arms, so that her tight golden bracelets flashed, she fled down the penthouse stairs and out of sight. This time, after an interval of slightly stunned silence during which the others present looked mainly at their toes or, in the case of Sir Richard Lionnel, out of the window, the front door was heard opening and shutting.

Isabelle was the first to break the silence. 'Idiot gir-r-rl!' she exclaimed. 'Where will she go? Dressed up like that at lunchtime, after all I have taught her.' But there was a gleam of satisfaction in her eye. Isabelle smelt victory. Jemima thought the expensive suitcases would soon be making the return journey from Adelaide Square.

'Why don't the rest of you all sit down?' Jemima spoke with determination before the spell of their silence could be broken. At this, she was faintly amused to see that the four remaining participants in the mystery conference reacted exactly according to character. Kevin John relapsed rather than sat back into the large white armchair he had previously occupied.

Sir Richard Lionnel ushered Isabelle towards the white sofa, helped her to sit down with a certain solicitousness, and then, remarking politely: 'Thank you, I myself prefer to stand', took up his station with his back to the balcony. He had already lit one of his black cigarettes, which he was smoking rapidly, flicking the ash in the direction of the grey and white plants. Whether by choice or chance, he was situated so that his expression could not be checked.

Adam Adamson, without saying a word, sat down exactly where he had been standing, not far from the doorway; he descended cross-legged as though he were a piece of furniture which had been neatly folded up to save space. Then he murmured *sotto voce*: 'Speak, goddess.'

Jemima seated herself beside the sitting-room cupboard, in an oatmeal swivel-backed office chair which she had never occupied. It was – had been – Chloe's writing chair. In her brief interlude of peace in the flat, Jemima had instinctively avoided it. Now it seemed the right place from which to speak in her capacity of recording, if not avenging, angel.

'First of all, this is a story of love,' Jemima began, without further preamble. 'Love and of course later on death. But primarily a story of love. I thought we were dealing with hatred, and all the time we were dealing with love. Until I got that emphasis right, thanks to a chance remark by one of you quite recently, I never began to understand the truth about the death of Chloe Fontaine. Oddly enough the police – Detective Chief Inspector Portsmouth – got that right from the first. All the stabs. He said to me: "sign of a lover, more likely than not".'

At this point Sir Richard Lionnel threw away his black Sobranie and immediately lit another one.

'Miss Shore, if I understand you right' – he spoke still with urbanity, but the impatience was not totally disguised; the drags on his cigarette were also faster – 'you have asked us all here on a Saturday morning to tell us about the death of poor Chloe Fontaine. If that is so, aren't you rather pre-empting the work of the police? And possibly, if I may say so, rather embarrassing our friend here?'

'I'm not your friend, you bastard,' said Kevin John thickly. '*She's* my friend and my darling, Jemima Shore, Investigator. I asked her to solve the mystery of the universe and she has. As for the police' – he made an extremely rude gesture – 'that's for them, all of them, the long and the short and the tall of them. I need a drink.' He rose heavily to his feet and shambled off to the kitchen, returning with a bottle of wine and one glass which he proceeded to fill, drink down and fill again. No invitations to share the wine were given, and no one present appeared to regret this fact.

'A story of love,' resumed Jemima as though none of these interruptions had taken place. 'And all of you here, in your different ways, loved Chloe. It's what you properly have in common, it's what links you together, much more than your common implication in her death.'

Isabelle frowned. 'But Jemima, my darling,' she began in a puzzled voice, ''e did it. Ver-r-ry sad. A cr-r-rime of passion – 'oo does not understand it? But 'e did it.' She indicated Kevin John, proceeding at that moment relentlessly to his third glass of wine. ''E was drunk, of course; *mais quand même.*' Isabelle shrugged her shoulders.

Jemima ignored her. 'That's why it's as well that Laura has left us. Because Laura Barrymore certainly did not love Chloe Fontaine. She would have been the odd one out in our chain, broken the links. But for the rest of you: let us take you first, Sir Richard. No, Isabelle, let me speak. You, Sir Richard, loved her. She fascinated you; she was your romantic type, as you told me yourself, wayward, emotional, unpredictable as she was in everything except her work, the exact opposite to those strong sensible women with whom you take care to surround yourself on the domestic front, your wife, his sister' – she pointed to Adam. 'No, Isabelle, let me go on.

'She, Chloe, represented danger, didn't she? That was half the point of it all. The penthouse flat in your own building, the secret holiday. Unfortunately Chloe saw things from exactly the other angle. When Chloe decided that you represented for her security, money, protection and the abandoning of the endless struggle to support herself in the world's most precarious livelihood, novel-writing, in favour of ease and luxury, including luxury to write if she so wished – well, you weren't interested were you?'

'You're right about one thing, Miss Shore,' Sir Richard spoke without emotion. 'In my own way, I did love her. Having said that, as far as I'm concerned there's really no more to be said on this rather distasteful subject, so if you will excuse me—'

'Ah, but forgive me, there is. Quite a lot more to be said. You see, Chloe – in her own way a very determined woman even if her objectives were sometimes a little ill-defined – had decided that nothing would satisfy her but security, the security of marriage. And that meant obliging you to leave your wife, something you were manifestly loath to do. For one thing, Lady Lionnel is an extremely jealous woman not likely to relinquish her husband of many years' standing without a struggle. Then you, particularly at the present time, had a great deal to fear from scandal, with a grand new job coming up.'

'No, Sir Richard, it was a delicate operation to make you get a divorce. Chloe knew that. Then, when fate dealt her an unexpected card in the shape of pregnancy, she made the mistake of thinking it was an ace. She thought she could persuade you into marriage by the lever of the child. Whereas in fact the card was not an ace, but the most diabolical kind of joker – for not only was the child not yours, as she herself was well aware, but it also *never could have been* yours—'

From Adam's startled expression, Jemima realized that he had not know Chloe had been pregnant. He looked rather white.

'She was a liar,' said Lionnel rather gruffly. 'And – well, that's enough. I still loved her.'

'Yes, you loved her. You loved her enough to come round to Adelaide Square, hot foot, that fatal Saturday. You came to warn her about your wife, didn't you, Sir Richard?'

'Don't deny it! I saw you, you murdering bastard.'

For a moment it looked as if Kevin John, having interrupted, might spring at Lionnel. But Jemima went relentlessly on. 'You worried that Lady Lionnel, who had come up from Sussex to "The Little Athens" to confront you, would come here to Adelaide Square and find Chloe. So you hurried round, on the pretence of getting a taxi, hurried round – it's not far, and you had the alibi, it's always difficult to get taxis in the Tottenham Court Road, especially on a Saturday.'

'Clever of you to work that out, Miss Shore. Stavros, I suppose. I should never have taken the risk of taking a woman of your intelligence to the same restaurant. Do the police know?'

'Not yet.'

'But I'm going to tell them,' Kevin John threw in belligerently.

'On the contrary,' interrupted Jemima. 'Even at the end of this mystery conference, you have nothing to tell them about him. Nothing at all. Because you see, Sir Richard Lionnel did not kill Chloe Fontaine. Shall we say he did not love her enough to kill her?'

There was a silence while Jemima watched the vein beating in Kevin John's temple.

'For having reached seventy-three Adelaide Square so rapidly, he veered away,' she continued. 'Yes, Kevin John, he veered away as though he had seen someone he knew. Your own words to me last night – or was it this morning? Having come round to warn her about his wife, having telephoned her first but got no answer (you told the truth about that telephone call to the police, Sir Richard, if not the whole truth), you saw someone you knew, someone dangerous to you, outside the building. At that sight, you veered away. You rushed back to "The Little Athens", getting a taxi on the way. Chloe was never warned, and Lady Lionnel, for all her threats, satisfied with the scene she had made, went back to Sussex. No, Sir Richard, it was not you who came back.'

'True. All perfectly true.' Sir Richard extended the immaculate white cuffs from his tweed jacket and inspected them gravely, as though confirming them rather than Jemima Shore in the truth of their remarks.

'Then who did the bastard see?' enquired Kevin John truculently. 'Who are we talking about? Me, by any chance?'

'No, not you, Kevin John. You didn't kill Chloe Fontaine: a point you've made over and over again – to the police, to me, and to anyone else who would listen, and it's true. Perhaps in the end you didn't love her enough, or desire her enough, to pursue her through to the end. You could leave a new happy life in Devon – Cornwall? sorry – with a new young happy girl, whom Chloe called "submissive", and come up to London on a bender, try and seek her out, the ever elusive she, Chloe, the one that got away, the unsubmissive one.

'But in the end, when all that was over, when you'd delivered a few blows, when you'd drunk more than a few drinks, you were prepared to go back to Cornwall, weren't you, into the embraces of another, and forget her. In short, when she delivered her final ultimatum – that fatal Saturday—'

'"Get out of my life, you drunken slob!" That's what she said. She never had a lover as good as me, she knew that.' Kevin John sounded both childish and indignant. 'And now: you drunken slob, that's all I was to her. There's gratitude for you, there's women for you. I used to screw her all night, and at the end of it all – you drunken slob.'

There was a change of tone. 'Added to which, she'd got away with my best picture, the best damn picture I ever painted.'

'And you went. The police didn't believe it. But I did. You went. No, Kevin John, you didn't love her enough to kill her.'

Isabelle Mancini rose and, as though about to sing, settled her flowing grey veilings round her, then clasped her fine strong hands together. Silver bracelets, looser, heavier than the constricting golden serpents which adorned Laura Barrymore, clanked down her arms as she did so and gradually settled like hoops over a fat peg at a fair.

'Thees is absur-r-rd, dulling.' She sounded hysterical, and there were tears in her eyes. But Adam's swift uprising from the floor forestalled whatever metaphorical aria she would have sung.

'In case there's any doubt in your mind,' he said in a careful voice, very different from the usual carefree richly embroidered tone he affected, 'I did love her – a little. I find it very easy to love people a little. I love you a little, Jemima Shore, Investigator, for that matter. But more than that at the present time is outside my present capacity.' He spoke as though he had measured himself out like a medicine, and found the vessel destined to receive it not large enough. 'In theory I regret her death, and the death of her unborn child, quite as much as the destruction of the buildings Sir Richard Lionnel has murdered. Whether or not it was anything to do with me, is immaterial since it was a life. In practice I can express myself much more freely about the buildings. You can take it from that, Pallas Athena, that I did not kill Chloe Fontaine.'

'I know that, Adam.' Jemima thought it unnecessary to add that she also knew, had in a sense witnessed first hand, the exact nature of his alibi. 'No, be quiet, Kevin John, let me continue.' She turned to Isabelle, down whose cheeks tears were now freely flowing.

'The fourth person who loved Chloe, was you, Isabelle. Yes, you did love her. I suspect in your heart of hearts you love her still, for all her disloyalty, her treachery in using your letters in her novel, her cruel threat to publish those letters in the anthology Valentine Brighton commissioned. That's because you, with all your concentration on disloyalty, are loyalty itself – I think you gave your warm heart to her and never quite managed to withdraw it.

'For it was you, Isabelle, who gave me the clue to the true killer of Chloe Fontaine. That day in "The Little Athens", when we talked about Chloe's need for violence, even from those she loved. There was someone you mentioned – do you remember; a fifth person who loved her, but could not by temperament provide that violence? If only he had been able to give her something like that – the violence she craved, you said, "life would have taken a different turn for Chloe". Isabelle, do you remember? You were right. For that person, that lover, did in the end, provoked beyond all endurance, find the violence in him to proceed, the violence she wanted. And in so doing he killed her.'

'Valentine,' said Isabelle in a sad far-off voice, 'Valentine Brighton. Poor boy.'

19

'Tell me who to kill'

'Yes, Valentine Brighton. Valentine: the lover in the gardens.' Peace, a strange resigned calm, had been restored. Jemima and Sir Richard between them had had to restrain Kevin John, who at her words had bounded out of his chair with surprising force considering his condition, fists doubled, his attitude expressing what he scarcely needed to put into words: 'Tell me who to kill.'

The knowledge, when it penetrated, that Chloe's murderer was beyond his personal vengeance, caused him further furiously expressed anguish. It was some time before all this turmoil subsided.

'I told you that this was a story of love. Love unrequited, love exploited. Valentine Brighton, inhibited, repressed, the only child of a dominating mother, fatherless from an early age, a classic text-book case perhaps; with a very low sex drive indeed, if any drive at all – that fact was far more important than whatever direction it took – from the first he was utterly fascinated by Chloe Fontaine. You saw the truth of that, Isabelle, with your own knowledge of love.

'Never mind all his little throwaway pretend-snobbish jokes, the ones that made us all wonder secretly whether they weren't for real, whether he wasn't at heart a great deal more snobbish than he admitted: "Mummy wouldn't like it, Chloe wouldn't go down well with the neighbours" and so forth. Mere persiflage to disguise feelings which were all the more violent because he couldn't express them – physically, that is.

'In the meantime he makes do with his double role of confidant and publisher: confidant while Chloe goes to bed with half London, or so it seems to him, the outsider, the observer. But still in a sense he still possesses her, doesn't he? He's the only one, for example, who knows

478

the truth about her liaison with you, Sir Richard, because he's so safe, or rather Chloe thinks he's so safe, which is rather a different matter.

'Chloe-watching, for that is what it was, became an obsession with him. And then a mania. For Chloe, courtesy of Sir Richard Lionnel and Lionnel Estates, actually came to live in Bloomsbury, the next-door square to his office, the actual square where he had his own small London flat. And this square, Adelaide Square, has gardens, thick shrubby deserted gardens, to which only residents have the key.

'Chloe's move to Bloomsbury gives new life to Valentine's passion. It brings death to Chloe.

'To begin with, Valentine can see so much more of her comings and goings; it's easy for example to observe the entrance to seventy-three Adelaide Square from the gardens; I know, I've done it – I saw you, Adam, on the afternoon of her murder ... As an occupation, Chloe-watching was probably often difficult to resist for a lonely man on a hot summer's evening. I expect he always swore to himself he'd never do it again. We all plan, don't we, to resist our secret self-destructive pleasures the next time?' Jemima thought back to past loves of her own, married loves, telephone numbers dialled without hope or reason and answered, predictably, by wives; houses with lighted windows, and other windows even more hauntingly un-lighted, hopelessly regarded from a taxi at night ...

Jemima went on, wrenching her thoughts back: 'But Chloe too had the right to use these same gardens. A right on the whole, she didn't exercise – too busy elsewhere, a cynic might say. Until one fine day, one fine night rather, Chloe forgot the keys to number seventy-three ... We shall never know the circumstances under which she forgot them, as a result of which she climbed into the square gardens (the key to the square was with the flat keys). She had the idea of sleeping out there, it was after all summer, and it was very hot. But it is tempting, is it not, to think she sought her own fate? Perhaps her story to me afterwards wasn't true; perhaps she didn't forget her keys   Chloe in that respect was the reverse of careless; perhaps after a dull evening out, she glimpsed Valentine lurking and the spirit of devilry took over; it's not important – and, I repeat, we shall never know. They're both dead now.'

'What is important is the fact that that night, that fine wild summer's night, evidently inspired something new in Valentine, extinguished some long-held fear, conquered some inhibition, lit the vital fire so long laid. And Valentine – the resident lover, the lover with the key, became the lover in the gardens.

'They had what Chloe afterwards called "a casual encounter" – a surprising one, short-lived, because she by this time was utterly determined to marry you, Sir Richard. It was also a carnal encounter. A very brief one. That short duration must have caused Valentine enough pain in itself, but cruellest of all was the fact that Chloe continued to tell him, her erstwhile lover for at least one passionate night, all about her plans for Richard Lionnel.

'It was at this point that Valentine's Chloe-watching took a desperate turn. First he discovered a route up to this flat by the fire escape, at the back of the building. Again, was this discovery choice or chance? He told me the latter. But it's not important. What is important is that he also found a loose brick in the back wall, or loose enough, Sir Richard, with due respect to Lionnel Estates, for him to prise it away.

'He did so. He probed further. He was confronted by a picture. Or rather the back of a picture whose front he knew well. This picture was called "A Splash of Red".' Kevin John gave a kind of groan.

'It hung in her bedroom. He'd often seen it, as we see it now.' Jemima uncrossed her dark legs in their scarlet sandals and walked unhurriedly towards the bedroom doors. She opened them in the same deliberate fashion. The painting stared down at them, the violence of the subject matter made more shocking by the fact that the bedroom itself was now empty – clean, white, virginal – except for the white-shrouded bed.

Isabelle shuddered. She said something which sounded like: 'R-r-repulsive.' She might have been referring to Valentine's behaviour.

Jemima continued: 'In this picture Valentine cut a hole. To put it bluntly, a spy-hole.' She did not look to see if Kevin John, or for that matter Richard Lionnel, winced. 'And so Chloe-watching took on another dimension. Did she know? In this case I think it unlikely, but once again, we'll never know.

'I'll pass over speculation and cut to Saturday, the fatal Saturday of her death. Several things happened on and around that day, leading up to her murder, and I'll try and put them in order, so that you, like me, can understand the tragic progression. On Friday evening Chloe installed me in the penthouse flat as caretaker and cat-sitter in her absence; this was primarily because Lionnel was worried that the Press would pick up his affair with Chloe, and she had the brilliant idea that I, of all people, being a member of the media, would be able to fend them off. I was of course quite innocent myself as to the true nature of her holiday. Then Chloe herself departed to spend the weekend – the weekend only – on the first floor while you, Sir Richard, took in your Downing Street meetings.

'In the meantime I received two telephone calls, or rather two *types* of telephone call: the first came from Chloe's parents, who had expected to see her in Folkestone and never received the letter putting off the visit. The second came from Valentine and I think were obsessional calls no longer directed necessarily towards Chloe, or even towards me who received them; they were the measure of the madness which was now enveloping him.

'Because, you see, Valentine had taken vengeance into his own hands and had tipped off Lady Lionnel in Sussex about her husband's secret little holiday with the pretty lady writer. There can be no question that that information was passed on deliberately. Whereupon Lady Lionnel insisted on coming up to London to confront her husband. And Valentine, he too was in London. He was here, not to warn Chloe as he pretended to me, but to gloat. You, Sir Richard, tried to warn her. But Valentine, the watcher, wanted to observe in his twisted way, his darling, his loved one, receiving her come-uppance at the hands of the woman he had deliberately set upon her.

'Unfortunately it is now, quite independently, that Chloe has her inspiration about her parents. If the wife can stage a scene, so can the mistress. She's pinning everything on this holiday, but so far Sir Richard isn't rising to the bait – just invoking the name of his notoriously jealous wife. However, Chloe knows that her stepfather is still quite strong-minded enough in his late seventies to express himself forcibly on the subject of pregnancy and marriage to the highest in the land – in this case exemplified by you, Sir Richard. She had planned to tell you about her pregnancy while you're both abroad, but now this seems a better way to do it, more difficult for you to back out, a gambler's throw, perhaps, but then Chloe in her personal life was ever a gambler.'

Sir Richard did not react, merely drew on his black cigarette. Against the light his expression remained unreadable. Jemima passed swiftly on: 'Chloe has written to her parents with a view to a visit and breaking the news to them personally. But Sir Richard's weekend session at number ten changes all that. She puts off her trip to Folkestone. Then she telephones her parents to invite them to London instead and discovers to her horror that her second letter putting off her visit hasn't arrived. In fact her first letter, confirming her visit, has arrived only that morning. She hasn't thought about them for so long, or written or visited them – hasn't needed them, you might say – that the normally careful Chloe has failed to note their change of postal address. They're so worried that they've already telephoned me to check up. Still, the dramatic news that Chloe is pregnant overrides everything. Her mother's too frail, but her step-father agrees to come up on Saturday afternoon.'

Isabelle gave a gasp.

'*Mais c'est incroyable,*' she exclaimed. 'She 'ated babies. Books not babies, 'ow many times 'ave I 'eard 'er say it?'

'Not this baby, Isabelle. Because she thought it would help her in her plan. But it's now that there's a hitch. One thing she doesn't know about – you, Kevin John, you who have erupted back into her life like the splash of red you are – only she doesn't know it yet.

'Kevin John, quite unknown to Chloe, had made an early-morning appearance in the penthouse and found me there. We'll draw a veil over that. He came back again at lunchtime. This was the fatal return. For this was the return which Valentine unexpectedly witnessed. Yes, Kevin John, he saw you. Through the hole in the picture. The hole he had made to spy on Chloe.'

A reference to his own picture did at least penetrate Kevin John's consciousness. His fists clenched again and he swivelled his blue eyes in that direction. Then he delivered a stream of obscenities about the late Lord Brighton, which left Sir Richard unmoved, caused Adam to yawn, and provoked Isabelle to murmur something Gallic and disgusted.

'You, Kevin John,' went on Jemima, 'the force of sexuality, of violence, all he could never be, all of which he confidently believed had been rejected from Chloe's life; Sir Richard – security – that he could understand. But your kind of rampant sexuality, never. It cracked something in him, to see you there, sent him mad. It was you who came back, Kevin John, just as the police thought, except you didn't kill her. You're so fatally at home, aren't you, or so he thought, with a razor in your hand. So she'd lied, lied all along, the one thing she never did to him, swore she never did. "I always tell the truth to Valentine, he can't resist that" – her own words to me.

'Never mind that Valentine wrongs Chloe. It's actually *your* razor, Sir Richard. She hasn't gone back to you, Kevin John. Far from it. She's not even present. Later, when she does return, she calls you a drunken slob, in effect throws you out. Valentine doesn't know that, for at this point he leaves, goes away, back into the gardens where you, Sir Richard, later spot him watching the house. Yes, it's Valentine Brighton you saw, Sir Richard, your country neighbour, the friend of your wife, the trouble-maker. From him, and his gossiping malicious mother, you flinch away.

'Valentine Brighton waits in the square gardens until he sees you, Kevin John, leaving. From something you said to me earlier, I think you may also have glimpsed him. But you thought he was harmless, "that's impossible" you told me—'

'Bloody harmless, was he?' exploded Kevin John. 'If I hadn't been such a' – more obscenities followed, applied equally to Kevin John himself and to Valentine Brighton – 'I'd have spotted what he was up to. Yes, I saw him in the gardens, lurking in the bushes, he was just the type, wasn't he? Not even a pansy, just a neuter. Impossible, yes I damn well did think it was impossible that *he* should be anybody's lover let alone banging away like that in the middle of central London—'

'Then Valentine can't bear it any longer,' continued Jemima, thinking it prudent to cut short this tirade. 'He rushes back into the building. Runs up the front staircase this time. The front door of the penthouse is still open. Chloe's surprised. She's still in her white petticoat. Why?

'Now the answer to that one is in fact very simple, although for a long time I didn't spot it. Like you, Kevin John, like Valentine himself, I thought she must be having a rendezvous in the penthouse with a lover, and that baffled me. The police of course thought she indulged in some kind of love scene with you, Kevin John. Or at least the preliminaries to it.

'Then suddenly it came to me. When does a woman take off her clothes? Down to her petticoat. In the daytime. The reason is obvious. Not to receive a lover but to change them! She was in her own flat, wasn't she? She knew I was out. She'd come up to the flat simply to *change* her clothes. And why did she change? Why, quite simply to receive her stepfather suitably dressed for the occasion, for the confrontation. You all remember how meticulous Chloe was about that kind of thing – neat, the right clothes for the occasion.

'You see, she only had holiday clothes downstairs with her. She wouldn't have wandered up the staircase in her petticoat. She came up here and merely took off her dress beside the sitting-room cupboard, where she had stored her London clothes to make room for mine in the bedroom.

'At this point, before she has a chance to choose a dress the cat escapes and, frightened of the traffic outside, she dashes after it, all the way down to the basement, just as she told you, Kevin John. Which means she misses you coming up the stairs; you're by now in the bedroom; she returns, is about to put on another dress, when you, Kevin John, surprise her. Being Chloe she has already hung up the dress she has removed. But the cupboard, which she had locked the previous evening in my presence, is still open.

'After your departure, Valentine rushes in. We'll never know exactly what happened then, since they're both dead. Perhaps she taunted him, teased him, flirted with him a little in her provocative way, not realizing the seriousness of the situation, of his madness. I think it more than likely she taunted him with her pregnancy: babies, as he once told me, horrified him. It was her, Chloe, that he wanted.

'And so he killed her, killed her with one of your long sharp knives, Isabelle.' Isabelle gave a gasp and the tears started to flow again. 'The knives you gave her, before she cut your friendship to pieces.'

'Cruel, poor little Chloe,' whispered Isabelle.

'One stroke killed her: he was strong, expert, a sportsman, brought up in the country even though he had rejected it. The other stabs were for passion and love, and pain and frustration, and perhaps for all the other people she had loved and, in his tortured mind, betrayed him with.'

'He left her. He left her dead in the bedroom, so that we know she must have led him in there, gone willingly. But it was no part of his plan to be discovered. No, it was now that the cold, detached, clever part of his mind took over. No scandal for Valentine Brighton – above all, no scandal which would break his mother's heart. Those last words of his to me in the Reading Room – "Poor Mummy, how will she bear it?" – not about his voyeurism after all, but the horror of her only son being a murderer. So away with the prints, the evidence, and even when you, Kevin John, are arrested, he still feels no compunction, no desire to protect you from the consequences of his own deed. For he summons me to the Reading Room again explicitly to reveal your presence at the scene of her death.'

'But I'm jumping ahead. After he's killed her, the madness leaves him, he has to establish an alibi and fast. So he goes to the British Library, where he knows he'll find me. In fact he strikes lucky, sees me in the street on the way from the Pizza Perfecta, and tails me. It's easy then to sit down, deliberately clear the seat next to his (despite the fact its officially occupied) and rely on me discovering him, theoretically asleep. Then he talks of Lady Lionnel, of warning Chloe. He looked terrible then, ghastly. No wonder. He had just killed the one person – other than his mother – that he felt anything for in the world, and he knew he was sending me back to find her lacerated corpse.'

'So that bastard set me up!' shouted Kevin John, brandishing a bottle which was nearly empty. 'He would have testified against me. And all the time he knew I hadn't killed her, because he'd fucking well done her in himself.' There was bewilderment as well as rage in his voice, as though he found such diabolical adult villainy directed towards himself hard to comprehend.

Why pretend, thought Jemima. 'Yes, Valentine hated you,' she said directly to him. 'He was also deranged where you were concerned. He loved her but he hated you. Afterwards it was you he wanted to kill, extinguish, punish, as he had already punished her.'

'May one enquire how you are going to prove all this?' asked Sir Richard coolly. Of them all he remained the most detached. Adam still looked white, shocked, and as a result, even younger. But Sir Richard was once more inspecting his splendid cuffs with their agate links. 'That policeman of yours, Inspector Portsmouth, isn't it? Is he going to be much impressed by all this analysis. What proof do you have after all? The man's dead. I did see him in the gardens – fair enough – but that's no evidence that he was about to commit a particularly revolting crime.'

'The police *have* to believe her: she's Jemima Shore, Investigator!' Kevin John put the bottle to his lips and drained it, then leaping up, he rushed over to Lionnel. The latter stepped calmly backwards and sideways onto the balcony to avoid his rush.

Kevin John took him by his tweed lapels.

'You adulterous fascist shit. They have to believe her. I'm innocent, innocent, can't you understand that?'

Lionnel, with continuing aplomb, merely plucked Kevin John's fingers from his coat, and stepped further away. He acted sharply but not violently: Jemima was reminded of his treatment of Tiger that Saturday evening – 'cats in their place'. Artists too, it seemed.

'He's not guilty. That's clear,' said Isabelle reprovingly as though Sir Richard had somehow suggested that he was.

'I believe you. It figures. But I hope you can prove it, because – otherwise, well – a dead man. A dead Lord. A dead Lord with, I take it, a live mother. Will the fuzz buy that one? I doubt it.' Adam spoke, not very loudly, but loud enough for Jemima to hear.

'But you saw him there – in the gardens.' Kevin John, wielding the now empty bottle, was still menacing Lionnel; on the balcony, shouting at him, his face red, almost purple, his voice roaring; he looked quite out of control. 'You'll tell the police you saw him.'

'Will I, indeed?' Sir Richard, moving one more pace away, sounded highly remote from the whole affair. 'I'll have to talk to my lawyers about that. Naturally I shall cooperate as and when may be necessary; but otherwise I see no need to be mixed up further in this filthy business.'

He paused. 'Besides, I'm not at all sure that you're *not* guilty – please forgive me, Miss Shore, but I knew poor Valentine Brighton well, and of course Hope Brighton is one of Francesca's closest friends. We're country neighbours, you know what that means, one really gets to know people well, doesn't one, in the country, quite unlike these rather intense *urban* relationships.'

Another pause. Sir Richard had moved; he no longer had his back to the light, so that the expression on his face was once more visible. Afterwards Jemima would always remember that there had been something mocking, malicious, cruel about that expression, as though he was the controlled matador to Kevin John's maddened, helpless bull. For the first time she saw the ruthless tycoon who had torn down the beautiful houses of Adelaide Square and built for profit the modern horror which had become Chloe's tomb, and might become the tomb of Lionnel's own reputation, were he to weaken.

'Charming fellow, Brighton, in my opinion very much one of us,' he went on. 'Wouldn't hurt a fly, hated shooting, any kind of blood sports; Francesca, who's much to that way of thinking herself, used to have wonderful talks with him about it. And Chloe, herself, she used to laugh about him. My tame tabby, my other pussy-cat, she used to call him. Whereas our friend here—'

'Is that me you mean?' Kevin John was bellowing.

'Yes, my good man, indeed I mean you. Quite the brute, aren't you, with your great fists and muscles, and your obscenities, quite the murdering type, I would have said myself. Do you really think she found that kind of thing attractive just because you're some kind of stud, she, Chloe? Why she loathed it, loathed the memory of all your repulsive violence, the beatings, to say nothing of your endless sexual boasting, she used to tell me about it—'

The virulence with which Sir Richard Lionnel spoke was so unexpected, so outside his usual calm diction, that Jemima was still too startled to react, while Sir Richard continued in the same tone of rising venom: 'I wouldn't be a bit surprised if you didn't do her in after all, poor little thing; anyway it's clear she wouldn't have died, we wouldn't all be in this appalling mess, if it wasn't for your blundering return, you disgusting drunken oaf – take your hands off me—'

Isabelle screamed loudly, but stood immobile in the sitting room wringing her hands. Adam leapt lithely off the floor and darted forward, but even so did not reach the balcony until too late. Jemima too rushed forward. She also was too late.

For Kevin John, at Sir Richard's last words, first hurled the bottle over the balcony, its crash only just audible over the fracas which followed, and then flung himself at the tycoon.

'Murdering type, am I? We'll see about that.' The rest of his words were more or less lost, although afterwards Isabelle was prepared to swear that he had said something like: 'I didn't kill her but I will kill you.' Jemima was less certain.

In the end all any of them knew for certain was that Sir Richard, taken off guard, standing against the concrete parapet which fronted the balcony – that Lionnel fancy, the parapet just slightly too low for safety – was forced back against it, onto it, over it, still with Kevin John shouting and shouting while at his throat. And quite suddenly Lionnel was no longer there. Kevin John was there. Standing, panting, great fists now hanging at his sides. But the substantial figure of Sir Richard Lionnel had vanished.

A strange sound reached their ears as he disappeared, not so much a scream, as a huge sigh or a cry, perhaps merely the sound of his body rushing through the air. The noise of its landing far below was almost extinguished by the hysterical screams of Isabelle Mancini. Nevertheless the disseminated thud indicated that, far below, something heavy had met its end.

20
The last word

'A murdering type', commented Pompey with satisfaction afterwards, when Kevin John Athlone had been charged with the wilful murder of Sir Richard Lionnel – this time there was to be no bail. Even Punch Fredericks did not suggest it. In view of this Pompey was really quite restrained in his private comments on solicitors, who believed in bail-for-everyone – even murderers, and the consequences of their rashness.

'A murdering type. Didn't I say so all along?' It was an echo of the dead man's last – fatally provoking – words.

'But he didn't kill Chloe Fontaine,' retorted Jemima. 'Didn't I say that all along?' Charges against Kevin John for this crime had been withdrawn, a fact which had passed almost unnoticed in the Press, in view of the welter of publicity which had surrounded the death of Sir Richard Lionnel, the Lion of Bloomsbury, hurled – as the Press liked to put it – from the top of his own notorious building.

'How about that for a victory for the feminine instinct?' Jemima added.

'Ah, my dear, always let a woman have the last word.' Pompey shook his head sagely. 'That's what twenty happy years with Mrs Portsmouth has taught me. Above all, never argue about her instincts. Shall we settle for the fact that we were both right?'

'You do have your murderer,' Jemima pointed out. 'Or rather, your alleged murderer. If not precisely for the crime you were investigating.'

'Very true. And I must tell you that sometimes in the watches of the night I wish we did not – or rather I wish we did not have this particular crime. What with enquiries from number ten, very polite mind you, just interested, and Lady Lionnel, now *there's* a terror for you, and the dead man's secretary or whatever she calls herself, another terror, and sister, by the way, of your friend the squatter – I don't know what the world is coming to. Give me the Dowager Lady Brighton every time. She may be a terror, but she's a lady too.'

It seemed doubtful, at the time of Pompey's chat with Jemima, whether the murder of Chloe Fontaine would ever receive an official solution. This was partly due to the activities of Hope Lady Brighton, who on the one hand threatened dire penalties if her dead son's name was blackened on such slender evidence, and on the other made a series of heart-rending appeals as a grief-stricken mother. It was also due to the extreme reluctance of Mr Stover, on behalf of his wife, the dead woman's next of kin, to press for any form of revenge. The attitude of Valentine Brighton's mother, in which despair and authoritarianism were mingled in roughly equal parts, found an answering echo in Mr Stover's own breast.

There was a last interview with Jemima Shore, in which Mr Stover, grown suddenly much older and even smaller, began by sounding more bewildered than aggressive. But on the subject of the Press, for whom his full hatred was reserved, he still managed to express himself with something of his old strength. He for one was clearly immensely relieved that there would be no murder trial centred exclusively round the lives and loves of his stepdaughter.

'The things they wrote about Dollie!' he exclaimed to Jemima. 'Did they not think of her mother, her mother and me?' He broke down a little. 'Despite her change of name. Always made it quite clear who she was, when she was on television, and so forth, the relationship, told the neighbours, and now—'

'At least her books are selling well. At long last. And they're thinking of televising *Fallen Child*. She would have liked that,' put in Jemima.

It was a bald statement but true. Chloe's premature death, under hideous circumstances, had in a strange way bumped up her literary reputation. Dr Marigold Milton, whose moral enthusiasm in a good cause terrified her intellectual inferiors, pointed triumphantly to her long advocacy of Chloe's novels in a major piece in *Literature*. Other critics, honorably determined not to consider the scandal which surrounded her name, but their attention drawn to it nonetheless, found themselves pondering on Chloe's books as a whole for the first time. After all, her work, as well as her life, was over. In all this, the avidity of the public for further details concerning Chloe Fontaine was no disadvantage. In future, while her frozen body was freed at last into the obliteration of burial, her work would flourish.

'And we've got to know you,' Mr Stover spoke with perfect confidence. 'Her mother said that this morning before I left. The last thing she said – "We've got to know Jemima Shore, haven't we, Dad?" She'd like to give you that picture, the wife, not sell it back to them as the gallery suggested. "Why don't we give it to Miss Shore," she said, "to remind her of Dollie?" '

'No, no,' Jemima interrupted hastily. 'The gallery is quite right. Sell it.' She had no wish to introduce 'A Splash of Red' into her own life.

'You'll visit us, I expect', Mr Stover continued remorselessly. 'When you're our way. We'll talk about memories – Dollie – Chloe, I mean.' It was one of the touching things about Mr Stover that latterly he had made a determined effort to refer to his stepdaughter by her literary name. 'You can tell us about what goes on in television, books, well it's all the same thing isn't it? She knew all about it, Chloe, our girl.'

Mr Stover went on: 'And if you ever wanted to make a programme about Dollie, Chloe, all of this, well, you would need us, wouldn't you?'

'I'll visit you,' said Jemima Shore gently. She said it with a slightly heavy heart because she knew she would keep her word. Dollie Stover might have left her parents coldly unvisited, but she, Jemima Shore, would keep in touch with them. A sense of duty and sadness would not let her neglect them.

In the meantime Tiger, the golden Lion of Bloomsbury transplanted to Holland Park, graceful, wild and ultimately unknowable, would remind her of Chloe Fontaine.